## Praise for The Queen of the Dead:

"*Touch* is a novel I've been looking forward to for some time. *Silence*, its well-received predecessor, was Michelle Sagara's first foray into Young Adult waters: a story of ghosts and friendship, grief and compassion, and higher stakes than are initially apparent. As a sequel, *Touch* more than lives up to expectations. . . . Reflecting on *Touch*, in some ways I'm put in mind of Buffy The Vampire Slayer in the early years. Not the humor, not the apocalypses, not the world—but the way in which a group of friends come together to support each other in the face of painful events. . . . More like this, please."
—Liz Bourke, Tor.com

"In *Touch*, Sagara paints an eerie and original picture of the afterlife as she continues the struggle of Emma and friends to free the dead from eternal imprisonment, while battling the necromancers of the Queen of the Dead. Beautifully written, with characters so real—even the dead ones—they could be any of us, *Touch* is an exceptional addition to a powerful series. Don't miss this."
—Julie E. Czerneda, author of *A Turn of Light*

"Sagara is back with the intensely emotional and thought-provoking conclusion to her Queen of the Dead trilogy. . . . A haunting yet ultimately hopeful tale."
—*RT Book Reviews*

"Lyrical, compelling, and beautifully poignant . . . I'll be waiting anxiously for the third book in The Queen of the Dead series to hit the shelves. *Touch* is an intelligent and compassionate novel that will enthrall you from the very first words."
—Fresh Fiction

"Anything but typical . . . Sagara's characters are extremely realistic and well drawn. [*Silence*] is a very atmospheric novel that gives off that eerie vibe that makes the hair on your neck stand up. It is chilling, yet full of underlying wisdom."
—Debbi's Book Blog

"A spooky and emotionally moving urban fantasy. . . . Sagara starts with some of the popular plot tropes, but doesn't take them in the directions you might expect, and the lovable characters and authentic emotion help set the book apart, too. It's a story of loss, grief, and the way life goes on after tragedy, sad at times, but hopeful rather than depressing."
—Fantasy Literature Review

D1589990

3 1526 05598520 1

# THE QUEEN OF THE DEAD

## SILENCE
## TOUCH
## GRAVE

WITHDRAWN

# MICHELLE SAGARA

DAW BOOKS, INC.

DONALD A. WOLLHEIM, FOUNDER

1745 Broadway, New York, NY 10019

ELIZABETH R. WOLLHEIM

SHEILA E. GILBERT

PUBLISHERS

www.dawbooks.com

SILENCE copyright © 2012 by Michelle Sagara.

TOUCH copyright © 2014 by Michelle Sagara.

GRAVE copyright © 2017 by Michelle Sagara.

Introduction copyright © 2021 by Michelle Sagara.

All Rights Reserved.

Cover art by Cliff Nielsen.

Cover design by Katie Anderson.

DAW Book Collectors No. 1903.

Published by DAW Books, Inc.
1745 Broadway, New York, NY 10019.

All characters and events in this book are fictitious.
Any resemblance to persons living or dead is strictly coincidental.

The scanning, uploading, and distribution of this book via the Internet or any other means without the permission of the publisher is illegal, and punishable by law. Please purchase only authorized electronic editions, and do not participate in or encourage the electronic piracy of copyrighted materials. Your support of the author's rights is appreciated.

First Printing, December 2021
1st Printing

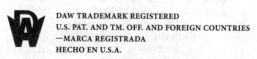

DAW TRADEMARK REGISTERED
U.S. PAT. AND TM. OFF. AND FOREIGN COUNTRIES
—MARCA REGISTRADA
HECHO EN U.S.A.

PRINTED IN THE U.S.A.

# Introduction

When I set out to write my first YA novel, I wrote it on spec. This came about because my editor asked if I happened to have a finished YA novel just lying around (this is almost an exact quote). As I had two books due that calendar year, I emphatically did not have any finished novels, mostly finished novels, or even partially finished novels on my figurative desk.

But I had an idea for one that I'd been mulling over for some time. It was even a contemporary, which meant I had some hope of writing a novel that was short (for me). I've always been drawn to stories about grief, loss, and the ways in which people deal with both. I wanted to write a ghost story, from the point of view of a young woman who had just lost the first love of her life.

So I sat down to write *Silence*. I had some idea of who the protagonist was, but I often discover nuances of character while writing. The prologue and the first chapter were exactly what I envisioned. The second chapter started in the same smooth vein.

And then chapter two took an abrupt detour, veering in a direction that I hadn't planned. I wrote:

*At 8:10, at precisely 8:10, the doorbell rang.*

*"That'll be Michael," her mother said.*

*You could set clocks by Michael. In the Hall household, they did; if Michael rang the doorbell and the clock didn't say 8:10, someone changed it quickly, and only partly because Michael always looked at clocks, and began his quiet fidget if they didn't show the time he expected them to show.*

Books have tone. They have voice. And I realized, as I paused at the end of that last paragraph, that I was about to veer wildly off-tone if I continued; that my careful, little paranormal would have an entirely different feel.

But I also suddenly understood where this new book was going. I understood, at that moment, who Emma was, and what had kept her moving during the almost crippling months of grief.

I knew that if I wrote this unexpected book, I was no longer writing a book that would be guaranteed to speak to the market—if any book can be said to do that with certainty—but I wanted to write this book. Because I could see the dedication, from that point on.

Let me explain why. I've had some experience with ASD (Autism Spectrum Disorder) as a parent. I've experienced the difficulties school can cause—even an incredibly supportive school, which we were lucky to have. I witnessed firsthand my oldest son's inability to parse social cues, and to miss simple things like people saying "hi!" with enthusiasm—an enthusiasm that waned when he all but ignored them. He didn't hear; they didn't know he couldn't.

We are terrified, as parents, for our children; we are terrified that they won't fit in, they won't find friends, they'll be made fun of, they'll be isolated. Because my oldest son was diagnosed ASD (Aspergers at the time) I was prepared for this, but not less terrified, and it broke my heart to know that my son was terribly lonely when I could see the children in his class trying very hard to make connections with him. If I was present, I could point them out—but I wasn't going to be present for most of his school day.

He struggled through two years of kindergarten with some limited success, and then came the full day of grade one. And in grade one, he met the girls, the ones to whom the first book is dedicated. The teacher treated my son as if his behavior was normal *for* my son, and at six, children's ideas of normative behavior are very flexible. The girls took their cues from his teacher that year, and perhaps with a different teacher they would have picked up different cues. I don't know.

What I do know is this: My son hated the noise of the stairwell and his class was on the third floor, so he was required to use the stairs. He almost always entered dead last, when the stairwell would be mostly empty. On this day (half-way through the year), he was trudging up the stairs, and the stair monitor, a woman of middling years, shouted at him.

He failed to hear her, so she marched up the stairs and shouted in his ear. And he still failed to hear her; he pretty much tuned out all the noise until he left the stairwell. I started to approach the stair monitor to tell her as much, and stopped as a young girl with platinum blond hair caught her by the elbow.

"He can't hear you, you know," she told the woman. "He's daydreaming. He always daydreams when he walks up the stairs."

She was six years old. She was six years old and entirely fearless when it came to correcting a much older and much larger authority figure. And she had done so without prompting from anyone. My son, of course, didn't even notice. But I did.

She was part of a group of friends, and they kept an eye out for my son. They also came to his birthday parties from grade one through grade six, although by that time three of them were no longer in the same school.

When my son was in grade three, we took karate together. Karate made us late, and one night there was a school open house, so we went directly from the dojo, in our gis, to the school. We entered his classroom and found two girls there, and my son approached one of them—in his karate outfit—and started to talk.

The other girl said, with a sneer, "As if we care about your stupid karate." This is the type of reaction I feared, as a parent, especially given that ASD children can go on for an hour about any topic that engages their interest.

But the first girl turned to her friend and said, "Well, I *do* care." And proceeded to talk with my son about his karate progress. She was, of course, one of the six.

Did they spend their whole days doing nothing but babysitting my son? No, of course not. They spent most of their time socializing with each other. But they continued to keep an eye out in all the little ways that made my son's life easier. I'm not even certain, these many years later, that they would remember the incidents that I remember so clearly and so gratefully.

Michael appeared at Emma's door at exactly 8:10 in the morning.

And I thought: Why not these girls? Books are written about shy outsiders or social outcasts all the time; books are written about mean girls just as frequently, and often books are a combination of these two extremes. And there is nothing wrong with that.

But why not these girls? Girls who were best friends and who supported each other (often by phone even in the early years) and who, while having lives entirely of their own, also had the compassion to keep an eye on an awkward ASD child? It's a paranormal, it's contemporary, but why can't the story be about girls like these?

*Silence* is that book.

SILENCE:
This is for the girls:
Callie – Katie – Caroline – Molly – Alexandra – Rada
With thanks, with gratitude, although admittedly they might
not understand why.

TOUCH:
This is for the teachers:
Carol Morgan – Manjit Virk – Lisa Adams – Carolyn Watt – Sara Cheng
– Eric Chelew – Ashley Marshall – Ed Hitchcock
Because you chose to see all difficulties as challenges, and you worked to
meet—and even exceed—them. Teaching is a vocation; it is an incredible
gift, and it's given day-in and day-out.

GRAVE:
This is for Jane Fletcher.
She made school as sane and bearable as it could possibly be for my son
when it was absolutely essential, and I can truly say that he is as much a
product of her guidance and leadership as he is of mine.
No matter how difficult things were, he knew that he could go to Ms
Fletcher, talk to her, be heard. He knew that ultimately, at the top of the
chain, there was both accountability and trust. She made school feel safe.
And that is so very, very rare.

# Silence

## Emma

Everything happens at night.

The world changes, the shadows grow, there's secrecy and privacy in dark places. First kiss, at night, by the monkey bars and the old swings that the children and their parents have vacated; second, longer, kiss, by the bike stands, swirl of dust around feet in the dry summer air. Awkward words, like secrets just waiting to be broken, the struggle to find the right ones, the heady fear of exposure—what if, what if—the joy when the words are returned. Love, in the parkette, while the moon waxes and the clouds pass.

Promises, at night. Not first promises—those are so old they can't be remembered—but new promises, sharp and biting; they almost hurt to say, but it's a good hurt. Dreams, at night, before sleep, and dreams during sleep.

Everything, always, happens at night.

Emma unfolds at night. The moment the door closes at her back, she relaxes into the cool breeze, shakes her hair loose, seems to grow three inches. It's not that she hates the day, but it doesn't feel real; there are too many people and too many rules and too many questions. Too many teachers, too many concerns. It's an act, getting through the day; Emery Collegiate is a stage. She pins up her hair, wears her uniform—on Fridays, on formal days, she wears the stupid plaid skirt and the jacket—goes to her classes. She waves at her friends, listens to them talk, forgets almost instantly what they talk *about*. Sometimes it's band, sometimes it's class, sometimes it's the other friends, but most often it's boys.

She's been there, done all that. It doesn't mean anything anymore.

At night? Just Petal and Emma. At night, you can just be yourself.

Petal barks, his voice segueing into a whine. Emma pulls a Milk-Bone out of her jacket pocket and feeds him. He's overweight, and he doesn't need it—but he wants it, and she wants to give it to him. He's nine, now, and Emma suspects he's half-deaf. He used to run from the steps to the edge of the curb, half-dragging her on the leash—her father used to get so mad at the dog when he did.

*He's a rottweiler, not a lapdog, Em.*

*He's just a puppy.*

*Not at that size, he isn't. He'll scare people just by standing still; he needs to learn to heel, and he needs to learn that he can hurt you if he drags you along.*

He doesn't run now. Doesn't drag her along. True, she's much bigger than she used to be, but it's also true that he's much older. She misses the old days. But at least he's still here. She waits while he sniffs at the green bins. It's his little ritual. She walks him along the curb, while he starts and stops, tail wagging. Emma's not in a hurry now. She'll get there eventually.

Petal knows. He's walked these streets with Emma for all of his life. He'll follow the curb to the end of the street, watch traffic pass as if he'd like to go fetch a moving car, and then cross the street more or less at Emma's heel. He talks. For a rottweiler, he's always been yappy.

But he doesn't expect more of an answer than a Milk-Bone, which makes him different from anyone else. She lets him yap as the street goes by. He quiets when they approach the gates.

The cemetery gates are closed at night. This keeps cars out, but there's no gate to keep out people. There's even a footpath leading to the cement sidewalk that surrounds the cemetery and a small gate without a padlock that opens inward. She pushes it, hears the familiar creak. It doesn't swing in either direction, and she leaves it open for Petal. He brushes against her leg as he slides by.

It's dark here. It's always dark when she comes. She's only seen the cemetery in the day twice, and she never wants to see it in daylight again. It's funny how night can change a place. But night does change this one. There are no other people here. There are flowers in vases and wreaths on stands; there are sometimes letters, written and pinned flat by rocks beneath headstones. Once she found a teddy bear. She didn't take it, and she didn't touch it, but she did stop to read the name on the headstone: *Lauryn Bernstein.* She read the dates and did the math. Eight years old.

She half-expected to see the mother or father or grandmother or sister come back at night, the way she does. But if they do, they come by a different route, or they wait until no one—not even Emma—is watching. Fair enough. She'd do the same.

But she wonders if they come together—mother, father, grandmother, sister—or if they each come alone, without speaking a word to anyone else. She wonders how much of Lauryn's life was private, how much of it was built on moments of two: mother and daughter, alone; father and daughter, alone. She wonders about Lauryn's friends, because her friends' names aren't carved here in stone.

She knows about that. Others will come to see Lauryn's grave, and no matter how important they were to Lauryn, they won't see any evidence of themselves there: no names, no dates, nothing permanent. They'll be outsiders, looking in, and nothing about their memories will matter to passing strangers a hundred years from now.

Emma walks into the heart of the cemetery and comes, at last, to a headstone. There are white flowers here, because Nathan's mother has visited during the day. The lilies are bound by wire into a wreath, a fragrant, thick circle that perches on an almost invisible frame.

Emma brings nothing to the grave and takes nothing away. If she did, she's certain Nathan's mother would remove it when she comes to clean. Even here, even though he's dead, she's still cleaning up after him.

She leaves the flowers alone and finds a place to sit. The graveyard is awfully crowded, and the headstones butt against each other, but only one of them really matters to Emma. She listens to the breeze and the rustle of leaves; there are willows and oaks in the cemetery, so it's never exactly quiet. The sound of passing traffic can be heard, especially the horns of pissed-off drivers, but their lights can't be seen. In the city this is as close to isolated as you get.

She doesn't talk. She doesn't tell Nathan about her day. She doesn't ask him questions. She doesn't swear undying love. She's *done all that*, and it made no difference; he's there, and she's here. Petal sits down beside her. After a few minutes, he rolls over and drops his head in her lap; she scratches behind his big, floppy ears, and sits, and breathes, and stretches.

One of the best things about Nathan was that she could just sit, in silence, without being alone. Sometimes she'd read, and sometimes he'd read; sometimes he'd play video games, and sometimes he'd build things; sometimes they'd just walk aimlessly all over the city, as if footsteps were a kind of writing. It wasn't that she wasn't supposed to talk; when she wanted to talk, she did. But if she didn't, it wasn't awkward. He was like a quiet, private place.

And that's the only thing that's left of him, really.

A quiet, private place.

# ✎ Chapter 1

AT 9:30 P.M., CELL TIME, the phone rang. Emma slid it out of her pocket, rearranging Petal's head in the process, flipped it open, saw that it was Allison. Had it been anyone else, she wouldn't have answered.

"Hey."

"Emma?"

*No, it's Amy*, she almost snapped. Honestly, if you rang her number, who did you *expect* to pick it up? But she didn't, because it was Allison, and she'd only feel guilty about one second after the words left her mouth. "Yeah, it's me," she said instead.

Petal rolled his head back onto her lap and then whined while she tried to pull a Milk-Bone out of her very crumpled jacket pocket. Nine years hadn't made him more patient.

"Where are you?"

"Just walking Petal. Mom's prepping a headache, so I thought I'd get us both out of the house before she killed us." Time to go. She shifted her head slightly, caught the cell phone between her chin and collarbone, and shoved Petal gently off her lap. Then she stood, shaking the wrinkles out of her jacket.

"Did you get the e-mail Amy sent?"

"What e-mail?"

"That would be no. How long have you been walking?"

Emma shrugged. Which Allison couldn't see. "Not long. What time is it?"

"9:30," Allison replied, in a tone of voice that clearly said she didn't believe Emma didn't know. That was the problem with perceptive friends.

"I'll look at it the minute I get home—is there anything you want to warn me about before I do?"

"No."

"Should I just delete it and blame it on the spam filter? No, no, that's a joke. I'll look at it when I get home and call you—Petal, come back!" Emma whistled. As whistles went, it was high and piercing, and she could practically hear Allison cringe on the other end of the phone. "Damn it—I have to go, Ally." She flipped the lid down, shoved the phone into her pocket, and squinted into the darkness. She could just make out the red plastic handle of the retracting leash as it fishtailed along in the grass.

So much for quiet. "*Petal!*"

Running in the graveyard at night was never smart. Oh, there were strategic lamps here and there, where people had the money and the desire to spend it, but mostly there was moonlight, and a lot of flat stones; not all the headstones were standing. There were also trees that were so old Emma wondered whether the roots had eaten through coffins, if they even used coffins in those days. The roots often came to the surface, and if you were unlucky, you could trip on them and land face first in tree bark—in broad daylight. At night, you didn't need to be unlucky.

No, you just needed to try to catch your half-deaf rottweiler before he scared the crap out of some stranger in the cemetery. The cemetery that should have bloody well been deserted. She got back on her feet.

"*Petal, goddammit!*" She stopped to listen. She couldn't see Petal, but he was a black rottweiler and it was dark. She could, on the other hand, hear the leash as it struck stone and standing wreaths, and she headed in that direction, walking as quickly as she could. She stubbed her toes half a dozen times because there was no clear path through the headstones and the markers, and even when she could see them—and the moon was bright enough—she couldn't see enough of them in time. She never brought a flashlight with her because she didn't need one normally; she could walk to Nathan's grave and back blindfolded. Walking to a black dog who was constantly in motion between totally unfamiliar markers, on the other hand, not so much.

She wondered what had caught his attention. The only person he ran toward like this was Emma, and usually only when she was coming up the walk from school or coming into the house. He would bark when Allison or Michael approached the door, and he would growl like a pit bull when salesmen, meter men, or the occasional Mormon or Jehovah's Witness showed up—but he wasn't much of a runner. Not these days.

The sounds of the leash hitting things stopped.

Up ahead, which had none of the usual compass directions, Emma could see light. Not streetlight, but a dim, orange glow that flickered too much. She could also, however, see the stubby, wagging tail of what was sometimes the world's stupidest dog. Relief was momentary. Petal was standing in front of two people, one of whom seemed to be holding the light. And Emma didn't come to the graveyard to meet people.

She pursed her lips to whistle, but her mouth was too dry, and anyway, Petal probably wouldn't hear her. Defeated, she shoved her hands into her jacket pockets and made her way over to Petal. The first thing she did was pick up his leash; the plastic was cool and slightly damp to the touch, and what had, moments before, been smooth was now scratched and rough. Hopefully, her mother wouldn't notice.

"Emma?"

When you don't expect to meet anyone, meeting someone you know is always a bit of a shock. She saw his face, the height of his cheekbones, and his eyes, which in the dim light looked entirely black. His hair, cut back over his ears and shorn close to forehead, was the same inky color. He was familiar, but it took her a moment to remember why and to find a name.

"Eric?" Even saying the name, her voice was tentative. She looked as the shape in the darkness resolved itself into an Eric she vaguely knew, standing beside someone who appeared a lot older and a lot less distinct.

"Mrs. Bruehl's my mentor," he said, helpfully. "Eleventh grade?"

She frowned for a moment, and then the frown cleared. "You're the new guy."

"New," he said with a shrug. "Same old, same old, really. Don't take this the wrong way," he added, "but what are you doing here at this time of night?"

"I could ask you the same question."

"You could."

"Great. What are *you* doing here at this time of night?"

He shrugged again, sliding his hands into the pockets of his jeans. "Just walking. It's a good night for it. You?"

"I'm mostly chasing my *very annoying* dog."

Eric looked down at Petal, whose stub of a tail had shown no signs whatsoever of slowing down. "Doesn't seem all that annoying."

"Yeah? Bend over and let him breathe in your face."

Eric laughed, bent over, and lowered his palms toward Petal's big, wet nose. Petal sniffed said hands and then barked. And whined. Sometimes, Emma thought, pulling the last Milk-Bone out of her jacket pocket, that dog was so embarrassing.

"Petal, come here." Petal looked over his shoulder, saw the Milk-Bone, and whined. Just . . . whined. Then he looked up again, and this time, Emma squared her shoulders and fixed a firm smile on lips that wanted to shift in entirely the opposite direction. "And who's your friend?"

And Eric, one hand just above Petal's head, seemed to freeze, half-bent. "What friend, Emma?"

But his friend turned slowly to face Emma. As she did, Emma could finally see the source of the flickering, almost orange, light. A lantern. A paper lantern, like the ones you saw in the windows of variety stores in Chinatown. It was an odd lamp, and the paper, over both wire and flame, was a pale blue. Which made no sense, because the light it cast wasn't blue at all. There were words on the shell of the lamp that Emma couldn't read, although she could see them clearly enough. They were composed of black brushstrokes that trailed into squiggles, and the squiggles, in the leap of lamp fire, seemed to grow and move with a life of their own.

She blinked and looked up, past the lamp and the hand that held it.

An old woman was watching her. An *old* woman. Emma was accustomed to thinking of half of her teachers as "old," and probably a handful as "ancient" or "mummified." Not a single one of them wore age the way this woman did. In fact, given the wreath of sagging wrinkles that was her skin, Emma wasn't certain that she *was* a woman. Her cheeks were sunken, and her eyes were set so deep they might as well have just been sockets; her hair, what there was of it, was white tufts, too stringy to suggest down. She had no teeth, or seemed to have no teeth; hell, she didn't have lips, either.

Emma couldn't stop herself from taking a step back.

The old woman took a step forward.

She wore rags. Emma had heard that description before. She had even seen it in a movie or two. Neither experience prepared her for this. There wasn't a single piece of cloth that was bigger than a napkin, although the assembly hung together in the vague shape of a dress. Or a bag. The orange light that the blue lantern emitted caught the edges of different colors, but they were muted, dead things. Like fallen leaves. Like corpses.

"Emma?"

Emma took another step back. "Eric, tell her to stop." She tried to keep her voice even. She tried to keep it polite. It was hard. If the stranger's slightly open, sunken mouth had uttered words, she would have been less terrifying. But, in silence, the old woman teetered across graves as if she'd just risen from one and counted it as nothing.

Emma backed up. The old woman kept coming. Everything moved slowly, everything—except for Emma's breathing—was quiet. The quiet of a graveyard. Emma tried to speak, tried to ask the old woman what she wanted, but her throat was too dry, and all that came out was an alto squeak. She took another step and ran into a headstone; she felt the back of it, cold, against her thighs. Standing against a short, narrow wall, Emma threw her hands out in front of her.

The old woman pressed the lantern into those hands. Emma felt the sides of it collapse slightly as her hands gripped them, changing the shape of the brushstrokes and squiggles. It was *cold* against her palms. Cold like ice, cold like winter days when you inhaled and the air froze your nostrils.

She cried out in shock and opened her hands, but the lantern clung to her palms, and no amount of shaking would free them. She tried hard, but she couldn't watch what she was doing because old, wrinkled claws shot out like cobras, sudden, skeletal, and gripped Emma's cheeks and jaw, the way Emma's hands now gripped the lantern.

Emma felt her face being pulled down, down toward the old woman's, and she tried to pull back, tried to straighten her neck. But she couldn't. All the old stories she'd heard in camp, or in her father's lap, came to her then, and even though this woman clearly had no teeth, Emma thought of vampires.

But it wasn't Emma's neck that the old woman wanted. She pulled Emma's whole face toward her, and then Emma felt—and smelled—unpleasant, endless breath, dry as dust but somehow rank as dead and rotting flesh, as the old woman opened her mouth. Emma shut her eyes as the face, its nested lines of wrinkles so like a fractal, drew closer and closer.

She felt lips, what might have been lips, press themselves against the thin membranes of her eyelids, and she whimpered. It wasn't the sound she wanted to make; it was just the only sound she *could*. And then even that was gone as those same lips, with that same breath, pressed firmly and completely against Emma's mouth.

Like a night kiss.

She tried to open her eyes, but the night was all black, and there was no moon, and it was *so damn cold*. And as she felt that cold overwhelm her, she thought it unfair that this would be her *last* kiss, this unwanted horror; that the memory of Nathan's hands and Nathan's lips were not the ones she would carry to the grave.

## ᗧ Chapter 2

The rottweiler was whining in panic and confusion. His big, messy tongue was running all over Emma's face as if it could, by sheer force, pull her to her feet. Eric watched him in silence for a long minute before turning to his left. There, sprigs of lilac moved against the breeze.

He had been waiting in the graveyard since sunset. He'd waited in graveyards before, and often in much worse weather; at least tonight there was no driving rain, no blizzard, and no spring thaw to turn the ground to mud.

But he would have preferred them to this.

He felt the darkness watching. He knew what lived inside of it.

"It can't be her," he said.

*She saw me.*

"It's a graveyard. People see things in a graveyard." He said it without conviction.

*I could touch her.*

He had no answer for that. His fingers found the side of Emma's neck, got wet as dog-tongue traveled across them, and stayed put until he felt a pulse. Alive.

"It can't be her," he said again, voice flat. "I've been doing this for years. I *know* what I'm looking for."

Silence. He glanced at his left pocket, half-expecting the phone to ring. If the rottweiler couldn't wake her, nothing would, at this point. She was beyond pain, beyond fear. If he was going to do anything—anything at all—this was the time; it was almost a gift.

But it was a barbed, ugly gift. Funny, how seldom he thought that.

"No," he said, although there was no spoken question. "I won't do it. Not now. It's got to be a mistake." He glanced up at the moon's position in the sky. Grimacing, he began to rifle through her pockets. "We can wait it out until dawn."

But the dog was whining, and Emma wasn't standing up. He flipped her cell open and glanced at the moon again. He knew he should leave things be; he couldn't afford to leave the graveyard. Not tonight. Not the night after.

But he had no idea how hard she'd hit the tombstone when she'd toppled, and had no idea whether or not she'd wake without intervention.

Emma opened her eyes, blinked, shook her head, and opened them again. They still felt closed, but she could see; she just couldn't see well. On the other hand, she didn't need to see well to notice that her mother was sitting beside her, a wet towel in her hands.

"Em?"

She had to blink again, because the light was harsh and bright in the room. Even harsh and brightly lit, Emma recognized the room: it was hers. She was under her duvet, with its faded flannel covers, and Petal was lying across her feet, his head on his paws. That dog could sleep through anything.

"Mom?"

"Open your eyes and let me look at them." Her mother picked up, of all things, a flashlight. The on switch appeared to do nothing. Her mother frowned, shook the flashlight up and down, and tried again.

Emma reached out and touched her mother's arm. "I'm fine, Mom." The words came naturally to her, even if they weren't accurate, she'd used them so often.

"You have a goose egg the size of my fist on the back of your head," her mother replied, shaking the flashlight again.

Emma began a silent count to ten; she reached eight before her mother stood. "I'm just going to get batteries," she told her daughter. She set the towel—which was wet—on the duvet and headed for the door.

Mercy Hall was not, in her daughter's opinion, a very organized person. It would take her mother at least ten minutes to find batteries—if there were any in the house. Batteries, like most hardware, had been her father's job.

If her mother were truly panicky, the kitchen—where all the odds and ends a house mystically acquired had been stowed—would be a first-class disaster. It wouldn't be dirty, because Mercy disliked dirt, but it would be messy, which Mercy barely seemed to notice. Emma looked at her clock. At six minutes she sat up, and at six minutes and ten seconds, she lay back, more heavily. Petal shifted. And snored.

She was still dressed, although her jacket hung off the back of her computer chair. Her fingers, hesitantly probing the back of her head, told her that her mother was, in fact, right. Huge bump. It didn't hurt much. But her eyes ached, and her lips felt swollen.

She gagged and sat bolt upright, and this time Petal woke. "Petal," she whispered, as the rottweiler walked across the duvet. His paws slid off her legs and her stomach, and she shoved him, mostly gently, to one side. He rewarded her by licking her face, and she buried that face in his neck, only partly to avoid his breath.

It was fifteen minutes before her mother came back, looking harassed.

"No batteries?"

"Not a damn one."

"I'll stop by the hardware store after school."

"I'm not sure you're going to school. No, don't argue with me." She came and sat down on the chair. "Em—"

"I'm *fine*, Mom."

"What happened?"

Her mother didn't ask her what she'd been doing in the cemetery. She never did. She didn't like the fact that Emma went there, but she knew why. Emma wanted to keep it that way.

"Allison phoned, I dropped Petal's leash, and he ran off." Petal perked up at the sound of his name, which made Emma feel slightly guilty. Which was stupid because it was mostly the truth.

"And you ran after him? In the *dark*?"

"I wasn't carrying scissors."

"Emma, this is not funny. If your friend hadn't been with you, you could have been there all night!"

"Friend?"

"Eric."

"What, he brought me home?"

"No, *he* was smart. He called me from your phone. I brought you home."

She hesitated and then added, "He helped me carry you to the car, and he helped me carry you to your room."

"He's still here?"

"He said he was late and his mother would worry."

"What, at 9:30 at night?"

"10:30, and it's a school night." But her mother seemed to relax; she slumped into the chair. "You sound all right."

"I told you—"

"You're fine, I know." Her mother's expression was odd; she looked slightly past her daughter's shoulder, out the window. "You're always fine."

"Mom—"

Her mother smiled that bright, fake smile that Emma so disliked. "I'll help you get changed. Sleep. If you're feeling 'fine' in the morning, you can go to school."

"If I'm not?"

"I'll call in sick."

There was no way that Emma was not going to school. "Deal," she said.

The only thing in the room that shed light was the computer screen; the only words were voiceless, silent, appearing, letter by letter, as Emma's fingers tapped the keyboard.

*Dear Dad,*

*It's been a while. School started last month, and it did not miraculously become interesting over the summer. Mr. Marshall, on the other hand, still has a sense of humor, which is good, because he now has me.*

*Marti moved when her dad got a job transfer. Sophie moved when her parents got divorced (why she couldn't just live with her dad, I do not know; she asked). Allison and I are still here, holding it down, because Allison's parents are still married. Takes all kinds.*

*Michael is doing better this year. He had a bit of a rough time because he's always so blunt when anyone asks him anything, and he doesn't remember to be polite until someone is threatening to break his nose. Oh, and Petal's going deaf, I swear.*

*I wish you were here. I must have tripped in the cemetery; Mom's freaking because she thinks I have a concussion. I think. I had the world's worst dream before I woke up, and I'd be*

*sleeping now, but, frankly, if it's a choice between sleep and that
dream? I'm never sleeping again.*

*And we have no batteries.*

She stopped typing for a moment. Petal snored. He had sprawled across
the entire bed the minute Emma had slid out of it, but he always did. Every
night was a battle for bed space because technically Petal wasn't allowed to
sleep in her bed. He'd start out at the foot of the bed. And then he'd roll over,
and then he'd kind of flatten out. Half of the time, Emma would end up sleeping on her side on six inches of bed with her butt hanging just off to one side
of the mattress.

She rolled her eyes, winced, and went back to the keyboard.

*But I'm fine, Mom's fine. She doesn't say it, but I think she
misses you.*
*I'll write something more exciting later—maybe about drugs,
sex, and petty felonies. I don't want to bore you.*

*—Em*

She hit the send button. After a few minutes, she stood and made her way
back to the bed, nearly tripping over the cord of the desk lamp that was probably going to be hulking on the footboard of her bed for the next six weeks.
Her mother didn't really use it; she did most of her work on a small corner of
the dining room table.

She hadn't lied, though; she really, really did not want to sleep.

In the morning, she was fine. She was fine at breakfast. She was fine watering
and feeding her dog. She was fine clearing the table and loading the dishwasher.
She was even fine pointing out that the dishwasher was still leaking, and the
ivory and green linoleum beneath it was stained yellow and brown.

Mercy Hall looked less than fine, but Emma's mother had never, ever been
a morning person. She looked at her daughter with a vaguely suspicious air,
but she said nothing out of the ordinary. She watched her daughter eat, criticized her lack of appetite—but she always did that—and asked her if it was
entirely necessary to leave the house with her midriff showing.

Since it wasn't cold, and since Emma was in fact wearing a blazer, sleeves
rolled up to her elbow, Emma ignored this, filing it under "old."

But she hugged her mother tightly as they both stood up from the table,
and she whispered a brief *thanks* to take the edge off her mother's mood. She

put her laptop into her school bag, made sure she had her phone in her jacket pocket, and looked at the clock.

At 8:10, at precisely 8:10, the doorbell rang.

"That'll be Michael," her mother said.

You could set clocks by Michael. In the Hall household, they did; if Michael rang the doorbell and the clock didn't say 8:10, someone changed it quickly, and only partly because Michael always looked at clocks and began his quiet fidget if they didn't show the time he expected them to show.

Emma opened the door, and Petal pushed his way past her, nudging Michael's hand. Michael's hand, of course, held a Milk-Bone. No wonder they had the world's fattest dog. He fed Petal, and Petal sat, slobbering and chewing, just to one side of the doorframe. "Be right there," Emma told Michael. "Petal, don't slobber."

Michael looked at Emma. He had *that* look on his face. "What?" she asked him. "What's wrong?"

"Is it Friday?"

"No. It's Wednesday."

He seemed to relax, but he still looked hesitant. Michael and hesitant in combination was not a good thing. "Why are you asking?"

"Your eyelids," he replied promptly.

She lifted a hand to her eyelids. "What about them?"

"You're wearing eye shadow."

She started to tell him that she was wearing no such thing but stopped the words before they fell out of her mouth. Michael was many things—most of them strange—but he was almost never wrong. "Give me a sec."

She stepped back into the house and walked over to the hall mirror.

In the morning light her reflection looked back at her, and she automatically reached up to rearrange her hair. But she stopped and looked at her eyes instead. At her eyelids. Michael was right— they were blue, the blue that looks almost like bruising. Her lips were . . . dark. Reaching up with her thumb, she tried to smear whatever it was on her eyes.

Nothing happened.

She grimaced. Okay, it looked like she was wearing makeup. It did not, however, look like *bad* makeup, and she didn't have time to deal with it now; Michael had a mortal terror of being late. She picked up her backpack again and headed out the door.

They picked up Allison on the way to Emery. Allison was waiting because Allison, like Emma, had known Michael for almost all of her school life. Ally could be late for almost anything else, but she was out the door and on time in the morning. Mrs. Simner stood in the doorway and beamed at the sight of

Michael. Most parents found him off-putting, or worrying. Mrs. Simner never had, and Emma loved her for it.

There was something about Mrs. Simner that screamed *mother*. It was a primal scream. She was short, sort of dumpy, often seen in polyester, and she *always* thought that anyone who walked anywhere near her house must be, you know, starving to death. She could listen sympathetically for hours on end, and she could also offer advice for hours on end—but somehow she knew when to listen and when to talk.

She never tried to be your friend. She never tried to be one of the guys. But in her own way, she was, and it was to the Simner house that Emma had gone in the months following Nathan's death.

Allison was sort of like her mother. Except for the polyester and Allison's glasses. When you were with Allison, you were, in some way, in the Simner household. It wasn't the only reason they were friends, but it helped. She carried the same blue pack that Emma did, with a slightly different model of laptop (for which official permission had been required). They fell into step behind Michael, who often forgot that he was tall enough to outpace them.

"Did you get a chance to read Amy's e-mail?"

Damn. Emma grimaced. "Guilty," she said quietly. "I'm sorry I didn't call you back last night—I kind of fell asleep."

"I guessed. She's having a party next Friday."

"Why?"

"I think her parents are going out of town."

"The last time she tried that—"

"To New York City. Without her."

"Oh. Well, that would do it." Amy was famed for her love of shopping. She was in particular famed for her love of shopping in NYC, because almost everything she was willing to admit she owned—where admit meant something only a little less overt than a P.A. announcement between every class—came from NYC. "How big a party?"

"She invited me," Allison replied.

Emma glanced at Allison's profile. She thought about saying a bunch of pleasant and pointless things but settled for, "It's not the only time she's invited you."

"No. She invited me to the last big party as well." Allison shrugged. "I don't mind, Em."

Emma shrugged, because sometimes Emma minded. And she knew she shouldn't. Allison and Amy had nothing in common except a vowel and a gender; Amy was the golden girl: the star athlete, the student council representative, and the second highest overall GPA in the grade. She was also stunningly beautiful, and if she knew it, the knowledge could be overlooked. When people are tripping over their own feet at the sight of you, you can only *not* notice it by being disingenuous.

Amy also never suffered from false modesty. In Amy's case, *any* modesty was going to be false. "Are you going to go?"

"Are you?"

Emma, unlike Allison, had managed to find a place for herself in Amy's inner circle of friends. Emma could, with relative ease, hit a volleyball, hit a softball, or run a fast fifty-yard dash. She had decent grades, as well, but it wasn't about grades. It had never been about grades. If people didn't cause car accidents when they saw Emma in the street, they still noticed her. She had no trouble talking to boys, and no trouble not talking when it was convenient; she had no trouble shopping for clothes, and when she did, she bought things that matched and that looked good.

Allison, not so much.

Allison was plain. In and of itself, that wasn't a complete disaster; Deb was plain as well. But Deb could do all the other things; she knew how to work a crowd. She had the sharpest tongue in the school. Allison didn't. Allison also hated to shop for anything that wasn't a book, so after-school mall excursions weren't social time for Allison; she would simply vanish from the tail end of the pack when the pack passed a bookstore en route to something more interesting, and frequently fail to emerge.

But Allison, like Nathan, was a quiet space. She didn't natter and she didn't gossip. She could be beside you for half an afternoon without saying two words, but if you needed to talk, she could listen. She could also ask questions that proved that she was, in fact, listening—not that Emma ever tested her. They'd been friends since the first grade. Emma knew there was a time when they hadn't been, but she couldn't honestly remember it.

Emma didn't always understand what Allison saw in her, because Emma was none of those things, even when she tried. "Do you want me to go?"

"Not if you don't want." Which wasn't a no.

"I'll go. Friday when?"

"I don't think it matters."

Emma laughed.

There was a substitute teacher alert, which passed by Emma while she was pulling textbooks from her locker. Why they had to have textbooks, instead of e-texts, Emma didn't know.

She dropped one an inch to the left of her foot but managed to catch the messenger, Philipa, by the shoulder. "Substitute teacher? Which class?"

"Twelve math."

"Ugh. Did you tell Michael?"

"I couldn't find him. You want to check on him on the way to English?"

Emma nodded. "Who's the teacher, did you catch the name?"

"Ms. Hampton, I think. Or Hampstead. Something like that." Philipa cringed at the look on Emma's face. "Sorry, I tried, but it wasn't clearer."

"Never mind; good enough." It wasn't, but it would have to do. Emma scooped up the offending book and headed down the hall and to the left, where the lockers disappeared from walls in favor of the usual corkboards and glass cabinets. She narrowly avoided dropping the books again when she ran into another student.

Eric.

"Hey," he said, as she stepped to one side of him and started to walk again.

"Can't talk now," she replied, without looking back. Had she had the time, she would have admitted that she didn't particularly *want* to talk to him, because he reminded her of the graveyard, and she didn't want to think about that right now. Or ever.

He fell in beside her. "Where are you headed?"

"Mr. Burke's math class."

"That's a twelve, isn't it?"

She nodded. "But Michael's in that one. I need to reach him before the teacher does, or at least as soon as possible."

"Why?"

"Because," she said, cursing silently, "Mr. Burke is not actually teaching the class today."

"Who is?"

"A substitute teacher. Ms. Hampton or Ms. Hampstead." She reached the math twelve door and peered through the glass. Michael was standing beside a desk that already contained another student. It was, unfortunately, the desk that Michael always sat at, and Emma could tell the student—Nick something-or-other—knew this and had no intention of moving. Grinding her teeth, Emma pushed the door open.

Michael was not—yet—upset.

Emma reached his side, handed him her pack, and then dropped a book on Nick's head.

"What the fuck—"

"Get your butt out of the chair or I'll upend the desk on you," Emma said tersely. She would have asked politely if she'd had more time. Or if she felt like it, and honestly? At this moment she *so* did not feel polite.

He opened his mouth to say something and then stopped. Eric had joined Emma. He hadn't said a word, and from a brief glance at his face, he didn't look particularly threatening, but Nick shoved the chair back from the desk and rose. He added a few single and double syllable words as he did.

"Michael," Emma said, ignoring Nick as she pushed the chair back in a bit, "Mr. Burke's not here today. He's ill. Ms. Hampton or Ms. Hampstead—I didn't hear her name clearly, but it's only one person—will be teaching the class today. I don't know if she has Mr. Burke's notes, so she might not be covering the same material."

"What type of illness?"

"I'm sorry, I didn't ask."

Michael nodded. Emma was very afraid that he was going to ask her what Ms. Hampton or Ms. Hampstead actually looked like. "You shouldn't have dropped the book on Nick's head," he said instead.

Emma said, "If it were up to me, I wouldn't have." She did not add, *I would have slugged him across his big, smug face*, because when Michael gave a lecture, it generally lasted a while, and it was hard to interrupt him. "I was in a hurry, and the book slipped. I've dropped it once today already."

Michael nodded, because he could parse the words and they made sense. As a general rule, Emma did not go around the school dropping books on people's heads.

"I'll see you at lunch?"

He nodded, and she said, "The substitute teacher probably doesn't understand everything about you."

"No one understands everything about anyone, Emma."

"No, but she probably understands much less than Mr. Burke. If she does the wrong things, remember that. She doesn't know any better. She hasn't had time to learn."

He nodded again and sat down, putting his own textbook on the table and arranging his laptop with care so it was in the exact center of the desk. She left him to it, because it could take him ten minutes.

Eric followed her out. He hadn't said a word.

"What was all that about?"

"Michael's a high-functioning autistic," she replied. She had slowed down slightly, and while she didn't have the time to have this conversation unless she wanted to add to her late-slip collection, she felt that she owed it to him. "I've known him since kindergarten. He does really, really well here," she added, half defensively, "and he hasn't needed a permanent Ed. Aide since junior high. But he's very particular about his routine, and he doesn't react well to unexpected changes."

"And the person you dropped the book on?"

"He's an asshole."

"You go around dropping books on every asshole in the school, you're not going to make many classes."

In spite of herself, Emma smiled. "Michael always sits at the same desk in any class he's taking. Everyone who's in his classes knows this. All the teachers too," she added. "But substitute teachers might not know. If Nick had stayed in that chair, Michael would have probably blown a fuse before the teacher showed up, and a strange teacher on top of that interruption—" she shook her head. "It would have been bad. And Nick knew it."

"And you really would have upended the desk on him?"

"I would have tried. Which, to be fair, would probably have upset Michael just as much. He's not a big fan of violence." She added, "Thanks."

"For what?"

"For coming in. I'm not sure Nick would have moved if you hadn't been there."

It was Eric's turn to shrug. "I didn't do anything."

"No. You didn't have to." She smiled ruefully. "I'm not always this . . . aggressive. Michael doesn't sit in on all of the normal classes. He has trouble with the less academic subjects, but he also hates English."

"Hates?"

"There's too much that's based on opinion, and he has to make too many choices. Nothing is concrete enough, and choice always causes him stress. You should have seen him in art classes. On the other hand," she added, as she stopped in front of a door, "*I'm* expected to attend all the regular classes."

"So am I," he told her, and he opened the door to the English class.

"Emma, are you okay?"

Emma blinked. Half of English had just passed her by. Normally, anything that made English go by faster was a good thing. But she'd missed the good thing—whatever it was—and was left looking at a clock that was twenty minutes ahead of where it was supposed to be.

"Emma?"

She turned to look at Allison, who was watching her with those slightly narrowed brown eyes, which her glasses made look enormous. "I'm fine."

Allison glanced at the computer on Emma's desk. The screen on which notes were in theory being typed was a lovely, blank white. "I'll e-mail you what you missed."

"Don't worry about it. I can read up on it." She put her fingers on the home row of her keyboard and listened to Ms. Evan's voice. It was, as always, strong, but some of the syllables and some of the words seemed to be running together in a blur of noise that was not entirely unlike buzzing. This, Emma thought, was why the word droning had been invented.

She tried to concentrate on the words, to separate them, to make enough sense of them that she could type something.

"Em?" Allison went from expressing minor concern to the depths of worry by losing a single syllable—but that was Allison; she never wasted words in a pinch.

Emma looked at her friend and saw that Allison was not, in fact, looking at her. She was looking at Emma's laptop screen. Drawn there by Ally's gaze, Emma looked at it as well. She lifted her hands off the keyboard as if it had burned her.

She had typed: **Oh my god Drew help me help me Drew fire god no**

Reaching out, she pushed the laptop screen down. "E-mail me your notes."

"Emma?" Allison was worried enough that she almost walked into the edge of a bank of lockers in the crowded between-classes hall.

Emma shook her head. "I'm—I'm fine." Nothing had happened in art, and nothing had happened in math; her computer hadn't suddenly sprouted new words that had nothing to do with either her class or her. But she felt cold.

"Emma?" Great. Stereo. She glanced up as Eric approached. "You okay?"

Closing her eyes, she took a deep breath, made sure she had her laptop, and made double sure it was closed. "Yeah. Allison," Emma said, "this is Eric. He helped me out when Nick was being a jerk in Michael's math class this morning. Eric, my best friend, Allison."

Allison smiled at Eric, but she would—he was new, and he'd helped Michael. Which, Emma had to admit, was part of the reason she found him less scary. She started to walk more quickly. "We've got to hurry," she told him. "We meet Michael for lunch."

The cafeteria, with its noise and its constant press of people, wasn't Michael's favorite room. It was also not a room in which a table could easily be marked out as his. The first day he'd come to Emery, Emma had found him loitering near the doors. He hadn't been waiting for her. He'd been walking in tight little circles.

Shouting in his ear when he was like that did nothing. Touching him, on the other hand, always got his attention; she'd put a hand very firmly on his shoulder, and when he said, "Oh, hi, Emma," she had steered him into the cafeteria. Philipa and Allison had pulled up the rear, and Amy had gone on ahead, clearing a path by simply, well, telling everyone to get out of the way. They had found a table with enough space, deposited Michael at one end, and had taken turns braving the lunch line.

The big advantage to having Amy as the unofficial spokesperson on that first day? It made clear that she, too, was watching out for Michael, and anyone who chose to pick on his strangeness was going to have social difficulties that lasted pretty much until they died, which would probably not be that far in the future. And it worked reasonably well, at least where the grade nines had been concerned.

It was harder to control the other grades, though, and they had made Michael's life a little less smooth.

After the first day, Allison and Emma explained that if Michael found a space at a table and sat there, they would get lunch and join him. He did that, although he always chose the empty table closest to the door.

Michael brought a bagged lunch from home. Given the food in the cafeteria, this was probably for the best. He would sometimes eat other food if it was offered to him, but he was—no surprise—enormously picky. He would also join in a conversation if the topic interested him. Given that it was the cafeteria that was seldom. But he had made a few more friends since ninth grade, and one of the things that fascinated him was *Dungeons and Dragons*. He also liked computers, computer games, and web comics, and by tenth grade, Oliver and Connell frequently took up spots beside or facing Michael.

This had continued into the eleventh grade, and a long and tortuous discussion—to those who were not interested in *D&D*—was well under way by the time Emma reached their table. She frowned because there was someone sitting beside Michael, and she didn't recognize the student. He wasn't in their year, but she knew most of the grade twelves on sight. Maybe he was new?

But he was sitting beside *Michael*, he was a total stranger, and Michael didn't even seem to be concerned. One glance at the table made clear he hadn't braved the cafeteria lines for what passed for food, either.

"Emma?" Allison asked. Emma stood holding her tray, and Allison shrugged and sat down.

She sat down on top of the stranger—and passed right through him.

For a moment the strange student and her best friend were superimposed over each other. Emma blinked rapidly as the lines of the stranger's face blended with Allison's, the cafeteria tray listing forward in her hands. Eric caught it before she lost her grip completely.

"Emma?"

She shook her head as the stranger stood. Allison's expression slowly untangled from his as he moved. His eyes widened as he met Emma's, and then he smiled and waved. She opened her mouth; he shook his head, and as she watched, he faded from sight.

# ✍ Chapter 3

Eric set Emma's rescued tray down across from Allison's and took a seat himself.

Emma stared at her food. There was no way she was now up to eating any of it.

"Em?"

She smiled across the table at Allison; it was a forced smile, and it obviously didn't make Ally feel any better. "I'm fine. Honest, I'm fine—I have a headache, that's all."

Michael turned to her. "You have a headache?"

This was not exactly what Emma needed. She could lie to Allison in a pinch. She could lie to Eric, because she didn't know him and didn't need a near stranger's obvious concern. Lying to Michael, however, was different. She could tell Eric—or Allison—that she had headaches all the time, and they'd pretend to believe her; Michael would call her on it, and if she argued, it would upset him because what he knew and what she was claiming was true weren't the same.

"I tripped when I was walking Petal last night. I hit my head on something."

Allison's brows rose, but she said nothing.

Michael, *Dungeons and Dragons* forgotten, frowned. To no one's surprise except Eric's, he began to question her about possible symptoms. Emma interrupted to ask what, exactly, these might be symptoms *of*, and he very seriously replied, "Concussion. I think you should go to the doctor, Emma."

Emma didn't particularly like visiting the doctor. Neither, if it came down to it, did Michael—but Michael persisted in being logical. And if you wanted him to persist in being calm, you had to toe the same logic line.

Rescue came from an unexpected quarter. "Hey, don't waste your time on Emma," said the clear and annoyingly perky voice of Deb McAllister, who, accompanied by Amy and Nan, had paused in her walk to the exit.

"Oh?" Eric asked, turning on the bench.

"She's not looking for anyone."

Eric glanced at Emma, who shrugged and nodded. "It's true. I'm not."

Eric returned the shrug. "Neither am I." He smiled politely at Deb and Nan, smiled in an entirely different way at Amy, and turned back to what was left of his lunch. He was not, unlike most of the guys, a fast eater.

"Too bad." Deb's voice was friendly. In fact, given Deb, she was probably trying to be helpful. In her own special way.

Nan smiled shyly and introduced herself to Eric, who—as if he were someone's grandfather and not their classmate—actually *got up* from the table to *shake her hand*. This caused a little ripple of silence, but it was a pleased silence. Nan was not, in the classical sense of the word, beautiful, but she had long, thick, straight black hair that was the envy of every girl in the school who wasn't Amy, and her eyes were a perfect brown in equally perfect skin. She could speak Mandarin, but she hated doing it unless she was with her cousins, five of whom attended Emery. Emma had asked her why once, and Nan had said, "I'm not someone's exotic pet seal. I don't want to bark on command."

And Amy?

"Eric, what are you doing Friday night?"

"Why?"

"I have a big—I mean *big*—open house planned at my place. Pretty much everyone in our year should be there, if you want to meet them all. I would have invited you by e-mail," she added, "but you're new enough here that I don't have yours yet.

"Are you coming, Emma?"

"Yeah."

"Good. Can you tell Eric where and when, and send me his e-mail address if he has one? I have to go to the yearbook committee meeting—I'm running late."

"Sure." She watched Amy head out the cafeteria doors and then said, "Pull your tongue back in. You're drooling."

Eric laughed. "That obvious?"

"Well, you're male. And at least you didn't try to eat and miss your mouth."

He laughed again.

"Don't laugh," she told him with a grimace. "I've seen it happen at least once every semester."

When history was over, school was done for the day. Emma went to her locker, deposited her textbooks, and then stood leaning against the narrow orange door.

"Emma?"

She looked up. Eric, pack hanging loosely from his left shoulder, was watching her.

"Are you feeling all right?"

"Yeah, I'm fine." She pulled herself off the locker door and grimaced. "I have a bit of a headache."

"Should you be walking?"

Emma shrugged. She slung her backpack over her right shoulder and started to head down the hall. "I'll be fine," she told him, when it became clear he was following her. "Allison will walk me home."

"Did your mother take you to a doctor?"

"I did not, and do not, have a concussion. I have a headache."

"Migraine?"

"Eric, look, you are not my mother, for which I'm grateful because I can barely handle the *one* I have now." She gritted her teeth and lifted a hand, palm out. "No, look, I'm sorry, I know that was unfair. I have a headache. I will walk home. I will sleep it off."

Eric lifted both his hands in surrender. If her waspish comment had bothered him at all, it didn't show, and if her head had not, in fact, been pounding at the temples, and if the light in the halls had not begun to actually hurt, she would have smiled.

"Tell you what. You can follow me at a discreet distance, and if I collapse, you can call my mother again. She might take a little longer to show up, though, because she's at work."

Allison was waiting for her on the wide, shallow steps from which less adventurous skateboarders leaped. The one thing Emma missed about winter was the lack of skateboards.

Allison bypassed the usual quiet and concerned questions she liked to open with and went straight to the single syllable. "Em?" She held out a hand, and Emma took it. Clearly, from the way Allison's expression changed, she had gripped it a little too hard.

"Sorry," Emma managed to say. "The light is killing my eyes, Ally. And the noise—it's making me dizzy. I feel like someone is stabbing the top of my spine with—with hot stabbing things. I think I'm going to throw up."

"Let me call your mom."

"Are you *kidding*? I'll throw up in the car, and you *know* who's going to have to clean it up later." Not that her mother wouldn't try. "Just help me get home." She paused and then managed to say, "Where's Michael?"

"He's talking to Oliver."

Going home from school had never been as stressful for Michael as getting there. Which made sense—going to a very strange place from a safe one was always worse. "Ask him if he needs us to wait for him?"

Allison nodded and then said, very softly, "You need to let go of my hand. Sit down on the steps so you don't fall over." She helped Emma lower herself to the steps and then hovered there for a minute.

Emma heard steps behind her. Actually, she heard steps in all directions, but the ones behind her were louder. Allison hadn't really moved, so they couldn't be hers.

"Emma," Eric said, speaking very, very quietly. "Let me take you home."

"I'm fine."

"No, you are not. I have a car," he added.

"You drive?"

"Depends on who you ask. I have a license, if that helps."

"No, look, I—"

"And if you throw up in the car, I can clean it up. Go ask Mike if she needs to wait," he added. Emma couldn't see Eric; at this point her eyes were closed, and her hands were covering them. But she could guess who he was talking to, and she did hear Allison's retreat.

"Don't call him that," she said.

"What?"

"Don't call him Mike. It's not his name, and he doesn't recognize it as his name." She wanted to weep with pain. She stopped talking.

"I'm driving you home," he said, in the same quiet voice.

She didn't have the energy to say no again. She did, apparently, have the energy to throw up.

The car was agony. Curled up in a fetal ball, Emma almost cried. Almost. She did throw up again, but Allison was in the backseat beside her, and she was holding something in front of Emma's face. Eric was either the world's worst driver, or *any* motion caused waves of nausea.

She tried to say Michael's name, but it really did not come out well. Mostly, it was whimpering, and Emma decided not to talk.

"Michael's here," Allison said quietly. "He's in the front seat with Eric." Allison's hand was cool when it touched Emma's forehead. She wanted to lean into it.

"Make it stop," she whispered, to no one. Or to everyone. "Please, make it stop."

And she heard Eric's voice, cool and quiet, drop into the noise that was so loud it should have been making her ears bleed. "It will, Emma. I'm sorry."

Eric had lied. He didn't drive her home.

Emma survived the painful and endless stops and starts that were Eric's driving, and she must have arrived in one piece, because she felt the agonizing crack of a car door opening, felt the change of light as she left the car, her eyes clamped shut. Eric lifted her; it must have been Eric. Allison and Michael wouldn't have been able to carry her that far between the two of them.

But he didn't take her up the familiar walk to her home; he didn't take her to where Petal would be barking or whining. Instead, he carried her up a different stretch of road into a familiar building: the hospital and its emergency waiting room.

She could hear the short, harsh stabs of conversation that passed between Allison and the person at admitting. She couldn't see the person, but the voice registered as female, crashing in, as it did, on all the other unfamiliar voices that were screaming—literally—for attention.

She wanted to pass out because, if she did, she would be beyond them. But she didn't, because that would have been a mercy. Instead, she heard Michael's clear voice answering questions. She couldn't hear the questions nearly as clearly, but it didn't matter; Michael had come for a reason, and he would make himself heard. Even if, in fact, the questioner had no desire to hear any more. You had to love that about Michael, because if you didn't, you'd strangle him.

She shifted, attempted to sit up, and ended up curled forward in a chair, trying desperately not to throw up for a third time. At some point, she felt familiar arms around her shoulders and back, and she knew that her mother had been called and had somehow arrived.

She tried to apologize to her mother, failed, and also gave up on not throwing up. Because her mother was there. There was something about being sick that made it so easy to turn your whole life over to your mother. Even when her father had been there, it was her mother who had spent hours by the sickbed, and her mother who had cleaned her up, made sure she drank, and monitored her temperature.

It was her mother who was here now, losing work hours and work time. Emma tried to sit up again, tried to open her eyes, tried to tell her mother she was, as always, fine. Even if it was a lie. Some lies, you could *make* true, if you said them enough.

But she couldn't say them, now.

She tried. She tried to make them loud enough to drown out all the other sounds, all the other words. She felt a hand in hers and couldn't tell whose it was. She wanted to grip it tightly, but even that movement made her wrist ache, made the skin of her arm shriek in protest.

She wanted it to stop. She didn't care if she died; it would be better than this. Better. Than. This.

It wasn't the first time in her life that she'd wanted something to stop this badly. But that time? The pain had been different. She wanted to weep. But it was as if old pain and new pain combined by some strange alchemy to allow her to remember, to allow the images a lucidity and clarity that the pain denied everything else.

Nathan's funeral. Nathan's death.

She could remember standing and watching by the side of an open grave. She had thought to help, to dig at the earth with a shovel, to roll up her sleeves—or not—to stand in the dirt as it yielded, inch by inch, becoming at last a resting place, a final stop. But there were no shovels. When she'd arrived there, no shovels. Umbrellas, yes, because the sky was cloudy and overcast, but the umbrellas had yet to be wielded; they were bound tightly, unopened, waiting for rain. Instead, there was a hole, beside which a tall mound of dirt had been heaped over a large tarpaulin. And beside that, in a bag—a *bag*—a small container, a nondescript wooden one.

Her mother had said she didn't have to go to see the ashes interred. As if. Nathan's mother, eyes red and swollen with weeping, voice raw, had turned to her, hugged her, hanging on for a second to the only other female in the cemetery who had loved Nathan so much. That was why she'd come. That. To stand, to be hugged, to acknowledge a loss that was different from, and almost as great, as her own.

Emma did not weep. Emma did not wail or speak; she had been invited to say something at the funeral service, and she had stared, mute, at the phone while Nathan's father waited for a reply that would never come. Emma had never been a drama queen. Why? Because she had cared what other people thought. Of her. That caring, it was like a fragile, little shield against the world; things broke through it all the time. Things hurt.

But not like this. The shield was gone; shattered or discarded, it didn't matter.

Watching. Distant. Seeing the truth of headstones. No name of hers engraved in rock. Dates, yes. Birth. Death. Nothing at all of the in-between. Nothing about love. Nothing about quiet spaces. Nothing about who he was, who he'd been. Because it didn't matter. None of it mattered anymore to anyone but Emma. Emma and Nathan's mother.

She had wanted to die. She had wanted to *die*. Because then it would be over. All the loss, all the grief, all the pain, the emptiness—over. And she had said nothing, then. Nothing. Nor had she crawled into her room and swallowed her mother's pills, or crawled into her bath and opened up her own wrists. As if death were somehow personal, as if death were somehow an enemy that could be faced and stared down, she would not give it the satisfaction of seeing how badly it had hurt her. Again.

She wanted to scream. She opened her mouth.

She felt the movement, felt the stabbing pain of it, felt the press of sound against her skull, as if her fontanels had never closed, and her head could be crushed by carelessness, not malice.

And then, suddenly, all the sound and all the pain seemed to condense into one point, one bright point, just outside of her body. She felt, for a moment, that she was falling, that the only thing holding her up had been sensation. A cool—a cold—breeze touched her forehead, like soft, steady fingers gently pushing hair out of her eyes.

*Sprout, Sprout, you shouldn't be here.*

She felt the pain condense, all sound becoming a single point that fled the whole of her, and she was suddenly sitting up, her body light with the lack of pain.

"Dad?"

*Em,* he said.

She opened her eyes. The room wasn't dark; it was fluorescent with light and half full of people in various states of health. She could see Michael sitting beside Allison, could see Allison beside her mother. She could see other people, strangers, sometimes sitting beside people and sometimes entirely alone. And, in the light of the emergency admitting room, she could also see her father.

She stood, freeing her hands.

"Dad."

He turned to face her. *Em,* he said again, and then his gaze drifted away from her face and fell, slowly, to her mother's. Her mother's worried face, her mother's pained expression. Emma started to say something and then stopped. Her mother was trying not to cry.

"She can't see you, can she?"

*No.*

"Dad . . ."

Her father's eyes were faintly luminescent; they *were* his eyes, but they were subtly wrong. He watched his wife. Emma turned again to look at her mother. To see that her mother's hands were *holding her daughter's,* even though Emma was now standing five feet away from the chair into which she'd curled. She tried to look at herself, at the her that her mother was still holding onto so tightly. She couldn't. She could see a vague, blurry outline that might, or not might not, be Emma-shaped.

It was very, very unsettling.

"She can't see me right now either, can she?"

*No, Em.* He looked back to his daughter, his expression grave. *You shouldn't be here, Sprout.*

"No. I shouldn't. Does this mean I'm . . . dead?"

His smile was quiet, weary; he had some of Mercy Hall's worry embedded in his expression. *No.*

"Does this mean I'm going to *be* dead soon?"

*No.*

"Dad—what's happening to me?"

Her father turned to look at Eric, who was standing very quietly in the center of the room.

Eric, arms folded across his chest, looked at Brendan Hall. At him, not through him. Emma glanced at her other friends. They were still sitting beside her mother, or each other; none of them had noticed the standing-Emma.

But Eric, clearly, did. He was, Emma realized with a bit of surprise, taller than her father, and he had lost the friendly, easygoing smile she associated with his face. His hair looked darker, the brown of his eyes almost the same color as his pupils.

*Tell her.*

"Tell me what? Eric?"

Eric met her gaze, held it a moment, and then looked away.

"Eric, I don't mean to be a bitch, but you know, if I wind up being one, I think I'm entitled. What the hell is going on?"

He said nothing, and she walked toward him, trying not to ball her hands into fists. When she was three feet away from him, she stopped. "Eric," she said, her voice lower. "Please. Tell me what's happening to me because I cannot spend every day from now until I die doing this."

He closed his eyes, but when he spoke, it wasn't to Emma. It was to her father.

"You're the one who shouldn't be here," he said quietly.

Her father said nothing.

"It's not too late," Eric continued, his voice lower than Emma's had been, the words quietly intense. "She's standing on the edge. She doesn't have to fall over it."

*She can't continue like this,* her father said at last. *Do me the favor of allowing me to know my own daughter.*

"I do. I am."

Emma thought her father would say nothing; he had that expression. She'd seen it often enough to know it, because he used to wear it when he argued with her. And when he argued with her mother. But he surprised her. *I couldn't stand back and do nothing. She can't survive hearing all of the—*

"She can," Eric said. "She only has to do it for three days. Maybe you don't understand what her life will be like," he added. "Maybe you're as shortsighted as she is and you can only see the now. But you're doing her no kindness. You shouldn't be here."

Her father nodded, slowly. He took a step back, and Emma shouted, wordless, and ran past Eric.

Eric called her name, and she felt it like a blow; it slowed her, and it hurt her, but neither of these was enough. Her father was there, and somehow, somehow he understood what she was going through and had tried to spare her some of the pain.

And she wanted that.

She wasn't willing to let him go. And he was going to leave; she saw that too. *No. No.* She'd done that. She'd done that once. She saw her father's eyes widen as she ran toward him, and she saw him lift his hands, palms out, telling her, wordlessly, to stop. She slowed, but again, not enough.

"Dad—"

*Emma, don't—*

She reached out and grabbed the hands he had put up to fend her off. His hands were cold. His eyes widened, rounding; the light that burned so strangely in them dimmed.

And she heard, from right beside her, and at the exact same second, from behind her, her mother's single shocked word.

"Brendan!"

## ᗡ **Chapter 4**

Everything happened slowly, and everything happened at once; it was as if Emma were two people, or two halves of one person. The one, sitting beside her mother, holding her mother's hands, heard her mother's sudden shift in breath: the sharpness of it, the strange fear and hope.

The other half, holding her father's cold hands, turned to look at her mother and realized that her mother could suddenly see her father. Could see Brendan Hall. She could see the color ebb from her mother's face, because fear had always done that to her.

She could see Allison stand, could see her mouth the words, "Mr. Hall?" although no sound came out. And she could see Michael. Michael's gaze, on her father's face, was unreadable. It always was when he was processing information that he hadn't expected and wasn't certain how to deal with.

He lived in a rational universe. He had to. All the irrational, unpredictable things made no sense to him, and, worse, they were threatening *because* they made no sense. Things that could be explained, in however much exhaustive detail he demanded—and he could demand quite a lot—were not things he had to fear.

But things like . . . Emma's dead father . . . How could she explain something like that to Michael? When she didn't understand it herself?

She said, felt herself say, "Michael, he's still my father. He's the same person he was. He's not dangerous."

But Michael didn't appear to hear her. He probably had; it had taken him years to learn to look at people when they talked. She remembered—and what a stupid thing to remember now, of all times—telling him that he had to look at people when they spoke so they knew he was listening. And she remembered the way he had looked at her, his expression serious, and what he'd said.

"Emma, I don't hear with my eyes."

"Well, no. No one does."

"Then why do I have to look at people so they'll know I'm listening?"

She wasn't always very patient, and it had taken her three days to come up with a better phrasing. "So that they'll know you're paying attention." She'd been so proud of herself for that one, because it had worked.

"Brendan?" her mother whispered.

Her father—the expression on his face one that Emma would never forget, said, "Mercy." Just that.

She wanted to let go of her mother's hands. She couldn't.

Instead, watching Michael, she let go of her father's.

The room collapsed; the lights went out. Emma felt a sudden, sharp tug, as if she'd been floating and gravity had finally deigned to notice her. She fell, screaming in silence, to earth—but earth, in this case, was a lot like cheap vinyl, and it didn't hurt when she hit it. Much.

She opened her eyes, blinking in the harsh fluorescent lights of the emergency waiting room. Lack of feet caused a moment's panic before she realized they were curled beneath her. She looked to her side and saw her mother's profile, her slightly open jaw, her wide eyes circled by dark lack of sleep.

"Mom," she croaked. "My hands." Her fingers were tingling in that pins-and-needles way, and they looked gray. Or blue.

Her mother shook her head; Emma's voice had pulled her back. "Oh, Em, I'm sorry," she said. It was pretty clear she had to work to free her hands, or to free her daughter's. Their hands shook, but Emma curled hers in her lap; her mother lifted hers to her face, and very slowly let her head drop into them.

"Mom—"

Mercy Hall shook her head. "I'm sorry, Em—I'm—I've had a long day."

Emma looked away from her mother. "Michael?" she said, slowly and distinctly. Michael didn't appear to hear her. He was staring straight ahead. "Allison?"

Allison, on the other hand, turned to meet Emma's gaze.

Emma gestured in Michael's direction, and after a second, Allison took a deep breath and nodded. She turned and walked over to Michael, calling his name. Michael was still staring. When Allison stepped in front of him, he didn't stop; what he was seeing, Emma could only guess.

Allison knelt in front of Michael and picked up his hands, one in each of hers. "Michael," she said again, voice softer.

He blinked, and his gaze slowly shifted in place, until he could see Allison. He was rigid. But he was quiet. Emma wished it didn't resemble the quiet of a rabbit caught in headlights quite so much. He blinked.

Emma slowly pulled her feet out from under her. They were tingling as well, and she grimaced as she flattened them against the floor. But she tried to stand, and as she did, Eric moved. She had almost forgotten him, which was stupid.

He crossed the room and offered her his hand; she stared at his palm until he withdrew it. He was silent. She was silent as well, but her look said, *We're going to talk about this later.*

His said nothing, loudly.

She walked over to Allison and Michael, and stood beside Allison; she would have crouched beside her, but she didn't trust her knees or her feet yet. "Michael?"

He looked up. He was still seated, and that was probably for the best. "Emma," he said. She smiled, and not because she was happy. It was meant to reassure.

"I'm here," she told him, while Allison continued to hold his hands.

"Emma, that was your dad." It wasn't a question.

Had he been anyone else, she would have lied, and it would have come cleanly and naturally. Lies were something you told other people to make things easier, somehow—hopefully, for them, but often more selfishly for yourself. Lies, Emma realized, as her glance flicked briefly to her mother and back, were things you told yourself when your entire world was turned on its end for just a moment, and you needed to put it right side up again.

But Michael? Michael hadn't even understood what a lie was supposed to do until he'd been nine years old. He hadn't understood that what he knew and what other people knew were not, in fact, the exact same thing. Emma didn't remember a time when she didn't understand that. And she wasn't certain why, at nine, Michael began to learn. But he had; he just didn't bother lying because he could see the advantage of honesty and of being known for it.

Not lying, however, and not being lied to were different. Emma could have lied, but that—that would have pushed him over the edge he was clearly teetering on. Because he knew what he'd seen, and nothing she could say was going to change that.

She took a breath, steadied herself. "Yes," she told him quietly, just as Eric said, "No."

Allison turned to stare at Eric. She rose, still holding Michael's hands. She passed them to Emma, who could now feel her feet properly. Michael looked at Eric and at Emma, and Emma said, quickly, "Eric doesn't know, Michael. Remember, he never met my father. He's new here."

Eric opened his mouth to say something, and Allison stepped, very firmly, on his foot. She didn't kick him, which Emma would have done. Allison hated to hurt anyone.

Michael, however, was nodding. It went on too long. Emma freed one of her hands and very gently stroked the back of Michael's hand until he stopped.

"He's dead, Emma."

"Yes."

"He used to fix my bike."

"Yes."

"Why was he here?"

She started to say *I don't know*, because it was true. But she stopped herself from doing that as well. Things were always more complicated when Michael was around. But they were cleaner, too. "He was trying to help me," she said, instead.

"How?"

"I think he knows what's causing the—the headaches."

"It's not a concussion?"

"No."

"Oh." Pause. "Where did he go?"

"I don't know."

"Will he come back?"

"I don't know, Michael. But I hope so."

"Why?"

"Because I miss him," she said softly.

Michael nodded again, but this time, it was a normal nod. "I miss him, too. Was he a ghost?"

"I don't think ghosts exist."

"But I saw him."

She nodded. "I saw him, too. But I don't know what he was."

"He looked the same," Michael told her. "And you said he was the same."

She had said that. She remembered. "I think ghosts are supposed to be scary," she offered. "I think that's why I don't think he's a ghost. Was he scary?"

"No. Well, yes. A little."

Emma could accept that.

"He doesn't want to take you away?" Michael continued. "You aren't going to die, are you?"

"Everyone dies," she told him.

"But not now."

"No, Michael," she managed to say. "He doesn't want to take me away. And even if he did, I'm not leaving." She knew, suddenly, where this would go, and she *did not* want to go there.

Michael closed his eyes. Emma braced herself as Michael opened them again and asked, "Will Nathan come back, too?"

And, after a moment, Emma managed to say, "I don't know."

Emma knew her mother was upset. But upset or not, Mercy Hall insisted on waiting for a CAT scan. Emma told Allison she should go home with Eric and Michael, but that fell flat as well. They huddled together in silence. Emma's mother said almost nothing to anyone who wasn't a doctor, and Michael sat quietly, thinking Michael thoughts. Allison was worried, but she didn't say much, either; it was hard to find a place to put words in all the different silences in that waiting room.

The CAT scan was a four-hour wait. The results, they were told, would be sent to the Hall family doctor, which meant, as far as Emma was concerned, that they hadn't found anything that constituted an emergency. To confirm this, the doctor filled out discharge papers, or whatever they were called, gave Emma's mother a prescription for Tylenol, but stronger, and also gave her advice on headaches. Emma was tired, and her body still felt strangely light, as if part of her had gone missing. But she was no longer in any pain.

Not physical pain.

Eric said nothing. He waited. When Emma's tests were done, he offered Allison and Michael a ride home. Emma would have preferred to have their company, but it was clear that her mother wouldn't. Michael and Allison went home with Eric.

Emma went home with her mother in a car that was as silent as the grave. It was worse than awkward. It was painful. Mercy kept her eyes on the road, her hands on the steering wheel, and her words behind her lips, which were closed. Her expression was remote; the usual frantic worry about work and her daughter's school were completely invisible.

Emma, who often found her mother's prying questions difficult, would have welcomed them tonight, and because the universe was perverse, she didn't get them. She got, instead, a woman who had seen her dead husband, and had no way of speaking about what it meant. Possibly no desire to know what it meant; it was hard to tell.

When they got home, it was 8:36.

Petal greeted them at the door with his happy-but-reproachful barking whine.

"Sorry, Petal," Emma said, grabbing his neck and crouching to hug him. She knew this would get her a face full of dog-breath, but didn't, at the moment, care.

Emma's mother went to the kitchen, and Emma, dropping her school backpack by the front door, followed, Petal in tow. They briefly, and silently, held council over the contents of the fridge, which had enough food to feed two people if you wanted to eat condiments and slightly moldy cheese. There were milk and eggs, which Emma looked at doubtfully; her mother often stopped by the grocery store on the way home from work.

Today, she had stopped by the hospital instead.

"Pizza?" Emma asked.

Her mother lifted the receiver off the cradle and handed it to her daughter. "Pizza," she said, and headed out of the kitchen. It was a damn quiet kitchen in her absence, but Emma dialed and hit the button that meant "same order as previous order." Then she hung up and stared at her dog. Her dog, the gray hairs on his muzzle clearer in the kitchen light than they were in the light cast by streetlamps, stared at her, his stub wagging.

She apologized again, which he probably thought meant "I'll feed you now." On the other hand, she did empty a can of moist food into his food dish, and she did fill his water bowl. She also took him out to the yard for a bit; she hadn't walked him at all today, but she knew that tonight was *so* not the night to do it. From the backyard, she could see the light in her mother's bedroom window; she could also see her mother's silhouette against the curtains. Mercy was standing, just standing, in the room.

Emma wondered, briefly, if she was watching her or if she was watching Petal. She kind of doubted either.

When Emma was stressed, she often tidied, and god knew the kitchen could use it. She busied herself putting away the dishes whose second home was the drying rack on the counter. She had homework, but most of it was reading, and like procrastinators everywhere, she knew that tidying still counted as work, so she could both fail to do homework and feel that she'd accomplished something.

But when the doorbell rang, Mercy came down the stairs to answer, and she paid for the pizza and carried it into the kitchen. She looked tired but slightly determined, and she had that smile on her face. "I'm sorry, Em," she said. "I'm not sure what got into me there. Things are stressful at work."

Emma accepted this. She usually asked what was causing the stress, but she didn't actually enjoy listening to her mother lie, so she kept the question to herself and nodded instead. She also got plates, napkins and cups, because her mother didn't like drinking out of cans.

They took these to the living room, while Petal walked between them. The pizza box was suspended in the air above him, of course. He was too well trained to try to eat from the box when they put it down on the table in the den. He was not, however, too well trained to sit in front of it and beg, and he had the usual moist puppy eyes, even at the age of nine.

Emma fed him her crusts.

He jumped up on the couch beside her and wedged himself between the armrest and her arm, which meant, really, between the armrest and half her lap; she had to eat over his head.

Her mother didn't like to eat while the television was on, but even she could take only so much awkward silence before she surrendered and picked up the remote. They channel surfed their way through dinner.

Eric stood in the graveyard, beneath the same dark willow that he'd leaned against for half of the previous night. He carried no obvious weapons, and he hadn't bothered to wear any of the less obvious protections because he didn't expect to need them. He wanted to need them. He wanted to need them right now, in this place, but what he wanted didn't matter; almost never had.

The graveyard was silent. The distant sound of cars didn't change that; they blurred into the background. His night vision was good; it had always been good. But he stared at nothing for long stretches. Once or twice he turned and punched the tree to bleed off his growing frustration.

*Not Emma*, he thought bitterly.

*Emma.*

He tensed.

*I have never been mistaken before. I am not mistaken now.* She approached, emerging from a forest of headstones.

*She is powerful, Eric.*

"You've got to be wrong," he told her, grim and quiet. He expected an argument, was surprised when it failed to come.

*I will . . . leave it up to you*, she said at last. *I will not call the others yet.*

"Why?"

*Because she* is *different, to my eyes, and I have reasons to doubt that feeling. You know why.*

Eric swallowed and turned his attention back to a graveyard that remained empty for the rest of the night.

# ⌐ Chapter 5

Emma woke up on Friday morning, which had the advantage of being formal day at school. This meant, among other things, that she didn't really have to work out what she was going to wear; she was going to wear a plaid skirt, a blazer, and a white shirt. Ties were optional if you weren't male, although most of the girls wore the non-stupid thin leather ones. They often wore makeup on Fridays as well, because, face it, there weren't too many other things you could wear to set yourself apart.

Emma, for instance, didn't wear earrings. Watching a toddler grab a dangling hoop and rip through the earlobe—literally—of a friend in grade seven had cured her of the growing desire to ever have her ears pierced. Admittedly, this was viewed as a bit strange, but they were her ears, and she wanted to keep them attached to the rest of her face.

She did spend more time in the bathroom on Fridays, which was worked into what passed for an early morning schedule in the Hall household, partly because her mother did everything she could to stay in bed until the last minute.

Emma finished dressing and went downstairs. She expected the kitchen to be quiet, and it was; Petal was hyper but not yappy. Her mother was not yet in the kitchen. Emma glanced at the clock and winced. She put the coffee on, because if her mother was still not here, she was going to need it, and she took milk, blueberries and cereal to the table, which she also set.

She stopped on the way to get napkins and hollered up the steps, waited for five seconds to hear something like a reply, failed to hear the wrong words—of which there were several—and continued on her way. When her mother came thundering down the stairs in a rush, she handed her mother the coffee and ushered her to a chair. This would have been awkward had Mercy actually been awake.

Then again, given the last few days? Being awake was highly overrated. They ate in relative silence, because Petal had emptied the dry food dish and was trying to mooch. He didn't actually like any of the food his two keepers were eating this morning, but that never stopped him.

Emma, who had marshaled her arguments, waited, with fading patience, for her mother to tell her that she was not going to school today. When it was dangerously close to 8:00, she gave up on that, and instead said, "Don't forget, I'm going to Amy's party tonight."

"Amy's? Oh, that's right. You mentioned it yesterday. You're going straight from school?"

"What, dressed like this?"

Mercy seemed to focus for a minute. "You look fine to me," she said, but it was noise; Emma would have bet money that she hadn't actually noticed what her daughter was wearing. "Are you going to be home for dinner?"

"Why, are you working late?"

Mercy nodded slowly.

"I'll grab a sandwich or something if you're not here." Emma pushed her chair back from the table and gathered up her empty dishes. "I won't be too late," she added.

"When is not too late?"

Emma shrugged. "Midnightish. Maybe 1:00." She waited for any questions, any comments. "Mom?"

Her mother looked up.

"Are you feeling all right?"

"I'm fine," her mother replied. Emma thought dying people probably sounded more convincing. They certainly did on television.

"You're sure?"

Mercy looked at her daughter and shook her head. "Of course I'm sure. I'm always fine the morning after I've seen my dead husband in a hospital."

The silence that followed was profoundly awkward. It was worse than first-kiss awkward. "Mom—"

Her mother lifted a hand. It should have been a familiar gesture; Emma used it all the time. But coming from her mom, it looked wrong. "You can mother Michael," Mercy Hall said firmly, and with a trace of annoyance, "and any of the rest of your friends. I already have a mother, three bosses, and any number of other helpful advice-givers in the office. I don't need mothering."

Emma, stung, managed to stop herself from saying something she'd probably only feel guilty about later. Guilt, in the Hall household, was like the second child of the family. The secret one that you tried to lock in the attic when respectable people were visiting.

Instead, she turned and walked into the hall, where she gave herself the once over in the mirror, frowned at both her eyes and her lips, which were slowly returning to normal, and then picked up her backpack to wait.

Michael rescued her at 8:10.

The walk to school would have been the same type of awkward that breakfast had been, but it was made easier by Michael, because Michael didn't worry that someone would think he was crazy. Michael, by dint of understanding his own condition, also understood that he saw the world in entirely different ways than the rest of the students in his grade did; he was used to this. Because he was, he didn't really question what he saw, and he didn't second-guess himself; he second-guessed (and third, fourth, and fifth for good measure) everyone else.

So he asked Allison if she'd seen Mr. Hall, as they all still called Emma's dad, and when Allison reluctantly admitted that she had, he was silent for a half a block.

When Michael was silent, it didn't mean anything in particular. It didn't mean that he was trying desperately to think of something to say, and it didn't mean that he was worrying about what you might say behind his back, because for the most part, he didn't worry about that kind of thing. It didn't mean he was really thinking about the last thing he'd asked about either, because he could slide into a segue so quickly you had to wonder if you'd heard the first part of what he said correctly.

But for the first time in years, Emma privately wished that she didn't have the responsibility of walking him to school, because she didn't want him to pick up the conversation from where it had left off last night. Guilt came and bit her on the backside; clearly, she hadn't left it in the attic this morning.

"Do you think Eric saw him?"

Since this was so much better than the question she'd been dreading, Emma pounced on it. "I'm sure Eric saw him."

"Oh. Why?"

"Everyone else did. Probably," she added, "everyone in the waiting room. Most of them wouldn't notice or care."

"Until he disappeared?"

"Until then, yes." She shrugged and added, "but they probably wouldn't really notice that either unless they were staring right at him. People in emergency rooms are usually thinking about other things."

Michael nodded. "But Eric?"

"Eric saw him."

"He's worried about you, Emma," Michael told her.

Allison winced.

"Oh. Why? Did he say something in the car last night?"

"Yes."

"What?"

"That he was worried about you."

Of course. This was Michael. "Did you ask why?"

"No." He stared at her for a minute and then added, "Your father is dead. And he came to the hospital. I think most people would be worried about that."

"I'll talk to Eric," she said, with feeling. She turned to Allison and added, "Did he say anything else?"

"Not very much," Allison offered. "It was a pretty quiet car ride."

\*　　\*　　\*

Emma skipped English that morning. Eric also skipped English that morning. It wasn't a coincidence; she collared Eric before he entered the class. The way she said "Can I talk to you for a minute?" would have made teachers throughout her history proud.

Eric, to give him credit, didn't even try to avoid her. He met her eyes, nodded without hesitation, and took his hand off the doorknob. "Here, or off-site someplace?"

Off-site sounded better, but it made the chance that they'd be attending any of the rest of the morning classes a lot slimmer. Given everything, Emma reconciled herself to absence slips and parental questions and said, "Let's go somewhere where we won't be interrupted." She grimaced and added, "And if I collapse again, just drive me home."

They went to a very quiet cafe around the corner. Where around the corner meant about ten blocks away. Emma chose it out of habit, but at this time of day, almost nothing was crowded.

She took a seat by the window; a booth was at her back. Eric sat opposite her. They waited until someone came to take their order; Emma ordered a cafe au lait and a blueberry scone; Eric ordered black coffee and nothing. He glanced out the window, or perhaps at Emma's reflection; it was hard to tell. His normal, friendly expression was completely absent. It made his face look more angular, somehow, and also older. His eyes were clear enough that she couldn't quite say what color they were, although she had thought them brown until now.

When their order had come and the waitress had disappeared, Emma cupped her bowl in both hands and looked across the table. She took a deep breath. "Eric," she said softly.

He was watching her. His hands were on the table, on either side of his coffee cup, and she noticed for the first time how callused they were, and how dark compared to the rest of his skin. He wore a ring, a simple gold band that she hadn't really seen before. It looked . . . like a wedding ring.

"What happened last night?" she asked when it became clear that he was waiting for her. Waiting, she thought, and judging. She didn't much care for the latter.

"What do you think happened last night?"

*If I knew, I wouldn't be asking.* She forced the words to stay put, but it was hard. Instead, taking a deep breath, she said, "Something happened the other night in the graveyard. You were there."

He said nothing.

"I don't know if you saw—saw what I saw." She hesitated, because it still made her queasy. "I thought you couldn't have. Now I think you must have and that you understood it."

"Go on."

"But I don't. I know that I saw my father last night." She took another, deeper breath. "And there were two of me. You saw both. No one else in that room did. But when I touched my father, everyone saw him." She added, "And he was cold." She wasn't sure why she'd said it, but she couldn't claw the words back. "The headache has nothing to do with my falling."

"You're sure?"

"No. But you are."

He picked up the coffee cup as if it were a shield. And then, over the steam rising from it, he met her eyes. "Yeah," he said, not drinking. "I am." He turned just his head, and looked outside. Emma watched his face in the window. "Why were you in the graveyard, Emma?"

It was her turn to look out the window, although it wasn't much protection; their gazes met in reflections, both of them transparent against the cars parked on the curb outside. "It's quiet there," she said at last.

"Don't ask me questions," he replied, "until you're ready to answer them."

"I'm ready to answer them," she said, more forcefully. "I'm not willing to share the answers because they are none of your goddamn—" She bit her lip.

He shrugged. "No, they're not. They're not my business."

"But this is my business."

"No, Emma. It's not. I'm trying to spare you—"

"Oh, please."

His jaws snapped shut, and his eyes—if she hadn't been so angry, so surprisingly, unexpectedly angry, she would have looked away. But really? She had been so many things since Nathan had died. Self-absorbed. Even self-pitying. Desolate. Lonely. But furious? No. And right this second, she wanted to reach across the table and slap him. Emma had never slapped anyone in her life.

She swallowed. She picked up her bowl. Held it, to steady her hands, to keep them from forming fists. He sat there and watched.

"I was at the graveyard," she said, words clipped so sharply they had edges, "to visit Nathan's grave."

"A friend?"

She laughed. It was an eruption of sound, and it was all the wrong sound. "Yeah," she said bitterly. "A friend."

He put his own cup down and laid his hands flat against the table. "This . . . is not going well. Can we start again from the beginning?"

She shrugged. She could carry any conversation; it was a skill, like math, that she had learned over the years. Sometimes she tried to teach Michael. But it was gone. Whatever it was that had made her carry pointless conversation, underpinning it with a smile and an attentive expression, had deserted her.

She tried to make herself smile. She could manage to make herself talk. "We can try."

"I'm sorry. I didn't mean—"

"It doesn't matter. If I talk about it, if I don't. If I cry or I don't. It doesn't change anything." She shook her head, bit her lower lip. Tried to make the anger return to wherever it had unexpectedly come from. It fought back. "I go there," she added, "because it doesn't change anything. I don't expect him to answer me if I talk. I don't expect to turn around in the dark of night and see him. I don't expect him to—" She looked across at Eric, really looked at him.

Something about his expression was so unexpected, she said, "You lost someone too?"

It was his turn to laugh, and his laughter? As wrong as hers had been. Worse, if that was possible. He turned his hands palms up on the table and stared at them for a long time.

*Begin again*, Emma thought. There was no anger left. What she felt, she couldn't easily describe. But she wondered, watching him in his silence, if this was what people saw when they watched her. Because she wanted to say something to ease his pain, and nothing was there. It made her feel useless. Or helpless.

"You're right," he said softly. "It's none of my business. I don't even know why I asked." He took a breath and then picked up his coffee. This time, he even drank some of it, although his expression made her wonder why he bothered. Which was a whole lot safer than wondering anything else at the moment.

"Can you see them?" Emma asked, trying to shoulder her part of the conversation.

"The dead?"

She nodded.

"Yeah. I can see the dead."

"Does it help?"

He gave her the oddest look, and then his smile once again spread across his face. It made him look younger. She wanted to say it made him look more like himself, but what did she really know about him?

"No. It doesn't help anything. It doesn't help at all." He paused and then said, "Did it help you?"

She nodded. Lifted her hands, palms up. "He's my dad," she said. "It was almost worth it—the pain. To see him again."

He grimaced. "Don't go there," he said, but his voice and tone were different. Quieter. "You're not dead. He is. Emma—" he hesitated, and she could almost see him choosing the right words. Or choosing any words—what did right mean, now? "I know the pain is bad. But you can get past it. It stops. If you can ignore it for two more days, you'll never be troubled by the dead again."

Thinking of Nathan's grave, she was silent.

"Why can I see them? Is it because of—"

"Yes." He didn't even let her finish the question. "It's because of that. You can see them," he said, "and you can talk with them." He hesitated, as if about to say more. The more, however, didn't escape.

"And it's only that?"

He looked out the window again. After a long pause, he said, "No."

Emma hesitated. "I can touch them," she said, a slight rise at the end of the sentence turning it into a tentative question.

He nodded.

"My dad—people could see him because I touched him."

"Yes. Only because of that. If you hadn't, he would have stayed invisible and safely dead."

She wanted to argue with the use of the words "safely" and "dead" side by side, but she could see his point. "Can you?"

"Can I?"

"You can talk to them. You can see them. Can you touch them?"

"No."

"Oh. Why not?"

He didn't answer.

"Eric, why is it important to you that I—that I stop seeing the dead?"

"Because," he replied slowly, "then I won't have to kill you."

## ⤢ Chapter 6

Emma blinked. "Can you say that again?"

"I think you heard it the first time."

"I want to make sure I heard it the first time. Sort of."

He merely watched her. She watched him right back. It was almost as if they were playing tennis and the ball had somehow gotten suspended in time just above the net; she wasn't sure which way it would fly when it was released.

"Why were you at the graveyard?" she finally asked.

"I can see the dead," he replied. "And oddly enough, there are very few dead in the graveyards of the world. It's not where they lived," he added, "and it's not where they died. They're not all that concerned about their corpses. I like graveyards because they're quiet."

"But—but you were with someone."

"Yes. Not intentionally," he added, "but yes. I expected some difficulty. I did *not* expect you." He picked up his coffee again. Set it down. Picked it up.

"Eric, it's not a yo-yo."

And he actually smiled, although it never reached his eyes.

"What did you expect?"

"Trouble," he finally said. "Not Emma Hall and her dog. Which she calls Petal for some reason, even though he's a rottweiler."

She winced. "My dad called me Sprout. Petal was a puppy when my father brought him home, and it seemed like a good idea at the time. Because of his ears. And my nickname." She looked at Eric and said, "You were expecting me."

"Emma—"

"You didn't know *who*, but you had some idea of *what*."

He shrugged.

"Why did you phone my mother? Why did you help me home? Eric, what were you planning to do in the graveyard?"

He continued to say nothing. But at length, he replied. "I watched you, in school. All of you. Amy, with her ridiculous entourage, her obvious money."

"And her fabulous body?"

"That too. But not just Amy. Philipa. Deb. Nan. Allison. Connell and Oliver. Michael. You all have your problems, your little fights—but you also have your generous moments, your responsibilities. This may come as a surprise to you, but your thoughtless kindnesses made being in a new school a lot more pleasant."

"Thoughtless kindness?"

"Pretty much. You do it without thinking. There's not a lot of calculation, and I can't see how most of it directly benefits any of you." He paused again and then added, "I did *not* expect to see any one of you in that graveyard. Even when I saw you, I didn't expect what happened."

"If it hadn't been me, or any of us, what would you have done?"

He looked at her for a moment and then shook his head, and something about his expression was painful to look at: not frightening, not threatening, but almost heartbreaking.

"What I should have done, I didn't do. What I should be doing, I haven't done. Instead, I'm sitting here in a cafe in the middle of a school day drinking coffee that isn't very good with a confused, teenage girl."

"Teenage girl?"

"And talking too damn much," he added. He drained the coffee cup.

"Eric, you're not exactly ancient, yourself."

He laughed. It was not a good laugh. "Come on," he said, as if the bitterness of the dregs of the coffee had transferred itself to his voice. "You shouldn't have touched your father." He grimaced. "Emma, understand that what I know about—about what you can do was learned only so that I could prevent most of it. I can't tell you what you can do; I don't want you to know. I want you to turn your back on it and walk away."

"So you won't have to kill me."

"I told you you heard me."

She managed to shrug.

"I don't want to draw your mother into this; I don't want to draw your friends into it, either. Usually that's not much of a problem; most of the people who are affected by this are loners."

"Like you?"

"Like me. You're not. You're tied to your life, and you take it seriously." He looked out the window again. "I shouldn't be talking to you, and you shouldn't be skipping school. Let me pay for this, and I'll drive you back."

"Are you coming to Amy's party tonight?"

He looked at her as if she were almost insane, and she had to admit that as a non sequitur, it was pretty damn ridiculous. "I'm probably driving you home, where you'll sit in the dark until all this has passed. But yes, I intend to go to Amy's." He stood.

She stood as well. He waved the waitress over, and they had a small argument about who was paying, which Eric won by saying, "You can get the next one."

As they were heading to his car, he asked, "Will you try?"

She didn't pretend to misunderstand him. "Yes."

He nodded, as if that were the most he could expect.

Allison caught up with Emma in the lunch line-up, looking slightly anxious. "You missed English. Is anything wrong?"

Emma grimaced. "My mother has given up pretending she didn't see my father in the hospital, if that's any indication."

Allison winced. "Is she okay?"

"She's the Hall version of okay, which is to say, she's *fine*."

"What's she going to do?"

"If I'm lucky it won't involve joint trips to the nearest psychiatrist." Emma paused and pointed at the macaroni and cheese, which was one of the hot meal choices. "You know what my luck is like."

"And English?"

"I was talking to Eric," Emma replied. She hesitated and then added, "And

I'll tell you all about it tonight. If I'm not curled up in the dark someplace whimpering." She reached out and caught Allison's hand; it was a gesture she'd learned to use with Michael over the years, and it meant, more or less, *I'm serious, pay attention.* Allison, who had also learned the same gesture, understood. "I'll tell you everything, but you have to promise that you will do your absolute best not to worry at me."

Allison nodded. "I'll try."

"I'm going to try to go to Amy's tonight because I *like* having a social life, and I already told her I'd be there."

"Michael's going to go."

Even the horrendous background noise that was the cafeteria didn't disguise the utter silence that followed this statement. Michael was always invited to the larger gatherings, he just never went. Ever.

"Oliver's going," Allison told Emma, nudging her to get her moving. "And I think Connell might go as well."

"How's Michael getting there?"

"I'm not sure. We can figure it out when we get back to the table."

Eric seemed to have decided that their table—that being whichever table Michael sat at—was also his table. Even given his concerns, most of which she still didn't understand and most of which she was now certain she didn't *want* to understand, he was pleasant and low-key company. He listened to Michael without eye rolling, which was pretty much the only requirement in a lunch companion at this table.

Not, Emma thought, if she was being fair, that she didn't sometimes engage in eye rolling, but she felt she'd earned that, and Michael understood what it meant when she did it. Michael didn't ask her about her father, for which she was grateful. It was a normal day, and Emma wanted to hold on to the normal for as long as she could.

But as they were filing out of the cafeteria, Emma noticed that Allison was hanging back, and she was doing it in front of Eric. She started to say something and thought better of it, following Michael out of the cafeteria instead.

Allison was clearly nervous. Determined, but nervous.

Eric, leaning on the warped wood of the stair railing on portable D, watched her, waiting. He didn't look bored, and he didn't look angry; he didn't seem confused. He just . . . waited. When it became clear that waiting was going to be rewarded with a lot of awkward silence, he cleared his throat. "You wanted to talk to me?"

She nodded. And then said "Yes," just in case.

He waited for a bit longer. "Allison—"

"I'm sorry," she said, and looked at her feet. "It's about Emma." She looked up in time to see the way his expression changed. It closed up, like a trap.

"Ah. I'm not interested in Emma in that way," he said carefully.

"She's really not looking for anyone," Allison said, at the same time. The words collided. It was all so awkward.

"Why don't you start at the beginning?"

"Beginning?"

"You want to tell me why she's not looking for anyone. Or anyone special." When Allison nodded, he took his arm off the railing and shoved his hands into his front pockets. And waited. Then, when it became clear the awkwardness wasn't going away anytime soon, he very quietly took the threads of the conversation into his own, figurative, hands.

"You've known her for a long time?"

"Since we were six. Well, I was five."

"You've been friends since then?"

Allison nodded.

"You're not really like her, though."

"No."

"And you're not really interested in the same things."

"Some of the same things, but . . . no." Allison hesitated. "You've met Amy."

"It's impossible to be a student at Emery and *not* meet Amy."

"Do you like her?"

Eric shrugged. "She's a girl."

"I hated her, in junior high."

Eric's brow lifted slightly, as if in surprise.

"I hated that age," Allison added softly. "I thought she was so full of herself, and so cruel. But Emma liked her," she added.

"Emma liked you."

"Out of habit. But it was Emma who told me that Amy's not cruel on purpose. She doesn't enjoy being mean—she's just thoughtless; she's caught up in her own life and in her own problems. Just as I was then. To Emma, Amy was important. Amy's friendship was important. You've seen Em," Allison added. "Emma fits in with them. She always has."

"She doesn't seem to spend much time with them, now."

"No. She worked hard," Allison said, staring out into the field, or into a memory. She lost the nervous look, and her hands fell to her sides. "She worked hard to belong. She did what they did, went where they went. I was so afraid of losing her. I was jealous. Of them."

"Ah."

"But . . . we survived. It was even harder, for me, when Emma started seeing Nathan."

"Nathan?"

"Her boyfriend. He died this summer, in a car accident. They were always together. Things she'd do with me—things that she couldn't do with Amy and her friends—she started doing with Nathan instead. She spent all her time with him. Even Amy was getting annoyed. Nathan was quiet, though. He was never mean, and he was never showy. I liked him," she added, "and I hated him. I never told her about the hate part."

"I won't," he said softly.

"But when he died . . . It was bad. I don't even remember who told me, but it wasn't Emma. She came to school and she did her work and she hung out with Amy, but . . . she'd stopped caring. She always seems so self-confident to people who meet her now. It's not that, though—she just doesn't care anymore. She says what she's thinking because she doesn't care what other people think about her. None of it matters.

"And I felt guilty for a long time, because I sometimes wanted Nathan to *go away*. I wish he hadn't," she added, her voice still soft. "Because Emma is always "fine" now. Even at the burial, she was fine." She took a deep breath. "And Amy, who I always thought of as selfish? After Nathan died, she gathered all of us together, and she tried to arrange a different schedule for Michael, so that Emma would have time to grieve and pull herself together."

"She offered that to Emma?"

"No. But she was thinking of Emma, of what Emma had lost. They treat her a little differently now than they used to. They understand, and they try to give her space. All the stupid social games they used to play? They don't play them with Emma anymore." She frowned. "They still play them with each other, though."

"So if Amy arranged for someone else to meet Michael, why is he coming to school with the two of you?"

"I told them no."

He stared at her, his expression odd. "Why?"

"Because Michael hadn't changed. He still needed Em. And I think Emma needed the responsibility of watching him, the way she'd always done. Besides," she added, with a grimace, "Michael would have taken three months to readjust to a new routine, and Michael needed to know that Nathan, not Emma, was gone. Nathan understood Michael. It was why Emma started to like him in the first place."

"You're worried about her."

Allison nodded. "Emma has always gotten along with Michael because Emma *sees* Michael. She doesn't see what she wants him to be; she doesn't see what he lacks. She just sees what he is, and she understands it. She sees me the same way. She doesn't think about "normal." She just sees what we are. Mostly only the good parts," she added. "But they're still true.

"When Nathan died, Emma's mother always tried to offer comfort, and Emma didn't want it. She spent a lot of time at my house, because my mother didn't. My mom didn't need Emma to cry or scream or be angry or grieve. She let Emma be. And that's what Emma needed. It's hard," Allison added. "Sometimes it's hard. But I try to do the same."

"And you're telling me that's what I have to do?"

Allison nodded.

History was the last class of the day, and Emma approached it warily, watching for any signs of the odd dislocation that could be mistaken for concussion symptoms. Allison was watching her as well. They made their way to their seats.

Emma blinked.

"Em?"

She heard the word from a long way off; it was a tinny sound, something small and so stretched she could tell it was Allison talking only because Allison used that single syllable so effectively. She could hear the droning of Ms. Kagayama, but that, too, could barely be resolved into a familiar voice; there were no words.

No, that wasn't true. There were no familiar words, and the words that she *could* hear were spoken in so many voices, all overlapping, they almost made her dizzy. But the voices were clearer, and if it seemed as if there were thousands of them, they were distinct. This time, instead of fading into painful noise, they stayed at the edge of a shout, a chorus of shouts.

She blinked again, and she realized why.

She had thought that light hurt her eyes. Yesterday and the day before, she would have sworn it. But she realized now that it wasn't the light, it was the images that swirled around her vision, sharpest at the periphery. They formed an aurora of scintillating colors—but they had shapes now, textures that she recognized.

Clothing. Hair. Faces.

None of them stayed in one place long enough for her to really *look*. But she had the sense that she was standing still and they were streaming past, shouting, screaming, or crying as they did.

"Em?"

She lifted a hand. She couldn't speak and look at the same time. And she wanted to look. She had told Eric she would try, but she *wanted* to see her father. Or hear him. She wouldn't touch him again, she promised herself that much. But it was *hard*. Her head began to pound with the effort it took to keep looking, to *listen*, to break out one voice from the multitude.

But she managed, somehow.

And realized, as she did, that it was not her father's voice that she had reached for and not, therefore, her father that she could see.

Instead, she saw *fire*, and she shouted, bringing her hands up to cover her face. She would have let go, then. She would have let go and slid into oblivion and nausea and darkness. But she could see, wreathed in fire, the face of a small child, and she could hear, in the distance, the screams. No, the scream. One voice. One voice shouting words that were familiar because Emma had typed them, in a half-trance, on the day of the first headache.

**Oh my god Drew help me help me Drew fire god no**

She stood—she managed to stand.

Allison was standing as well; she felt Allison's hand on her arm. And then she felt a familiar arm encircle her shoulder. It was tight, meant to brace her and hold her up. She swallowed, closed her eyes, and forced them open again.

She heard Eric's voice, and his voice was blessedly clear. "Strength, Emma." It was a whisper of sound, a tickle in her ear. But she could hear it. She nodded and managed to say, "Take me home."

She felt herself being lifted.

"Strength," Eric said again.

She nodded.

She threw up in the parking lot. Eric seemed to expect this, and although he set her down, he hovered. "Where's Allison?" she asked, as she pushed herself to her feet.

"I told her to stay. There's not much she can do."

"And she listened?"

He chuckled. "Very reluctantly. I'm not sure she trusts me."

"She's smarter than I am," Emma said. She caught his arm. Her knees felt like rubber, but they held. "I think I can walk," she told him, as he put an arm around her shoulder.

**Drew**

She closed her eyes. "How can you live like this?" she whispered.

"I don't see what you see now."

"Oh. Did you ever?"

"Never. I am not what I fear you are, Emma."

**DREW**

One voice in the maelstrom. She opened her eyes to fire; fire and black, thick smoke. She could almost taste it, and fell to her knees against the asphalt.

Eric picked her up. He had never looked particularly large to Emma, but he carried her as easily as Brendan Hall had when she had been a small girl.

"Eric."

His arms tightened, but he continued to walk. "Em," he whispered. "Don't do this. Please."

She opened her eyes; she could see his profile, because her head was resting against his shoulder. His eyes were faintly luminescent in her vision, although they were also dark brown; his jaw was tensed, as if with effort. She said, "Eric, there's a child—"

He almost missed a step, but he caught himself—and Emma—before they both fell.

"There's a child, in the fire."

"What fire, Emma?" He asked it as if she were a fevered child. It should have irritated her, but it didn't. She wasn't sure why.

"I don't know. There's a fire and a child standing in it. There's smoke, it's thick and heavy. And I can hear *one* voice, over all the other voices."

He had reached his car, and now set her down close to the front passenger seat. He unlocked the door manually, and then put an arm around her waist as she slid into the car. She felt the vinyl against her legs; it was warm.

"But, Eric," she continued, as he closed the door gently and walked around the front of the car to the driver's side. She waited while he slid behind the steering wheel. "Eric?"

"I'm here. Take this," he added, and handed her a small bucket. "I thought you might need it."

"The voice I hear sounds different. It's not—it's not like the other voices."

"How is it different?" He spoke patiently and slowly.

"I don't know for certain—I can't shut the other voices out, not completely, so it's hard to listen." She grimaced, and added, "and I can see the child."

"Now?"

"Yes." She'd already nodded a couple of times, but this time remembered that speaking was less painful.

**Drew oh my god oh god**

He started the car.

"He's not very old. I think he's four. Maybe a bit older, maybe a bit younger, it's hard to tell." And she was concentrating now. Her vision was a strange collage of things she expected to see and things it should have been impossible to see.

The phone rang. She blinked. The fire wavered, its roar diminishing to a crackle. She automatically reached into her pocket before she realized that the ringtone was wrong; it wasn't her phone.

It rang again. "Eric, I think that's your phone."

He said nothing, and Emma listened to it ring three more times before it fell silent. When it did, the roar of the fire returned.

The child's eyes were wide, and she could see black tears trace the delicate lines of his cheeks. He was staring *at* her, his lips slightly open.

"Yes," Emma said, although she couldn't say why. "Yes, I'm coming." She turned to Eric. "Go left here."

The car rolled to a halt. He opened his mouth, and shut it when the phone rang again.

"Are you going to answer that?"

"No. I know who it is."

"Without looking?"

"Not many people have my number. What do you mean, turn left here?"

"We have to drive that way," she replied, lifting a shaking arm.

"Why, Emma?"

"Because we—we just have to drive that way."

Eric lifted a hand to his face. "All right. All right, we'll play it your way for now."

Eric followed Emma's ad hoc directions. Emma concentrated on staying upright. She gave right, left, and straight calls, and he followed them, paying attention to the lights. But she must have given him the wrong direction, because he turned instead of going straight, and Emma screamed as the car drove up a curb, over an unwatered lawn, and *into* a large shed.

"Eric!"

His knuckles whitened on the wheel, and she watched as the shed and the car converged. The car passed right through it, leaving no wood, boards, or broken glass in its wake. She turned to look over her shoulder; there was nothing at all behind them but a two lane residential street.

He glanced at her once, but said nothing.

"I'll just stick with directions," she said, shakily. "Sorry for screaming."

One-way streets made the drive more difficult. Eric attempted to follow her directions, but told her curtly that he found having a driver's license convenient when he was forced, by street signs, to ignore Emma. "It would help," he added, as his phone began to ring again, "if you knew any of the street names."

She did. She just didn't know *these* streets. "Eric, can you answer the damn phone?"

"No."

"Then give the damn thing to me, and I'll answer it."

"No."

She rubbed her temples. It didn't help, but it gave her something to do with her hands other than try to strangle Eric. Given that Emma didn't have her license, strangling the only driver in an increasingly unfamiliar part of town seemed like a bad idea. As if to argue with that, the phone started ringing again immediately after it had stopped.

Eric ignored it. Emma gritted her teeth and tried to do the same. "Has it ever occurred to you that it could be an emergency?" she asked, through those gritted teeth.

"Just keep your mind on the road."

She did. She found it easier as the driving continued. It wasn't that the light, and the quality of its shifting images, lessened; the opposite happened. But as those phantasms grew more concrete and she could hold the images in the center of her vision as if they were just another part of the landscape, the pain decreased.

And the voices dimmed as well, until there was only one voice, screaming to be heard against the cracking of timber and the roar of fire.

Emma said, "Here, Eric."

But the car had already rolled to a stop.

The phone rang.

It was pretty difficult, in the city of Toronto, to find any patch of land that did not have a building on it. This one was a partial exception; it had what looked like the remnants of several buildings, with partly blackened walls, a total lack of glass in window frames, and boards over where the doors would have been.

Emma experienced, for a second time, the sudden cessation of noise and light. This time, though, she could feel the movement of all of these things as they left her in a rush, condensing, at last, to a single point that existed outside of her head. She shook her head, partly to clear it, and partly because sitting this close to a row of burned out townhouses wasn't something she did every day.

Eric turned the engine off and glanced at her.

"Here," she said quietly. She started to tell him that she no longer had the headache and then gave up; his expression made clear that he knew. And that, unlike Emma, he wasn't happy about it.

She opened the car door and slid out of the car. "Do you want to wait here?"

"Wouldn't dream of it," Eric replied. He opened his door, and his phone rang. Again.

"Look, if you don't want to answer it, and you don't want me to answer it, why don't you just throw it away or step on it or something?"

He looked as if he was considering it, and then shrugged. "I'll turn it off."

Emma's phone had only ever been off when she'd forgotten to recharge the batteries. She grimaced. "Or that," she said.

She made her way off the road, over the dead patch of lawn that was usually bracketed by sidewalk and curb, and onto the sidewalk itself, and then she began to walk toward the second house from the end.

"Where are you going?" Eric asked, following her.

She pointed to the house. "Do you know what street we're on?"

"Rowan Avenue."

Emma took her phone out of her pocket, and made a note to herself.

"It's two words," Eric said, raising a brow. "You're not going to remember two words?"

"Probably not." She slid the phone back into her pocket and headed up the walk. "Do you think this is safe at all?"

Eric said nothing. It was a lot of nothing. And to be fair, the obvious answer was No. "Emma, what are you going to do?"

"I don't know," she said quietly. "But I think—I think the child's in that building."

"He's dead."

"Very funny."

"Only by accident," he replied.

"Stay here."

"Emma—"

"Just let me check the floor." She moved very slowly up the walk, and then detoured to the lawn, to get closer to the ruined building. It was at least two stories in height; a third floor might still exist, small rooms cramped beneath the peak that was suggested by the buildings, farther down, that seemed in better repair. The fire must have occurred recently; the building was still standing. There was no evidence of bulldozers; no evidence of people's handiwork beyond the haphazard boarding that had been put up. As she approached what had once been windows—the facade was damaged enough that the frames on this floor looked a lot like big, black holes—she felt heat and saw, for a moment, fire.

They weren't ghostly flames; they were hot, and high, and adorned by billowing smoke as air moved from the outside of the house toward them.

She heard, again, the screams. But she heard them at a distance, and she turned to where Eric was standing, expecting to get a glimpse of the woman—for it was a woman's voice—that had once been capable of uttering them. The street, except for Eric and a couple of cars, was quiet.

"Eric?" She waved him over.

He shoved his hands into his pockets and walked slowly toward her.

"Pretend that you won't have to kill me if you answer my questions."

"Emma, do you understand how serious this is?"

She looked up, to the second story. "Yes. I need to know something about the dead."

He waited, and after a minute of silence, she said, "I saw a student in the cafeteria the other day. He *looked* alive to me. I realized something was really wrong when Allison sat *through* him."

"Go on."

"But he seemed to notice *me*. He smiled at me," she added, "just before he disappeared. I can see the fire," she added softly. "I can feel its heat."

"You're right. It has to be recent."

"What I need to know is if the child—"

"The dead child?"

"The dead child. Will he be able to see me and react to me?"

The silence was longer and more marked, but Eric eventually said, "Yes."

"Will he be able to see you?"

"Yes."

"Anyone else?"

"Not unless you touch him."

"Why?"

"I'd rather not say."

"Is he stuck there?"

"He's dead."

"*Eric.*"

"Emma, it may come as a surprise to you, but I'm not dead." He took his hands out of his pockets; they were fists. He relaxed them slowly, but it looked like it took effort. "But yes, there's a good chance that *he* feels he can't come out."

"Can we make him come out?"

"Why?" The word was sharper, and harsher.

"Because he's stuck in a *burning house*, and he's *four years old*."

The phone rang.

Emma's eyes widened. "I thought you said you shut it off?"

Eric shrugged. "I did. Welcome to my life." He slid his hand into his jacket pocket—school jacket, for formal day—and took the phone out. "I can't talk right now," he said, as he lifted the phone to his ear. "No. I left early. Someplace downtown." He rolled his eyes. "Rowan Avenue. No, I'm with another student. Yes. No." He glanced at Emma, and then said, "It might not be a problem. Look up Rowan Avenue. No. Because I'm not near a computer. Look, I can't talk right now. I'll call you as soon as I can."

He hung up and slid the phone back into his pocket.

It started to ring again. Eric raised a brow in her direction and she grimaced and threw up her hands. "You win," she told him. "Ignore it."

"Why, thank you."

She walked up to what was left of the house and raised her arms to shield her face as the flames leaped out of the windows, driving her back and into Eric. He put his hands on her arms to steady her. "Fire?"

"You can't feel it?"

"No."

"See it?"

"No. You may need to wait this out," he added softly. It was loud anyway; his lips were beside her ear.

"If you can't see it," she told him, gritting her teeth, "it's not *real*." She shook herself free of his hands, and approached the building again. She forced herself to approach the fire. It singed her hair, and she jumped back again.

"Emma—"

"I don't understand," she whispered.

"The fire *is* real, in some way, for you. It's not real for me." He exhaled sharply and then said, "In twenty years, you'll see it, but it won't sustain the ability to burn you. Or it shouldn't."

"Twenty *years*?"

"More or less. Come on, let me drive you home."

"You mean that child is going to be trapped in a burning building for *twenty years*?" She turned to face him, and grabbed one arm to prevent him from walking away. "Eric, if the fire isn't real *to you*, you can enter the building."

"If the building has any structural integrity, yes."

"If you can make it in without feeling the fire, I might be able to go with you. And if I collapse because of smoke inhalation, you can drag me out."

She heard the screaming again and turned. Street and cars. Nothing else. Frowning, she said, "I don't think the voice I can hear is a dead person's voice."

Eric said nothing, which was starting to get old.

"I think—I think it might be his mother's voice."

"Emma, let it go. Please. If it's strong enough that you can hear her voice, he is *too* strong for you."

"He's four."

"A living four year old and a dead four year old are not the same. Trust me."

"I can't."

Silence. Then, "No, I don't suppose you can." He looked away, toward the house. "Even if I get you into the house, I probably won't be able to get you up the stairs. I don't think enough of them are left standing to support my weight."

"But enough is left standing to support mine?" The quality of his silence was as good as an answer. "Because it was standing, or almost standing, when he was trapped there. I'm where he is, when I approach the house. Some part of me is walking to where he is."

"Yes. And no. You're here," he added softly. "This isn't like the hospital."

"No. In the hospital there were two of me." Her eyes widened slightly. "The one part sees the dead," she said softly, as if testing the words. "And the other part sees the living. Why aren't there two of me now?"

"You only get that dislocation at the beginning," was the quiet reply.

She looked at the burning house carefully and then said, "All right. We need a ladder. A big, solid ladder." And she turned and walked back to the car.

"Why is he trapped in the house?"

"He's not."

"Why is he *staying* in the house?"

"Better question. I honestly don't have the answer."

"Why are any of the dead here *at all*?"

Eric glanced at her in the mirror, but otherwise kept his eyes on the road. He had to, since Emma had no idea at all of how to get home. "Where should they be?" he asked at length.

He was testing her somehow, and she knew it. She had always been good at tests, but this test was decidedly unfair; she didn't even know what the subject was. "I don't know. Heaven? Hell?"

"I'm not dead. I don't know either."

"And you don't care."

"No. I care. But there's nothing I can do about it."

"There must be something *I* can do about it."

His silence was long, and she watched the way his jaw tightened into it. "If this is your idea of trying to stay out of things," he told her, "you fail."

"Full of fail. That happens when a four year old is going to be trapped forever in a burning house, reliving the moment of his death."

The phone rang, but it had been doing that on and off since they'd gotten back into the car. "You could change the ringtone," Emma suggested.

"This is the shortest ring I could find."

# ⌒ Chapter 7

Eric drove Emma home and parked on the street. Emma opened the car door and then turned to Eric. "If you need to go home before Amy's party, I can send you the directions to get there."

He blinked. "Amy's party?"

"Remember? We spoke about it before we left school?"

He shook his head. "You're crazy."

"If you think she looks good in school, you've never seen her when she's actually trying."

He didn't smile. "And what are you going to do?"

"I'm going to go hit the computer and then call Allison."

"And?"

"Get ladders," she replied quietly. "And go back to Rowan Avenue. If we're lucky, we can figure out what needs to be done before Amy's party."

"And if you're not?"

"If I'm not," she said starkly, the half smile deserting her face, "I don't think we're going to have to worry about it."

"Emma you can't go in there blind. You have no idea what you're doing!"

"No, I don't. I'm going to try to find out more before I head out there." She turned toward the door and then turned back again. "I don't understand what you're afraid of, Eric. I don't understand what's going on with you. What I understand, at the moment, is that that child is somehow stuck in that house. And I want to get him out."

"To what end?"

She stared at him. And then she got out of the car without looking back, and shut the door.

The phone rang. Eric listened to it, his hands still gripping the steering wheel, knuckles white. Prying his fingers free, he picked up the phone and stared at the screen while the ring died into silence. He looked up to see Emma and got a brief glimpse of her ridiculously named rottweiler before her front door closed.

When the phone rang again, he answered.

"Yeah."

"Eric—"

"Rowan Avenue?"

"Ten days ago."

Eric whistled.

"Eric?"

"Ten days. I would have guessed three, tops."

The silence was cold. "And why would you have guessed that?"

Eric shrugged. He realized that this wasn't likely to convey itself over the phone and decided he didn't care enough to put the gesture into words.

"Eric, what is happening there?"

"Not much. I'm going to Amy's party tonight," he added, just for the momentary amusement of silent outrage on the other end of the line. It came and was followed by brief spluttering, an added bonus.

"Eric, *did you find the Necromancer*?"

Eric counted four uses of his name in six sentences, which was about as far as he could push it without things getting ugly. "Yes."

"Good. Dead?"

"No."

"No?"

"No."

"You arrived too late." It wasn't a question.

Eric was not one of nature's natural liars. He said nothing, which was neutral. It was also not enough.

"Eric, did you arrive too late?"

"No."

The silence that followed his monosyllabic confession was long. ". . . No. And the Necromancer is not dead."

"No."

"You need backup."

"Not really."

"And I'm sending it."

"If you send Chase, I won't guarantee he'll survive."

"If he doesn't, I'll come myself."

Fuck.

Emma had to work not to put her fingers through the keyboard. It was almost not worth the trouble. Yes, Eric was a stranger. Yes, they had no history. Yes, he knew something about her that she *did not know herself*, and he wasn't about to share. And yes, if it came down to it, she *knew* somewhere in the back of her hindbrain that if she did something wrong, somehow, he would kill her.

She also didn't doubt that he could, and that was strange, because it wasn't something she usually worried about. What she usually worried about was saying the wrong thing, alienating her friends, or pissing off her mother or her teachers. And it was beside the damn point. He knew that there was a child trapped in that house, and he didn't *care*.

Google was not slow to load answers to her query, and she looked at them, opening the first five in tabs. She began to read, and as she did, anger at Eric dimmed. She didn't like to hold on to anger, and she let it go.

Only one person had died in the fire—Andrew Copis, four years of age. Cause of fire: under investigation. From the sounds of it, though, the fire hadn't started in Andrew's home; it had started one house down. The walls were not cinderblock, and the fire had spread. Maria Copis, Andrew's mother, was twenty-eight years of age. She was a divorced single parent; her ex-husband was not in residence. She had—oh.

Three children. Andrew was the oldest; she had an eighteen-month-old girl and a two-month-old boy. She had picked them up, and carried them both out of the house. The little girl had suffered smoke inhalation.

She had not been able to carry Andrew at the same time, and she had screamed at him to follow her. And he had screamed at her to *carry him*. A brief moment of outrage at all news reporters came and went. How could you *ask* a mother something like that?

Emma closed her eyes. She knew, now, why Andrew stayed in the house.

It was a few moments before she could read again, but she did. Andrew had died of smoke inhalation; the screaming, the deep breaths required *to* scream, hadn't helped. He had suffered burns as well by the time the firefighters reached him, but it wasn't direct fire that had killed him.

The firefighters had gone into the building; the building at that time had supported their weight. They were all heavier than Emma, especially with the gear they wore. They'd gone in through the second story windows. Check.

She sat back in her chair and rubbed her eyes with the heels of her hands. How was she going to talk a terrified, hysterical four year old out of a burning building if she was trapped in the same burning building?

She pulled her phone out of her pocket and called Allison.

She told Allison everything.

Everything except the part about Eric not having to kill her—which of course implied that he *might* have to kill her— because there was no way to say that without causing panic. Then she waited while the silence on the other end of the phone stretched out.

She finally said, "I know it sounds crazy."

Allison replied, "Em, I *saw* your father. We all did. I don't think *you're* crazy. But it does sound kind of crazy."

Emma reminded herself, as her shoulders eased down her back and she relaxed, that there were reasons she loved Allison. "What are you doing?"

"Googling. I've got your article on the fire," she added. "Oh."

"Three kids. Two of them had no hope of walking out of that place on their own," Emma said softly.

"Did you write down where Andrew's buried?"

"I don't think I know," Emma replied. "I think there was a service that was open to the public, but I don't think it mentioned the burial site. Why?"

"Because," Allison replied, "I don't think you're going to be able to get Andrew to leave that house without his mother."

A *lot* of reasons why she loved Allison. "You don't think so, either?"

"No. We can try," she added. "With what we've got here, we can try. But . . ."

"I know." Emma got out of her chair and walked toward the window. "We could probably find her in the phonebook. She's a divorced single parent, now. How many Copises could there be?"

"There could be an unlisted one." Allison hesitated—her breath was different when she was trying to figure out which words to say. "But I have no idea how we're going to approach her."

Emma had avoided thinking about that as well. Pacing in her room, her phone against her ear, she thought about it now. And grimaced. "Me either. But even if we look like a couple of lunatics, wouldn't it be worth listening?"

"We're not going to look like lunatics. We're going to look worse. We're going to look like the meanest, most vicious, malicious people *ever*."

Emma tried to imagine Allison in this context and failed utterly. "We have to try," she said quietly.

"I know. But we have to find her first, and we're probably not going to manage that tonight. If we knew where the grave was, that might be the best way to meet her in person."

"It'd be the *worst* place to approach her, though." She glanced out the window again and saw that Eric's car was still parked in the street in front of her house. She turned, and ran into Petal, who had decided that it was time to be taken for a walk. "Not now, Petal," she told him, scratching behind his ears.

But dogs can be particularly dense when it comes to understanding English. He padded out of the room and appeared again two minutes later, dragging his leash across the carpet and wagging his stub. "I have to take Petal for a walk," Emma said, surrendering.

"Call me when you get back?"

"I will. Maybe I'll have thought of something useful by then. Maybe we could pretend to work for the insurance company or something. I mean, we only have to *get* her there."

"Single mother of two."

"Ugh. Later," she added, hanging up. She picked up the leash that was attached to her dog in the wrong way—mostly by his mouth—and changed that.

Eric's car was still in the street, and he was still behind the wheel, when Emma left the house and locked up behind herself. Most of her anger had evaporated, but a small core of it remained, and she hesitated while Petal tried to drag her down the walk.

Then, squaring her shoulders, she dragged her dog down to the street and rapped on the front passenger window. Eric turned his head to look at her, and then he nodded and got out of the car. "You're walking your dog?"

"I'm about to be walked by my dog. Subtle difference."

He smiled at that, and it was the comfortable and genuine smile that she liked on his face. She surrendered the rest of her anger, then.

"You want company?" Eric asked.

She shrugged. "If you're going to just sit here in the car, you might as well join us."

She didn't realize where she was walking. Petal was doing his usual intense inspection of anything that might be a garbage can. Given that it wasn't a collection day and he wasn't always the brightest dog, that took him a little too close to the actual houses.

Eric laughed, and Petal was thankfully old enough not to find this flattering. He did find it slightly encouraging, but that was probably a Hall fault; if people were laughing, they were a lot less likely to order you to heel.

"No ladders?" he asked, as Petal decided that forward was better than sideways and actually let them gain half a block of sidewalk before he started barking at a squirrel.

"No . . ."

"No?" When she looked at him, he shoved his hands in his pockets and continued the slow, meandering stroll that was walking her nine-year-old dog.

"We'll need them later," Emma told him.

"I didn't think you'd given up, if that's any consolation."

"Not really."

He shrugged. "Later?"

"Allison doesn't think that Andrew will leave the house if his mother's not there."

"You *told Allison*?"

"She's my best friend. There's not a lot about my life that she doesn't know."

"And she didn't think you were insane." It wasn't really a question, but the last few words did tail off in a slight rise.

"She's my best friend," Emma said again. "Look, Eric, she sees the world in a way I don't. She picks up things I might miss. I do the same for her when she asks." And even when she didn't, sometimes, but Emma had gotten better since junior high. "And she wasn't saying anything I hadn't thought, she was just more certain."

Eric shook his head again. "Emma," he said, raising his face to the bower of old maples that lined the street. "I give up. I just . . . give up."

Petal tugged at the lead, and they picked up their pace a little, coming to rest at the side of a busy street. Petal turned left, and Emma turned with him. "Is that a good thing?"

"What?"

"Giving up."

"Depends on you who you ask, but I can guarantee that some people aren't going to like it." He looked at her. "How are you going to contact the child's mother?"

"His name is Andrew. Drew for short."

"You didn't get that from him."

"Google is your friend," she said. "But the nickname? His mother is screaming it. Or was. He can hear her, and I'm almost positive that's what *I'm* hearing."

"He's strong," Eric said quietly.

"He's dead. What difference does strength make to the dead?"

"Well," he said, sliding his hands out of his pockets as Petal ran back. "There are always ghost stories. You've heard them. I've heard them."

"Yes, but when *I* heard them, I didn't think they were *true*."

His smile was both faint and genuine. "The sightings are often false," he told her, "if that makes any difference."

"Not much at this particular moment. And besides, I don't want to hear about the false ones."

"All right. The real ones, then. Ghosts don't tend to haunt things. Your father doesn't, for instance, but he's here."

She spun on her heel. There was no sign of her father.

"Sorry. By 'here' I mean he's dead, and of the dead, but he's not throwing furniture at people's heads in a fury."

"Got it. Can he just show up whenever he wants?"

"You mean can he visit you?"

She nodded.

"I'm not entirely sure it's that easy. He's not without power," Eric added as the lights changed and they crossed the street, "but what he has is nothing like what Andrew has."

"Andrew's age doesn't matter?"

"No. And before you ask? I have no idea why some of the dead have more power than others. There used to be theories that said the manner of death defined the amount of power the dead would have, but that's been debunked." He looked moodily into the distance, and his eyes narrowed.

*By whom?* Emma wondered. But Eric was talking, and she didn't know how long that would last; she didn't want to interrupt him, and judging by his expression, she wasn't certain she wanted the answer.

He shook himself. "But there are some ghosts who are powerful. Powerful enough to affect the living world."

"Andrew's not."

"No. He's a step down. The ones that are, though? Those are your ghost stories, your poltergeists. They're dangerous," he added softly. "But Andrew is powerful enough. He is, however, still four years old. What he creates out of what he remembers is something you'll have to walk through to get to him— at all. To get him to *listen* to you, or anything you have to say, is going to be very, very difficult."

"Probably impossible," Emma said quietly. "I think our best chance is his mother. If she could go in there—with me—and I could touch her son, she'd be able to see him and hear him. I think he would follow her out."

"Which brings us back to the original question: How are you going to contact her?"

"Cold calls," Emma said. "We'll think of something because we *have* to think of something. I know he's already dead," she added softly, "but it seems so wrong to leave him there for god knows how long, just burning."

"Emma," he said gently, "even if you do manage to get him out of the house, he's still dead."

"So?"

"What do you think you're going to do with him once he's outside?"

She stopped walking. "Do with him?"

"He's dead, and he's lost," Eric replied, looking at Petal's back. It seemed deliberate to Emma. "If you can talk him out of the house, he'll still be both dead—and lost." He looked at her then; she was standing still, although Petal was causing a bit of a tilt.

"What do you mean, lost?"

"I mean lost. There's nowhere for him to go."

"But—that can't be right."

"Ask your father sometime. *No*, not now."

"Wait."

"Petal is going to pull your arm off."

"He'll try. Can the dead see the other dead?"

"Not always, not clearly, and not at first."

"So he couldn't see my dad?"

Eric looked at her oddly. "Not in his current state, from everything you've said. Why?"

She lowered her eyes because they suddenly stung her. "My dad," she said softly, "is good with lost kids."

He rolled his eyes, but he also smiled.

"I really don't understand you," Emma said, dredging up a smile from somewhere and surprising herself because it was genuine.

"Lucky you."

She didn't realize where Petal was headed because she was engrossed in conversation and thought. But when he led her to the fence that bordered the cemetery, she knew. She stopped walking for a moment, compressing her lips in a thin line.

"Not here," she told Petal. Petal came back to her, his tongue hanging out of his mouth. He cocked his head to one side, and after a moment she fished a Milk-Bone out of her pocket and offered it to him.

"I wasn't lying," Eric said quietly. "Graveyards really are one of the quietest places on earth."

She shook her head. "I can't," she told him.

"Why?"

"I don't want to—" She grimaced. "They're not quiet *enough*." Squaring her shoulders, she looked straight at Eric. "What did you see the night you met me here?"

"Not what you saw," he replied. It was evasive, but he didn't look away. "I saw the ghost," he continued, when she didn't speak. "She spoke to you."

"She did *way worse* than speak to me."

"What did she do?"

"I don't want to talk about it."

He laughed. The laughter grew louder as she glared at him. It was hard to glare at Eric when he was laughing.

"I didn't bring it up," he said, when he could finally stop. "But I didn't see anything other than that. She talked to you, you backed up, tripped, and banged your head."

"She handed me something," Emma said quietly. This much, she wasn't too embarrassed to say.

Eric could get so still when he was already mostly standing there. "What did she hand you?"

"A lantern. I think it was made of . . . ice."

Eric looked at her for a long moment, and then he shook his head. "Emma," he said softly, "if you ever meet any of my friends, fail to mention that."

"I haven't mentioned it to anyone but you." She paused, "And Allison."

They walked down the path into the cemetery. At this time of day, the gates weren't shut, and cars could drive in as well. Petal loved it.

"She was so old, Eric. *So* old."

He said nothing for a long moment.

"Is that how you saw her?"

"No," he said quietly.

"She looked like a bag lady out of nightmare. Why did you see her differently?"

"Some of the dead can choose their form."

"You mean they don't look the way they did when they died?"

"I mean they don't have to. Andrew, in a few decades, will probably be able to appear older, if he thinks about it."

"Why would he bother? Why would any of them bother?"

Eric shrugged. "I'm not dead," he told her. "Remember?"

"That could be arranged."

Eric laughed. Petal decided that this was his cue to get lots of attention, where attention at his age meant another Milk-Bone.

"Who was she?" Emma asked, when Petal once again decided to test the tensile strength of his leash.

He looked at her, and then looked away. "The mother of a friend," he said, in the wrong tone of voice.

She thought of the ring on his finger and said nothing. And this nothing? It was comfortable. She knew how to give him this space because in some ways, it was the space she herself needed.

Still, she hesitated as Petal began to crawl, sniff, and occasionally piss his way across the cemetery. She had never come to visit Nathan with any company but Petal before. *Nathan*, she thought. For just a moment, she wanted to see him, and she wanted it so badly she forgot to breathe.

But she remembered to breathe after a few seconds, and she remembered to keep her mouth shut. It didn't happen often, but it did happen. She covered her eyes with her hand for a few seconds, and then, when she dropped that hand, she was fine.

Eric was watching her.

"Don't," she said softly.

"Nathan?"

"I said don't."

He lifted both hands and took a step back. "I surrender. *And* I'm unarmed."

"And that," an unfamiliar voice said, "is really strange. On both counts."

Emma frowned and looked past Eric's shoulder. A boy was leaning, with one hand, against the hem of an angel's long, flowing robes. Admittedly the angel was on a pedestal on top of a tombstone that would have been at home over a dozen graves.

The stranger was taller than Eric, and his hair was an orange-red that would have been at home on Anne of Green Gables. He had green eyes, and his skin was the same pale that redheads often have, but it was dusted with freckles and rather puckish dimples.

He wore a jacket, the type of navy blue that said School, but in a cut that said Money; it had no crest. Beneath that? Collared shirt and a thin wool pull-over. He also wore gray pants, with perfect pleats.

Eric grimaced and turned, slowly, to face the stranger. "Chase," he said.

"Eric." Chase grinned broadly. "I came to lend a hand; the old man said you wanted some help. Who's your friend?"

"A classmate," Eric replied tersely. "And the old man was wrong. Why don't you go play in traffic?"

"Not much traffic to play in around here, frankly. And I am bored out of my mind."

"You're always bored. Did no one ever tell you that bored people are generally also boring?"

"You have. About a thousand times." He straightened up, his hand leaving the angel's hem and falling into his pocket. His jacket pocket. "But I'm rarely bored when you're around," he added, with a grin. "So, come on, introduce us."

"I'd rather not."

Chase clucked. "Well, then, unless you're going to kill me here and now—"

"Seriously considering it, Chase."

"—I'll just introduce myself, shall I?"

Eric said, to Emma, "You don't have to be friendly. I try to offend him frequently, but he's so dense none of it sticks."

She laughed. "Are you brothers?"

They both snorted with obvious derision and then glanced at each other.

"I'll take that as a yes."

"It's a definite no," Chase said. "If he were related to me, I wouldn't let him out in public dressed that way. He's often rude, frequently sullen, and generally unfriendly."

"And Chase," Eric added, "is often rude, frequently whiny, and never shuts up. Emma, this is Chase Loern. Chase, this is Emma Hall."

"Pleased to meet you," Emma said. "I think."

Chase laughed. "You *have* been hanging around our Eric, haven't you?"

She shrugged. "He's never been rude, he's never been sullen, and he is unfailingly helpful and friendly."

"Which is another way of saying boring."

"Only to teenage boys with too much time on their hands."

Chase's red brows arched up into his hairline. "On the other hand," he said, "maybe you're meant for each other."

The silence that followed these words was both awkward and telling.

"If you'll excuse me for a moment," Eric said to Emma, recovering first. He grabbed Chase by the arm and began to drag him away, "I'm going to kill someone."

It was almost true. Eric pulled Chase around the trunk of a messy weeping willow. Chase allowed this with apparent good humor until his back was against the tree. Chase and humor were funny things, if you liked black humor liberally laced with violence. Eric often referred to him as Loki.

"What the hell are you doing?" Eric pushed him, and when Chase brought both of his hands up, let go and stepped back, finding his feet.

"You need backup," Chase replied. "I'm here."

"I don't need backup. And I don't need to babysit."

Chase's pale skin darkened. "You found the Necromancer. The Necromancer is not dead. Ergo, backup."

"I found the Necromancer; the Necromancer is not dead. I'm not dead either, and as you can see, not close. Backup doesn't equal cleanup. I don't want to have to clean up after you again."

"Is it Emma?" Chase asked. He waited for a half-beat and then said, "Don't be stupid, Eric."

Eric said nothing.

"You've historically had a weakness for the girls." A brief grin animated Chase's mouth.

Eric didn't try to break his jaw, but that took effort.

"Well?"

"Don't make me kill you."

Chase laughed. He would. But he could laugh just before he killed, and he could laugh a good deal after, as well. "I think that's a yes." His amused expression vanished, as if it had just run for its life. "What's your game, here?"

Eric really did not want to kill Chase. "She's not what—or who—I expected."

Red eyebrows disappeared into hairline. Chase was genuinely shocked. Eric could tell, because Chase didn't have anything to say for almost two minutes.

"You need to take a vacation," was all he could manage.

"After this."

"Now. Are you *out of your mind*? She's *not what you expected*?"

"Keep it down," Eric said quietly, nodding in the direction of Emma, which also happened to be in the direction of the willow.

"Pardon me for being outraged. If they find her—and you know damn well they will—you *know* what she'll become. What she *is* now doesn't make a god-damn difference. She's a fucking *Necromancer*, Eric!"

"The rest of her life is about what she is," Eric replied quietly. This usually didn't work with Chase; Chase generally spoke as if conversational volume had to be a constant.

Chase was still shocked. He reached into his pocket and pulled out his phone. Eric pivoted and kicked it out of his hand; it flew, like an ungainly silver bird, in an arc past the tree.

"How many times have I saved your life?"

"About as many," Chase said, still staring in the direction of the phone, "as I've saved yours."

Eric snorted. "Good to see you're still incapable of counting." He lowered his hands. "Give me a week."

"A week to do *what*? She's not going to get *less* dangerous in a week!"

"Give me a week, Chase."

"Fuck that." Chase started to move, and Eric blocked him.

"Give me a goddamn week, or we can finish what we started the first time we met."

The silence was profound. They had so much history, these two. They argued like the brothers they technically weren't, but beneath those arguments they had always shared a single, common goal.

"I'm not going back to the old man," Chase finally said.

"No. You're not."

"Eric, he'll know. We're the two best agents he's got. If we don't call in, if we don't tell him the Necromancer is dead, he'll come himself."

"I'll deal with that if it happens."

"*When* it happens. What the hell is so special about that girl, anyway?"

"Nothing that would make any difference to you."

"And what's going to happen in a week?"

Eric tensed and stepped back slightly, adjusting his stance. Chase saw, and he noted it, drawing himself in as well. "She's going to try to talk a four-year-old ghost out of the burned-out wreck of his home."

"What?"

"You heard me."

Chase laughed. "Are you *kidding* me?"

"No."

"Does she even know what you are?"

"No. She doesn't care, either. I can stay away," he added, "or I can be there; she's going to try anyway."

"And you intend to help her."

"How? I've got nothing to help with. She's already singed her hair," he added, "and she's determined to keep going."

"So you get out of killing her when she dies."

"Pretty much."

Chase put his hands down. "You're taking too many risks."

It was true. Eric didn't deny it because he couldn't. He also didn't relax his own stance, because he was dealing with Chase.

"I understand why you're pissed off," Eric said. "And I understand why she's a threat. But I would rather she died that way than—"

"Than by your hand."

"Pretty much. I don't want to kill her, Chase. I can't think of the last time that happened."

"Because, clearly, you were *still sane* before. Look, buddy, don't weaken here." Chase stretched. "I'll give you the week." And he held up his pinky.

Eric grimaced. He *hated* this part.

"Shake on it, pinky shake, or we don't have a deal."

"You're an asshole," Eric told him.

"Pretty much." He waited until Eric did, in fact, lock pinkies with him.

"But you know," Chase added, "You owe me a phone if that one's broken."

"I'll buy you another phone."

"And there better be someone around here to kill. I don't like to get dressed up for nothing."

## ◜ Chapter 8

Emma, who could recognize an argument-in-the-making when she saw it, had retreated, skirting the stone angel with its ostentatious pedestal and heading toward more familiar markers. Daylight transformed them, as it often did, but Petal didn't seem to notice. He paused in front of standing wreaths, sniffed his way across the mostly shorn grass, and headed more or less straight to Nathan's grave.

Emma approached the headstone quietly. It looked so new, compared to many of the others; light glinted over the sheen of perfect, polished stone.

Eric could see the dead. Eric said that the dead didn't gather in graveyards.

She knelt, slowly, in front of the headstone. Usually she sat farther back, but today she chose to sit within touching distance. She could see her reflection across its surface, broken only by the engraved grooves of letters and numbers.

Her reflection. His name, yes. But she was alone.

Petal padded over and sniffed at her pockets, and she pulled a broken Milk-Bone out and held it in her open palm. He ate it, of course, and then dropped his head into her lap. She smiled and glanced up again. She was alone except for her big, old, stupid dog. On impulse, she wrapped her arms around his neck and hugged him.

Nathan wasn't here.

But then again, she hadn't come here for his sake. And it *was* quiet, in the graveyard. She'd missed that the past few days. She certainly wasn't going to experience any of it tonight.

Petal's head rose and reminded her that on some days, quiet was a lost cause. On the other hand, he was a good early-warning system. She stood, straightening her jacket and rearranging the pleats of her skirt, and then turned to see who he was barking at.

She felt both guilty and relieved when it wasn't Nathan's mother. Eric, standing about twenty feet away, slid his hands into his pockets, and waited for her to leave the space she'd created for herself here. She did, walking carefully between the headstones.

"Do you think Amy would mind if Chase tagged along tonight?"

"Probably less than you will," she offered.

Chase laughed.

"If she called the police on him, I'd be grateful." Eric was smiling.

"If he does anything that would make a police visit worthwhile, there probably won't be enough of him left to take into custody."

Chase lifted a hand. "Bored with being talked about in the third person now."

"Sorry," Emma said, cheerfully.

"That's sorry? Try harder."

"I'll work on it," she promised. "I have to get home and get changed. Do you want to meet me back at my place, or do you want me to text you Amy's address?"

"We'll meet you at your place," Chase said cheerfully.

Eric hesitated, then shrugged.

"You gave me a week."

Chase, sharpening his knife, shrugged. "We can't afford to lose you, too."

Eric stiffened. "What happened?"

"The old man sent Else and Brand out hunting. Brand didn't make it back."

Else and Brand worked on a different continent. "They found the Necro-mancer?"

"Yeah. He wasn't alone." Metal scraped against stone in a way that was both soothing and dissonant. "Eric—"

Eric started to clean the kitchen.

"Don't wash anything," Chase said, putting the knife down.

Eric ignored him.

"You don't put the cutlery in the water *first*. Glasses. Glasses first." He elbowed Eric to the side. "This is your idea of hot water?"

"Chase—"

"You had to choose the only house in the neighborhood without a dishwasher?"

"It was the only one in range for sale."

Chase ignored this and turned on the hot water. "The old man's worried," he said to the rising steam. "I think he's done with solo hunting assignments for a while."

"You haven't talked to him?"

"I gave you a week. And I'm not going to be the one to tell him the Necro-mancer's still not dead, and we're going to a *party*."

"Amy's party," Eric said, giving up on the washing.

"Where are you going?"

"To get our jackets." He wasn't really looking forward to Chase's reaction when he saw them.

Emma fed and watered Petal before she went foraging in the fridge for something that resembled dinner. Although Emma could cook, and sometimes even enjoyed it, she seldom bothered when it was only herself she was feeding. It was too much like work. And it wasn't as if there wasn't going to be food at Amy's. It was almost 7:00 by the time she headed up the stairs to get changed.

She phoned Allison first. "Hey, Ally, how is Michael getting to Amy's?"

"Philipa's picking him up."

"Isn't that a little far for her to walk?"

"She's driving."

Philipa was not, perhaps, the worst driver known to man. She was, however, in the running. "We needed new lampposts anyway. Are his parents coming to get him, or are we supposed to get him home?"

"I told his mother we'd get him home. When are you leaving?"

"I'm not sure. Eric's meeting me here, and we'll leave when he shows up. Did you want us to pick you up on the way?"

"Philipa's also picking me up."

Emma laughed. "I hope Michael appreciates this."

"It's Michael," Allison replied.

There was a long pause.

"Emma? Em, are you there?"

"Yes," Emma said softly, "but I have to go. My—my dad's here."

Brendan Hall was standing in front of the computer, his arms folded. He didn't move, but the computer screen blinked on, and the screen began to flicker as windows opened. Emma watched in silence for a moment, the hair on the back of her neck beginning to rise.

"Dad?"

He nodded without turning, and Emma knew what he would be looking at: the Letter Graveyard. The place where anonymous people—or people who used handles like **imsocrazy** and **deathhead666** at any rate—sent letters that would never be read.

Except that these *were*.

"Sprout," he said quietly, reading—of course—the letters she had sent him over the years. She tried to remember if anything in them was horribly embarrassing, but she couldn't.

"I missed you," she said softly, answering the comment he didn't—and hopefully wouldn't—make. "Sometimes it helped. To write. Even if you couldn't read it."

"Your mother knew about this?"

"Of course not. She'd just worry. I mean, worry *more*." Emma paused and then asked, "Were you always watching?"

"No. Not for the first year. Not really for the second."

She hesitated. She wanted to touch him. To hug him. But she remembered the cold of his hands, so much like the lantern, and instead curled her fingers into fists and kept them at her sides. "Dad, can I ask you something?"

He sat in her chair, and she turned it so that he was facing her. His eyes were still oddly colored, and they suggested a light that burned beneath the surface of what looked, to Emma, to be perfectly normal skin. There was no translucency to him, nothing to mark him as a ghost, although if she were being truthful, she didn't *want* to see him that way. "Ask," he said, in that quiet father's voice of his that meant he was serious and paying attention.

"Is it true that after you died, you had nowhere to go?"

The silence was lengthy. In Hall parlance, this usually meant yes.

"Em," he finally said, "I'm dead. You're not. You should concern yourself with the living."

"I concern myself," she replied tightly, "with the things that concern me. Is it true?"

"What did Eric tell you?"

"Pardon?"

"What did Eric say about this?"

"He told me to ask you, if you want the truth."

Her father nodded as if this made sense. "Yes."

She almost laughed, but it would have been a strained laugh; she kept it behind her lips. "So . . . you've been stuck here for almost six years, with nowhere to go?"

"Yes."

"And what about the others?"

"The others?"

"The other dead people. The other ghosts."

"There are people," he told her quietly, "that have been trapped here far longer than I have. I have you," he added. "I have your mother. I can watch you, sometimes, and see how you've grown. How both of you have grown. I've never been able to speak with you before, but—your presence here attracts me. It binds me," he added.

"Binds you?"

"It keeps me here."

Emma was silent for a few minutes. At length she said, her voice thicker, "What about the others?"

"When the people they knew in life die, there's nothing to keep them where their lives once were."

"And they move on?"

He was silent. It was not a good silence.

"Dad, where do they *go*?"

He rose, as if the chair were confining, but he didn't turn to face his daughter; instead, he walked to the window. Shaking his head, he let his hands drop. "Emma, can you understand that I don't want you involved in this if it's at all possible?"

"No. I'm not eight years old anymore," she added, feeling slightly defensive. "And I *am* involved. I can see you. I can talk to you." She took a deep breath. "I don't want you to leave," she said starkly. "I'm selfish enough to be happy that I can still talk with you. It's been so long."

"But if you're trapped here, if you're trapped in this—this half-life, I don't want that. I want you to be here because you want to be. I don't want you to be here because you have no place else to go." She hesitated, then said, "There's a four-year-old boy who's trapped in a burning house."

He did turn his head to look at her then.

"I don't want him to stay trapped there. He—Eric says his memories are strong enough that he stays in the burning building and strong enough that when I approach the house, it burns *me*. But he's four. And I want him to come out of that house. I don't want him to stay there forever.

"And I'm going to *get him out*. Don't even think of trying to talk me out of it."

His smile was rueful, but she saw the pride in it, and it was brighter, for a moment, than the odd luminescence. "I wouldn't dream of it, Sprout."

"But Eric says . . . if I manage to get him out somehow, he's still lost. He has nowhere to go. Dad," she added, her voice dropping to a whisper, "he's *four*. I don't want him to be stuck wandering the streets alone until his mother finally dies. Is that going to happen to him?"

"If he's lucky," her father replied. He shoved his hands into his pockets. But he looked at the curtains, and after a moment, Emma crossed the room to open them herself. To let the light in.

"It's not that we're not drawn," he told her. "It's not that we don't know *where* to go when we die. There *is* a place for us. We can't *get there*, but we're always aware of it."

"Can't get there?"

He nodded. "It's like looking through glass. But it's not glass; we can't shatter it. We can't pass through it."

Emma folded her arms tightly across her chest. "Where is it?"

"It's not a geographical location, Em. I can't pull up Google Maps and point it out."

"But you could find it?"

"I could find it now. I could find it now without moving." He rose and made his way to the window that Emma had revealed. "But it's painful. To see it, to see what I can only describe as light, and to be shut out forever. The dead, especially the newly dead, will often gather there, wailing."

She didn't ask her father if that's what he'd done because she didn't want to know. Her father had been the pillar of the world with his patience, his quirky humor, his ability to override anger. "If you free your four year old, that will be where he's drawn, if he's lucky. He won't see the others," her father added. "Not immediately. But he'll linger, for a year or two."

"It's got to be better than burning," she whispered.

"It's better," he agreed. But his tone said *it's the same*.

"What's on the other side of the glass?"

"Home," he replied softly. "Peace. Warmth. I would say love, but I don't think any one of us can say for certain because we can't reach it. We're like moths, Em," he added.

"And this is *lucky*?"

He glanced at her, then, and she knew he had come to the end of the words he was willing to share. But she'd lived with him for years. "Dad?"

"Yes?"

"When I touched you in the hospital, Mom could see you."

He closed his eyes.

"Why?"

"I won't answer that either, Em. Don't ask."

"Why?"

"Because Eric, if I'm not mistaken, is already having some difficulty with you, and I would like very much that it not get harder for him."

"For *him*. Why?"

"Because," her father said, "he'll have to kill you, or try, and while I want to see you, I want you to have a life. You've only just started," he added softly.

"But *why* will he have to kill me?"

"Because he'll see only what he fears in you. He won't see what he admires." Her father lifted one hand. "I can't judge him," he added softly. "I can hate him, but I can't judge him. Don't touch me. Don't touch *any* of the dead."

"If I don't touch the child, his mother won't be able to see him."

His father looked at her, his expression darkening. But he knew her, knew her far better than Eric did; he said nothing. Instead, he began to fade.

Conversation over.

When Eric came to the door, Petal was already there, barking his lungs out. The Hall household didn't need an alarm system; they had Petal. On the other hand, alarm systems didn't require feeding, watering, walking, and endless cleanup.

Emma opened the door and let herself out, locking the door while Petal's barking deteriorated into a steady, guilt-inducing whine.

"Michael?" Eric asked, and she smiled. He was wearing a gray collared shirt and dark jeans but otherwise looked entirely like himself.

"Allison's got that taken care of."

Chase, on the other hand, had decided to go insane. His red hair was a mass of gel, he wore incredibly angular sunglasses, and he wore a tank under a black leather jacket that looked more like studs than coat.

"You," she told him, "don't get to tell Eric how to dress."

He lowered the rim of said glasses. "Thank you. You don't clean up badly yourself. Are we ready to go?"

"One of us was ready half an hour ago," Eric told him.

"Two of us," Emma said helpfully. They headed down the walk to Eric's car. She stood by the back passenger door, and when the locks clicked, she got in. Chase took the front passenger seat, and Eric got behind the wheel of the car.

"I should warn you," Eric told Emma, "that I will kill Chase if he divulges any personal information of an embarrassing nature. So if you like him at all, don't ask."

Emma laughed.

"Easy for you," Chase muttered, "since he's not going to kill *you* for asking."

It had been such a long week. It felt as though Tuesday night had happened months ago. Emma stared out the window as the streets moved past, thinking about her father. Thinking, as well, about Nathan, and where Nathan might be. It was hard. She worked *not* to think about him, but she wasn't used to it; there had been no reason not to think of him before.

A year, her father had said. Maybe two. Two years, and then he'd drift back, either to his home or to hers.

"Emma?"

"Hmmm?" She looked up. "Oh, sorry. I forgot." She started to give him the directions he needed to get them to Amy's.

If there had been any question about which house the party was at, it was answered definitively the minute the car doors were opened: You could hear the music from the street. Emma listened for a few tense minutes and then relaxed.

"DJ?"

"Yeah. Last time she did this, she hired a band."

Eric laughed.

"I'm not kidding. The band was louder," she added, "and they kind of had to be escorted out of the house when one of them got dead drunk and started hitting on anything that moved. And I mean *anything*."

"Escorted how?"

"Oh, the usual. Someone called the police before things got really ugly." She shrugged and added, "Not that it wasn't ugly afterward. Mr. Drunk and Amorous really didn't appreciate the shabby treatment and he broke a few things to make his point."

"She does this often?"

"Not too often. Depends on what her parents have been doing—or not doing, in this case."

"Not doing?"

"Not taking her to New York City, for a start."

Eric glanced at Chase, and Chase shrugged. "What's so great about New York City?" he asked.

"Everything, basically. Look, if you can avoid saying that anywhere where Amy can actually hear you, things will go a lot smoother."

"What?" Chase shouted, as they approached the front door.

"Good point," Emma grinned, shouting back.

Amy's house was huge. If palaces had been built in a modern style, they would probably have been only slightly larger; Emma's whole house, from top to bottom, would fill only two of the rooms. The grounds—and really, only Amy's house had grounds, everyone else being stuck with simple lawns—extended back into a forested ravine, and the front was only disturbed by a circular road that was too wide to be called a driveway. There was, of course, a sidewalk beside the road.

Chase whistled.

"Amy's family is pretty well off," Emma admitted.

Chase knocked on the door, and Emma hit the doorbell instead. Had Allison been standing beside her, they would now be betting on how many times she would have to hit the doorbell before someone actually heard it. But Eric and Chase were not Allison.

And the answer was five.

Amy's brother answered the door, which surprised Emma enough that her smile froze on her face.

"Hey," he shouted.

"Skip?" This was not actually his name, but for some reason, it was what all of Amy's friends called him. Emma suspected that this was a leftover artifact from elementary school excursions through the mansion that was Amy's house, but she couldn't remember for certain. "Aren't you on the east coast?"

"Something came up," he replied. "I had to come home for a few days. Good damn thing I did," he added, although she saw the beer in his hand. "Someone needs to keep an eye out. If the neighbors call the police again, Amy'll be homeless. These friends of yours?"

She nodded. "Eric's in our year, but he's new to the school. Chase is his cousin."

"Chase? What kind of a name is that?"

"Skip?"

He laughed. "Good point. *Amy!* The last member of the Emery mafia is here!"

Eric looked at Emma, who reddened slightly.

"Mafia?"

"Don't ask. Skip has no sense of humor. Unfortunately, he still tries."

Eric laughed, and they entered the house as Skip left the door and wandered away. Emma caught up with him before he got too far. "Skip, do you know where Allison is?"

"Who?"

"Never mind."

Amy's house was huge. It had five bathrooms, not including the powder room in the main foyer—a powder room that even without shower or bath was still bigger than the main bathroom in the Hall household. The foyer itself was larger than the living room and dining room in the Hall house combined, but at the moment, the rows upon rows of shoes and fall boots that lined the walls near the door made it look slightly less palatial.

"I'm *not* taking my boots off," Chase said loudly.

"Why? Someone's going to steal them?"

He bent down and picked up a pair of running shoes. "They're better than *these*," he said, with obvious disdain. "Or these," he added, choosing a different pair. "Or these."

Eric smacked him on the back of the head.

Unfazed, Chase pointed at Eric's shoes. "Or those. And Eric would definitely steal these."

Emma said, "Suit yourself. But Amy's pretty particular about the shoes in her house, and if she sees you wearing those, you'll probably be waiting outside in the car."

"But you can wear yours?"

"Mine," she replied, "are part of the outfit. And I don't wear them outside much."

"So are mine, damn it. I'm wearing *white socks!*"

She raised her eyebrows. "What, white socks in *that* get-up?"

"They're all Eric had!"

"You did *not* get that crappy jacket out of Eric's closet!"

"Kids," Eric said, putting a hand on both of their shoulders. "Could we maybe save this for Amy?"

Emma grimaced. "If you make it a fashion question, Chase might be able to get away with the boots." She shook her head and added, "White socks."

Finding Amy was not as easy in practice as it was in theory, which, given that she always stood out, said something. As Emma was mostly concerned with finding Allison, this didn't bother her too much.

"You recognize all these people?" Eric shouted. Everything, at the moment, had to be shouted, but you expected that at Amy's big parties.

Emma shook her head, because she didn't really enjoy shouting all that much.

"Do you recognize *half* of them?"

She nodded, because it was more or less true. You *also* expected that with any of Amy's big parties. "Just look for Allison."

"What?"

"*Allison.*"

"No, but I see Michael."

"Where?"

He pointed into a crowd so dense there seemed to be more people than floor space. Before she could tell him—loudly, because there wasn't much choice—how helpful this wasn't, he rolled his eyes and grabbed her by the arm.

Two people trying to snake their way through a thick crowd are notably less coordinated than one. Emma, who felt she already knew this, didn't really appreciate the refresher course. On the other hand, she had to admit that it would have taken twenty minutes to cut across this particular room, and Eric had just carved about fifteen minutes off that. He had also almost knocked four people over, although the sound at her back implied that almost was no longer the correct word for at least one of them.

She looked around and realized that he was actually heading toward the large, enclosed sunroom. Or, more accurately, the sliding doors that led from the slate-floored, sparsely decorated room, with its wicker chairs and foot-rests, to the patio. She realized, again, that Eric was actually taller than she thought, because he could see Michael standing outside in the floodlights. Even in her shoes, she hadn't.

Michael was, not surprisingly, talking to Oliver. He was also, therefore, not paying much attention to anything else that was going on around him. But Allison was standing just to one side of them, out of the worst of the lights' glare, and Emma shook herself free of Eric and ran over to her.

"Sorry," she said. "But you and Michael are still in one piece, so I'm assuming there was no menace to telephone poles."

"And we didn't run any stop signs, either. Philipa's really gotten a lot better behind the wheel of a car. You didn't have any trouble?" There was a slight tinge of anxiety in the question.

"Us? No. We're late because Chase took his time getting dressed."

"Chase?"

Emma nodded in Chase's general direction. "The redhead in the studs."

"I heard that," Chase said. In the bright lights of the patio, he looked even worse. His skin was washed out, and his hair looked like a bad edifice that might just topple if you breathed on it the wrong way.

"Allison, this is Chase. He's a friend of Eric's. Chase, this is Allison, *my best friend.*"

Chase immediately put both of his hands up in the universal gesture of surrender. Allison laughed, and to Emma's surprise, Chase—in his black leather—smiled. "I'm not stupid. Eric's afraid of Emma," he said to Allison.

Eric glared at him.

"I'm not technically allowed to embarrass him in public," Chase added, by way of explanation. "Like the jacket?"

"It's . . . interesting," Allison replied.

"I can't stand it either."

Allison laughed again. Emma turned to stare at Chase.

"What, do I have an enormous zit or something?"

"She is staring at you," Eric replied, when Emma failed to answer, "because you are actually capable of charm, and this is the first time you've shown any."

"I figured she's used to no charm." Chase's smile was very smug. "She's spent the week with you, after all."

Allison was polite enough not to laugh out loud at this but amused enough not to be able to keep the smile off her face. "Are you sure you're not brothers?"

"Please," Chase said, at the same time as Eric said "Positive." He turned to glance at Michael, Connell, and Oliver, who existed at the moment in their own world.

"I don't suppose you play Dungeons and Dragons?" Allison asked Chase.

"Not often."

Emma stared at him again.

"What?"

"Fourth edition rules, if you want to join the discussion," Allison said politely.

Emma gave Allison a look, and Allison laughed. "Or not."

"Have you seen Amy at all?"

"Sort of. Her brother showed up yesterday, with a friend from law school in tow."

"Good looking?"

"Very. And impeccably dressed. I think. Do you want to meet him?"

"No."

"Well, then, I suggest we move," Allison replied. "And quickly, because they're heading this way."

"Emma!" Amy's voice—which was, like the rest of her, exceptional—cleared the distance between them as Emma squared her shoulders and fixed a friendly, party smile to her lips. She turned in time to see Amy step through the open doors, followed by the sound of very loud music, Skip, and a stranger.

Amy was wearing a black and white dress. It was cut to suggest, in some ways, a harlequin, but it was fitted, and the black diamonds that trailed from throat to hem glittered; the white was soft and pale in comparison. Her hair framed her face and fell, in a thick drape, down her back. Her shoes were the inverse of the dress; black with a single white diamond.

She looked, in short, fabulous. Emma, who had long since given up any attempt to compete with Amy, repressed a sigh. Which, Amy being Amy, was noticed anyway. "Well?" she said, demanding her due.

"You are *gorgeous*. And I love the shoes!" Emma, on the other hand, was perfectly willing to grant what was due.

"Notice the earrings?"

"No—come here."

Amy did. The earrings were also black and white—but they were the yin and yang symbols, not the straight lines of trapezoids. "Nicely understated," Emma told her.

Amy nodded, satisfied. "I like your dress," she added. Which, to be fair, was a genuine compliment, because if Amy *didn't* like your dress, the best you could pray for was silence.

Because she had perfect timing, Amy paused and then looked at Chase. Whose dress, for want of a better word, she didn't care for. "Emma?"

"This is Chase," Emma said quickly. "He's a good friend of Eric's."

"Really?"

"Eric doesn't dress him," Emma said, with a perfectly straight face.

Chase, on the other hand, had fallen silent. While Emma was used to this reaction when a new guy was put in the vicinity of Amy, it was the wrong type of silence for someone like Chase. She glanced at him and then turned to look at Eric.

Both of them were utterly still. And both of them wore the same expression, or the same lack of expression; it was as if something had sucked all the life and warmth from their faces. What it left was disturbing.

Amy noticed it as well, but, being Amy, she ignored it. She turned as Skip and his friend joined them. "Skip," she said, "this is Eric, a friend from school. He's new here," she added helpfully. "This is his friend, Chase. Eric, Chase, this is my brother. And this is his friend, Merrick Longland. They met at the beginning of term at Dalhousie."

Merrick Longland stepped into the light, standing with his back to Michael and his friends, who remained entirely unaware of encroaching strangers. He was, as Allison had said, impeccably dressed. The dress in question was casual, not formal, but there was something about the crisp lines of a loosely fitted coal jacket and the collarless white shirt beneath it that suggested formality. The shirt was partly unbuttoned, and the telltale gleam of a gold pendant lay across his exposed chest. Emma didn't notice what kind of pants he wore. She noticed that his hair was a short, clean-cut brown, that his cheekbones were high, that his chin was neither too prominent nor too slight; she noticed that his brows were thick.

But mostly, in that quiet moment that exists just after you've drawn and held breath, she noticed his eyes. They were gleaming, faintly, as if lit from behind, and she could not honestly say, then or later, what color they actually were.

Merrick smiled, and it was a deep, pleasant smile; it transformed the lines of his face without exactly softening them.

"Merrick," Amy said, although her voice now sounded quiet and slightly distant, "this is Emma Hall. She's one of the Emery Mafia," she added.

"Emma?" Merrick said. He held out a hand.

Emma stared at it, as if she couldn't quite remember what to do. Shaking her head, she grimaced. She held out her hand in turn, and he grasped it firmly in his.

His hand was *cold*. Not like ice, but like winter skin. She started to pull back, which no amount of apology could excuse or convert into good manners, but his hand tightened.

"Oh, Emma," he said softly. "We've only just been introduced, and I think we have a lot to say to each other."

"I—I'm here with friends," she replied, knowing how lame it would sound even before the words left her mouth.

"Ah. Yes. That could be awkward." His eyes, the eyes that were somehow luminescent, flared in the dark of night sky, becoming what the soul of fire would be, if fire had a soul.

And then the world stopped.


## ∽ Chapter 9

In the bright lights of the patio, all the shadows cast against the stonework suddenly stopped moving. The music, transformed by solid glass into the thumping of loud bass, continued its steady, frantic beat—but no one was shouting to be heard.

No one, it appeared, was talking much at all. She couldn't tell if they were even trying; she couldn't look away from his face. She knew. She'd tried. But she could see their shadows—Amy's, Skip's. Allison, Eric, and Chase cast shadows that fell past her line of vision.

"Better?" Merrick Longland asked.

"No."

He smiled. It wasn't meant as a threatening smile; Emma was certain he meant it to be friendly. But her hand was cold, and she could have shaved her dog with the edges around that smile. She tried to dredge up an answering smile from somewhere, and she managed. Unfortunately, it was the same as the smile you offered a dangerously furious dog while you were carefully reaching for a big stick.

"What have you done?" she asked, speaking softly because the unnatural quiet almost demanded it.

"I've provided us with a little bit of privacy."

"I don't think we need it." It was hard to keep her voice even.

"It's better. For them," he added. "There are things I have to tell you—things about yourself—that they don't need to hear."

"Need to hear?"

He nodded. "I'll be brief, because I have to be; this is costly. When Skip mentioned that his sister was having a party, I didn't realize I would have to control a small village's worth of teenagers."

She laughed; it was a thin sound, and it quavered too much. "It's one of *Amy's* parties." From his expression, it was clear that there were people in the world who hadn't heard of Amy's parties. And while Emma knew this was in theory possible, it wasn't often that she met them.

"We can explore the delights of Amy's party in a few minutes." He was clearly underimpressed. "What I have to say to you is important. Your life is in danger. I was delayed some few days in my arrival," he added, "but so were our enemies, it appears."

"What do you mean?"

"You're alive. The delay might have cost you your life. There are people who will be hunting you, and if they had found you before I did, you'd be dead. But I have some measure of defense against them."

She nodded carefully. "I'm willing to talk about this, but I want you to let go of my hand."

"I imagine you do. And I will. I mean you no harm," he added. "I traveled here, at some risk to myself, to save your life."

"Who would want to kill me?" But she knew. And it seemed very important at this minute that she keep that knowledge to herself.

"No one you would know. But they know what you are, Emma. And I know what you are. Shall I show you?"

She started to say no. She wanted to say no. But she said nothing, mute, as the hair on the back of her neck began to rise. She felt as if she were at the science center again, one hand on either of two balls that produced enough static to literally make all the hair on her head stand on end.

It wasn't as bad as that. But it *felt* that way.

"Come," he said, in a commanding tone of voice. "Show yourself."

Emma frowned, her brows drawing together. She even started to speak, but she lost the words. Beside Longland, thin tendrils of what looked like smoke began to appear in the air. He spoke a word that was so sharp and curt she didn't catch it. Didn't want to. Eyes wide, she watched as the smoke began to coalesce into a shape that was both strange and familiar. A woman's shape. A young woman.

Her eyes were the same odd shade of light that Brendan Hall's eyes had been; her hair was black, and her skin was pale, although whether that was because of the lighting, Emma couldn't say. She wore a sundress, the print faded, the material unfamiliar—although Emma had no doubt that Amy would recognize it instantly if she could see it.

"Hello," Emma said to the girl, speaking quietly. It was an entirely different quiet than she had offered Longland, because the girl was afraid.

The girl looked at Emma but did not speak.

"You see her, don't you?" Longland asked.

Emma nodded. "Who was she?"

Longland frowned. "Who was she?" It was clearly not the question he expected.

"When she was alive." Remembering that she actually had manners, Emma turned her attention to the girl. "I'm sorry, that was rude."

The girl's eyes widened slightly.

"My name is Emma Hall," Emma continued, lifting her left hand, because she couldn't actually offer the girl her right one; Longland hadn't let it go. "What's yours?"

Longland's frown deepened. He glanced at the girl; it was a cold glance and a dismissive one. "Answer," he said curtly.

The girl remained mute.

Longland's expression shifted again. "Answer her."

"If she doesn't want to answer, it's okay," Emma said, raising her voice.

Longland said, "When you understand your gift better, you will understand why you are wrong." Each word was clipped; he was angry. "*Answer her.*" When a name failed to emerge, he suddenly lifted a hand.

"Merrick, don't—"

But he didn't strike the girl. He *yanked*, and when he did, Emma could see a thin, golden chain around his fingers. It was fine, like spidersilk, and she had missed it because it was almost impossible to see. But she *had* seen it, and she was now aware of it and determined to remain so. The strand ran from his hand *into* the heart of the girl. The girl staggered, her face rippling—literally rippling—in pain.

"Emily Gates," the girl replied, and the sound of her voice was so *wrong* Emma almost cried out in fear. Before she could think, she slapped Merrick, and even as his eyes were widening in shock, she reached out for that golden chain, and she *pulled*.

The chain snapped in her hand, and she held its end.

Merrick Longland still held her right hand, however. All smile, all friend-liness, was gone. "You will give that back to me," he said, each word distinct and sharp. "Now."

In answer, Emma tried to yank her right hand free. Longland didn't move. She tried harder, and reaching out with his left hand, he grabbed her by the chin. "Give it back, Emma. Don't force me to be unpleasant. No one can hear you," he added, lowering his voice. "And at parties of this type, bad things sometimes happen."

His fingers tightened as he drew closer.

She tried to pull back.

And then she heard a familiar voice in the silence, and she froze.

Michael said, "Leave her *alone*."

Longland's brows twisted in a mixture of confusion, anger, and surprise, but he released Emma, shoving her back before he started to turn.

"Michael! No!"

A familiar and much-maligned book suddenly and unexpectedly con-nected with the side of Longland's face. It was—Emma could see the title flash by beneath the bright lights—the 4th edition Dungeon Master's guide. She promised that she would never *ever* roll her eyes at that book again.

Noise returned as Longland staggered back. Emma, hands free, began to run to Michael's side, but Eric grabbed her around the waist and yanked her off her feet.

"Allison!" he shouted, "Grab Michael! Grab Michael now!"

Allison's familiar form darted slightly in front of Emma. She didn't grab Michael, but she did touch his arm and his shoulder with both of her hands; he was panting, heavily, his precious book clutched in knuckles that even Emma could see were white.

She saw Chase run past them, reflecting more light than the glass doors did.

"Michael," Allison said, in her steady, even voice, "It's dangerous. Come stand with Emma and me."

"He was trying to hurt Emma," Michael said, still staring at Longland.

"Allison!" Eric shouted.

"He was trying to hurt Emma," Allison agreed, "but he didn't. Emma is safe with Eric. Come back, Michael." She drew him toward Eric and Emma. Emma could see that her hands were shaking. "Emma—what's happening?"

"I don't know. But it's bad. Michael, Allison—" she stopped speaking be-cause Chase had reached Longland. Emma suddenly knew exactly why he had refused to take off his boots; his leg snapped out, and he kicked Longland in the head. Longland staggered and then threw up his arms.

The grass around the patio burst into white and green flame. So did Chase. "Emma!" Longland shouted. "Come!"

"Fuck," Eric said, under his breath. Had his mouth not been so close to her ear, she wouldn't have caught it. "Emma, stay *here*. Do *not* interfere. Do *not* run away." And then he was gone, racing across the patio stones toward Chase.

For ten long seconds the flames burned in silence. Eric ran, and Emma, watching him, felt the ghost of his arm around her waist, the tickle of his words in her ear. She saw Chase moving through the fire; saw that it followed him like white shadow. She couldn't see his expression, couldn't hear his voice—if he said anything at all. But he moved *slowly*, and she thought she could see the black curl of burning hair rising from his head.

Eric would help him, somehow.

Lifting her hands to her mouth, cupping them on either side of her lips, she shouted. "Oliver, Connell! Come here!" She glanced quickly at Michael and saw that Allison was holding onto his arm.

"Emma?"

She'd forgotten Amy. Under normal circumstances she would have bet that wasn't possible. "*Oliver!*" Turning, she glanced at Amy. Amy was pale, but confusion in Amy seldom gave way to raw fear.

"Tell me," she said, "that our back lawn isn't burning."

Emma swallowed.

"Never mind. Skip, call emergency. *Everyone else,*" she added, raising her voice into the stratosphere, "*get back into the house.*"

Years of obeying Amy had engendered a purely Pavlovian response to her commands. They all started to head toward the door taking slow, jerky steps, looking at the fight, at the lawn.

But it was Amy who held them up at the door. "Skip?"

Emma glanced at Skip and saw that he hadn't moved.

"*Skip.*"

He was standing there, teetering. Amy ran back to him, looked at him closely, and then slapped him across the face. He turned, slowly, to look at her, his brows gathering, his eyes widening in confusion. "Amy?" He spoke slowly.

"Give me your phone," she said, holding out her hand.

"My what? What are you doing here?"

"I live here, remember?"

He blinked. Emma saw the color of his face, and she shouted a warning to Amy just before his eyes rolled to white, like a screen whose projector has just died. He crumpled at the knees, and Amy managed—barely—to stop his forehead from smacking into the flagstones.

"I *do not* believe this," Amy said, under her breath, as Emma ran back to help her. "Tell me my brother's friend is not fighting with Eric and Chase near the hedges."

"Let's just get Skip inside."

"Rifle his pockets for his damn phone," Amy replied, grunting as they each grabbed him under an arm. "My mother is going to murder me if they burn down the garden."

Emma laughed. It was entirely the wrong type of laughter, and she wouldn't have been surprised if Amy had slapped her as well. Hysteria had that effect on Amy.

Longland had retreated to the hedges. Blood trickled down his forehead, and his lip was swollen. His eyes widened as he saw Eric approaching at a run, but they narrowed quickly as he crossed his wrists over his chest.

Chase was caught in the soul-fire, slowed by it; it hadn't yet managed to eat its way past his defenses. But it would if the Necromancer wasn't brought down soon.

Stupid, stupid, *stupid*. Eric hadn't expected to find a Necromancer at Amy's party. He hadn't been prepared. His damn shoes were in the endless hall of shoes that was Amy's vestibule. Chase had kept his head, Chase had stayed focused. He hated it when Chase was right.

Eric slid the one weapon he always carried out of its sheath beneath his shirt. Chase, being paranoid, was probably bristling with knives, but he could only wield two, and even in the stretched warp and weft of space around the Necromancer, Eric could see that he carried one knife in each hand.

Longland hissed a word that broke in three places, and Eric threw himself to the side as the air above the garden grass crackled. He saw night and soul-fire expand in a bubble, stretching and twisting the earth beneath it as it grew. He felt the edge of it catch his arm, and he cursed, shoving himself off the grass and into the air as it spun him around. As he landed, he twisted the dagger around, catching the bubble's edge.

It resisted, and he threw himself back as Longland spoke again.

This time, the hedge itself grew, its branches thickening and widening as they twisted, groping in the air. He felt leaves slice his cheek, and he swore again. He wasn't certain how many of the people at Amy's party had been affected by the Necromancer's first spell. But it encompassed everyone standing outside, and he had held it for some time.

They hadn't sent just anyone to gather Emma; they'd sent someone powerful.

Chase had reached Longland. He didn't throw his daggers, but at this speed, they wouldn't have pierced paper if it was held out as a shield; he kept them close, cutting tendrils of fire, and shedding them as he could. But he was slow.

Eric, trying to avoid the same slowness, grunted as the hedges bit again; he cut the one branch that had secured itself tightly enough to cut shirt and tear skin. It shrank before it hit the ground. Longland, damn it, was *good*. Two to one, and he wasn't panicking. But he was breaking a sweat.

*Come on, Chase,* Eric thought. He cut in to the right, and when Longland brought his arms up for a third time, he caught his wrist with the dagger, breaking the sweep of his arms. Narrowing his eyes, he *looked*. Longland was glowing faintly, but there was no other white shadow surrounding him: no nimbus of death, of the dead.

He jumped and rolled along the ground nearest the base of the hedges, came up and cut through two branches. Six feet. Five.

He swung, low and up, and his dagger clanged off metal.

Longland cursed again, and then, instead of reaching up with those arms, he reached *back*, grabbing the hedge with both hands. All along the row, its carefully cut and manicured lines broken everywhere by the touches of Necromancy, fire blossomed. White fire. And green.

Longland pulled all of that fire *into* himself, absorbing, as well, the fire along the grass and the fire that clung to Chase. Chase screamed—more in frustration than pain—as Longland pulled the entire hedge *around* himself and vanished.

Chase swore. He swore loudly.

Eric pushed himself to his feet. "Well," he said, "that could have gone better."

"Did you recognize him?"

"No."

"He's going to recognize us if he sees us again."

Eric nodded. "But we're going to have other problems," he added.

"What's a problem compared to a prepared Necromancer?"

Eric turned toward the house.

"You're joking, right? You don't intend to go back there. Eric, don't be an idiot. You're not worried about your Peter Parker identity, are you?"

"We're not done here," Eric replied. "And I want to check on Emma."

"On Emma. The *other* Necromancer."

"Don't even think it, Chase."

Chase hadn't sheathed his daggers.

"You gave me a week."

"It's not a game anymore."

"It was never a game. She didn't help him. She didn't even try."

Chase just shook his head. A moment passed, and then, glaring, he put the knives away. "Sorry about your jacket."

"Not a problem—but we're going to have to get those stupid studs repaired."

Chase looked at the jacket; the studs had smeared into running, flattened blobs of silver-crusted iron. "We're going to have to get a different jacket."

"Maybe. And maybe this time you can buy your own."

Eric wished, for just a moment, that he could let Chase take his ire out on the DJ. Chase on the other hand, didn't even appear to notice the sudden increase in volume. Before entering Amy's house, he had carefully peeled off the ruins of his jacket and had folded it in half with the lining facing out.

Not that many people had seen the fire on the lawn, and the fire was now gone. The hedges would probably look a lot worse in the morning light then they did at the moment, but Eric wouldn't have to be there for that. Hopefully, by Monday morning's first class, Amy would be distracted.

Or, he amended, as he entered the sunroom, distracted by something else. Michael was waiting for them as they entered the room, Allison by his side.

"Where's Emma?" Eric asked them. If they noted the tears the leaves had made in his clothing, they stopped themselves from actually mentioning them.

"In the kitchen with Amy and her brother. They asked us to wait here in case you couldn't find it. Chase, are you all right?"

Chase grimaced and reached up gingerly to touch his hair. "I've been better," he admitted. "But I've been a hell of a lot worse. You two are okay?"

"Michael is *not* happy about hitting someone across the side of the face with a heavy book," Allison said. "I'm fine. Confused," she added, in a way that suggested that honesty, however hard it was to get at, was important to her. "But not injured. What happened?"

Eric lifted a hand just as Chase opened his mouth. "I'd rather not have to explain it a dozen times," he said curtly. And loudly. "We can save it until we get to the kitchen." The sunroom was directly adjacent to the very large living room. It was also adjacent to the hall that ran along the back of the house. People filled both of these spaces. "Why are all these people still here?"

"Why wouldn't they be?"

He stared at her for a moment as if she'd just spoken in French. "Because we just had a—"

"Take your own advice," Chase said, swatting him on the back. "It's a big, *loud*, crowded house. Things didn't last that long. I'd bet you even money that most people here didn't even notice; it's not as though they're standing here with their faces pressed against the windows."

Great. The day not only held a powerful Necromancer and a powerful Potential—it also held a moment in which he had to listen to advice from Chase when Chase was right.

Emma looked up as Allison and Michael entered the kitchen through dark, swinging doors.

"Did you find them?"

"See for yourself," Allison said. Chase and Eric entered the kitchen behind her.

Amy was kneeling on the floor with a cold cloth in her hands. Her brother's head was in her lap. The last time that Emma had seen Amy with something wet in her hands near Skip, it was because he had turned the hose on her and she had chosen to retaliate. It was also the last time, Emma thought, that Skip had been home, and the Emery Mafia had, in his words, taken over the entire place. He'd then packed up and left for Dalhousie and law school.

Emma had been solidly part of the Emery Mafia then. Nathan had still been alive.

Amy looked at Eric and Chase. She was, of course, still beautiful—she always commanded attention just by existing—but she was also that peculiar shade of white that comes from anger. Amy was seldom angry. Even when her parents had, in her own words, ditched her for New York City, she'd only managed to reach annoyed. Or irritated. She was beyond that now.

But Emma understood why. Amy was frightened, and Amy Snitman did not *do* fear.

"What," she said, making a stiletto of the word, "is going on here?"

Chase shoved his hands into his pockets and looked at Eric. "Your show," he said, shrugging.

Eric looked at Amy. He glanced at Emma and Allison and hesitated when he came to Michael. Oliver and Connell, on the other hand, were not in the kitchen, and Michael's book was no longer in his hands. It was in the backpack that was across his shoulders. Emma understood why he hesitated; she would have done the same.

But in the end, she would have surrendered to the inevitable, because in a pinch, Amy was her friend. They might disagree on some things, but when it was an emergency, Amy was a person she could trust at her back. She couldn't make that decision for Eric, and she knew it was a decision he was trying to make for himself.

"How long has he been out?"

He's stalling, Emma thought.

Amy's lips thinned, but to Emma's surprise, she answered the question. "Since just after the fire."

"Did he say anything before he collapsed?"

"He asked me what I was doing here."

Eric glanced at Chase, whose hands were still in his pockets. Chase nodded.

"Why?" Amy asked sharply.

"Did he say where he thought he was?"

"No." The pause between that word and the next few couldn't quite be called hesitation, but only because it was Amy. "But I don't think he thought he was home. He might have thought he was at school," she added, her brows furrowing slightly.

"How far away is his school?"

"On the east coast."

"How long would it take him to get here, assuming he had the plane tickets booked?"

"Hours. I'm not sure. It would depend on where he was, what the traffic was like, how long it took to get his baggage."

"Hours is good enough." Eric walked over to Skip and knelt. He pushed one eyelid up and then lifted a limp arm. "He should come out of this in the morning. He won't expect to be home, though. He'll probably be a bit disoriented, and he'll think he had a very unpleasant dream."

"And his so-called friend?"

"He isn't likely to see Merrick Longland again."

"But you're sure he'll be okay?"

"I don't know what level of compulsion was placed on him. They don't normally do this," he added. "It's costly."

"What would they normally do?" The sharp edge was back in her voice.

"Normally? They'd suggest that he wanted to go home to visit his friends or his family. They'd make it his idea, and they'd just happen to be prepared to go with him. He'd feel like an idiot, after, but he'd remember almost everything."

"Almost?"

"He wouldn't remember the friend in question. He'd just remember the stupid idea—of going home on no notice—and wonder what the hell he'd been thinking."

Amy looked at Emma, who had been watching the conversation in silence. "Is Eric sane?" she asked.

"More or less. I won't vouch for Chase."

"And you knew about this?"

"Me?" Emma lifted her hands, palms out, in front of her. "No. Not this. Not the fire, either. But . . . I'd trust him."

Amy nodded and turned back to Eric. "What you've left out is why."

"Why?"

"Why would someone compel my useless brother to come home? Why didn't Longland just come here on his own?"

"Good question," Eric replied, frowning. "I've been wondering that as well. Longland clearly wanted to be in on this party." The frown deepened. "Chase?"

"Amplifiers," Chase said. If Emma hadn't been standing closer to him than to Amy, she might have missed it. She might also have missed the two words that followed, but they were just swearing. "I'll check."

"Check now," Eric told him roughly.

"Excuse me?" Amy said, and Chase paused in the half-open door.

Eric cursed under his breath. "Amy, it's important."

"How important?"

"He might have needed your brother here to have easier access to your house."

"Which would help him how? We're here alone," she added. "If he could force Skip to leave law school on zero notice—and forget all about it later—he could probably get anyone to do anything he wanted."

"Some people are easier to compel than others," Eric told her, giving her a very pointed look.

She chose to take it as a compliment, but that was Amy all over. "Emma, go with Chase and help him find whatever he's looking for. Don't," she added, "let him find anything he shouldn't be looking for."

"Chase," Eric said, before he could make it out the door, "remember what you said."

Chase rolled his eyes toward the ceiling.

"Where do you want to start?" Emma asked him, when they were finally on the other side of the kitchen door.

Chase glanced at her for a moment and then shrugged. "Any place there aren't four hundred people."

"So you want to start next door."

"Ha-ha."

"We can start upstairs. No one's supposed to be there, and if we happen to interrupt someone making out, Amy will thank us."

"Great. They won't."

"Probably not," she agreed cheerfully. "Besides, you need to get to a mirror and look at your hair."

"My hair?"

"Well, what's left of it." She waved at Nan and Phil, who were closest to the stairs, said hello to a couple of people she vaguely recognized but didn't know by name, and made her way to the main stairs. "Amy didn't even notice your boots."

"Don't sound so disappointed."

They cleared the top of the stairs and headed down the hall. It wasn't a short hall. The rooms that crowded around it weren't small rooms. "Bathroom's over there," Emma said, pointing to the farthest door in the wall to the right. She could feel the bass of the sound system pounding beneath the parts of her feet that were actually against the ground; given that these were dress shoes, that wasn't much. But she walked farther down the hall and then turned to face Chase.

"What, exactly, are we looking for?" It was a reasonable question.

Chase was not in a reasonable mood. "I'll let you know if I see it."

"I'd rather have some warning."

"You probably won't—"

"See it?"

He frowned. "No," he finally said. "You probably *will* see it. But it probably isn't anything that you would recognize as dangerous."

"Do you see the dead as well?"

His brows rose slightly, and then he grimaced. "Can I just say I don't know what you're talking about?"

"If you like lying to my face, sure."

"You don't know what you're talking about." He headed toward the bathroom, and she followed him in. The room was almost painfully brightly lit, but the skylight was dim and dark, although one edge of slanted glass reflected the light. "Yes," he said, as he pushed the door open. "I can see the dead. But not the same way Eric does. Eric's naturally talented; I have to work my ass off for even a glimpse. I'm lazy," he added, just in case this wasn't obvious. "God this room is *huge*."

Since that had been her own first reaction, Emma didn't laugh. Barely.

"What you're looking for," she asked quietly, "could it be planted quickly?"

"If by quickly you mean in less than one day, yes. If by quickly you mean five minutes, no. Not unless the—never mind. No." He stopped to look in the mirror, and froze. The mirror was most of the wall. The parts of the wall that weren't mirror were occupied by a sink with a lot of smoky marble countertop.

"I *told* you," Emma said. And then she realized that he was not, in fact, looking at his reflection—or more precisely, his hair—at all. "Chase?"

"Get Eric."

She looked, instead, at his reflection. It mirrored him; his eyes were slightly wider, and his expression was frozen in place. His hair was a frayed mass of singed ends, and his previously pale skin was the red that usually requires way too much exposure to sun.

"Chase?"

"Get Eric, Emma."

She hesitated in the doorway and then said, "Not without you."

"Emma, I am not joking. Get Eric."

"I'm not laughing, you'll notice. I'm not going to get Eric without you." She couldn't say later why she wouldn't budge. Chase had clearly shown that he was not afraid of much, and that he could handle himself. She forced her face to relax into a smile, and added, "Amy will kill me."

His expression did change, then, to one of frustration and, surprisingly, resignation. On the other hand, he swore a lot as he turned away from the mirror.

Chase and Eric went up the stairs, and Emma followed them as if she were an afterthought. They didn't talk at all. Chase didn't tell Eric what he'd seen, and since Emma had seen nothing, she couldn't fill him in either. But what was most disturbing was that Eric didn't *ask*. He just pushed himself up off the kitchen floor—where Skip was still unconscious—and followed.

But he stiffened as he touched the bathroom door.

"Eric?" Emma asked softly. Eric spun, and what she saw in his face made her take a step back. He reined it in, but she could see that he had to work at it, and it made her nervous.

He had spoken about having to kill her before, and they had been just words to Emma. For the first time since he'd said it, they weren't. He saw that in her face, as well, and his mouth tightened as he gripped the doorknob and turned away.

Without looking at her, he said, "It's too much to hope you'll go back downstairs and stay with your friends."

It almost wasn't, but she didn't say this.

"But stay in the doorway, Em. Keep your feet on the carpet, and keep your hands on the walls if you have to grab anything. Whatever you do—or see—stay out."

She nodded. She would have asked him why, but in emergencies, why was the first thing to go, and everything about Eric at this point *screamed* emergency. "Wait—what about Chase?"

The tension left his shoulders, and he shook his head. "Chase," he told her softly, "can take care of himself. You've known him for what? Minutes?"

"People I've never met die all the time."

"And you worry about them?"

"They're not standing in front of me. There's nothing at all I can do to help them."

"Believe that there is nothing at all you can do to help Chase. Or me." Eric shook his head. "I give up," he said, to no one in particular.

"You already said that."

"I'm continually optimistic by nature. Shut up, Chase." Taking a deep breath, he entered the bathroom. Chase was standing to one side of the mirror, his arms folded across his chest. The lack of leather jacket didn't detract from the attitude of his posture, which said a lot about his attitude and only a little about the jacket.

Eric stepped up to the counter, looked into the mirror, and froze.

Emma, her feet pressed against the carpet, her hands pressed against the wall, froze as well. She could see Eric's reflection in the mirror; she could see the welt across his cheek, the dark slash of dried blood, but those had been pretty clear in the fluorescent kitchen lighting as well.

What she hadn't seen until this moment were the reflections that had no physical counterparts: the pale, almost translucent profiles of a middle-aged man and a young girl. They stood to either side of Eric, their arms raised above their heads, their eyes open in the glassy stare of people who no longer take in the world that's passing around them.

"Chase?" Eric said, voice both soft and sharp.

"Two. If there's a third, I can't sense him."

"Did you touch the mirror?"

"Do I look like a moron?"

"Usually. Ready?"

Chase nodded, his arms folding slightly more firmly around his upper body.

Eric reached out with his palm and laid it flat against the mirror's surface. The mirror—and Eric's reflection—rippled. Emma felt it; it was as if, in rippling, the mirror had disturbed not only its own surface but the surfaces of every other solid thing in the room as well. Chase grimaced at the same time as she flinched; even Eric clenched his jaws.

Only the two silent people who extended their arms in the mirror seemed entirely unmoved, and Emma knew, then, that they were dead.

But if Eric saw them, he gave no sign; the whole of his attention was focused on the mirror. As the rippling stilled, he withdrew his hand; it fell to his side as if he no longer cared whether or not it was part of him. His reflection was gone. So, too, was the background to it: the tiled walls, the large, in-ground bath, the standing shower stall.

In their place were the walls of an entirely different room, with red rugs, dark-stained wood-plank floors peering out at their edges, globes of light on standing sconces, and one central figure.

Sitting in a tall-backed chair directly opposite Eric, wearing a dress that not even Amy at her most ostentatious could have carried off—too many beads, too much fabric, too many frills, and too much damn *gold*—was a woman Emma had never seen.

Not even in a nightmare.

## ༄ Chapter 10

Nightmare was an odd word to apply to the woman seated on what was, Emma thought, a throne. Nothing about her suggested the monsters that dwelled across the boundary of sleep. She was not beautiful in the way that Amy was beautiful, but she was striking in a way that Amy was not, at least not yet. She wore a dress that reminded Emma of pictures of Queen Elizabeth I. Her hair was pale, not gold and not platinum, but closer to the latter, and bound in such a way that nothing escaped—no tendrils, no curls.

She wore a thin diadem just above the line of her hair, which contained a single sapphire; this set off eyes that were a remarkable blue. Her lips were, in Emma's opinion, unnaturally red; it was the only thing about her that made her look old.

Or rather, it was the only thing Emma could point at, because no one who wasn't old wore that color. But something about this woman radiated age. Nothing about her seemed remotely friendly. Not even when she smiled. Especially not then.

And she smiled, the left corner of her lips twitching upward, as she looked at Eric. Emma could see only his back, but his whole body had tensed.

"Well met, Eric. Am I to assume, from the unexpected pleasure of your company, that Merrick is dead?"

Chase said nothing. He said it very loudly. Eric's nothing was quieter.

"I thought you might make an appearance," the woman added, when it became clear that no one else would speak. "And here you are. And you've brought your pet with you." Her smile deepened. "If there are two of you, the situation must be dire, indeed. It is seldom that you go hunting these days." The smile slid from her face. "But you will play your games, won't you? Experience teaches you nothing. You should stop, Eric. You should end this game. What can you do, after all, that does not, in the end, add to *my* power?"

He said nothing.

"What can you do at all?" She lifted an arm; it glittered in the globes of light at her back. "Come back to me. Come back. Everything else is dust and illusion." Her expression had changed as she spoke, her eyes rounding slightly as she leaned forward in her chair. Her voice had softened, losing the brittle edge that made it seem too cold.

Eric stood there for a long, silent moment, and then he turned away. Emma saw the expression on his face, and her eyes widened, her mouth opened. But words wouldn't come; she was as mute, in her way, as he was. She would have walked over to him, she would have pulled him away, but he had told her very clearly to stay put, and that much she would do.

But it was hard.

"Eric," the woman called.

He didn't turn back.

"*Eric!*"

Those beautiful eyes narrowed; those red, full lips closed. The arm that had been lifted in what was almost a plea fell once again to the arm of the chair, and even at this distance, Emma could see the way the knuckles of both hands suddenly stood out in relief.

"Chase," Eric said quietly, his back to the mirror, "come on."

Chase, however, was staring at the woman. His back was not turned to Emma, and if Emma had ever needed any proof that Eric and Chase were two entirely different people, she had it here. His expression was as white as the woman's. White with rage.

He took one step forward, just one, and Eric spun and caught the fist he'd lifted before Chase could slam it into the mirror. "*Chase.*"

Chase's arm was shaking, and Eric's hand was shaking as well, and they stood there while the woman watched, her fury not lessened by the malice of her smile. But feeding that malicious smile was more than Emma could bear to watch Eric and Chase do.

Keeping her feet on the carpet and anchoring herself with the doorframe, she pivoted into the room and reached for the lights, her hand slapping the wall until she felt the familiar switches beneath her fingers. She turned them off, and night descended through the skylight.

After a few moments of silence, Emma said, "Is it safe to turn the lights back on?"

"More or less."

"I'd prefer the more, if it's all the same to you." She waited for another minute, and then she flipped the switch back on. Chase and Eric were no longer locked in a struggle to prevent Chase from punching the mirror. Better, the mirror now reflected them. She waited, watching them look at each other.

*Who was she?* Emma wanted to ask, but given the tension of their expressions at the moment, she couldn't. Had they been Allison—or Michael—those would have been the first words out of her mouth, and they would have been angry, protective words. But Eric and Chase were not friends of a decade; she wasn't sure how they would take it—but she could guess. Badly.

"Guys."

They both turned to look at her.

"Is she what you were looking for?"

"She is *so* not what I was looking for," Chase replied.

"So that means the house search is still on?"

Eric nodded. "I don't think we'll find anything else," he added. "But we might as well be thorough."

He was wrong. He wasn't happy to *be* wrong, but he was wrong.

And it happened that the person who proved him wrong in this case wasn't Chase. It was Emma. Emma knew the house pretty well; it was hard not to know a house that you'd played extended games of hide-and-seek in from elementary school on. Amy's house, it was agreed, was the best house for hide-and-seek because there were so many places to hide, and you could hide on the move if necessary. It changed the whole feel of the game.

So Emma knew the house as well as anyone but Skip or Amy, and once she'd decided to take charge, she led, and Eric and Chase were forced to follow.

She hesitated on the threshold of Amy's bedroom, but that was the only dangerously sensitive area upstairs, and it was, in Chase's opinion, clean. Mindful of Amy's ability to notice when a hairpin had been moved half an inch, Emma supervised Chase like an angry principal conducting a locker search.

Skip's room had never been off limits in the opinion of anyone but Skip, and none of the girls took him seriously anyway. Since Skip barely noticed his closet—and evidence of this could be seen by the shirts and the pants that were nowhere near it, and should have been—she relaxed and let them both poke around.

"Clean," Chase said.

"In a manner of speaking," Eric added.

The room that had been Merrick's was one of four guest rooms. It was almost self-contained, in that it had a bathroom, a small study, and a very large bedroom (certainly larger than any of the rooms in the Hall household) behind a set of off-white double doors. It had a walk-in closet as well. The only thing it lacked was a kitchen. They approached this room with care—enough care that Eric caught Emma's arm as she reached for the doorknob and pulled her back.

"Let Chase open it."

"Why me?"

Eric glared, but Chase was—mostly—grinning. They really were like brothers. Chase opened the doors that led to the guest room. The rooms were empty, which was more or less what they expected. They weren't entirely tidy, but given that they'd been occupied by a so-called friend of Skip's, Emma didn't expect tidy.

The bathroom had the usual things in it—toothbrush, electric razor, deodorant. It had a mirror that was not nearly as dramatic as the one in the hall bathroom, but Emma hesitated at the doorway just in case. Chase, however, didn't seem worried. Eric was that type of quiet that doesn't let much out into the world; she couldn't tell if he was worried or not.

The bathroom was clean. The bedroom contained one very large suitcase and one carry-on bag; the bed was made.

"Was he planning to stay a while?" Eric asked.

Emma shrugged. "I didn't ask," she replied. "But Amy takes something that size on day trips." In case it wasn't clear, she indicated the large suitcase. "Longland looked like he was a bit of a clothes horse, so it might mean nothing."

Eric tried to open the suitcase. It was locked. So was the carry-on.

"Chase?"

"This," Chase told Emma, "is what we call job security." He opened both suitcases, using what looked like long wires.

"Can you unlock doors that way as well?"

"Not easily. A baby could do this, though. At least a baby not named Eric."

The carry-on was full of books. And two large chocolate bars. They were not, however, good chocolate, which said something. Chase pocketed them anyway, which also said something. She looked at the books as Chase lifted them out of the bag.

Eric had opened the larger suitcase. It was, not surprisingly, full of clothing. But this clothing? It was almost like studying geological strata. The first layer? Shirts. One T-shirt, one sweatshirt. Underwear and socks could be found under two pairs of gray pants. No jeans. But beneath the expected layer of clothing? The unexpected.

"What is that?" Emma asked. She had assumed it was either a jacket or a very heavy shirt, but it just kept unfolding as Eric drew it out of the suitcase. In the end, it was a dress. No. Not a dress. A robe.

"Looks like a robe to me," Chase said.

"Seriously?" She reached out for a fold of the draping cloth and saw that it was not quite gray, as it had first seemed. It was a slate blue, embroidered lightly in curling fronds of gray. Gold thread decorated the sleeves and the hem.

"Eric?"

Eric nodded at Chase.

"What, they have a uniform?" Emma asked.

"Not exactly. But my guess? This wasn't meant for his use."

"Whose, then?"

"Yours."

"Why?"

"Because there's another one. Look."

She reached into the suitcase and pulled out a robe that was similar in cut. It was, however, rust red. She held it against her shoulders and watched the hems flap around in folds across the ground. "I think I like the red better."

As a joke, it fell flat. Chase glanced at her and then at Eric; Eric deliberately didn't meet his gaze.

Emma's hands, still clutching red cloth, became fists. She looked at the two of them, and if Eric was avoiding Chase's gaze, he was *also* avoiding hers. Chase followed suit.

"Guys."

They both looked at her, then. "Can we just stop this right now? You know things you aren't telling me, and they're *about* me. You know what I'm facing, and *I don't*. Tell me."

They exchanged a glance, and Chase shrugged. Eric took a breath, held it for a little too long, and exhaled. "Let's keep on looking."

"Eric."

"Emma—"

"At least explain this." She lifted the robe. "These aren't exactly what you or I would call everyday wear. They're not formal, either. I could put that on," she added, pointing to the slate blue robe, "if I were playing a priest in a badly staged school play."

He nodded.

"I could not put it on and just blend in here, for any value of here that didn't include Amy's Halloween party."

"Amy has Halloween parties?" Chase asked. Eric hit him.

"Your point?" Eric asked Emma.

"My point is that I couldn't wear this anywhere here. If I was meant to wear this, where exactly was I supposed to *go*?"

"Emma—"

"Was I meant to go where *she* is?"

Eric flinched. "No," he said, almost too softly. "Never that, Emma."

But Chase said, "God, Eric."

Eric looked at Chase and said, No. But without the sound.

"Idiot. She's right. She's absolutely right. Eric, wake the hell up."

Eric was silent. Chase turned to Emma. "Find us a big room," he told her.

"How big?"

"Damn it, just—*big*."

She bit her lip and nodded. "Come on. There's one up here, and there're two downstairs that might do. They don't *look* as big when they're full of people."

She led them to the master bedroom. It was at the end of the hall, it was fronted by the largest doors on the second floor, and it had always had an invisible sign across it saying: *Keep out or Amy might kill you.* Not that this had always worked.

Tonight was one of those nights when fear of Amy was not as strong as fear of the utterly nameless future that included Chase, Eric, and a man who could suddenly turn the entire backyard into an eerie blaze of silent white and green fire. She opened the doors.

To either side of the doors were large, walk-in closets; beyond those, mirrored vanities with small—for this house—sinks and very large counters. There were also two bathrooms, one beside each vanity. Emma passed between the mirrors and grimaced, but the mirrors were just mirrors. She headed on into the depth of the bedroom. The bed, which was so huge that it would not have fit around the bend in the stairs in the Hall household, looked tiny.

Chase scoped the room out with care, and Emma watched him with growing unease. "Nothing," he told Eric.

"You're sure?"

Chase nodded and then looked at Emma. "Emma," he said quietly, "have Amy clear the house out."

She stared at him. "Chase, it's barely nine o'clock. You want me to tell her to kick everyone out *now*?"

He said nothing.

Eric, understanding Emma's problem, said, "Let's check it out. The noise and the people won't get in the way if we're looking."

"No. Only if the Necromancer comes back."

Necromancer. Emma stared at Chase for a long moment and then turned and headed toward the stairs. "It's one of two rooms," she managed to say. *Necromancer.*

"Any chance any one of those rooms is empty?"

"Depends. If you get the DJ to put on the wrong damn music, he'll either get lynched or people will leave really fast."

There was a lot of quiet swearing. None of it was Emma's. She was still stuck on the word *Necromancer*. She headed down the stairs, clinging to the railing; they followed. She turned one sharp right at the end of the stairs, and came up against the expected press of bodies; this slowed their progress by a lot. This time, however, Eric didn't just grab her arm and drag her through people.

He did catch her hand, and he did hold it, but it was probably either that or get left behind. The music got louder, and the talking was now that level of shouting that's needed just to say hello in a loud room.

"Chase!" Emma shouted

"What?" he shouted back.

"Where?"

"Go to the back of the room. The DJ."

Emma nodded and headed that way. The music got louder; the bass was like a heartbeat—but a lot less welcome—by the time she had made it most of the way there. She'd chosen to try to sidle along the walls, because the people standing there were less likely to accidentally elbow her or step on her feet.

But she stopped well before she reached the DJ. Eric walked into her. Chase walked into him.

Standing against the far wall were four people.

Not a single one of them was alive.

"Emma?" Eric asked, his mouth close enough to her ear that she felt the words trace her spine. "Emma, what is it?"

"Can't you see them?" She lifted her hand and pointed. When Eric failed to answer, she turned—and it was hard—to look at him. His eyes were narrowed, and he was scanning the back wall, but no shifting expression told her that he saw what she could easily see.

"Chase?" She had to shout this.

Chase shook his head slowly. He moved closer, which meant that they were all standing on almost the same square foot of floor. "What do you see?"

Emma didn't like the words "dead" or "ghost" because they didn't look like her preconceived notions of either. They were, for one, too solid; there was a faint luminescence around their eyes, and even their skin, but without it, she might have mistaken them for living people.

Although perhaps not in those clothes. She hesitated, then said, "The dead. There are four, two women, one boy and one girl. Eric—I don't understand why you can't see them. They're dead."

Chase closed his eyes, and his shoulders tensed. Eric finally let her go so he could put a hand on one of those shoulders. "Not now, Chase."

"Fuck, Eric—" He took a breath, steadied himself. "You can't see them?"

Eric shook his head.

Emma said, quietly, "They're chained."

Eric looked at her. "Chained?" She almost couldn't hear the word.

She nodded.

He swore, but it was background noise, now. She started to walk again, and after a minute, he followed. The DJ shouted something and pointed at the floor, but Emma couldn't see what he was pointing at. She smiled at him, and he grimaced and shrugged.

She passed him, reached the wall, and approached the closest of the dead women. She was, Emma thought, a good deal older than her mother—older and stouter. She wore a dress that might have been acceptable business dress twenty or thirty years ago, and her hair, which might once have been a mousy brown, was shot through with gray. She didn't appear to see Emma, which, since Emma was standing in front her, was a bit disconcerting.

Emma lifted a hand, waved it in front of her eyes. Nothing.

She felt Eric's hand on her shoulder and turned. "They don't see me. Eric, why are they here?"

He didn't answer. But Chase said, brusquely, "Tell her, Eric."

"Not here."

"Tell her, or I will."

Eric reached out and grabbed Chase's shirt, Chased shoved him, and Emma snorted. "*Guys,*" she said, through clenched teeth. "While I would love to see you pound each other senseless, it's not actually *helpful.*"

They both looked at her.

"You really are brothers. I don't care what you say." She took a deep breath and stepped up to the woman until she could touch her. Her hand hovered just above the rounded contours of the pale cheek, before she let it fall. It wasn't—wouldn't be—like touching her father; it would be like touching a corpse.

Instead, she looked at the chains. They were slender, golden chains, much like the one Merrick Longland had held. She'd snapped that; she thought she could snap these as well. "I'm sorry," she said to the woman, who might as well have been a statue for all she seemed to notice.

"Emma, what are you doing?" Eric asked her.

"Not trying to strangle Chase," she replied curtly. The chain was thicker, and she could see that it was like rope and that the woman was bound several times by its length. Those loops disappeared into the wall and emerged out the other side, gleaming faintly. One strand—only one—passed from this woman to the next, and from her to the two children. It seemed to be looped several times around each person.

"Emma?"

"Just let me figure it out." She touched the chains that bound the woman to the wall; they were pulled so tight they had no play at all. Fine. She walked to the woman's right, and put both hands on the taut, single strand. It was slightly warm, and although it looked metallic, it felt . . . wet. Slippery. If the

chain that had bound Emily Gates had been slippery, Emma hadn't noticed.
That was one of the advantages of adrenaline.

She tugged at it, and all four of the trapped people shuddered. She pulled
her hand back as if she'd just grabbed fire.

Eric must have seen her expression. But he had come to stand by her side,
and he said—and asked—nothing. Chase came to stand on her other side; they
were like bookends. Probably better that she was standing between them,
though. If they *did* start pounding on each other here, Amy would kill her later.
Amy put great stock in civil behavior when it wasn't her own.

But that was people: you could always justify what *you* chose to do, because
you made sense to yourself.

"I'm really, really sorry," she said softly, to four people who didn't seem to
be aware she existed. "I'm sorry if this hurts. I don't know what I'm doing."

She put her hands on the chain again, both hands this time, and she tried
very hard to keep the strongest of the pressure between her hands. She saw the
chain stretch and thin, saw the four shudder again, but this time she kept
going.

The chain snapped.

Eric swore. As the chain unraveled slowly, the women began to blink. They
looked at Emma, and Emma exhaled.

"I see two," Chase told her. Or Eric; she didn't look at them.

"There are two at the end. They're younger." She left the slowly waking
women and walked to the children. She found the single strand that stretched
between them and broke it.

They blinked, recovering more quickly than either woman had.

"Are you okay?" she asked the girl. A girl who looked to Emma to be about
six years old. She was very viscerally glad that the dead didn't look like their
corpses.

The girl blinked again and then looked at Emma, her eyes that faint and
odd luminescence that seemed to contain no color. She nodded slowly but
didn't speak. Neither did the boy. He was taller than the girl, and his hair was
an unruly dark mass that suggested hairbrushes had been no part of his cul-
tural norm; he didn't, however, look significantly older. Emma worked her way
through the slowly building rage their presence here invoked.

She didn't reach out to touch them; she lifted her hands and then forced
them back down to her sides, remembering what had happened the last
time she had touched her father. Four very oddly dressed strangers appearing
out of nowhere in the middle of the room was probably not going to
cause a big stir in a place this loud and crowded, but if it did, she'd be at the
center of it.

Instead, she asked them all to follow her, and they nodded again in silence.

"Follow you where?" Eric asked her, as he and Chase fell in behind.

"Outside. We can check on Skip and pick up Allison as we go."

Picking up Allison was a bit of a production that involved literally lifting Skip and dragging him up to his very messy room first. Chase and Eric did the heavy moving, and Amy came along to stage-manage. Michael, Allison, and Emma hovered behind the hard work, glancing at each other. Emma's arms were firmly folded across her chest.

"Bad?" Allison asked.

Emma nodded. "And confusing."

"More confusing than anything else that's happened this week?"

"Good point. Maybe. Certainly not less confusing." She glanced at Michael. She had expected Michael to be fidgeting—and he was—but he wasn't yet possessed by the all out frenetic movements that meant he had outlasted his best-before date and needed to be gently nudged home.

"Michael, do you want to go talk to Oliver and Connell while we figure things out?" Emma asked.

"No." He had the slightly vacant expression that meant he was thinking. It was harder to stop him from thinking than to stop a moving subway train by standing in front of it and pushing.

"Okay, then."

Eric, Chase, and Amy descended the stairs. Emma, seeing them coming, headed out to the backyard. It was too much to hope that Amy wouldn't follow, so she didn't bother. She did, however, hope that Amy wasn't as angry as she looked. But she did look angry, and when Amy was *that* angry, it was very hard not to cringe when she did anything. Like, say, speak. Or look at you.

When they were safely outside—and this took a few minutes as people approached Amy, saw the look on her face, and hurriedly backpedaled—Amy shut the door and then turned, hands on hips, to glare at them all.

Eric took this moment to tell Michael, gently, that it would probably be best for him to go inside and join the party. Michael stared at Eric blankly.

"Emma, help me here." Eric said, out of the corner of his mouth.

Emma grimaced. "He's staying."

"I don't think this is going to be helpful for him."

"It's probably not going to be helpful for me, either." She exhaled. "He's not an idiot, Eric. He saw what happened with Longland. He saw more, I'm guessing—I don't think anyone else was moving until after he hit Longland with the book."

"They weren't moving," Michael said. His hands were slightly balled fists at his sides, and his feet didn't stay in the same spot for more than a few seconds. "No one was moving but Emma and Skip's friend."

Emma nodded but continued to speak to Eric. "This is strange for all of us, and we all want explanations. Michael does more than want: he needs them."

"He doesn't need these."

"Yes," Amy said, quietly coming to the rescue—not that it was needed. "He does. Don't bother to argue with Em about this. She won't budge."

Chase started to speak, and Allison cut him off by simply raising her hand. The funny thing was that Chase actually paid attention. Allison then added her voice to the discussion. "He's always processed information differently than the rest of us do—it might be why he wasn't completely affected by whatever it was Longland did. Because he knows he doesn't understand some of the same things we do, he needs the explanation; if we don't give him one, he'll come up with one on his own—one that doesn't resemble reality."

"Which can be even more frightening than the truth usually is. If he knows what's actually happening, he can work with it." Allison reddened slightly. "Sorry."

"And he clearly doesn't mind being talked about in the third person, as if he weren't here," Eric observed.

Michael frowned. "But I am here," he told Eric. "Everyone knows it."

"Yes?"

"Then they're not talking about me as if I weren't here."

Emma almost felt sorry for Eric. Almost. "He's staying, Amy's staying in case you were about to be stupid enough to suggest she leave, and Allison's staying because I'm going to tell her everything anyway, and it's just easier not to get who-said-what confused. That about covers our side of things." She glanced at Allison. "Did you fill Amy in on everything?"

Allison nodded, looking slightly relieved.

"Then we're good to go with *your* side of things."

Eric and Chase glanced at each other; Chase shrugged.

Amy cut in. Given the number of sentences they'd managed to get through uninterrupted, this was more than expected. "What exactly did Longland do to my brother?"

"We're not sure. Not exactly. Which is to say, we don't have a good way of explaining how it works. We've seen it before," Eric added, speeding up slightly as Amy opened her mouth, "and as I said, it's a compulsion. A control."

"You said he normally wouldn't do something like this—he'd just make it look like it was Skip's idea. Skip's not the brightest guy in the world. This is the type of stupid he might believe could be his own."

Eric nodded, wary now. Emma liked that about him. He wasn't stupid.

"But if he needed to do something in the house, he'd do something worse. Which he clearly did."

"More or less." On the other hand, he looked distinctly uncomfortable.

"So Chase and Emma went upstairs to search the house, and Chase came back and pulled you in. What did you find?"

They looked at each other again, and any sympathy Emma felt for either of them evaporated. Michael, however, had stopped fidgeting so badly. She reached out and put a hand on his shoulder.

"Nothing."

"Nothing?"

"Nothing upstairs," Emma interjected. "Chase, you called Longland a Necromancer. Maybe we can start with that."


## ⌒ Chapter 11

Amy turned to look at Emma. "A . . . Necromancer."

"Pretty much."

"So . . . what Allison said about your dad in the hospital—that had something to do with Necromancy?"

Emma frowned. "I don't think so. I think he's just dead."

"Oh. Okay then."

Emma winced. "Yes, yes, I know it sounds insane."

"It sounds worse than insane, but at least it hasn't descended into B-movie badness. Yet. We checked the hedge while you were upstairs; Longland broke a few branches. The grass is mostly okay."

"How mostly?"

"I *think* I'll survive. I'm not sure Skip will, if we don't have an explanation that won't get us both thrown into an insane asylum. And no, before you ask, I am *not* telling my parents about any of this unless they absolutely need to know." She added, "You haven't told your mom, have you?"

Emma shook her head.

"Allison?"

"No."

They all turned to look at Michael. Michael looked mildly confused. "I told my mother about Emma's dad. Why aren't you telling your parents?"

"Our parents will worry so much they probably won't let us out of the house again, except for school," Emma told him. "What—what did your mother say?"

"Not very much. She asked me not to tell my dad. She told me I must be mistaken. I told her she could ask your mother. Did she?"

"No." Emma thanked god for small mercies. "But she probably doesn't want your dad to worry." *Because she doesn't believe you, and she's pretty certain he won't either,* Emma thought. This was not, however, something you could say to Michael unless you wanted to upset him.

"When the rest of you have finished, you can tell me when you'd like me to start."

The girls turned to look at Eric. He lifted his hands in instant surrender.

"Start with Necromancers, if you can't start with Longland. What, exactly, is a Necromancer, anyway? Some special type of—of dead person?" Emma tried unsuccessfully not to rest her hands on her hips; she was aware that this made her look a little bit too much like her mother. Or an Amy wannabe at this moment.

"No. They're not dead. They're very much alive."

"Alive and something that no one else has ever heard about."

"Not and survived, no. Possibly not and died; they don't really feel the need to explain their existence to ordinary people."

"So . . . they're like a secret society?" Amy walked over to the patio furniture, snagged herself a chair, and dragged it back. She sat down.

Chase and Eric exchanged another glance. Chase was clearly torn between finding this hilarious and finding it infuriating, and he hadn't decided which.

"Ye-es."

"And people who can see the dead, for whatever reason, are naturally Necromancers?" Emma decided that a chair was a good idea. She did not, however, move.

"No," Eric said, as Chase said, "Yes."

"Eric can see the dead. Eric is, I'm assuming, not a Necromancer."

Silence.

"We all saw your dad," Michael offered. "I don't think I'm a Necromancer. Eric, what is a Necromancer? I know what they probably are in D20 rules," he added, to be helpful.

"They're not like that. They can't summon an army of zombies or skeletons. Science will get there first. And no, Michael, you are definitely *not* a Necromancer. Neither is Mrs. Hall or Allison or the other people who probably saw Emma's dad."

"But Emma?" he added, with just a trace of anxiety.

"Emma," Chase said, while Eric was struggling for words, "is a Necromancer."

If, as they say, looks could kill, Chase, or what was left of Chase, would have fallen over on the spot. Chase, however, squared his shoulders and met Eric's furious glance without blinking. "She is," he said quietly, shoving his hands into his pockets.

"Are you telling this story, or am I?"

"You are, of course. If I were, I wouldn't have taken this long to get to the damn point."

Emma thought Eric was going to punch him, and Chase, judging by the way he shifted his stance, thought so too. "Eric," she said.

He lowered his hands. He didn't manage to uncurl them.

"I'm a Necromancer?"

The look he gave her made her turn away for a moment. Sometimes you couldn't look too closely at another person's pain.

"Yes."

"And this means you have to—" she broke off, looking at her friends. "Tell me."

"The headaches weren't headaches. They weren't a concussion. Some people have a lot of trouble adjusting to what they see when they're first coming into their power. Your brain builds new channels, new ways of assimilating visual information, but it's complicated and it hurts. While you're doing this, you can often hallucinate, hear voices, see things. It's both painful and confusing, but if you have no guide, if you have no information, those will shut down on their own as your brain learns to ignore the incoming information. It's almost natural."

"That's what you were hoping for."

He nodded, closed his eyes, turned his face away.

"He knew it was too late," Chase told her. "He just doesn't want—"

Eric stepped on his foot, hard.

"What is it that Necromancers can do that makes them so dangerous?" Emma found it easier to ask this of Chase. Possibly because it didn't seem to hurt him so much to answer, and possibly because he was still recovering from the very necessary stomping.

"You can ask that after tonight?"

She grimaced. "Good point. But—how can they do it?"

"They take their power from the dead."

"From the dead." Emma's eyes widened. "You mean like the dead in the room?"

"Like the dead that are following you, yes."

Amy said, "Allison, do you see any dead people?"

"No."

"Michael?"

"No."

"Okay. Just checking, because *neither do I.*" Amy shifted in her chair.

Emma had to give her this: when she wasn't in the mood to be impressed, it took a lot to impress her.

"With the dead you have following you," Chase continued, "you could probably destroy this whole block without blinking and still have power left to go home."

"I can walk home from here."

"That's not the home I was talking about."

"It's the only home I have." But she turned to look at the dead. Because Chase was right. They were following her. She frowned. "Emily," she whispered.

A fifth ghost appeared, almost shyly. "Yes?"

"Sorry. I—I almost forgot about you, and I wanted to see if you were still here."

"I can't leave," the girl replied.

"Why not?"

"You hold me."

"Emma," Amy said sharply, "You are creeping me the hell out. Who are you talking to, exactly?"

Emma grimaced. "I don't know if this will work," she said.

Eric said, "Don't. Em. Don't."

But Emma reached out with her hand, palm up, to Emily, who hesitated for just a minute before she reached out and grasped Emma's hand with her own. Hers was *cold*. To Emma's eyes, nothing had changed.

But Amy's intake and Allison's soft rush of breath—exhale or inhale, Emma couldn't tell—told her that things had changed for her friends.

Michael said, "She doesn't look dead."

"No. Thank god. I don't think I could stand to see corpses everywhere. This is Emily Gates. Emily, these are my friends. This is Michael," she added, because Michael had walked toward Emily. He was tall, certainly taller than Emma, Amy, or Allison.

"Hello," Michael said quietly. He held out his hand.

Emily looked at it and then shook her head. "I can't," she told him.

"Oh." He let his hand drop. "It's okay," he added because she seemed to be unhappy about the admission. "Emma, why can we see her now?"

"I don't know. But in the hospital—I touched my dad."

"No, you didn't."

"She did," Eric replied. His voice was very quiet. "But not in a way you could see, not then. Until she touched him, you couldn't see him."

"Why does her touch make them visible?"

"It doesn't. Not exactly. She's using a very, very small part of their power to make them visible to you. To everyone here."

Emma's hand tightened slightly, and then she let go. "Emily, how do I let you go? What am I holding?"

Emily frowned. "I don't know."

"It doesn't matter." Eric's voice was rough. "You can't let them go here, even if you could figure out how to do it. Longland's still alive, and he's still out there. You let them go, he'll probably be able to pick them up again, and we cannot face him when he's wielding that kind of power. It's not *easy* for him to pick up the dead this way. It is not trivial."

Emma nodded and turned to the other four. She introduced herself, and she received their names. The children were hard for her. They were just too young to be caught up in all of this. Too damn young, she thought, to *die*.

But they were dead. "Do you want to meet my friends?" she asked them softly.

"Don't." Eric again. "Emma—don't do this."

Setting her jaw, she touched each by the hand, and she introduced Georges, Catherine, Margaret, and Suzanne, to her friends. She introduced the two women, Margaret and Suzanne, first, and then the children, because she knew what effect they would have on Michael.

Michael liked children, possibly because there was something in children that was not yet entirely fettered by social convention, and he responded to it. Her hands—she introduced Georges and Catherine at the same time—were numb by the time he had finished asking them questions, because he did ask. They answered, slowly at first. But as they talked, they grew more animated, and Michael, forgetting for a moment that they were dead, started to play, to make faces, to try to get them to laugh.

It was heartbreaking to watch him. It was worse to watch them absorb this playfulness, because they wanted it so badly, and this fact was completely obvious to Emma.

It was obvious, Emma thought, glancing at Allison and Amy, to all of them. Allison approached them as well, but she was more reserved. She retreated because Michael was making them laugh, and when they laughed—they didn't seem dead.

But when Allison turned to Emma, her eyes were filmed with tears that she was trying not to shed. "Em."

Emma nodded.

"How can we help them?"

"I don't know."

"There's got to be something we can do. Is the little boy in the burned out building like this?"

"I think he would be, if we could get him out of the fire."

"And if we don't?"

"He'll be a four year old trapped in a burning building at the moment of his death for decades, if not forever."

Amy said, "What four year old?"

Allison told her.

"You were going to tell me about this, right, Emma?"

Emma shrugged. "It sounded crazy," she said. "But I probably would have; we need really big, solid ladders, and a car that can carry them, without the parents that would probably insist on coming along."

"Right. Ladders. Car. Parents out of town. Check."

"Emma."

She turned to look at Eric. "Michael, I have to let go of their hands, now. I can't feel mine at all."

"Oh. Why?"

"Their hands are very, very cold. It's like grabbing ice, but without the wet bits."

"I don't think they want to go away."

They didn't. She knew they didn't. She managed to nod, but she had to force herself to unclench her jaw. "Eric, I'm using their power?"

"Yes."

"Does it hurt them?"

"Ask them," he replied.

"Georges? Catherine?"

They failed to hear her, the way children who are having fun frequently fail to hear the parents who want them to leave the place in which they're having it.

"I'm going to take that as a no," Emma told Eric. "I'll let go when I can't feel my arms."

"Emma—"

"Did Longland come here to find me?"

"Yes."

"How did he know where I was?"

"Probably the same way we did. It's not exact," he added, "but the dead . . . some of the dead know."

"And he expected me to just pick up and go wherever he wanted me to go."

"That's what usually happens."

*Unless you kill the Necromancer first.* She wanted to say it, but didn't. Throwing murder into the mix, while her friends were standing around her, was something she wasn't up to doing.

"Michael, don't do that, you'll get grass stains on those pants." Emma shook her head, because Michael, like the two six year olds, wasn't really listening.

"And the four in the dance room?"

"They're amplifiers," Chase replied. "I think that room was meant to serve as a road."

"A . . . road."

"A road."

"To where? Hell?"

"Pretty much. That's not what they call it," he added.

"What do they call it, and what *is* it?"

"I don't know what they call it."

Emma suppressed a strong and visceral urge to strangle Chase. She probably wouldn't have managed if she weren't still holding onto two children who were leeching the heat out of her body by inches. "What do you call it?"

"The City of the Dead."

"Great. And Longland thought he could just come here, screw around with my friends, and cart me off?"

"He doesn't know you very well, does he?"

"No, Michael, he certainly doesn't." She paused, then said, "If I had gone with him, what would have happened to these four?"

"He would probably have sucked all the power out of them at that point. Creating a road like that takes a lot of power."

"And this power—if it were gone, what would happen to them?"

Chase just stared at her, as if she were making no sense. "What do you mean, what would happen?"

"What I said. I can try to use smaller words, if it'd help."

"They're dead. They'd still *be* dead."

"Sucking the power out of them can't be good for them. They must need it for something. What do they use the power *for*?"

"How the hell should I know?"

"Eric, I'm going to kill Chase now."

Eric just looked at her. "Emma—" He exhaled, and then shook his head, lifting his hands as he did. "I give up."

To her surprise, she started to smile, and it was a genuine smile, even though her hands ached, and her arms were now tingling. "You say that. A lot."

"Without their power, they still exist. You might even see them, although it's not a given. They can't *use* the power they have, not on purpose. Andrew Copis *is* using power, but not consciously. They can't use it to defend themselves. They can't use it to free themselves. They can't use it to manifest and play with Michael on their own.

"To do any of that, they need you."

"They need a Necromancer, you mean."

"No. A Necromancer would never, ever do what you're doing now. Any of it. I meant you." He smiled, and it was the smile that she liked best. It was warm, if slightly weary, and it changed the lines of his face. Made him look more open. "Chase."

"Is she crazy?" Chase asked.

"Oh, probably."

"And the rest of you," Chase continued, looking at Amy, Allison, and Michael, although Michael was not paying attention. "Are you all crazy, too?"

"Dude, you see the dead and you talk about Necromantic magic and the City of the Dead, and *we're* crazy?" Amy shot back.

Eric walked over to Emma. "Emma, you are letting go of the children. Now."

"But they—"

"You can always let them out to play with Michael later. But you need to let go now."

"Why?"

"Because your teeth are starting to chatter, and you're turning blue." He reached out and caught her hands, and he forced them out of their numb, frozen curl. "We can come back and visit Michael again tomorrow," she told Georges and a crestfallen Catherine. "I promise."

His hands? Weren't cold. They were so very, very warm. And he cupped them around both of hers and held them.

"Is the house safe?" Amy asked Eric.

He nodded. "We can search the rest of the rooms if it makes you feel better."

"Not really. If it's safe, I have a party to attend." She stood, scraping concrete with the legs of her chair. "Emma?"

Emma nodded.

"I'm going to check on Skip. I don't see any reason to kick people out. So far, no one's called the police to close us down."

Chase's eyes almost fell out of his head, which made Emma laugh.

"What?"

"You're going to keep the party going?"

Amy shrugged. "Why not? Longland won't be back tonight."

"How the hell can you say that?"

"He's not an idiot. Allison and Emma make a habit of trying to see—and say—only good things. I don't."

"No kidding."

She rolled her eyes. "He didn't like the odds or he wouldn't have run in the first place. You're still here. You know who he is now, or what you think he is, at any rate. Eric said he can't gather his power base at all quickly. He's not going to come back to face the same odds. Because I think you'll kill him, if he does. Or try. You can correct me when I'm wrong," she added. "Not that it happens often. Emma, did he wear those boots upstairs?"

"Sorry."

"Never mind. I'll kill him myself if I find dirt. Speaking of which, you should take Chase upstairs and do something about his hair." Amy grimaced. "Which, at this point, would probably involve shaving his head. We can talk in the morning, maybe go to this burned-out house you saw earlier."

Emma nodded again. Amy, in her perfect mock-harlequin getup, slid the doors to one side, letting noise out and herself in. Only when she was gone did Emma turn to Chase and Eric. "You're sure the house is safe?"

"Where did you find her?" Chase asked.

Eric, on the other hand, nodded.

"Good. We might as well go inside and see if there's any food left."

He shook his head. Emma caught it out of the corner of her eye as she turned to face Michael, who was standing, head bent, hands at his sides. He wasn't moving around too much, which was either a good sign or a very bad one.

"Michael?"

Michael nodded. "I want to go with you," he told her quietly.

She could have pretended to misunderstand him, but if she had, he would have asked again, with more words. "We won't go without you."

He nodded again, and this nod went on in a little bobble of head and hair. Allison touched his shoulder, and he stilled.

"I want to help them," Michael told her. "They shouldn't be here."

"No," she agreed softly. "They shouldn't. But I don't think Eric or Chase know where they *should* be. And I don't know how to get them there."

"But there's someplace they should go?"

"I think so, Michael."

He paused, but she knew him well enough to know he wasn't quite finished. "Will they be happy there?"

Remembering her father's words, Emma nodded. "Happy and safe."

"Then we should help them go there. Can you see it?"

"No. I think only the dead can."

"I don't want you to die, Emma."

She nodded again.

"But I guess sometimes what we want doesn't matter. You can't make them alive again, can you?"

She felt Eric's hands stiffen as they covered hers, as if he'd been stabbed or struck, hard. Her own tightened, catching his fingers.

"No," she told him softly. "I can't. If I could—" She closed her eyes. "I can't. I don't think anyone can."

"Would you?"

"Yes."

He nodded again, but this time, she thought he was done. He surprised her, but he often did. "What should I do?" He asked her quietly, in a voice she hadn't heard since he was twelve.

"Go find Oliver and Connell. And your books. We're going to stay here until one, and then we'll head home. But we'll call your house in the morning. Try—try hard—to finish your homework in the morning."

"But I watch—" he stopped, swallowed, and nodded. "I'll do homework in the morning."

"Michael?"

"Yes?"

"You did good. Georges and Catherine were happy, and I don't think they've had much to be happy about for a long time."

He smiled, then. Michael's smiles were always some mix of heartbreaking and beautiful, partly because they had their roots in a childhood he could still reach back and touch. It wasn't the same as Emma's or Allison's, because he saw it more clearly.

Only after he had shuffled inside did Allison speak.

"So, Eric. You and Chase hunt Necromancers."

They glanced at each other, and Eric winced slightly. This was probably because Emma had just crushed one of his hands in hers, in warning. Even Chase, who didn't seem, to Emma, to be the sharpest knife in the drawer, hesitated before he nodded.

"And you kill them, if you can."

"Ally, it doesn't matter," Emma said urgently.

"Yes, it does. Because if I'm not mistaken, Chase thinks you're a Necromancer."

The silence was notably chilier. Allison let it go on for a bit before she started again. "Longland was looking for Emma. But so was Eric, the 'new student.'"

"Ally."

"Were you looking for her to kill her?"

"Ally, *please*."

"Is that a yes or a no?" When Eric didn't answer, she looked at Chase. "Well?"

"Yes," Chase replied. "She's a Necromancer."

"She's a Necromancer who *hasn't done anything wrong.* You were just going to kill her because in the future she *might*?"

Chase's eyes had narrowed. "We were planning to kill her before she figures out how to use the power she has and starts killing hundreds of *other* people, none of whom have our training."

"Because you could just assume that she's going to turn into a mass murderer?" Allison's face had gone from the healthy side of pink to the unhealthy side of crimson. "And how many other times have you *saved the world* by killing someone who is *entirely* innocent of any crime?"

"Have you ever met a fucking Necromancer?"

"Apparently yes—I have one for a best friend!"

"So maybe she's a freak!" Chase was also red now. The color didn't suit him.

"So *maybe* other budding Necromancers were freaks too—and you'll never know it because they're dead!"

"Allison," Eric said, shaking his hands free from Emma's and turning toward her, "don't judge him. You don't know what he's been through."

"I don't know what he's been through?" Allison took a deep breath. It was not a cessation of hostility, however. She needed it. "You're right. I don't. And you know what? I'm not going to kill *him*. He has *no idea* what Emma's been through, and he intended to kill her."

"When he speaks of hundreds dead, he speaks from experience. He's seen what Necromancers can do."

"Fine! Then kill the Necromancers that *do*. Killing Emma means there's one less decent person in the world! Or does he only try to kill Necromancers who can't do anything to defend themselves first?"

"Ally, he did go after Longland."

Allison looked at Emma, and then shook both her head and her hands to prevent a familiar half-shriek of frustration from escaping. "Em, this is serious."

"I know. Believe that I know. But Eric? He's not going to kill me."

"Chase?"

Chase had shoved his hands into his pockets, and his shoulders were at about the same level as his ears.

"Well?" Allison's hands were in tight fists at her sides.

"No," he said, as if the word had been dragged from him, and judging by his expression, had broken his front teeth on the way out. "No, I am not going to kill Emma. Satisfied?"

"Not really."

"What *would* satisfy you?"

"Help us."

"Help you do what?"

"Free the dead. You can start with the little boy on Rowan Avenue."

Chase gave the little shriek that Allison had managed to swallow. "What's the *point*? He's *dead*!"

Allison just stared at him. After a moment, she said, "I would rather spend eternity wandering up and down an empty street than burning to death without actually dying. I'm assuming that the same is probably true of a *four year old*."

Chase stared at her for a moment and then turned to Emma.

"Don't look at me for support. I'm so much in Allison's camp we might as well be sharing a brain."

"Eric?"

"You can go back if you want; I know enough to know this is going to be hard on you. But I'm staying until this is resolved, one way or the other."

Chase opened his mouth. Closed it, shoved his hands into his pockets. Opened his mouth again. Emma liked that Chase was always so expressive, except when she didn't.

Before he could say anything—or before he could figure out which of the many things he was going to say first—a phone rang.

Emma recognized the ring.

"Fuck." So, apparently, did Eric.

"Are you going to answer that?" Allison asked him.

Emma almost laughed.

"No."

"At this time of night? It could be an emergency."

"If I answer it, it will be. Come on, let's get something to eat."

Chase shrugged as the phone stopped ringing. They made it to the door before it started ringing again. "You know he's just going to keep trying."

"Let him. It's loud enough inside I won't hear it."

"Answer it, Eric."

"No."

"If you don't answer it, he'll just call *me*."

"You don't have a working phone."

Chase laughed. "You think of everything."

"Someone," Eric said, sliding the door to one side, "has to."

They dropped Michael off first, swung around to Allison's house, and then dropped Emma off by her front door. The time was just a little past one-thirty, which in the Hall household was still within the bounds of "on time."

Emma stopped by the driver's window, and Eric opened it.

"Do you have my number?" she asked him.

"No."

"Do you want it, or do you just want to come by in the morning?"

Chase said something about morning, which Emma pretended not to hear.

"If you come, I'll feed you. I might even feed Chase. I don't know when Amy will call, so you might be cooling your heels for a while."

"Any chance she won't call?"

"None."

"We'll drop by. When's good?"

"Any time after eight-thirty." She turned toward the house, stopped, and turned back. "Thanks."

"For what?"

"For tonight. You can thank Chase, too."

"You could thank me yourself!"

"Too much trouble," she said, but she smiled. She was tired, and even the hot and stuffy house hadn't taken the edge off the chill in her hands. "We need to find Maria Copis, and we need to get her to Rowan Avenue. I don't think all the ladders in the world are going to help us get that child out if she's not there."

"Let us figure out where she went after her house burned down. You get some sleep."

She nodded, and headed to the front door. The walking, black alarm system was already gearing up on the other side of it.

When the house door had closed on the glimpse of a frantically barking rottweiler, Chase turned to Eric. "Do you have any idea what you're doing?"

Eric shrugged. After a moment, he said, "Do you really want to kill her?"

"I think we should. You didn't tell her that she's now carting around more power than most Necromancers *could*."

"No." Eric was restless enough to open the car door; the lights went on. "They're not power, to her. There's no way she's going to *use* them."

"She didn't even have to *try* to get the dead to show. She just did it."

"I know, Chase. I was there, remember?"

"You didn't warn her about Longland, either."

"If I had warned her about Longland's power, she'd've figured it out. She's crazy but she's not stupid. And warning her wouldn't give her any useful information." He looked at Chase, got out of the car.

Chase sighed—audibly—and slid out the other door.

"Do you want to kill her?" Eric asked again.

"Does it matter? I'm not going to try."

"Yeah, it matters."

"I think we should."

"Not an answer, Chase."

"Asshole." Chase slammed the car door shut, turned his back, and after a minute, walked around the back of the car and slammed the other door shut as well. He leaned against the driver's door, his back to Eric. "I understand why you didn't. Kill her, I mean. She seems so *normal*."

"Yeah. Normal. Happy. Has friends she actually cares about who are actually still alive. So."

Chase pushed himself off the car. "You want me to take the first shift, or do you want to take it?"

"Up to you."

Chase detached himself from the car. "I need a new coat." He glanced at the house and added, "Any chance that dog won't go insane if I park myself inside?"

"He's a rottweiler."

"Figures."

"You sure you want the first shift?"

"Yeah. I don't want to go back and hit the radioactive button on the answering machine."

Eric grimaced. "Fine. I'll be back in four hours."

"It'll probably take at least that long to wade through the messages."

"Thanks. Don't," he added, "do anything stupid. If Longland does show up here, he's not going to kill her. He will, however, kill you without blinking."

"He'll try." Chase smiled. Even in the scant light, it wasn't pleasant. But it was, Eric had to admit, all Chase.

## ᕲ Chapter 12

Emma's mother hadn't waited up, which was probably for the best. The lights were off in the house; the only light in the hall was the light that shone in through the little decorative windows in the front door. Emma doused that when she shut off the front door's light. She stood in the hall, absently patting Petal's head until her eyes had acclimated to the darkness; the only place it was ever truly dark was the basement.

When everything had become a dark gray, she slid out of her shoes, picked them up by the back straps, and headed up the stairs. The stairs were carpeted, but the house wasn't exactly new; they creaked as she walked. They creaked as

Petal walked, but he jingled anyway. No one in the Hall house could be easily woken up by either sound. Not if they actually wanted to get sleep, ever.

She made her way to her room, dropped the shoes in front of her closet, and began to fiddle with the straps of her dress. Her hands were cold; she rubbed them together, but it didn't help. Bed—and the large, down duvet—might. Petal jumped up on the bed, somewhere near the foot, and waited, his head resting on his forepaws.

"Sorry, Petal. I know it's late." She slid out of her dress, grabbed pajamas, slid into them, and sat on the side of the bed, scratching behind his ears.

Something made her look up. It wasn't sound, exactly, and it wasn't light— but it caught her as if it were both, and loud and bright.

Her father stood in the center of the room. "Sprout."

She wanted to get up and run into his arms. She didn't. She was cold enough, and she knew that there was no warmth waiting. Love, yes, and affection—but also cold. She pulled the duvet up and around her shoulders, resting her hands in her lap.

"Dad." Petal tried to get under the covers as well, but as he was sitting on the outside of one end, he had no luck.

"Sleep, Em."

"Why are you here?"

He shook his head and looked out the curtained window. What he saw, given that the curtains were drawn, she couldn't tell.

"To see you, Emma. To see that you're okay."

She smiled, shivering. "I'm fine," she told him.

He stared at her and then folded his arms across his chest. If hands-on-the-hips when angry came from her mother, this folding of arms—and raising of one brow—was definitely learned from Brendan Hall.

"You need to let them go, Em."

She could have pretended to misunderstand him, but that had never gone down well. "I don't know how."

"How did you bind them?"

"I didn't! They were already bound."

"They're bound to you."

"How do you *know*?"

"You're my daughter," he replied.

His words made her yearn for the days when she was four years old, parents lived forever, and her father knew *everything*. The yearning was so strong that she was out of bed and almost across the room before she caught herself and froze. He'd opened his arms as well, and at the last moment, stepped back, failing to catch her.

"It's hard, being dead," he told her, his lips curved in an unfamiliar and bitter smile.

"Is it worse than being alive when the people you love go and die on you?" She stopped speaking and looked away. After a moment, when she could trust her words again, she added, "Sorry, Dad."

"Nathan?" he asked her softly, and she startled.

"You know about Nathan?"

"Daughter, remember?"

She tried really, really hard to believe that he hadn't seen anything that would embarrass her. Or him.

If he had, he was kind enough not to mention it. But he'd mentioned Nathan. She went back to her bed, pulled enough of the duvet free of Petal, who'd begun his midnight sprawl, and wrapped it tightly around herself. "I miss him.

"I keep hoping—I keep *wanting*— to see him." She looked at her father, then. Waited until her voice was steady. That took a while. "Just to talk to him. Just to hear him again." And to touch him again, even if her hands numbed at the shock.

"But . . . what if he's like the others? What if he's on some golden leash, and he's being drained of any power he might have that could—that could bring him *back* to me?"

"Emma." Her father started to say more, and stopped.

She was cold, cold, cold. She couldn't, at this moment, remember what being warm felt like.

"You need to let go of them. At least a couple of them. Chase and Eric didn't say enough. Maybe because they don't understand it. I can see it in you, now. It takes power, to hold the dead. If you can't pull power from them to do it, the bindings take power from you."

"How do I let go?"

"Unwind the chains, Emma."

"I broke them."

"Yes. And no. You couldn't break them; you grabbed them. You're holding them."

"Oh." She looked at her hands, at her empty palms. "Dad?"

"Yes?"

"What else can you tell me about being a Necromancer?"

He said nothing.

"What can you tell me about the City of the Dead?"

His arms, which had fallen to the sides in his abortive hug, now folded themselves across his chest again; his hand curled, for just a moment, around the bowl of a pipe that he couldn't smoke. When she had been young, he had called it his thinking pipe. "Not very much," he finally said. "But it's there."

"Where?"

He lifted an arm, his sleeves creasing slightly, and pointed.

"Give me something I can Google."

That smile again. She hated it.

"Can the dead at least talk to each other?"

"Some can. It depends."

"On what?"

"Power, Emma."

"But Eric and Chase said—"

"They're not dead."

She was shivering, and the duvet didn't help. His arms fell to his sides, and then he walked across the room to the side of her bed and knelt there, as if she were four years old again, and sick, and awake in the middle of a long night.

He touched her forehead with his hand, and his hand passed through her. Or it started to. She reached up and grabbed that hand. And *yes*, it was cold. But she felt something at the heart of that ice, something that shed warmth the way the sun sheds light. She brought her free hand around, caught his, held it, and felt her hands, without the painful tingle, for the first time since she had introduced the dead to her friends.

And then she cried out, and pulled both of her hands back, as if the warmth had scorched her. "Dad, no!"

"Emma, you won't survive a week otherwise. I'm dead," he added softly. "And in this world, that means only one thing: sooner or later, someone is going to harvest whatever power I have. I would rather give it to you now, because when I give it to you, I'm saving the life of my very stubborn, very precious daughter.

"I can't do anything else for you. Let me do this."

"You can. You can talk to me. You can come to me more often. You can tell me I'm not insane."

"Talk is cheap."

"Fine. It's cheap. It's better than *nothing*."

He flinched.

But she wouldn't touch his hands again, and she realized that she had to be the one who initiated the touch. He could touch hers, but there was no actual contact. She knew this because he tried. "I'm not cold now," she whispered, and it was true. But she felt like a—a vampire. Or worse. The cold had to be better than this.

Eric and Chase came by at 8:30 in the morning.

Had it not been for Emma's father, her first clue would have been Petal jumping off the bed, running down the stairs, and barking in an endless loop.

But even in her sleep, she was aware of Brendan Hall, and he returned at 8:00. Which was good, because on a good weekend, her mother didn't lever herself out of bed until 9:30 or 10:00. Given the shock of seeing her dead husband, Emma expected that this would be a *bad* weekend. For her mother.

Which would be useful, but made Emma feel guilty.

Swinging around the bottom of the banister she headed to the kitchen, checked milk, eggs, and bread with a slightly anxious frown. All there. She also checked sugar, brown sugar, maple syrup, cinnamon, coffee, and tea. That done, she fed Petal, who was as usual slightly anxious because she'd done things in the wrong order. If he could talk, he would say *feed me* pretty much all day long.

It was too early to phone anyone, and she had no idea exactly when Eric and Chase would show up, so she sat in the living room, legs curled beneath her on the couch, Petal's head in her lap. Thinking about Necromancy. About Necromancers. And about the dead, her absent, longed-for dead. It wasn't a cheerful way to spend the time, but it was also the way she frequently spent a lot of the weekend. Except for the Necromancy part.

When Petal bounced off the couch and headed to the door, she rose and went with him. She didn't bother to tell him to be quiet, because it never worked; instead she inserted her legs between as much of his body and the door as she could, while opening it.

Chase and Eric were almost at the front step.

"Can you guys hurry?" she said. "I don't want Petal to wake up my mom."

"She can sleep through that?" Clearly skeptical, Chase looked at Petal, who could be heard barking through two closed doors and a stretch of walk.

"Not for more than ten minutes."

They hurried into the house as Emma slid a Milk-Bone into the palm of her hand. The rottweiler stopped barking and started chewing instead. Eric crouched down and patted his head. Because Petal was a very sweet-tempered dog, he didn't assume that Eric was trying to steal his food, and Eric got to keep his hand.

She busied herself in the kitchen and was surprised when Eric and Chase ambled in.

"Can we do anything to help?" Eric asked.

"The answer to that is no, trust me," Chase told Emma. "Because I see the table is already set."

Emma, breaking eggs, spared Chase a glance. "Oh?"

"He can set the table and dry the dishes. And take out the garbage, if you nag him. He can't, on the other hand, be trusted with food."

"Because he eats it?"

"Because he ruins it. I've had eggs he's forgotten were in boiling water; you could bounce them off walls."

"That happened *once*," Eric told Emma.

"Because we never let him try it again."

"Chase likes cooking because it gets him out of cleaning up."

Chase grinned. "Also true."

Emma looked at the two of them and laughed. Felt a pang of only-child sneak up on her, even though they weren't actually brothers. It was hard not to like them, even knowing what they did. On the other hand, if she needed a reality check, Allison would be coming sometime soon. She glanced at the clock. Not time to call Michael yet.

Chase picked up an apron.

"No, honestly, I don't need help."

"Don't get all kitchen territorial on me," he told her cheerfully.

"Why not? It's my kitchen."

He turned enormous, puppy dog eyes on her. Petal would have been jealous, if he'd noticed. Chase's hair was a good deal shorter—and a good deal less frizzled and sooty—than it had been the previous evening, although a tiny, red braid trailed down the side of his neck.

She laughed in spite of herself. "That's not an answer."

Eric leaned against the counter and stretched.

"Well," Chase told her, "We hardly ever get the chance to cook like this. Mostly, we fight, drill, buy ugly jackets we can modify, fight some more, bleed a lot, and narrowly avoid dying."

"And kill people?"

"That, too."

"Chase," Eric said, "Don't be an asshole."

"What? I'm asking Emma for a chance to pretend—for, like, half an hour—that I'm a normal person."

Eric grimaced as Emma glanced his way. "Half an hour is the most he can manage."

"You're better at it?"

"Mostly. Sometimes I forget my manners."

"Your manners are good."

"Yes. Often too good."

She thought about that for a minute, and nodded. "Fine. Make the pancakes." She regretted this about two minutes later, because apparently Chase had strong religious issues about using an instant pancake mix. He also had some issues with the lack of bacon, and when Emma said "Nitrates," he snorted and sent Eric to the store.

\*       \*       \*

Emma called Michael after breakfast and asked him to wait for Allison. She
called Allison next and asked her to pick Michael up on the way. Eric, who was
standing beside the phone, handed her a folded piece of paper. She opened it.
It was an address.

"What's this?"

"Maria Copis' address. Her phone number's unlisted."

"How did you get this?"

"Don't ask."

She set the phone down almost hesitantly.

"What's wrong?"

"I'm afraid."

"Of what, exactly?"

She waved the address in the air. "We don't know what we're doing," she
told him, as if this needed saying. "And if we go and get Andrew's mother, and
drag her to Rowan Avenue, and we can't even reach her son, we'll have hurt
her for no reason."

"And if you can reach him, somehow, and she's not there, there's no
point?"

"Something like that."

"I think you're taking too much of a long view."

"Why?"

"Because you're going to need to get her there first. Work on that," he
added.

"I think we can only get her there once."

Chase appeared from around the kitchen. "Eric, dishes?"

"Don't worry about the dishes." Emma told them both.

"What? I cook, he cleans. Those are the rules."

"You didn't *have* to cook, and he doesn't *have* to clean."

"If I don't want to listen to Chase bitch about this for the rest of the week,
I do." He headed back into the kitchen. Emma started to follow him, but Chase
positioned himself in the arch.

"Chase, I helped you cook. I can help him clean."

But Chase's expression had shifted, the smile that accompanied his banter
deserting his face so cleanly it was hard to imagine that it had been there at
all.

"I understand what Eric sees in you. In all of you."

"And that's a bad thing."

"For us? Yeah, it is. It reminds us of the life we don't have." His face tightened, jaw clenching a moment as he closed his eyes. "My sister," he said, eyes
still closed, "would have liked you." Something went out of him, then. "Allison

reminds me of my sister. Same unexpected temper. My sister would have said the same damn thing she said last night. But," he added, slowly opening his eyes, "she would have smacked me."

She swallowed. "Chase—" Reached out to touch him, and then pulled back. "Your sister's . . . not alive."

He shrugged, shirt creasing and draping again in a way that suggested silk. "No." He turned, and then turned back. "You're right. You don't know what you're doing."

"I know."

"What you don't know? It can kill you."

Remembering the heat of the fire, she nodded.

"It can also kill anyone you take with you. Your friends. Michael. Allison."

"Amy?"

"I don't think anything can kill Amy." He grimaced. "Look, you're what you are. I can't talk you out of it—and I'm not Eric. I'm not going to try, because unlike Eric, I have no hope. But Michael and Allison are *not* what you are. You drag them into this, they have no protection. You might think on that," he added, "because you seem to care about your friends."

"They—they want to help." Her mouth was dry.

"A toddler wants to play in the middle of the road, too. I'm not telling you what to do, Emma. I'm pointing out that it has costs."

"But you and Eric aren't Necromancers, and you do this all the time."

"Emma, what you're going to try? We've never done that. We've never tried it. And what we are? This is our *life*. If Michael and Allison had led *our* lives, they wouldn't be *your* friends." He swore. "And it wouldn't make it safe for them anyway."

"So . . . you're saying both you and Eric are at risk."

"Anyone there is at risk." He looked as if he would say more, but he didn't, and this time when he turned and headed into the kitchen, he didn't turn back.

Michael and Allison arrived less than half an hour later. Petal was all over Michael two seconds after the screen door opened—Emma knew this because she counted. She had to nudge them both out of the doorway so that Allison could actually get into the house without having to step over the huddle of rottweiler and Michael, but Emma took a minute to watch them. Michael would probably have a small fit if someone walked up to him and licked his face, but he barely grimaced when Petal did it. And she knew what her dog's breath smelled like.

Still, watching Michael with Petal was normal. She needed a bit of normal.

She handed Allison the piece of paper that Eric had handed her; Allison knew what it was immediately. She also had the same concerns that Emma had. But she had more faith in Emma than Emma did at this particular moment.

"Are you worried about getting her there?"

"No. I can do that."

Allison didn't ask how. "It's not just Andrew, is it?"

"Mostly."

"Em."

Emma grimaced. She had learned, over the years, that she could lie to Allison about little things—probably because Allison didn't care enough to pick at them—but never about anything big. Why she still bothered to try, she didn't know. "Chase thinks you're all in danger if we do this."

"We probably are. So?"

"Life-threatening danger."

"Emma Hall, do not even think of leaving us behind. You promised Michael you wouldn't," she added.

"I know. I just—I shouldn't have promised him that. I wasn't thinking."

"Yes, you were. You were thinking that you go through enough alone as it is. You don't need to prove anything. You don't know what you're doing, and neither do the rest of us—but we've always managed to come up with something when we work at it together. Besides, you're going to phone Amy and tell her you don't need her help?"

"Chase says that nothing can kill Amy."

Allison laughed. "Probably not."

Amy called at 10:00. She dropped by the house with a loaded SUV at 10:30 and honked, loudly. Emma, flipping the drapes back, saw the big gray vehicle they affectionately called the Tank, and motioned for everyone to head out.

Amy was not, however, alone. In the passenger seat, elbow hanging out the open window, was Skip. He looked better than he had the last time they'd seen him—he was at least conscious—but not by much.

"This is not a fucking barbecue," Chase muttered under his breath.

"Hi, Skip!" Michael said. He was cheerful in part because Chase's comment and Skip's presence seemed entirely unrelated to him. "Emma, are we bringing Petal?"

"No." Emma headed over to the driver's side of the car and glanced pointedly at Skip. Amy shrugged. "He wouldn't give me the car keys unless I brought him."

"If we were the secret service," Emma said, "the country would be doomed. How much does he know?"

"Enough," Skip replied, before Amy could—and given it was Amy, that was impressive, "not to have to be talked about in the third person."

Since ignoring Skip was a bit of a specialty, Emma said, "We always talk about Skip in the third person." She didn't, however, stick out her tongue.

"I'm coming along to keep you guys out of trouble."

"Oh, like *that* ever worked."

He grimaced. "Fine. I'm coming along because I'd like proof that my sister has lost her tiny little mind. I have a camera. I'll take pictures." When Emma hesitated, he added, "I'm going, or the car and the ladders aren't. You can take Amy."

Amy rolled her eyes at him in the mirror. "If you're finished? He can help with the ladders," she added. "Where are we going first?"

Emma grimaced. "We're going to get Maria Copis."

"That's the mother?"

Emma nodded. She gave Amy the address, waited until Amy had fiddled with the talking map, and then took it back.

Maria Copis lived well away from the downtown core, in a neighborhood of semi-detached homes with uniformly neat lawns and trees that had grown to a reasonable height, obscuring the boulevards. Emma looked at them as the car slowed, and Eric said, "Her mother's house. Number sixty-two."

"Oh."

"Where did you think she would go?" Chase asked.

Eric took one hand off the wheel to slap his shoulder.

"No," Emma told Eric. "It's fair. I didn't think."

"Listen to Emma," Chase told Eric. To Emma, he said, "Did you think about what you were going to say?"

When Emma didn't answer, Chase snorted. As the car rolled to a stop, he opened the door.

"No, you don't." Eric grabbed his shirt. "You're not going anywhere near that house. Emma, Allison, this is all yours."

Emma nodded and glanced at Allison, who nodded back and opened her door. She got out first, waiting for Emma to join her. Emma's hand was shaking on the car's handle as she pushed the door open. She got out slowly.

*I don't want to do this.*

"Emma?"

Emma glanced at Allison.

"I think we should get Michael."

"We look more harmless without him."

Allison said nothing, and after a moment, Emma nodded. She almost regretted it, but it bought her time. *I don't want to do this.*

Allison walked over to Amy's car as it pulled up, and after a minute, she returned with Michael. "She's got kids," Allison told him. "An eighteen month old and a baby. We might need you to help with them while we talk."

Michael nodded and looked at Emma, who hadn't moved.

Emma shook herself, took a deep breath, and started up the driveway. Yes, she didn't want to do this.

But she couldn't let that stop her.

As she walked, she thought of how she would feel if two strangers—of any age, any description—had shown up at her door, promising her they could take her to Nathan. Telling her that unless she believed them and went with them, Nathan would be trapped in a miniature version of hell for a long damn time.

She knew that she would stand in that door, Petal practically under her feet, staring at them as if they were either insane or unspeakably cruel. Knew, as well, that while most of her would want to slam the door in their faces, some stupid part of her would *want* to believe them. Not about hell, but about the necessity of *her* involvement.

And that part of her?

That stupid, selfish part would want to believe it because then she'd see him again. Just once. Just one more time. She could say good-bye. She could tell him she loved him. She hadn't been able to do that. He hadn't survived long enough for Emma to reach the hospital.

"Em?"

"Sorry." She'd stopped walking. Wrapping her arms around herself, she started again. But she was aware, as she walked, that it was the stupid, selfish part of herself that she needed to understand here: the part that hoped in the face of the worst possible loss even when it knew all hope was pointless.

Emma approached the bright red door. Flecks of peeling paint showed that it hadn't always been bright red, and this was exactly the type of detail she noticed when she was nervous. She cleared her throat, straightened her hands, reached for the doorbell and hesitated for just a moment.

Allison said nothing. Emma was fiercely glad that Allison was beside her; if she'd been Amy, she would have already pushed the doorbell and taken a step back. "Sorry, Ally," she said. "I'm just—I'm not certain what to say."

Allison nodded. Because she wasn't, either. But she had just enough faith in Emma that Emma *could* push the doorbell. Heard from the wrong side of the door, the chime was tinny and electric.

They waited together, listening for the sounds of footsteps. They heard the sound of shouting instead, and it got louder until the door opened.

A woman with a red-faced child on her hip stood in the doorway, dark strands of hair escaping from a ponytail and heading straight for her eyes. She was younger than Emma's mother; she looked as though she wasn't even thirty. The child's voice gave out in the presence of strangers, and she—Emma remembered the eighteen-month-old daughter—shoved a balled fist into her mouth.

"We're sorry to bother you," Emma said quietly, "but we're looking for Maria Copis."

The woman's dark eyes narrowed slightly. "Why?"

"We're not trying to sell anything," Emma said quickly. "Are you Maria Copis?"

The child reached out and grabbed a handful of her mother's hair, which took some effort, and made clear why so much of it had escaped its binding. "Don't do that," the woman said and, catching the perfect little fist, attempted to retrieve her hair without tearing it out. "Yes, I'm Maria Copis. As you can see," she added, "I'm a little busy. What can I do for you?"

"We just want a—a moment of your time," Emma replied. "I'm Emma Hall, and this is Allison and Michael. Do you mind if we come in?"

The answer was clearly yes. Maria set her daughter down inside the hall. The child immediately grabbed the edge of her mother's shirt and tried to drag her away from the door. "I really don't have time to talk right now," Maria said. "Maybe you could come back when my mother's home from work."

"I'm afraid we won't be here, then," Emma told her.

Before she could answer, her daughter let go of her shirt and walked in that precarious way that toddlers do, half leaning forward as if taunting gravity. She reached the edge of the front step and pointed up—at Michael. Michael knelt instantly, putting his hands in reach, and she leaped off the step to the sound of her mother's quiet shriek. Michael caught her, and she caught his nose. He laughed and said ouch, but not loudly enough to discourage her.

"Cathy, don't pinch people's noses," her mother said.

"I don't mind. It doesn't hurt," Michael told her. Cathy grabbed his ear instead, and he stood, lifting her off the ground. He also let her pull his head to the side until she was bored, which, since she was eighteen months old, didn't take too long. She went on to discover the pens Michael sometimes carried in his pockets, when he was wearing shirts that had them. She grabbed one, and they had a little tug of war over it.

Maria Copis stood in the door for a minute, watching Michael with her daughter. Her shoulders relaxed slightly, and she glanced at the two girls, shaking her head in wonder. "She's going through a shy phase. She won't even let my mother pick her up."

"Michael likes kids," Allison said. "And they've always liked him. Even the shy kids."

"I guess so." She exhaled. "You might as well come in, then. It's not going to be quiet," she added. "And the place is a mess."

The place, as she'd called it, was undeniably a mess, and they had to pick their way over the scattered debris of children's toys just to get out of the doorway. Michael tried to put Cathy down, but she grabbed his hair. So he sat crouched in the hall, surrounded by toys that were probably hers. He picked up a stuffed orange dinosaur and tried to exchange it for his hair.

When she ignored it, Michael made baby-dinosaur noises, which was better seen than described, and Cathy laughed when the baby dinosaur tried to lick her face. Emma glanced at Maria Copis, who was watching while a smile tugged at the corner of her lips. It was a tight smile, and it faded into something else as Emma watched.

She wanted to leave, then, because she knew what the expression meant, and she hated invading this woman's privacy—and her grief. But still, watching her daughter play with Michael was peaceful, and Emma remembered watching Michael play with Petal in just the same way. Life went on.

Some lives.

She let it go on for a while, because she was a coward and she still didn't want to do this: bring up Andrew, her dead son. Add to the pain.

But Andrew was waiting, and he was waiting for his mother. Emma found courage from somewhere, and she spoke.

"I know this is going to sound bad," she said quietly, and Maria started slightly and turned to face her. "And I want to apologize for that up front. I almost didn't come here today."

The woman looked confused. Not suspicious, not yet; that would come. Emma glanced at the living room, which was also mired in toys, and after a pause, she walked toward it, forcing Allison and Maria to follow. Michael, absorbed in little shrieks of laughter, would notice eventually, and even if he didn't, Maria could still keep an eye on him if she wanted.

"What did you want to talk to me about?" Her eyes narrowed. "You're not reporters, are you?"

"No! I mean, no, we're not. We're still in school," Emma added.

"I'm sorry," the woman replied. "The only strangers recently who've wanted to talk to me have been reporters. Or ambulance-chasing lawyers. And no," she added, again looking at Michael, or more accurately, at her daughter's face, "you really don't look like either."

Emma bit her lip. "We might as well be," she replied quietly. "Because we *are* here to talk about your son."

## ᴄ Chapter 13

The ease—and there hadn't been much of it—drained out of Maria Copis' face. What was left was raw and angry. Emma flinched, even though she'd been expecting it.

"I think," the woman said evenly, "you'd better leave, now." Her hands, Emma noted, were balled in fists, and they were shaking slightly.

Emma raised both of her hands, palms out. "Please, hear me out. Please. I don't—I wouldn't do this to you, I *would not* be here, if there were any other way. I lost my father a few years ago. My boyfriend died this past summer in a car crash. Both times people let me grieve in peace. They gave me privacy, and I needed it. I *know* just how much I'd hate me if I were in your shoes.

"Please, just let me say what I came here to say. If you—if it makes no sense to you, if you don't believe it, we'll leave and we will never, ever bother you again."

The edge of anger left Maria's dark eyes, but her hands were still clenched, still shaking. Michael, behind her, was crawling around the floor on all fours, barking like a dog.

"Your boyfriend died last summer?"

It wasn't what Emma had expected to hear, and she flinched again, for entirely different reasons. But she swallowed and nodded.

"Were you there?"

"No. I would have been, if I could have. I went to the hospital the minute his mother called me to tell me—but none of us made it there in time." She closed her eyes and turned her face away for a moment, remembering the industrial gloss of off-white halls and the klaxon sound of monitors in the distance. She shook herself and looked back to Maria Copis.

"I'm sorry to hear that," the woman said quietly. As if she meant it. Her eyes were ringed with dark circles, and she lifted a hand and pushed it through her hair. No fists, now. No obvious rage.

"It was the worst thing that's ever happened to me," Emma replied. "And even so, I can't imagine what it must be like for you. I can try. I can *think* I understand it—but I don't." It was hard for her to say this, because she wasn't even certain it was true. Just one week ago, she would have said that no loss was greater, or could be greater, than the loss of Nathan. But . . . for just a moment, she thought Maria Copis' loss might be.

"Why did you come here, Emma?" The question was quiet, weary.

Emma took a deep breath. "I can see the dead."

*        *        *

Cathy shrieked with delight; it was the only noise in the house. It was followed by Michael's voice. Neither of them erased the heavy weight of the words Emma had just spoken.

Maria Copis said, "Pardon me?"

"I can see the dead," Emma repeated. She swallowed. "I know it sounds crazy. I know it sounds stupid, or worse. But I'm not pretending to be a medium or a—a whatever. I'm not going to tell you that I can reach the afterworld and put you in contact with your son, or offer to do it if you pay me. I don't want your money, and I'll never ask for it."

"You . . . can see the dead."

Emma nodded.

"And you're going to tell me you've seen my son."

"Not—not exactly."

Maria Copis lifted a hand. "I'm crazy tired," she said, and she obviously meant it. "And I'm either hallucinating, or I've lost my mind. I need a cup of coffee. Would either of you like one?"

"No, thank you," Emma replied. Allison didn't drink coffee.

"Come into the kitchen with me."

"Should we tell Michael to follow us?"

Maria lifted a hand to her eyes and rubbed them a couple of times. "No," she said. "My mother would call me an idiot, but—he's not going to hurt her, and he's not going to let her hurt herself. And this is as happy as I've seen her since—since. She deserves to play in peace while he's willing to play with her." She turned and walked into the kitchen, and, stepping around toys, Emma and Allison followed her.

She made coffee in silence, opening the various cupboards to find filters, coffee, and a cup. She kept her back to Emma and Allison the entire time, grinding beans first and then letting coffee percolate. When it was done, and when she'd added cream and sugar to the cup in very large amounts, she turned to them, leaning her back against the kitchen counter as if she needed the support.

"So. You two can see the dead."

"Oh, no," Allison said quickly. "Just Emma."

Maria's eyes reddened, and she bit her lip. She rubbed her eyes again with the palm of her hand. Emma looked at the floor, because it was hard to look at someone whose grief was so raw and so close to the surface she was like a walking wound.

Hard because Emma had been there. Had hidden it, as much as she could, because she *needed* to hide it. She'd told everyone she was fine—everyone except Petal, because Petal couldn't talk. When Maria Copis spoke again, however, Emma looked up.

"So, Emma, you can see the dead. But you haven't seen my son."

Emma grimaced. "Not yet."

"And you're trying to see him for some reason?"

"No." She swore softly. "Yes."

"Which is it?"

"Yes. We're trying to see your son." Emma spread her hands, again exposing her palms. "I—I heard you," she whispered. "From midtown, I heard you shouting his name. Drew."

Maria stiffened.

"And I followed it. The shouting. It was—" Emma took a deeper breath. "I'm sorry. Let me try this again. I *can* see the dead. Some of the dead are strong enough that I can see where they are. Or where they were when they died. Some of the dead are strong enough that they think they're still there, and I can see and feel what they see and feel."

Maria put the coffee cup down on the counter and folded her arms across her chest, drawing them in tightly.

"I could hear the shouting while I was in school, and I followed it, while a friend drove and took my lousy directions. When we finally got to Rowan Avenue, I tried to go into what was left of the house. I couldn't. Fire was gouting out the windows."

"There's no fire there now," Maria said.

"No. In theory there wasn't any fire when I went, either. No one else could see it," she added quietly, "because no one else can see the dead. Only me. It singed my hair.

"I didn't know who was trapped in the house. I only knew that the fire was recent because it looked recent, and the buildings were still standing. I went home, because I couldn't get into the building, and I looked the address up, because I hoped it would tell me what had happened or what was happening." She swallowed. "And when I read his name—Andrew—I realized that the shouting I'd heard wasn't his. It was yours."

Maria lifted a hand to her face for just a moment. When she dropped it, she wrapped her arm around herself again. She didn't speak.

Emma did. "He could hear you. He could hear you shouting. He still can.

"He thinks the house is burning. I couldn't get to him because I couldn't get through the fire, not then. So, no, I haven't seen your son."

Silence.

"I am *trying* to see your son," Emma continued, her voice thickening, "because I think he's trapped in the burning building. I'm not even sure we can safely get into the building; I'm not sure if we can reach wherever he's standing. But I have to *try*. And I came to you because—" She couldn't say it. She couldn't say the rest of the words. She turned to Allison, and Allison was blurry, which was a bad sign. Emma Hall didn't cry in public.

Allison caught her hands and squeezed them, and Allison saved her.

"We think," Allison told Maria Copis, "that Andrew won't—or can't—come out of that building if you're not there. He's waiting for you," she added quietly. "He has no idea that he's dead."

And there it was. When Emma could see again, when she could see clearly—or as clearly as she was going to be able to see—she could see the hunger in Maria Copis' eyes as plainly as if it were her own. She could see the suspicion, as well; she could see the way Maria's expression shifted as she tried to figure out what their angle was. What they wanted.

As if to quell those suspicions, she walked to the edge of the kitchen and glanced out into the hall where Michael was still playing with her toddler. She stood there for minutes, and then, arms still tightly wound around her body, she turned back.

She was crying now, but she didn't raise her hands to wipe the tears away; they fell, silent, down gaunt cheeks. "Why should I believe you?" she whispered.

This, too, Emma understood. But she could do something about this. She lifted one hand, and she whispered a single name. *Georges.*

In the air before Emma, a golden chain extending from the palm of her hand to his heart, Georges shimmered into existence. The sunlight through the kitchen windows shone through his chest, casting no shadows. But he looked at Emma almost hopefully, and she cringed.

She held out her hand to him, and he took it in his own.

Maria Copis gasped and covered her mouth with one hand. She swore into her palm, her eyes widening, her brows almost disappearing beneath the fringe of loose, dark hair.

"Georges," Emma said, "I'm sorry. Michael can't play right now, but I wanted to introduce you to Maria Copis. Maria," she added, "this is Georges."

"He's—" Maria hesitated and then took two firm steps toward Georges, who looked dubious but stood and waited. Georges didn't look like a ghost. He felt like one, to Emma, whose hand was already beginning to sting at the physical contact. Maria tried to touch Georges and her hand passed through him, as Emma had known it would.

"Oh, my god. Oh, my god."

Georges turned to Emma. "Where's Michael?"

"He's babysitting right now."

The look of disappointment across those delicate features was its own kind of heartbreak, in a day that had already exposed too much of it.

"I'm sorry, Georges," Emma said, kneeling so that she was closer to his eye level. "I promise as soon as I can, you can see Michael again. But we're trying to help another little boy—"

"They caught him?"

"No. No, Georges. He's trapped inside a burning building."

Georges frowned. "Did he die there?"

Emma nodded.

"I don't think you should go there."

"We have to try to help him," Emma said quietly. "He's a little boy. Much younger than you."

"Oh." Georges nodded. And then, while Emma watched, he quietly disappeared.

And Maria Copis looked at Emma.

"I'm sorry," Emma said, rubbing her hand. "Even dead children like Michael."

The woman's laugh was brief and brittle.

Emma swallowed air. "I can't promise anything," she told Maria Copis. "And I won't try. I'm not sure we can even get past the fire—but I can't leave him there without trying. We came here to ask you to come with us—but we might not be able to reach him at all. It might all be for nothing."

"When are you going?"

"We're going now. If you give me your phone number, I can call you if we can actually get far enough into the building to reach him."

Maria laughed again, and it was the same thin laugh.

"But we have two cars," Allison told her, correctly interpreting that laughter. "If you can't find a babysitter, we can all go. Michael would stay if we asked him."

"I can call my mother. I can ask her to come home from work. I can—" she stopped as Emma stiffened, but Emma said nothing. ". . . I can sound like a crazy, grief-stricken, hysterical daughter."

Emma winced. But she didn't disagree. "I could ask Georges to come out again for your mother," she began.

"No. You're right, even if you didn't say it out loud. We could call her, she could come home, and she could be terrified enough that she wouldn't be fit to babysit, if she even let me out of the house. How long do you think—" She lifted a hand. "No, sorry. I'm just being incredibly stupid. I can't call anyone else, either. Do you have enough room for two car seats?"

Emma nodded. "We have two cars—and a couple of other friends as well."

"There are more of you?"

"We needed help with the ladders. You'll come with us?"

"Yes. He's *my son*. There's no way I'm going to stay here just waiting beside the phone while you try to help him. Yes, Emma. I'll come. Maybe Michael can help with the kids while we're there."

If Emma's world had changed overnight—and, with the appearance of Longland and the ghosts, it had—Rowan Avenue had continued in blissful ignorance. If, by blissful, one meant a raging fire and billowing dark smoke from all the downstairs windows. Emma got out of the car slowly, and approached the sidewalk, where she surveyed the ruined buildings. Only one of them was burning, which made it a bit easier to spot, given the lack of numbers on the front facade.

She glanced at Allison, who had also emerged, and at Michael, who was half in and half out of the car, struggling with the straps of a car seat and a toddler who did not, apparently, like being stuck in one. Amy had pulled up by the curb, parked, and flipped the back hatch of her vehicle up; she was already giving Skip—and Eric and Chase—instructions about the ladders.

Maria Copis emerged last, holding her baby while Michael carried Cathy. She stayed beside Michael, possibly because Cathy was attached to him with that toddler force that allows for no quiet separation, and possibly because it was hard for her to approach the ruins of her home, the place where her son had died.

Emma glanced at her and found it hard to look away. Maria was holding her baby as if the baby was some kind of life buoy and she was on the edge of drowning.

"Maybe this wasn't a good idea," Emma said softly to Allison.

Allison shook her head. "It's going to be hard for her. Even if she weren't here with us—even if she weren't trying to help her son. Her oldest child died here. I don't know if Cathy remembers the house or not—she's still glued to Michael—but . . . Maria had to walk out of the house without Andrew and pray that he followed."

"I know—it's just . . . the look on her face, Ally."

Allison didn't tell her not to look. Amy would have, but Amy was busy shouting at Skip. Skip, not shy, was shouting back. Eric, not stupid, was quietly avoiding getting between two siblings who were arguing, and Chase—well, it looked as though Chase was *trying* not to be stupid and mostly succeeding.

Emma spread her hands out, palms up. "I feel like I should say something to her or do something for her, but I can't think of a damn thing I could do that won't somehow make it worse."

"Except this," Allison said quietly.

"Except this."

"What do you see, Em?"

Emma grimaced. "Smoke. Black smoke. And fire."

"Can you hear anything?"

Emma frowned. After a moment, she said, "Beyond the fire? No."

"No shouting?"

"No. It's the first time—" She grimaced again and wondered if the expression was going to be stuck there permanently, she'd used it so often lately. "Not that I've been here that often. But . . . no. I don't hear her voice."

"Is that a bad sign?"

"I don't know."

"Emma!" Amy, hands on her hips, had turned. "Are you going to sit there chatting with Allison all day, or are you going to get this show on the road?"

Allison touched her shoulder. "We needed the car and the ladders," she whispered.

Emma nodded, shoved her hands into her pockets, and headed toward the facade, where Chase and Eric were now positioning ladders. Or trying to keep them in position. The front of the building was not entirely cooperating, because there was a small porch on the second floor that hovered just over the door. It wasn't terribly wide, but it was—almost—in the way of at least one of the ladders.

They did, however, manage to set the ladder against the wall just to one side of the overhang. How, Emma had no idea, and she wasn't about to look a gift horse in the mouth. No one lived here anymore, so any external damage to the building wasn't likely to get them in trouble.

"Eric," she said instead, as she approached him, "I think something's changed."

He raised a brow, and left Chase and Skip. "What's wrong?"

"I—when we were here last time, I could hear his mother shouting his name. I can't hear her now. Is that because she's here?"

"Emma, please don't take this the wrong way, but I don't know. I've never done this before. Chase sure as hell hasn't, and neither have any of your friends. This is a first, for all of us." He glanced over his shoulder at Amy and then back. "On the other hand, at least one of us isn't fazed by it at all."

"Amy doesn't believe in dwelling on difficulties."

"There's a lot Amy doesn't believe in. I'm surprised she believes in the dead."

Emma laughed. "If she's seen it, she believes in it. And if she believes in it, it's not safe to question her."

"I think I got that." He smiled, but it faded. "Can you see the fire?"

Emma nodded. She glanced at Skip, and winced. "I don't think I've ever seen Skip so angry."

"He's not gaining much traction with Amy."

"No, but he's lived with her all her life; he's got to be used to that. He mostly trusts her. If he's pushing, he knows she'll push back, and *he's* the one who's skipping Dalhousie to come to Amy's party."

"That's not his fault."

"His parents won't care, unless he can convince them—and no one's in a hurry to drag parents into this." She failed to mention Michael. "They can't do anything but die." She turned back to the fire, although she'd never really left it; it was loud.

"Bad?"

"It's bad. But firefighters did get in through the upper windows, and the worst of the fire seems to be coming out of the downstairs ones. If it's true that I'll be in whatever Andrew sees, I should be able to get to him through the second story as well."

"Without the asbestos and the oxygen."

"Thank you, Eric."

He grinned, but the grin didn't reach his eyes. "You don't have to do this," he told her, reaching for her hand and gripping it surprisingly tightly.

She looked over her shoulder at Maria Copis, still clutching her baby. Then she looked back, and briefly squeezed his hand. "Sorry. You don't have to, though."

"As if." He shook his head, but he hadn't expected a different answer, and she wondered why he'd tried. She would have asked, but Maria now approached her. Emma made way for her at the base of the first ladder.

"What do we do, now?" Maria asked.

"I go up the ladder," Emma told her, striving for certainty. "I'll take a look around."

"And what do you want me to do?"

"Give the baby to Amy or Allison. Or Skip. You can climb up on your own, but you won't see the fire—at least I don't think you will—until I find Andrew."

"You don't think?"

Emma winced. "I'm not entirely certain how this part works. I'm fairly new to all this—"

"Is there anyone here who isn't?"

Emma didn't answer that, but continued, "—but new or not, we all feel we need to at least try." She tried to keep her voice smooth.

Maria Copis frowned. "This isn't safe, is it?"

"It should be."

"For you. This isn't safe for you."

Eric, bless him, said nothing.

"Does it matter?" Emma asked Maria, squaring her shoulders slightly, and taking the meager scraps of courage she could from defiance.

"Yes. You're not dead. He is." Maria swallowed and glanced away, but only for a second. "I don't want to be responsible for—for killing you."

"You're not. This was my decision, start to finish, and we're going up there with or without you."

Eric cleared his throat. "I think you're getting left behind," he told them both.

Emma frowned and turned toward the ladders. Chase was already at the top of the rightmost one. He turned and blew her a kiss, and she grimaced. He missed it; he'd already braced himself against the ladder—with a pause to shout instructions to Skip and Amy, who had managed enough of a truce to hold the ladder steady between them—before crawling in through the window. "Chase," she told Maria, "is very easily bored and has no sense of self-preservation."

"Chase," Eric corrected her, "is testing the floor to see if it'll hold weight. It probably won't," he added quietly, "and if it doesn't, you're going to have to hold her hand before she enters the building."

"But the fire—"

"Yes. She'll see it, too."

Maria's glance bounced between Eric and Emma a few times. She didn't speak. Instead, she withdrew for a moment. Emma almost asked why, but she stopped when Maria pulled up the edge of her shirt and nudged her baby awake.

"I'll feed him," she told Emma quietly. "And change him. Hopefully he'll sleep until after—after we've finished."

"What if he wakes up?" It was Allison, who had joined them quietly, who asked. Which made sense, since it was Allison who was going to be holding him.

"Walk him around. Or bounce him—gently." She didn't ask Emma how long things would take. She didn't ask anything. Instead, she told Allison, "There's a bottle for Cathy in the diaper bag and a couple of teething biscuits; if she's fussing—and she won't until she's tired—have Michael give her both." She took a breath, held it, expelled it. "I don't suppose any of you have changed diapers?"

Eric raised a hand. "I have."

"If she needs—"

"We'll take care of her. If we're down here."

Chase came down the ladder and found Eric and Emma.

"Well?" Eric asked him.

Chase grimaced. "It held, at least part of the way in. I'd recommend that you let Maria risk it," he told Emma, "but make sure she's standing almost on top of you. If the floor buckles, grab her hand or her arm, and pull her in.

Unless the fire doesn't seem too bad when you get up there. In which case, just pull her in right away."

He hesitated for a minute, and then he addressed Maria. "I'm going to go up with you both, if that's okay. I'm crap with babies, and Eric's practically a wet nurse, but without the breasts. If Emma has problems, I'm going to have to pull her out. I'll be walking behind you, hopefully far enough back that my weight won't be a tipping point if the joists are going to collapse. But I'll need to risk a bit, because I won't be able to reach her if she needs help.

"She'll be walking into the burning house," he added. "It won't look like that to either of us, but . . . she might catch fire, her hair might burn. I don't know if the effects of the—of—" he had the grace to flush. "I'm sorry. I don't know if your son is strong enough to actually burn her clothing."

Maria nodded gravely. "If she looks like she's being burned, or if she starts to cough or choke, you'll pull her out?"

"Got it in one. But I might need help. Don't try to help me unless I ask for it; stand your ground, because the floor's not solid. When I touch Emma," he added, "the floor will be solid for *me*. But so will the fire. If you can avoid that, avoid it. Wait for my word.

"Got it, Emma?"

Emma nodded. "Maria, was he in his bedroom?"

Maria swallowed. The words were slow to come, and they came in a heavy rush. "Yes. I left him there and headed to the stairs. It's the room to the side of the hall, not the back room. These windows open onto my bedroom. If you head out the door into the hall, his is the first room on the right."

"Good. It's not far."

Chase said, "Far enough."

Eric stepped on his foot. "Here, Em. Maria. Take these." He handed them damp towels. "Cover your mouths, if it comes to that. I don't know how much time you'll have; I don't know how much time you'll *need*. Buy what you can."

Emma nodded.

"Come out the same way you entered, if you have that much control."

"We should be able to do that."

"Yes. You should. But right now, Andrew is in the driver's seat, and it may mean you won't have the choice." He hesitated and then added, "Even if you can touch him, and she can see him, she can't touch him, Emma." The words were soft and final.

Emma, who had not thought of it until that moment, felt the world shift—in a bad way—beneath her feet. His mother couldn't touch him, and couldn't pick him up, and he hadn't moved the first time when she'd shouted and pleaded with him. He had waited for her to carry him out.

And that had killed him.

\*       \*       \*

They started up the ladders. Emma went first, and she moved slowly, covering her mouth and nose with a damp towel. It was hard to see much, because the smoke from the lower windows was so dark and so acrid; it stung her eyes, and clung—she was certain—to her hair. She felt the heat, but the actual ladder was cool to the touch. It wasn't much of a comfort, but here, you took what you could.

Beneath her, struggling in her own way, Maria Copis followed. Chase was climbing the other ladder in parallel, shouting encouragement. At least, that's what Emma thought he was trying to do; what he was actually achieving was more irritating. Then again, an irritating Chase was a whole lot better than a deadly fire if she had to choose something to dwell on.

There was still broken glass in the window frame. Only the bottom of the frame, which was black with smoke, was an issue, if they were careful. Emma, who had dressed to visit a bereaved parent, winced—she had old painting clothing, most of it her mother's, and after she'd finished here it was going to look a whole lot better than what she was wearing now. And she *liked* these clothes.

Chase helpfully told her to be careful of the glass.

She helpfully told him that she was; she might have said more, but Maria was here. Maria, whose face was a little like the shards of glass that nestled in what was left of the window's frame; you could cut yourself on her expression if you weren't careful.

Emma was careful enough to hold the cloth to her face and to partially cover her eyes, and then she wasn't worried about Maria anymore. The room wasn't burning, but smoke was wafting up the stairs and through the open door. It was hard to avoid the glass when she couldn't clearly see it, but she came up on the window's edge on the soles of her shoes before jumping lightly down. The floor held. It was hot, but it held.

Chase had told her to wait for Maria, but it was hard. This was where Andrew had died, and this was almost when—and what killed him, could kill her. She dropped to the ground, staying as close to the floorboards as she could to avoid the smoke.

Maria came up through the window next, and she took a lot more care getting down from the frame. Chase, in the window beside hers, was doing the same. "You're okay?" he asked. Emma wasn't certain who he was asking; she couldn't see, clearly, where he was looking.

"Emma?" Maria said.

"Avoiding the smoke," she barked back. "Hurry, please."

But it wasn't as easy as that; it never was. Maria was stepping gingerly across the boards, testing how much give they had; she was stopping to listen to Chase, and she was following his directions. He was less careful than she was.

Emma couldn't see what Maria was stepping on; she could only see what she herself moved across, and she wondered just how different they were. Grinding her teeth, and staying as low to the ground as possible, she crawled along the same path that Maria Copis was walking. She crawled faster.

By some miracle, they reached the hall door, then the hall itself. Emma didn't bother to get to her feet, because the smoke here was at its thickest. Instead, she scuttled across the floor, holding her breath; she could only barely see the dim outline of the door in the hall; she couldn't tell what color it had been painted. She thought, at first, the poor visibility was due to smoke, but then she realized that it was night in Andrew's world. The fire had occurred at night.

Breathing through her nose and keeping her lips tightly pressed together, she made her way to his bedroom door. She couldn't and didn't look for Maria; there was too much smoke, and she was too afraid. She had never been in a fire before, and if she survived this one, she would never, god willing, be in one again.

The door was slightly ajar, and over the crackle of burning, she heard Andrew Copis for the first time.

He was screaming.


## ᕯ Chapter 14

Emma had to fight the urge to get to her feet and run into the room; she crawled toward the door and nudged it open just enough that she could fit through it. Andrew Copis was standing—in his bed—screaming for his mother. It wasn't a scream of pain; in some ways, it was worse. He was utterly terrified, and his voice was raw with the weight and the totality of that terror.

As long as she lived—and she wondered how long that would be—she would remember the sound, the feel of it; it passed right through her, leaving some of itself behind.

She didn't fight to stay on the floor after that; she couldn't. She got to her feet, and she ran to the bed, and to the child who stood there, his eyes wide with the horror that came from a growing realization that he'd been utterly and completely betrayed—and abandoned. He had, she realized, his mother's dark hair, and part of it was plastered to his face; the bangs were wet with either sweat or tears, and gathered in clumps near his eyes and across his forehead. Emma reached out for him.

He was *cold*. He was so damn cold to the touch she pulled back as if she'd been burned. He didn't seem to notice that she'd touched him; he didn't seem to notice that she was there at all.

She heard footsteps behind her, and shouted. "Chase, shut the damn door! Keep the smoke out!"

The door did close. She heard his muttered apology.

"Emma?" She also heard Maria's voice. It was hard to listen, though; Andrew had not fallen silent, and Emma thought, short of exhaustion, he wouldn't. No, not short of exhaustion. Short of death. This was how he had died.

She felt it like a blow, and she almost turned to throw up. But turning, she caught sight of his mother's face, and that was just as bad.

She looked at Chase instead. Chase, whose face was shuttered, whose expression was grim and closed. She wanted to ask him to help, but she couldn't force the words out. Or not all of them.

"Chase . . ."

He grimaced, which cracked his expression. "What is it?"

"He's so damn cold. I can't—" She lifted shaking hands. Numb hands. "It's not like—"

"Emma," Chase said, cursing. He walked to her, caught her hands in his. Crushed them, briefly. "He's powerful. You *knew* that."

"I didn't know what it meant." She swallowed. Chase was angry. And, she realized, he probably should be. Andrew was here—and he was in worse than the hell she'd imagined. She'd tried to touch him once, and she was almost in tears. How pathetic was that?

"Sorry, Chase," she told him. She squeezed back, feeling her fingers.

And then she squared her shoulders, took as deep a breath as she could, regretted it briefly, and approached Andrew again. This time, she held out her hands slowly, waving them in front of his open, sightless eyes. Nothing. If he was aware of her at all, he made no sign.

"Maria," Emma whispered, aware that the smoke was thickening in the room, aware that—for herself and Andrew—there was a growing lack of time, "brace yourself."

She didn't know how Maria responded, wasn't really certain she'd been heard at all. Emma reached out with both of her hands and grabbed both of Andrew's.

The cold was so intense it defined pain; she forgot about fire, about heat, about the smoke of things consumed by either. She tasted blood and realized that she'd bitten her lip. Knees locked, she stood, rigid, in front of him.

But even with his hands in hers, the screaming didn't stop. Emma realized she'd bitten her lip to stop from joining him. She dropped to her knees by the bedside, coughing; she'd dropped the cloth during her first rush to reach him, and she couldn't hold it anyway; both of her hands were in his.

"Drew!"

*Emma.*

Maria could suddenly see her son. And Emma could see her father.

"Drew!" Maria darted forward, closing the gap between them. She blinked, coughing, as the truth of fire rushed in, along with the lack of sunlight that spoke of night. If her son was trapped here, so, now was Maria Copis—but Emma understood, from the look on her face, that she had been trapped here ever since the night her son had died. She reached for Drew, and her hands passed through him. Emma shuddered; she couldn't help it.

Maria reached for Drew again. A third time. A fourth. There was no fifth, but there were now tears, leaving a trail across her cheeks. "Emma—he doesn't see me."

It was true.

"I don't know why," Emma forced herself to say. The words were shaky and uneven, but she managed to get them out clearly. "This has never happened before." She turned and looked up at her father.

*Emma.*

"He can't see her. He can't see his mother. I—I don't even think he can see me, and he's so *cold*."

*Sprout.* Brendan Hall stood in the wafting smoke. He watched Maria and her son, and after a moment, he closed his eyes. *I was spared this*, he told his daughter softly.

"You were never in a fire."

*No. That's not what I meant. I was spared your death. I got to die first. This*— he shook his head. *This is our worst nightmare, Em. As parents, there is no fear that's stronger. It's still my worst fear. If it were up to me, you wouldn't*— But he opened his eyes again, and he looked at Maria Copis' face. He didn't bother to say the rest.

"Help me, Dad. I don't know what to do. I can't leave him here—"

Her father glanced at Chase.

"I honestly do not give a damn what Chase thinks or what he's afraid of right now. We'll all die here if I can't get him out. His mother's not going to leave him a second time."

It was true. It hadn't occurred to her until this moment, but it was true. She could tell Maria that she had two living children who needed her, now more than ever, and she knew that Maria, like Andrew, would be deaf.

Her father reached up with both of his hands, and he cupped her cheeks. His hands were not cold. Emma remembered what he'd done—what she'd taken from him—and she tried to pull her face away. "No, Dad—"

He couldn't touch her unless she touched him first. She remembered that. He couldn't touch her unless she *wanted* him to touch her. But he did, and maybe that said things about her that she'd never wanted to admit. She said no, but she let him do it anyway.

Chase started forward, hand outstretched. But he stopped, and he dropped the hand, where it curled in a fist at his side. "Emma—"

"Shut up, Chase. Just—shut up."

"Is he trying to *give* you power?"

She said nothing, because what she wanted to say would have irritated the hell out of her father. At least it would have when he was alive.

*Sprout,* he said quietly, *let me help you.*

"I don't want—"

*Sprout.*

"I don't want you to leave."

He smiled, the indulgent smile that had always been given only to her. And sometimes Petal. *I won't leave. I've nowhere else to go.*

"But I—"

He bent down and kissed her forehead gently. Where his lips touched her skin, warmth traveled, carrying with its slow spread something that felt like the essence of life, which was strange, because he was dead. She tried to hold on to the cold, but she couldn't. Maybe she was that selfish. Maybe, in the end, all children were. But this warmth reminded her of what love, being loved, felt like, and she leaned into it.

The cold drained out of her hands, although she still held onto Andrew Copis. Andrew, who still wailed, unseeing and terrified.

Chase was watching her in silence. Watching, she realized, her father as he stood, bent over her. When her father unfolded, he vanished slowly; for Chase, Emma realized, he had vanished the instant his lips had left her forehead.

She met Chase's gaze and said, "That was my father." Her voice was thick. She swallowed, then turned back to Andrew.

"Your father."

"He came to help me. He—it *does* help me. Even if he didn't—even if I didn't—" She couldn't force herself to say the words. "It helps me to know he's there. And that he's always been there, watching me." But she flinched as he continued to stare. "I think I know why you hate Necromancers," she whispered. "Because I'm afraid. What he gives me, Chase—I take it. I'm afraid I'll take it *all.* I'll use him up, somehow. There'll be nothing left."

Chase was utterly still. After a moment, he slid his hands into his pockets and swore. Neither Maria nor Andrew noticed; Emma couldn't make out the actual words herself. She could make out the smoke and the heat of the floor. Time was passing in Andrew's world, and time here was not kind.

Finally, Chase said, in a flat, cool voice, "You need more power."

She shook her head.

"You do. And it's standing there screaming on the bed."

This was a test. Emma thought it, and wanted to slap him. But she couldn't withdraw her hands. Even if they were no longer so cold she couldn't feel them. Perhaps especially then.

Instead, she turned her attention to Andrew Copis, who was choking. He might have been choking because he'd screamed himself raw. He might have been choking because of the cost of that screaming in a house that was filling with smoke. It didn't matter.

"Andrew," she said, raising her voice as his sputtered, momentarily, out.

He stared straight ahead. He stared *through* her. Through his mother, whose hands were shaking. She'd not made fists of them; she still held them out, palms up, as if to show how empty they were.

Emma turned to Chase, still holding the boy's hands, and said, "Chase, I don't care if you think you'll have to kill me. I need you to tell me what I need to do here."

"If you keep this up, I won't. Have to kill you," he added. He looked around the room. "It'll just be a matter of time."

"I notice that you're standing here anyway."

"It was me or Allison."

"Allison wouldn't—" she bit her lip.

"Or Michael. Emma, I'm not what you are. You need to pull some of his power."

"I'm doing that now, according to Eric—if I weren't, his mother couldn't see him at all."

"If what I'm seeing is any indication—and remember, not an expert—you're not doing it *at all*. You're giving him whatever *you* have. Emma, he has power for a reason." He grimaced. "He's stuck here. It's that power that will unstick him, and the only person who can use it is you."

"He's not exactly *giving* it."

"No. But you can—exactly—take it."

"And what the hell am I supposed to *do* with it?"

"Fuck, Emma! You came here without even thinking?"

"I came here because I *was* thinking—about him! It's not like there are a lot of experts I can just ask to show me what to do!"

Maria Copis cleared her throat. Loudly.

Emma and Chase both startled, and both had expressions of similar guilt as they looked at her.

"I need to be able to touch him," she said quietly.

"Lady," Chase said, "he's *dead*. There's no way—"

"I can't bring him back to life," Emma told Maria. "And I am *not* letting you die. I'm not even sure the dead can touch each other."

"I need to be able to touch him," Maria said, in the same reasonable, flat voice.

Emma took a shallow breath and counted to ten. She got to eight, which is about as high as she ever reached in her own home. But it wasn't words or temper that killed the count; it was sensation.

The hands that were holding Andrew began to tingle, and as Emma looked down at them, they began to glow. The glow was golden, but it wasn't even; her hands looked as if she'd slid them into delicate, lace gloves. She could see her fingers beneath the winding strands of light; could see, beneath the forming lattice, the veins on the back of her hands and the slight whitening of her knuckles where her hands were clenched that little bit too hard.

She glanced at Maria Copis, but if Maria noticed at all, she gave no indication. Chase, on the other hand, was watching her hands with narrowed eyes.

"What do you see, Chase?"

He shook his head.

"Andrew," she whispered. But Andrew, like his mother, was in a different world, a different time.

"It's not Andrew," Chase told her.

She frowned. Then she looked at her hands again. The strands of light were strands of gold; they were the chains that she had broken and wound around her palms. She could follow them, now, tracing filigree from skin to the air around her.

Georges materialized first, pulling himself slowly into the world. He reached out to touch Emma, and Emma let him.

Maria Copis flinched. That was all. Whatever pity or kindness she had to spare for the dead was being entirely absorbed by her son. Georges was not her problem because he wasn't *hers*. Following Georges came Catherine, and she appeared in the same slow, almost hesitant, way. But she also touched Emma gently.

"Margaret and Suzanne can't come unless you call them," Georges told her. "And neither can Emily. She's almost here," he added, "but she's kind of stuck."

Chase stared at the two children. "You came here for Emma on your own?"

Georges nodded solemnly. "Margaret didn't think Emma would call us," he added. "I told her we could come. And," he said, with the serious pride of a six-year-old boy, "we *did it*. The fire can't hurt us," he told Chase. "We're already dead. But it *can* hurt Emma. We like Emma."

"But she's a Necromancer."

Georges shook his head forcefully. "No, she's *not*."

Chase lifted both hands in surrender. "This is fucking *insane*," he told Emma, out of the side of his mouth.

"We can still hear you," Catherine told him, with all the vast and vulnerable disapproval a six-year-old girl has in her arsenal. Having been one, Emma was familiar with the tactic.

"I thought . . . you couldn't talk to each other."

"We couldn't, before," Catherine condescended to tell him. "We couldn't until Emma. But now we can talk to each other. Georges can talk to Emma's dad," she added. "I like *him*."

Georges faced Emma. "You need to call the others," he told her. "Margaret is really smart. She can help you. She's been in the City of the Dead for a long time."

"Does she want to come?" Emma asked him. She tried to keep hope out of her voice.

Georges nodded. "She says it's dangerous, though."

"Why?"

"Necromancers."

Chase swore. A lot.

"Chase, do you want to go?"

"Fuck." He reached into his pocket and swore more loudly. "The fucking phone! If we survive this, I'm going to kill Eric."

Emma grimaced. "I've got mine," she told him. She glanced significantly at both of her occupied hands. "It's in the left pocket. Dig it out."

He did as she asked, although it was slightly awkward, and when he'd flipped it open, he punched the buttons hard enough it was a small miracle they didn't come out the phone's back. "If Eric doesn't answer this—Eric?" He moved a little away from Emma, and covered his mouth. "Emma, get this show on the road—we don't have time. Yeah, it's me. Who else?

"We might have a problem. No, shit for brains, a serious problem. One of the ghosts says we've got Necromancers. No kidding. No, they're not talking about Emma. No, how the hell should I know? They're not talking to *me*. You want me to leave?" He glanced at Emma.

Emma called Margaret, Suzanne, and Emily. They came quickly, and far more easily than either Georges or Catherine had done. But they came because Emma summoned them.

"Maybe. How the hell should I know? Look—you need to get the others the hell away from the house. Yes, I'll stay. I think it's a waste, but I'll stay." He looked up at Emma. "Emma—when your ghost said Necromancers, plural, was that just a figure of speech?"

"I don't know. Give them a sec, we can ask."

"A second is about all the time we have. We didn't manage to kill Longland."

"Margaret?" Emma's voice was soft and shaky. She couldn't reach out to touch the older woman because she didn't want to let go of Andrew, even if touching him didn't seem to be doing any good. Margaret, who was not six, made no attempt to touch her.

Margaret was the oldest of the four who'd been trapped along one wall in Amy's ad hoc dancing room. Her hair was an austere blend of gray and brown, and her eyes were the same noncolor, the slight odd glow, that the eyes of all of the dead seemed to be; she wore clothing that would have suited business-women thirty years ago. Or more.

She looked at Chase. "It was not," she said, in a deep and precise voice, "a simple figure of speech. But you may tell your hunter that one of those Necro-mancers is Merrick Longland."

Chase looked back. Margaret was visible to him, even though Emma couldn't touch her. "How do you know?"

One gray brow rose. Emma had seen teachers with less effective stares.

So, apparently, had Chase. "How long do we have?"

"Minutes," Margaret answered. "Possibly ten."

"How many?"

"I can be certain only of Longland. And Emma."

"Then you're not certain there are more."

"There are more. At least one other, possibly two. I can't tell you who they are, but I can tell you they're with Longland."

"Fine. Eric, you still there? No, it wasn't a figure of speech. Yes, we're screwed. You still don't want backup?" The silence lasted a minute too long, and Chase flipped the phone shut. "Emma—go. Whatever you need to do, do it *now*."

"Chase—"

"Because if the fire doesn't kill us, the Necromancers will. Eric's our best," he added. "But even Eric can't stand against more than one Longland. Not alone."

"Then go. Help him. You can't do anything here anyway."

Chase hesitated. "He'll kill me."

"Probably. And I'd like him to be alive to do it." She turned only her face— her body was aligned with her hands—and added, "Maria's children are out there. Allison and Michael. Skip and Amy. You were right," she added, her voice dropping. "*Go.*"

Chase shoved the phone back into her pocket and then sprinted for the door. Smoke billowed in when it opened, and the air seemed to be sucked out, into the hall. He slammed the door shut behind him, for all the good it would do.

"I'm of two minds about that boy," Margaret told Emma. She then glanced at Andrew, whose screaming had quieted. It hadn't stopped; he'd just lost volume as the minutes passed. "But I think you'll win him over, in the end."

Emma clenched her teeth. She'd met women like Margaret before, however, and she forced herself to speak politely and clearly when she trusted herself to speak at all. "Margaret, if we don't manage to reach Andrew, we're—Maria and I—not going to leave this place. Not alive."

Margaret nodded, and her expression softened; it added years to her face, but those years weren't unkind; she had the bone structure that made a lie of youthful beauty. "Can you bind him, Emma?"

"Can I what?"

"Bind him. Bind him the way we're bound to you."

"How do I do that?"

"How did you bind us?"

"You were already tied to a wall. I just—I broke the chains around you and they kind of stuck to me."

Margaret closed her eyes and shook her head, and Suzanne gently touched the older woman's shoulder. "Well?" Margaret said, opening her eyes and looking to Suzanne. Suzanne glanced at Andrew, who was standing and shuddering on the bed. "I don't think so," she said, after a pause. "He's too young, Margaret, and too new."

"He is very, very powerful, though."

"He is."

"Emma, can you touch that power at all?"

"I can touch him. I—no." She gave up on excuses. "No. I can't."

"Well, then." Margaret turned to Maria Copis. "I'm sorry for my lack of manners, but the situation is somewhat dire," she said, speaking slowly enough that the words seemed to run counter to their content. "I'm Margaret Henney. You are Andrew's mother?"

Maria managed to pull her glance away from her son. Her face was streaked with trails, and those trails were now dark gray. "I am. I—"

Margaret lifted a hand. "I know, dear. My son drowned in a crowded lake at the height of one summer. I understand guilt. And loss. I also understand that you wouldn't be here at all if it weren't for Emma.

"But neither would we. I am about to suggest that we try something that may not work. And it may leave some permanent scars."

Maria Copis laughed. "You think I care about *scars*?"

Emma, listening, shook her head. "She's not talking about that kind of scar," she told Maria. "I think she means it might change you somehow."

"Will it get my son out of here?" Maria said, still looking at Margaret.

"It might. It's the only thing I can think of that has any chance, unless you're willing to wait another ten years."

Maria's eyes widened. Answer enough. "Emma, what is she suggesting?"

"I'm not sure." Emma hesitated, thinking. It was hard, because Andrew had found a second—or third, or tenth—wind. "Is it something you can do, Margaret?"

"No, Emma. Not I."

"Me, then."

The older woman nodded. "What do you see, when you look at us?"

"The dead." Emma shook her head. "No. Truthfully, you wouldn't look dead to me at all if it weren't for your eyes." And the fact that they could appear out of thin air.

"What do you see when you look at Maria?"

"I see Maria." Emma started to describe her, and stopped as Margaret's words finally came into focus, over the endless wails of a bereaved four-year-old boy. She swallowed, coughed. "Margaret—"

"Look at her, Emma. Look *carefully.*"

Emma shook her head, almost wild. "She's *alive*, Margaret." She glanced at the door, as if seeking some kind of guidance from Chase, who was no longer in the room. "I can't—" pause. "Do Necromancers—can they—"

"What you are, and what they are, are not yet the same. You can become them," Margaret added, in her crisp, clear voice. "Or you can become something different. But, yes, Emma. If they were willing to pay the price, they could touch the living."

"What price?" Maria asked Margaret. She was pale, the way old statues are pale.

Margaret looked at Maria, and her expression gentled again. "You cannot pay it for her, although you may suffer in the process. You are willing to suffer; I don't doubt it, and in the end, neither does our Emma. But Emma is afraid of losing what she is."

"Will I?" Emma asked starkly.

Margaret didn't answer. But Georges came to stand by Emma's side, and he wrapped his arms around her, briefly. Catherine did the same, looking first to see whether or not Georges' gesture was met with disapproval.

"Margaret, will it kill her?"

Margaret said nothing for a long moment. When she did speak, she said, "Trust yourself." Which was so far from comfort, she might as well not have bothered. "Catherine, dear?"

Catherine detached herself from Emma. "Yes?"

"Please. The young boy?"

Catherine nodded. "He's very loud," she said. But she walked over to Andrew Copis, and she put both her arms around him, as if she were his older sister. He started, looked at her, and then screamed *MOM* at the top of his little lungs.

The world slowed, then. The smoke seemed to freeze in place.

Margaret looked at Emma again, as if this had been some sort of proof, at the end of a long theorem. In a way, it was. Because Emma now thought she understood exactly what Margaret hoped she could achieve. She took a deep breath, nodded, and then let Andrew Copis go.

Maria darted forward and stopped. She took deep, deep breaths while she stood rigid.

Emma looked at Maria Copis. She saw a woman who was not quite thirty, in a sooty shirt, baggy jeans. Her hair was dark, her eyes were dark, and her face was that kind of gaunt that makes you feel like a voyeur just seeing it. Emma shook herself, took a much shallower series of breaths than Maria had, and looked again.

Her eyes were dark, yes. Her cheeks were stained. This wasn't helping. She was alive, her son was dead; they were divided by that state. Just as Emma and her father had been divided, as Emma and Nathan had been divided. Death was silence, loss, guilt. And anger.

But life led that way, anyway. From birth, it was a slow, long march to the grave. Who had said that? She couldn't now remember. But it was true. They were born dying. If they were very lucky, the dying was called aging. They reached toward it as if they were satellites in unstable orbits.

And when they got there, they were just dead. Like the unfamiliar student in the cafeteria. One moment in time separated the living from the ghosts. Emma looked for that moment now.

She tried to age Maria in her mind's eye, the way she avoided aging her mother. It didn't help, and she discarded the attempt, wishing—briefly—that she'd brought Michael with her. Michael, with his rudimentary social understanding and his ability to see beyond almost all of it, would have had a better chance of arriving at something useful than she did.

Michael would have asked her the important questions. *What is death? What are the dead? Why are they here? Do people have souls, Emma? Can you prove it?*

Well? Did they have souls?

She glanced at Margaret, at Suzanne, and at the two children.

Did it matter? They looked as they must have looked in life. Not in death; the death itself didn't seem to define them. But the life they'd lived? That did.

In the clothing, the names, the style of their hair, the way they spoke to her. They remembered what they had been; it was, in essence, what they still were.

If Maria Copis died now—today, here—this is what she would look like, to Emma. Because this is what she would look like to herself. It was *there*. It was in her. People couldn't predict death most of the time. Maybe ever.

"Maria," Emma said. "Give me your hand. Just one."

Maria held out a hand. She hesitated for just a moment, then firmly gripped Emma's in her own.

Emma *looked* at her. Not at her face, her hair, or her clothing; not at her expression. "Georges," she said, not taking her eyes off Maria, "come here and take my other hand."

Georges shuffled along the planks, and then she felt his hand in hers. It wasn't cold, but she knew why. Her father's gift. She used it now, without pause for regret or guilt.

When she touched the dead, the living could see them. Eric had said this was because she was using some of their power—some very small part—to make them visible. To give them a voice. But now, just now, she tried to see *how* she was taking that power. What she was actually touching when she reached for what looked like a hand.

She closed her eyes, because actually looking wasn't helping her to see at all.

She heard Maria say, "Hello, Georges."

She heard Georges reply. Where, in his words, was Emma's power? Where, in that quiet, child's voice, was some evidence of her work? There. In the palm of her hand. A small tendril, a string, a chain. Something that bound him to her, but something that also bound her to him. It went both ways.

It was cool; the way ice was cool when touched through thin gloves. Colder when she pulled, because she could pull at it if she concentrated. She tried, and Georges said, "Yes, Emma?"

She hadn't built it. It had existed before her. But she'd used it. She was using it now, in some ways. She let go of Georges' hand in the darkness, and whispered, "Dad."

She couldn't see him, but she could feel his sudden presence growing. With it came memories, some good, some bad. They were hers, but they were his as well, seen on opposite sides and from different angles.

*Sprout.*

"Dad, take my hand?"

He did. She heard him say, "Hello, Maria. I'm Brendan Hall, Emma's father."

She touched her father. If she tried, she could feel the cold—but it wasn't as sharp as Georges; it was the difference between a winter day and solid ice.

She tried to pull at him in the way she had pulled at George, and it was harder. But it was—barely—possible.

But his power had flowed *into* her when he wanted it to.

*We're bound, Em,* he told her, and she could hear the affection in his voice so strongly it almost hurt. *I love you.*

She looked at him, then, and her eyes teared. She started to tell him it was the smoke, then stopped and smiled instead. It was a weak smile, and she added, "I'm fine, Dad," before she could stop herself. "I miss you."

He touched her face for just a second, and his smile deepened.

She looked, last, to Maria. Maria, whose chain she didn't hold; Maria, whose love she didn't have. The only thing they had in common was the desire to save a four-year-old boy from decades of terror and pain—and Emma knew her desire was nowhere near the equal of Maria's.

But the desire to try was as strong, and that would have to do. She took a breath, and she tried to reach for Maria Copis. All she felt in her hand *was* Maria's hand.

She reached for her father again, and she felt the cold. This time, she was more careful. She approached the fact of his death slowly, as if he were not, in fact, dead at all. She could see him. She could speak with him. She could, if she wanted, hug him. He still loved her. He still worried about her.

What he couldn't do, she didn't think about—not now.

She felt the cold. But instead of shying away from it, she reached into it, and then, as if it were a wall, she pushed beyond it. For a moment, the cold was sharp and cutting, and then she felt a slow and steady warmth. She opened her eyes and stared at her father, who said, and did, nothing.

"I think," Margaret said in the distance, "she might have it, Suzanne."

"He's dead," Suzanne very correctly replied. "The boy's mother is not."

"No. You make a point. But still."

Emma let go of her father's hand, and the warmth receded. She wanted to call it back, because in it, for a moment, she felt safe. She felt safe in a way that she couldn't remember feeling, even as a four year old; what pain could touch her, there? What worry, and what loss?

"Maria," she said, and she held out her free hand.

Maria took it.

"Think," Emma told Maria, "of the good things. The good things about Andrew. Not his death, not his loss, but all the reasons you feel the loss so strongly. Can you do that?"

"I . . . I don't know. I'll try."

Emma had never doubted it. She watched Maria's face, and after a moment, Maria grimaced and closed her eyes; she'd been staring at the spot in midair where Andrew stood because she could no longer see—or hear—him.

And this was probably for the best, because there was no way she could have done what Emma asked, otherwise. As it was, climbing Everest with toothpicks for pitons would probably have been easier.

Emma watched Maria's face. Her eyelids flickered and trembled, and her lips turned at the corners, tightening and thinning. The smoke was thick in the room, and Emma sat; she wanted to lie flat across the floor, remembering her elementary school lessons about moving in fires. But she crouched instead, waiting, and trying not to feel the passing time.

Bit by bit, Maria's expression relaxed, her lips losing that tight, pained look, the lines around her closed eyes slowly disappearing as she bowed her head toward Emma. Emma, both hands locked around Maria, just as they had previously been locked around her son, closed her eyes as well.

She reached out for Maria Copis the way she had reached out for her father; she didn't move her hands, didn't open her eyes, didn't try to physically grab anything.

And doing so, she remembered the first night that she had seen—and touched—her father. Her *body* had been in a chair, beside Michael. But *she* had been standing in the middle of the waiting room in front of Brendan Hall, her hands outstretched, her palms and fingers splayed wide to catch him before he vanished.

That part of her—it was inside her now, and had been ever since that first night. Maybe it had always been inside her. Maybe what she saw, somehow, was not actually what was *there*. Maybe it wasn't something eyes could actually see—but her mind was doing the translating and giving her images that she could recognize and hold.

Eyes closed, she looked for her father.

And she saw him, standing in the darkness, limned in light, his face bright with that smile that meant she'd done something that made him proud. She looked for Georges, and she saw that he was standing beside Catherine; they were holding hands, and where their hands met, the light was bright and unfaltering.

She nodded at them but didn't speak; instead she moved on, searching now for Maria Copis.

She saw Andrew first, his face tear-stained, his hair matted to his forehead, his eyes wide and wild. He wasn't solid; he wavered in her vision like a—like a ghost. But he stood in the way, and she felt that if she could move past him somehow, she would reach Maria.

Instead, for the first time in this darkness of closed eyes that had nothing at all to do with her living, breathing body, she held out a hand. Or at least that's what it felt like she did; when she looked, she couldn't actually see her hand. Or her arm. Or anything at all that looked like Emma Hall.

But for the first time, Andrew seemed to sense her. Chase had called him powerful, and maybe he was—but not here. Here, he was weak, wavering like a heat mirage in the air before her; here he was so damn lost it was hard to see him at all. She held out her hand again.

This time, he reached for it.

*Come on, Andrew,* she told him, as gently as she knew how. *Let's go find your mom.*

## ᗕ **Chapter 15**

"Amy. Skip. Grab the ladders. They're not coming down any time soon." Eric turned to speak to Allison; he turned back when he realized that the ladders weren't coming down. "We need to move. Quickly."

"And if they need to come down in a hurry?" Amy's hands lodged themselves on her hips, and she shifted her stance.

Eric resisted the urge to point out that she was not, in fact, holding the ladder at this moment. "Skip," he said, over her, "it sounds as though your friend Longland is going to make an appearance. I'd suggest you get ready to hightail it out of here with your sister, if you can get her to leave."

Skip let the ladder go and turned to his younger sister. For the first time, Eric saw the similarities between the siblings, not the very obvious differences. Amy was obviously angry; on her, it looked good. "Amy."

She turned so her back was squarely facing his voice.

"Amy, we're leaving."

"I'm not leaving Emma—"

"Eric's staying."

"Eric's barely known her for a month. I'm not—"

Skip grabbed one of the arms that was attached, by her hand, to her hip. "You're leaving. You can carry a ladder, or we can leave the ladders behind— but I'll be carrying you."

Her eyes rounded in an almost operatic way; Eric thought she was going to slap her brother. "The kid's dead." Skip spaced the words evenly and slowly, as if English were not Amy's native tongue. "If what you said about last night is even halfway true, you're going to join him if we can't get away before Longland shows. I personally don't give a shit if you die here," he added. "But it'll kill Mom and Dad."

"Amy—" Eric began.

She lifted the arm that wasn't gripped by Skip. "Fine," she told her brother. Skip pulled the ladders down as Eric turned to Allison.

"Allison, take the baby. You and Michael get as far away from this house as you possibly can." He glanced at Michael, who was in Cathy's world and had failed to hear anything, and he decided that Michael and his compliance were going to have to be Allison's problem.

"I'll take Amy and Skip," Allison told him, after a small pause.

"Michael's not—"

"Michael is the only person who seemed to be unaffected by whatever it was Longland did at Amy's."

Which was interesting. "Probably because his brain's wired differently. It'd be worth some study—at another time. This is not that time. If Longland is aware that Michael somehow resisted the very, very expensive compulsion that affected everyone else in that house, he won't bother with subtlety. He'll kill him, probably quickly.

"Once he's committed to that, he'll kill all of you," Eric added.

"But Emma—"

"Emma has Chase."

"Why is Longland here?"

"If I had to guess? Andrew Copis has a lot of raw power, and Longland has, at the moment, a need for raw power."

"He—"

"If he's adept, he can sense it. He can't sense the rest of us; we're probably not his target here. That'll change when he arrives, and I'd rather not risk any of you." He slid his hands into his pockets. Nestled against his thigh were iron rings, warmed by constant contact with his leg. He pulled them out and slid them on. "If he's done any research at all, he'll have some idea of what he's facing."

"Could he go into a burning building and drag Andrew out?"

The fact that Emma, Maria, and Chase had failed to emerge passed without comment, but the worry was there on her face.

"Hard to say. It wouldn't be his first choice, if our own records of Necromancers are anything to go by. If we're away from the building, and he sees the same fire that Emma sees, he might try to find a different power source. He probably hasn't had the time to gather any."

"But you're not coming with us. You don't think he's going to leave."

"If he decides to risk it—" He shook his head. "If he decides to risk it, he'll have safer passage than Emma did; he knows how to use the dead, and he only has to reach Andrew. No, I'm not coming with you. Emma isn't close to his match yet, but she has *all* the others. Even if he gives up on Andrew, Emma's got what he needs—he can just take that. I'll hunker down out of sight, and I'll see what he does. But the rest of you have to leave *now*.

"Ally," he added, when she failed to move, "I'll have enough to worry about. If you all stay here, you'll slow me down when I can't afford to be slowed."

She hesitated again, and Eric looked, very pointedly, at the baby she held in her arms. He could see that she wanted to argue. She didn't. But she shifted her grip on the baby, and she bent to grab the diaper bag before she retreated as far as Michael. She tapped Michael on the shoulder, and he looked up instantly; Eric couldn't hear what she said. But he saw Michael's expression darken in utterly open concern.

Eric understood why Emma valued them both so highly. Why, in fact, she loved them, even if that word was out of vogue among the young. He had thought, watching Emma, Allison, Amy, and the rest of Amy's mafia, that Michael was simply a burden they'd chosen to adopt.

But he watched Michael pick up Cathy, as if Cathy were his baby sister, and he watched as Michael's mouth moved over words that distance silenced, and he understood that the burden of care, if that's what it was, was not by any means shouldered on just one side.

He could see only Allison's profile, but she was, at this distance, measured and calm for someone who was also, clearly, in a hurry.

Michael lifted Catherine, and they headed down Rowan Avenue. Skip and Amy joined them, and Amy's denunciation was the clearest sound in the street. Skip was ignoring her, rather than engaging. Arguing was, admittedly, hard to do when they were both lugging ladders.

He hoped they weren't heading in the wrong direction. He couldn't be certain. He didn't have time to check; Longland would come to number twelve. Now if only number twelve weren't lacking anything remotely useful behind which he could hide. If, he thought grimly, hiding would do any good at all. Longland wasn't alone. He wouldn't feel the need to be that cautious.

There were no bushes here; no obvious cover, no neighbor's yards, and no roof that he was certain would bear his weight, if he could climb that far up. Eric glanced at the boards nailed in a large X across what remained of the doorframe. He grimaced and started to pull them off.

They splintered from the inside as he worked, and he jumped back, pulling daggers. He got both a face and an ear full of pissed off Chase for his troubles.

"Chase, what the *hell* are you doing here?"

"Same old, same old," Chase replied, looking past Eric's shoulder. "Someone moved the fucking ladders. Where were you going?"

"In." Eric bit back every other angry comment he wanted to make, because, in the end, he was happier to have Chase than to stand alone. "They're not here yet, and outside is a total bust."

The hair on his neck started to rise, and he swore. "Scratch that," he said, pushing Chase back into the house, and flattening himself against the wall with its shattered windows. "They're here."

Andrew's hand wasn't solid. But even insubstantial as it was, Emma could reach out and touch it. She did, and he allowed it.

*The house is on fire*, he told her, the last syllable stretching out as if it were about to birth a scream.

"Yes, I know." She kept the words simple and forced them to be gentle. Here, she missed Michael, because Michael could have distracted—or better, calmed—Andrew.

*I want my mom.*

"I know. She's here, somewhere. But it's smoky and she's lost. Let's go find her."

He reached up for her, then, and she tried to pick him up. He stiffened, and the scream that she'd managed to subvert started in earnest. She didn't so much hear it as feel it. As gently as she could manage, she put him down again.

*Only Mommy.*

She nodded. "Let's find your mother. She's been very worried."

*I waited for her.*

Emma's eyes were already closed, or she would have closed them. She held out her hand again, and when he placed his palm in hers, she closed hers over it gently.

This time, she reached for Andrew, while she held this small part of him. She reached for him, and then, she reached through him. All she felt was a little boy who was close to hysteria—on the wrong side. Four years old.

Since the day her father had died, so many years ago, she had accepted that life wasn't fair. When Nathan died in the summer, she had hated it. Life. The grayness. The ache. The loss of future. All of it.

Watching other people's happiness, other people's dreams, had been so damn hard, she'd withdrawn from most of her life. Only Allison and Michael had remained a central part of that life because they wouldn't let her go. Everyone else had made space for her grief; they'd given her the room in which to mourn.

They could give her *years*, and it would never end.

*Are you crying?* Andrew asked, in that curious but detached way of children everywhere.

"A little."

*Why?*

"Because it's dark, and it's scary, and I'm lonely."

*Oh.* The pause was not long, but it was there. *Me too. Are you a grown-up?*

Two years ago she would have answered yes without hesitation. Now? "Not quite. Almost."

*Can you get out of the fire?*

"I think so."

*It'll kill you, you know. If you don't.*

"I know."

*Where's my mom?*

"She's here." Emma took a breath and looked down at her non-hand. This time, when she reached out, she reached out for Maria Copis.

She felt the skin of the older woman's hand in her palms, and knew that that was a real sensation; it was distinct, almost overwhelming in its sudden clarity. Andrew cried out, and she flexed her hands; felt Maria's response.

*Don't go!*

"No, Andrew. I'm not leaving." She took another breath. It hurt.

"Emma?"

"Margaret?" She blinked. Margaret stood in the shadows, Suzanne by her side.

"Yes, dear."

Emma hated being called "dear" by anyone under the age of seventy. She grimaced but said nothing.

"You're almost there, dear, but I wanted to warn you—you don't have much time. You've reached the boy, and the fire has slowed; you've got his attention. But . . ."

Coughing, Emma nodded. She reached for Maria Copis again, but this time, eyes closed, she reached out with her other self. With the self that had left her body in a chair in a hospital emergency triage room.

"Hold on, dear. Hold on for as long as you can."

She would have asked Margaret what she meant, but she didn't have time. Fire engulfed her hands, searing away skin, sinew, tendon. She bit her lip, tasted blood, stopped herself from screaming—but only barely, and only because she was also holding Andrew, and Andrew was terrified.

Andrew had never stopped being terrified.

The soul-fire came to sickly green life in the frame of the door, lapping around the sharp edges of newly broken boards.

They were out of its range, but only barely, and the floors here looked suspiciously unstable.

"Where did the fire start?" Chase hissed.

"Basement. Back of the house one over." Eric rolled along the floor against the wall. The wall would have provided more than enough cover had it not been for the large gap a windowpane had once occupied. Here, everything was blackened; paint had peeled and curled, and just beyond the windows, the carpets were the consistency of melted plastic.

But the soul-fire didn't burn in that particular way. Something to be grateful for. "Chase?"

"I'm clear."

Eric felt the soul-fire bloom just above his head. These damn homes with their huge windows. Even the cheap homes had them all over the place.

"I'd say they know where we are," Chase added.

"No kidding." Eric drew daggers.

Chase pulled a mirror out of his shirt pocket. "You've got yours?"

"No."

"Fuck, Eric, what were you thinking?"

"Never mind. It'll only piss you off."

Chase angled the mirror so that it caught light through the ragged hole that was now the door in these parts. "Three."

"Longland."

"Yeah. Two others."

"Dressed?"

"Street clothes. No robes."

"They were already in Toronto, then."

"Either that or the old lady's getting lax."

Eric winced. "Don't call her that, Chase. You know it pisses her off."

Chase shrugged and pulled the mirror back. "We've got trouble," he told Eric grimly.

"How much trouble?"

"Longland has Allison."

Emma had never been terrified of fire. It had always fascinated her. Candlelight. Fireplaces. Bunsen burners. Even the blue flames of the gas stove. But all of those other times, she'd been far enough away to feel only warmth.

Here, there was no warmth. Warmth was too gentle.

She'd broken her arm once, and that snap of bone had been quick and comfortable compared to this. She almost let go, but she realized that the fire burned only her *hands*.

No. Not even her hands, not her real hands. The fire had not yet reached this room. She dimly remembered that Andrew had died of smoke inhalation; it was possible that this type of fire would never reach these rooms.

Remembering Margaret's words, she held on. It was like holding on to a stove element when it was orange. It was almost impossible, and she would have screamed and pulled back in defeat, opening her eyes and falling back into her body and the grimness of reality, if it had not been for Andrew Copis, who waited by her side in the darkness, where the pain was strongest. For his sake, she held on.

But it wasn't enough just to hold on.

She realized it, tried to cling to the thought, until pain washed it away, again and again, as if she were the shore and pain was the ocean that reached for her. It wasn't *enough* to hold on. Hold on. No, it's not enough.

It was like breath, like heartbeat, this pain and this realization, but it wore grooves in her thoughts, until the pain couldn't dislodge it anymore. And when that happened, she reached into, and through the fire, as she had reached into, and through the cold.

On the other side of the fire, she finally found the warmth she hadn't even realized she was seeking.

"Maria."

The urge to throw herself into that warmth, and away from the fire itself, was so strong it was like the gravity that takes you—quickly—to the bottom of a cliff from its height. But she'd stood on the edge of a lot of cliffs, and she'd never once thrown herself off. She heard, in the distance, the sudden gasp of shock or pain in Maria's voice, and she knew what the warmth was.

Emma had never tried anything like this before, but she had a pretty good idea that throwing yourself entirely into another person's life—any other person, no matter how you felt about them—was not a good thing. But it was hard. She'd tried it once before, and then? It had been joy, until it was loss, and pain. Finding boundaries, with Nathan, had been so difficult; accepting the boundaries he sketched for himself, more so.

She didn't love Maria Copis. She didn't even know her.

But not loving, not knowing, she was still drawn into parts of her life. The parts were good, because she had asked Maria to think about happy things—as if she were the Disney channel—and Maria had done her best to oblige. Emma could feel love, fear, and frustration for her children, and all of these were mixed and intertwined. She couldn't, in her own mind, see what the joy of changing a dirty diaper was, but apparently, Maria could.

She could hear Andrew's first words, although she couldn't understand them at all. Maria could. Or thought she could. Parents with small children were often stupid like that. She could see Andrew take his first steps. See him run—and fall, which he didn't much like—and see him insist on feeding himself.

Cathy came next, but Andrew was entwined with Cathy, and a brief glimpse of someone Emma had never met and yet now both loved and hated intruded. He was taller than Maria, and he was young, even handsome, his hair dark, his eyes dark, and his smile that electric form of slow and lazy that can take your breath away. The children loved him. Maria loved him.

And him? He loved them, maybe. He loved himself more. Emma watched the expressions on his face when he thought no one was looking. Saw the phone calls that he took, the false joviality of casual conversation no blind at all to Maria. The easy way he lied.

The hard way the truth came out.

Shadows, there. Anger. Loss. The slow acceptance of the death of need. Or love. It was complicated, and Emma tried very hard not to look at it, and not only because she was afraid of walking unannounced and uninvited into the Copis bedroom.

But she could see the man leave—and that still hurt—and she could see the struggle to be a reasonable, sane parent with almost no money and two children with a third on its way. The struggle to find the joy in the townhouse, with its narrow walls and its crowded, cluttered rooms, was both hard and somehow rewarding. Emma felt it, but she didn't understand it.

But she saw the turn happen, and she knew that she couldn't withdraw; she followed Maria, holding on as lightly as possible and riding her back like an insect. Andrew was walking. Talking. Arguing. Saying a lot of unreasonable *No*. Andrew was trying to stick six slices of bread, side by side, in the toaster. Andrew was grabbing Cathy's toys, and Cathy was pulling his hair, a trade that didn't seem fair to his outraged, little self.

Andrew was trying so hard to be a Big Brother, even if he didn't quite understand what that meant when it came to toys.

Andrew was standing in the line-up to junior kindergarten, glancing anxiously back at his mother before the doors opened to swallow him and the other twenty-six children. Andrew was—

Andrew was—

Dead.

Just like that, the warmth twisted; Emma held it, but it was *hard*. Because to hold it, she had to hold on to the fire, and the smoke, and the screams of her daughter and her son; the baby was sleeping, thank god, the baby was hardly awake. She had to pass through the smoke, the thickening of it, the heat of the floors, the sudden, horrible realization that she had slept through death, and death was calling.

But Emma had done despair, and loss, and guilt. She'd lived with grief until it was silent unless she touched it or poked it. She'd lived with its shadow, lived at its whim, gone through the day-to-day of things that meant nothing to her anymore—the gray, pointless chatter of her friends, the endless nothing of her future.

Emma knew these things well enough that she could endure them, because she already had. Even if this was *worse*.

The baby was sleeping in her room. Cathy was down the hall—at the farthest end—in her crib. Andrew was in his bed in the room midway down. She grabbed the baby, and she ran, covering her mouth, the panic sharp and harsh. She woke Cathy, she grabbed Cathy, lifting her in one arm, lodging her on her left hip; the baby was cradled, awkwardly and tightly, on her right.

She kicked Andrew's door open; Andrew was waking, and Andrew *never* woke well. Andrew woke, crying. Disoriented, the way he often was when wakefulness didn't come naturally. She kept her voice even—god knew how— and she told Andrew to follow her quickly.

He stood up in bed, and he saw smoke and his mother's harsh fear, and he froze there, in the night, the glowing face of a nightlight the only real illumination in the room. *Andrew, follow me—the house is on fire!*

Andrew, understanding her panic, was terrified.

She'd done it *wrong*. He could hear the raw fear in her voice, and he could see—oh, he could see—that she carried Cathy and the baby in her arms. He was a *child*. He could see that she carried *them*, while the house was burning. He could understand what this meant about her love for *him*.

And as a child, he started to cry, to whimper, to lift his arms and jump up and down on the spot, demanding to be carried. It wasn't petulance; she saw that clearly. It was terror.

She'd done it wrong. If she had just stayed *calm*—

But she hadn't. She tried to lift him somehow, Cathy screaming in her ear, the baby stirring. But she couldn't do it. She couldn't—she shouted at Andrew, told him to follow, begged him to follow, and she realized that he couldn't do it either. Not newly awake. Not in the dark with the fire eating away at the promise of life.

She turned, ran down the stairs. Fire in the living room, fire in the hall. The front door clear, but covered by the smoke shed by burning things. God, she had to get them *out*. Just—get them out, come back in before it was too late, get Andrew, bring him out as well. Running as she'd never run, through the smoke, past the fire, coughing, as Cathy was coughing in between her cries.

And then, night air, smoke rushing after her as she raced along the path in her bare feet, picking up small stones and debris. Her neighbors, she could see, were standing in the darkness, except it wasn't dark; it was a bonfire. Not her house, not her house—

She handed Cathy to the lady next door, handed the baby to the lady's husband, turned to the house again, ran back up the path.

And fire, in the hall, near the door, greeted her—

Emma broke through the fire, the memory of fire, the scream that was swallowing all thought and all rational words. "Maria," she said, in a voice that was outside of memory, but strong enough to bear the pain and the despair, "Come. It's time to rescue your son."

She held out a hand—a hand she could actually see—to Maria, and Maria stared at her, her face white and blistered from heat, and she paused there, on the crest of the wave, and realized that all hope was already lost.

She was not in the fire.

She was in the daydream of the fire, the one to which she returned, night after night, and in every waking minute: the one in which she had done things *right*, or the one in which fire hadn't spread so damn fast, the one in which she could make it up the stairs to her son's small room, to her son's terrified side, the one in which she could pick him up and carry him. Not back to the door; that was death.

But to the window that overlooked the gable above the porch. To her bedroom, where he'd slept until he was almost a year old. To those windows, which she could break and through which she could throw one screaming child because even if he *broke something*, he'd still be alive.

And standing beside her, Emma Hall was also in her daydream.

Maria looked at Emma's hand and understood in a second how damn much Emma had seen.

Andrew was screaming.

Emma's hand was steady.

Maria grabbed it, and together they walked through the fire and up the stairs, where smoke lay like a shroud. They walked into Andrew's room and saw Andrew standing on the bed, screaming and coughing, and his eyes widened as he saw his mother.

Emma opened her real eyes to Maria's real expression, to the wet and shining veil of tears across both cheeks. Maria opened her eyes on Emma, and then she looked past Emma's shoulders, and her eyes widened.

"Andrew!" She could see him, although Emma wasn't touching him.

"Mommy!"

Maria pushed herself off the floor and ran to him, arms wide; she picked him up, and he hit her face and shoulders before his arms collapsed around her neck, and he sobbed there while she held him, her lips pressed into his hair, her body the shield through which nothing—nothing at all—would pass.

"We have to go," Emma told her softly.

Maria swallowed and nodded. "The fire—"

"I think—the fire won't kill us now."

"You're not sure."

"No. But we need to leave."

Maria's arms tightened around her son. "What happens when we leave?" she asked Emma.

"I don't know. I'm sorry."

Maria nodded again, and Emma understood why she hadn't moved. This was her son, her dead son, and these might be the only moments she would ever have with him again. They were a gift—a terrible, painful, gift—and she wanted to extend them for as long as she possibly could, because when she opened her arms again, he would be gone.

Emma Hall, who didn't cry in public, struggled with her tears, with the thickness in her throat, as she understood and watched.

"Emma," Margaret said at her back.

But Emma lifted a hand, waving it in a demand for silence. For space.

"Just . . . give them a minute," she finally managed to say.

Maria, however, turned, her eyes widening. "Margaret?" Her voice was soft; it was the first time since she had lifted her son that she'd taken her lips entirely from his hair. "I can see you."

Margaret nodded. "Yes."

"But Emma's not—"

"No. You will be haunted all your life by glimpses of the dead. I'm sorry, dear."

Maria's arms tightened around her son. "I'm not." She kissed his hair, his forehead, his wet little cheeks, held him, whispered mother-love words into his ears until he told her she was tickling him.

"Emma," Margaret said again.

"What?"

"Longland is here."

Emma closed her eyes.

"And Emma?"

She didn't want to hear more. But she listened, anyway.

"He has Allison and Maria's baby."


## ꙮ Chapter 16

"How—how do you know?"

Margaret said nothing for a long moment, and then she glanced at Emma's father. He slid his hands into his pockets—it was odd that the dead would have pockets, since they couldn't actually carry anything—and said, "Someone else is also watching."

Which made no sense.

"I know what happens to you," Brendan Hall told his daughter. "I watch you. I'm not—yet—like Margaret, but I have some sense of what you've seen, what you're worried about."

Emma lifted a hand and looked at Maria. Maria looked mostly confused, but an edge of fear was sharpening her expression. Emma hadn't bothered to mention little things like Necromancers to her, because it hadn't occurred to Emma that they would actually meet them.

The only child that was in danger here was supposed to be Andrew, who was already dead. But the baby that Allison carried was alive. And in the hands of a man who, if you believed Chase, and, sickeningly, Emma did, had no trouble at all killing anyone.

She took a deep, steadying breath. Panic was not her friend, here.

"Margaret," she said, as her father's words finally sunk in. "Someone you knew in life is out there as well?"

"Yes, dear."

"Can he help them?"

She didn't answer.

Emma ran to the door and pulled it open; the doorknob was warm but not yet hot. She yanked the door wide, and smoke billowed into the room; it was all she could do not to turn and shout at Andrew. *We've brought your mother here, she's carrying you, damn it—*

*Damn it, he's four years old, Em. Think. Just think.* She headed down the hall to Maria's bedroom, which was only a few short steps away; the door was ajar, as they'd left it. Fire was playing out against the height of the stairs, but how much of the stairs had been consumed, she couldn't say.

It didn't matter. She made her way to the front windows, the bedroom windows, and some instinct made her flatten herself against the floor. The air here was cleaner, but at this point not by a whole lot. She rose slowly to one side of the window frame, and she looked out into Rowan Avenue.

She could see Longland in the street. His hand was on Allison's arm, and Allison's arms—both of them—were curled protectively around the baby.

No Michael, no Amy, no Skip. Emma felt sick, literally sick, with sudden fear. Where were the others? Were they even alive? Chase had warned her. Chase, who'd been so angry, so self-righteous, and so damn *right*.

*Emma.*

She looked up and saw her father standing in the center of the room. Beyond him, Maria stood, her son in her arms, her face so pale her lips were the same color as the rest of her skin. The others were nowhere in sight.

Emma swallowed. "Dad," she said, her voice still thick. "What do I do?"

"Just think, Em."

She wanted to scream at her father, and screaming at her father was something she'd done, in one way or another, since she was the age of the baby in Allison's arms. But it wouldn't help anything, and it wouldn't change anything.

"Maria," she whispered. "Stand to one side of the window; don't stand in front of it. Don't let them see you."

Maria hesitated and then nodded, crossing the room to where the windows, open to night, let in air that was breathable and relatively clean. "What's happening? Who has my— Allison and my son?"

"His name is Merrick Longland, but his name doesn't matter. He's a—" Emma grimaced. "They're called Necromancers. I don't know a lot about them, but I do know a couple of things."

"Share."

"They feed on the dead."

"But—"

"Not on their corpses. I think they'd be called ghouls. Or zombies." God, she could say the most idiotic things when she was frightened. "They feed on the spirits of the dead."

Maria was not a stupid woman. Her arms tightened around her son. "What does it give them?"

"Power."

"Power?"

Emma nodded. "And with that power they can do a bunch of things that we'd technically call magic."

"Please tell me he's not here for my son."

"I'd like to. But I don't know why he's here, and your son—" she swallowed. "Your son could maintain a fire that could burn me even if I couldn't see him and couldn't touch him."

"What does he want with Allison?"

"I don't know. But if I had to guess, probably me."

"But—but why?"

"I have something he thinks of as his. He probably wants it back."

"Can't you just give it to him?"

"No. No more than you could just give him Andrew."

Maria really wasn't stupid. "You're talking about the others," she said, her voice flat. "Georges, Catherine, Margaret—and the other two. I'm sorry, I don't remember their names."

Emma nodded. And then, because she was a Hall, added, "Suzanne and Emily."

"He can use them because they're dead."

"Pretty much. It would be like handing a loaded gun to a man who's already promised to kill you." She grimaced, and added, "Sorry, Margaret," aware that it was all sorts of wrong to talk about people as if they were simply strategic objects. *That* made her more like Merrick Longland than she ever wanted to be.

"Emma?"

From her position on the floor, Emma glanced up at Maria.

Maria could see street in the narrow angle between the wall and the window. Her gaze was now focused in that distance. "I think your two friends are out there as well."

"Who?"

"Eric," she said. "And Chase."

"What—what are they doing?"

Silence, and then, in a much quieter voice, "Burning."

"Is the fire green?" Margaret asked.

They both started, but Maria nodded. "It's green, yes. It *looks* like fire, but filtered badly."

"It's soul-fire. They've some experience with that fire," Margaret said at last. "It may not kill them yet; it is not, technically, fire at all."

"Maria, is Allison—"

"I don't know. Longland—that's the name of the one who's holding her, right?" When Emma nodded, Maria continued, "Longland is speaking. Or shouting; I think I can almost hear his words."

So could Emma, but the fire made it difficult; it was louder.

"Emma, dear," Margaret began.

Maria said, "Eric and Chase have stopped moving. They're carrying knives," she added. "But they're not approaching Longland."

"Has he done something to—"

Maria's breath was sharp and clean as the edge of a knife. She didn't speak. She didn't have to.

Emma rose. She stood, forgetting any warning she had given Maria, because she had to *see* and had to *know*. Longland had his hands on Allison, yes, but Allison was struggling because he was also now touching the baby. He frowned and then almost casually lifted his hand from the infant's chest and slapped Allison, hard, across the face. Allison staggered, and were it not for his grip, she would have fallen.

It would have been a bad fall; she still held tightly to the child. Would hold tight until the end of the world—or the end of her life. It was Ally all over. It was why Emma loved her.

She swallowed, and she looked, hard, at Longland. Looked at the two people who stood to either side of him. One was male, and older; the other was female, perhaps Maria's age, if that. Emma's gaze narrowed as she watched them all.

"There's at least one ghost," she said out loud. "Maybe two. Longland doesn't have one."

"How can you tell?" Maria asked. Her voice sounded soft—but it wasn't. It was strained, as if speaking loudly would break it.

"The Necromancers bind the dead somehow, and to me it looks like—like a golden chain. I can't see the dead, but the links are pulsing," she added. "They're using that power."

"They would have to, dear. Against Eric, in particular, they would have to. Longland must have recognized him at some point."

Emma shook her head. "He talked to some lady in a mirror. *She* recognized him."

Margaret was utterly, completely silent. Emma would have glanced back, but she couldn't force herself to look away. She had felt helpless before, but never like this.

"They'll kill Eric," she said, almost numb. "They'll kill Chase."

"If Longland has Allison, yes," Margaret said. In a much gentler voice, she added, "You've always had a rather large amount of power on hand, dear."

"Margaret?" Emma swung away from the window and lifted her hands, palms curved and empty, as if she were begging. Which was fair; she was about to start.

Margaret turned to confer, briefly, with the other ghosts—all save Brendan Hall, who stood, arms folded, expression watchful. She turned back to Emma. "You know you don't have to ask," she began. She lifted an imperious hand when Emma opened her mouth, and Emma snapped it shut again in deference. "But you do ask. It's the difference," she said quietly, "between making love and rape.

"We'll let you take you what you need."

"Georges—"

"He's not a child, dear. He's dead."

"I saw him with Michael," Emma replied.

Margaret shrugged, a motion that was at once both delicate and crisp. "You know what to do."

"But I don't—"

"You don't know that you know. But you managed to walk the narrow path when you altered Maria's perception. And you changed very little—in her. What you've done to yourself remains to be seen, but that's for another time. Touch the lines, Emma. Touch all of them."

"Lines? You mean the chains?"

Margaret nodded.

Emma frowned, and then she turned to Andrew, still lodged in the safety and heaven—for him—of his mother's arms. "Andrew," she said, without looking up at his mother, "there are men outside. I don't know if you can see them, but they're—they're not good men. One of them wants to hurt your baby brother. And he will hurt us—all of us—if we're not very careful."

"Emma—" Maria began, her voice as sharp and cutting as only a mother's can be when her child is threatened.

Emma forced herself to ignore this. "If they try to reach your mom, you need to look at the fire," she told him.

He buried his face in his mother's neck, and Emma looked away. "I'm sorry, Andrew," she said softly. "But the fire—it's doing what you want it to do, even if you can't see it, yet. If they come, try—try really, *really*, hard."

She turned back to her ghosts, and this time, when she lifted her hands, she lifted the right one in a loose, grasping fist. From that fist, streaming from her folded palm to the five who now watched her in silence, ran lengths of golden chains. They stretched, as they had the first time she'd seen them, from her hand to their hearts, glowing with a faint luminescence, just as their eyes—all of their eyes—did.

She swallowed.

"Your friends will die, if you don't, dear."

She hesitated, because she knew these lines and their life force, if it could even be called that given they were dead, were the dividing line. If she did what she *must do*, she *was* a Necromancer. What she'd done for Andrew, what she'd done to Maria—it was different, and she knew it.

This? This was using the exact same power that the Necromancers did. It didn't matter, in the end, why. All of the Necromancers must have believed they had their reasons, and all of them must have believed those reasons were *good* reasons, because people were just like that. They could justify anything they did themselves. Things only looked wrong or evil when seen from the outside.

She turned to look out the window in desperation. She saw green fire lapping at Eric and Chase and saw it distorting the green-brown of the lawns on the boulevard; she saw Longland, both hands on Allison, and she saw the other two Necromancers, both hands splayed out in the air, as though the fire that surrounded Chase and Eric was coming directly from their hands.

Eric. Chase. Allison.

She didn't know what had happened to her other friends.

She took a deep breath to steady herself, and then she opened her hand.

"Emma—"

The chains lay against her palms. "I can't," she said starkly. "Not this. But I *can* break the power they're using, the way I did with Emily."

"If you try, he'll kill Allison."

"If he kills Allison, he'll die." Emma said nothing else, because there was nothing at all she could say. And as she started to find a handhold on the windowsill, to lever herself up onto it, she felt her hands began to pulse. With warmth. With heat that was both intense and intoxicating.

"You'll do, dear," Margaret said, her voice a bit deeper. "You'll do."

"Margaret!"

"Oh, hush. You've said what you had to say, and you even believed it. That's all we could ask for. Suzanne?"

"I agree."

"We would have let you take the power," she said. "But we can also—like your father—give. Go, dear. Do what you have to do. We'll be with you."

Because they didn't have any choice.

The warmth stretched up from her hands, traveling through her arms, her shoulders, and from there into the whole of her body. She closed her eyes for just a minute because the sensation itself was so powerful it was almost embarrassing.

And when she opened her eyes again, the whole world looked different.

The street was dark, although it was the middle of the day. The sky was an angry red—not the red of sunset or sunrise; it was too deep for that, and there was no other color in the sky. It took a moment to understand why, in that light, the street was so dim.

The grass was gray. The trees were gray. The cars—which were translucent and ghostly—were also gray. Even the clothing they wore—the pants, the shirts, the jackets—were different shades of the same damn color.

Emma pushed herself up into the window's frame and balanced there a second.

Only the people—Eric, Chase, Allison, Longland and his two companions—looked normal. Even the baby was a dull shade of puce, because he'd woken, and he was not happy about it.

She balanced a moment in the window, looking down at the small roof that covered the porch. It wasn't much of a roof; it covered the door and a few linear feet of concrete, no more. The ladders had been placed beside it, and one had run up to the first window, with only a little difficulty. The second window had been clear. There were no ladders now, however.

She slid out of the window and landed on the roof of the porch so hard that her knees buckled. The small roof, however, held her weight. She took a deep breath and looked at the street again, now somewhat closer to it. Chase was in pain, and he was breathing hard. Eric's face was a mask. If it had ever had any expression at all—and it must have, because she remembered his gentle smile so clearly—he'd shed it completely. Emma couldn't tell if the fire, which still surrounded him, caused him any pain at all.

He watched Longland as if Longland were the only thing in the street.

"Emma," Margaret said. Her voice drifted down, carried by a breeze that smelled faintly of cinnamon and clover.

Emma nodded.

"Look at the soul-fire. Look at it carefully. Longland doesn't see you yet— but the minute you act, the minute you use power, he will. Eric has the whole of his attention," she added.

"Does Eric know I'm here?"

There was a brief hesitation. "Almost certainly," Margaret finally admitted.

"But he's not looking—"

"No, dear, please try to pay attention. If Eric looks here, so will Longland. Eric is a bright boy, and he—and Chase—are buying you time at some cost."

"But—"

"He's willing to trust you. I don't know why. He's sensitive enough that he knows there's a lot of power behind and above him, and if he knows where, he's almost certainly guessed whose power it is."

Emma nodded, only partly because it made sense. The other part wanted Margaret to stop with the lecture. She didn't ask, because the lecture had followed useful information. Instead, she acted on that information, and she looked with new eyes at green fire.

It was no longer, strictly speaking, green. It wasn't exactly gray, either; it looked at base like gray, but as she watched it, she realized that it was almost opaline. The colors grew brighter as she watched them, and she realized they were responding, in part, to the movements of the Necromancers, who were concentrating from some distance away on maintaining them.

And when she looked at the Necromancers again, she could see the chains, not as chains but . . . as the attenuated bodies of the dead. Long, thin, their forms stretched out around the Necromancers, as if they were on a rack; they were pale, as if they'd never seen sunlight—which wasn't surprising in a ghost, or wouldn't have been had Emma not seen any.

But as she watched, she saw that the color was being leeched out of them for the sake of that fire.

She saw, as well, that the fire was clinging to Chase in a way that it had not yet managed to cling to Eric; that the colors of that fire were attempting to match his skin, his hair, the flush of his cheek. She didn't know what would happen if they finally did reach the same hue, but she could guess.

"Ready?" she asked Margaret softly.

Margaret didn't answer.

Emma grabbed the lip of the porch roof in her hands, held it tight, and lowered herself as far down as she could go. It was awkward; her legs dangled above the concrete steps before she forced her hands to let go. They came, with the addition of a bunch of small splinters, as she fell the last yard.

When her feet hit the ground, she saw the grass ripple as if it were water and she had just broken its surface. Waves of green traveled out from her feet in fading concentric circles, and when they stilled, the green remained, an odd splotch of color against the gray background.

Longland frowned. She saw that much because she had to look to see if Allison—and the baby—were okay. More than that, she didn't take time for, because she could see the dead, stretched out now between Necromancers and fire, and she could see which of them powered the fire that was, even now, destroying Chase.

"Emma—what are you—"

Emma reached out. She reached out while standing still, as she had done with Maria Copis. As she had done the first time, with her father. This time, she felt herself leave her body. It was not a comfortable feeling; it was work. But the last time, she hadn't had the power of five of the dead behind her. She wasn't sure why it made a difference, and didn't have time to ask.

Instead, she ran—across grass that still turned green beneath her nonfeet— toward the Necromancers. Toward Longland, who held Allison. She touched Ally's arm, briefly, brushing it with her fingertips. She whispered two words, *I'm sorry,* and then she let go and turned to face the Necromancer. The woman. Her hair was a pale gold, and it was wrapped in so many fine braids it looked fake.

But she herself looked young, and strong, and utterly wrong. Her eyes were not the luminescence of the dead—but they weren't living eyes, either; they looked as if shadow had pooled permanently where there should have been whites. Emma reached out, not for the Necromancer but for the long, pale form of her dead.

The face of the ghost twisted at an odd angle to look at Emma as she touched him. Him, yes. Beard.

"What's your name?" she whispered.

His eyes widened, and he looked straight at her, as if she were somehow something entirely unlike the Emma Hall she had been in the process of becoming for all of her life.

"Please," she added.

"Morgan." The two syllables were stretched and slow.

"Morgan, come to me." She closed her hand around his arm, and she pulled with all her insubstantial might. She felt the snap of chain, although she couldn't see one, and then he was standing, hand in hers. His hand was cold. She smiled briefly. "Margaret?"

"Here, dear."

"This is Morgan; keep an eye on him?"

The man looked confused, but Emma had no more time. She glanced at

Chase and saw, even at this distance, that the fire was going out. She moved, then, to the other Necromancer; the woman was frowning.

"Longland," she said. "I—the power—I think it's gone."

"On *that?*"

Emma moved around Longland's back and reached, again, for the long, thin stretch of a person that was anchoring the fire that lapped against Eric. When they were this elongated, this distorted, it was hard to say much about the dead; she couldn't quite tell if this one was male or female. But it didn't really matter.

She reached out and touched the ghost's arm. "I'm Emma," she said, striving now to be as unthreatening as possible. "And I'm here to free you."

She saw eyes that were six inches long, and very, very narrow, swivel to focus on her. She couldn't really tell if they widened. "What's your name?" she whispered, trying not to flinch.

"Alexander."

"Alexander," she repeated. Her grip tightened, and she pulled. Again, she felt something snap. It was a clean, quick sensation. Alexander appeared by her side, his hand in hers. His hand was also cold, and again, she smiled.

Alexander was younger than Morgan; he was older than Georges or Catherine, but younger, she thought, than Emily; his face hadn't yet hardened into the jaw, nose, and forehead of an older boy. "Emma?"

She nodded. "Emma Hall."

"You're in danger," he told her, shivering. "You shouldn't be here."

"My friends are here," she told him quietly. She looked at Eric. He staggered as the fire guttered, as if he'd been playing tug-of-war with it and it had suddenly let go. He turned and he looked straight at Emma, something neither Longland nor Chase had done.

She saw him nod; it was slight and almost imperceptible.

"Alex," she told the ghost, "you're going to have to wait here for a minute."

She turned to look at herself. At Emma Hall, who was standing, motionless, just before the front steps of a burning house. In the window, she caught a glimpse of Maria Copis' face through the smoke; she didn't, however, appear to be either burning or choking, and her young son, with his wide, luminescent eyes, was staring down at the street.

Emma started to approach herself, which was simultaneously comforting and really, really creepy, when she heard Longland speak.

"I have your friend," he said. "And I advise you both to keep your distance if you want her to remain alive. Leila, take the baby."

She ran the rest of the way to her body, and leaped *into* it. It enclosed her like a womb. For just a moment, she felt it: heavy, solid, inertial, so unpleasantly confining she wanted to leap out again, and be free. But she didn't, because she knew that without a body, she was just another one of the dead.

*No*, Margaret told her. *Not the dead*. But she felt both surprise and approval radiating from this internal voice.

She opened her eyes—her real eyes—and the world was the right color again. The grass was green-brown, the cars were solid, the houses were brick and stone and aluminum siding in various shades. The people wore clothing that didn't suggest that gray was the new black.

The Necromancers were powerless. That's what Emma thought, and that was her first mistake.

The woman drew a gun. She held it to the side of the baby's head, and she told Allison, coldly, to *let go*.

And Allison, who might well have held on had the gun been pressed against her own temple, shuddered and slowly unlocked her arms. Eric and Chase froze, and the other Necromancer—a man whose name was unknown—pulled a second gun, while the woman Longland had called Leila grabbed the baby. Her ability to point a gun while juggling a crying child was poor; she was clearly not a parent. Or not Michael, who, if he could ever bring himself to *touch* a real gun, could have done both.

Longland was still in control, because he had Allison.

From the window above the street, the window from which Maria Copis watched, Emma heard a scream.

It was not, however, Maria's scream. Emma started to turn and something hit her, hard. It wasn't painful, but it was so large, it drove her to her knees fast enough that concrete abraded her skin. Her hands tingled, and her hair rose as if caught in an electrical storm. She felt something leave her, something that she was not entirely in control of—and for better or worse, she let it go.

Leila *screamed*.

Fire erupted around her, and it was not green fire but red and orange, the heart and heat of the flames that had destroyed Rowan Avenue and, with it, so much of Maria's life.

Eric shouted, Allison turned. From her place on the steps, Emma could feel the fire's heat, and Allison was standing right beside it. She shouted and grabbed the baby just before he toppled out of Leila's grip. Longland almost lost her, then, but he managed to hold on.

But the baby wasn't burning.

The other man shouted something, loudly, and then he turned and pointed the gun—not at Eric or at Chase, but at Emma.

Even at this distance, she could see the barrel so clearly it might as well have been a few inches from her forehead.

Longland turned in the direction the gun was pointing, and his eyes widened enough that she could see the whites. "Emma!" he shouted, "you fool! What have you *done?*"

She had time to cover her face or to duck, but she did neither. Instead, almost horrified, she watched Leila burn. Burning was horrible, and although she'd known that, watching it was worse. Any other death, she thought, almost numb. "Andrew!" she shouted. "Andrew, enough! Enough!"

But he didn't hear her, and even if he did, she understood that it wasn't entirely his doing. It couldn't be; he was dead. She understood that what she'd felt was some part of Andrew's power, pushed through her—but it shouldn't have worked that way. And she had no idea how to stop what she'd let go, either.

Paralyzed, she knelt, staring at the barrel of a distant gun.

Wasn't terribly surprised when she heard it fire.

## ᐧ Chapter 17

The bullet failed to reach her.

Confused, she stared as the gun wavered, dipped, and fell. This was because the man who was aiming it staggered and then toppled, part of his face a sudden red blossom.

"Emma, dear," Margaret said urgently, "Call me now. Call me out."

The words made no sense. Emma watched the man topple and watched Longland suddenly curse, spinning, Allison almost forgotten.

Ally kicked him, hard, in the knee, still grabbing the baby tightly. He reached for her with his free hand, and then let go, because he had a knife in his upper arm.

Allison *ran.* She ran, in a straight line, toward Emma, holding Maria Copis' youngest child as if both their lives depended on it. Emma, still on her knees, looked up as Allison reached her, and then she pushed herself off the ground.

Another gunshot.

Merrick Longland cursed, turned, and light flared in the street.

Emma rose and opened her arms and hugged Allison fiercely; they were both shaking. "Ally—"

"Michael's okay. Amy and Skip are okay. Longland left them—" Allison swallowed. "They were okay when we left them."

Emma nodded. "Thank you."

"Emma," Margaret said. "Call me. *Now.*"

"Margaret—"

"Do it, dear. I can't emphasize this enough at the moment."

Another gunshot. Emma looked; Longland was staggering. Without Allison to stand behind, he had to face Chase and Eric, and she knew they would kill him. But death was supposed to happen quickly and, at best, painlessly. Years of watching television had taught her that.

The truth was visceral and ugly, and although she hated everything Longland had done in the brief time she'd been aware of him, she couldn't watch. But she also couldn't look away.

"He would have killed you all without blinking," Margaret said quietly. "And Emma, *call me out now.*"

Emma lifted a hand. She whispered Margaret's name into the noise of fighting: the sullen sound of flesh against flesh, the grunts, the swearing. She knew Margaret had arrived when Allison's eyes widened slightly.

"Thank you, dear. I'm sorry to be so pushy. It's always been a failing of mine."

*No kidding.* Emma, however, was too weary to be unkind. "Could he have—could he have defended himself against them if I hadn't—"

"If you hadn't taken Emily, yes. And more."

Emma was silent for a long moment. "How are Alexander and Morgan?"

"A bit dazed, dear, and a bit confused. They'll be fine, I think."

Emma nodded without looking at Margaret. It seemed important to her to watch, to bear witness, to truly understand the scope of the events she had put into motion. She didn't regret them. She wouldn't change much. Or maybe she would change everything, if she knew how.

Andrew Copis would still be alive. Her father would still be alive. Nathan would still be alive. People like Chase and Eric would be out of work.

But life didn't work that way, in the end. You lived it, and it happened around you. If you were very lucky—and thinking this, she hugged Allison again—it happened while you still had friends. She had to let go of Allison because the baby was screaming his lungs out, and if Allison bounced him up and down and moved around a bit, he quieted. He didn't sleep, though.

"I think he's hungry," Allison told Emma.

"Which we can't do anything about right now."

When Longland finally fell, Emma looked up to the bedroom window. "Maria," she said quietly, "we'll get ladders and we'll get you both down. I think the baby's hungry, and we've lost the diaper bag."

From high above her head, Emma heard Maria Copis' laugh. It wasn't an entirely steady laugh, but there was a thread of genuine amusement in it, along with relief and a touch of hysteria.

Eric had the decency to clean the blood off his hands before he approached them. Chase? Well, he was Chase. And he looked bad; his face was a mess of blisters, and Emma thought it likely other parts of his body—all thankfully hidden by clothing—looked about the same.

"Your poor hair," she told him softly. "If I were you, I'd do it a favor and just shave it all off."

He reached up and touched his hair, because his hair, unlike his skin, had simply curled and shriveled.

"Allison," Chase said, the word a question.

Allison took a deep breath and nodded. "I'm good. I'm," she added, glancing at Emma, "*fine.*"

"You?" Eric asked Emma. He moved toward her, standing beside Allison and a little closer. It was a bit strange, but Emma had seen so much strange she didn't worry much about it.

"I'll be better once I actually set eyes on the rest of my friends. And the diaper bag," she added, wincing, as she glanced at the baby. "Oh, and the ladders."

He shook his head.

"You knew I was there."

He shoved his hands in his pockets, shrugged. "You got out."

"I did. Maria and Andrew are still up in Maria's room."

"She—"

"It's complicated. Don't ask." Then, taking a breath, she added, "but Andrew is fine, and he's almost out of the fire. Thank you. And Chase?"

"What?"

"I owe you an apology. You were right."

He shrugged and glanced at Eric. "Yeah, well. Eric is still one up on me."

"So, I have a question. If you and Eric were fighting with knives, who shot the other Necromancer?"

Eric and Chase exchanged a glance.

"I did. And now, Eric, and you, young lady with the baby, if you'd care to move out of the way?" An older man, possibly fifty, possibly sixty, was standing about five yards away on the sidewalk. He was dressed in some version of summer casual that had to be decades old, but it suited him, and his clothing was sadly not the most notable thing about him. The gun that he held in his hand was. It was not—yet—pointed at anyone, but Emma stiffened anyway.

She glanced at Eric and saw the expression on his face: this man was the reason he'd moved in so close. Eric was taller than Emma, and broader. "Stay behind me," he told her, and then he slowly turned.

"Is that the person whose phone calls you keep ignoring?" she whispered.

He laughed. "You ask the strangest questions, Emma. But yes, it is."

"I'm not sure I'd dare."

"Eric," the man said, waving his gun. "Please step aside. And you, young lady."

"Ally," Emma whispered, "move."

"I think he wants to shoot you," Allison replied, voice flat.

"Oh, probably. At this point, I wouldn't mind shooting myself." Raising her voice slightly, she said, "Chase, help Allison find a safer place to stand."

Chase nodded and reached for Allison's arm. Allison gave him A Look. Chase ignored it. "I didn't almost get fried alive," he told her through gritted teeth, "so you could be shot by the old man. He'll kill you if he feels he has to," Chase added. When Allison failed to move, Chase swore. "Allison, let Eric handle it. If anyone can handle the old man, it's Eric."

"Allison, *please*," Emma whispered. "You've got the baby."

"Chase can hold the baby."

Silence. "Ally, think about what you just said."

Allison looked at Chase's blood covered hands and grimaced.

"Look, go and get Michael and the others. Tell them that everyone's safe. Well, everyone who wasn't trying to kill us. And get them to bring the ladders."

Allison hesitated for just another minute, and then she nodded, and she let Chase lead her away. Chase didn't return; he went down the street with her, as if he couldn't quite trust her not to turn back. It was surprising sometimes when Chase wasn't stupid.

This left just Eric and Emma, standing in the street in front of the house as if it were one giant tombstone, while above the street, Maria and Andrew waited.

Allison and Chase were halfway down the street when the man fired. Allison turned back instantly, and Chase caught her by one arm, spoke something that no one could hear except Allison, and then dragged her down the street.

Emma flinched, instinctively closing her eyes. Eric, however, didn't move.

The bullet hadn't hit him; it had struck the poor grass and dug a runnel through it. The older man and Eric watched each other in a silence that lasted long enough for Chase and Allison to turn a corner. And then some.

"Eric," the man finally said.

"No."

"You don't realize what the girl *is*."

"I realize, better than you know, who Emma is."

"And you're not enspelled."

"Not more than usual, no."

"Longland was not the threat that this girl—Emma, you called her?—will be."

"She has no training."

The old man looked as if he were about to be sick. He lifted the gun and pointed it at Eric. "She *has no training,* and she burned a Necromancer alive? And you're standing there and telling me not to *shoot*? Eric, what the hell is wrong with you?"

Emma was almost grateful that she couldn't see Eric's face. The stench of charred flesh still wafted on the breeze, such as it was, in the street.

Margaret cleared her throat and stepped forward.

The man's eyes widened. When they narrowed again, his face had lost the look of angry confusion, but the cold fury that replaced it was worse. He would shoot Eric, Emma realized. He would shoot Eric just so he could kill her.

She wanted to be brave enough to step out of Eric's shadow, to stand exposed, to let herself be shot, because if he was going to shoot her anyway, it would at least save Eric's life; she had no doubt at all that he could use the gun—she'd seen him blow off the side of a man's head.

She wanted to be that brave, but she couldn't. The most she could manage was to peer around Eric, in as much safety as she could.

"Ernest," Margaret said, in a tone of voice that had made even her most imperious commands seem friendly and mellow by comparison. "If you shoot either Eric or the girl, I will find some way to haunt you horribly for eternity."

The man's jaw dropped slightly, and his face lost a trace of the look of deadly, implacable fury that had made him seem so terrifying. "Margaret?" Fury, however, was tempered now by suspicion.

"I admit that I wouldn't be so drastic if you put a bullet in your Chase, because that boy has *no manners,* and it would probably do him some good." Margaret folded her arms.

The man—Ernest—looked past Eric to Emma. He was no longer entirely suspicious, but he was a far cry from friendly. "Let her go," he said coldly.

Emma cringed. "I don't know how," she told him. "I'm not sure how I'm even holding her. She kind of does what she wants."

Eric, on the other hand, said, "You know Margaret?"

"He does, dear," Margaret replied. "We were rather close while I was alive, although I admit it was somewhat fraught."

"Margaret—"

"But not without its rewards. Ernest," she said, unfolding her arms, and letting them drop to her sides—Margaret not being a woman who seemed to know how to plead, "Emma does hold us. Emma, dear, do be good and call out the others. Oh, I see that Georges and Catherine are already here. Give Emily a hand."

Ernest's jaw opened very slightly—an old and controlled person's version of shock—as Emma obeyed Margaret. It was, however, true that Georges and Catherine had already come out. "Emma?" Georges asked, Catherine standing slightly behind him and letting him do the dirty work, as usual.

"Now is not a good time, Georges," she told him firmly.

Georges practiced the selective deafness of determined children everywhere. "Can we play with Michael now?"

"Michael's not even here, Georges, and if he were, he'd still be babysitting."

"Yes, he is."

"No, he—oh." She could see them all coming down Rowan Avenue, and in spite of the fact that only Eric stood between her and a madman with a gun, she smiled. "Well," she said carefully, "we have to wait until Ernest decides he's not going to shoot me. Or Eric."

"Andrew would be angry," Georges told her confidently. "I'm sure he'd burn him up, too."

"We *do not want* Andrew to burn anyone else," Emma told Georges quite severely. "But we need to get Andrew and his mother out of that house first. After they come down, you can play with Michael."

"Me too?" Catherine asked.

"You too."

Ernest was staring at the dead in utter confusion.

"You see, Ernest," Margaret said, in a slightly less frosty tone of voice. "Emma is not a Necromancer."

"But she killed—"

Margaret shook her head. "No. She was the conduit, no more, and she was the conduit out of her own ignorance."

"I don't understand."

"Margaret—please." Emma's life goals had never included blaming a killing on a four-year-old boy. "I could have stopped it. I didn't."

"Dear," she said, annoyed at being interrupted, "you didn't even know what it was."

"I knew it was power. I knew it was passing through me. I could have held it in." She paused, and then she lifted both hands where Margaret could see their open palms; she didn't have the ferocious dignity of Margaret and didn't feel that she needed it. "He's four. The Necromancer had a gun pointed at his baby brother. He saw it, and he was upset."

"You have a *four-year-old Necromancer*?" the old man almost shouted. He looked at Eric.

Eric shook his head. "No," he said, and his shoulders relaxed ever so slightly in Emma's view, "the four year old is already dead."

Chase told everyone to stop about thirty yards away. Amy, of course, ignored him entirely. And where Amy went, everyone else followed, tagging along in her wake like intimidated younger siblings. Or like Catherine with Georges.

Ernest paused, the gun hand still steady. "The boy who died in the fire here?"

Eric nodded.

"She bound him?"

"Not exactly."

"Ernest, if you are not going to shoot, put the gun away. You're going to scare the other children." Margaret glanced, significantly, not at Georges and Catherine, but at the rest of Emma's friends.

Ernest, on the other hand, glanced at the three corpses on the lawn.

Margaret grimaced. "Yes, you have a point, there. Will they bring the ladders, Emma?"

"Skip has one of them. He's going to get his head bitten off if he's lost the other one," she added. "Let's get Maria down. If," she added politely, "you're okay with not shooting us until we at least get someone out of a burning building?"

Since the building was clearly not burning, and the world seemed to have slid sideways on the way to upside down, the man slowly holstered his gun. Which, given the heat of the barrel, struck Emma as either brave or stupid.

Not much about the man suggested stupid, though.

While Chase held the ladder, Eric went up it, and he helped Maria Copis navigate her way down the rungs. She was still clinging tightly to Andrew, who in return was clinging tightly to her, and she was forced to climb with one hand and two feet, which was highly awkward.

Eric did not, however, complain.

"Is it over?" Maria asked Emma as she finally put her second foot down on solid ground.

Ernest was staring at Andrew.

"It's mostly over," Emma told her quietly. "I'm sorry about—about the . . ."

Andrew looked at Emma. "She was going to hurt my brother," he said, with special emphasis on the last two syllables. That and not a little anxiety.

"Yes, she was," Emma told him. "You saved your brother's life." She smiled at him. "Andrew—"

Maria shook her head and hugged him tightly.

Ernest, however, said, "I can see the boy."

Allison nodded. "We can all see him, I think."

"It's because Maria is holding him," Emma replied.

"Maria is a Necromancer? Is the entire *city* full of Necromancers?" Ernest said this, with some heat, to Eric.

"Maria's not a Necromancer," Emma replied. "She's just a very, very determined mother." Emma looked at Andrew and at Maria, and knew that she wasn't quite finished here yet.

Maria paused, and then, looking at her red-faced infant, and her slightly worried two year old, she finally set Andrew down. He was less reluctant to go, but he watched her as she took her infant from Allison, sat down on the concrete steps, and began to quietly nurse him.

"He's hungry," Andrew said.

"Yes," Emma told him.

"Emma?"

"Yes, Andrew?"

"Am I dead?"

Maria didn't look up at the question, but she flinched.

Emma sucked in air and then said, "Yes."

"Oh." He turned to look at his mother, his brother, and then his younger sister. "I don't like the fire," he finally said.

Emma said nothing. She said nothing when Andrew's gaze lifted until he was looking up at a point beyond her left shoulder, his eyes widening slightly. While he looked, Emma reached out for Catherine and Georges' hands, and they came, cold to the touch, appearing in front of Michael.

She let them play with Michael, as much as they could, and Michael, understanding that they needed this, obliged, although he was very, very upset at the dead people. Playing with the children did help, though; it was something he knew, understood, and could do well.

But Emma was cold when at last she told the two very disappointed children that it was time for Michael to rest and time for Emma to do something else.

"What?" Georges asked her quietly.

"Open a door, if I can," she replied.

Margaret, who had been conversing with Ernest, who seemed to see her regardless of whether or not Emma was actually touching her, looked up at that. Ernest, his conversation broken, looked as well.

"Dear," Margaret began.

"I have to try," Emma told the older woman. "How long have you been trapped here?"

"Long enough. It's the nature of the world, and the nature of the dead."

"But it wasn't always."

Margaret was notably silent.

"What are you talking about, Emma?" Eric asked. He was still keeping a very watchful eye on Ernest, although Emma had long since relaxed.

Emma turned to him. "Andrew. Sort of." She exhaled. "He's going to be trapped in empty streets for god only knows how long—and it's not supposed to be like that."

"What is it supposed to be like?"

"I don't know. Heaven. Maybe. But something *else*. He's done here. They're all—" she added, extending an arm to take in the dead who now gathered as if it were a company barbecue, "done here. My dad told me there's somewhere else they should be able to go."

Margaret winced and looked away—away from Emma, from Ernest, from Georges and Catherine.

"They can find it from anywhere," Emma continued. "But they can't reach it. It's closed. It's blocked."

"Emma—"

"I want to try to unblock it."

"You can't."

"I might not succeed, but I can try."

Ernest was staring at her. He turned to look at Eric. Neither of the two said anything, but it wasn't their permission she wanted, anyway.

She turned to Maria Copis, who, having finished feeding—and changing— her baby, looked desolately at Andrew. Andrew, who was crouched at her feet looking up.

Allison came to take the baby, who was now both clean and asleep, and Maria reached down to pick Andrew up and draw him into her lap. Then, her chin resting on the top of his head, she looked at Emma.

"He'll be here," Emma said quietly. "He'll be trapped here, like all of the dead are trapped."

"I want more time," Maria whispered.

"We all do," Emma whispered back. They were both silent for what seemed like a long time.

But Maria unfolded, still carrying her son. "I heard what you said to Eric. If you do whatever it is you're going to try, will he—"

"He'll be able to leave."

"But to where?"

"Someplace where there's no pain," Emma replied. "I haven't seen it. I don't know. But my father has. All the dead have. They feel that it's home—no, more like the ideal of home, a place where they're wanted, a place where they belong and where they're loved."

Andrew said, quietly, sitting in the arms of his mother and still looking up, "I want to go there. I'm dead, Mom."

His mother closed her eyes and nodded. "I'm so sorry, Drew. I'm sorry."

But he reached up with one hand and touched her cheek, although he didn't look away from whatever it was that drew his attention. "I can wait for you, there," he told her in a faraway voice.

"Will you?"

He nodded. "I'll wait forever. I'll wait for Stefan and Catherine, too."

Maria swallowed and smiled. She was crying. Emma was not, by sheer force of will. "Yes, Emma," Maria said quietly. "We're ready."

Emma told the others what she wanted to do, but it only made sense to the dead. They stared at her for a moment with something that looked like hunger but was really just a deep and terrible longing, sublimated because it was so pointless.

"Dad?"

"He's not here, dear," Margaret told her.

"But—"

"If you accomplish what you intend, I think he feels he'll have to leave you. The pull is very strong."

"But he said he could find it no matter where he was."

"He hasn't just walked down the street." In a more gentle voice she added, "He's not ready to leave you yet, and he doesn't trust himself to stay. You can't know what we've seen and what we long for. Because you can't know, you don't know how very hard it will be for him. But he does know. And he's not willing or ready to leave you, not yet."

"Is that because I don't want to let him go?"

Margaret's smile was almost gentle. It was also sad. "Partly, dear. I'm sorry."

"How do I—"

But Margaret shook her head. "Only partly. The dead are what they are, and if you will not make decisions for them, respect his. You'll need power for this, dear. And it will be more power than you held when you faced Longland."

Eric sucked in air. "Emma, don't do this."

"Why not?"

"Because she's not telling you the whole truth."

"Then you tell me."

"You can't—you might not—survive the taking of that much power. And even if you do, it might change you."

"You mean, more change than seeing the dead and being able to leech the life out of them?"

He grimaced.

"She has a point," Chase told him. Chase's expression throughout had been very, very odd, and it wasn't an odd that could be attributed to blistered skin and patchy red hair.

"Fuck you," Eric said.

"Why? Eric, she's going to try it anyway. You've known her for long enough to know that. You might be able to interfere—but she won't thank you."

"She can't do it."

"Then she'll fail. What's the big deal?"

Eric turned, then, to Margaret. But whatever he saw in her face gave him no strength and no hope. "I didn't save you from the old man so you could commit suicide."

"No. But that's not what I'm trying to do."

"You'll need the dead, dear."

"I have—"

"More."

Emma deflated. "I have no idea how to bind the dead. I don't even think I want to know."

"No, you don't. But you already know. It's a different binding," Margaret added, "and it's costly, for you, child. You pay for it, and we—the dead—touch a little bit of life again. But what you'll need to do this is far more than we gave you. If we give you everything we have, if we drive ourselves beyond the point of speech or perhaps even thought, we will still not give you enough.

"You need the dead," Margaret added firmly.

She turned to the others. "Will you help me?" she asked them. "Will you help me even if it means you have nothing left?"

As one, transfixed, they nodded.

"I think there are very, very few who would say no," Margaret told her.

Emma nodded. "Then I have to find a way to—to summon the dead. I can gather them, if I find them." She glanced at Maria. And swallowed.

*No.*

She frowned. She could hear a voice, and she felt it as if it were a dead person's voice, but none of them had spoken a word.

*You have what you need, Emma Hall. Be what I could not be. Be what she could not be.*

And then she saw the almost translucent image of an ancient, ancient woman, dressed in rags, her flesh like another layer of grimy cloth upon her skeleton. It was the old woman from the graveyard. Emma lifted a hand to cover her mouth, but she managed not to take more than a step back.

Margaret turned toward the old woman, and she bowed and fell silent, moving to allow this most ancient of ghosts to pass her.

"You're not going to kiss me again."

"No."

Emma lowered her hand. Allison was staring at the side of her face, and she reddened. "Who are you talking about? Who couldn't be, and what?"

The old woman shook her head. "If I had survived, I could not do what you will try now. There is only one, in our long history, who could."

"And she?"

The old woman fell silent.

"Emma—"

They both, young and old, living and dead, turned to look at Eric. He also fell silent.

"It is dark, where the dead live. The light they long for has been denied them. But you have other light. Use it."

Emma frowned, and then her eyes widened. She looked at her hands, at the hands that had gripped, for moments, the sides of a lantern in a distant graveyard. As she looked, she saw the sides of it appear, like a layer, against her skin. She saw the writing first, and then the wires, the folds of textured paper. She felt the ice and the cold of it, and it burned her as if it were fire.

But she'd held on to Maria Copis for longer, and that was worse.

Margaret was again utterly silent.

Eric flinched.

Ernest swore under his breath. "You gave her that?"

"I did not give it to her intentionally," the old woman replied, her gaze held by the growing light in Emma's hands. "She took it."

"You *allowed* it."

The old woman did turn, then. "It was meant to be used," she finally said. "It was meant to be used *this* way. She knew *nothing*, and it was the light she reached for." Turning once again to Emma, she continued. "Sometimes they exist shrouded in darkness; they cannot find the way. And then, Emma Hall, we find them, and we lead them home."

When the lantern was solid, Emma lifted it. She shifted position, one hand at a time, until she held it by its top wire; it swung wildly back and forth as if caught in a strong wind.

Georges whispered in a language that Emma didn't understand. She meant to ask him what he saw but fell silent as the lantern began to glow. Its light, which had been so orange and then so blue, became a white that was almost blinding. Almost.

It was brighter than the azure of clear sky; it was brighter than the sunlight. It spread as she watched it, touching the houses that were closest and passing beyond them as if it could blanket the entire city, yard by yard, as it traveled.

Georges came to stand by her side. She thought it was because he was nervous, but when she spared him a glance, she realized that he wasn't; he was standing as close as possible to her because she was the center of that light, and that was where he wanted to be.

And in the distance, as her eyes acclimated to yet another change in color and texture, she saw that he wasn't the only one. From every street she could see, growing larger as they walked—or rode, or ran—the dead came.

## ↶ Chapter 18

They came in ones and twos, to start, but as the time passed, the numbers grew. Eric swore, because Eric could see the dead. Maria didn't swear, but a quick glance at her face told her this was more because she was holding a four year old than from any lack of desire.

Emma didn't know the names of the dead, but she thought she should. They looked, or rather, felt, familiar to her. She saw the young, and the old, the strong and the infirm, the men and the women; she saw different shades of skin, heard the traces of different languages. From the language she did understand, she thought that the voices were raised in prayer.

What these dead didn't do, apparently, was see *each other*. They saw her. They saw the lantern that she held in her hand. It was enough to draw them, like moths to flame. And Emma very dearly did not want to be the flame that consumed them.

"This is going to take a while," Eric told Ernest.

"Meaning?"

"You'd better start cleanup detail or Emma and her friends are all going to be on the inside of a jail, which we can't afford."

"Ah. Right."

She asked them their names. She touched them, briefly, as she did. They answered, even the ones who didn't apparently speak English, and she absorbed their names. Not their beings, and not their power, but the simple fact of the syllables that had identified them in life.

She started by telling the first few of the dead what she intended and by asking their permission and their help to do it; she finished merely by taking their quiet, hushed—and heartbreaking—assent. They knew, somehow. They understood.

They gathered in a crowd that made the most exuberant of concerts or political rallies look paltry by comparison. But they gathered almost on top of each other, occupying physical space as if it meant nothing to them. It became hard to look at them and see the mismatch of face and chest and shoulder as they overlapped.

She closed her eyes instead.

With her eyes closed, she could see again, and she knew that, without effort, she had once again slid out of her body. She looked at a world that was gray and at the dead, who were not. She could barely see houses; they were sketched against the horizon as if by an impressionist. The cars and the trees were gone; the plain spread out forever. And above it, on a spiral of stairs that glimmered, she could see it: a door.

"Maria," she said, although she could no longer see Maria Copis.

But she heard, at a great remove, Maria's steady voice.

"Give Andrew to me," she told his mother, as gently as she could.

She didn't know if Maria hugged him or kissed him or spoke to him, although she was certain she had, but after a long moment, she felt the weight of a four year old placed, gently, in her arms. The arms that were extended and carrying the lantern. Andrew Copis materialized, and smiled at her.

"Are you ready?" she asked Andrew.

His eyes were shining.

She held the lantern by her fingers and Andrew in the curve of her arms, and she began to climb those stairs as the crowd that gathered all around her took—and held—a collective breath. The dead didn't need to breathe, of course, but maybe they'd forgotten they *were* dead. Her feet were the first to touch the steps.

As she ascended, they followed. They were much more orderly than a concert crowd; they didn't push and didn't shove and didn't swear at each other. But then again, they didn't have to. She thought, for a moment, that they might not need to touch the stairs at all—and wondered if what she was "seeing" was entirely something created for her own benefit.

But it didn't matter. She could climb stairs, and the dead could climb whatever it was they saw in their individual, unconnected worlds. She rose, and they rose, until she was at the top of the steps on a platform that led to a single door.

It wasn't a fancy door; it wasn't pearly gates. It was a simple, thick wood of a kind you didn't see much anymore. It had no handle, no doorknob, no knocker, no bell. It was just there.

She put Andrew down, and then she reached out to touch the door. Her hand stopped an inch away from its surface.

"You're not dead," Andrew told her calmly. He reached out with considerably smaller hands, and his hands did touch the wood. He frowned, though, and looked as if he might cry. "I can't get through."

"Well, no. You have to open it first."

"Open *what*?"

So, she thought, it wasn't just the stairs that were for her benefit. Her father had said he could see light, and Emma demonstrably couldn't. It should have worried her, but she found it oddly comforting. The closed door was like another metaphor, and all she had to do was open it.

Without being able to actually touch it.

She shook her head, and reached for the surface of the door again.

"Emma—"

"Hush, Andrew. I'm not dead—but right now I'm not exactly alive either. I'm here, I'm with you, and with all the others."

He looked up at her for a moment and then nodded. "You brought my mom to me."

"She wanted to come."

He nodded. "She was sad."

"Yes. She's been very, very sad. I think seeing you has made her happier, though. Now, let me try this." This time, when she reached out with her palm for the door's surface, she pushed. The inch between her hand and the flat planks gave way very, very slowly, and even as it did, she felt her hands begin to tingle and ache. It was a familiar sensation, but it grew stronger as she pushed.

She looped the lantern around the crook of her elbow, and she freed up her other hand. She applied that one to the invisible barrier as well, and it continued to give slowly. Sweat started to trickle down her neck, although she felt it at a great remove.

The inch became half an inch, and then a quarter, an eighth, a sixteenth. Every tiny increment required more power, and she took the power that was there, gathering it as if she were breathing it in and exhaling it through her hands.

But when she finally—finally—touched the door, she knew. She felt it, and she felt what lay beyond it, so clearly she could almost *see*. She heard the faint, attenuated cries at her back, and she knew that what she could almost see, they could clearly see. They had given her this, and it had robbed them of the power of their voices, muting them.

She *pushed* hard.

The door gave slowly, fighting her every inch of the way.

But it gave, and when it did, she renewed her efforts because she could see what they saw: the light, the sense of comfort, of home, of belonging. The sense of perfect ease, of place. She felt it like a blow, and she felt herself, somewhere, stagger back at the force of it.

It was like the very best parts of loving Nathan, and it tore at her because she had thought they were gone forever and she wanted them so badly. Badly enough to hold that door against the force that was trying to keep it closed. As she struggled, she felt the dead begin to pass by her. Andrew was the first to go, and this felt right to her, but he was only the first.

The others streamed past as well.

She couldn't count them. She didn't try. She became the struggle, and she knew that all she had to do was keep it open for long enough. How many of the dead would pass through, she didn't know. Not all of them, unless she could somehow wrench the door wide open, and free of all restraint.

But she didn't have to do that. All she had to do was hold it for long enough, and then?

She could go, too.

She could go to the light, and the peace, and the lack of pain and loss, and she could find comfort there, and she could give over all grief, all numbness, all of the horrible gray and guilt and anger that had clouded the last months of her life.

*Emma!*

It would be so easy. It would be so much easier.

The last person slipped through, and her hands now ached with effort, and with cold. She knew she'd run out of power; there was no one left to give it to her. But she could—

Could go. But Nathan, she knew, would not be there. He hadn't been among the dead; she would have known him anywhere. His name, his face, the sound of his voice. Even if she couldn't touch him without the cold. She could pass through this door, and he would be trapped here, and she would spend eternity without him.

And, she thought, she would be dead, and she wouldn't *have to care.*

She swallowed, her fingers slipped, and she moved an inch forward.

And then, clear as a bell, she heard a familiar, quiet voice, uncertainty and fear etched into every word. *Emma, I don't want you to die.* Michael's voice.

She knew that he would be fidgeting, that he would be in that physical state that was one step short of out-and-out panic, and she knew that if she walked through this door, the one short step would be crossed the minute he understood that what he wanted didn't matter.

She didn't love Michael the way she'd loved her father. She didn't love him the way she'd loved Nathan. But she accepted the responsibility of the love she did feel for him, and she let the door go, weeping. Understanding, as she did, that the Maria Copises of this world were doing the same thing.

The door slammed shut with so much force it should have shattered, and while Emma watched it reverberate, it grew eyes.

Shadowed, dark eyes, scintillating with color the way black opals did. They were not—quite—human eyes, although something about them implied that they might have been once, and they were rounded with effort and, Emma thought, fear.

*I will kill you for this.*

She heard the voice and knew that it was the second time she had heard it. The first time had been in Amy's house, when Eric had spoken to an image in the mirror.

She should have been afraid. Later, maybe. Right now she was too caught up in grief, and when she opened her real eyes again, she was weeping. In public. She couldn't even find the strength to tell anyone that she was fine.

Eric drove her home. She left him at the door when Petal emerged, barking in his stupid, loud way. She'd run out of Milk-Bones, and anyway, feeding Petal was not exactly what she needed at the moment.

But need it or not, it was what she had to do, and she walked into the kitchen and found a can of dog food, a can opener, and his dish.

"Emma." She looked up, and she saw Brendan Hall standing in the kitchen, where in any real sense he would never stand again. She'd recovered just enough that she could turn her face away. She did, but then she turned back to her father, as if she were eight years old. She had nothing to say, and he waited.

"You didn't leave," she whispered, when she could speak at all.

He shook his head. "While the door is closed," he told her, his voice heavy with worry and yet somehow warm with pride, "I'm staying."

"Why?" She had to ask, because she'd come so close to not staying herself, and she, at least, was alive.

"Sprout," he said quietly, and Petal looked up and barked. It wasn't a "strangers-at-the-door-man-the-cannons" bark, which was his usual form of noisemaking; it was tentative and hesitant.

Brendan Hall bent and stroked his dog's head. His hand passed slightly through fur, and he grimaced. "Because," he told his daughter, not looking at her at all, "you're here."

She nodded, and then she reached out blindly for him, and he hugged her. His arms were cold, but she didn't mind.

Her mother was in the living room.

Emma discovered this when she at last let her father fade into whatever world he occupied when he wasn't with her, and she tried to walk, stiffly, up the stairs. She needed to remove a dozen splinters from her palms, and she needed to change. She probably also needed to burn or dispose of the clothing she was wearing, because it looked as though she'd already tried and had done a truly bad job.

But when her mother called her name, she froze, one hand on the rail. Petal, always hopeful that any spoken word meant food, came out of the kitchen and tried to tangle his blocky body around her legs. She grimaced, looked down at her clothing, and then turned. "Mom?"

Her mother rose. She was pale, and she had that I've-got-a-headache look. Emma realized belatedly that she'd been sitting on the same spot on the couch that Emma often occupied when she was thinking about Nathan. Or thinking, more precisely, about his absence.

The headache look, on the other hand, vanished as Mercy Hall approached her daughter. "Emma!"

Emma started to tell her mother she was fine—because, among other things, it happened to be true—but she stopped. "There was a bit of fire," she said instead.

Her mother's brows rose most of the way up her forehead.

She glanced at the hall mirror. From this angle she could see only a quarter of her body. "It's not as bad as it looks," she added quickly. "But I would like to get changed."

"What *happened*?"

"There was a fire," she repeated. "We were—we tried to help."

"Who is we?"

"Ally, Michael, me. Eric and his cousin, Chase."

"Was anyone hurt?"

How to answer that? "No. No one was hurt." Lie. She should have felt guilty; she didn't. "Let me get changed," she added. "And showered. And maybe you could help me take these splinters out of my hand before—"

"They get infected?"

"Something like that."

Mercy Hall folded her arms across her chest, and her lips thinned. But she drew one sharp breath and nodded. "I swear," she said softly, "It was so much easier when you were two. Then, I *had* to keep my eyes on you all the time. Now? I never know what's going to happen."

Emma, who had walked away from death and its peace, nodded. Her mother would worry—but her mother always did that. What her mother wouldn't have to do, not this time, was stand by a grave and bury her only child. She thought of Maria, then, and she turned and surprised her mother: She wrapped her in a tight, tight hug.

"I *am* fine, Mom," she said, when she at last pulled back.

Her mother's eyes were filmed with unshed tears. "I'm sorry I wasn't here earlier—"

Emma shook her head. "Don't be," she said quietly. Knowing that her mother was thinking about her father. And missing him. Emma wanted to call him out then, to call him back—but she had a strong suspicion that he wouldn't actually listen. He'd always believed he knew what was best for both Emma and her mother.

But he was gone, at least for the moment; Emma and her mother were still here. They had each other. "I'll come back after I've showered. Maybe you can find the tweezers?"

Monday at 8:10, Michael came to the door.

Emma, her bag ready, her hair brushed, and her clothes about as straight as they were going to be for the day, opened the door, waited while he fed Petal a Milk-Bone, and then joined him on the front steps.

The good thing about Michael was that she didn't need to apologize for anything. Whatever had happened, they'd both survived it, and he held nothing against her, not even her near death. He did ask a lot of questions, but she answered them as truthfully as she could, often resorting to "I don't know" because it was true.

They picked Allison up on the way to school. Allison looked surprisingly cheerful, but it was the kind of forced cheer that hid worry.

"I'm fine, Ally," she told her.

"You're always fine," Allison said. "But are you okay?"

Emma nodded. "Mostly," she added, mindful of Michael.

"Maria left you her phone number. She had to get the kids back."

Emma winced. "I'm surprised she'd ever want to speak to me again. She almost died there."

"You almost died there as well."

"Yes, but I can't get away from me."

Allison laughed.

They made it to school, and when they did, Emma saw that Eric and Chase were waiting for them on the wide, flat steps of the school. Although skateboarding was strictly prohibited, people were skateboarding anyway. Business as usual.

But Eric came down the steps to meet them.

"I'm fine," she told him, before he could speak.

"You're always fine," he replied.

She glanced at Allison and surprised herself by laughing. Allison laughed as well.

"Can I talk to you for a minute?" Eric asked her.

"Maybe five. Why?" Allison raised an eyebrow, and Emma nodded in response. She stood still, in front of Eric, while Allison dragged Michael through the doors of the school.

"Are you leaving?" Emma asked him.

"Leaving?"

"School. You aren't really a student here."

He hesitated and then said, "No. If it's all right with you, I'd like to stay."

This surprised her, but she covered it by saying, "Not if it means we have to keep Chase, too."

"I heard that."

Eric chuckled, but he looked pained. "You have to keep Chase, too. He's enrolled."

"But—"

"The old man insisted."

"The old man who was going to shoot me? And probably shoot you as well?"

"That one."

"But—but why?"

"Because he's decided he's not going to shoot you. Or me. Well, not for that at any rate. Emma—"

She looked at him for a long while, and then she smiled.

His turn to look slightly confused. "What? Have I got something on my face?"

"No. But you know, you *did* stand between me and a loaded gun. That's not a bad character trait in a guy." She nodded toward the door. "Unless you want to beat my late-slip collection, we can talk about this later."

She started up the stairs, and Eric fell in beside her; Chase pulled up the rear. "You realize," he said, sounding aggrieved, "that you're forcing me to *go to school* and listen to a bunch of boring teachers talk about crap that has nothing to do with my life?"

"So sue me."

Eric laughed, and Emma smiled again, less hesitantly. It wasn't all despair and loss, this whole living business. Sometimes, it was good. It was important to hold on to that.

On Tuesday night, Emma went to the graveyard. She took Petal, her phone, and Milk-Bones, and she made her long and meandering way through the residential streets, where lights were on in different rooms.

Petal was, of course, offended by the nighttime excursions of the local wildlife, and Emma caught a glimpse of raccoons when she was almost yanked off her feet because she was foolishly holding the lead. She continued to hold it, however.

She looked for ghosts, for patches of strangeness in the architecture, but the dead—at least in this neighborhood—were sleeping. And Eric had said graveyards were peaceful because the dead didn't go there.

Emma, who was not dead, did.

She had thought that, with the realization that Nathan was somewhere else, she could give up these nightly excursions, but she'd come to understand that she didn't go for Nathan's sake; she went for her own. For the quiet that Eric himself seemed to prize.

It was a place in which she never felt the need to say *I'm fine*. She didn't feel the need to talk, or be interesting, or be interested; she could breathe here, relax here, and just be herself. Whoever that was.

She found a wreath of flowers standing on a thin tripod, just in front of Nathan's grave, and she swept a few fallen leaves from the base of the headstone before she settled into the slightly dewy grass. It had started here.

Petal butted her with the top of his broad, triangular head, and she made a place for him in her lap, scratching absently behind his ears. The sky was clear, and the stars, insofar as any city with profuse light pollution had stars, were bright and high.

She could pretend, if she wanted, that the entire past week hadn't happened. She couldn't as easily pretend that the last few months hadn't happened, and that hurt more. But . . . maybe she was selfish. Seeing Maria, meeting her, had left her with the sense that she was not entirely alone; that she was not even the only person to suffer the loss she'd suffered.

It helped. She scratched Petal's head, fed him, and looked at the moon for a bit. It was good to be here. It was good, as well, to be home. To be with friends. She rose, picked up Petal's leash, and began to head there.

But as she started toward the path, she stopped, because someone stood in the moonlight. There wasn't a lot of other light here, but it didn't matter. Emma didn't need a flashlight to know who it was.

She walked, slowly, toward him, and when she was a couple of feet away, she stopped.

She hadn't expected to see him. Not here, and not for years. Certainly not in the graveyard where she had come for the silence and privacy that he had given her while they were together.

She wanted to hug him. She was afraid to blink. But his lips turned up in that familiar little half-smile as he waited, as if he knew she couldn't decide what to do. She wanted to say so much, ask so much. But in the end, because he was dead and she knew it, she held out her hand. He took it, and cold blossomed in her palm, spreading up her arm.

She wondered what he felt, if he felt her hand at all.

"Hello, Nathan," she said quietly.

"Hello, Em."

# Touch

## Nathan

When you slide into the car, it's empty. Stuffy. You roll down the windows, sit for a minute in the garage. It's quiet, in the car. It's like a bubble world. You're in it; it's your space. It's your space until you park, turn off the engine, and get out.

Sitting in the garage won't get you anywhere you want to be, and you want to be somewhere, but you're not in a hurry, not yet. You start the car, back out of the garage, think about where you're going.

Radio says there's an accident on Eglinton you want to avoid. You're not the only one to take that advice; traffic is slow.

Here's a thing about cars. In the summer, when the humidity is 98%, you might as well be in an oven if your dad's air-conditioning is dead. Intersections are not your friend. Windows are. Still air becomes breeze, and breeze becomes wind—but only when the wheels rotate.

Here's another thing about cars. They have history.

Some of the history is in rust and nicks and dents and the taillight that's sketchy. Some of it's in stains on the vinyl; some of it's wedged between the seat back and the bench. Some of it, though, is memory. Where you went. More important, with who. You can think about the empty passenger seat on the hot, humid drive, and you can imagine that Emma is sitting beside you, hair trailing back in the cross-breeze, elbow on the doorframe.

You can remember the first time you kissed her, when she got out of the passenger side and walked around to where you sat, behind the wheel, looking for words. Words have never come easily to you, but Emma gets that. She doesn't make you say anything you're not ready to say.

It was dark, but her eyes looked so bright. You didn't even get out of the car; you looked up to tell her you'd see her tomorrow, and her face was inches from yours; she was leaning into the open window, into where you were. And then you didn't want to start the car at all.

And maybe you didn't.

When you're on the inside of a car in motion, you're not really thinking about physics. When you're behind the wheel, you pay attention to red lights, green lights, stop signs, walk signals. If you don't, you've got no business being behind that wheel. But there's room for Emma in that, and you think about her when you're waiting for lights to change. You want to see her. You're going to see her.

But here's the big thing about cars: They're a couple of tons of metal and extraneous bits. Add wheels, and you get momentum. It's pure physics. You get momentum even if your car isn't moving, because the car that *is* moving doesn't stop until half your car is crushed between its SUV hood and the wall of a building.

The front half.

You see the SUV.

You see the SUV a dozen times.

You see it a hundred times. You're trapped in a loop where time slows down or speeds up randomly. You can see the license plate. You can see the driver. You can see his passengers, and you can count them. He's not much older than you are. They're not much older than he is.

You can see the front grille getting closer and closer. You know the license plate number by heart; it's burned into your memory. You can feel the car crumple around you, can see the windshield crack and shatter. You don't feel pain. It happens too fast for pain.

And you don't feel heat. It's summer, the sun made the car seats too hot to touch. Now it's cold in the middle of July. Cold, dry, endless July. It's still a bubble world, and you know you're trapped here until you can open the door—but you can't. There's not enough of a door left. Not enough of you.

You are dead.

You come to realize you are dead. It only happened once, the dying; this stupid looped repeat has nothing to do with life. Nothing to do with you, except you're *in it*. You don't know where you are. You know that people talk about heaven—or hell—and this is hellish, except you feel no pain. Only confusion and anger and cold. You don't know how many times their car has hit your car. You can't begin to count.

But until you realized what it *meant*, you had to live it over and over again. Now you know.

Now you can leave the car. You don't even try to open the door. You just slide to the left of the steering wheel, and you pass through the car door. You're out.

Your car still gets crushed against the wall, but this time, you're not in it.

Your ears are ringing. You can see the street. You can see pedestrians, freezing, turning; you can hear the sound of a woman screaming. That grabs you, makes your blood freeze, but you don't recognize the voice, and you can move again.

The thing is, you can't see very well. You know people are here, but they're blurs. You shout. They can't hear you. You stand in front of them. You jump up and down like a four year old, but nothing changes. They're still blurry. Some of them move. But they move past you, around you, as if you're not there. As if they're not here.

There's no sun here. No heat.

You spend an hour screaming. You can scream forever. No one hears you. You jump up and down, you try to throw things. You go nuts. You haven't gone nuts like this since you were five. There's no reaction. No one sees you. You can barely see them, they're so fuzzy. It's like you died and you suddenly need glasses. Or worse.

You need to get out of here. You need to leave.

You can go home. That's what you should have done. You should have gone home. You didn't even think of home. Why?

Thinking of home. Mom. Dad. Gotrek the hamster. You'll go home.

You don't recognize the street you're on. You don't recognize the intersection. You *know* how to get home. You know this part of the city. But . . . you don't. The streets are too long. The buildings are the wrong shape, the wrong size. You can see them more clearly than the blurred smudges that are people—but they make no sense.

You've had this nightmare before. You leave school, exit by the front doors, and stare out at a totally unfamiliar neighborhood. It's as if the entire building had been teleported to some other borough while you were in history or math. In those nightmares, you end up wandering the streets, lost, until you wake up.

But you can't wake up here. You've never been lost like this.

When it gets to be too much, you sit down. Just sit, in the middle of the road, staring at nothing, wondering where the hell the sun is. Wondering why there's no blood on your clothing, no dirt on your hands. Wondering why you're even here at all. This isn't how death is supposed to work.

You have no sense of time, because time makes no difference. You have no idea how long you've been sitting on your butt in the middle of this street. You are cold, you are silent. You don't scream anymore. You don't move. The world moves around you, leaving you behind. You miss Emma. You miss Emma, but you're terrified because you don't remember what she *looked like*. You don't remember sunlight.

So when sunlight comes, it's almost too much. You curl in on yourself, because it's too much. But it gets stronger and brighter. It's not going away. You stand, you turn, you face it; it is so bright and so warm and so close you can almost touch it. And you can *hear* it. If you can reach it, you know you will never be cold again.

You won't be lost, either. Maybe this is why you couldn't find home when you tried: you can't live there anymore. You can walk toward the sun. You don't need the road. You can run, and you do.

Scattered throughout your childhood are memories: *Cover your eyes. Don't stare at the sun. Do you want to go blind?* Different voices, different ages, same advice.

So you know this isn't the sun because there's no pain. Your eyes don't water. Your vision doesn't blur. The light doesn't become a spread of painful brilliance; it takes shape and form. And you have no words for the form. It's not round; it's not square; it's not flat. It's not person-shaped, but . . . it's alive. You are certain it's alive. It's alive the way home is alive: it promises warmth. It promises what you need—what you've always needed: quiet space, and company in which you can be entirely yourself.

No defenses. No shields. No prescriptive behavior. No need to define yourself by other people's desires, by other people's approval or disapproval. No need to talk if you've got nothing to say, no need to shut up if you've got too much. People are waiting there, on the other side: people who see you and know you and accept everything about you until your fear of the things they can't accept becomes meaningless.

You can't see that—how could you? You're not even certain what it would look like, if you were still alive. You've seen glimpses of it in Emma. In your parents. In moments of time. You can't put a shape to it. But it's solid, and you understand that you only have to reach it, touch it, and you will be fully, finally, home.

But as you approach, you hear wailing. It is the most distinct sound you've heard since your car collapsed around you.

You can hear it as if it's your voice; it's inside you, inside your mouth and your ears. Your hands freeze with the strength of it because it is loss. It is loss; it is death.

You thought you were dead. No, you *knew* you were dead. But until this moment, you didn't understand what that meant.

The light is where you belong. It's where you want to be—it's the only thing you want. But you can't reach it. No one—you understand this as the screams take shape and form—can.

You can see shadows moving in the light. You know what they're doing: They're trying to touch it. They're trying to reach it. You want to do the same. You don't. You don't because you know you'll be up there screaming with the rest of them if you try and you fail.

And it's true. You would be. You'd scream for years, and you'd feel every passing second as if it were a century. It's what the dead do. This is their birth, their rebirth; this is when they come, at last, to accept their eternity. Like any birth, it's painful and of interest only to parents—but, of course, yours aren't here.

If they knew what awaited the dead, would they have children at all? It's a question that no one has asked. The living who can speak to the dead don't care, after all. The dead are dead, and they serve at the whim of their Queen, when they are at last presented to her.

Rare indeed is the dead boy who does not need to journey to the city to greet her. How many times do you think she has left her palace within that city and walked the paths the living walk to find the newborn dead?

Ah, but you *are* newborn. You don't know. You have no idea of the honor done you.

You know only that there is a light that reaches for you, a light you can touch. In form and shape it is familiar: human, only slightly taller than yourself. But it casts no shadow, and it offers warmth—the only warmth you've found in the land of the dead.

Is she beautiful? To you, yes; you are dead. You see what lies beneath the surface of life, and you see it purely. No age, no experience, no prior vision blurs your sight. You would kneel, if kneeling made sense; you are immobile, instead, staring; you are afraid to blink, because in blinking, you might lose sight of her. Thus do all of the dead who understand their state stand before her: transfixed. Helpless.

Here. Take the Queen's hand, and she will lead you to the only real home you will have for the rest of eternity.

~

Some people cry in public. They're champion criers. They cry when they see a familiar name in a phone book, or when they're signing yearbooks, or when they're talking about anything more emotional than grocery shopping. It's as though all of life is a big box of tissues.

Nathan's mother has never been one of them. Nathan's never *seen* her cry. Maybe her mother did, when she was a kid; if she did, she never shared. Nathan learned about crying from his mother, but it took him longer.

Maybe that's why he fell for Emma. Emma was a total failure as a crier. She wasn't like his mother in any other way, except gender. Which is also why he liked her.

But she and his mother had this in common. It wasn't that they didn't *want* to cry; it was that they chose not to and made it stick. No tears in public. Nathan never understood why.

"If it's the way you feel, why hold back?"

"If I feel like punching Nick in the face," Emma replied, "I don't see you encouraging me."

"Your fists, his face. Not practical. Get a tire iron." He shrugged. "It wouldn't bother me if you cry."

"It would bother *me*."

"Why?"

She kissed him instead of answering, which was a cheat. But it was a *good* cheat.

He knows the answer now. He knows, and he should have known it then, would have, if he'd known how to think about tears the same way he thinks about circuit boards. He is standing in his house. He is standing in his room. His room hasn't changed. Transistors, wires, solder, tweezers, in neat boxes, like a wall at the back of his desk. His clamps, his light, his computer. It's been three months.

He knows because the date is marked on his calendar, the calendar that hangs from the corkboard to one side of his bedroom window. Someone's been marking the date. He watches as his mother puts a neat, red line through a square box in October. She doesn't need it; her calendars exist in the ether.

But she puts the pen on his desk, draws his curtains shut. Stands behind the closed curtains, her shoulders curving toward the floor, her arms bending at the elbows until she wraps them around her upper body. They're shaking. No, she's shaking. Her head drops. Nathan stands frozen for one immobile moment, and then he reaches out for her back in a kind of terrified wonder.

She cries.

God, she cries. It's a terrifying, horrible sound. No quiet tears; it's like someone is trying to rip the insides out of her, but they've got nowhere to put them. It's paralyzing; it's worse than walking into his parents' bedroom when the bed was heavily occupied. He feels like he's violating her, just standing here in his own room.

And then the guilt and the paralysis break, and he's reaching out for her, he's trying, *trying*, to put his arms around her—from the back, he's not an idiot—but he *can't*. He can't. They don't *go* anywhere. He calls her. He shouts. He shouts louder than he's ever shouted—and she hears nothing, and her knees give, and her forehead is pressed against his goddamn desk, and it is the worst thing he's ever seen.

Worse than an SUV driving toward the side of his car.

He can't *do* anything. He knows, watching her back, that no one can. She's here, in his room; his door is closed. She *isn't* crying in public. There's no public here, because no one lives in his room anymore. And he knows she won't cry like this outside of her own house. Because it would have to practically kill anyone who could see her and hear her; a sound like this could burn itself into your brain, and the only way you could avoid it would be to plug your ears and run screaming.

You couldn't help her. You couldn't do anything to make the pain go away—and you'd *want* to. You'd be immobile, your own helplessness and uselessness made clear. You couldn't escape it unless you avoided her, avoided any hint of her grief, and let what you witnessed fade.

She doesn't cry in public because of what it would do to everyone *else*. It's not because of what other people will think of her—that's what he assumed, once—it's because of what they'll think of *themselves*, afterward. He knows because he *hates* himself, now. He hates himself for dying. He hates the people who killed him—first time, for everything—and he hates that he can't *touch* her, can't *reach* her, because if he could, it would stop. Or change.

This is the first time Nathan's been home since he died. He wants to flee. He almost does. But he waits it out, because in the end, he has to know that it does stop. If he leaves now, he won't believe it; every other memory of home will be buried beneath this one.

It does stop.

It stops. The rawness of grief peters into an echo of itself—but the echo speaks of pain as if pain were an iceberg, a colossal structure beneath surfaces that hide nothing if you know how to look. When it's once again submerged, she stands, slowly and awkwardly, as if she's spent months living on her knees, her forehead propped up against the edge of his desk.

Her father died when Nathan was a child. He remembers it clearly, now. He remembers the phone call; he remembers her eight-hour absence. He remembers arguing with his dad about bedtime because he wanted his mother. His mother did not come home that night. When she returned the next day, she told him his grandfather had died. He wanted to know why, because death made no sense. Death had no impact.

He asked her if his father was going to die.

"No," she told him softly. "Not for a long time. But, Nathan, everyone eventually dies."

She didn't cry. He didn't cry because she didn't. He asked her if she would miss Grandpa, and she said, "Yes, very much."

She carried him—at five years of age—for most of her father's funeral. He thought it strange, because babies were carried and he was a Big Boy. But she still didn't cry. For the whole, long day, she didn't cry.

People came up to talk to her. He recognized some of them; some were strangers—but not to his mother. They told her they were sorry (But why? They hadn't killed him). They told her he'd had a good life. A full life. But some of them told her stories about her father, instead, and they made her smile.

No one tells his mother stories in this room. He knows. No one can tell her that her son had a full life, or a good life. There is nothing to make her smile, here. Seeing her gaunt face in the evening light, he wonders if she's smiled at all in the last three months. He thinks she must have—but he can't make himself believe it.

She straightens her clothing. No one can see it, but she straightens it anyway. Then she turns, walks to the door, opens it, and turns again. Into the darkness that contains her son, she says, "Good night, Nathan."

She closes the door.

Nathan has learned a few things about being dead.

He's learned, for instance, that the dead don't eat. They can't. They don't feel hunger, and physical pain is beyond them. They never get thirsty. Snow, hail, storms, and blistering desert heat don't bother them. He assumes that bullets won't hurt; knives don't.

He's learned that the dead have their own version of sleep. It doesn't involve beds, and it doesn't hold dreams—or nightmares. It's a kind of darkness and stillness in which even memories fade. It's the ultimate silence. The silence of the grave.

It's not boring, this sleep. It's not confining. It's . . . nothing. Just nothing. But sometimes, nothing is good; right now, he's not keen on the alternative.

Because tonight, he's learned that the dead are useless. They can't touch anything. They can't change anything. In any way that counts, they've got no voice. They can speak—but no one can hear them.

Not no one.

*I want you to go back to your home, Nathan.*

"Why?"

*Because there, you will find an opportunity that most of the dead will never have.*

He didn't ask what the opportunity was. Even the first question had been a risk. The Queen of the Dead doesn't like to be questioned.

*Go home. I will give you no other orders yet. Just go home. Watch your family, watch your friends.* Her smile was winter, her eyes sky blue. They were wide, and looked, in the radiance of her face, like windows. Beyond those windows: clouds, lightning, destruction. As if she were the only thing that kept the storm out.

∽

*Promise me, when we're old, you'll let me die first.*

*What kind of a promise is that, Em?*

*The only one I want. I don't want you to die first. I don't want to be left behind again. Promise?*

Emma's house is half lit. Her mother's office lights are on the second floor, but her mother's probably working—as she usually does—in the dining room. Emma's bedroom is dark. Nathan stands between two streetlights, looking up. He wants to see Emma. He wants more than that, but he'll settle for what death has left him.

The moon is high. The night sky is a different shade of gray. Nathan slides his hands into his pockets and waits. He's got nothing but time, and he hates it. But he hates it less when the front door of the Hall house opens and Emma steps out, surrounded by Petal, the rottweiler who refuses to stand still. Nathan can't take his eyes off her; for one long moment, she is the only thing he sees.

He watches her lead Petal toward the sidewalk in silence.

Nathan joins her, stopping when she stops and moving when she moves. He can pretend, for a few minutes, that he's still alive, that this is a normal night, a normal walk. He doesn't have to fill the silence. Silence has never bothered Emma.

There's a difference between being alone and feeling lonely. Emma is alone. Nathan? Doesn't want to think about it.

The breeze lifts Emma's hair. Petal's name leaves her lips. She keeps walking. Nathan watches her go. He wants to talk to her. He doesn't try.

The problem with death—this version of death—is that it feels pretty much like life, at least to the dead people. He's not dragging bits and pieces of corpse around, because he's pretty sure that's what he'd be doing if the manner of death defined him. He's not spouting blood. He's not a poltergeist.

He's Nathan. She's Emma. They haven't seen each other for three months, and the last thing Nathan did was break a vow. He left her. He left her behind.

It was a stupid promise. He knew it was stupid before he made it. But she was there, lying in his arms, curled against his chest, her hair tangled, her eyes wide. She wasn't joking. She wouldn't *let* him make a joke of it.

He promised. He promised because to him it was just a different way of saying *I love you*.

And he does. He meant every word of it. She knows—she *must* know—that dying wasn't his choice. It wasn't his fault. She must know that he'd be out here by her side, walking her half-deaf dog, if it had been up to him.

He shakes himself, hurries to catch up with her, and stops when he finally realizes where she's going. The cemetery.

Emma. Oh, Em.

Nathan has no desire to see his grave. He'd had no idea, until he followed Emma from her house, where he'd been buried. But he knows now, and he almost leaves. He doesn't want to see Emma cry. He doesn't want to see her go to pieces the way his mother did. He can't comfort her. He's got nothing to offer her at all.

But when she slips behind the fence, he walks through it. He keeps her in sight. The night sky is clear. If there's a breeze, he can't feel it; he can feel the cold, but it's always cold now. He doesn't read the headstones. He doesn't read the markers.

To his surprise, Emma does. She reads them. She lingers. But she doesn't stop; she hasn't reached the gravestone with his name on it. Petal's tongue is hanging out of his mouth as he trots back and forth between the markers. He's happy. Emma is silent. She's not in a hurry.

Emma finds a standing wreath of white flowers before one marker. She kneels in front of it, picks up a petal, blows it off her fingers. Tucking her legs to the right, she sits; Petal flops down to her left and drops his head in her lap. She scratches behind his ears.

She doesn't speak. She doesn't weep.

Nathan listens to the ever-present sounds of passing cars. Mount Pleasant isn't a small cemetery, but it's in the middle of a city. He looks up, as Emma does, to see the stars. To see the moon in the night sky. To know that they're seeing the same thing.

He's never minded waiting for Emma. He could wait for her forever. He doesn't interrupt her. He doesn't talk. He knows she'll come to him in her own time.

She picks up Petal's leash as she unfolds, straightening her hair and brushing petals off her legs. Her head is bent as she walks back the way she came; Nathan knows, because he's standing there.

But she lifts her chin, and as she does, she slows. He can see her eyes so clearly, even though it's dark. He can see their shape, the way they round; he can see the edge of her lashes. Her mouth opens slightly as she approaches. Her eyes are brown. They've always been brown. But they're also luminescent. It's not an exaggeration: They glow; they're alight. He's seen light like that twice since his death. Only twice.

And he knows, then, that Emma can see him. He knows how to hide from the sight of anyone but the Queen of the Dead; if she's looking for someone among the dead, she'll find them. But he can make himself so still, so quiet, that no one else who can see the dead will see him.

It never occurred to him to worry that Emma might see him. It doesn't occur to him now. If he's afraid at all, it's of the sharp edge of ridiculous hope. He has never loved anyone the way he loves Emma. When she lifts a hand, palm up, it's the most natural thing in the world to reach out to take it.

It's the most natural thing in the world, but he's dead, and she's not. She can *see* him. He can see her. Touching doesn't happen, for the dead; it's too much to hope for.

He feels the shock of her palm beneath his. His hand doesn't pass through hers. Before he can withdraw, she closes her fingers around his, tightens them. And, god, she is so *warm*.

"Hello, Nathan," she whispers.

"Hello, Em."

There's so much he wants to say to her. So much he wants to explain. There's so much groveling to do, for one. Maybe he'll start with that. But the words stick on the right side of his mouth, and as he stares into her eyes, his gaze drifting to her parted lips, they desert him.

He hugs her, instead. He reaches out, pulls her into his arms, tucks her head beneath his chin. He's dead. He's dead, but he can *feel* her. She smells of shampoo and soap.

He wants to apologize. He doesn't. He holds her instead, amazed at the warmth of her. But he always was. They stand together in the darkness until Emma begins to shudder. He thinks she's crying, but he pulls back to catch her chin, to pull her face up.

She's not crying. Oh, she *is*, but she's not weeping. She's shivering. She's shivering as if it's winter and she's caught outside without a coat.

He lets go of her. He feels the loss of her touch as a profound physical pain. He feels cold again, but this time, the cold is harsh. Isolating. And he understands, as her eyes widen, as her brows gather in the way they do when something confuses her, that the warmth he feels—he's stealing it.

Emma . . . Emma is like the Queen of the Dead. Like her, and nothing at all alike.

*I want you there, Nathan. You have an opportunity that very, very few of the dead will ever have.*

Nathan is afraid. Three months ago, Emma was his quiet space—one of the few in which he could be entirely himself. She knew him. He knew her. He thought he knew her. But the Emma Hall he fell in love with couldn't touch the dead.

Emma is a Necromancer.

Petal whines, and Emma glances at the wet nose he's shoved into her palm. She feeds him a Milk-Bone, but she tries not to take her eyes off Nathan, as if she's afraid he'll just disappear. Nathan knows the look.

Emma is a Necromancer with a whiny, half-deaf dog. She goes to school. She lives alone with her mother. She visits her dead boyfriend's grave. She lives *here*, among the living. And her eyes are still round, and she's still shivering. And grieving.

"You promised," she whispers. She's not smiling. There's no humor in her voice.

"This is the best I can do." He almost hugs her again, but balls his hands into fists instead.

Her face is wet with tears, shining with them. He always hated making her cry. Being dead hasn't changed that. He can't stand so close to her without touching her. He wants to kiss her. He wants to cup her face in his hands.

He heads toward his grave instead. The wreath of standing flowers is new. The petals that adorn Emma's legs—the few she hasn't managed to brush off—are scattered across the ground in ones and twos, but the flowers themselves haven't wilted or dried. He recognizes his mother's hand in this. His mother. He closes his eyes.

When he opens them, Emma is standing by his side. She's still shivering.

"Does my mother come here often?"

"Often enough. I don't see her. I think she must come after work."

"You?"

"It's quiet, here. Good quiet."

Which isn't an answer. He doesn't press. It's never been hard to talk to Emma before. It's hard now. What can you say to your girlfriend when you're dead? Apologies won't cut it, but beyond apologies, there's not a lot he can offer.

She holds out a hand. Nathan keeps both of his in his pockets. When she says his name, he shakes his head. "I'm making you cold. I'll walk you home."

"I'm not sure I want to be home right now."

Home, for Nathan, is where Emma is. God, he wants to touch her. He finds it hard to look at her; she's always been beautiful, to him. Now, she's luminescent.

# ⌒ Chapter 1

"Get your feet off my dashboard."

Chase, slumped in the passenger seat, grinned. "What? My boots are clean." The skin around his left eye had passed from angry purple to a sallow yellow; it clashed with his hair. In Eric's opinion, everything did. "And I'm wearing a seat belt."

"Seat belts," Eric said, sliding behind the wheel and adjusting its height, "are supposed to be worn across the hips, not the ribs. What did the old man say?"

"Long version or short version?"

"Shorter the better."

"Tell me about it." Chase's grin sharpened. "But I had to sit through the long version. No reason why you should get off easy."

"I'm driving. Don't make me fall asleep at the wheel."

"Couldn't make your driving any worse."

Eric pushed a CD into the player.

"You bastard." Chase was flexible enough to remove his feet from the dash and hit eject before more than two bars had played. He wasn't fond of perky singers. Gender didn't matter. Eric ignored them, but Chase couldn't. They were fingernails-against-blackboard painful to him. "You know I'd rather you stabbed me. In the ear, even."

"I'm driving or I'd seriously consider it. What did the old man want?"

"We've got a problem."

Eric reached for the CD again. Chase grabbed it and threw it out the window, barely pausing to open the window first.

"We've got three Necromancers, just off the plane. Old man thinks there's a fourth." Chase appeared to consider throwing out the rest of Eric's collection as well.

"Thinks?"

"Yeah. He can't pin him down."

Eric grimaced. "Why does he think there's a fourth?"

"Margaret insists."

Shit. "She recognized him."

"I wasn't the one questioning her. The old man was in a foul mood. You want to tell him he's wrong?" Chase fished in his pocket and pulled out a phone. Eric glanced at it.

"Driving, remember? When did they get in?"

"Yesterday. We had two addresses; neither was good."

"They take a cab?"

"Yeah. They were careful," he added.

Eric swore.

"He also reminds you we've got two midterms tomorrow."

"Midterms? Are you kidding me?"

Chase dangled the phone under Eric's nose again.

"This is getting unreal."

"Tell me about it. I've got the same midterms, and apparently my marks are crap compared to yours." Chase slid his feet back up on the dashboard. "We've got two addresses. Margaret supplied them. We're supposed to head over to the first one tonight." He frowned as he glanced out the window. "Is that Allison?"

Eric glanced at the side mirror. Allison Simner, in a puffy down coat, head bent into the wind, walked through the crisp November air beside another classmate. "And Michael."

"Stop the car and let me out."

"Chase—"

"What? She took notes."

Allison walked Michael home after school, as she had done for most of their mutual school life. It wasn't that he needed the company or the implied protection of another person, although he might once have. Now it was just part of their daily routine, and it was almost peaceful.

But Emma usually joined them. For the past two days, she hadn't. She'd explained her absences to Michael, and Michael—given his natural difficulty recognizing subtle social cues, such as white lies—accepted her yearbook committee excuses at face value. Allison tried. She wasn't her mother; worry was not her middle name, maiden name, or, on bad days, her entire name.

But her mother's best friend hadn't developed the ability to see the dead. She hadn't been targeted by Necromancers. She hadn't almost died in a fire that no one else could see, let alone feel, in an attempt to save a child who was *already* dead.

Allison's best friend, Emma, had. And it wasn't just that Emma could see the dead; if Emma touched ghosts, everyone else could see them, too. They'd learned that the hard way, at the hospital: Emma had grabbed onto her father's ghost because she didn't want him to leave.

And who could blame her? She hadn't seen her dad for the eight years he'd been dead.

But Allison had seen him, that night in the hospital. Michael had seen him. Emma's mother had seen him. And Eric. Eric had seen him as well. It had been disturbing, but—being able to see your dad, when he wasn't dangerous and he didn't look much different from the last time you'd seen him—wasn't inherently scary.

All the stuff that had happened after was.

Well, not Andrew Copis, the child who had died in the fire. And not his grieving mother, because if Emma wanted or needed to see her dad, Maria Copis was a hundred times worse: She *needed* to see her son. Emma was willing to walk through fire—literal fire—to help that happen, and Allison got that. She understood why.

What she didn't understand were the parts that happened directly afterward: the Necromancers. Two men and one woman, armed, had stopped their car outside of the house in which the child had died, gotten out of it, and pulled guns. Allison had been carrying Maria Copis' youngest child, a son. They had pointed the gun at the *baby*, and they had dragged Allison to Andrew Copis' burned-out house—in order to threaten Emma.

To threaten Emma, and to—to kill Eric and Chase.

Eric and Chase had survived. The Necromancers hadn't. But it had been so close. And the death of the Necromancer in charge, Merrick Longland, if he hadn't lied about his name, had been anything but fast. Chase had been covered in blood before he'd stopped stabbing and slashing at him.

Allison didn't watch horror movies. She found the violence in most of them too intense. She knew people who loved them, and she'd never understood why. Now she felt as if she were living on the edge of one. Predictably, she hated it.

She hated it because Michael was trapped on the same edge, and Emma was at the center of it. Allison could step away. She could turn her back. She could hide under the figurative bed with her hands over her ears. But if she did that, she was walking away from Emma. And Emma was no better prepared to be the star of a horror movie than either of her friends. Allison's fear was intense, and it made her feel so guilty.

Michael didn't know how to walk away. Michael didn't talk about the Necromancers—but Emma had asked him not to. Allison didn't talk about them because to talk about them, she had to think about them.

Then again, when something wasn't actively distracting her, it was hard not to think about them.

There had been no new Necromancers, but Chase had made it clear that it was only a matter of time—and at that, not a lot of it.

Allison usually walked Michael to his door, where she would wait to say hello to his mother. As a much younger child, she would then give his mother a report of the school day; as a teenager she'd continued more or less out of habit. She filled Mrs. Howe in on the positive or outstanding things, upcoming field trips, or perturbations in Michael's schedule.

Allison had avoided that at-the-door conversation for the past couple of weeks.

Michael's mother, being a mother, was worried about her son, because she knew there was something wrong. Michael didn't lie, so he'd told her he couldn't talk about it. His mother was not an idiot; she was pretty certain that Emma and Allison had some idea what was going on.

Allison wasn't Michael; she could—and on rare occasions did—lie. But she'd never been great at it, and it left her feeling horrible about herself for weeks afterward. She did the next best thing—she avoided the questions.

It was only as she was scurrying away from Michael's driveway, like a criminal, that Chase caught up with her.

Chase was almost a head taller than Allison.

Allison had never been tall. Emma was taller and more slender, with straight hair that fell most of the way down her back. On bad days, Allison envied her and wondered what Emma saw in her. Emma had a lot of friends.

Stephen Sawoski, in eighth grade, had answered the question. "Pretty girls don't want to have pretty friends—they hang around the plain girls 'cause it makes them look better." He'd sneered as he said it. Allison could still see his expression if she tried. She didn't really avoid it, either, because of what happened next: Emma had taken her milk, in its wet, box container, opened it, and then poured half of it into Stephen's lap.

The expression on his face then was *also* one Allison never forgot.

"If I wanted to hang around ugly people just to look better," Emma had said to Stephen, while Allison gaped like a fish out of water, "I'd spend more time with you. Come on, Allison, Michael's waiting."

Allison was plain. It was true. Emma offered, every so often, to help her change that if she wanted to do the work. But she didn't. No amount of work would make her look like Emma. Stephen was obnoxious, but he wasn't wrong—about the being plain. He was wrong about the friendship. She held on to that.

She glanced up at Chase.

He smiled. "You took notes," he said.

"I did. I can email them, if you want them. Biology?"

"And English. You're heading home?"

She nodded. "I have a pretty boring life."

"Not recently."

"I *like* having a pretty boring life." She started to walk. Chase shortened his stride and fell in beside her, hands in his jacket's pockets. Fire had singed his shock of red hair, and he'd been forced to cut it—but even short, it was the first thing anyone noticed.

"You really do," he replied. "Look—things are going to get crazy."

She didn't miss a step. "When?"

"Does it matter? You're not cut out for this shit. You, Michael, the rest of your friends—you've never lived in a war zone."

She had a pretty good idea of where this conversation was going: straight downhill. Allison didn't like confrontation. She didn't like to argue. Usually, there wasn't a lot to argue about. "None of us are cut out for this."

"Eric and I are."

Allison nodded agreement and stared at the sidewalk. She was three blocks away from home.

"Emma's part of this."

She shoved her hands into her pockets, which weren't really built for it, and lowered her chin. Chase had saved her life. She had to remember that Chase had saved her life. He'd almost died doing it. What had she done? Nothing. Nothing useful. "Emma didn't choose to be part of it."

"Choice doesn't matter. She has none."

Allison started to walk more quickly, not that there was any chance of leaving Chase behind if he was determined. He was.

"But you do. You've got the choice that I didn't have."

She stopped walking, her hands sliding out of her pockets to her hips. "And I am *making* a choice."

It was clear, from his expression, that he thought it was the wrong choice. "You think you can just duck your collective heads and the bullets will miss."

"No, I don't. But I know Emma."

"Really? I haven't noticed she's spending a lot of time with you recently."

That stung. "I'm her friend, not her cage."

"You don't understand how Necromancers work. You don't understand what they *become*."

"I understand Emma. Emma is *not* going to become a monster just because you're afraid of her!" Straight downhill. Like an avalanche.

"Why don't you ask her what she's been doing the past couple of days?"

"Because I trust her. If she wants to tell me, she'll tell me."

"And will she tell Michael?"

She could see him switching lanes. She let him do it, too; she was angry.

"If you're capable of making the decision to put your life on the line, is he? Are you willing to let him make the same choice?"

"Michael. Is. Not. A. Child."

"That's why he needs an entire clique of babysitters?"

"If Michael hadn't been at Amy's party, Emma would already be lost. In case you've forgotten, Merrick Longland had us *all* ensnared. None of your party tricks saved either you or Eric!"

". . . Party tricks?"

"Training. Whatever. Michael wasn't affected by Longland—but *you* were. And Michael knows it. We all know it. I get that you don't understand how we work—but if you try to break it, I'll—"

He folded his arms across his chest and stared pointedly down at her. "Yes? We're finally getting to the good part. You'll what? Scream at me? Cry?"

She wanted to punch him. Sadly, she'd never punched anyone in her life; if she'd thought she had any chance of landing one, she might have tried.

*Chase saved your life. He almost died saving your life.* "Probably both."

He looked down at the top of her head, and then he laughed. It was almost rueful. "You understand that I don't want to see you hurt, right?"

She did. But she also understood that there were all kinds of hurt in life, and he didn't count the one that she was most afraid of: losing her best friend. "I have to go. My mom's staring out the window."

"And she's not going to be happy that her daughter's shouting at a stranger?"

"No." She took three deep breaths, because deep breaths always helped. Chase made her so angry. She'd never met anyone who could make her so angry. Stephen Sawoski had made her feel ugly, invisible, unwanted—but never angry. Not like this. He'd made Emma angry though.

And maybe that made sense. Allison wasn't much good at sticking up for herself. She never had been, not when it counted. But she could stick up for her friends. She trusted her instincts where they were concerned.

"Your mom just disappeared," he told her.

Allison exhaled. "You might as well come to the house," she told him. "Because if you don't, she's going to come out."

"I really don't need to meet your mother."

"You should have thought of that before you followed me home."

Chase could be friendly. He could be charming. Allison had seen both. He had a genuine smile, a sense of humor, and a way of turning things on their side that mostly suggested a younger brother. Someone else's younger brother. Allison, however, was full up on younger brothers, given Tobias, the one she had. She searched the windows of the upper floor with sudden anxiety. If he embarrassed her in front of Chase, she'd have to strangle him. No Toby was visible from the street.

Allison headed toward her front door. Chase lagged behind, losing about three inches of height at the top of the driveway. She looked back at him. "Don't even think of running."

"Is it that obvious?"

"You smile when you're facing armed Necromancers. You charge *into* green fire. Compared to that, meeting my mother is terrifying?"

"I don't meet a lot of mothers."

"No, you don't, do you? Mine doesn't bite. Mostly. I'd suggest you drop any discussion of Emma, killing Emma, or abandoning her, though. I come by my temper honestly." She put her hand on the doorknob and added, "She also approves of Michael."

"Everyone does."

"Not really. But Michael's a kind of litmus test. People who see Michael as a person are generally people you can trust. People who dismiss him or treat him like he's a two year old, not so much."

"I don't follow."

"People who treat him as if he's a child see what they want to see; they don't see what's there."

"Me being one of those people."

"Not sure yet. You might have been trying to be manipulative."

"And that's not worse?"

"It's bad—but it's not worse. Not really. I know how to handle guilt."

Chase laughed as she opened the door. Her mother was buttoning up her coat. "Mom, I'd like you to meet Chase Loern. Chase, this is my mother."

Her mother held out a hand; Chase shook it. "I'm one of the new kids," he told her. "Allison finds me when I get lost between classes. I'd have built an impressive late-slip collection without her."

"He's lying," her daughter added cheerfully.

"Lying? Me?" The slow smile that spread across his face acknowledged a hit with a wry acceptance and something that felt like approval.

Allison's mother took her coat off as Allison removed her scarf. "Chase is behind on assignments," she said. "And he hasn't figured out how to use the electronic blackboard—yet." The last word was said in a dire tone. She took off her coat as well, reaching for a hanger to hand to Chase. He stared at it.

"You're not wearing that jacket in here—my mother will turn the heat up twenty degrees if she thinks you're cold, and the rest of us will melt."

He slid out of his jacket. Allison noticed that his eyes were sharper; he surveyed the hall—and the stairs and doors that led from it—as if his eyes were video equipment and he was doing a fancy perimeter sweep. She should have found it funny. Or annoying. She didn't.

She wondered, instead, what Chase's life was actually like. She didn't ask; her mother had headed directly for the kitchen, and Allison was about to drag Chase up to her room, which was the one room in the house in which her younger brother was unlikely to cause *too* much embarrassment.

Chase followed, looking at the staircase the same way he looked at the rest of the house: as if it were alien, and hostile at that. She didn't know a lot about Chase. Except that he made her angry and that he'd saved her life.

She headed straight for her desk when she reached her room and counted her pens. "I don't really need a brother, do I?"

Chase laughed. "What did he do?"

"He seems to think that he's working in an office, and stealing office supplies is a perk. This," she added, pointing to the penholder, "would be the office supply depot."

"He's younger?"

"Yes, or he'd already be dead."

"None of you seem to use pens much."

"It's the principle."

He laughed again. He had an easy, friendly laugh. Hearing it, it was hard to imagine that he'd killed people. But she didn't have to imagine it; she'd seen it. She took her tablet out of her backpack and plunked it on the desk, plugging it in before she opened it. "Biology and English. You'll actually get these? I notice you didn't bring your computer with you."

"I'll get them. I don't have much study time in the queue tonight." And there it was again: the edge, the harshness.

*Wouldn't you be harsh? If your entire life was devoted to killing mass murderers, wouldn't you?* But . . . he'd come to kill Emma, and Emma was not a mass murderer. And maybe he was staying to find proof that she would never become one. That was the optimistic way of looking at it. The pragmatic version was different: He was staying until she did, at which point he'd kill her.

Which meant he'd be here a long time.

She turned around; Chase was standing in the middle of the room, staring at the walls. The walls in Allison's room were not bare. She had posters, pictures, and one antique map, which had been a gift from her much-loved grandfather, covering everything that wasn't blocked by furniture. Even her closet door was covered; the one mirror in the room was on the inside of the door.

"This is a scary room," Chase finally said, staring pointedly at the *Hunger Games* poster to one side of the curtained window.

"Scary how?"

"If that bookshelf falls over, it'll kill you in your sleep. Who thought it was a good idea to bolt it into the wall *above* your head?"

She raised a hand.

"Have you read all of these?"

"Yes. Multiple times. I don't keep everything, just the ones I know I'll re-read. My brother knows better than to touch my books," she added, as he reached for the shelf.

He grinned. "I'm not your brother."

"No. You're a guest, so you get to keep your hand." She smiled as she said it, but he wasn't looking at her; he was looking at *Beauty*.

"So . . . you come home, you do homework, and you read a lot."

"Mostly." Her phone rang. She fished it—quickly—out of her bag because she recognized the ringtone. It was Emma. Or someone who had stolen Emma's phone.

"Hey, Ally—are you doing anything after dinner?"

"Studying a bit."

"Want to come walk a deaf dog with me?"

"Not a random deaf dog, no—but I'll come for Petal."

Emma laughed. "He's the only one I have. Is something wrong?"

"No. Nothing. Want to come pick me up or should I meet you at your place?"

"I'll head over there. Mom's not home, so I'll make something to eat here." She paused. "I have something to tell you. It's not a bad thing," she added quickly, because she knew Allison came from a long line of champion worriers. Petal started to bark in the background. When Petal set up barking, it never stayed in the background.

"I'll talk to you later," Allison said.

Chase was apparently still perusing her bookshelves, but Allison wasn't fooled. "That was Emma?"

She almost didn't answer. *Chase saved your life, but he also probably saved Emma's.* "Yes. She wants to talk—later. You've met her dog."

Chase nodded, putting the book back on the shelf and withdrawing.

"We're going to walk him. Look, can you sit down? I don't care where. It's hard to talk when you're standing there looking down at me."

He sat on the edge of the bed—probably because it was the farthest away.

She turned to her computer and found the Biology and English notes he'd asked for. She wasn't sure they'd do him much good; Chase didn't really understand how to study. But she sent them to him anyway before she turned.

He was sitting absolutely still, watching her, his elbows on his knees, his hands loosely clasped between them. "I don't hate Emma," he said.

"No?"

"Let's pretend that I believe you. That Emma—the Emma you know—is never going to become another Merrick Longland. She's never going to learn how to use the power she has. It's never going to define her."

This was not a surrender, and Allison knew it; the tone of his voice was too measured for that. But she nodded, waiting.

"They're not going to leave her alone." He exhaled, running his hands through his hair. "They know—roughly—where she is. They'll know exactly where she is, soon."

This, Allison believed. "How do we stop them?"

He stared at her, his eyes rounding, as if he couldn't believe the stupidity. "Eric's spent his entire adult life trying to do just that. So has the old man."

"Yes, but you're hunting proto-Necromancers, if I understand anything. You're stopping their numbers from growing. How do we stop them, period?"

"Kill their Queen," he replied. He might as well have said, *kill their god*, given his tone.

She stared at him.

"It's complicated. I'd say it's impossible."

"If we kill their Queen, it stops?"

"If we kill their Queen, the dead are free," he replied. "Wherever it is the dead go, they'll go."

"Andrew Copis—"

"Yes, there'll always be some who get stuck or trapped. But they won't stay that way forever, and they won't be able to hurt anyone who isn't a Necromancer by birth. But it's not going to happen."

She swallowed.

"I don't think you have it in you to kill. Not yet. Probably not ever. It's not a problem the Necromancers have."

"I noticed."

"Good." He lifted his chin, exposing his Adam's apple. "Emma might not have it in her, either. But they won't stop. So let's go back to that: Emma is in danger here."

"And because she's in danger, I'm in danger."

He tensed; he heard the edge creep into her voice. She tried to stop her hands from balling into fists, since she wasn't going to use them anyway.

"If you can't step away, yes. I know you don't want to do it. If you were the type of person who could, I probably wouldn't be here. I mean, here, in this room, in this house. I wouldn't be having this moronic conversation. I wouldn't be—" he fell silent, and his expression was so raw, Allison had to look away.

## ⌒ Chapter 2

Chase with downcast eyes was probably for the best; the door—which was ajar—swung open, and her mother walked into the room carrying a tray. "I didn't ask what Chase drinks," she said apologetically.

Chase shook his head. "I don't drink when I'm working."

Her mother laughed, because Chase was grinning. "And I don't serve alcohol to minors." She set the tray on the desk beside Allison's computer, which was conveniently open at a screen full of biology notes.

"I'm going to walk Petal with Em after dinner," Allison said.

"Make sure you wear a heavier coat. It's not getting any warmer out there."

Allison reddened but nodded, and her mother left. "It's hot chocolate," she told Chase. "And bagels; there's jam. And apples."

"I can see that." He took his phone out of his pocket. Allison hadn't heard it ring. He glanced at the screen and grimaced dramatically.

Allison laughed.

"I'm disappointed," he said, with mock gravity. "You didn't strike me as someone who mocks the pain of others."

"You laughed."

"I did not. And if I did, it's gallows humor." He took the mug she handed him and held it cupped in the palms of his hands—something Allison couldn't do, because the mugs were too hot. He also took the snacks and ate them. He was not a slow eater.

"You didn't eat lunch?"

"I did. All of mine and half of Eric's." He looked around the room again, his expression shifting into neutral. "If gets bad, we're going to have to run." Before she could speak, he said, "Yes, 'we' includes Emma."

Allison was silent. She didn't want to be left behind. But the future as Chase painted it was grim. If they had to leave the city on short notice—and short could mean none—where were they going to go? What were they going to do?

"I want to go with you, if you go."

"I know. I don't want to take you. If it were up to me, we'd already be gone."

"Where?"

Chase shrugged. "Wherever the old man sends us. He has the wallet. He doesn't normally hang around for this long—and he doesn't trust Emma, either."

"Did the old man train you?"

"Yeah. He and Eric."

"Could he train us?"

To her surprise, Chase didn't sneer; he didn't dismiss the idea out of hand. But he did empty his mug. He was tidy; he placed it back on the tray, along with the empty plate. Allison suspected he would have taken the tray back down to the kitchen if she'd finished as quickly.

She couldn't. She'd never been good at eating when upset.

Chase didn't have that problem—but he wouldn't, would he? All of his life, seen from Allison's vantage, was nothing *but* being upset. Any uneasiness Allison felt was probably trivial in comparison. And any pain. "Chase?"

"Yeah?"

"Promise you won't leave me behind?"

"I can't. I can promise I won't kill your best friend unless she deserves it. I can promise to be polite to your mother. I can promise to ask the old man about training you on really short notice. I don't know *why* I'd promise any of this—but I will. I can't promise to drag you out of your home and away from your family just so you can be a fugitive until the day you die." He ran his hands through his hair again and stood. "Don't ask.

"In return, I won't ask you to promise me that you'll keep your distance from Emma. I won't ask you to promise that you'll warn me when—if—things with Emma start to go downhill."

"Promise you'll stop nagging me?"

He sucked in air. "That's a borderline case. I can only promise to try." He exhaled again. "If Emma cared about you at all—"

Allison's expression tightened. "If she cared about me at all, she'd stay as far away from me as possible, is that it? She'd leave me because that was safest for me?"

"Yes."

"And if that wasn't what I wanted?"

"If you knew what we face pretty much continuously, you *would* want it."

The conversation was, once again, going straight downhill. "Chase, what's the worst thing that's ever happened to you?"

He stared at her for a long moment and then looked down at his phone. "I've got to run. Hopefully I won't see you tonight." He headed toward the door, then turned back, his brow an oddly broken line across the bridge of his nose.

"The worst thing that's ever happened to me? Not dying."

*Not dying.*

Allison saw Chase to the door and even saw him out; after he left the house, she watched him from the window, as if she were her mother. His hands were in his pockets, his shoulders hunched slightly against the brisk wind.

She brought the snack tray down to the kitchen, set the table, and ate dinner with her family while Toby grilled her about the redhead she'd brought home.

"Is he your boyfriend?" he asked, in the highly amused, singsong tone that annoyed older sisters the world over.

"No."

"Mo-om, is he Ally's boyfriend?"

"Eat your dinner, dear."

"Allison's got a boyfriend! Allison's got a boyfriend!"

"Tobias," her father said, coming—in one word—to her rescue. He did give Allison the careful once over, but asked none of the questions he was probably thinking.

"Allison is about to be minus a brother," Allison told the brother in question, through gritted teeth. This had the predictable effect—none. But aside from Michael, which boys had she ever brought home? Nathan, but he'd come with Emma.

She finished dinner in slightly embarrassed silence and retreated to her room. She even picked up a book, but her mind bounced off the words instead of sinking beneath them.

*Not dying.*

Emma had said that, once, two weeks after Nathan's death. She hadn't used the same words, but it didn't matter. What Chase saw when he chose his words was what Emma saw when she looked into a future that, now and forever, had no Nathan in it.

There had been nothing she could do for Emma, and she'd hated it—fluttering helplessly to one side, uncertain whether or not any comfort she tried to offer would be intrusive or make things worse. She understood Emma's loss, she understood Emma's grief—but she'd never known how much room to give. When did giving someone space become abandoning them or ignoring them?

What saved her was understanding that it was Nathan, not Emma, who had died. Allison knew she couldn't fill the empty, collapsing space that Nathan had left in Emma's psyche—but Allison wasn't Nathan. She didn't *have* to fill it. She just had to make sure that the space she did occupy in the same psyche was a safe one. It was best-friend territory, not love-of-life territory, but it was important.

Allison had watched Emma withdraw. It wasn't completely obvious to begin with; Emma went through all the motions. She took care of her appearance, she did all her schoolwork, she spent time at school with her friends, she watched as their relationships began or fell apart. But none of it mattered anymore.

Michael mattered. Allison mattered. Petal mattered.

Why? Because the three of them needed Emma, and she couldn't just turn and walk away from them.

Nathan was a shadow that could fall, unexpectedly, over any conversation. A line of a dialogue. The punch line to a joke. A piece of familiar clothing on an entirely unfamiliar body. Snatches of music. Even food. Emma would flinch. She always withdrew when it happened, but she didn't always leave.

Both of Allison's parents were still alive. So was her brother. The Simner family didn't have pets, except goldfish, and while burying goldfish had seemed enormously heartbreaking in kindergarten, she knew it didn't and couldn't compare. The only death she'd experienced had been her grandfather's, and she had been younger. Death hadn't seemed real. Her grandfather hadn't lived with them. She had come to understand that death meant permanent absence—but it hadn't shattered her.

She could sometimes hear the echoes of his voice, and pipe smoke pulled his image from her memories, because she'd liked his pipe. Her mother, not so much.

Emma had lost her father and her boyfriend. She'd had eight years to recover from the loss of her father. She'd had less than four months to recover from Nathan. And Allison didn't lie to herself: Those months were *not* a recovery. They were a tightrope act, an effort to find and maintain emotional balance when you'd just lost half of yourself.

Now, Emma could see the dead.

She could see the father she'd missed and longed for for half her life. And she knew that if she waited long enough, she could see Nathan as well. There was no balance in that. She could see Nathan. The fact that he was dead and she wasn't wouldn't matter. Not yet.

Maybe not ever. Emma's dad had told her that it took two years for the dead to find their way back to their old homes and old lives. Allison knew Emma. Emma would wait.

The wind was loud beyond the windows, but Emma would be here soon; Allison headed downstairs to get ready.

She was worried. She hadn't told Chase she was worried, because he wouldn't understand, and it would only make his suspicions more unreasonable.

Petal came to the door, dragging Emma behind him; he'd never been clear on the concept of leashes. When he approached a door from the outside, he wagged his stump and bounced up and down, but he didn't bark. Allison wasn't Michael; she didn't have a ready supply of doggie snacks in the house. Petal liked her anyway.

Emma, dressed for the cold, looked nervous. Nervous but happy.

It was a kind of happy Allison recognized, although she hadn't seen it for four months. She stepped outside, closed the door at her back, and smiled as they headed down the driveway.

*I haven't noticed she's spending a lot of time with you.*

Allison had noticed. Seeing Emma's expression, seeing the way her gaze slid to her right—Allison was on her left and Petal, as always, was in the lead—she knew why. She knew exactly why. It wasn't the first time she had come second to Nathan.

But she also knew it hadn't *been* two years.

Chase was already suspicious. The old man—Ernest, if she remembered correctly—was suspicious. If Nathan was here only four months after his death, what did that say about Emma?

She bit her lip. It said nothing bad about Emma. Necromancers used some essential part of the dead—Allison hesitated to say "soul"—for power. There was no way Emma would do that to Nathan. Even if she knew how, and she didn't, Nathan would never become that source.

But he was here. He was here, by her side, and he shouldn't be.

*Well, where should he be?* she thought, in some disgust. Emma was happy. It was the troubled happy of early love—anxiety mixed with euphoria. Allison braced herself for Emma's news, and was surprised when Nathan's name wasn't the first thing out of her mouth.

"I don't understand my mother."

"My mother gave me a lecture about wearing warm clothing in November. In front of a guest."

Emma laughed. "It's different when someone else's mother does it."

It always was. Mercy Hall could worry at Emma like a pit bull, and Allison never found it embarrassing. Mercy Hall could worry about Allison, and she still didn't take it personally.

Petal took offense at a raccoon, which diverted Emma's attention. But she had something to say, and she came back to it, slightly sideways. "Have you talked to your parents?"

Allison was certain her eyes looked liked they were about to fall out of her face.

Emma laughed. "I'll take that as a no."

"My mother would never let me out of the house again. Ever. Why? Have you?"

The reply took longer. "I tried to talk to my mother. About my dad." She glanced at Allison. "She saw him, Ally. We all saw him, the first time."

"What did she say?"

"The first time? That she had an early morning meeting."

Mercy Hall was so not a morning person.

"The second time, that she had work to do. It was after dinner. The third time she came right out and said she didn't want to talk about it because she had nothing to say."

"She didn't ask you about . . ."

"Being able to see the dead? No. She asked me nothing. And I don't understand. I don't understand why."

Conversations with Chase went straight downhill. Sometimes they started at a very steep incline. Conversations with Emma were different. They went off the map. But not all terrain off-map was safe. It's not that Allison and Emma had never had a fight; they'd had a few. But fighting wasn't what they did. Allison could see the direction this conversation might take. She wanted to avoid it.

"Why doesn't she want to know?" Emma almost demanded.

"Is she pretending she never saw him?"

Emma frowned. "More or less. She won't out and out deny it. She just won't talk. It's like—like she doesn't care. Like she doesn't *want* to see him." She shoved her hand—the one that wasn't holding Petal's leash—into her pocket and lowered her chin against the wind, in a frustrated, moody silence.

"She doesn't know about the dead." Allison spoke because the silence was growing uncomfortable. Most silences with Emma were peaceful. This wasn't. Allison had known her for long enough to pick up on the difference. "She doesn't know why she saw her husband. You know. I know. And honestly, Em? Sometimes even I find it disturbing."

"But—if she listened. If she listened to me, she could *talk* to my dad. He's right there, Ally. He still keeps an eye on both of us."

"Have you asked your dad?"

Emma was silent. It was still not the good silence. Petal made enough noise for two. Toronto had a *lot* of garbage-raiding raccoons.

"Do you know what I would have done?" Emma asked.

Allison looked at her best friend's face in the streetlight. The outer shell of socially adept, polite Emma had cracked.

"I would have done *anything*. If it'd been me—if I'd been my mother and I'd seen Nathan at the hospital—I would have done anything just to be able to talk to him again."

"Em, your dad died eight years ago."

"And that's all it takes to forget him? Eight years? He wasn't just a grade school crush, Ally. He was her husband. It's been eight years for me, too, but *I* wanted to see him. I wanted to talk to him again."

When a conversation was going straight downhill, you could still control your descent. You could just stop talking. Going off-map sometimes revealed surprising cliffs in the conversational landscape. Allison felt the edge of one beneath her feet. She wasn't certain how steep the drop would be.

"He's dead. Even if your mother could talk to him again, he'd still be dead. She can't touch him without freezing. She can't talk to him without you. If you're there, she can't say any of the personal stuff."

"It would still be better than nothing."

Allison wasn't so certain.

\*     \*     \*

"Chase, pay attention."

Chase frowned. He didn't argue; Eric was right. He wasn't paying attention. Not to the streets and the dwindling stream of people getting in the way of their stakeout. Not to the cars that were parked on the street, and not to the ones that had slowed to leisurely crawls in search of parking.

He wore three rings, all etched with symbols; one was solid silver, and two had iron cores. He passed his hand through the air; nothing wavered. There was no visible distortion. He slid his phone out of his pocket.

"What's with you?"

"Checking to make sure you got the right address." He slid the phone back into his jacket pocket, because nothing had changed. They'd been sent to midtown to check out two addresses. "We're up," he added, as the door to the apartment building swung open.

There were multiple ways to get into a building. Chase had been an electrician, an apprentice plumber, a cable technician, a phone technician—in short, one of the invisible people who kept things running. It was easiest, when necessary. In countries like this, it was mostly necessary. Money opened doors—but only figurative ones.

He vastly preferred to hunt—and kill—Necromancers in the streets of the city. Any city. Buildings were too easy to trap, too easy to bug, too easy to monitor. The Queen of the Dead didn't care much for modern life—and modern life was therefore their best advantage.

But they didn't catch all of the proto-Necromancers, as Allison called them. And some of the ones that slipped through their fingers were also part of the modern age. Given that most of them were teenagers, their understanding of the finicky bits of modern life only scratched the surface; most of them didn't know how their phones worked or where their internet connections came from.

Then again, Necromantic magic was generally more useful than cell phones when it came to communication.

They entered the apartment. "Number significant?" Chase asked, nodding at the door.

Eric shook his head. "I don't think they had the time." He nodded toward the kitchen and the dining room beyond it. Chase headed that way; Eric headed to what were probably bedrooms and closets.

The living and dining area was clean. Eric whistled, and Chase headed to the bedroom. "Got something?"

"They're here." There was a mirror in the room, on the desk; Eric had already covered it.

"All of them?"

"Two." He lifted passports, tossed them to Chase, who frowned. One of the two was twenty. One appeared to be in his thirties. "Not high in the upper echelons of the Court."

"Good. They didn't leave much."

"You think they've already gone hunting?"

Eric nodded. "Grab their passports."

"Cash?"

"Some. Not much. They didn't leave wallets here."

"Robes?"

Eric shook his head. "They're either wearing them or they don't intend to grab and run."

"You think they're going to kill her?"

Eric frowned. "Emma opened the door," he finally said.

"She'll know."

Eric nodded. "Every other Necromancer alive might have missed it, but the Queen will know. She won't know how Emma managed it, but she has to suspect."

"The lamp."

"The lamp. If Emma dies, she won't get her hands on the lamp." Eric was examining the phone. He swore.

"What?"

"Car. Now."

The only person Chase worried about was Chase Loern. That had been his truth for a long time now. Eric was his equal—or, on a bad day, his better; he could take care of himself. So could Chase. Anyone who couldn't was dead and buried in some unmarked grave somewhere.

Chase wasn't afraid of death—he just wanted the bastards to *work* for it. So far, they hadn't worked hard enough. Rania had called him suicidal, back in the day. She'd been a lot like Eric—proper, well mannered, well educated. Unlike Eric, she'd become a casualty.

Chase had no illusions about death. Death was not a peaceful end. It wasn't a release into the great, happy beyond. There was no heaven waiting, no divine presence. Only the Queen of the Dead. If she found Chase, he'd be a figurative lamppost in her city—if he was lucky. Rumor had it she held a long grudge.

Then again, so did Chase. But he wasn't a Necromancer. His grudge wasn't worth much; he made it count by killing Necromancers. But it was a stalling action. Sooner or later, they were all going to end up in the same damn place.

*　　*　　*

"My mother's not like yours," Emma said. "We don't talk about important things in the Hall house. I don't know if that would be different if my dad hadn't died. I kind of doubt it, though. But she talked to me about Nathan. After he died. She talked about my dad. It was the first time I'd really thought of him as her husband. I mean, I knew—but he was my dad first.

"He was her husband. She lost him. She had me—but it wasn't the same. I have Petal," she added, with a wry smile.

"You're more important to your mother than Petal," Allison said. "Sorry, Petal."

Emma smiled. "We had that in common. The loss. The way we understood it. I knew she'd survived. So I knew I could." Her smile faded. "On some days, I didn't want to."

Allison knew.

"Maybe Dad wasn't as important to her as Nathan is to me. Have you ever noticed that people seem to love less as they get older? I don't want that to happen to me." She swallowed. "If I forget him, Ally, if I reach a point where talking to him, seeing him, isn't important enough—what was the point?"

"Emma—"

Emma smiled. "Hold this?" she asked, handing Petal's leash to Allison without waiting for a reply. Allison took it in gloved hands; they were numb. It was a cold night, even for November.

Emma removed her right glove; Allison held her breath as Emma held her hand out to the night air. She held her breath when Nathan materialized beside her best friend. He wasn't dressed for November; he was dressed for summer. The cold wouldn't touch him now. Aside from Emma and people like her, nothing could.

"Hey," Nathan said. It was dark enough she couldn't see the color of Emma's eyes, although she knew they were a lighter shade of brown. She couldn't see the color of Nathan's, either.

For a long moment, she said nothing. And then, exhaling, she said, "Hey, Nathan."

The problem with being Emma's best friend was that Emma understood her. Allison smiled. She *did*. But the expression was half-frozen; it was like a mask. Emma knew. Emma needed Allison to be happy for her, and the best Allison could do was try.

But it was November, it was cold, and Allison knew that touching the dead sucked warmth and heat out of Emma. "We should—we should go inside," she suggested. It was a compromise.

Emma's smile was fragile, and it broke. Her hand—her bare, gloveless hand—twined with Nathan's, tightened.

"It's cold," Allison said again. "And you're not going to get any warmer if you—if Nathan—" She shook her head. She had Petal's leash, but Petal was no longer tugging at it; he'd doubled back. Allison watched as he headed toward Nathan, whining anxiously. His stub of a tail was still. He wasn't growling. But he wasn't happy, either—and he'd always liked Nathan.

They all watched as he walked back and forth through Nathan, as if he were a particularly solid shadow. He whined, and Emma eventually tried to feed him—but for once he wasn't interested in food.

Allison took the leash more firmly in hand and began to walk; Emma followed, Nathan held just as tightly.

It was quiet. It was the wrong type of quiet. Emma said nothing, but Allison knew the look. She wasn't happy, but she didn't want to start an argument about Nathan in front of Nathan. Allison didn't want to start an argument at all.

But she understood why Mercy had no desire to see her dead husband again. She was certain that Emma wouldn't see it the same way—and who could blame her? Ghosts didn't age. They didn't change. Their touch was cold enough to numb. They couldn't work. They couldn't eat. They couldn't *live*, or they wouldn't be dead.

Emma wasn't dead, but she stood in death's shadow—and she wanted to stay there.

*You don't understand*, Allison thought, because she knew that's what Emma wanted to say to her. And maybe it was true. But Nathan was dead. He was always, and forever, dead. She was afraid that Emma would join him.

And she couldn't say that. Not now. Maybe not ever. *Who is it hurting?*

*You, Emma. It's hurting you.*

But Emma would tell her she'd lived in a world of hurt since last July, and this was the first time she could see an end to that pain. There weren't many things you couldn't say to your best friend—but Allison was facing one of them now.

Emma's phone rang. Emma fished it out of her pocket without letting go of Nathan's hand, which was awkward; she was trembling with cold. Nathan watched her as she fumbled and then looked past her to meet Allison's eyes.

Allison wanted to talk to him about Emma—but that couldn't happen now. Anything Nathan heard, Emma would hear by default; she was his only conduit to the rest of the world. He knew she was worried. He probably even knew why; Nathan had never been stupid.

And he'd never been selfish, either.

"Em," he said, as she brought the phone to her cheek. "Let go. Ally's right. It's cold."

She ignored him. "Hello?" To Allison, she mouthed, *Eric.* "We're just out walking Petal. I'm with Allison. No, we're near the ravine, why?" Her eyes rounded. The phone slid from her face as she turned.

"What's happened?" Allison asked, voice rising.

"Eric says—Eric says we have two Necromancers incoming. He wants us to head to the cemetery. Now."

"Why the cemetery?"

"It's closest to where he and Chase are. They'll meet us there."

"I don't understand what the Necromancers want," Allison said, shortening the leash and picking up the pace.

Emma was silent for half a block. One phone call from Eric had turned quiet night shadows into dangerous omens. "Ally, I want you to go home."

Allison stared at her.

"They're not—they're not after you. If you go home now, you should be safe."

Allison felt a pang of something that was like anger. Or hurt. Hadn't she just had this argument? Coming from Emma, it was harder. Her hands were shaking. Her throat was dry. Speaking over the fear took work. "Don't."

"I don't want you hurt."

"Don't say it."

"If they're here, they're hunting me or Eric or Chase—"

Adrenaline made Allison's hands shake; it wasn't just the cold. The last time they'd seen Necromancers, they'd had guns. Allison never wanted to see them again. "If I go home and something happens to you—"

"Ally, what are you going to do if you don't go home and the Necromancers find us?"

"I don't know. We'll figure that out if it happens." Her eyes, made much larger by her glasses, narrowed.

Nathan reached up to touch Emma's cheek; his hand stopped an inch from skin and fell, curling into a brief fist. "Em, listen to Ally. She's right more often than she's wrong."

"You shouldn't be here, either," Allison told him. "You're dead. Necromancers use the dead for power—and if they don't have enough, they'll grab whatever they can reach."

Nathan shook his head. "I'm not in danger. I'm already dead. There's not a lot they can do to me to change that. There's a lot they can do to you—but you're staying." He hesitated, and then said, "If the dead have power to give to the living, I'm willing to give all I have to Emma."

Allison couldn't argue. She didn't tell Nathan that Emma didn't know how to take that power, and didn't know how to use it. Emma believed that—but Allison wasn't certain. Emma had walked into the phantasm of a fire that no one else could see unless she touched them. Emma had walked out again, hair singed, clothing black with soot.

Emma had given Maria Copis the ability to see her dead son—and the ability to pick him up and carry him, at long last, out of the fire that had killed him. If Em wasn't trained in magical, Necromantic magic, she could still do things that Allison couldn't explain. And could never hope to do herself.

But Emma's question hung in the air between them. Nathan at least had the sense to stand on the far side. *What can I do? If Necromancers come, what can I possibly do?*

They picked up the pace in the uncomfortable, heightened silence.

Emma didn't have to drag Petal with her; he hunkered down by her side, like a portable, living tank. The streets were dark; the streetlamps were high and unevenly spaced, and there were no houses on this side of the street. There were graves just beyond the fence that bounded the cemetery, and moonlight, although the background of city lights caused stars to fade from view on all but the clearest of nights.

Petal's growling grew deeper.

Allison stopped walking. In the street ahead, in the middle of a road that cars traveled on shortcuts, stood two men.

Had they just been walking, she wouldn't have noticed them. They wore normal winter coats, hats, faded jeans; one wore boots, the other, running shoes. One of them seemed to be about their age; the other was older.

They weren't walking, though. They were waiting. Their hands hung by their sides, and in the shadowed evening light, Allison saw that they wore no gloves. Emma slid her gloved hand out of her pocket and held it out to Allison who understood what she intended; she pulled Emma's glove off and shoved it into her own pocket for safekeeping.

"The dead are here," Nathan told them.

Emma knelt to let Petal off his leash and rose quickly. The rottweiler was growling now as if growling were breath.

"Emma Hall?" One of the two men said, after a long pause.

Emma nodded.

He lifted his hands, palm out, as if in surrender. Or as if he was trying to prove that he meant her no harm. As if. "We've come a long way, looking for you," he said. He took a step forward.

So did Petal.

"You're in danger, here," the younger man added. "We've come to bring you to safety."

"Why am I in danger?" Emma asked, as if meeting two strange men who knew her by name in the middle of the night near the cemetery was a daily occurrence. Allison heard the tremor in her voice, because she knew Emma so well.

Her own throat was dry.

"You're special, Emma. *We're* special, and you're like us. You're gifted. People won't understand what you can do. They'll fear it. If they can, they'll kill you. We're here to make sure that doesn't happen."

Allison was stiff and silent. The two men said something to each other; it was quiet enough that the feel of syllables traveled without the actual words. Emma swore. She let go of Nathan's hand, lifting hers as if to surrender. Nathan seemed to disappear. But Allison knew Nathan. He wouldn't leave Emma. Not now.

Neither would she.

"They have the dead with them," Emma whispered to Allison, although she faced straight ahead. Her voice dropped. "Four."

Allison wasn't Emma. She couldn't see the dead. But she didn't need to see them to understand what Emma meant. Necromancers derived their power from captive ghosts. Four was bad.

## ᔐ Chapter 3

Emma's hands were shaking; one was numb.

Allison had been right about one thing: Touching Nathan was no different from touching any other dead person. It leeched heat out of her hands, numbing them.

There were four ghosts chained to the two men who now approached. Two of them were women, one only slightly older than Emma or Allison and the other older than Emma's mother. The two boys, however, were exactly that: boys. One looked as if he could pass for six on a good day. The other she guessed had been nine or ten at the time of his death.

The dead, to Emma's eyes, looked very much as if they were still alive. There was one significant difference, though. She could never tell, looking at the dead, what color their eyes were. It didn't matter if she knew what the color had been before their death, either. Her father's eyes—and, more significant, Nathan's—were the same as the rest. They seemed slightly luminescent in the dark of night, but that luminescence shed no color; it was like an echo of the essence of light. Maybe it was pure reflection. Her father had told her that there was a place to which the dead were drawn and that, for roughly two years, that place was all they could see.

All they wanted to see.

Eye color wasn't the only thing the four dead people were missing. They lacked any expression at all as they stood silent, still, unmoving. In that, they looked like corpses. Emma knew she could scream at—or to—them, and they would hear as much as an actual corpse, and respond the same way. She thanked whatever god existed that Allison couldn't see them.

Nathan, however, could.

"Stay back," she told him, voice low. "Stay with me."

With the dead as escorts, the two men began to move; they walked slowly. Nathan started whistling the theme song to an old Western his dad used to watch. Emma wanted to laugh. She also wanted to run.

One of the two men gestured; white fire rose on either side of the road. It stretched from a point just behind the men to a point well behind where Emma, Allison, and Petal were. They now stood in a tunnel.

Allison's sharp intake of breath made it clear that the fire, unlike the ghosts, was visible.

"So," Emma said, backing up. "This is supposed to make me trust you?"

"No," the taller of the two men replied. "It's supposed to keep us safe." His eyes were now the color of a dead man's eyes, he'd absorbed so much power.

Emma stopped moving.

Eyes narrowed, she could see the delicate strands of golden light around the Necromancers' hands and wrists. If she were closer—and close was *so* not where she wanted to be—she would see those strands as chains, like the chains of a necklace or a delicate bracelet. Unlike jewelry, the chains ended in the figurative heart of a person—a dead person. If she could grab those chains, she could break them, depriving the Necromancers of the source of their power.

Petal was growling nonstop. Emma felt the hair on the back of her neck rise; she felt the howl of a sudden, arctic wind and turned, leaving her dog to keep watch.

The road behind her back was gone. In its place, rising up past the boughs of the old trees that lined the street on the wrong side of the fence, was a standing arch composed almost entirely of the same fire that blocked escape on two sides.

"We don't have time to explain things here," the tall man continued. "So we've arranged a little trip." He frowned, said something to the man beside him. Emma reached out and caught Allison's hand, pulling her close. As she did, strands of white flame shot out from the right side of the road and wrapped themselves around Allison. The fire was *cold*.

"Stop it!" Emma shouted. "Let her go!"

The taller man shook his head. "I'm sorry," he said, in a calm and reasonable voice. "But she's seen us, and she's not one of us. In future, you'll understand why it's important to leave no witnesses behind."

Emma grabbed the white strand that was tightening its grip on Ally's throat. It was bloody cold; ice would have been warmer. Contact with it numbed her fingers instantly.

*This is why I wanted you to run!* she thought, struggling—and failing—to get a grip on the tendril of fire. Ally was turning purple; her knees buckled. Petal leaped at the man who'd been doing most of the talking, and Emma couldn't even watch; she was trying—and failing—to force the fire to let go of her best friend's throat.

"Em," Nathan said. He caught her hand in his; his hands, like the hands of all the dead, were cold. She didn't try to pull away; she knew that Allison's only hope lay in Nathan. In his hands and in hers. Nathan was dead. Emma was a Necromancer. If she could use his power, she could save Ally.

"I'll go with you," she told the Necromancers. "I won't fight—but you've got to let her go."

"You'll go with us anyway," the younger of the two said.

The pressure of the strand didn't let up. Emma swallowed and began to pull the only power she had access to: Nathan's. He offered it; he offered it willingly. As she took it in, her hands began to tingle. No white glow gloved them; it wasn't that kind of binding. But it didn't matter. Emma could now see how the strand was connected to Allison, and she could—and did—melt it off. Allison was gasping for breath as Emma turned. The men were closer now; the younger of the two looked both annoyed and surprised.

The older just looked weary.

"It was the least painful way for her to die," he told Emma, in a gentle voice. "But there are others, and they are more certain." He gestured again, and this time—this time she recognized the fire that lay in his palm, like a roiling ball. It was green. Chase had called it soul-fire.

It had almost killed him—and it would kill Allison if it hit her.

Emma didn't *know* what to do with the power she had. She didn't know how to use it, how to defend herself—or anyone else—with it.

"Please," she said, voice low and shaking. "Just let her go. I'll go with you. I won't fight. Just—let her go."

The taller of the two shook his head, although there was a weight to his expression that hadn't been there before. "I can't," he replied. "It's against the law."

"Everything you're doing now is against the law!"

"Mortal law doesn't concern Necromancers, Emma Hall. It doesn't concern you anymore, although you don't understand that yet. You have a gift—"

"It's the same as yours," she said quickly, her hands now warm in Nathan's because she was drawing power from him. "It's the same as yours—and this is *not* how I want to use it!"

"You'll learn. All your friend loses is a few years. A few years, in the existence of the dead, is nothing."

"She's not dead—"

"She will spend far, far more of her existence dead than she will alive, even if she lives to see old age. Come, Emma. If you feel you must, in the decades to come, you can return here and find her; if you grow in power and stature within the City, you can command her, and she will come to where you wait."

He threw the fire.

He threw it, and Emma reached out and caught it with her arm; it splashed, as if it were liquid, and spread instantly across the whole of her coat. Real fire wouldn't have done that.

The Necromancer's eyes widened in either shock or horror. He was still too far away to tell.

Allison was nearer, and she started to reach out, but Nathan barked at her, and she stopped. She could see Nathan now. Emma was holding onto him.

Emma was doing more than that. The fire wasn't hot, but it wasn't cold. It burned, but it didn't burn hair or skin; it burned something beneath it.

"You fool!" the Necromancer shouted. Power spread out from him in a fan; it was distorted by the rising waves of green.

She reached for Nathan almost blindly, and she set what he gave to her, his very presence, against the spread of the fire itself. She didn't tell Allison to run—there was nowhere to run to. She didn't look to see if her dog lay dead in the streets, because there was nothing at all she could do about him now.

Where Nathan's power surged through her, the fire stopped its painful spread. But it didn't bank; it ate away at what he'd given her. She could take everything he offered—everything—and she might extend the fight with the flame for long enough to put it out. And then? He'd be here, unable to talk or interact or do *anything*.

But she couldn't stop herself; she couldn't disentangle their hands; she took what he offered, fighting every step of the way.

She wasn't prepared for the way the green fire suddenly guttered, and she stumbled, still holding Nathan's hand. She was surprised that his weight supported hers, but she didn't have time to think about it: Looking up at the Necromancers, she saw that the one who had thrown the fire had fallen to his knees. His eyes were wide; she could see their whites from here.

Behind him, she could see Chase.

\*     \*     \*

Eric swore. Chase heard the words at a distance because he left them behind at a sprint. Two men stood side by side in the street. Beyond them, Emma and Allison were backing up. Emma appeared to be talking; she'd lifted both of her hands, as if in surrender.

Allison was silent.

Chase saw the white-fire corridor spring up to either side of the two girls. He saw the hazy swirl of visible light behind them, and he swore himself; he knew what it meant. The Necromancers didn't intend to head back to their apartment for passports and plane tickets; they intended to walk home, with Emma between them.

Allison would be a footnote. Allison, who stumbled. Emma stopped immediately, huddling at her side; she lifted her face. He was close enough to hear her words. Close enough to see the white filament around Allison's neck as it melted. He sucked in air, picked up speed, lightened his step as much as he could; he wouldn't have much time before the Necromancers became aware of him.

But he wouldn't need it.

He gave up on stealth the minute he saw the green-fire globe form in the Necromancer's hand. He wasn't going to make it in time. He wasn't going to be able to drop the Necromancer before he threw the fire.

"Allison!"

Necromancers didn't spend years learning how to throw; aim, when it came to soul-fire, didn't matter. Blindfolded, they could still hit their targets. There was only one certain way to douse soul-fire: Kill the Necromancer. There were less certain ways—but Chase knew whom the soul-fire was meant to kill. And he knew that Allison had no protection against it.

No protection but Emma and Chase. He knew which of the two counted.

He threw one of his two knives; it struck the man cleanly between the upper shoulder blades. He made it count, leaping to grab the handle of the knife as the Necromancer's arms windmilled. Chase twisted the knife.

He yanked the blade out as the man fell forward, blood spreading across the new gap in the back of his jacket. Chase looked up, then, to see that Allison was not on fire. Emma was—but the fire, like the Necromancer, was dying. He grudgingly revised his estimate of Emma's usefulness.

The second Necromancer turned. The white walls on either side of the street faded as he pulled his power back. He made no attempt to help his partner; he had no hope of saving him, and they both knew it.

Instead, he ran. If he could make it past Allison and Emma, if he could make it to the portal, he'd survive. He thought he had a chance. As Eric leaped past Chase in the night streets, Chase grinned.

*       *       *

Allison's skin was red where the white filament had twined round her throat. Her fingers, on the other hand, were blue, and her hands were shaking. She'd managed to half-knock her glasses off her face.

"Ally?"

"I can breathe." Not without coughing, though; her voice sounded hoarse.

"Allison!" Chase had saved Allison's life. On television, rescue usually came in the form of someone a lot less blood spattered. Chase was, once again, wearing a variant on the world's ugliest jacket.

Allison lifted one hand; it was shaking. "I'm alive," she said. "We're both alive. Where's Petal?"

"Here," Eric's voice came from somewhere behind Chase; Chase was close enough it was hard to see around him. Petal was whining, which meant he wasn't dead.

"We need to get out of here," Eric told them. He was staring down the road, and Emma turned to look that way as well. The arch was slowly fading, its cold light giving way to the night of streetlamp and road.

"Where did it lead?" Emma asked.

"To the City of the Dead," he replied, without looking at her. Petal's tail started to move, and he set the dog down. The Necromancers hadn't killed him. He glanced at the two dead bodies that lay in the middle of the street. "Chase, give the old man the heads up."

Chase, however, was kneeling beside Allison. Allison felt dizzy and nauseated, but she knew, looking at his expression, that this wasn't the time for either. She smiled. She forced herself to smile at him.

He grimaced and rolled his eyes. "Don't even try," he told her. He practically shouldered Emma out of the way. Allison caught only a glimpse of Emma's expression before Chase's shoulder covered her face.

"It wasn't Emma's fault," she said, between clenched teeth.

He slid an arm beneath hers and lifted her to her feet. "I didn't say it was."

"Chase—"

"Not here," he told her. "Not now."

She would have argued—she almost did—but she realized that part of the trembling she felt wasn't her own. The fact that Chase, spattered in blood, was shaking, silenced her.

"Emma?"

Emma smiled wanly. "I'm fine."

Eric's brows rose. "I haven't known you long," he finally said. "But 'fine' in Hall parlance doesn't mean much."

"No?"

"No. You're just closing the door in the face of external concern."

She grimaced. "I'm *fine*, Eric. Allison was the one—" She exhaled. She couldn't see her best friend; Chase's back was in the way. Pointedly in the way.

"I'm okay," Allison said. Her voice was shaky. No surprise, there. The Necromancers hadn't tried to kill Emma. Just Allison. Because Allison had been stupid enough to join Emma while she walked her dog.

Her dog bounded toward her, and she felt a surge of both guilt and gratitude. She knelt and let his wet nose leave tracks across her face. People were often put off food by danger; Petal proved that in some ways, he was all dog. She offered him a Milk-Bone, and he ate it.

"Eric's worried about you," Nathan said. Emma startled, which was embarrassing. She ran her hands through her hair and then turned toward Nathan. He didn't *look* different.

"He's like that," Emma replied. "Chase—the redhead with the broad shoulders—doesn't care if I die."

"I wouldn't bet on it. He was worried about Ally, though."

"It's why I can't hate him," Emma said, speaking quietly so Allison wouldn't hear her. "He's attractive, he's confident, he's—I don't know. A guy. But he does like her. He didn't even notice Amy—and I can't think of another living male who hasn't."

Nathan smiled. "It's hard not to notice Amy. If most women are bullets, Amy's a nuclear bomb—overkill on all levels."

Emma didn't even feel a twinge of jealousy; she would have, once. Eric glanced at Nathan.

"Oh, I'm sorry." She was. She'd forgotten that Eric could see the dead. Eric, who wasn't a Necromancer, who wasn't suspicious, and who Chase had not come to Toronto to kill. "Eric, this is Nathan. Nathan, this is Eric."

"Pleased to meet you," Eric said. He didn't hold out his hand.

Neither did Nathan; they stood sizing each other up in an almost painfully obvious way. Emma cleared her throat. "We were going to leave?"

Eric nodded. "The old man's coming to clean up. But you're not going home yet."

"Where are we going?"

"Our place."

Chase was pissed off. Emma wasn't in the best of moods herself, but she wasn't angry with Chase; he, however, was clearly annoyed with her. He inserted himself firmly between Emma and Allison and made clear by the direction his shoulder was turned—toward Emma—that that was where he was staying, period. Ally didn't notice; Chase had his *arm around her shoulder* and she wasn't saying anything. She was white as a sheet.

Nathan walked on the other side of Allison, glancing at her from time to time. He made no attempt to touch her or speak with her—it was pointless—but seemed to take comfort from offering her his entirely invisible support.

Petal stuck like proverbial glue to Emma's side. He did attempt to eat a Milk-Bone through her pocket; she shoved his nose aside—his wet, warm nose—to save her jacket from saliva and teeth marks.

For a group that had survived death by Necromancy, it was pretty grim. The blood really didn't help. Eric's hands were still red; his shirt, his coat, and part of his face were sticky with blood. It wasn't his—which did help—but it was disturbing. Mostly, it was disturbing because he didn't appear to notice or care. Both he and Chase acted as though this sort of thing happened every day. Or every night.

"Eric," Chase said, "I'm taking Allison home."

Emma stopped walking. "No, you're not. Not looking like *that*."

Chase bristled. "Would you like to keep her here so someone else can try to kill her?"

Allison made a strangled sound and ducked out from under Chase's arm. "Don't say that!" She was trembling, she was white, and she was—and this hurt—frightened. But she was also angry, and that added a bit of welcome color to her cheeks.

Chase grimaced. "Allison—"

"Don't ever say that again. Emma didn't want me to stay—*I* wanted to stay."

"And now you know why it's a very bad idea. Look, Allison, I know the two of you are friends—"

"Best friends."

"Whatever. But she's a Necromancer. You're *not*. Even if there's something you could in *theory* do, you don't have the training, you don't have the experience. The best you can do is die painlessly. The Necromancers don't always aim for best case. They don't care about you. They care about Emma because they think she'll become one of them. But they don't spare friends or family. Trust me."

Emma's throat tightened. Chase was right. She knew he was right. Forcing herself to speak lightly, she said, "If you take her home right now, her mother will see you, covered in blood, and have a coronary. If you're very lucky, she won't call the police. And I know you—you're never going to be that lucky."

Allison winced and managed a strained laugh. "She's right."

Chase swore. "Fine. Come with us to Eric's and hope that we don't get traced."

"Emma," Allison said, in a much more subdued voice, "I'm sorry."

That was the worse of it. She apologized and she *meant* it.

"Why?" Emma said, wanting to grab her by the shoulders and shake the words so far out of her they never came back. She was surprised by the anger, by how visceral it was.

"Chase is right. I didn't do anything. I couldn't do anything."

"Ally—neither could I." Emma glanced down at her hands. At the hands that both Allison and Nathan had grabbed. "I couldn't do anything, either. I thought you—" she stopped speaking; it took effort. "It's not you who should be apologizing. It's me. I—I should have at least as much power as they do— and I couldn't do anything, either. If Chase and Eric hadn't arrived, you'd be dead, and I'd be god only knows where.

"But I'd never, ever, forgive them."


## Nathan

Nathan's surprised at how much Chase seems to hate Emma, and how much Chase seems to care about Allison.

Most of Emma's friends at Emery are like Emma. They're comfortable in crowds; they fit in; they find energy talking about similar things. Clothing. Boys. Music and Drama. They go shopping in packs, roving the malls with bright eyes and easy laughter; not all of that laughter is kind, but it has an energy that's fascinating at a distance.

None of those girls is Allison. Allison wanders into bookstores and paper stores. She sits to one side of the group, buried in words that she didn't write and won't have to speak out loud. She's moved by things that are imaginary. Her head, as Nan once said, is permanently stuck in the clouds.

What Nan doesn't see is where Ally places her feet. Yes, her head is in the clouds, but she's rooted, grounded; when she can be pulled out of them, what she sees is what's there. Maybe, Nathan thinks with a grimace, that's *why* she likes clouds.

There are no clouds for Allison now. Her eyes are dark and wide. There's a livid bruise around her throat, and her hands are shaking. She snaps at Chase, Chase snaps back. Emma flinches with each exchange, although she stays out of it.

Allison feels guilty. Nathan recognizes it; it's twin to his own sense of guilt. She was there. She was *right there*. And she couldn't do anything. She couldn't stop the Necromancers. She couldn't even protect *herself*. She was dead weight. Worse. She was terrified.

She was afraid she'd die. That part's simple. But the fear itself has branches.

Death is frightening to the living. Hell, it's no walk in the park for the dead either. But it's not just that. Ally knows what her death would do to Emma.

Because Ally's seen what Nathan's death did.

Nathan's seen it as well. He's spent days watching Emma at school, like some kind of crazed stalker. She's still Emma—but she's quieter. She still talks to Amy and the Emery mafia, and they still talk to her—but it's different. No one mentions Nathan's name. They're careful not to talk too much about boys or boyfriends when she's in the group; they wait until she's gone.

As if she understands this—and she probably does—she drifts away. She doesn't want to be a wet blanket. She doesn't want to pretend that Nathan never existed. She doesn't want to force her friends to acknowledge him the way she did, because they didn't love him the way she did, and she's fine with that.

But Allison almost never talked about boys. She talked about books, and with the same happy, riveted intensity. She talked about Michael and his friends, about schoolwork, about stray thoughts brought on by too much Google and not enough time outside. None of that has changed.

Nathan is afraid that tonight, it has. Allison feels guilty.

And Emma feels guilty as well. Because Emma is a Necromancer, and if it weren't for Chase and Eric, Allison would be dead. Being a best friend has suddenly become a death sentence. She didn't *need* company, tonight. She had Nathan.

But she wanted company. She wanted to tell Allison that Nathan had returned.

Allison was not happy about his reappearance. Emma was surprised. Hurt. Allison recognized that. So did Nathan—but Nathan weighs Allison's unhappiness differently. She's worried. She's worried *for* Emma.

And she should be.

"You can drive us home after you change. And shower. Get the blood out of your hair and your hands."

They're still arguing. Chase, in the overhead light above the door, is the color of chalk; his red hair makes him look even worse.

"Fine. Eric can drive us home. My mother will never let me out of the house again if she sees you looking like that!"

"And that's bad how?"

If Chase could see Nathan, Nathan would tell him to stop. He can't. Allison always seems meek and retiring to people who don't actually know her. She's uncertain in social situations. She's afraid she's just said the wrong thing even when she hasn't said anything.

But once she's made a decision, she doesn't bend, and she is not bending now.

Emma, arms wrapped around her upper body, is exchanging glances with Eric, who looks as much of a mess as Chase but without the red hair to top it off.

Eventually, they enter the house, where eventually means Chase shouts, "Fine!" and opens the door and slams it shut behind him. Allison is practically shrieking with outrage; Nathan laughs. He can; she can't see him.

"I always liked her," he tells Emma.

Emma gives him a shadow of a smile. But she's not with him right now; she's in Allison's orbit. When Allison yanks the door open and marches in—a sure sign that she's angry—Emma apologizes and follows her.

That leaves Eric on the porch.

Nathan doesn't want to talk to Eric. He avoids Eric where at all possible. But given tonight, given Allison's reaction both before and after the Necromancers, he knows it's time to stop.

Eric folds his arms across his chest; Nathan lets his hang loose by his sides. There's nothing Eric can do to harm him. Not directly.

Eric gets straight to the point. "Why are you here?"

"I could ask the same question." Nathan shrugs. "Did you come here to kill Emma?"

Eric's a tough audience. He doesn't even blink. "Yes."

"She's not dead."

"I changed my mind."

"Why?"

Eric's gaze never leaves Nathan's face. "Your girlfriend isn't a Necromancer."

"That's not what Chase thinks."

"And I'm not Chase. I've been doing this a lot longer than he has. Long enough to know you shouldn't be here."

"Allison knows I shouldn't be here?"

"She knows you're here?" He exhales, loosens his arm, and runs a hand through his hair. "Never mind. Of course she knows. She's Emma's best friend."

Nathan chuckles. He can't help it. He's not much of a sharer; it took him a while to get used to the fact that there were no secrets between Emma and Allison. Something about the chuckle loosens the rest of Eric's expression.

"Why are you here?" He asks again, in an entirely different tone.

Because he does, Nathan can answer. "I don't know."

Eric glances at the closed door. "Walk with me," he says. He moves—rapidly—away from the front porch, and Nathan follows.

*      *      *

"It usually takes the dead time to recover," Eric says, as they walk. The chill in the air is lessened by the start of snowfall, but it's a gentle fall. Flakes cling to Eric's jacket and begin to dust sidewalk and road. "Two years, give or take a month. Sometimes it's longer."

"But never four months."

"No. You want to tell me why?"

"Not really. I will, though. I—" he glances at Eric. "I don't know how much you know."

"About the door?"

"Is that what you call it?"

"It's what Emma called it, when she saw it."

Nathan stops walking, frozen for a moment at the idea of Emma lost there.

"Emma hasn't told you this?"

"I haven't asked." But the answer is no, and they both know it. He stumbles over words; it's not like he can stumble over anything else here. "I was there. I don't think of it as a door. It's a window—a solid, bulletproof window. You can see through it. You know what's waiting. But you can't ever reach it."

Eric nods.

"She came to find me there."

He stiffens. "Who?" he asks, but it's clear he already knows the answer.

Nathan gives it anyway. "The Queen of the Dead."

Eric says a lot of nothing for a few blocks. "Why did she send you here?"

"I don't know."

"What did she tell you?"

"She told me to go home."

"That's it?"

Nathan hesitates. Eric catches it instantly. "No," he finally says. "She also told me I'd be safe from her knights."

"Her . . . knights?"

"That's what she calls the Necromancers."

"*Knights*?"

"Sorry. Now that you mention it, it's kind of stupid. She summoned her Necromancers to her throne room."

Eric is quiet. It's a controlled quiet, a veneer of stillness over something so large it might burst at any moment. "Does she spend all her time in her throne room?"

Nathan says, more or less truthfully, "I don't know."

"How much time did you spend there?"

"I don't know." He exhales out of habit, Nathan's version of a sigh. "You know where I was when she found me."

Eric nods. It's a tight, leashed motion.

"She was the only other thing I could see. She's like a bonfire. I'm like a moth. She's terrifying—but she's *there*." He hesitates, then doubles down. "I see Emma the same way, except for the terror. She's luminous. When I'm near Emma, I don't think about what I can't have or where I can't go. I don't think about an exit. I just think about Emma. And that's natural, for me."

"How do you see the others?"

"The others?" For a moment, Nathan thinks he's talking about Allison. Michael. Even his mother.

"The rest of the Necromancers. Do you see them the same way?"

"Only in comparison to my friends. They're brighter, sharper. They catch the eye—but they wouldn't have been able to catch my attention in the beginning. Not the way the Queen did."

"And Emma would." It's a question without any of the intonation.

"Yes," Nathan replies, voice softer. "But I can't be objective."

Eric's brow rises. "I don't believe that."

"What do you see when you look at Emma?" Nathan strives for casual, now. For objective observer. Eric can touch Emma without burning.

Eric closes his eyes. "I see a naive, bleeding heart with a collection of scrappy friends, a deaf dog, and a dead boyfriend." He exhales, opens his eyes, and adds, "I see what you see. Tell me what the Queen of the Dead said to her . . . knights."

"She introduced us, more or less. She told them that if they touched me, if they mentioned me at all in any capacity, they'd be serving her in a 'less advantageous way' for the rest of eternity."

"She meant for you to come to Emma," Eric says, voice flat.

Nathan doesn't argue. He wants to, but it's the only thing that makes sense.

"Have you spoken with the Queen since you arrived home?"

"Yes. Once. She summoned me." He slides hands into his pockets and regards Eric for a long moment, trying to decide whether or not to say what he's thinking.

Eric knows.

"She's waiting for you," Nathan tells him. He's not sure why.

Eric slows; eventually he comes to a dead stop. Nathan's not surprised to see that they've returned to the cemetery. There are no corpses in the street, no obvious signs of blood. No dead that Nathan can see.

"Did she tell you that?" Eric asks, hands in his jacket pockets, balled in fists.

"No."

"How do you know?"

"There are two thrones in the throne room. They're identical, at least to my eyes. I don't know what the living see—the only living members of her Court are Necromancers, and it didn't seem safe to ask. The Queen sits in the left-hand chair, if you're facing her—and no one stands at her back."

"The chair on the right is empty?" When Nathan fails to answer, Eric turns.

"Yes. And no."

"Which is it?" Eric asks, hands in pockets, eyes on the sidewalk just ahead of his feet.

"It's empty. But you can see an image—like a storybook ghost—seated in the chair. It's her magic," he adds softly.

"You can tell that?"

"Yes. By the light, the quality of the light."

"Whose image?" he asks, his voice dropping, his breath a small cloud of mist.

"Yours."

Eric turns and walks away.

Nathan drifts to his grave. It doesn't feel familiar, but it bears his name, and it's where Emma was waiting for him. He touches the headstone, or tries; his hand passes through its marbled surface. Beneath his chiseled, shiny name, there are flowers.

Eric eventually returns, as if Nathan is actually alive and can't be deserted. "It's not my image," he says.

"No. He's not dressed the way you are."

"Please don't tell me I'm wearing a dress."

Nathan laughs. "No. You're not wearing armor, either. You are wearing a crown, though."

Eric snorts. "A crown."

"A big, heavy, ornate, impressive crown. There's less blood and more gravitas."

"I bet. We'd better head back. Chase and Allison probably need a referee by now." He starts to walk, stops, and says, "What have you told Emma?"

Nathan follows, borrowing part of Eric's silence. "Nothing," he finally says. "When I'm with her, I can almost forget I'm dead. I don't want the reminder. I don't want a Queen. I don't want to remind Emma of what the Necromancers represent." It's all true, but there's more, and it's harder. "I don't want to think that my presence here is a plot against Emma."

"If you found out that it was, could you leave?"

"Yes. But I'm not you. I don't think there's anywhere I can go that the

Queen can't find me." He lays out his fear. "If I left, if she knew, she'd send me back. If I couldn't, or wouldn't, stay, she might even come here in person."

"She won't leave her city."

"Why? She left it to find me."

"No, Nathan, she didn't. Her city is the only place she's built where she feels safe."

"You probably understand the Queen better than anyone. Why am I here, Eric? What does she want from me?"

Eric says nothing.

There's a question Nathan wants to ask, but he doesn't, because if Eric answers, Nathan will know—and if the Queen thinks to ask, Nathan will tell her what Eric said. Maybe not immediately.

He contents himself with thinking it as they walk back to Eric's house.

*Could you kill her, Eric? Could you kill the Queen of the Dead? Could you kill someone who loves you so much?*

Eric drives Emma and Allison home. Nathan hitches an uncomfortable ride in the front seat. He still doesn't have the hang of sitting. He passes through chairs and seats. A lifetime's gravity habit is apparently hard to kick.

Nathan missed the beginning of the conversation, but he's not concerned. He can read a lot in their physical closeness. Allison has obviously shared information that's upset her—but the sharing, the spreading of that pain across two sets of shoulders, diminishes it. It's something he's often envied about girls: Talking actually makes a difference to them.

"Chase didn't mean it," Emma says.

"He meant some of it. The part he did mean is still—"

"Making you angry."

Allison nods. Anger isn't her natural state; most people find it hard to believe she has a temper. "I hate it when he talks about killing you—about killing anyone—so casually."

"Amy does it all the time."

"Amy's never killed anyone." Allison gives Emma the Look. "Chase has."

"Good point." Emma concedes with grace whenever she's in a losing position. "But I think he's genuinely worried—about you."

"He's worried about my safety."

"Same thing."

"It's *not*, Emma. He doesn't care about anything *but* that. Do you know how I'd feel if I just walked out on you, now? Let's pretend you're not you. Or you're not involved. You're some other, random Best Friend I've known since we were five years old."

"Okay."

"He's not asking me to walk out on my Best Friend; he's asking me to walk out on my own life. He's asking me to be so afraid for my own safety that I'm willing to just leave you behind. And I could," she adds. "But it would change what friendship means—to me—forever. I could never, ever throw my whole heart into it, because if things were too dark or too scary, I'd know, in advance, that I'd be ducking, hiding, and running for cover.

"It's not about you, not really. It's about *me*. It's about being able to look myself in the mirror. I'm not five years old anymore. I need to do this—for me. Can you live with that?"

"I'm not exactly a disinterested observer," Emma finally manages to say. Nathan knows the tone; she's close to tears. Emma doesn't cry in public. Even the good tears, and these would be good.

He understands what Emma sees in Allison. He understands that Allison mostly doesn't. He knows that Allison wasn't happy to see him, and given Eric's reaction, he's terrified that she's right.

Nathan knows Emma. He knows that Emma's not nearly as certain as Allison; he knows that Allison's belief in Emma is way stronger than Emma's belief in herself. But he could turn it around: Emma's belief in Allison is stronger than Allison's belief in herself. They shore each other up when the insecurities bite them.

They could, if they were different people, break each other down instead.

"Don't hate Chase," Emma says instead. "I can't. I know you think he doesn't care about what you need—but Ally, he does care about you. He's a guy. He's just got a crappy way of expressing it."

Eric clears his throat, loudly, to remind them there's a captive guy behind the steering wheel of the car.

"I want to slap him, and I want to spend an hour screaming in his ear, but—I don't hate him. If I hated him, I wouldn't care. No, I'd care because I care for you—but I wouldn't be so *angry* with him. I don't know why, but I expect better."

Emma laughs. "Having spoken with Chase, I don't know why either."

## ⌁ Chapter 4

This evening had contained Necromancers, near death, and death; it contained Allison and her anger at Chase—Chase was almost always angry, so his anger in response didn't matter as much. It contained the difficult nonconversation about Nathan—a conversation Emma was no longer certain she wanted to have.

But another unexpected surprise was waiting in the driveway of Emma's house. It was a car. Technically, it was an SUV. The night was too dark for her to tell immediately what color it was, but Emma instantly knew three things: It wasn't a Hall car, she'd never seen the car before, and the driver wasn't sitting behind the wheel. Even if her mother had somehow been talked into buying a new car—which they couldn't really afford at the moment—there's no way she wouldn't have spoken to Emma about it first.

"New car?" Nathan asked, when she'd been staring at the license plate for a little bit too long.

"No. It's not ours." Her left hand was numb. She hadn't held on to Nathan for most of the evening, but she hadn't recovered from the early contact, and she rubbed the numb hand absently. She took two steps up the drive, turned, and said, "I'll see you again tomorrow?"

He nodded. "I'll hitch a ride to school in the morning, as long as you promise you won't make me speak to anyone—I think I still owe Brady some money."

She laughed, but the laughter lost ground as she looked at the strange car. "I have to go talk to my mom."

He nodded, leaned in closer, and then stopped himself. She wanted to kiss him. She didn't want to go into the house with blue lips.

The lights were on. It was dark because it was November, not because it was late, although it was closing in on nine o'clock. Petal bounded into the house, his stump wagging in a way that implied he'd been homesick for *so* long. He couldn't be hungry—scratch that. He was always hungry, but he couldn't need food yet; she'd fed him dinner before they left for their disaster of a walk.

The lights in the living room were on. The lights in the dining room were on—but Emma paused in the arch that led to the dining room because she could actually see the tabletop. The perpetual stacks of paperwork that defined half her mother's home life had been removed. There were flowers—real flowers—in a slender crystal vase atop a table runner.

"Okay, Petal," Emma told her dog. "This is really creeping me out."

She looked at this new incarnation of a dining room. It could have walked straight out of *Coraline*. Clearly this didn't bother Petal as much as it bothered Emma. Worse, though, was the sudden sound of her mother's laughter. It came from the kitchen.

Emma's mother did not love the kitchen. Some of her friends were foodies, and while Mercy Hall enjoyed eating as much as the next person, she didn't enjoy the cooking; she often forgot ingredients or petty things like timers. Emma was a better cook than her mother. Brendan Hall had done most of the Hall family's food preparation in the early years, and he had started teaching Emma.

But that was undeniably her mother's laughter, and unless the kitchen had suffered the same transformation as the dining room, she was in the Hall family's kitchen. Emma hesitated for a long minute and then headed toward the sound of her mother's voice.

Mercy Hall was laughing. She was wearing, of all things, a dress, and faint traces of makeup. She looked about ten years younger than she normally did, which wasn't the shock—although admittedly, it was a bit surprising. The shock was the person who was standing beside her—standing *way* too close, in Emma's opinion. She'd never laid eyes on him before, but he was clearly laying eyes on her mother.

He looked up first. It figured. He also took a step back from her mother, who noticed and looked up as well. "Emma, you're home late," she said, the happy, open smile on her face fading into a more familiar expression of concern.

"We ran into a couple of friends," Emma said automatically.

"I was hoping you'd be home a little earlier. I wanted to introduce you to someone." She turned to the strange man. "This is Jon Madding. Jon, this is my daughter, Emma."

Emma tried to dredge up a smile. She might as well have kissed Nathan; her lips felt frozen anyway. She extended a hand as Jon Madding—what kind of a name was Madding, anyway?—stepped forward. He took her hand, shook it; she thought his grip was a little on the weak side. He was taller than average, but sort of balding, and he had a beard. Emma wasn't all that fond of beards.

"I'm so pleased to finally meet you," he said, with a broad smile. "Mercy's told me a lot about you; you must be so proud of your mother."

Emma smiled and nodded. "Oh, I am. So, how did you meet my mom?"

"At work."

"You work in the same office?"

"No, I work for one of her firm's clients. But we've crossed paths a number of times." He smiled at Mercy and added, "She's got a sharp tongue when she's under a deadline, but she focuses and she gets things done."

"Oh, don't say that to Emma," Mercy told him, reddening. "She has to live with me; she knows what I'm really like." She smiled at her daughter. Her smile was more genuine than Emma's, but because Emma *did* know her mother, she could see anxiety start to surface.

Keeping her own Hall standard smile plastered to her face, Emma asked, "How long have you known my mother?"

"Three years? Four? Mercy?"

"Four and a half."

"Your mother's never mentioned me? I'm hurt," he said, laughing.

"No, my mother's never mentioned you. I guess she's been too busy.

Speaking of which, I've got a ton of homework to do, and I won't get it done if I don't start an hour ago." She turned, stopped, and turned back. "Nice to meet you, Jon."

"Maybe we'll get a chance to talk on a night you don't have homework," he replied, turning back to her mother.

Emma couldn't force herself to say something equally pleasant. She headed straight to her room, pausing only to lift her schoolbag from its perch in the hall.

"Em, that was unkind."

Her back was against her bedroom door; her eyes were closed. She didn't want to open them because she knew damn well who was speaking. "What was unkind?"

Her father was silent, as he often was when disappointed. It had been one of his most effective weapons in the intermittent war that was childhood; she'd forgotten just how much she'd hated it. She forced herself to look at her dad, afraid that she would see pain in his expression. It wasn't there; there was plenty of disappointment to make up for it, though.

"You *knew*," she said, voice sharpening.

He said nothing.

"Dad—you knew she was seeing someone."

"Em—"

"How long has this been going on? How long as she been seeing *Jon*?"

"I think that's a question you'll have to ask your mother. If it helps, this is the first time she's brought him home."

It didn't. It didn't help at all. Petal interrupted the conversation from the other side of the door, mostly by scratching and whining. She managed to pry herself off the door and let him in. He padded pretty much through her father's ghost and headed straight for the bed.

"You're not supposed to let him do that," her father observed; Petal was rolling in the duvet, having pulled off the counterpane he detested.

"I have more important things to worry about at the moment. Why won't you answer the question?"

"Because," he replied, folding his arms across his chest, "it's none of my business."

"P-pardon?"

"It's none of my business, Em. It's been eight years. I didn't come back here to watch Mercy wallow in grief and misery; I came because I wanted to know that you were both okay."

A peal of laughter rose in the distance. Mercy's. If Jon was laughing, his register was too low to carry as far. Emma hated it anyway.

"Have they—"

Brendan lifted a hand. "Do not even think of asking me that question. Don't ask your mother either."

"Because it's none of *my* business? Dad, in case it escaped your notice, I live here too."

"Yes, Emma, but he doesn't. You didn't tell your mother everything about Nathan; she didn't ask. Do her the favor of extending her the same respect."

Emma was silent. She was cold. She hadn't lied; she did have some homework. She sat at her desk, opened her bag, and pulled out her laptop. Flipping it open, she stared at a white, white screen with a menu bar somewhere on top of it.

Petal whined. He knew she was unhappy because he could clearly hear her side of the argument. He couldn't hear her dad's, and that was just as well, since Petal had never been fond of the Disappointment, either.

"Emma."

"I have homework, Dad."

"And you're getting so much of it done."

She swiveled in her chair. "What do you want me to say?"

"Your mom's dating choices aren't the only thing in your life at the moment," he replied. "To my mind, they're not even the most important."

"Thanks." She bit her lip, staring moodily at her screen.

"Give him a chance."

"I thought you said there were other things to talk about."

His silence was heavy, but after a moment he abandoned it. "What happened tonight?"

"Allison nearly died." She looked down at her hands; they were shaking, and the left was still numb. Her father walked over to her, reached for her hand, and then pulled back with a grimace.

"Sorry," he said. "Sometimes I forget."

"That you're dead?"

He nodded. "If I were alive, I'd be able to help, somehow."

But Emma shook her head. "If you were alive, you wouldn't be in my room, and even if you were, I wouldn't be talking to you about—about Allison. Or Necromancers. I'd be talking about homework."

"Jon wouldn't be here either."

". . . I know. Dad—"

"Sorry, that was unfair of me."

It bloody well was, but Emma suspected she deserved it. "Two Necromancers came after Ally and me while we were out walking Petal. Dad—they were going to just kill her."

He closed his eyes. "I wasn't there."

"No—but you can't be."

"Actually, I pretty much can; I don't have a lot else on my plate. But Nathan—"

She swallowed. Looked back at the screen that was only a little less white. It was true. She did want—she did *need*—some privacy.

"What happened to the Necromancers?"

"Eric and Chase killed them."

He looked away again. "You were there, for that?"

She nodded. "I didn't even mind it at the time."

"Emma—"

"Maybe this is how it starts. I didn't mind that they'd killed the Necromancers, and the Necromancers are human too. But if they hadn't, Allison would have died. Chase was pissed. He wants Allison out."

"Out?"

"Of my life. Of danger. I can't blame him. But if she's not going to leave me—and she won't—then I have to be able to do something if it happens again."

"You mean you have to learn how to kill."

She felt the shock of his words as they settled around her. She wanted to deny it, but she couldn't. She had no idea how far she'd be willing to go to save the life of someone she loved. She could imagine herself killing someone. But even thinking it, she could hear the sound of a knife hitting flesh and bone, and she almost stopped breathing.

He watched her, his eyes that noncolor of dead eyes, his expression painfully familiar. After a long moment, he breathed in, like the inverse of a sigh, and the line of his shoulders softened. This time, when he reached for her, he didn't hesitate, didn't pull back; he caught both of her hands in his.

He was *so* cold.

And then, for a moment, she was warm.

She wanted to cry, to tell him she didn't want or need this, not from him. But the truth was, at this very moment, she felt she *did*. She wasn't a child anymore, and she'd been nothing but a child the last time he'd hugged her when she was—as he put it—down. She let him fold her in his arms while she drained something from the touch that went both ways.

"Remember," he said, into her hair. "Remember, Emma. What Eric or his friends ask of you, what they think they want—it's not the only way. It's their way, but you're not them."

"I don't understand," she said, into his chest. "I don't understand what the Necromancers get out of this. I don't understand why they do what they do."

"No. But you will." His voice was softer.

*       *       *

In the morning, Jon's car was not in the drive. Emma knew; it was the first thing she checked when she crawled out of bed. She was grateful for small mercies. Large ones seemed to be beyond her, at the moment.

Her mother's door was closed, but that wasn't a big surprise; her mother and mornings weren't the best of friends. She wondered if her mother would drag herself out of bed if Jon had stayed, and the thought soured the optimism that lack of his car had produced. She climbed into the shower, hoping to wash the uglier bits of her mood down the drain.

Getting dressed, making breakfast, and feeding the animal that was dogging her heels, helped. Making coffee for her mother helped as well, because it was normal.

Her mother came down the stairs straightening her blouse and holding a pair of nylons in one hand. She looked as bleary-eyed as she normally did, but there was a thinness to her lips that was new. Or rarer, at any rate.

"Emma," she said, as she entered the kitchen.

"Coffee," her daughter replied, handing her mother a large mug with a chipped handle. "Blueberries are on the table with the granola. There's milk as well, but we need more."

"I'll get it on the way home from work. Emma—"

The doorbell rang. Emma had timed breakfast and coffee with a merciless eye toward the very accurate clock because she knew Michael would show up at her door, the way he did every day on the way to school. It was precisely 8:10 in the morning. Emma kissed her mother on the cheek and said, "I've got to run, sorry breakfast was late."

"Emma—"

She answered the door; Michael was mobbed by Petal—if one dog didn't normally constitute a mob, Petal tried really hard to make up for it—and Emma grabbed her hat, her scarf, her gloves.

Mercy knew better than to start an argument—or a discussion—when Michael was on the clock, as it were. "Will you be in tonight?"

"Tonight? Did you forget I'm going to Ally's for dinner?"

Mercy grimaced. "Clearly."

"I won't be home too late after that. Have a great day at work," she added, shrugging her shoulders into her coat and heading out the door.

Allison's mother came to the door to see them off, and she had a very open, very obvious expression of parental worry etched into the corners of her eyes and mouth. Allison kept a cheerful smile more or less fixed to her face as she turned to wave, but to her friends it looked hideously forced; she only relaxed it once they'd turned the corner, which Emma did as quickly as possible.

"You can stop smiling now. If your face freezes like that, it's going to be scary."

Allison's grimace was far more natural. "I told her as much of nothing as I could get away with. But apparently *I* look worried. Or not cheerful enough. And she noticed the bruising."

Emma wilted as Allison's jaw snapped shut. Michael, however, said, "What bruising?" in exactly the wrong tone of voice.

Emma and Allison exchanged a look that Michael couldn't have missed had he been sleeping. And while Allison *was* a better liar than Michael, it was only by chance; anyone over the age of three who was still breathing was, after all.

It was—it had always—been tempting to treat Michael like a child; it was also both unfair and a mistake. But it was Allison who made the executive decision as they walked the rest of the way to school.

"Emma and I took Petal for a walk last night," she told him quietly. "And we met two Necromancers just outside the cemetery."

Michael's eyes widened. After a moment, they narrowed. "They hurt you?"

"They tried."

"Bruises don't—"

"Yes, they hurt me—but not badly. I'm just bruised, and it's not a big bruise, either." The executive decision had clearly faltered.

Emma picked up the slack. "They tried to kill her."

It was Michael's turn to miss a step, but when he righted himself, he'd stopped walking.

"Talk while we walk, Michael; you'll be late if you don't."

For once, the panicky prospect of being late didn't move him, much. "What happened?"

"Eric and Chase showed up."

He took a deep breath and began to walk again. "They killed the Necromancers?"

"They did." Emma watched him out of the corner of an eye; Michael didn't like violence, much. To be fair, neither did Emma or Allison.

This particular violence, however, didn't shatter his equilibrium; he nodded as if he hadn't heard. "Emma will need to learn how to defend herself," he finally said.

The girls exchanged a glance; this one had higher eyebrows.

"But I guess she'll have to be careful not to—not to be like them."

"Emma could never—" Allison began, hotly.

"But, Allison, they couldn't have started out that way either, could they?"

"Why not?"

Michael looked confused. "When they were born—"

Allison lifted a hand. "I'm sorry," she said quickly. "You're probably right. They probably weren't like that to start, but it doesn't matter; they're like that now, and Emma's *not*."

"Of course she's not." His look of confusion deepened.

Poor Michael. Emma caught his arm. "Ally and Chase had a very loud fight about me last night. Pretty much about this."

"Oh." He turned to Allison. "I'm sorry."

Michael wasn't Chase; Allison couldn't be enraged at him if she spent all day trying. "It's fine. We're going to Eric's after school today, though." She paused. "Do you want to come with us?"

It wasn't clear that Michael had even heard the question until they reached the entrance of Emery. They were used to this. "I think I would like to go with you," he told them, "if Eric doesn't mind."

"I'm sure Eric won't mind," Emma replied.

"Are you *crazy*?"

The lunchtime cafeteria was, as usual, loud enough to deafen—but not apparently loud enough to completely blanket Eric's voice. People—a handful of whom knew Emma fairly well—swiveled in the lunch line to stare. Emma pretended he was shouting into someone else's ear and kept both hands on her tray as she headed to the cashier.

Eric recovered pretty quickly and followed, but he'd clearly lost all appetite for food. Since Michael was waiting at the emptiest table in the cafeteria, Emma slowed down to allow Eric to catch up with her.

"Michael is *not* Allison."

"If it weren't for Michael, I'd have disappeared at Amy's party. I know he seems like a child or a simpleton to you," she added, "but he's not. He's capable of very complex thought and action—just not complex *social* action. It's just going to bother him, and he'll have no outlet for it, otherwise."

"How, exactly, is it going to bother him? Never mind. Let me guess. You told him what happened."

"We didn't plan on telling him, but it came up while we were walking to school. Sorry."

"Emma—"

"He's been a part of this since it started."

"I get that—but this isn't a goddamn party. Allison almost died. Michael will be at risk in the same way. I don't want to be responsible for—"

"You're not. Tell him the risks—when we get to your place—and let him decide. He may decide to bow out; there's a lot of stuff he won't join in on because he doesn't like the possible consequences. But let him make that decision. He's not four; you don't have to make it for him."

Eric fell silent; it didn't last. "He's not four," he said, speaking through clenched teeth, "but he still needs to be walked to school every morning."

Eric had saved Emma's life not once, but twice—and at the moment she wanted to slap him anyway. She couldn't recall being so angry with him before, not even when he'd discovered the truth about Andrew Copis and hadn't cared enough to try to help the child. Her hands were full of tray, and she wasn't close enough to the table to set it down. She embedded the edges into both of her palms and kept walking instead, trying to keep the momentary expression of murderous rage off her face, because Michael was watching.

Eric didn't seem to notice; he was looking pretty angry himself. That much anger at a cafeteria table wasn't comfortable; Allison, watching them approach, fell silent, which was unfortunate because she'd been halfway through a sentence to Michael. Michael looked at Allison's less than familiar expression, then looked at Emma and Eric.

"Is something wrong?" he asked.

"No," Emma said curtly, as Eric said, "Yes."

They exchanged a glare, but Eric still waited until Emma was seated before he took a seat himself. This took about four minutes longer than usual and was followed by a tense silence, because the sound of chewing didn't carry far in the uncarpeted acoustics of the cafeteria.

"There's nothing wrong with you," Emma finally said. "It's our problem."

Eric said nothing, but he said it loudly. Allison started to push her food around her plate. When she wasn't angry herself, she was quite uncomfortable around angry people.

Rescue came from the outside. Two of Michael's D&D friends—Connell and Cody—saved them by descending on the table and taking seats on either side of Michael, which forced Allison to move over. While they didn't have Michael's autism spectrum diagnosis, they were frequently socially clueless; silent, uncomfortable anger didn't hit their radars at all. They were deep in the middle of a technical discussion about a game of some sort, which involved cards, numbers, and strategies that seemed far more like math and statistics than fun to Emma. Michael was drawn to the magnet of the game, though, and as he began to enter the state of animated compulsion that was most of his focused discussion, Emma felt her jaw relaxing.

She still couldn't have this conversation in front of Michael; she wasn't certain she could have it at all at the moment. She was angry enough that her food now tasted like sawdust—undercooked sawdust; it caught in her throat.

"He's wrong, you know," a familiar voice said. She looked up; standing just over Michael like a slightly ratty Angel stood Nathan. He was smiling down at the top of Michael's head, and that smile deepened around the edges as he met Emma's eyes. "Michael's not a child. In some ways, he's more responsible than most of us."

Emma felt part of her anger cool. "I know he's wrong. It's just that—what if something happens—" Allison nudged her under the table, and she realized that she was, to all intents and purposes, talking to thin air, which wasn't something she wanted to be seen doing. She grimaced as Nathan laughed.

Nathan had never treated Michael like a child. It was one of the first things she'd noticed about him and one of the first things she'd appreciated. She bent her head over her lunch as Nathan began to walk around the cafeteria, occasionally passing through people as he looked around, hands in pockets that looked physical but couldn't be.

She wanted to leave lunch behind and walk with him, to hear what he had to say because Nathan was perceptive, and he could afford to be blunt at the moment; no one else would hear him. No one but Eric.

She glanced at Eric and saw that he was watching not Nathan, but her. "I'm not wrong," he told her softly. "It's not his age. That's not what it's about."

"You didn't say that about Allison."

"No. I didn't." He looked at Allison and then offered Emma a pained, lopsided grin. "She'd've killed me."

"I would have, too," Ally said.

Emma accepted this gesture of partial surrender. She was still angry, but what had she expected? Eric didn't *know* Michael; he didn't know what Michael was capable of. He *did* know that the posse of girls who'd all drifted from the same school kept an eye out for Michael; he *did* know that the teachers made allowances for Michael's particular peculiarities.

He could learn the rest. She told herself that firmly. He could learn.

But she looked past him, through the crowds in the cafeteria that were slowly dwindling as the lunch hour passed, and she thought that Nathan had never had to learn; he'd just known. He'd just accepted.

## ⤳ Chapter 5

After school, Allison and Michael met Emma at her locker. They walked to Eric's in silence; there was enough snow on the ground that Allison regretted her decision not to wear boots. Emma spoke very little, and Allison was too annoyed at Chase to try to carry a conversation without a lot of help.

Annoyance was better, by far, than worry. Worry was better than all-out fear. She held on to her anger as if it were a talisman, noting that Emma wasn't walking beside them; she was trailing behind. Michael, thinking, didn't notice. Allison knew that Emma wasn't alone.

Michael didn't. He accepted that the impossible had happened: Emma could see the dead. But he accepted it because he'd seen it himself, and he had no other reason to doubt his sanity. In that, he was practical. He was almost unswerving. If Michael believed something to be true, he had all the facts lined up, and it was nearly impossible to move him; social censure certainly couldn't do it, and that was the lever most people tried to use.

"Michael," Emma called.

Allison tapped his shoulder to get his attention, and he turned. So did she.

Standing beside Emma, left hand in her right, stood Nathan, conspicuously dressed for summer when all the rest of the gang was in heavy November clothing.

"Hey, Michael," Nathan said, when Michael failed to say anything.

Michael nodded. He glanced at Emma, who was watching him with an uncertain smile on her face. "I promised you you'd be the first to see Nathan when he came back."

Technically, she had broken that promise, but best friends didn't count.

"Did Emma find you?" Michael asked, after a long thinking moment had passed. The sun was heading to the horizon, and it wasn't getting any warmer.

"I found Emma," he replied.

Emma began to move, and Nathan came with her.

"Have you come to take her away?" Michael asked.

Emma's eyes widened in the silence that followed. Allison started to answer, but no words came out of her open mouth.

Nathan, however, shook his head. To Nathan, it was one of Michael's questions: the kind no one else would ask, even if they were thinking it. Some people found it off-putting; Nathan had always accepted it entirely at face value. It was one of the things that Allison had respected. Nathan wasn't Mr. Popularity; he was low key, but he got along with pretty much everyone.

"Emma's alive," Nathan said quietly. "Just like the two of you. I wouldn't wish being dead on anyone I loved."

Michael slowly relaxed. "What is it like?"

"Being dead?" Nathan asked.

Michael nodded.

Nathan frowned. "It's hard to explain," he finally said. It sounded lame to Allison, which surprised her. Nathan didn't generally try to protect Michael by simplifying or hiding facts. For one thing, it was condescending, and for another, it didn't work. Michael was young for his age in a lot of ways, but he

had the base practicality of a much older person. He was certainly more practical than Allison on a bad day.

"Do you remember what it's like to be alive?" Case in point.

"Oh, yes."

"How is dead different, then?"

Nathan grimaced. From the expression on his face, he was trying to decide
whether or not he wanted to answer the question; he wouldn't lie to Michael,
but he had very few problems declining to answer Michael's questions if he felt
they crossed a line. To Michael, the idea that a line could be crossed wasn't
natural, but he accepted it, although a gentle reminder was often in order. To
be fair, there were very, very few questions that could offend Michael and very
few he wouldn't answer.

"Dead is a bit like sleeping," Nathan finally said.

"Sleeping's not bad," was Michael's hesitant almost-question.

"Not regular sleep. Have you ever had an operation? In a hospital?"

Michael shook his head. Hospitals were a source of morbid fascination, as
long as there was no chance whatsoever that Michael himself would be the
patient.

Nathan grimaced. "Wisdom teeth? Did you have yours pulled yet?"

"Not everyone needs to have theirs removed," Allison added quickly, just
in case.

Michael, it appeared, was still in possession of those teeth.

"Well," Nathan continued, aware that as an example this was going to fall
a little flat. "It's like that. You go under. You wake up confused. It takes a while
to get your bearings, and the waking is cold—very cold—and unpleasant.
Once you're awake, once you realize where you are and why you're here, it's
fine."

"So you're fine, now?"

Silence.

Emma, who'd been watching Michael, turned to look at Nathan; had they
not been walking side by side, Allison might have missed it.

"You don't stay awake, do you?" Emma asked, in the quiet Hall voice that
was loud in every way but volume.

Nathan glanced at her, then away.

She squeezed his hand. "Nathan."

Without looking at her he said, "No." It was almost inaudible.

Michael started to speak again; this time, Ally ran interference, leaving the
question in Emma's hands.

"Do you get any choice in when you—when you fall asleep again?"

"Em—"

"Answer me, Nathan. Please, answer me."

"You already know the answer."

"Only because you won't say it."

"Em, if I don't want to say it, and you know what it is I don't want to say, why is it important that I say it at all?"

Emma fell silent then.

But Michael said, "Why is it important that you don't?"

The conversation came to a halt not because it was finished—although as conversations went, Nathan's refusal to answer the question had kind of killed it—but because Eric's house was now in view. In the daylight, it looked like a perfectly normal house. Nothing about it hinted at the occupations of those who lived within, but then again, did it ever, really?

Nathan extracted his hand. Michael's frown indicated that Michael, at least, could no longer see him.

"Is Nathan still here?" he asked Emma, as they approached Eric's door.

Emma smiled stiffly and nodded. She pushed the doorbell and stepped back.

Before Michael could speak again, someone opened the door. It was, to her surprise, Ernest—called the old man by Eric and Chase when he wasn't actually present—looking much more modern than he usually did. The rustic and ancient jacket was gone; the button-down shirt had joined it. He was older than Emma's father would have been, had he lived, older than her mother. He wasn't as old as some of the teachers, nearing retirement, who taught classes at Emery.

Emma had met him a grand total of once. He'd been on the wrong end of a gun he'd been pointing at her; he'd have fired it, too, if Eric hadn't been standing stubbornly between them. She knew, however, that he was responsible for keeping information about both the Necromancers and their hunters from spreading; he could—and did—move corpses and somehow keep them out of sight of local authorities.

At the moment, he looked like a normal parent, not a man who dealt with bodies and owned at least one gun.

"Is something wrong?" His question was almost the definition of curmudgeonly.

It was Emma who said, "You look—you look very different."

He raised a brow. "Do *not* ask me. If you want to pester someone with trivial questions, you have my leave to grill Margaret."

Emma dared a glance past him into the empty hall. Margaret Henney was one of the dead; a woman who had died sometime in her fifties, and who had the distinct advantage of intimate understanding of Necromancers, because she'd once *been* one.

If she was giving Ernest fashion advice, she was doing it on her own time; the hall behind Ernest was empty.

Chase was in the living room, or what passed for the living room; he was arranging logs in the fireplace, but took a chair when they entered the room, slumping into the cushions as if he weighed about three times more than he should. He wasn't wearing a jacket, although studded black leather adorned the arms of the room's largest chair; he had nothing to do with his hands, so he fidgeted, in silence, with his keys.

Chase kept glancing at Ernest, as though he was either suspicious or expected a tongue-lashing at any minute; he wasn't entirely comfortable.

Eric, on the other hand, was doing something practical; he was lighting a fire in the fireplace. Allison was surprised; many homes had fake fireplaces or none at all. She preferred none; she couldn't see the point in a fireplace that didn't actually burn things.

"I suppose smoking is out of the question," Ernest said.

Michael's brows rose; Allison grimaced. Emma, however, said, "We'd really prefer if you didn't, but it's your house."

"Technically, it's Eric's house."

"He doesn't let *me* smoke here," Chase pointed out.

"You don't have to deal with the two of you," was Ernest's more acid reply.

Chase muttered something under his breath.

"We need to talk about self-defense." Eric, satisfied with the stability of the small fire burning between the new logs, rose. "The reason we wear these jackets," he said, lifting one of the uglier ones that lay over the arm of a chair, "are the studs." He hefted the black leather blob in both hands and tossed it to Allison.

Allison's eyes widened. "This is heavy."

"There's a chain of iron sewed into the hem in the lining. It's a bitch on the fabric; we replace a lot of linings. If you look at the collar—"

She was already turning it up.

"That would have effectively stopped the problem you had last night. You might have felt uncomfortable; there might have been a tightness about your throat, but the iron works to prevent the grip of Necromantic magic. Silver cuts it better, but in the case of silver, the contact has to be direct.

"It's not much in the way of armor," Eric continued. "It's not meant to be bulletproof—and bullets can be a problem. It'll slow down a small knife; it won't stop a sword."

"No one carries swords," Michael pointed out.

"Necromancers don't, no. They don't carry many knives, either. If you see a Necromancer pull a knife, you know he—or she—hasn't reached the height of their power yet. But the knives are still a danger if you don't know how to fight."

Chase snorted and said something rude under his breath, which caused Allison's hands to turn into white-knuckled fists. She didn't respond in any other way because she was practical: She *didn't* know how to fight, and knew it.

"So a getup like this," Eric continued, as if Chase didn't exist, "is meant for the heavy duty Necromancers who usually hunt us. They don't send out the scrubs when they're looking for us."

"We can't wear these in school," Allison said. She handed the jacket to Michael, who'd been staring at it with some fascination. He touched the interior fabric and relaxed. Michael was sensitive to weaves and cloth; he couldn't, for instance, stand real wool and never wore it.

"No. We're hoping we never face a Necromancer in the school."

Emma turned widening eyes on Allison, who looked grim. Just grim.

"They don't want to be discovered," Eric told her. "And we don't want them to *be* discovered either. If they know their cover is blown, they generally feel they only have one recourse."

"Kill all the witnesses?" Michael asked.

"Yes."

"Can they?"

"Yes. I don't think they could take out the entire city of Toronto. They can—and will—take out dozens of people if necessary."

"One school's worth of students?" Emma asked, voice tight.

Eric said nothing.

Chase opened his mouth, and Allison glared at him; he snapped it shut. It was audible.

"The Queen of the Dead isn't one of the dead," Eric finally said. "She's alive. Anything living can be killed. If she destroyed a city or a large town, a lot of people would suddenly be looking for her."

"So the City of the Dead is a physical place?"

Eric nodded.

"Where is it located?"

Eric and Chase exchanged a glance. "It doesn't have a fixed location."

This answer confused Michael, which was fair; it confused Emma and Allison as well. On the other hand, Michael was the only one to press the issue. "How can it be a physical city without a fixed location?"

"Look, Michael—" Eric caught Emma's pointed stare, and ran his hands through his hair. "All of you already know too much. If she thought you knew this, she *would* nuke your city just to make sure you couldn't share the information. I understand you need to know things. Understand that there are some things no one living should know. If you ever have the misfortune to visit the City of the Dead, you'll have all the answers you need."

"I doubt that," Allison said quietly.

Eric grimaced. "I didn't say you'd be able to do anything useful with them. Necromancers can travel to the City of the Dead. In very rare cases, they can travel elsewhere, but someone at the other end has to have a *lot* of power prepared as a terminus. The Queen could anchor that kind of transport, but I don't think many of the others could. They can open gates *to* the city—but even that requires a lot of power, and some preparation on the part of the Necromancers. It's also harder to do in the presence of iron; it's hard to do in a building with, say, steel-beam construction. If the gate is aligned properly, it will work, but modern construction makes it more challenging. Again, it's not trivial."

"Then the two men—"

"Yes. They didn't intend to fly home; they intended to grab you and run. The portal wouldn't have to be open for long. If they had to leave a functional door between here and their City, they'd have to find a lot of the dead on very short notice."

"They can see the dead."

"Yes—but the dead who have the most potential often don't want to be seen." He hesitated again, then looked at Emma. "The Queen of the Dead can find the dead if she needs them; she's extraordinarily sensitive."

"And powerful," Michael added.

"Yes." Eric lifted another jacket and tossed it to Allison; she'd passed the first jacket to Michael, who had let it pool in his lap as he focused on the conversation. "Try it on."

Before Allison could answer, he picked up a third jacket and tossed it to Emma. "You too. How does it feel?" Eric asked Emma.

"Heavy. Kinda ugly."

Chase snorted and corrected her. "It's hideously ugly, but we don't ask Eric for fashion advice unless we *want* to look like Goth clowns. That's not what he's asking."

Emma frowned. The frown deepened.

"Can you still see Nathan?" Eric asked, correctly divining the source of her surprise.

She nodded. "He's—he looks less solid."

Eric said, "There's almost nothing you could do that would make the dead invisible to you."

Emma recovered quickly, for Emma. "Could we get a less ugly jacket?"

"Sure," Chase said. "But by the time we finished with it—or *you* finished with it, because you're going to be doing some of the damn work—it'd be almost as ugly. I never buy decent jackets anymore—hurts too much to ruin them."

"Allison?"

She was less amused by his rationale than Emma, but she did try the jacket on. It was *heavy*. It was heavy and about two sizes too large. But she slid her arms into loose sleeves, and the very ugly jacket let gravity pull it more or less straight.

"Well?" she asked Emma.

"I think it looks better on you than it does on Chase."

Chase opened his mouth, looked at Allison, and frowned. After a pause of several seconds, he said, "Damn it, she's right."

Emma's brows rose. "You agreed with something I said?"

"You've got a better eye than Eric. For fashion."

"And friends. Don't forget the friends."

"I've never criticized your taste in friends—except for Eric."

Allison cleared her throat, loudly, before he could continue. "Better on me than on Chase isn't really saying much. How bad does it look?"

Emma winced. "We can try a better jacket once we can figure out—"

"You need some kind of leather," Chase said, voice flat. "Thicker is better. No kid glove leather, no Napa—you'll rip the coat to shreds trying to put it all together. You might be able to get away with trench coats. We don't use 'em."

"Why?"

"Too cumbersome. When we need to move, we need to move; we can't afford the hems getting caught on any protrusions. I think they'd work for you."

Allison removed the jacket. "Is this all?"

"Hell no. We're just getting started."

An hour later, they were wearing necklaces of silver, with weighted pendants that were some combination of silver and iron. The pendants themselves were simple but heavy, and hard to hide under anything other than a loose knit or blouse. Emma asked if they could use a longer chain; Eric shook his head. Chase snorted and pointed out that it was the *pendant* that was important, and if silver could be made into a comfortable choker, that was best.

"So that stupid dog collar you were wearing wasn't ancient, bad Goth?"

"No. Don't look at me like that; I make sacrifices like this all the time. We've got rings; the rings are easy. Wear 'em. They're not there to protect your hands; they're there in case something like last night happens again."

"If I'd been wearing these rings, I could have pulled the—the tentacle away?"

"It's not guaranteed but you'd have had a much better chance."

"Why do silver and iron work against Necromancy?" Michael asked. He accepted the weight of the jacket, accepted the necklace, but cast a dubious glance at the rings. Michael didn't like having things on his hands. Even gloves in the winter, although he'd wear them if it was cold enough.

Chase shrugged. "Does it matter? They work."

"It matters to Michael," Allison said quietly.

Chase opened his mouth and closed it before more words could fall out. "Eric," he said, "it's all yours."

Eric grimaced. "We don't know, Michael. We weren't given a lot of explanations. We were told that it disrupts Necromantic magic—but not why. It made no sense to me the first time, but it worked. It wasn't complete negation; I'm not sure that exists unless you're a Necromancer yourself.

"I'd explain it if I had the answer. I don't. Old Man?"

Ernest, who'd been silent throughout, shrugged. "It's something to do with earth, with the bones of the earth."

Which made about as much sense to Michael as it did to Allison. Emma turned to Michael. "They can't explain it themselves. But I think we need to trust them."

Michael *did* trust them. He didn't understand them, and lack of understanding always made following instructions vastly more difficult. If you could explain something to Michael, he had no trouble following orders. It's what made people so difficult for him. A smile did not mean the same thing to two different people; laughter didn't either.

He looked at the rings again. Emma looked at them as well; they were *not* subtle. They were large, thick, and on the ugly side.

"If these are mostly silver, is there any reason we can't find silver rings of our own to wear?"

Chase rolled his eyes. "Something is better than nothing," he conceded. "These have the advantage of being both free and heavy."

"Probably their only advantages. Did you make these?"

"The old man did."

Emma grimaced and offered Ernest an apology. Ernest was looking wintery and less than amused. "It hasn't escaped my attention," he said, although he was looking at Chase, "that some people find my work less than aesthetically pleasant."

Michael took two rings. Allison took two. Emma sighed and took two as well; there were dozens, after all.

"Is there anything else we can learn in an evening?"

"No. Not in a single evening. These are the most useful things we can give you at the moment. If you're amenable, we can begin to train you in basic self-defense. But as Eric has pointed out, the Necromancers don't generally resort to brawls and physical beatings to kill people. They will—and they have in the past—but it is not their preferred method." Ernest rose. "In other circumstances, we wouldn't remain here. Part of the ability to survive Necromancers who come hunting is not being present when they arrive. We move."

"A lot," Chase added.

Allison started to shrug the jacket off her shoulders, but Chase caught it before it could fall. "Promise to wear it home," he said, pulling it back into place by the collar. "Wear it to school. Wear it shopping. I know it's not what you'd normally wear—but wear it."

She met his gaze and let her arms fall to her sides.

"Give me your phone," he said.

She frowned. After a moment, she handed Chase her phone.

Chase turned it on and fiddled with it for a bit. "It's a speed dial," he said. He called his own phone from hers. "If something or someone looks suspicious, call. I don't care if nothing comes of it—*call.* Eric and I patrol most nights." He hesitated, exhaled, and finally said, "You're not a Necromancer-in-waiting; they won't have an easy way to find you if they don't know what they're looking for. But we killed two, and there was either one or two more on that plane with them."

Ernest surprised everyone by ordering pizza. It was really strange to be in a living room with paper plates, cups, and pizza, discussing the ways in which total strangers would try to kill them, but their lives had been strange since October.

They agreed to meet up at Eric's in three nights, provided no immediate emergencies prevented it. Emma and Allison walked Michael home; he was silent, although he was fidgeting with the rings on his fingers. Emma was almost surprised he'd chosen to wear them.

But Michael had seen the Necromancers in action. Michael knew they'd tried to kill Allison. He hadn't been there when Allison had almost died, but that didn't change the facts. Being utterly defenseless against a known danger was a greater threat than having things encircling his fingers.

Emma was tense; she was nervous. She couldn't help it. But they looked so *ridiculous* in these jackets, she had to laugh. Ally, seeing the direction of her gaze, started to chuckle as well. Michael didn't. He knew them well enough to know they weren't laughing *at* him, but he honestly didn't see anything worth laughing about.

"Does this make me look like Chase?" he asked, pointing at his own jacket.

Allison, by dint of will, didn't laugh louder. "No. Maybe a little more like Eric. No one else looks like Chase."

"It's his hair," Emma added. She glanced at Nathan, who was smiling in Michael's direction.

Nathan had hardly spoken a word for most of the evening. He'd stayed, as he'd promised, but he'd looked distinctly uncomfortable—and that wasn't Nathan. She wanted to talk to him, but it was cold enough tonight that she didn't want to hold his hand so Michael and Allison could also participate.

She waited instead, walking Michael home and dropping Allison off next. Ally wasn't happy about the order.

"Eric and Chase are close," Michael told her before he entered his house.

Allison immediately swiveled to look over her shoulder; Emma, squinting into the darkness, couldn't see them. "They are?"

Michael nodded. "I think Chase is worried about you."

"Chase isn't worried about me," Allison said, with more than her usual heat.

Michael frowned. "He isn't?"

"He is," Emma said. "Allison doesn't like the *way* he's worried, that's all."

"Why?"

She bit back a sigh. It was Michael. "Chase doesn't think Allison should spend time with me anymore, because of what happened. He doesn't think it's safe."

"He doesn't want you to be friends?"

"No, he really doesn't. He thinks if I *were* a good friend, I would stop seeing Allison until this was all over."

"But . . . but when is it going to be over?"

That, of course, was the million-dollar question. Emma squared her shoulders. "Chase isn't completely wrong." Before Allison could interrupt, she continued. "It would be safest for Allison if she wasn't with me. The Necromancers don't want to kill *me* yet. My life's not in danger. But Ally—"

"Wants to help you."

"Yes, Michael. Yes, she does." Emma smiled at Allison.

"Then it's her choice."

"Exactly," Allison said. "If it makes you feel any better, he's not all that thrilled that you're involved, either."

"He doesn't want Emma to have any friends."

"No," Allison agreed uncharitably.

# ⌒ Chapter 6

Emery's cafeteria sounded like a human hive. Stray syllables and the sound of sharp laughter permeated the buzz of too many conversations, but as most of those conversations weren't directed Emma's way, they could be safely ignored. Connell and Cody bracketed an animated Michael. Allison, beside Emma, was absorbed with Chase, and given the color of her cheeks, their conversation wasn't one Emma wanted to join. Eric was eating—slowly and meticulously as he usually did.

She could now look at Allison without thinking about Necromantic murderers, but it was hard. Allison hated guilt when it wasn't her own, and Emma's guilt was a burden; she tried to keep it to herself. Tried not to think about what Chase had said so often. Tried even harder to believe he was wrong. Friendship with Emma wasn't a death sentence.

"Lunch not edible?" Eric asked.

"It's not likely to kill," she replied. She turned to smile at him. He wasn't smiling back.

"We think we've got a few weeks in the clear before things get really messy."

She wanted to quibble with his definition of not messy, because the past few days defined fear for her. She said nothing. "Emma—"

She waited, hearing the start of a question in the way he said her name. The rest of the question failed to emerge. It was clear why; Allison's sudden increase in volume would have swamped it.

"And *I* think Emma would find it useful *as well*." Allison had been two bites into lunch, and given the set of her lips, no more food was going to enter her mouth.

"Emma isn't the *target*. She doesn't need to know this shit. She's—" He stopped and glared across the table at Eric. Emma guessed Eric had just kicked him sharply in the shins.

"Not the *place*, idiot," Eric said, with a friendly, casual smile. Given his tone of voice, it was forced. It didn't *look* forced.

"Fine," Allison said. She stood, abandoning lunch.

Michael stood as well. He had, of course, been listening. He could listen to two streams of conversation without losing either if both were interesting, although people who weren't used to him were often surprised or offended when he inserted himself into the conversation with no warning.

Allison, however, turned to Michael before he could leave the table. "Chase and I are going to have a fight. It will not be pleasant. I don't mind if you come, but—it's going to be loud and we're both going to be angry."

Michael sat down.

"Smart," Eric said, as he moved to follow Allison. He was surprised when Emma caught his hand.

"Sit down," she told him, smiling exactly the way he had.

"You don't want to leave Allison alone with Chase. He has an ugly temper."

"Are you saying he's going to hurt her?" Emma demanded.

"He has an ugly temper."

"Ally has a temper. He is not going to steamroll her. Eric?"

He stared at her for a minute and then turned to see Allison and Chase leaving the cafeteria by the back doors. "I'm not sure about this."

"You don't have to be. She's not your best friend. She *is* mine, though, and I *am* certain. Look, she's embarrassed when she loses her temper. Something about your friend makes her lose her temper. I think, overall, she'd be happier if we weren't there to witness it."

Eric sat. "I don't understand women," he said.

"You and fifty percent of the species."

By the time they reached a spot in the schoolyard that could be considered private, Chase's mouth was a compressed line that was white around the edges. He'd folded his arms across his chest and drawn himself up to his full height. He did not look friendly. When they stopped walking, he planted his feet half a yard apart and stared down at her.

Allison was not nearly as still or self-contained when she was angry. Most of the things that made her angry were things that embarrassed her. No one liked to think of themselves as small-minded or jealous or petty; Allison was not an exception. Or maybe she was; her sense of self-respect and consideration ran roughshod over that temper on most days.

There was nothing to repress her anger now. She tried. She tried to tell herself that she didn't *know* what Chase's life was like. She didn't know what she'd be like if she had to live every day knowing that random strangers with bigger weapons would be trying to kill her. But looking at him now, the little voice that struggled for civility was swamped.

"Well?" he demanded, as she struggled to find the right words.

"I know you don't trust Emma," she said, keeping her voice even and quiet with difficulty. "But *I* do."

Chase didn't reply.

"Chase, she risked her life to save a child who was *already dead*. She gave his mother a chance to find a little bit of peace. She had no reason to do it—she had nothing to gain and everything to lose."

He said nothing, but he said it loudly.

"You're afraid she has power. Fine. She has power. What good does it do her? If she'd understood what she's capable of doing, saving Andrew Copis wouldn't have been so risky. Putting power in Emma's hands is never going to be a bad thing!"

"You don't understand," he said.

"Then *make me* understand. I'm not going to take it on faith that she's going to become something evil and heartless. I'll take some things on faith—but not this. Yes, you have experience with Necromancers. But never as friends. Never as *people*. I *don't* have your experience—but I know Emma Hall. She is never going to become someone who kills because it's convenient. She's never going to be someone who undervalues life because we all wind up dead in the end.

"And I'm always going to be her friend. I want to learn how to be—how to be less helpless. I don't want to walk to my *own* death."

"If you cared about that, you'd leave her alone. Your life wouldn't *be* in danger if she wasn't your friend. If she cared about you more, she'd acknowledge that."

Allison's hands were fists. "So you want us to abandon each other. Me because I'm a coward and Emma because she's afraid she'll lose me anyway, and it'll be her fault."

"That's not what I'm saying—"

"Damn it, Chase—it *is*. It is what you're saying." She knew she was flushed; she always flushed when she was emotional. She hated it more than ever today. Because the ugly truth was that she *was* afraid. She'd had nightmares for two nights, and she found herself thinking about Necromancers and the thin line between living and dying when she wasn't actively thinking about something else. She could still feel the vine tightening around her throat. She could still feel the bruises it had left.

And she knew—she *knew*—that Emma was *this* close to retreating. To shutting herself off. To walking away from her friends for *their own* sake. She wanted Emma to walk away from Michael, but she wouldn't—couldn't—say it. Michael wasn't a child; he could make his own decisions, just as Allison could.

She held her ground as he took a step forward. Held it, getting angrier, as he took another. She stood entirely in his shadow by the time he'd stopped moving; there was almost no space between them. It would serve him right if she punched him in the stomach.

"I didn't start out as a hunter. Unlike Necromancers, we're not born that way. We train. We train hard." He lowered his hands to his sides. "We all have stories. Some of them involve the deaths of entire communities. Most of us were lucky; we only lost our families." He swallowed. His Adam's apple bobbed. She stared at it; she couldn't lift her gaze to meet his eyes.

"Do you know why I survived?" His voice was a whisper.

"No."

"She wanted to send a message. She wanted to send a message to someone, and I was it. I wasn't a Necromancer. I wouldn't be killed on sight. I watched, Ally." His hands were fists; his shoulders drew in toward his body, robbing him of inches of height. His skin was always pale, but this was different. "I watched. I screamed. I begged. Not for myself. For them. For my parents, my sisters, my little brother. They killed the dogs," he added. "Even the dogs.

"The only person they didn't kill was me. You understand why I'm a hunter."

She nodded. She did.

"I don't care if I die. I spent two years caring very much. But I couldn't kill myself. I couldn't do it. If I die killing them, I'll be grateful." He grimaced. "I have no idea why I'm telling you this."

"You want me to understand what Necromancers mean to you."

"Is that why?"

"Yes."

"I wasn't that keen on the rest of humanity, either. I don't care for most of the hunters, but at least I understand them. I work with Eric because I want to see him kill her."

"Her?"

"The Queen of the Dead." He ran a hand through his hair; it was shaking. "I wanted to kill her myself, but I'm not that lucky. In the end, I'll settle for second best. I don't want to care about other people's lives. I'm done with it."

She felt awkward and self-conscious; her anger had deserted her, and she couldn't claw it back. In its absence, she was shaking as much as Chase, and for far less reason.

"Chase?"

"What?"

"Be done with it." She swallowed. "Stay done with it, if you have to. Leave Emma alone. I'm not a child. It's my decision. I understand the risks, now."

"You would have died if we hadn't been there."

"I *know* that." She exhaled. "You hate yourself because you couldn't do anything for the people you loved. But you want *me* to accept that *I* can't—without even letting me try."

He stared at her, arrested. "I'm not—I'm not saying that."

"How is it different?" She had to look away from his expression again.

He stared at her for a long, uncomfortable moment. "I'll try."

"You'll try?"

"I'll try. I can't promise anything. I don't hate Emma. I hate what she *is*. You can't even see it." He turned back toward the school. "Allison—it's been a while since I was forced to spend this much time with other people. I'm not used to it anymore. I can't see them as anything other than walking victims. And no, Eric doesn't count." He stopped, his back still toward her as she started to catch up.

"I will never, ever forgive you if you get yourself killed."

Emma was waiting for Allison by the back doors. She was trying not to look worried and mostly failing—but failure didn't matter if no one could see it. When Chase strode toward the door, she put on her game face. She was surprised when he yanked the door open and headed straight for her.

"I don't know what you did to deserve a friend like Allison," he said.

Emma braced herself for the rest.

"She says I don't understand what you give her. I'll try. But Emma? I'll kill you myself if anything happens to her." The last words were soft; they were all edge. She met his expression without flinching.

"Deal," she said.

He blinked. "What?"

"It's a deal. If anything happens to Allison, you can kill me." Her smile was shaky but genuine, and it grew as his eyebrows folded together in a broken, red line. "I'll probably be grateful, in the end."

For just a moment, she thought Chase would smile. He didn't. Instead, he headed past her and into the post-lunch school. Allison was only a few seconds behind.

"What did he say to you?" she demanded.

Emma laughed. "He made very clear that you're important to him, and I'm not."

"Emma, it's not funny."

"No, probably not. But if I don't laugh, I'll cry, and I can't cry. I'm not used to people hating my guts out, but—he's worried about you, and I can't fault him for that." She caught Allison's arm as Allison began to stride—there was no other word for that determined step—in the direction of Chase. "He said he'll try, Ally. He promised he'd try. I'm okay with that. Don't ask him for more."

Allison exhaled. "He doesn't even *like* people," she said. "I don't understand why he cares so much."

"About you?"

Allison didn't answer.

Emma slid an arm through hers and dragged her gently back to reality.

*       *       *

Reality these days had its own problems. Amy Snitman careened around a corner, walking in the militaristic fashion that made people of any age move out of her way as quickly as humanly possible. Emma had already stepped to the side, but Amy came up short in front of her, glancing once at Allison and nodding curtly.

"Have you heard the news?"

"No—who died?"

"No one, but only barely. Mr. Taylor is in the hospital, and he's unlikely to be out of traction in the next three months."

"Oh, my god—what happened?"

"He was apparently driving under the influence."

Emma frowned. "Mr. Taylor drinks?"

"I'd've bet against it," was the curt response. "We're sending flowers," she added. "Your share is twenty dollars."

Emma immediately fished a wallet out of her computer bag. "Are you going to visit him?"

"Mrs. Esslemont says he's not taking visitors at the moment."

Which wasn't a no. In general, Amy expected the natural world to conform to her sense of generosity. "What's happening with the yearbook committee?" Mr. Taylor was the supervising teacher; all school committees and clubs required one.

"It's up in the air. Mr. Goldstein has offered to step in."

Emma hoped she didn't look as horrified as she felt. Mr. Goldstein was *this* close to retirement, and most of the students privately felt it was on the wrong side. He was also condescending in a parental way, and it grated.

"You're right," Emma said.

"Of course I am. Which particular flavor of right?"

"It's an emergency." And in a peculiar way, Emma felt grateful for it. It didn't involve dead people. It didn't involve the near murder of her best friend. "Have you talked to Mr. Hutchinson?"

"Not yet. Heading that way."

"I'll come with you." She turned to Allison, who wasn't on the yearbook committee but was well aware that Amy was in a foul mood. "I'll see you in class?"

Allison nodded.

Mr. Hutchinson was the principal. Amy believed in going straight to the top when she wasn't happy with a situation. Since it was impossible to teach at Emery—or to be breathing anywhere in its vicinity—and *not* know Amy Snitman, most of Amy's friends were assumed to be caught up in Amy's tide.

Teachers might hope for and expect a certain amount of intellectual indepen-dence, but they weren't idiots; they knew that peer pressure counted for a lot. Emma had never been on Amy's bad side.

Then again, you didn't land on Amy's bad side unless you were extraordi-narily stupid or thoughtless. If it weren't for the social pressure exerted by Amy Snitman, Michael's life might have been a lot harder at Emery. If you were the idiot who was stupid enough to bully Michael, that spelled the end of your social life for a few weeks.

And the petty pleasure of bullying Michael was not worth the price.

Mr. Hutchinson was in his office; he was eating lunch there. His desk was a fabulous clutter of slips. Emma caught sight of an application for transfer floating on top of them. The principal was almost as old as Mr. Goldstein, but on Hutchinson, the age didn't show. He met all of Emery's many inhabitants as if they were people, rather than excuses to draw a paycheck.

"What can I do for you, Amy?" he asked. He nodded at Emma, but he was busy, and he knew who was in charge. Emma didn't resent this. One couldn't and remain Amy's friend.

"I'm here on behalf of the yearbook committee."

His smile faded. "Yes?"

"I've heard rumors that Mr. Goldstein has volunteered to oversee it."

"He has."

"If I can find you another teacher, will you take him instead?"

"Amy, Mr. Goldstein—"

"Yes, I know. He's experienced and well-respected." She folded her arms across her chest.

"As it happens, I'll be interviewing the temporary replacement for Mr. Taylor. He's new to teaching, and he's been working as a substitute; he could start, without causing difficulty for another school, within the week. He's in-dicated a willingness to undertake Mr. Taylor's extracurricular activities within the school."

Amy's arms tightened. She couldn't exactly demand to be present for the interview. She could find adults who served as trustees, and they could bring pressure to bear where necessary—but it wouldn't be immediate.

"Give him a chance, Amy. If you have concerns after you meet him, we can talk about a suitable replacement."

"Fine."

By the time school dragged its way to a close, the entire student body had heard of Mr. Taylor's accident. Michael was concerned because he took a class with Mr. Taylor, and he was comfortable in that class. A new teacher often created a mess of subtle problems until he or she was accustomed to Michael.

It was Emma's job to speak with whoever the replacement was about Michael's current classroom needs—not that Mr. Hutchison wouldn't have most of them covered. Pippa had offered, but Amy turned her down; she felt that the replacement was likely to listen to Emma because it was already Emma's job to get Michael to school on time.

Not that he needed it anymore. But he clung to the familiar when things got strange—and given Necromancers and dead people, they were pretty damn strange at the moment.

Emma almost headed home but remembered at the last moment that her efforts to avoid talking about Jon Madding had her "eating dinner at Allison's." She walked Michael and Allison home and paused at the foot of Allison's drive, waving once to Mrs. Simner before she walked away.

What she wanted, even though it was November and it was cold, was to see Nathan.

And Nathan, as always, knew.


## Nathan

Emma looks lost and a little forlorn. It's an expression that's not at home on her face, but it's also a gift: it gives Nathan something to do. He slides an arm around her shoulder, but it passes through her jacket, stopping at nothing solid in between.

But she can see him; she can hear him. She was never big on public displays of affection. He can pretend—if he tries hard, and he does—that things are almost normal.

"What happened?" he asks, falling in to her left, on the road side of the walk.

"Mr. Taylor was in a car accident. They say it's lucky he survived."

He steers by walking ever so slightly ahead; he can tell by the flush in her cheeks that she's cold. They used to spend time at the local Starbucks, and it's close enough to dinner that it won't be crowded. He doesn't ask her why she's not at home; he knows.

He doesn't go home either. The reasons are different, but the end result is the same.

He passes through the door; he tries to open it and fails. It's frustrating. On a normal day—for a dead person—he's now used to the idea that everything is permeable. When he's with Emma, he regresses. He hates being dead.

Emma doesn't seem to mind that he can't open doors anymore. He can't buy her coffee. He can't do anything but pretend to sit in the seat across from hers and watch her while she drinks. The latte cupped between her palms steams, curls of white between their faces.

She starts to talk, but she realizes that while he's listening, so is half the cafe. Nothing about their conversation would be forbidden or embarrassing in public—but having one half of a conversation, no matter how innocuous, would be. She drinks her latte while it's still on the edge of too hot and then smiles at him. The smile is shadowed by death—his.

He often wanted to be alone with Emma, but he's sharply aware that there's a difference. The only time she can respond to him without causing concerns for her sanity is when they're alone. But most of her life isn't spent in isolation. She's isolating herself now.

She's doing it because of him.

If he were a stronger person, he'd leave. He knows Eric's right. He's seen enough of the Queen of the Dead to know his presence here can't be a good thing, not for Emma. But she's his entire world right now. There's no school. There's no worrying about college. There's no parental disapproval. There aren't even other friends. The friends he did have, he can't reach without Emma. She's the gate that stands between Nathan and the pain of eternity, and she is incandescent.

Even in her pain or her fear.

He wants to touch her. He wants to take her in his arms. He wants to kiss her. You'd think being dead would get rid of all that; it doesn't. It hones it, makes it sharper. When he was alive, Nathan thought Emma was the most important person in the world. Now he *knows* it.

But he also knows that if her touch warms him and makes him feel alive, it has the opposite effect on her; it chills her. It's like he's frostbite. What Eric said bothers Nathan, and it's hard not to drown in the worry; there's not much he can do to distract himself.

He can read over someone's shoulder. He can slide into a movie theater and watch. He can't talk while he's watching it, which is probably a good thing—but he can't talk to anyone about it afterward. He can't drink, not that he did that much drinking while alive; he can't drive. Driving was one of his refuges.

But mostly he drove to get Emma or to take her home. Now he can only walk beside her as she leaves Starbucks.

"Em," Nathan says. "It's cold. You should go home."

She's silent for half a block, but she doesn't change direction.

"Em—"

"Do you want me to go?" she asks.

The truth is he never wants her to leave. He never did. But he had homework and parents, and so did she.

"I don't want you to freeze to death," is his compromise.

"Then I'm staying. I don't mind the cold." Her teeth are chattering. "I know I'm being unfair. But I don't want to see a stranger's car in the driveway. I just need a couple of days to get used to the idea. Is that too much to ask?"

"No." He watches the wind shuffle strands of her hair. He sees her breath in the white mist that dissipates. He's wearing a T-shirt and jeans. "No, it's not. But—"

"But not more than a couple of days?" Her smile is rueful.

"Not many more. Your mom's not an idiot. If you give Jon a chance, he might surprise you."

"He's like olives?"

Nathan laughs. He hates olives.

Emma returns home sooner than she'd planned, but it's not an act of kindness, not that way. She doesn't want to go home, and starts walking in that aimless way they often had. Nathan follows. He knows he should tell her to go home, but he doesn't want her to leave, not yet. Instead, they walk down roads where houses and lots get larger, and from there, they walk down sloped streets toward the ravine that occupies a large chunk of city real estate.

Emma's breath comes out in mist, adding visual weight to the sound of her breathing. Even though they're alone on the stretch of street that girds the ravine, it's not the only sound they can hear.

"Nathan?"

He frowns. "You're not imagining things. Someone's crying. I think whoever it is isn't very old."

"I don't suppose you have a flashlight?" she asks, with a grimace.

He smiles and shoves his hands into his pockets. "Next time, I'll try to die prepared."

She is silent for one frozen moment, and then she spins around to punch his shoulder. "That's not funny!"

"You're laughing." So is he.

"Because I have to laugh or I'll cry."

"Laughter's better. Do you want me to go down there and take a look?"

"You can come down with me."

"*I'm* not likely to slip, fall, and break anything on a tree I can't see. You might have noticed the snow in the ravine." Most of the snow on the roads has turned to salty slush, but in the ravine there's a thin blanket of white. It's the type of snow that often covers patches of ice.

"Neither am I." She laughs at his expression. He loves the sound of her laughter; he doesn't hear it so much anymore. "Okay, maybe. But you can't talk to the child if you do find him—or her; you can't help if he's lost or stuck."

"I could at least tell you whether or not he's *there*."

She shakes her head. "Come with me," she tells him, in a final-offer tone of voice.

"Em," he says, shaking his head in a way that once made his hair fly, "Don't change, okay? And be careful—I don't want to be with you so badly I want you to—"

She touches his lips. It sends a shock through his body, and he leans into the tip of her finger.

It's the dark gray that means night, but the moon is still silver. Emma begins to navigate her way through the snow, heading in the direction of the voice.

She freezes when the crying stops. She fumbles in her pocket for her phone. "I don't know where he is, but he can't stay out here. Not at this time of night."

"He might be with his parents—"

She gives him a look and turns back to the phone. The crying starts again, and she snaps the phone shut. "That way," she tells Nathan.

The trees don't so much open up as follow the line of a small stream that sometimes floods in the spring; Emma finds it easiest to follow the twisting line of the buried brook.

Cupping her hands over her mouth, she takes the risk of shouting. "Hello!"

Silence. The crying stops.

"I'm here to help you. Stay where you are, and I should be able to find you. I'm Emma," she adds. "Emma Hall."

Silence again. Emma bites her lip. "I know you're not supposed to talk to strangers," she says, in her loud, clear voice. "But it's very, *very* cold outside, and I think tonight, just this once, it would be okay."

It's a good guess. It's not a guess Nathan would have made.

More silence. Emma swears under her breath. "I should have gone home for Petal," she says, forgetting Jon Madding and her mother. "He could have found the child." She inhales and exhales a cloud, squaring her shoulders as she tries again.

Emma never gives up. Not when it's important.

"I was walking home from a friend's house when I heard you," she tells the invisible child. "I can just go home, if you want." She's lying. She isn't leaving until she finds this child, one way or the other. "I have a phone if you want to call your mom. You don't have to talk to me at all if you don't want."

Silence.

"But I'm freezing out here. It's *really* cold. I need to go home."

More silence.

"My mom won't let me talk to strangers either. I got lost on the subway once, and I was really afraid. I thought I'd never, ever get home again. I started to cry. But a woman noticed I was crying, and she stopped and asked me if I was lost. I answered her, even though she was a stranger and my mom had told me not to speak to strangers, because my mom had *also* taught me I should be polite to strangers.

"I never understood how you could be polite if you weren't allowed to talk at all. But that woman? She helped me get home. She was going home, too, and she was going to the same station I was supposed to go to.

"When I got home, I was very late, and I thought I'd be in a lot of trouble when I told my mom what happened. But my mom wasn't mad at me. My mom was grateful that someone was there who could help me.

"Your mom would be grateful, too. I'm sure she would."

Silence.

"Emma," Nathan says softly, nodding toward the trees on the far, far left. "Keep talking. I think I saw movement. I think he's following your voice."

Which is technically not breaking any rules about strangers. Children have the oddest notions; they take things so literally. Emma is sort of used to that, because Michael does it as well.

"My mom told me, afterward, that not all strangers are dangerous. In fact, she told me that *most* strangers are just like me—they want to help. They're nice people. The lady who helped me was a very kind person." Emma looks helplessly at the trees that Nathan indicated; she can't see what he saw. There is no movement of branches, no definitive crunch of icy snow—just the silence. The silence has become almost unbearable. She's stopped talking.

She picks it up, kneeling in the snow, trying instinctively to make herself seem smaller and less threatening. Her coat is long enough to cover her knees as she does.

"Because I remember that lady and how much she helped me, I try to help other children if I see them crying. I try to help them if I think they're lost. I think you're lost," she adds. "And I want to help."

She holds her breath as she finally sees what Nathan has seen: a flash of movement, a small change in the darkness to the left. She still can't hear much—the child must be really light or really small—but the glimpse gives her hope. She holds out both of her arms, and as she does, the child begins to cry again. The crying is different this time; the child is still frightened, but the fear has shifted from hopeless despair to something less heartbreaking.

"I'm lost," the small voice finally says. "You can take me home?"

But Emma, arms out, freezes completely as the child finally peers out from behind the trunk of a leafless tree. She finally understands why she'd heard the child so clearly from so far away: It is far too late to take him home. He is already dead.

# Chapter 7

"This is where I live," Emma said quietly. There was no strange car in the drive, which meant no stranger in the house. It should have been more of a relief than it was.

The dead child was a young boy. Emma thought him six at most, but he calmly told her he was eight years old. He was skinny and short for his age, and he had the same kind of calm vulnerability of—of Michael at that age. His hand was firmly in hers; if she could have, she would have carried him. Her hand had passed beyond pain three blocks ago; it was numb. Her upper arm was tingling from the cold of both winter and a dead child's hand.

The boy nodded as he looked at Emma's house. His name was Mark Rayner. He had one brother and one sister. He lived with his mother; his father mostly lived somewhere in America.

"Will we go to my house after this?" he asked.

Emma's careful smile faltered. She had asked Mark where he lived, and with whom. She had explained that her own mother might be worried if she was out so late in the cold. And she hoped that Mark knew he was dead. If he did, he wasn't sharing.

She managed to get the front door open with one hand, which took effort; she was afraid to let Mark go. Why, she didn't know; she didn't cling to Nathan in the same way, and she certainly didn't need to touch her father. But the boy seemed to take some comfort from the contact—and it might be the *only* comfort she could offer him. For her troubles, she got a face full of Petal as he ran full tilt at the door, his tongue wagging almost as much as his stubby little tail.

Mark's eyes widened, and he tried—still holding Emma's hand—to hide behind her.

"It's okay, he doesn't bite. He's a really friendly old dog. You can—" pat him? She was irritated at herself for speaking without thinking. "He won't hurt you. I don't think he's ever hurt anyone but himself; he's a bit of a klutz."

"Emma?"

This was *so* not what Emma needed. Mercy Hall walked out of the kitchen and into the front hall as Emma tried, very hard, to disentangle her hand. She didn't quite manage in time. Her mother blinked. Emma could still see Mark; Mercy Hall couldn't. But she'd probably seen something.

"Who were you talking to?" she asked, in exactly the wrong tone of voice.

Emma was too tired to lie; lying was a lot of work. She said nothing instead, removing her coat and her boots and putting them in the closet, her back—and her face—turned away from her mother. Composing her expression, she finished and turned around. "No visitors tonight?"

"No. I have a lot of work. You're alone?"

"I'm alone."

Nathan had left her, not at her house but in the ravine. *I don't want to scare him,* he'd said. *And he's already taken the risk of talking to one stranger. I think there's a chance he'll run if there are two of us.*

Mark was watching both Emma and her mother with a faint air of confusion.

"Emma, I wanted to speak with you about Jon."

*So* not the conversation she needed to be having right now. "You said you have a lot of work?"

"It doesn't have to be a long conversation."

"I have a lot of homework. Unless you're going to tell me you want him to move in, can we try this tomorrow when we both have more time?"

Mercy opened her mouth, shut it, and stood very still, as if she were counting. Then she nodded. "You'd like him if you gave him half a chance."

"I didn't hate him," Emma replied. "He seemed like a perfectly nice guy."

"He is."

The silence was awkward. The smiles that filled it were brittle, and not much better. Emma kept hers on her face until her mother slid back into the dining room. The dining table was once again a mess of scattered paper piles, which was all Emma saw of it before she turned to Mark.

"I'm sorry," she said quietly.

"That was your mom?"

She nodded. "She has a lot of work to do, and when she brings it home, I'm always careful not to disturb her too much."

"Mine, too."

"Come upstairs? My dad's not busy right now; I'll introduce you."

He clearly had no desire to meet strange men. Emma wondered how he had died. She couldn't ask, not yet. But she held out a hand, braced herself for the rush of cold as he took it, and led him upstairs to her room. Petal followed, whining.

Her dad was, in fact, in her room. He had a pipe in his hands and appeared to be inspecting the bowl. It wasn't lit, or if it was, ghost smoke had no scent. But he turned to face her as she entered the room with her visitor and set the pipe on the windowsill, where it vanished instantly without, oh, setting the curtains on fire.

"Emma," he said, smiling, his gaze on the stranger.

"Dad."

"You're late, tonight."

"I'm sorry. I—I heard someone crying in the ravine, and I climbed down to find him. This is Mark; he got lost there."

Mark was, once again, peering out from behind Emma. "Mark, this is my dad, Brendan Hall."

Mark said nothing, which wasn't a big surprise.

"This is my room. That's my computer—"

"You have your own computer?"

She nodded. "Do you want to see it?" Crouching, she hit the power button. She knew her dad could do something to make the computer respond and hoped it was a natural ability of ghosts, because Mark was going to be pretty disappointed, otherwise.

As it powered up, she glanced at her father and mouthed the word "help." Mark slid into Emma's chair, his hands hovering above the keyboard, his gaze riveted to the monitor. Brendan Hall gestured, and she quietly stepped away.

"What happened?" her father asked, his voice very soft.

She told him exactly what had happened, because at the moment, that wasn't her concern. "I don't think he knows he's dead, Dad. And I'm not sure what to tell him."

"How long has it been?"

"I don't know—I can't exactly start Googling for details about his death while he's on the computer."

"Go ask your mother if you can use hers."

"No way."

"Em—"

"I'm not explaining why. She doesn't want to know, but she'll ask. I'm too tired to come up with a decent lie."

"Emma—"

"She wants the dead to be dead," Emma continued bitterly.

"The dead *are* dead."

"Well, she wants them to be *safely* dead. And quiet. She doesn't want to know that her only daughter is touching their ghosts."

"Emma, I'll only say this once. What happens—or does not happen— between Mercy and me is none of your business. You are our child, but we're not one person. I'm dead, and I accept it. So, finally, does she."

"But you're *here*."

"Yes. And I shouldn't be. You know that." He nodded at Mark's back. "I think your young guest has some suspicions."

Emma frowned and looked over her shoulder to see a familiar Google logo on the screen; the rest of the type was too small, at this distance, to read. She walked, quickly, to the desk and did something she hated: She stood over Mark's shoulder, reading what his search had pulled up.

Mark Rayner.

She fished around in her pocket for her phone, pulled it out, and hit the first speed-dial button. Allison answered on the third ring.

"Emma?"

"Can you come here—with Michael—right now?"

There was a small pause, and Emma glanced at the clock; it was 9:45. "Never mind," she said. "I didn't notice the time. Don't come. Your mother will just worry at you."

"At me? I'm going to tell her it's your fault." She could almost see Allison's grin.

"No, Ally, I'm fine—"

"You're always fine. I'll call Michael's mother as well. We'll be there soon."

They arrived ten minutes later, which was fast enough Emma was instantly suspicious. Her suspicions were confirmed when she answered her mother's up-the-stairs summons: Allison and Michael stood in the hall, which she'd expected; Eric stood behind them, his back to the door. He looked over their heads and up the stairs at Emma.

Aware of her mother, Emma smiled a full-on Hall smile. "I'm sorry," she said, heading down the stairs, her father and a young boy safely ensconced in her room. "I didn't mean to drag you guys out so late."

"Eric drove," Michael replied.

Mercy Hall, like Eric, was looking at her daughter with question marks in her eyes. But she was a Hall as well; she kept them to herself while they had guests. Emma waited until shoes, boots, assorted mittens, scarves, and hats had been more or less closeted, and then led them all upstairs. "It's a bit of a mess," she told them before she opened her door. Petal joined the entourage, which guaranteed it would be even more of a mess in a handful of minutes.

He was the first one through the door, because he didn't wait for it to be fully open; he was also the first one on the bed, where he was technically not allowed to go. The duvet engulfed him, mostly because he was rolling in it. Allison and Michael walked in; Michael sat on the edge of the bed, nearest Petal; Allison sat on the ancient beanbag chair in the corner. Eric, however, stood in the center of the room, somewhere between Emma's dad and her visitor.

Emma took a deep breath, closed the door firmly behind her and glanced at Eric.

"I have a visitor," she said. She walked over to her computer; Mark was still seated in the chair, staring at a screen full of Google.

"Would his name be Mark Rayner?" was Eric's soft question.

The child turned at the sound of his name, his eyes widening as he saw Emma's friends. He had apparently failed to hear the door or see Petal, Allison, Michael, or Eric when they'd entered the room. It was almost as if he were a younger version of Michael. This impression was strengthened when he said, "Yes, I'm Mark Rayner," before turning back to the computer screen.

Eric raised a brow at his back. "Where did you find him?"

"In the ravine," Emma replied. She struggled with tone of voice, and lost. "I heard someone crying when we—when I was walking home."

"And you went into the ravine on your own in the dark to find him." Said like that, it sounded like an accusation.

The beanbag made its usual squeaking noises as Allison pushed herself out of it; Eric immediately fell silent.

"I did. It took me a while to find him. He's not supposed to speak to strangers, and I'm a stranger."

Michael stood as well. When Michael stood, it was generally a signal. "Emma, can I meet him?"

She nodded. She approached the chair in which Mark sat, and knelt beside it, bringing her eyes in line with his. He didn't look at her; he looked at the screen. His fingers hovered above the keyboard—or the mouse. Emma wasn't certain how he could use either, and now didn't seem like the right time to ask.

"I want to go home," Mark told her, without looking down to where she now crouched.

Emma closed her eyes. "Can I introduce you to my friends, first?"

"Yes."

"You'll have to get down from the chair."

"Why?"

She almost laughed. "It's important, when meeting people who don't know you and don't understand you."

"Why?"

"If you don't, they'll feel like you're ignoring them."

"Oh."

Since it appeared that he was ignoring them, and since Eric clearly felt he was, Emma gently forced the chair around. He came with it; she hadn't been certain he would. He frowned as she held out her hand. But after a long, silent minute, he placed his hand in reach of hers. "It feels different," he told her, sliding off the chair, looking for all the world like a living boy.

Her hand should have been numb at this point, but it wasn't, and the cold of his small palm burned.

"Mark, this is Allison, my best friend."

Mark nodded.

"This is Michael. I think Michael and you might have a lot in common. That's Eric."

Mark frowned as he looked at Michael. "Are you normal?" he asked.

It wasn't the question that anyone expected, but Michael was seldom floored by questions that weren't laced with anger or pain. "I'm normal for me."

"I'm not," Mark said quietly, staring at a fixed point on the floor. "I'm not normal."

A long silence followed. Emma had to resist the urge to put her arms around the child; she *also* had to resist the urge to ask him who'd told him this and, more important, why they'd said it. "No one is normal," she told him instead.

"Other people are normal."

"But you're not other people," Michael said, which was good; Emma was silent for a moment, struggling with a sudden surge of protective anger. Michael spoke calmly because he was stating simple, irrefutable fact.

Mark nodded, but he added, "If I were other people, if I were like other people, people would like me."

Allison's expression mirrored Emma's feelings; Ally had never been as good at the Hall face.

"Do you like dogs?" Mark asked.

Michael nodded.

"I don't like the smell. And their breath. I don't like the sound the lights make." These two statements were not connected. Mark really did remind Emma of Michael as a child.

"He doesn't smell bad, to me. He smells like dogs smell." Michael thought for a minute and then asked, "Do cats smell bad to you?"

"Not all cats. Some cats."

"Do these lights make bad noises?"

Mark frowned. He looked at Emma's hand, still entangled with his, and then tilted his head to one side. "No." He looked confused. "Emma's hand doesn't hurt. The lights here are quiet."

"Maybe it's different," Michael said, as Emma opened her mouth to speak, "because you're dead now."

Silence.

Mark proved that he was not like Emma, not like Allison, and not like other children. He blinked, then frowned. "Am I dead?" he asked Michael.

Michael nodded.

"Oh." He looked down at his hands, one of which was still wrapped in Emma's. "It doesn't hurt," he said. He sounded surprised. "Am I a ghost?"

Michael nodded again. "We can't see you if Emma's not holding your hand."

"Oh." Pause. "Why?"

"I don't know. Emma," he added, "can see dead people. But most of us can't."

"Why can Emma see dead people?"

"I don't know."

He turned to Emma. "Why can you see dead people?"

"I'm sorry, Mark, but I don't know, either. I can't—I can't always tell they're dead. They don't really *look* like ghosts look in stories or on television. I didn't know you were—"

"Dead?"

She nodded. "I could hear you—but I couldn't tell until I saw you."

"But you said—"

"When I could see your eyes, I knew."

"My eyes look dead?"

She shook her head. "It's their color." She paused, and then said, "My dad's dead, as well."

"Did you find him, too?"

"No." She hesitated, then looked at her father, who had been standing in the room the whole time. "No, he found me."

Mark's blank expression probably meant confusion; it's what it often meant on Michael's face.

"My father wasn't lost. He was dead, but he knew where he was."

"Oh. How did he know?"

"You'll have to ask him. You can see him, right?"

Mark nodded.

"Michael and Allison can't. They know he's there because I've told them, but they won't be able to speak with him until I hold his hand. I'm like a—like a window."

Allison shook her head. "Emma is alive, but Emma can see the dead, and when she touches the dead, she makes them visible for the rest of us."

Mark was silent for a full minute. Emma's father was watching him, hands in his pockets, his brow creased in concern.

"I want," Mark finally said, "to go home."

The silence was awkward, but there was no way to avoid that. Allison didn't exactly break it, but she did move toward Emma's computer. "Mark, what is the last date you remember?"

He frowned.

She tried again. "What was the date yesterday?" When he failed to answer, she said, "The day before yesterday?" She waited for another minute before she sat in the chair.

Ally moved to occupy the space in front of Emma's computer. The resultant sound of keys and mouse-clicks were audible.

Emma's hand was numb. Her lower arm was heading that way as well, but at the moment, the cold was painful. Eric was painful in a different way. Throughout the entire discussion he'd said nothing; he'd watched Mark and Michael in a stiff silence. Petal was agitating for Milk-Bones, and slathering Michael's hand in dog germs; Michael didn't appear to notice—hard, when a rottweiler was sitting *on* your feet.

"Three years ago," Allison finally said, into a lot of silence.

Emma, hand in Mark's, looked over her shoulder. She wasn't certain how much she could or should ask, given that Mark was in the room. But if Mark was like Michael, it wouldn't matter. "Exactly three years?"

"Three years in two months. He was eight years old, but on the small side for his age. He went out for a walk during the day and failed to come home. They mobilized most of a police division searching for him, but they didn't find him for two and a half weeks."

"Hypothermia?"

"Yes."

And he'd been there ever since.


"Are you cold?" Emma asked.

Mark frowned. He was wearing a simple ski jacket and equally simple shoes, neither of which he'd tried to remove on arrival. The shoes were in no way appropriate for tonight's weather—and it wasn't January yet, which was usually colder. "I'm not cold," he finally said. "But I'm not warm, either. My hand doesn't hurt," he added, looking at hers. "And the lights are quiet." He let go of Emma's hand, or tried; when he pulled, her hand followed.

"I'm sorry," she told him. "My hands—they get really, really cold when I'm touching a ghost, and my fingers get numb enough I can't really feel them."

"That's not good," he replied, as she pried her fingers free. He walked toward where Allison was still reading the computer screen, and stood to the left of her, reading as well. "I wasn't alone," he told them. Only Emma could hear.

Emma stiffened. "When, Mark?"

"I didn't go out alone. That part's wrong."

Emma turned; so did her father and Eric. She reached out and caught Mark's hand, and he allowed it, now that he was beside the computer.

"Mark didn't—didn't go out alone," Emma told Allison.

Allison's hands froze for a second. She turned to look at Mark, who was standing beside her. "You went to the ravine with friends?"

Mark seemed to shrink at that. ". . . I don't have any friends."

Allison's lips compressed. Emma started to say *everyone has friends*, but managed to stop those words as well. It didn't matter what she thought, after all; it was the truth as Mark saw it. It was just *so* hard to hear from the mouth of a child, especially a dead one; the urge to comfort him was visceral. But . . . when had meaningless, hopeful words been much of a comfort in her own life? Even with the best of intentions behind them?

Michael said, in all the wrong tone of voice for Michael, "Who took you to the ravine?"

Mark hesitated, and then said, "My mom."

## ⌒ Chapter 8

Emma had suffered awkward silences before; this one was charged. She took refuge, for a moment, in confusion. She wanted to cling to it. She might have even managed, but Michael was there, and Michael now walked to the computer. He was almost twitching, which was never a good sign. He looked over Allison's shoulder as if she weren't there, and didn't appear to notice when she moved, surrendering both mouse and keyboard.

He knew—they all knew—that not everything reported in the papers was exact; editors changed little things—like, for instance, dialogue—in the name of saving space. Why they did this for articles that were on the web, no one understood. Space wasn't an issue—maybe attention span was. But almost every article Allison had managed to find contained a quote from the grieving mother, and in each, she clearly stated that she had come home to find Mark had gone out.

Emma wanted to speak with her father, but she had Mark by the hand, and she couldn't think of a way to detach herself. She sent her father an imploring look and froze at his expression; he wasn't looking at her. He was, like the rest of the people in the room, looking at the computer.

"Mark," Emma finally said, "I don't think going home is a good idea."

He looked up at her. "You promised."

"I—" She swallowed. What was she going to say? She hadn't known he was dead? Her father approached Mark as she struggled to find useful words, and crouched—in much the same way Emma had when she'd coaxed Mark out of the ravine.

"Mark, why don't you come for a walk with me? You can show me where your house is."

Mark hesitated.

"He won't hurt you," Emma told the young boy.

"He can't," Michael added.

"My father lives in America," Mark told them. "Because of me."

Emma wanted to scream. "Sometimes my dad thought I was frustrating. We used to argue about Petal—that's my dog's name."

Brendan Hall chuckled. He didn't hold out a hand; he did rise. "I haven't been outside in a while. Let's take a walk." Glancing at Emma, he added, "Emma's not very good at reading maps. If she tried to find your house without help, she'd probably get lost for hours."

It was true. Emma didn't even mind that he'd said it. She wanted Mark to go with her father because she didn't want him to hear anything she had to say. *What will you be protecting him* from? she thought. *He's already dead.*

But dead, he was an eight-year-old boy who looked like he was six and spoke as if he were four. Dead, he'd been crying in the ravine for—for how long? He didn't have a body; he couldn't be murdered. He could no longer freeze to death, because according to Google, he'd already done that. But he could be afraid. He could be lonely.

He could definitely be hurt in all the ways that didn't actually kill you. Some of those, Emma thought, death was *supposed* to end. Clearly, it hadn't.

Mark still hesitated, and her father said, "I need to be able to find your house so I can tell Emma exactly how to get there from here. You don't want to be lost for hours, do you?"

Mark shook his head. "I want to go home," he whispered.

Emma knew her father would have picked Mark up if he could; he would have hugged him, or put him on his shoulders, or any of the things he used to do with Emma's friends when he was alive. He didn't try that with this one; she wasn't even certain he could. He couldn't touch the living—were there rules that governed the way the dead interacted?

Probably, she thought grimly. She had a good idea of who'd made those rules. She headed to the door and opened it, although it wasn't, strictly speaking, necessary. "He'll bring you back," she told Mark, "if you want to come back. He won't leave you, and he won't lose you."

Mark nodded. Brendan Hall walked through the open door. Staring at the floor—or at his feet, Emma wasn't certain which—Mark followed him out. She closed the door behind them and leaned back against it, thinking that bashing it a few times with the back of her head would actually feel *good* at this point.

Eric said, "You don't want to do this."

Emma and Allison both swiveled heads to look at him; Michael was in Michael-land. Allison gently pushed him into the chair she'd vacated. He sat without really paying attention, adjusting his posture in the same way.

They then moved toward the wall farthest away from Michael. Petal joined them for a bit, sniffing at their hands and whining like loud background noise. Emma scratched behind his ears because she could do that in her sleep; it didn't require a lot of attention.

She wasn't sleeping now.

"I told him I would," she said, keeping her voice low. "He's not wrong about that. I didn't—I didn't realize he was dead when I heard him the first time. He was crying; he sounded—" she bit her lip. "I didn't want to leave him in the damn ravine in this weather at this time of night. I almost called 911—" She stopped, aware of how badly *that* would have ended. "But I told him I would take him home."

Eric folded arms across his chest in silence.

"Don't even think of telling me it's not my business."

"I won't. I understand how you've made it your problem—" He held up a hand as Allison opened her mouth. "—And I sympathize. I don't fault you for trying to rescue a lost child. You didn't know he was dead, but Emma? Even if you'd known, you wouldn't have done things differently."

"I wouldn't have promised to take him home."

One dark brow rose. "Chase tells me I look stupid at least three times a day—but not even Chase would accuse me of being *that* stupid. If there was no other way to get him to come to you, you'd've done exactly what you did."

"Not if I knew—"

"Knew what?"

Her hands were shaking. This time it wasn't because of the cold, although the fact they weren't both bunched in fists was. She didn't want to say the words that were stuck in her throat.

Eric once again folded his arms across his chest.

Allison came to her rescue. "She wouldn't have promised to take him home to a mother who'd left him there in the first place." She now dropped her hands to her hips, the Allison equivalent of Eric's crossed arms. "No child needs to know—" she stopped speaking.

"If you can't even say it, how are you going to handle him while you're there?" He let his arms drop. "Emma—this is not a good idea."

"I *know* that. But I told him—"

"I know what you told him. I understand that you don't want to be the person who breaks her word—I don't usually consider that a bad thing. But in this case, what good will it do? This isn't about Mark—or not only about him. It's also about Emma Hall."

"He knows what we know. Or suspects what we suspect. It's already hard for him—if he *wants* to go home, how can I say no?"

"It's a single syllable. I think you can manage it."

"I don't think—"

"Tell him that you didn't know he was dead. He can't live at home, any-more. He can't live anywhere, period."

The breadth and depth of Eric's callousness robbed Emma of words for a long, long moment. The words that did come rushing in were words she was pretty sure she'd regret—sometime. At the moment, she was having a hard time seeing it. "Why do you think it's a bad idea?" she managed to get out.

"He's dead."

"My dad is dead—but he's here."

"Yes. But your mother can't see him. Only you can. He's had to come to terms with his near invisibility and his death, and he's had time to do that. Mark—from what I can tell—hasn't. He's had enough time to figure it out, but he didn't *take* that time; I don't think he was aware of the passage of time at all. What will home give him?"

"I don't know—what does it give my dad?"

Eric closed his eyes. When he opened them, he'd smoothed the edges off his jaw and out of his voice. "Comfort. He wanted to know you—and your mother—were doing all right. You both are."

"Maybe Mark—" But she couldn't say it. "We don't know what she said to him. We don't know how it happened. We know nothing, Eric. All we really know is we have a very young eight year old who's only just discovering he's dead. He wants to see the world he knew. And I—I promised I would take him home."

Eric slowly lowered his arms. "Emma—he's not alive."

"I *know* that—if he were, we wouldn't be having this problem."

"You'd have an entirely different problem."

It was true, but Emma was too tired for what-ifs and theory. She was too tired to argue with Eric. "Maybe my dad will have some luck talking to Mark. Maybe Mark will decide he can't—can't go home."

Silence. It wasn't Nathan's silence; it was built on accusation, anger, even guilt. Emma didn't want it; she wanted—briefly, ferociously—to see Na-than.

"Where will he stay, if he doesn't go home?" Allison finally asked.

Eric just shook his head. "Emma—I know you see the dead as people; you see them as more than dead. I understand that. But there's no orphanage for dead children. There's no place they gather—" he stopped.

Emma said, in a very soft voice, "The City of the Dead."

"They don't gather there by choice," was his cold reply. "They don't need food, clothing or shelter; they don't need school. They don't even need to take up space. Yes, they're part of the world you now see—but you're not trying to find a home for wind or rain."

"They're not forces of nature, Eric. They're *people*. They have feelings, and they're the same feelings *we* have. I don't know where he's going to stay," she added, looking around her room. "But there are worse places than this one."

Eric said nothing.

"My dad's here. My dad's great with kids. If Mark's parents are alive, why can't he stay with my dad?"

"You don't even know where your dad is, most of the time."

"I don't need to know—Mark does. But my dad would do that, for him."

"Or for you?"

It was her turn to cross her arms. "For him."

"Fine. Maybe it's genetic. I hope your dad can talk him into staying here, for your sake."

Michael rose, leaving the computer and the keyboard behind.

Emma glanced at the time; it was already past late. "Michael and Allison have to get home."

"I'll drive them. But Emma? Don't take him tonight. You're exhausted. It's late. If you have to go, go during the day, and take me with you."

Given his attitude tonight, she was absolutely certain she didn't want him there.

". . . Or take Allison and Michael if you won't have me."

"I highly doubt his mother is a Necromancer."

"So do I. If I thought she was, I'd approach it differently. Michael?"

Michael stood in the open door, one foot over the threshold, as if stuck there. He swiveled. "Emma promised," he said quietly.

"You heard that?"

Michael looked confused, but he nodded. "It's important. To keep your promises." But he looked at Emma and Allison and said, "I don't understand what happened."

They exchanged a glance. "Neither do we," Emma told him.

"Why did she take him to the ravine? Why did she lie to the police?"

"Michael—we don't know. We don't know what happened."

"We can ask Mark."

Emma felt a little like the floor had suddenly dropped out from under her. She swallowed. "Sometimes it's upsetting to be asked—"

"It's not more upsetting than being left in the ravine in January," he pointed out. His eyes were starting to rapid-blink. Allison walked over to him, put an arm around his shoulders. He leaned back into it.

"Tomorrow. Tomorrow, we can ask him. But, Michael—if he doesn't want to talk about it, we can't force him."

Since this seemed self-evident to Michael, he ignored it. Allison pulled him out the door. Eric watched them leave, and then turned to Emma with an expression she couldn't interpret on his face. "I'm sorry, Emma," he said. It didn't sound like he was apologizing for their argument.

"Send Chase to Siberia and we'll talk," she replied.

He laughed. Laughter, as Nathan had said, was better than pain.

"I went home."

Emma turned as Nathan appeared in her room. He was leaning against the back wall, his hands in his pockets, his head tilted up in a way that exposed his neck. She wanted to hold him. Or to be held by him.

"I went home," he repeated, "and I saw my mom. My dad. It was a totally different house. Do you know what she's done to my room?"

"She hasn't turned it into a guest room."

"No—it's like a small shrine. There's a picture of me on my pillow. The bed is made. All of my stuff is still on my shelves—but it's really, really tidy, now." He laughed. It wasn't a happy laugh. "She goes to my grave every day. She gets up in the morning before work. She stops by after work. If work was closer, she'd be there at lunch." He took his hands out of his pockets, lifting them in something that was like a shrug, but heavier. "She marks my *calendar*, Em.

"I can't talk to her. I can't touch her. I can't tell her I'm not in pain, I'm all right. She cries," he added, looking at the ceiling again. "I think she's driving Dad nuts."

"She did that anyway," Emma pointed out, and Nathan did laugh.

"True." The laughter faded. "It's not home. It's not home the way it is—everything in it is a reminder that I'm dead."

"That's not what she's trying to do—"

"I know. I know she wants to remember that I did live, I was there. But—I can't make her laugh, anymore. I can't stop the tears." He shoved his hands back into his pockets and looked directly at Emma. "But I don't know how I'd feel if there was no sign of her grief. I don't know how I'd feel if she was happy all the time. I don't know what I'd want if I—"

"If you were Mark."

He nodded. "It's different, for your dad. I think, right now, I want what he wants—I want my mom to be happy. I *know* that she loved me. I know that she misses me. I know that if her death could bring me back, she'd kill herself in a heartbeat. But it won't—and if it could, and she did, I would hate being alive.

"But I can think this and feel this because, right now, it's so clear that I was the center of her universe."

"You were the center of mine."

He actually winced. "I was only one of the foundations. You had Allison, you had Michael, and they both needed you at least as much as I thought I did. My mother—"

"Lived for you."

"Lived for me. I've gutted her life, and I hate it. But—"

"If she hadn't cared at all, you'd have hated that as well?"

"People are contrary. Yeah, I'd've hated it—if no one missed me at all, what would the point of my life have been?" A pained, quiet smile rippled across the stillness of his expression. "I don't want her to suffer," he said.

"But love causes suffering?"

He laughed. "Only when it ends."

"It never ends, Nathan. You're dead, but I still love you."

"You can talk to me."

"How do you think I know what your mother does? How do you think I know what she does for your grave? I was *there*. Not at the same time as your mother—but after. I saw the flowers she left, and the notes, and the Game Boy. Maybe she thought it would reach you somehow. She still loves you, Nathan— we both do. The fact that you died doesn't change that. It only changes—" she stopped. "She's never going to stop. I'm never going to stop."

"I don't want her to stop. I want her to move on."

"That's not your decision to make." She turned away.

"Emma."

"Yes?" She began to straighten her duvet, which was hard because Petal was flopped out in the middle of it and didn't want to move.

"Could you—could you let her—"

"Talk to you?"

"Yes."

"I could. If you want, I will." But she hesitated, and he caught it—he'd always noticed everything.

"You don't want to do it."

"I *do* want to do it," was her low, low reply. She bent a moment over the bed as the world became blurry. "I want to do it for her because it's what *I* would want. I'd want that last chance to say good-bye. I'd want to tell you all the things I didn't tell you because I didn't *know* it would be the last day. I'd *want it*, Nathan, because it would be peace."

"You don't think it would be peace for my mother."

"I do—but . . ." She looked down at her hands; they were shaking. "But if I knew that you could be called when I needed to—wanted to—see you, I don't think I'd ever let go. If she knows it's because of me, she'll be here. Maybe not the day after, but the week after, and every week after. She'll ask questions I can't answer—and she'll ask questions I *can* answer, but they'll put her life in danger.

"And I'll hate it—but I'll do it because I'll understand what she needs. I'm—I'm lucky. I *can* talk to you. I *can* touch you."

"Not without cost."

She laughed. It sounded like crying. "I don't want to deny her anything because what she feels—it's the closest to what I feel. My friends worry for me; Michael misses you. But they don't feel the loss the same way because they didn't—"

"Love me."

"Not like I did."

His smile was hesitant. If you didn't know him, it would have looked shy. Emma knew him. "Am I wrong?"

He shook his head. "No."

"But?"

He laughed. "But you were so angry at Allison for saying almost the same thing about *your* mom."

"I wasn't. She didn't say the same thing—"

"You were, Emma. It just didn't sound the same to you because you were talking about your mother, not mine. You don't want to give my mother hope when you can't guarantee you can carry it—but you want it for yours, anyway."

"It's not the same," she finally said, voice heavier. "Your mom wants to see you. I'm certain it's the only things she wants. My mom—"

He lifted a hand and touched her lips with his cold, cold fingers. "Don't. Don't say it."

"Why not? It's true."

"Not everything true deserves to be said."

"I'll do it, though. If you think it'll help her."

"It's not just what I think that counts here."

An argument was hovering in the air between them, growing denser and thicker as the silence stretched. Emma wanted to avoid it, but it loomed so large it was almost impossible to speak around it. It would have helped if she'd understood why; the last thing she wanted—the last thing she'd've said she wanted—was to fight with Nathan.

It was with some relief that she saw her father flow through the closed door and come to rest with his back against it. Her father looked aged and tired, even if the dead didn't change.

"Dad? Where's Mark?"

"He's outside."

"Outside the house?"

"Yes." The way he answered made it clear that it wasn't outside *this* one.

"What happened?"

Nathan had fallen silent, but he remained in the room; his hands were in his pockets, in fists.

"We went to his house," Brendan Hall replied. He left the door and walked toward the curtained windows, staring in the direction of the veiled sky. Back turned to Emma, he said, "If at all possible, Em, I think you should avoid this."

"How?"

"It's not—it's not like the last time. I don't think there's anything you can do at that house that will help Mark."

"Dad—" She knew it was bad; he kept his back toward her as she approached. She had to touch him before he would turn, and his elbow—the closest thing to her hand—was cold. To her surprise, he reached out and hugged her tightly; if his elbow had been cold, his hug wasn't. "I'm not telling you not to care," he told her. "I don't think you'll get rid of Mark any time soon; he's just come in from the—the cold; he needs company."

"But that part of his life is over. Maybe he can come back to it later—but not now."

"Then why is he there, Dad? Why didn't he come home with you?"

Her father's grip tightened for a moment; it was his only answer.

In the dark, Petal snoring on the foot of the bed—where foot, in this case, meant the entire lower half—Emma could hear the dead. She could hear them the way haunted people in movies did: they wailed, they cried, their words were stretched and attenuated. There was a hunger in their voices that distorted them so much they were barely recognizable as human. Emma knew; she tried.

One glance at the clock told her it was 2:30 in the morning, East Coast time. Sitting up, Emma slid her foot out from under Petal and swiveled on the bed. She had two tests tomorrow—tonight was *not* the night to listen to the wailing dead if she wanted better than a bare pass in either.

Explaining this to the distant voices, on the other hand, was a lost cause; all it did was wake up her dog, who assumed she wanted to take him for a walk. Loudly.

"Petal," she said, catching his face in her hands, which was always dangerous unless you *wanted* a whiff of dog breath, "we're *not* going for a walk, and if you wake Mom up, she'll bite *my* head off."

He not only breathed in her face, but licked her chin as well. She hugged him tightly, and only in part to avoid his tongue. The dead didn't bother him, he hadn't brought home a stray boyfriend, and he wasn't giving her advice she couldn't bear to follow.

The temperature in the room took a sudden dive; she tightened her grip around the rottweiler's neck before letting him go. He, on the other hand, had both large paws in her lap; he was whining. The room was dark enough that the sudden blink of the computer monitor made her shut her eyes. When she opened them again—slowly—she saw Mark's back. He was standing in front of the monitor, his hands by his sides. There were no key clicks, no mouse clicks, but the images on the screen were changing as she watched.

She remembered her dad reading a letter she'd written and posted; she couldn't remember whether or not he'd gone through the motions of touching the keys in order to make her more comfortable. It was something her dad would do—but Mark was not a child who would understand the need for that kind of make-believe. Neither, she thought, as she approached him, would Michael.

The light of the computer screen turned most of the nearby room a pale shade of gray and blue; it didn't touch Mark. The dead seemed to radiate their own light; regular light didn't change their appearance at all.

"Mark?"

His profile, silent and almost graven, didn't change. She wondered if he'd heard her. She almost reached out to touch him, but remembered that he didn't like to be touched. With Michael, it was the only certain way to get his attention when his focus was buried inside his own head. Mark wasn't Michael—but he reminded Emma of Michael in his childhood. Michael, however, was alive.

"Mark, shut it off. Come away. There's nothing there you haven't seen."

He didn't move at all.

She came to stand behind him, her palms hovering over his shoulders. His search terms—he was Googling—made her flinch. Mother. Kills. Child. Before she could find words, "Murders" was substituted for "Kills." On her best and brightest day, headlines like this were a horror she didn't visit.

She wished that Allison were here. Or Michael. Or her father. Anyone but her. At this time of night the only person who might wander by was her dad, and only because he no longer had to work in the morning. Brendan Hall remained conspicuously absent; Emma was alone with her slobbering dog and a boy who stood like a statue and read, and read, and read.

## ⤳ Chapter 9

At 8:10, Emma managed to be in the front hall, decently dressed but distinctly underfed. She hadn't made her mother's coffee but had managed to fill Petal's food and water bowls; her mother could buy a coffee at a dozen places on the drive in to work; her dog, however, couldn't open a can by himself. He *could* navigate the dry food bags and had in the past, but no one in the Hall house really *wanted* the contents of the bag spread across the kitchen floor.

Michael was on time, no surprise there. But he was tense, his eyes slightly wider than usual, his lips compressed. His hands were rigid by his sides—which didn't stop Petal from nuzzling them. It also didn't stop Michael from feeding the dog, but it took him a minute to zone back in.

"Emma," Mercy called from the top of the stairs, as they were just about to leave.

Emma turned.

"Jon is coming over for dinner tonight. You'll be home?"

"I'd love to, Mom, but I promised Allison I'd—I'd do some work with her at the library."

Her mother said nothing for a long minute. "Well. Don't be home too late."

"I won't." Emma escaped the house; she couldn't escape the tone of her mother's weary voice.

"Who is Jon?" Michael asked as they headed down the walk.

"My mother's new boyfriend."

"Oh."

"You can say that again."

Michael, who was watching the ground as if he expected it to break beneath his feet at any minute, said, "You don't like him?"

"I—" She held her breath for ten seconds. "I don't know him well enough to dislike him."

"But you don't like him."

She grimaced. No one else would have asked the question, because the answer was so clear. "It's not him, not exactly. I don't like the fact that he's my mother's boyfriend. I don't know him at all—I just don't want to *get* to know him. Not like that."

"But your mother likes him."

"Yes, clearly. And she doesn't care if I don't."

"She doesn't? Have you asked her?"

"No. We don't often ask questions in the Hall household," she added, speeding up slightly and hoping for rescue by Allison if she could just reach her house under the barrage of questions.

Allison was two minutes late and came careening around the Simner door, clutching the backpack she hadn't taken the time to loop over her shoulders, but Michael was so absorbed that he didn't notice. This should have told Emma something. Allison hit the sidewalk taking longer than usual strides—mostly to match Emma's.

"Michael," Allison said, before any of the usual morning greetings could be exchanged, "what exactly did you say to your mother last night?"

Emma froze in midstep, which, given the temperature of the morning wasn't as hard as it should have been. The shadows she cast in snow made brown by dirt, salt, and many feet had become desperately interesting. She turned to look at Michael, who was still concentrating on the ground. "I told her that we were late coming home from Emma's."

"That's all you said?"

"No. I told her about history and Mr. Taylor's accident."

Allison exhaled. "What did you tell her about—about Mark?"

This did get his attention, possibly because Allison's intensity was ratcheted up to a much higher level than usual. Attention, on the other hand, didn't mean that he shifted his gaze much. "I didn't tell her anything about Mark," he said. "You said it wasn't a good idea to talk about the dead."

Allison didn't relax much; Emma, who had started to, thought better of it when she looked at Ally's compressed lips. "Your mother called my mother this morning. That's why I'm late."

Michael did look at Allison then, possibly to see what her expression actually was. "My mother phoned your mother?"

Allison nodded.

"Why?"

"That's what I'm trying to find out," Allison replied. She now glanced at Emma, who shook her head. "Was your mother upset last night, Michael?"

"No."

"Did you—did you talk to her this morning at breakfast? I mean, this morning *at all*?"

"I always talk to her in the morning."

Allison, by dint of will and familiarity with Michael, did not pull her hair or shriek. "Did you talk about anything related to what happened last night at all?"

He was silent while he considered the question. "Yes," he finally replied.

Emma now stepped in. "Allison, what did she say to your mom?"

"She was worried about Michael. She asked if we knew of anything that had happened at school—at all—that might cause him to ask her about parents killing their children because their children weren't *normal enough*."

"Michael, we don't know that that's what happened," Emma said, voice low, glance sweeping the sidewalk for possible eavesdroppers.

Michael said, "We do. We do know that's what happened."

"No, we don't. We know that—that Mark's mother took him for a walk. We know that he—" she took a deep breath. "We know that he died. But we don't know why she left him there. It might be—"

"Emma, I'm not stupid."

Allison briefly raised her hands and covered her face with them. Michael, who was genuinely sweet most of the time, was not without a temper.

"I heard what he said," Michael continued. He'd stopped walking. "I understood what it meant. Were you listening to him?"

"I . . . I was."

"Why do you *think* his mother left him there?"

She had to look away from what she saw in his face. "I don't know, Michael. I can't ever imagine doing that to *anyone's* child—and I've babysat monsters." She tried to smile at the joke, but it was pathetic, even by Hall standards.

"I know I'm not normal—"

"Michael, *no one* is completely normal."

"I know that. But—"

"I'm a Necromancer," she said, digging hands into her hips. "How much *less* normal could a person be?"

That stopped him for a few seconds; it didn't, however, start him walking again. Allison glanced at her watch, but she didn't start walking either.

"People have already tried to kill Allison because I'm a Necromancer."

"Yes, but none of those people were her mother. Or yours. Do you think your mother would—"

"No!"

"Why?"

"She's my *mother*—" Emma lifted a hand because she couldn't stop the words that had just left her mouth, and she had no way to claw them back; not with Michael. "She knows *me*. She loves me, even when she brings strangers into *my* house that I don't want there."

"It's her house, too," Michael replied—as automatic in his response as Emma had been in hers.

"Yes. Technically it's entirely her house. But I live there, and she never asked me for permission. But even if she's disappointed at my reaction to her—her friend—she would never just lock me out to freeze to death."

"If she did," Michael replied, "You could come and stay at my house."

Emma smiled, and the smile was genuine, if pained. "Michael—your mother loves you. She always has. Yes, you're different. You've always been different—but different's not bad. You're normal for *you*. I'm normal for me. Allison is normal for Allison. None of the three of us are the same—but we're still friends, we still care about each other."

His shoulders slumped, half-inch by half-inch, as some of the tension left him. In the wake of tension, however, confusion opened up his expression. "Why did she do it, Emma?" His eyes were round; Emma thought he was close to tears. Michael had never been particularly self-conscious about them.

"I don't know, Michael."

"She couldn't have loved him."

"No."

"But he was her child!"

"Yes. If I could explain it, I would." She swallowed, and added, "I've been thinking of nothing else all night—because Mark wants to know as well. He wants to know more than any of the three of us do. It happened to him. I don't know what to say to him," she added, as she began—slowly—to walk. Michael was upset, yes—but being late wouldn't help that at all. "If you can think of anything—anything at all—"

"I have to understand it," Michael replied.

"There's not much to understand," Allison told them both. "His mother is a monster."

Michael was silent for a long moment before he turned and began to follow Emma. "She isn't," he said, his voice soft. "She's a person. If she were a monster, it would be easier."

"Mom?" Emma cupped her phone to muffle the pre-class noise in the hall and hoped she was audible.

"Em? Is something wrong?"

"I—I got my library date confused. I'll be coming home for dinner tonight. Do you want me to pick up anything on the way home from school?"

"Milk. And eggs. Not for dinner," she added. "But I think we're out." There was a pause, and then her mother said, "Thank you, Emma."

Emma felt a rush of something, a mix of guilt, affection, worry—and, ultimately, trust. Michael wasn't the only person affected by the morning's discussion. "I'll try, Mom. I don't always handle surprise well."

Allison waved her over as she ended the call. "Amy wanted me to tell you the yearbook committee is meeting after lunch."

"Is she still on the warpath?"

"It's Amy." Allison readjusted the necklace Ernest had given her. She didn't generally like things hanging around her neck. Her eyes widened in a particular way, and Emma turned; Michael was standing in front of his open locker staring vacantly at its interior. He hadn't removed his coat or his backpack.

Allison and Emma exchanged a single glance.

Michael had seen Necromancers. He had seen the dead. He'd even kept two dead children amused until Emma's arms were numb with the cold of making them visible. He'd seen men with guns, and he'd seen their corpses. But it was Mark that had caused the internal meltdown, because Mark's situation seemed so similar to his own, and Mark was dead.

"Michael," Emma said quietly, putting a hand on either shoulder.

He startled and turned.

"We're at school now. You need to take your coat off or you'll miss math."

Allison took his computer out of his pack, and waited until he'd removed his coat. She handed the computer to Michael, who stared at it as if it were a new and unknown object. No wonder his mother had been upset; Emma hadn't seen him this stressed since elementary school.

"Will you take Mark home?" Michael asked.

Emma couldn't even tell him that it wasn't safe to talk about Mark at school. "I don't know."

"You promised."

"I did. But I don't think his mother is going to be happy to see him, and I don't think that's going to help. What would you want, if you were in Mark's position?"

"I'd want to know *why*," was the low, intense reply.

"Math," she said quietly. "Whatever happens, it won't happen until after school."

"Can I come with you?"

Emma closed her eyes. She hadn't lied—one didn't, to Michael. She was afraid of what such a confrontation would do to Mark. He was eight, but a *very* young eight. His mother had taken him out for a walk on a literally freezing January day, and she'd left him in the ravine, returning to "normal" life without him.

What could she possibly say to Mark that would explain that? What could she do that would give him any peace?

"Yes," she said, after a long pause. Her voice was thick. "If I can't talk Mark out of it, you can come with me."

"Allison too?"

"And Nathan," Emma said, surrendering.

Michael inhaled and exhaled deeply. Then he straightened his shoulders and looked around the school halls as if they'd unexpectedly coalesced when he hadn't been paying attention. Emma steered him toward his class, just in case.

Lunch might have been awkward, but Emma only had to endure fifteen minutes of it. Given Eric and Chase, she wasn't certain she'd survive five; they were in a foul mood. They spoke normal sentences as if each word were a bullet, no matter who their target was. Michael, who brought his own lunch, had held the table. Nothing said in the cafeteria line—and admittedly, on committee meeting days, Emma got to jump to the head of the line—had indicated rage or fury.

But Michael was silent throughout most of lunch; not even Connell's question about mana decks could fully engage him.

Emma was hugely relieved when she had to leave the table to attend the yearbook committee meeting; she threw Allison one guilty look. Allison grimaced. Emma wasn't likely to be able to budge Chase, Eric, *or* Michael today. If she missed the yearbook committee meeting, she'd be adding angry Amy to the mix for no reason.

"I can't understand," Chase said, as Emma all but fled the cafeteria, "why everyone's so terrified of Amy."

"Given the caliber of your enemies, that's understandable," Allison replied. "But think about it on the inside of our lives for a minute. Amy is the reigning queen of the graduating year. She is gorgeous, she's on the Head's honor roll, she's talented, and she knows everyone. If she wants to make your life miserable, you will—while in school—be miserable."

"Amy can be nice," Michael interjected. "She's not a bully."

"I wouldn't call her a bully," Allison replied, realizing that she was skirting the edge of exactly that. "It's not that she makes people suffer because she enjoys random suffering. If she makes you suffer, she's absolutely certain there's a good reason for it. It just happens to be Amy's version of a good reason. But she's a steamroller. She's driving heavy machinery while the rest of us are digging ditches with our hands."

"Have you ever been on her bad side?" Chase asked.

Allison shook her head. "She mostly doesn't notice me. She's not looking for victims, but she has her friends."

"I would have guessed you were one of them."

"I like Amy the same way I like thunderstorms; she's a force of a nature. But . . . I'm not really Emery mafia material." She didn't generally talk about things like this, and she found herself almost embarrassed to say it so clearly to Chase. The embarrassment rattled her, but not enough that she wanted to hide the truth or, worse, lie.

"And Emma is."

Allison held up a hand. "I'm now instituting a rule."

"A rule?"

"You and I—that being Chase Loern and Allison Simner—are not going to discuss Emma Hall unless her life is in immediate danger and discussion will save it."

Chase blinked. So did Michael. With an air of someone who'd just remembered a question he'd forgotten to ask, Michael said to Chase, "Why don't you like Emma?"

Chase laughed at Allison's expression; when the laughter faded, some hint of it lurked at the corners of his lips and eyes.

"You're impossible," Allison told him.

"It's my middle name. One of my middle names. I have several."

"I'm not sure I want to hear the rest."

Eric said, "You really don't. Some of them aren't meant for polite company." Eric wasn't Chase; his smile didn't light up a room. He smiled now, and Allison realized, watching him, that he was tense. She almost asked him why, but she wasn't certain Michael needed more stress. She was fairly certain that she didn't.

"But why don't you like Emma?" Michael said again.

"I don't think I'm allowed to talk about Emma while Allison is in the room. Everyone else can be scared of Amy, but I personally think Allison is more terrifying."

Michael made the face he made when he was almost certain someone was joking. Sarcasm and humor had been hard for Michael when he was in elementary school; he was famously literal. But he'd become more comfortable with both as he'd marched through high school.

"Amy," Chase said, in a mock-sober tone, "has never hit me."

"I've never hit you either!"

"Not yet," he said, grinning. "I don't imagine it'll be long before—"

"Chase," Eric said, in the tone of voice reserved for emergencies that would inevitably lead to death.

The smile dropped instantly off Chase's face. Emma had just entered the cafeteria; Amy was by her side. Both of them were the color of chalk. Allison rose without thinking. When Amy looked frightened—when Amy looked even a tiny bit uncertain—it was big.

"Short committee meeting," Eric said, in the wrong tone, as they approached the table.

"We didn't go," Emma whispered. "We're heading out to find coffee."

Michael frowned; he rose as well.

"Em?" Allison said.

Emma shook her head and smiled brightly. It was, Allison realized, the same smile that Eric had been using throughout lunch—when he'd bothered to smile, that is. Allison nodded and headed toward the cafeteria doors.

"We're going to miss a period," she told Michael.

Michael hesitated. It didn't last. He accepted the disruption to his daily schedule as if it were the natural outcome of finding a boy who had in all probability been left to die on a winter hillside by his own mother.

There was no way to break this tension. Both Amy and Eric drove; Amy chose the venue. She wanted something a little farther away than normal lunch-hour traffic. The one thing about Amy that even Allison had to admire was that she never dithered. If given a choice, she made it quickly.

Sadly, this meant her patience for other people's indecision was practically zero. Had Amy been the type of person to rule by consensus rather than by fiat, it would have been a disaster. No one spoke in Amy's car; the silence was thick and uncomfortable.

No one spoke—aside from giving a waitress their order—until lattes and hot chocolate had hit the table.

For people who needed to find coffee, they didn't drink a lot of it; Allison didn't touch her hot chocolate either, although she made signs of finding it hot enough it needed time to cool. Amy didn't bother. She lifted her latte and set it down with an authoritative clunk, as if it were a gavel and she was calling Court to order.

"We know who the temporary replacement for Mr. Taylor is," she said, voice flat.

Emma glanced at her. She hadn't picked up her own drink; Allison guessed it was because her hands were shaking too much. She was willing to cede the floor to Amy; she looked almost grateful to be able to do so.

Eric waited. He'd taken his phone out of his pocket and placed it on the table; Allison wondered if he were recording the conversation. Amy didn't have any issues with being recorded.

"You'd recognize him." Even stressed, Amy knew how to draw things out. "All of you would."

"Emma?"

She shook her head.

"The last time we saw him," Amy continued, when Emma failed to interrupt, "he was a bloody, messy corpse."

Eric and Chase froze. It was clear from their reaction that this wasn't somehow impossible—to them.

"Merrick Longland. He's apparently just out of the faculty of education; he has a teaching certificate; he doesn't have a full-time job. He's been doing piecework and temporary work as it comes in, and this job is a godsend. He's grateful to have it and eager to work with new students."

Emma was white and silent while Amy continued to rattle off the talking points she'd pried out of the principal.

"On the off chance that Merrick Longland didn't have a twin, we decided to skip the yearbook committee meeting. So. What are the chances that our teaching replacement is the same Merrick Longland who took several wounds to various body parts and died? Judging by your reactions," she added, jabbing the air in front of Eric and Chase for emphasis, "the odds are damn high. What are these Necromancers? Vampires?"

"It's the middle of the day," Michael pointed out.

"So? He's not standing in direct sunlight."

"He'd have to walk in direct sunlight from his car."

Amy snorted. She understood Michael as well as Allison or Emma did, but didn't see any pressing need to treat him differently than she treated anyone else. It was one of the things Allison admired about her. She might expect everyone else to make allowances, but Amy's version of allowance involved very little condescension.

"We want to speak to your Ernest," Amy concluded, folding her arms across her chest.

Eric and Chase exchanged a glance.

"I *mean it*," she added. "He was supposed to be responsible for the cleanup, if I recall correctly. Cleanup doesn't generally involve hospitals and healing. Even if it *did*, that kind of knife work leaves scars. Our Merrick Longland would look like a more attractive Frankenstein monster; this one doesn't. I'm not sure he'd've recovered from extensive plastic surgery by now, either."

"Our Ernest, as you call him, works on his own schedule," Eric began.

Amy reached out and plucked Eric's phone off the table. Eric's eyes widened; he was the only person at the table who looked remotely surprised. She turned the phone on, while Eric's eyes rounded further, and after a few seconds, shoved it up beside her ear.

Even Chase now looked dumbfounded.

"Hi. Ernest? We met recently. My name is Amy Snitman. No, Snitman. Yes, that's right. I'm one of Eric's classmates. Eric and Chase are with me, and we are coming to your house to visit. We've got a few questions about your work and a possible emergency; we should be there in half an hour." She hung up.

"I take it back," Chase murmured.

Allison would have laughed, but Emma's expression killed all mirth.

## ◡ Chapter 10

Chase joined Emma and Allison in Amy's car; he provided directions. Amy was annoyed, and let it show—she had GPS installed. All she needed was the address. Chase told her he didn't remember the exact address.

No one, not even Allison, believed him.

Michael went with Eric. Amy's driving was always exciting and Michael had had enough excitement for a month. He believed that Emma and Amy thought they'd seen Merrick Longland—but he also believed that Merrick Longland was dead. As this was more or less giving Allison whiplash, she didn't expect anyone else to take it in stride; the only person who did was Amy.

Allison privately thought that Amy would prefer to be given a rational, logical, and above all believable explanation, which was why she was driving directly to Eric's. Chase's verbal directions guaranteed two things. The first, that Amy would be in a fouler mood, and the second, that Eric—with Michael in tow—would arrive first.

This wouldn't have been necessary if Amy had returned Eric's phone, but Allison kept that firmly to herself. She felt as if she were only barely treading water, now. Because she, like the rest, had seen Merrick Longland's death. She had nightmares about it. She kept them to herself.

Amy kept none of her thoughts to herself, which meant the ride wasn't silent. It was awkward, but given Amy was upset, awkward was as much as they could hope for.

She parked about three feet away from the curb, opened the door, and stormed out. Michael, had he been in the car, would have pointed out that she was too far out. No one else dared, but Allison suspected that no one else noticed. And if she were any kind of a decent best friend, she thought with guilt, she wouldn't have either.

She hurried to catch up with Emma; Emma was staring pointedly at a spot to her right. Allison guessed that Nathan was here. Or that he wasn't, and she wanted him. It didn't matter; she took up the position to Emma's left.

"Em?"

Emma smiled wanly. "I'm fine." It was the Hall version of fine: it meant, in more accurate English, shattered. She exhaled, and headed toward the door, which was already opening to allow Chase and Amy entry.

Allison hung back. She was afraid of leaving Emma on the front steps, because Emma looked at the door with an understated dread. "We don't have to stay," she offered. "It's not like we're going to be able to get a word in edge-wise."

That made Emma smile a real smile. "Amy's something," she said, shaking her head. "I'm so glad she was there. I don't know what I would have done."

"You wouldn't have gone to the meeting."

"I don't know if I would have noticed in time to back out. Longland didn't *see* us; she saw him first. Amy notices everything."

"And usually points it out loudly, just in case anyone missed it."

Emma laughed. She straightened her shoulders and added, "Should we go rescue Ernest? He won't know what hit him."

"He's got Eric and Chase."

Emma winced. "Exactly."

The living room was like a parent-teacher interview gone insanely wrong. Ernest was seated in the large armchair. His posture was stiff and his expression caught between bemusement and serious annoyance.

Eric was on the far end of the couch—as far from Ernest as the seating allowed. Michael, conversely, had taken the seat closest to Ernest and had left room for Allison and Emma. Chase hadn't bothered with a chair of any kind; he'd plunked himself down on the stone of the fireplace, crossing his legs.

Amy, on the other hand, was prowling the room like a tiger. Since she'd introduced herself on Eric's phone, she probably hadn't bothered with introductions either—she'd gotten straight to the point, which Allison and Emma, slower to enter the house and remove all the winter clothing, had missed.

"So let me get this straight," Amy said, her voice growing louder as Emma and Allison joined the awkwardness. "Merrick Longland was dead. You checked. You didn't convey him to an emergency ward anywhere in this city; you did not buy him plastic surgery, and you disposed of his body."

"I believe I've already answered all of these questions," Ernest said, in a clipped voice that clearly implied he was not the one who was usually on the receiving end of pointed, icy questions. "I fail to see why they're relevant."

"Leaving aside the fact that murder is illegal—"

"Self-defense is not illegal in Canada."

"Which the courts, not tweedy old men, decide—leaving aside that fact, it's relevant because the selfsame Merrick Longland has apparently taken a job at *my* school as a replacement for a teacher who's going to be in traction for a couple of months. He's taken over the supervisory role of *my* yearbook committee.

"Can we assume that he *is* the same Merrick Longland?" She folded her arms and came to a stop inches away from Ernest's feet.

Ernest was silent.

"Can we further assume that he retains memories of his death and all the stuff that led up to it, including our presence at the former Copis household?"

More silence.

It was hard to take eyes off Amy when she wanted attention, even if the attention she wanted wasn't yours. Tonight was no exception; she was *angry*. She wasn't angry with Emma, Michael, or Allison, but the full storm of her rage could easily encompass Chase and Eric, neither of whom wanted to meet her gaze. Allison knew. She was one of the few people present who could look at something else when Amy was on fire.

"If he's a teacher, he'll have access to our records. He already knows where *I* live," she added, each word a figurative bullet, "but he'll now know where everyone *else* lives. This would include Emma. And Eric and Chase."

Ernest failed to answer. He had at least thirty years on Amy, possibly forty. He clearly had experience in a variety of deadly situations; he could clean up savaged bodies without raising a brow. He owned at least one gun, and he'd shown no hesitance whatsoever in using it. But even Ernest looked distinctly uncomfortable.

"What are the chances we survive that knowledge?"

Ernest rose. "These are all very good questions," he finally said, in a voice that made November wind seem warm. "Or they would be, if you didn't already know the answers."

"I didn't, until now," Amy snapped. "Believe it or not, where *we* live, dead people don't come back to life. Among other things." She drew, and held, her breath, exhaling it in a burst of nonverbal anger. "If we kill Merrick Longland—no, if *you* kill Merrick Longland—will he stay dead this time?"

"He is already dead," Ernest replied, his jaws clenching.

"We want a definition of dead that only Emma can see," Amy shot back.

"If we, as you put it, kill Merrick Longland, he is likely to remain just as dead as he is now."

Someone cleared her throat. Allison, breath held, turned to look at Emma.

Emma had been beside Amy in a crowded school hall, and she'd watched as Amy froze in midsentence, all of the words she'd been about to say lost. Amy had said two words: Merrick Longland. She'd grabbed Emma's arm as Emma turned to stare, realization and recognition freezing her in place.

The dead looked alive to Emma. They wore the clothing they'd worn at the moment of their death, but they didn't sport the wounds or the other clear signs that their physical bodies were corpses. She'd seen enough of the dead to know that she couldn't easily differentiate between the dead and the living—but one of the dead she hadn't expected to see was Merrick Longland.

Amy wasn't an idiot; she'd seen the same thing.

This Merrick Longland, extraordinarily well-groomed and handsome, was *not* dead. Not in the way that Emma understood death.

Nathan had been standing in the hall; he saw what Emma saw. His eyes widened, and he turned immediately to Emma. "Leave," he said, voice low, urgency stripping it of the usual social graces. "Leave now."

Emma nodded. She didn't answer, not because she was afraid that talking to thin air would make her look crazy, but because she was afraid to speak a single word that might draw Longland's attention. She caught Amy's elbow and gave it an urgent tug, and Amy turned immediately, her face drained of color.

They'd retreated to the cafeteria, by which time Amy at least had found her voice.

And now they were here. They were at Eric's, Amy going toe-to-toe with the old man, Eric and Chase looking distinctly uncomfortable—or worse.

Amy was right: Longland would have access to all of their school records. He could, if he knew their last names, find their home addresses with pathetic ease. And at those homes were parents and siblings and half-deaf rottweilers.

Emma knew what would happen to their families if the Necromancers came to visit: They would die. Maybe they would die quickly and painlessly; maybe they would die horribly and slowly. But Necromancers didn't *care* about the living. Life was a cocoon state, as far as Necromancers were concerned; death was the eternity.

Death as a power source, with no voice and no choice in the matter.

She was nauseated. She wanted to throw up or cry, which was a first. Emma had cried tears of loss and grief; she had cried tears of humiliation, although she could be forgiven that act at the age of four or five; she had cried tears of joy. She had never cried because she was so terrified all other options were lost to her.

And she was *not* about to start now.

"How is Longland alive?"

Ernest glanced at her. It was the only sign he gave that he'd heard the faint question at all.

"I won't argue with you. If you say he's dead, I'll accept it. But—he's walking around in a way that the living can see. Clearly."

Ernest glanced once at the open arch. "We'll take care of Merrick Longland."

"Because it worked so well the last time," Amy cut in. Acid would be less corrosive.

"We would be pleased if you demonstrated how we could do better," Ernest snapped.

Emma was terrified that Amy would take him up on the challenge. She'd watched Chase finish Longland off. It still gave her nightmares.

"Ernest, that was uncalled for." From the direction of the kitchen, clothed in a way that suggested the fifties and coiffed the same way, walked Margaret Henney. Unlike Merrick Longland, she was a dead that no one could see.

No one but Ernest, Eric, and Emma.

Ernest didn't particularly care if the young people caged in his living room considered him sane or not. "It was not uncalled for," he said, an edge in his voice. "You've clearly chosen your usual brand of selective eavesdropping."

Margaret was not Amy, but in her own way, she was intimidating. She was also, judging by the tightening of an already unimpressed expression, ill pleased.

"Ernest," Emma said, her voice much softer than either the living Amy's or the dead Margaret's, "stop digging."

Chase laughed. He was the only person in the room who did.

"More dead people?" Amy all but demanded.

"Margaret Henney," Emma replied. "She was there when we rescued

Andrew Copis, but I don't know if you saw her directly. She's less than impressed with Ernest's response."

"That makes two of us."

"At least three," Allison said.

Emma said, quietly, "Margaret?" She held out a hand.

Margaret shook her head. "I don't need to hold hands to make myself visible. I need your permission, Emma. You hold me." Before Emma could reply,
Margaret added, "and I won't ask that permission, now. I've told you before: It
takes power. You won't use ours. You might not even understand how. But if
you won't, you're using your own life to sustain our appearance, and you can't
afford that at the moment."

"Margaret—how is Longland alive?"

"He isn't. Not in the sense that you or your friends are."

"But he's—"

"Yes. He is walking among the living as if he were actually alive. There are
differences, but they'll be noted only as time passes. For one, he will not age."

"Will he bleed?"

"Yes. He will also feel pain. He is a threat to you for precisely the reasons
your Amy states: He can interact with the real world. He can find information
that would not otherwise be immediately found. He can kill you—but he will
have to do it the old-fashioned way."

"Meaning the way Chase killed him the first time."

"Meaning exactly that, yes."

"That means he's not a Necromancer anymore?"

"It means, more precisely, that he doesn't have Necromantic powers or
abilities any more. He's dead. The dead don't."

"How can he be—"

"He is not alive, Emma," was her much gentler reply.

"Is the Queen of the Dead alive?"

Silence.

Allison was holding her breath. She exhaled slowly and quietly; unlike Amy,
she didn't use breathing as an act of aggression. She glanced at Chase and was
surprised to see that he was watching her.

She could only hear Emma's half of the conversation. But ever since Emma
had asked the question, it hung in the air like a nuclear cloud. *How is Longland
alive?* Allison had no idea if Nathan was in the room; she had no idea if Nathan had followed them to Eric's. She guessed that he hadn't, because Emma's
glance hadn't strayed to him.

But her thoughts had, even if she wasn't immediately aware of it.

Because if Merrick Longland had died a horrible death—and he had—so had Nathan. If Merrick Longland was, to all intents and purposes, alive, it didn't matter that Ernest said he was dead. What had happened to Merrick Longland *could* happen to Nathan.

It was Ernest, not Margaret, who chose to answer the question. "Yes. The Queen of the Dead is demonstrably among the living: she is a Necromancer."

"But—but—"

"Yes?"

"How old is she? You've been fighting Necromancers your whole life!"

"Not my whole life; I did, in the age of the dinosaurs, have a childhood."

Emma frowned. "I saw her. I don't—I don't mean to be offensive, but . . . she looked a lot younger than you do."

His smile was dry enough to catch fire. "She is much older than I am."

Amy, lips pursed, forehead momentarily lined, said, "So you're saying Necromancers are effectively immortal? Merrick Longland could be my grandfather's age?"

"Merrick Longland, as you've so bluntly pointed out, is dead. Before his death, yes, it's possible that he could have been as old as your grandfather. Or great-grandfather. It may come as a surprise to you, but we do not have an FBI style of dossier collection. Age is not necessarily an indicator of power."

Folding her arms across her chest, Amy said, "You're lying."

Margaret turned to Emma, "Dear," she said, which Emma was willing to tolerate given Margaret's age, "your friend—"

"Yes, she is my friend, and yes, she's very blunt."

Ernest met—and held—Amy's glare. Chase and Eric, who'd killed at least four people that Emma knew about, were looking anywhere else. "I am not lying; we do not have the resources to track every known Necromancer. But," he added, lifting a hand before Amy could break in, "Necromancers with Emma's knowledge—not her innate natural ability, but her actual, practical knowledge—will age at the expected rate. Lack of visible age is not a natural occurrence for Necromancers; it is a skill that can be learned with time. It requires an ability to harness the power of the dead on a continuous, low-level basis.

"It is a gift of knowledge that the Queen grants those in her Court who have done her service."

"You know this how?" Amy demanded.

Emma swallowed. "Some of the dead are Necromancers," she replied, aware that Margaret couldn't speak for herself. "When you're dead, it doesn't matter."

"That is not entirely true," Margaret replied softly. "If you have died in the line of duty—where by duty one refers to the demands of the Queen—you are elevated in her eyes. Should that be the case, you are declared off-limits for harvesting."

"Would most Necromancers care?"

Margaret's smile was all edge. "There have been breaches of the Queen's law in the past. There have also been challengers. Unless one wishes to join the dead, one does not break the Queen's law; it is absolute. In the mildest cases, she can refuse to teach you the arts of self-preservation—what you would call immortality. In the more extreme cases, she makes you an example—both at the end of your life and the eternity that follows."

"You betrayed her."

Margaret glanced at Ernest. "Yes."

"Did you attempt to kill her?"

"That's a rather personal question, but I'll answer you. No. I was not—I was never—a Necromancer with the raw power the Queen of the Dead possesses. I have only met one other who might rival her, in time. My treachery, such as it was, was simply to choose life.

"But it was a crime, and it was met with the inevitable penalty. I was caught, trapped, and given in service to Merrick Longland—a knight of the Queen's Court." When Margaret used the word "knight" it didn't sound inherently ridiculous. "I was rescued by you. I want to say unintentionally, but—on a visceral level, you knew what you were doing.

"Merrick Longland must have risen high in the Queen's esteem. She has cloaked him in flesh and form and sent him, once again, into the world. He serves her, and he will now do so until her death."

"He knows what I did."

"Yes. And if he knows, the Queen will know. It cannot be a coincidence that he has been sent here; this is the place where failure cost him his life. He lives, now, at the whim of the Queen—and if she so chooses, he will return to the ranks of the truly dead."

Amy said, "Em, you're talking to air here. Enlighten the rest of us." It wasn't a request, but Amy didn't do requests.

Emma obliged, haltingly repeating Margaret's words as if by doing so, she could understand them better.

"I think it best, until Longland is effectively neutralized, that alternate living arrangements be made," Ernest said quietly.

Emma stiffened.

"You said he's not a Necromancer now, right? He can't use his power to talk idiots into flying home on a whim without warning?" Amy demanded.

"Correct. But he is unlikely to be here alone. There is almost certainly at least one Necromancer in the field."

"Longland will report to him?"

"Longland will report directly to the Queen of the Dead," Eric said, speaking for the first time. "The dead communicate in ways the living can't trace. He'll need to use phones or computers to communicate with the Necromancer in the field—but we haven't found him yet. Or her.

"While the Necromancer's at large, any information Longland feeds him is possibly deadly—for the three of you."

"For two of you," Chase cut in. "Allison and Michael."

"And I'm chopped liver?" Amy demanded.

"You're a force of nature," Chase replied. "I wouldn't bet money on a Necromancer faced with you."

Emma smiled.

"You realize making your 'alternate arrangements' is going to be a huge problem if we can't tell our parents what's happening, right?" Amy said.

"If you tell your parents, they will in all likelihood die," Ernest replied. He fished about in his jacket pocket for a pipe. Amy gave it the dirtiest look in her arsenal, but didn't come out and forbid it; it wasn't her house after all. In Amy's house you were allowed to smoke only if you were actually on fire—and even then, it was dicey.

"And the Necromancers won't assume they already know?"

"Unclear. In their position, I wouldn't make that assumption. Understand that they are accustomed to secrecy and isolation. They believe, on a visceral level, that they are the misunderstood and the despised; they believe they'll be hunted with figurative pitchforks by angry mobs that will then burn them at the figurative stake. They trust the Queen if they trust at all—but in general, they don't. They trust their power. They work to amass a power base, and it's a power that's built on the dead.

"Not all of the dead have significant amounts of that power. Young lady, I am trying to explain, as quickly and clearly as possible, to those of you who have short attention spans. I would appreciate a little consideration."

Since Amy had not interrupted him, Emma felt Ernest was getting what he said he'd appreciate. Amy was, however, tapping her left foot, and her lips were one thin, white line. She said nothing, and after a pause, he exhaled and continued.

"Your young Andrew Copis had a *considerable* amount of power. If Emma understood how to bind him, she would have access to power that would immediately place her in the upper echelons of the Necromantic society, such as it is. But very few of the dead are Andrew Copis."

"Do Necromancers have more potential—as dead people—than the rest of us?"

"Not to my knowledge. There is a large line that divides the living from the dead. In the ideal universe, the dead would be free to leave the world the living inhabit. I am not a particularly religious man," he added, in case this was relevant, "so I have no opinion whatsoever on where they might ultimately arrive.

"Even absent Necromancers, the world would not be ideal. Your young ghost would have been trapped in the remnants of his burned-out building long after the building itself had been demolished and new homes built on the lots. Some of the dead get stuck this way.

"Only those who are Necromancers notice."

"And most don't care," was Amy's flat reply.

"I would not say that; most, however, are aware that there's a risk in such an approach. No one would have tried to harvest Andrew Copis in his current state; I am not even certain the Queen of the Dead would have taken that risk."

"But she could?"

Ernest glanced at Margaret.

Margaret, however, was watching Emma. "Emma could," she finally said.

"He almost killed Emma," Amy pointed out, although she hadn't heard Margaret's words.

"Not intentionally. But, yes, the fire was strong, and Emma is alive. There is a reason the divide between the living and the dead is so extreme. It was never meant to be crossed."

"Emma didn't bind him," Allison said, a slow heat in the words. "That's not why she—"

"We're aware that she didn't approach the child with the aim of adding to her power. It's almost a certainty that Longland *did*. Emma had effectively stripped him of his power; he had nothing to lose. I don't believe he expected Emma to be present; I do believe that when he discovered that she was, he chose to act. If she succeeded in binding Andrew Copis, she would have been a significant power—and he would have been much diminished. He knew that she had taken five of the dead from his grasp."

"That doesn't happen often?"

"No," Ernest replied. He eyed Amy as if she were a feral dog. Or a rabid one. Amy didn't particularly care, and if Amy wasn't going to take offense, it was never smart to take offense on her behalf.

"It shouldn't happen at all," Margaret said quietly.

Emma frowned. "Why?"

"It takes power to bind the dead. I know I've mentioned this before," she added, in a more severe tone.

"In theory, I *have* power," Emma said. "If it takes power to make the binding, it makes sense it would take power to break it."

Margaret was silent for a long moment. "Understand that I was rescued by the Queen of the Dead. I would have died—just as you should have—otherwise. Everything I know about my former power, I know through her teaching. She was not a particularly kind woman, as you might suspect. But in her fashion, she considers the Necromancers her only family.

"I don't know how she sees the dead. I know how I saw them, before Ernest. I didn't speak with them, Emma. I certainly did not stoop to rescue them. Had I known of Andrew Copis, I might have waited, watching the situation over the passage of a few decades. He would have been a coup. You couldn't—or wouldn't—see the power inherent in his condition, and even if you had, you wouldn't have kept him here.

"You set him free. You set all possible sources of power within the area free, as well. It is the one saving grace you will have should you choose to remain in your home—very, very few dead remain here. If you can break the bindings that give the Necromancers their power over the dead, they will be forced to retreat. They will, in all likelihood, be forced to flee using the normal methods of transportation available to the living."

"Merrick Longland—"

"Is no longer concerned with sources of power. He serves the Queen directly."

"Why did she send him?"

Margaret frowned. "I don't know. What will you do now?"

Emma exhaled. "Amy."

Amy nodded, although her glare didn't falter.

"If we can find the Necromancer, and we can free the sources of his power, Margaret thinks we'll be safe. She considers Toronto—or at least our parts of it—a wasteland as far as Necromancers and power are concerned."

"Allison?" Amy asked, still glaring at Ernest.

"I don't want my family hurt," Allison replied, after a long pause. "But I don't want to have to explain this to them. They'll think we're crazy. At best. If we prove we're not, they'll be terrified, and they'll call the police at the very least."

"Michael?"

Michael was silent for longer. "Emma," he finally said, "can you do it?"

She swallowed. Like Allison, she was afraid of the truth. Using it had costs. Hiding it had costs. "If Chase and Eric can tell us where—and who—the Necromancers are, I can break their power." But she turned once again to Margaret, who was silent and watchful.

"You're dead," she said, voice low. "And you were part of Merrick Longland's power base. If you didn't know—as a Necromancer—what it was like for the dead, you *do* know, now. What I did—what I shouldn't have been able to do, according to your teaching—why did it work?"

"You saw us as people," Margaret replied.

Eric rose. He was silent as he headed out of the room.

"What did she say?" Amy demanded.

"She said—she said I saw them as people."

"Well, duh."

"I'm not entirely certain your Amy is not like our Chase," Margaret said.

"She's scarier. Margaret—what do you mean?"

"You knew we needed help. You never doubted you *could*. Do you understand that most people would not be in a desperate rush to risk their lives just to save a child who was already dead?"

"He didn't know he was dead."

"No, but, Emma—you did. You knew that nothing you could do could change that."

Emma said nothing.

"What I did not realize as a Necromancer is that the dead still have some choice. It is slender, and against the brute force of Necromantic bindings, it is insignificant. But it was not absent. I was not aware of you until you touched what you describe as golden chains. When you did, Emma, I saw you. I understood in that moment that you saw me. I knew where I was; I knew that I was dead. But I felt as if you had finally found me."

Emma blinked; Margaret looked slightly embarrassed. "I know that sounds odd, dear. I didn't have a sense of who you actually were; I felt relief and warmth. The dead seldom feel warmth. I felt as if I had been offered a hand out of a very dark hole, and I took that hand and emerged.

"It's not a perfect analogy; there are some things you would have to be dead to experience. I could not have escaped Merrick Longland without your intervention, but you gave me the choice. I believe you did the same when you met Merrick Longland a second time.

"Even then, you would not take the power available in order to fight him."

"But I *did*."

"No, Emma. We gave. There is a difference. Even when you showed us the way by lighting the lamp, you *asked* and we *gave*. I believe, were you to hold that lamp, that any of the dead—no matter how weak or unaware—would see you and know you."

"Margaret," Ernest began.

Her look, in theory much milder than Amy's glare of death, did what Amy's couldn't: It silenced him.

"Longland is, of course, capable of killing without the power he defined himself by in life. But he is not of the living the way you now are. You must decide what you're willing to risk." She glanced at the rest of Emma's friends and added. "All of you. I'm sorry."

# ⤳ Chapter 11

Emma discovered something over the next uncomfortable half an hour: She was the only person present who was comfortable talking about a parent's death as if it were a reality. Amy was practical enough to consider it a serious risk, but she was arrogant enough to assume it happened to other people. Allison was subdued, probably because Chase was a whole lot of angry, even if he kept actual words to himself.

Michael was pale.

Eric offered strategies for essentially lying to their parents; he offered help if they wanted to disappear for the foreseeable future. He didn't offer advice, for which Emma was grateful.

Forty-five minutes later, there was still no solution that somehow made everything normal and safe again, and Amy decided she'd had enough for the day, which meant the discussion—and the visit—was officially over. School, however, was not. She left Eric and Chase to Eric's car, and gathered Michael, Emma, and Allison in her own.

"Do you want to keep having this discussion without Ernest?" Amy asked, as she pulled into the school lot.

"Any night but tonight," Emma replied.

"What's tonight?"

"I'm having dinner with my mother and her new boyfriend. I can't miss it. I can't be late for it. If something happens during dinner, my dad will be there to help me."

"With your mother's new boyfriend?"

"I know. It's awkward." But it felt less awkward, now. Emma and her mother had their differences—but Emma knew her mother was there for her. She was loved, had been loved, for as much of her life as she could remember. She didn't want to repay that with secrecy, lies, and death.

But she didn't want to leave home, either. Her mother would be beyond terrified—and she'd probably blame herself. The timing couldn't be worse. Maybe she'd assume Emma was running away from home because of the boyfriend. Her mother didn't deserve that. She didn't deserve that fear.

But she didn't deserve the fear the truth would give her either.

"Sometimes you get what you don't deserve," Amy said sharply.

"Did I say that out loud?"

"No. But it's all over your face."

Emma grimaced and got out of the car, wondering if this kind of worry plagued her mother. Probably, given the Halls.

"Let's see how long we can avoid Merrick Longland," Allison said quietly. Emma didn't answer.

There were two ghosts in the parking lot, and both of them were familiar. Her father was standing beside Mark, who stood slightly behind and to one side, his shoulders hunched and stiff. Emma exhaled. "You guys go in; I'll catch up later."

She waited until they started to move; Allison lingered, and Emma mouthed a silent "it's my dad," which was as much comfort as she could offer.

"Mark," she said, defaulting to the Hall smile.

Mark looked up—he had to. "I went home," he said, in a quiet voice.

She swallowed.

"I tried to talk to my mom. She couldn't see me. My brother and my sister couldn't see me either. You can see me."

Emma nodded.

"Your friends could see me because you wanted them to see me."

She knew where this was going; she could see it yawning, like a sudden chasm, inches from her feet. She looked over Mark's head to her father's drawn face.

"I want you to take me home."

"My father took you home and—"

"I want to ask her if she forgot about me."

Her father closed his eyes; Emma, however, slid her hands behind her back; they were bunched in fists. Did she pity him? Yes.

It was a tricky thing, to pity someone. There was a difference between sympathy, empathy, and pity. Pity was what you gave to injured animals, not people. Not even dead boys who looked like they were six years old.

"You already know the answer," she said, her voice calm and matter-of-fact.

Mark's gaze slid off Emma's left cheek. He wouldn't meet her eyes for a long, awkward moment.

"Mark."

He swiveled. "I want to go home," he whispered. She heard anger in the softly spoken words—and behind that wall of anger, nothing but pain and loss. Emma seldom hated anyone as much as she hated Mark's mother at the moment. And she knew it wouldn't help Mark now—but she couldn't think of a single thing that would.

Had she never known Michael, she might have tried lying. Lies—lies a person wanted to believe—could be comforting; they could be an act of kindness.

But they could also be an act of weakness. There was no way to minimize the wrong, no way to minimize the pain. Telling him that his mother wasn't worth this pain was the truth, but sometimes truth didn't change things, either. Not quickly.

Not at all.

The worst truth Emma had ever faced in her life was Nathan's death. For the first time that she could remember, she felt, viscerally, that Mark's truth was worse. There had been whole days when Emma had raged—in perfect Hall silence—against the pain of loss; hours when she had wished—and, oh, the guilt she felt—that she had *never* loved at all if all it amounted to was emptiness and endless pain.

But Nathan had loved her. She had been loved.

Mark's mother couldn't have loved him and done what she did. What kind of life had Mark known? What kind of death?

"Em," her father said softly. She looked up. "It's not that simple. Nothing ever is."

She wanted to argue; she would have. But Mark was standing between them, and she couldn't. The urge to somehow protect this child was so strong, he might have been alive.

"Pain and fear make us do hideous, ugly things. Love and joy make us do beautiful things. At base, we're all human."

"Dad, don't. Just don't." Mark was watching her intently. It didn't mean that he couldn't hear every word her father was saying.

"I know it's difficult, but it never helps in the end to make monsters out of people; it prevents you from seeing them as they are."

"I'm not making a monster out of her. She—"

"Em."

"You would never have done this!"

"No." He was silent for a moment. Had he been alive, he would have gone for his pipe; he had that expression. "Do you remember, when you were five, a friend of your mother's died?"

Emma frowned. Five was so far in the past it existed in fragmented memories. "Aunt Carol?" she finally asked.

"Yes. She wasn't an aunt; you called her that because you saw her so often. She died eight months after the birth of her first child."

"A boy. I remember."

"Do you remember that her son died as well?"

Emma nodded. "There was an accident," she began. She stopped, considering her father's expression. "It wasn't an accident."

"No."

"Her husband?" she asked.

"No, Em. She shut herself in her car in the garage with her baby. She turned on the engine. Paul was at work. She didn't call him. She didn't leave a note. When he came home, the garage door was locked; the remote didn't work."

Emma froze, arrested.

"He went into the house to find the key. His wife wasn't home. He assumed she'd taken the baby and gone out somewhere. He didn't understand why the garage door was locked. He found the key when he found her; he had to enter the garage through the house. He was too late for either of them. Too late for himself. He didn't kill them, but he did blame himself for what happened.

"Carol committed suicide. The doctor—after the fact—thought she must have been suffering from severe post-partum depression. It happens. You don't consider Aunt Carol a monster."

". . . No."

"But she killed her son."

"She killed *herself*, Dad."

"Yes. She was probably afraid of the pain her son would feel in future if she abandoned him by dying. She took him with her. But he was an infant, he was helpless, he had no choice, and he died." Her father slid his hands into his pockets.

Emma watched him.

"You don't think of Carol as a monster. In the worst case, you pity her. You don't think of what she did to her own son as murder. But her son could have had a life, much like yours, with his father."

"You can't possibly be defending someone who could do something like this!"

"No. I'm not. But I am profoundly *grateful* that I was never compelled to make such an ugly choice. I tried for most of my adult life to be what passes for a good man. But there were days when it was nothing but struggle. It's not something we talk to our children about—we want our children to live as happily and worry-free as they can. We don't talk about money. We don't talk about marital difficulties. We don't talk about struggles on the job front.

"And I wonder, sometimes, if the choice to remain silent serves anyone well. We want you to grow up in a safe space. We make it as safe as possible. But—if something breaks, it's one more thing to lose."

"What is?"

"The faith and belief your children have in you. There's a fair bit of ego in being a superhero in the eyes of your children," he added, with a wry grin. "Because god knows we're no superheroes in anyone else's. I'm not trying to excuse what Mark's mother did. But it's the act that was monstrous—and it was the act of a moment, a day. Pity her."

"Pity *her*?" Emma tried to remember that Mark was watching her. "What does she need pity for? She got away with—"

"It will haunt her for the rest of her life. Life is a test, Emma. A constant test. We want to believe certain things about ourselves, but as we see more and more of the world, we realize how small we are and how short our reach actually is. Things we swore we would never do, we find ourselves doing. It's easy to judge from the outside."

"Mom wouldn't agree with you."

He grimaced. "No. Had she been faced with the same choice Mark's mother faced, she would have killed herself, first." He turned to Mark, as if he'd never forgotten that Mark was part of the conversation. And maybe he hadn't. "Would that have been better?"

Mark stared, unblinking, at her father's face. When he finally answered, his voice sounded even younger. "I don't want my mother to die," he whispered.

No, of course not. What he wanted—even now, dead at her hands—was his mother's love and acceptance. He didn't even want to be alive again—he just wanted something he'd never had.

"Do you love your mother, Mark?" Her father asked. Emma felt her lower jaw drop in outrage and shock.

Mark looked down at his feet. "Yes," he said, voice very small. "I try to be what she wants. I always try. But I forget, and it hurts her."

"Dad—stop it. Stop it now."

"We all love our parents," he told his angry daughter. "Even when they don't deserve it. Sometimes especially then."

"She has other children," Emma said, voice low. "If she did this once, she could do it again."

"She won't hurt them," Mark told her. "They're normal."

Emma didn't swear in front of her parents. Her mother hated it—although she wasn't above dropping a few choice words herself when she was angry. She was fairly certain her father would have disapproved as well—but at eight years of age, she hadn't developed the habit. It saved her from saying exactly what she was thinking.

"She told me to wait for her," Mark continued, oblivious to the anger that rested beneath Emma's silence. "And I waited. It was cold. I was cold. I'm still cold."

"Does it hurt?" her father asked quietly.

Mark shook his head. "Not any more. But I want to talk to my mom."

"I have to finish school," Emma told Mark quietly. "I've already had to miss two classes." She hesitated, then added, "I have to be home for dinner as well. My mom's invited someone over, and I promised I'd be there."

"After dinner?"

She had homework. She meant to say she had homework. But excuses like homework seemed so pathetic and minor in comparison that she couldn't force them out of her mouth. She didn't want to take Mark to his mother's house. She couldn't see how it could bring anything but more pain to a child who had had enough of it. She didn't trust herself near Mark's mother.

And what could she do to Mark's mother? Call the police? Accuse the mother of murder—of abandonment—when the only evidence she had was the ghost of the dead child himself?

It wouldn't be the first time she'd proved her words with the help of dead children. But that had been different, and she knew it. Andrew Copis' mother had been forced to leave her oldest son in a house on fire because she'd been carrying an infant and a barely mobile toddler and Andrew *could* walk. His death haunted her; it had almost destroyed her.

But Mark's mother?

"Emma?"

She exhaled. "After dinner. We have a guest. It might be late."

Mark said, in an uncomfortably familiar tone, "I don't need to sleep, now."

The Halls of Emery Collegiate hadn't changed. They were the same paint-over-concrete; the floors were the same faux marble. The lockers, some dented by the boisterous set over the past decade, framed the occasional door and glass display cabinet; the teachers served as informal patrol as they headed between classes. Since the halls weren't carpeted, noise bounced; no conversation was muted—you had to raise your voice just to be heard.

The noise was a comfort today. It was normal. It didn't matter that snatches of unavoidable conversation were about television, boyfriends, and unreasonable parents. Emma wanted to hear them, even if she could no longer join them. She wanted a world in which her mother was annoying, motherly, and *safe*. Even if that mother brought a new—and unwanted—boyfriend into the house. There was nothing Mercy Hall could do that deserved death by Necromancer. Or death by anything, really.

But she didn't deserve to have her daughter disappear without warning—or forwarding address—either. She watched the doors to offices and classes closely, approaching them with caution; she didn't want to run into Merrick Longland. She caught up with Allison in social studies, just in time to avoid the late slip that should have been coming her way.

Allison's single glance held a question; Emma smiled in response. It was the silent version of "I'm fine," and caused Ally to frown. More than that wasn't possible. Michael sat at the front of this class, in part to avoid the chatting that often went on in the back. Emma wondered if he was absorbing anything the teacher said. She was having a hard time concentrating herself.

Boredom was highly underrated. She couldn't get Mark's expression out of her head, and when she tried, she was left with dinner, her mother, and her mother's new boyfriend. There was no resentment left in her, just a mouth-drying fear.

She'd accept the new boyfriend. She'd work hard to accept him. Just let everything else be okay. Let the Necromancers ignore her mother. Let Mark change his mind. Let her friends' families be safe.

*This is why Chase hates me*, Emma thought. She thought it without the usual sting. If it weren't for her, no one would be in any danger. She shook herself, took notes, and tried to find the discussion about willpower and its finite qualities interesting.

"Mark?" Allison asked Emma as quietly as she could in a very crowded stretch of hallway after the last class had ended.

Emma nodded. She headed straight for the front doors, without the usual social lingering. Allison was right behind her, and Michael was already outside. He'd chosen to wait in the usual place, but he watched the doors open and close with a twitchy nervousness. No one wanted to accidentally bump into Merrick Longland, and the minute Allison and Emma reached Michael, they began a hurried walk to put as much distance between Emery Collegiate and themselves as they could without breaking into an out and out run.

"Amy wants to meet at her house tomorrow after school," Allison said.

This surprised Emma. As a general rule, Allison and Amy didn't talk much.

Michael nodded, but Emma touched his shoulder anyway. When Michael was stressed out—and they were *all* stressed out at the moment—nodding came naturally; it didn't mean he agreed or even understood what had been said.

"I have track practice tomorrow," Michael told them.

"I'll talk to Amy. If it's okay with you, we can pick you up when you're finished." She steered him in the direction of his house. He was thinking, and sometimes Michael's thoughts became the whole of his geography; he could literally look up blocks from now in confusion, because he had no memory of walking them.

Today, Emma understood why. Walking down streets she'd seen all her life felt unreal. So much had changed in the past few months. She felt, on a visceral level, that the rest of the world should reflect those changes. It didn't.

And it made her question the life she'd lived up to now. It made every mundane street and every mundane corner sharper and harsher. Necromancers and their Queen had existed for longer than Emma had been alive, and until she herself had begun to see the dead, she'd never heard a word about them. Necromancers in the various games Michael and his friends played didn't have a Queen, and the dead were usually confined to the role of brain-eating, shuffling zombies.

The sun was low, but it wouldn't be dark for a couple of hours, and the lawns were, for the most part, buried under a pristine blanket of snow. Someone across the street was walking a black Labrador that didn't seem to be as deaf as Emma's rottweiler. Once, Petal had been that young.

She exhaled a cloud, shoving her hands deeper into her pockets. Maybe all of life was a little like this: You saw the parts of it you knew, and if no one pointed you in a different direction, that was the entire truth of your world. The different direction she'd been turned to face hadn't actually changed the world; it had just changed Emma's perception.

Her father had never been keen on ignorance; he felt that lack of knowledge was something to be alleviated, as if it were the common cold. She paused at the foot of Michael's driveway. "Don't forget to ask your mother about visiting Amy tomorrow," she told him, as she gave him a little nudge in the direction of his house.

"He wants to go home," Allison said, when Michael's front door had opened and closed behind him.

"Mark?"

Allison nodded.

"Yes. I don't want to take him," she added, although it was obvious. "And I waffled. I told him I couldn't do it tonight because I had important guests, more or less."

Allison winced on Emma's behalf, and Emma felt guilty. "I know my mother. I do. If Jon were a jerk, she wouldn't like him. But no, I'm not really looking forward to making nice at dinner. I don't know if I'm expected to impress him; I certainly haven't managed that so far."

"I think," Allison said quietly, "it's probably more important to your mom that Jon impress you."

"That's what I'm afraid of. I don't want my mom's new boyfriend sucking up to me. I don't know him. I don't have much to say to him." She held out a hand before Allison could speak. "I'll find something. I've always managed the small talk. I'm not even angry about him anymore. If things go wrong, a new boyfriend doesn't even register on the possible disaster scales.

"But I swear, if I walk into the house and there are any PDAs, I'm going to be ill."

*　　*　　*

The front hall was full of deaf rottweiler when Emma opened the door. Petal was happy to see her, although she suspected at the moment she looked like a walking food dish. Honestly, people who didn't know better would assume the Hall household regularly starved their poor, pathetic dog.

She wasn't immune to puppy-induced guilt and headed to the kitchen to remedy it. Unlike other forms of guilt in this house, food-related guilt was easily dealt with. When Petal had eaten enough—a rare occurrence—he left the kitchen and returned with a scratched, retractable leash in his mouth.

Emma shook her head. "Not tonight," she said quietly. This produced predictable whining. "I need to clean the kitchen and the dining room; we have guests coming for dinner."

She wasn't exactly lying; the kitchen and the dining room were in need of cleaning. But she needed the space of a few hours in which to think and make decisions—and if she took Petal out of the house, she was almost certain Nathan would appear.

Nathan.

She wasn't ready to talk to him again. Her mind was full of Merrick Longland, her mother, and the parents and siblings of her friends. It felt almost like betrayal, but she knew that Nathan—if he could hear her thoughts—would understand. The dead had time. Nathan had time.

And Emma had barely enough time to putter around the kitchen and the dining room in a silence broken only by dog whining. She didn't talk to herself as she worked because she had Petal, and Petal knew she was worried about something. He had stayed by her side during the long first month after Nathan's death, often with the leash in his mouth and his head in her lap.

He shuffled around her feet as she worked, and she let the work soothe her. It was normal. Meeting her mother's boyfriend, not so much. When the dining room was up to Hall guest standards—occupants having much lower ones—she headed up to her room to fix her hair and try to dress like a respectable daughter.

Her father did not show up, and given she was changing, that was a blessing.

When her mother arrived, Emma was in the television room, channel surfing in the hope that something would catch her attention. She set the remote aside when she heard her mother's car hit the driveway and caught Petal's collar before he charged up the stairs.

"Guests, remember?" she said, without much hope. She opened the door to see her mother fumbling with keys, a bag of groceries precariously cradled in her left arm. Jon was standing to one side, two bags of groceries in similar positions. Emma offered him her politest Hall smile, took the bag from her mother's arm, and headed toward the kitchen.

Jon followed, which wouldn't have been her first choice. But he didn't make himself at home in Emma's kitchen.

"Where did you want me to put these?"

"On the breakfast table," Emma told him, pointing. "I'll put them away." She hesitated, then added, "Can you reach the plates on the third shelf here?"

"With or without a chair?"

She smiled; it was less forced. She waited for him to say something stupid or awkward, because her mother had not yet entered the kitchen. He didn't. Instead, he got the plates and set them on the counter just in front of Emma. Emma tried to guess what exactly her mother intended to cook from the contents of the bags and came up with four possibilities. "I don't suppose she mentioned what was for dinner?"

"No. She bought desert, though." He looked at his feet and then up; he smiled. "She was nervous."

"It's a defining Hall trait," Emma replied. "That and guilt." She took a deep breath, held out her right hand, and added, "I'm Emma."

He took her hand as if he had never been introduced and said, "I'm Jon. Is your mother trying to give us time alone?"

Since it was the same thought Emma had, but with less annoyance and more genuine curiosity, Emma said, "Probably not. I know she's an ace at work, but she spends all her organization points in the office."

"Leaving the organization of the house to you?"

"More or less. If it helps, my locker at school is a class-A disaster."

"It helps a little. Look, I'm not great with small talk."

"Not great?"

"I suck at it."

Emma laughed.

Jon didn't. "I mean it. I'm seriously bad at making small talk. If I ask about someone's husband, they're in the middle of a divorce. If I ask about their family, their parents have cancer. If I compliment their clothing, they're wearing something their mother bought and they hate it." He held out both of his empty hands, palms up. "So mostly, I don't try."

"My mother's not bad at it."

"She's almost as bad at it as I am," he replied. He glanced toward the hall, which still contained Mercy, her coat, and, apparently, the family dog. "I'm not here to be your best friend. I'm not here to be your friend—that's presumptuous and probably unwanted." He ran his hands through his hair. "I care about your mother."

"Was this your idea or hers?"

"Pass."

"What?"

"I pass. I'll take question number two."

"Fine. Have you ever been married before?"

"How many passes do I get?"

She laughed. She couldn't help it. "As many as you need. This isn't an interrogation."

"You're sure?"

"Well, no, not really."

His smile deepened. The lines around the corners of his mouth were etched there; it made Emma realize that Jon smiled a lot. He wasn't a handsome man. He wasn't anywhere near as good-looking as her father had been. But she liked his smile. There were no edges in it.

"Teenage girls always make me nervous."

"You don't look particularly nervous."

"No. I'm better at hiding it. When I was a teenager, I kept my mouth shut. It mostly stopped the stupid from pouring out."

"Mostly?"

"I fidgeted more." He slid his hands into his pockets and leaned back against the edge of the counter. "I also suck under stress."

"You're under stress? Try meeting your mother's first boyfriend." She reddened. "I mean, first since . . ."

"You're always going to be your mother's daughter. If I screw up, I'm not guaranteed to hold the same position."

"You'd make a terrible daughter."

"If she's used to your caliber, probably. And I'm not willing to try—she's already got the only daughter she wants. So . . . what are our chances of eating dinner before ten?"

Emma pretended to consider the question. "Depends."

"On what?"

"If you want her in the kitchen right now, we could start shouting at each other."

He laughed. "I'll take dinner at ten, thanks."

To Emma's surprise, she wasn't in need of rescue. Jon looked just as surprised, because as it turned out, neither was he. When her mother entered the kitchen, she had the wary smile of a worried Hall attached to her face. It was brittle, and it was mildly annoying.

"I'm not bleeding," Jon told her.

Her mother had the grace to redden.

"He's not cowering in the corner either," Emma pointed out, with a little less humor than Jon.

Her mother winced. She didn't apologize, which would have been awkward, not that it wasn't already awkward. But Jon grinned. "She's your daughter. She's not going to wilt in the corner like a drama queen."

"Which proves," her mother said, in a more acerbic tone, "that you don't know the Halls well enough." To Emma she added, "I've given him plenty of opportunity to back out."

"And he's not bright enough to take any of them?"

"Apparently not." Her mother's smile was worn around the edges, but it was natural. "Jon, don't take this personally, but I need my kitchen."

"And your daughter?"

"Every chef needs a sous chef."

## ↜ Chapter 12

The kitchen with her mother in it was more awkward than the kitchen without her, an irony not lost on either of the Halls. "You don't have to love him," her mother began.

Emma, struggling with the theoretical sharp edge of a knife that clearly hadn't been sharpened in a decade, grimaced. "Good to know."

"You just have to understand that I might."

"Might? It's not decided?"

"I'm a little too old to fall head over heels in love," her mother replied. "It's been so long since I even considered being involved with anyone else at all." She set her knife down to one side of the cutting board and turned. "I didn't plan this. I wasn't even aware that he was interested in me."

Of all the conversations Emma could be having with her mother, this was the obvious one—but obvious or not, it was completely unexpected. Emma, who could cut and listen at the same time, nudged her mother away from the counter, but not before looking at her.

Objectively, her mother wasn't *old*. She wasn't young but then again, she had a teenage daughter. She dressed—and looked—like a middle-aged mother, to Emma. "You know," she said, half to Mercy and half to herself, "when I was four years old, I thought you were the most beautiful person alive."

"Were?" her mother asked. "Have I changed so much?"

Had she? "Well, after that I met Amy."

Her mother laughed. Hearing it, Emma wondered how long it had been since she'd heard that laugh. Her mother had laughed a lot more when her father had been alive. Emma finished slicing chicken and looked at her mother again. Her mother stood by the back screen door, her hands behind her. She thought about what her dad had said—the parts that didn't make her angry. Parents didn't *talk* to their kids; they wanted to give them a safe haven.

And safety was a myth.

"I know what I felt when I first got to know your father," her mother said quietly, looking out into the yard, her face reflected in the glass. She straightened her shoulders and headed back to the counter and their neglected dinner preparations. "I know this isn't the same. I'm not sure what I feel, but I don't want to overthink it."

"Mom—that's not the salt."

"What?" Mercy Hall looked at the glass jar in her hand. "Right. Sugar would be more interesting."

"Interesting food probably isn't the best choice for a first meal."

"I don't think Jon would mind too much. He's the better cook." That said, she put the sugar down and picked up the salt. "But Jon makes me laugh. He makes me laugh even when there's nothing remotely funny. Sometimes when I'm with him, I don't have to think." She turned to her daughter, who was silent.

"I know you miss your father. I miss him, too. I thought I'd spend the rest of my life in mourning. I don't know what I would have done if I hadn't had you."

"You'd've had an easier life."

"Easy and happy aren't the same—they only look the same when things are both hard and unhappy. I always thought your father was the better parent. He was more patient and more consistent. But I tried. I tried to live up to him."

"Tell her she did."

Emma closed her eyes as a familiar chill descended on the kitchen. She couldn't tell if her mother felt it or not; her mother was focused on dinner. And on the strange flow of words that Emma had never heard before. She turned to her father; her father was watching his wife making dinner for another man. His expression made Emma want to cry, but she was a Hall; she didn't.

She also didn't pass the words on.

"Tell her," her father continued when Emma failed to speak, "that she did better. I love her. I always have. And she's been lonely for long enough. She's not lying, Em. This *is* the first time she's ever been willing to risk opening up. To you," he said, in case this wasn't clear. "And to the possibility of life with someone else."

"I was too busy with you to be lonely," her mother said. She couldn't hear her husband's words, of course, but some instinct stopped their words from overlapping. "That's the truth. I knew we had to be a family, even if we were without a husband and a father. We still needed to keep a roof over our heads. Your grandmother offered to let us move in with her."

Emma grimaced but politely said nothing.

"But I had to know that we could make it on our own. And we have." She turned to the stove, wiping up invisible dirt from around the stovetop elements. "I don't know what happened the night we took you to the hospital."

Emma froze.

"I don't know if I was so frenzied with worry that I—" She shook her head. "No. That's not it. You saw—what I saw. Michael saw him. Allison did. I don't know if they remember. I don't know if they talk about it."

Emma started to speak, but her mother held up one imploring hand. "I need to say this, and if I don't get it all out now, I never will. Can you—can you let me do that? I'm asking for a lot, I know."

"Mom—" Emma swallowed. "You're not asking for much. You're just asking for me to listen." Who listened to her mother? She had a few friends she saw maybe twice a year—old university friends who now lived across the continent in different cities. Emma had Allison. Who did her mother have?

Not Emma, not really. Parents didn't talk to their children about anything important. No, that wasn't true. They listened and talked about things that were important to their *children*. But they didn't talk about their own lives. And it had never really occurred to Emma to ask. Why not?

"I saw Brendan. I saw him. I heard him." Her eyes were red, but—Hall. She didn't shed tears. They changed the timbre of her voice anyway. "He hadn't aged a day. He didn't look—he didn't look dead. But he looked the way he looked when you were a child and Petal was a puppy. And his expression—" She swallowed. "He looked so worried. For *me*. He looked—"

"You are *not* a disappointment to Dad," Emma said, with more force than she'd intended. She crossed the small space that divided them, forgetting for a moment that they had roles they were meant to inhabit. She slid her arms around her mother's shoulders and felt a shock as she realized how *small* her mother actually was.

"I'd just taken you to the hospital. I was terrified. If Dad were here—"

"Dad was alive when I broke my arm."

"A broken arm can't kill you."

"I'm sure Michael could come up with exceptions."

Mercy laughed. It was shaky. "When I came home that night, I felt so lonely. I haven't felt that way for so long. I felt as if the eight years and the work and the keeping things going—it was empty."

"Mercy," her father whispered. He was standing so close to them, all Emma had to do was reach out and touch him, and he'd be here too. But she didn't.

"And you hated yourself for feeling that way," Emma said softly.

Her mother blinked.

"I'm a Hall, remember? I know how this goes. You were *fine*. I was *fine*. There were probably days when you hated Dad for dying."

"Did you hate Nathan for dying?" her mother asked softly.

"Some days, I still do. Or I hate that I fell in love with him, because if I hadn't, life without him wouldn't be so bad."

Her mother nodded. "He cared for you."

"And Dad loved you."

Her mother put her arms around Emma. They stood together for a long, silent moment. "I don't regret a minute of the last eight years."

"The Candlewick project?" It had been one of Mercy's few—but significant—failures.

"Funny girl," her mother's voice was soft and fond. "But after I saw your father in the hospital, I couldn't shake that loneliness. I don't know if I love Jon, but when I'm with him, the world seems a little brighter and little more vibrant. He's so good at being who he is. It doesn't seem to matter if he's talking to an eighty year old or a toddler. He doesn't ask for anything, and he doesn't want a lot from me. He knows about your father, of course. He knows how important you are. He was nervous," she added.

"I know. I was nervous, too."

"I thought you were angry."

"I was." Emma tightened her arms. "I don't know Jon. But sometimes," she added, thinking about the conversation with her father earlier in the day, "I think I didn't really know Dad, either. I'll try, Mom. I will honestly try."

"I couldn't replace Nathan," her mother said. It sounded like an odd thing to say, but it mirrored what Emma couldn't put into words herself. "But I never doubted that you loved me."

"And I couldn't replace Dad."

"No one could. Jon isn't trying to be Brendan. He knows he's not your father. You only—and ever—have one." Her mother exhaled. "I'm not trying to replace my husband, either. He was my best friend and my pillar of support, and nothing Jon says or does will change that. But nothing anyone says or does can change the past. If I can't open up a bit, if I can't let go, the past is the only future I have.

"And you're almost an adult now. You don't need me anymore."

"I do, Mom."

"Not the way you used to. I miss it," she added, since this was a night for unexpected truth. "But no one gets to be a child forever—and no one should want to. You've grown. You've become so much stronger. I want you to keep growing up. I want you to go out into a world that doesn't include me. I want you to meet—" she stopped, stiffening at the words that had almost fallen out of her mouth, and the implication behind them.

At any other time, Emma would have been angry. But the anger wouldn't come. In a quieter voice she said, "I'm not ready to meet anyone new."

"No, of course not—I'm sorry, Em, I was just—"

"You took eight years, Mom. Eight years. Give me at least that long."

Her mother nodded and slowly disentangled herself. "We're going to have dinner at midnight at this rate," she said, running her sleeve across her eyes. Emma couldn't remember the last time she'd seen her mother cry.

"Jon won't care," she said.

"No, he really won't," her mother replied, smiling.

Dinner was late, even for the Hall household, but it wasn't midnight. It wasn't—quite—nine in the evening, although it only missed that mark by a few minutes. Allison texted before they'd even sat down, and Emma texted back a brief "I don't hate him." She avoided using the words "it's fine" because they always made Ally worry.

And the truth was, she didn't. She wasn't certain she *liked* him, but she was certain her like or dislike was irrelevant. Or it should be. But she lingered in the kitchen while her mother took the food out.

"Is this really okay?" she asked her father, who hadn't left the kitchen once.

"It's better than okay," he replied. "Nathan's death is too new to you. You can't see past it. You can't see a world that doesn't have him in it."

She almost said, *And I don't have to.* But she held her peace. She was in a strange state of mind; there was almost no fight in her.

"Your mother has had eight years of a life without me," he continued. "Sometimes she'd tell you that she missed me. But, Em—the life the two of you have now doesn't have a place for me in it. She's held that space empty, as if I might somehow return to fill it.

"It's not what I want for her. Maybe if I could come back—in the flesh, alive—I'd hate everything about this evening. But I think she's been in pain and been alone for long enough. I don't want you to compare Jon to me, because there's no point. Jon isn't me. Your mother is right—nothing will change our past. But it *is* past.

"If you can do one thing for me, help her."

"I've always tried—"

"Help her with Jon. He's a decent guy. He does care for Mercy. Maybe he can give her what I can't." He turned to his daughter, hands in ghostly pockets. "You were angry that she didn't ask about me. You were upset that she didn't want to speak with me. For you, speaking with Nathan is so much better than the silence and the absence.

"It's different for your mother. What she's seen of death is final; that door is closed. If she *did* speak to me, if she asked, it wouldn't make her life any easier because I can't be part of it." He closed his eyes. "What will you do?"

"I'll try to like Jon."

"No, Em, what will you do about the Necromancers?"

"I don't want to tell Mom. I think the worry would about kill her, if the Necromancers didn't do it first. But I don't want to run away without telling her anything—I'm afraid she'd blame Jon. Or worse, herself. This is the first boyfriend, and if I suddenly disappear, it'll probably be the last one. And . . . I don't want to leave home. I know she's not perfect, but I'm not perfect either." Exhaling, she said, "Tell me I'm wrong. Tell me she won't blame Jon or herself."

"You know your mother as well as I do. You probably know her better, by this point."

"Great. Sometimes I think life is just a way of accumulating guilt."

He chuckled. "For the Halls, it probably is. You should head out. Your mother's going to worry if she walks in and finds you talking to yourself."

Halfway through dinner, the doorbell rang.

Emma looked across the table at Jon. "Did you order pizza?"

He laughed as Emma rose. "I would never insult the collective cooking of the Halls; I like my teeth where they are." The smile faded slowly from his lips. "It's a little late for door to door salesmen."

"And we're not in the middle of election season. On the other hand, most people have probably finished dinner by now. Sit down, Mom. You have a guest. I'll get it." The last three words were said in a much louder voice, as Petal had set up barking.

She caught her dog by the collar and pulled him away from the front door, but she resented having to do it; at this time of night, random strangers who interrupted people at dinner deserved to have a face full of loud, suspicious rottweiler.

"Petal, sit. *Sit.*"

One hand on dog and the other on doorknob, she opened the door and froze in its frame as she met the eyes of Merrick Longland.

# Chapter 13

His smile was full-on teacher. "Just the young woman I wanted to see."

"Emma? Who is it?" Her mother's voice approached from the dining room. Emma swallowed and met Merrick Longland's eyes; under the light at the side of the door, they were faintly luminescent, but she couldn't describe their color. They were, in every way, the eyes of the dead.

But he wasn't dead. She knew. Her mother came out of the dining room and headed straight toward him, wearing her best, distancing business smile.

"Mrs. Hall?" he said, extending his right hand. "Have I caught you at a bad time?"

"We're in the middle of a late dinner," her mother replied, thawing slightly. "What can I do for you?"

"I'm actually here to speak with Emma. My name is Merrick Longland, and I have the privilege of being her supervisor on the yearbook committee." He held out a hand.

For one immobile moment, Emma wanted to slam the door in his face. But it was too late for that; her mother's expression had relaxed, and she was already shaking the hand Merrick Longland had offered.

If being dead made any difference to the physical body, it was too subtle for her mother. "I'm Emma's mother, Mercy Hall. We don't usually get teachers visiting at this time of night."

"It's eight o'clock," he said.

Her mother lifted a brow. "It's past nine."

He looked surprised, checked his watch and then looked sheepish. As acts went, it was beyond excellent.

"Mr. Longland is replacing Mr. Taylor for the rest of the year."

Her mother's expression became instantly more drawn. "That was a terrible accident. Mr. Taylor was quite popular at the school," she added.

"So I've discovered," he replied, still with the sheepish. "Look, I'm sorry. I lost track of time. I didn't mean to come here this late." He paused and then added, "You said I was interrupting dinner?"

"Dinner was a touch on the late side." She turned toward the dining room as Jon came into the hall. "Sorry," she said. "This is Mr. Longland; he's a new teacher at Emery."

"And he makes house calls at this time of night?"

"Not deliberately," Longland said. "I lost track of time. I'd hoped to have a word with Emma before the yearbook committee meeting next week."

"So you hunted her down at home?" Jon's smile matched Longland's, and in spite of herself, Emma was impressed.

"I live not far from here."

Impressed and terrified. She put on her best Hall smile. "Why don't the two of you go back to dinner? I'm sure this won't take long, and I'll join you when we're done." She did *not* want Merrick Longland in her house.

But she didn't want to leave her house with him, either. She accepted the obvious: Ernest had been right. Longland now knew where she lived. He probably knew where they all lived. And if she behaved in a way that worried her mother, he probably had ways of dealing with that.

Jon held out a hand. "I'm Jon Madding," he said. "I'm what passes for a dinner guest in these parts."

"Not her father, then?"

"No, as you well know," her father said.

"Mom, Jon—please go eat before the food gets cold." Emma nudged her mother back into the dining room, which was easy. Jon seemed reluctant.

"Not your daughter, remember?"

"Right. Not." He glanced at Mercy and then followed her as she left Emma, her teacher, and the ghost of the man whose seat he now occupied, in the hall.

Emma then turned to Merrick Longland. "Living room," she said, her voice even, her expression neutral.

Longland kept his game face on until there was no possibility of line of sight from the dining room. He then walked over to the couch and made himself more or less at home. His expression chilled instantly, which perversely made Emma far more comfortable.

"Yes, I do know," Longland then said—to Emma's father. "But she didn't strike me as the type of person who would use her own father as a focus."

"Meaning she's not you."

Longland darkened. "No. She's still alive." As he said it, he turned to face her, his eyes very like her father's but with more anger in them. "I came here the first time to *rescue* you. I came because I knew the hunters would kill you. I never threatened you.

"You're responsible for my death."

Emma stiffened. Words crumbled. Merrick Longland had defined monstrous to Emma—but it was true. He'd come to save her life.

"What, then, do you owe *me*, Emma Hall? Your life? The lives of your family?"

"Emma," her father said. "You are not responsible for this man's death. If he came to save your life, he didn't intend to give you a choice about where the rest of that life was to take place. He's responsible for the choices he made and the consequences of those choices."

"Thank you for the parental moralizing," Longland replied. "I don't believe this conversation is relevant to you. If you are truly free to go as you please, don't let us keep you."

"I'm also free to remain. This is more my home than yours." Her father folded his arms across his chest and looked down on Longland in, oh, so many ways.

Longland stared at her father, frowning. "Are you truly not hers?"

"I'm her father, but if you're asking if I'm bound to her, the answer is pretty obvious."

"If you're not bound to her, why are you still here?"

"It's his house," Emma said, more sharply than she'd intended. "He has every right to be here."

"That's not what I meant," Longland said, voice low. "And he knows it, even if you're too ignorant to understand."

She turned to her father because something in Longland's voice sounded like the truth. "Dad?"

"You're still here," Longland repeated. "There's no way you would be here if you weren't bound."

Her father was silent for a long moment, and then, of all things, he smiled. It was a sad smile, and it added lines to his face. "There are many, many bindings, Longland. I don't expect you to understand them all. Emma is my daughter, and I love her. No parent willingly turns his back—and walks away—from his child. Not when that child is in danger."

"My parents did," was the bitter—and unexpected—reply.

"And I'm not your father," Brendan Hall replied. "Nor is Emma you. The choices you've made might have been the only choices you saw, but there were always others."

"I would have died."

Emma had no desire to offer support to Longland in any way, but she remembered, in the silence that followed, the reason Eric had come to Toronto and the reason Chase had followed him.

Her father nodded. "Yes, in all likelihood." He knew what Emma knew. "But there's a world between dying and killing. A handful of people willing to end your life doesn't justify killing everyone else."

Longland closed his eyes. Emma wondered if closed eyes had the same effect for the dead that they would for the living. "You don't understand," he finally said, his shoulders sagging. "Death is forever. Life is so brief."

"Yet you valued yours enough to make the choices you did."

"There *are no choices.*" His voice was low, intent. "One way or the other, we serve the Queen for eternity. We can do it while we live, or we can do it afterward. But if we serve her *well*, we don't have to die. We don't have to age. The only people who are spared an eternity of *this*," he added, with loathing, "are the Necromancers."

"You don't look particularly dead," Emma pointed out.

"Not even to you?"

"The dead don't generally teach classes and supervise yearbook committees. Trust me on this. How are you alive?"

His answering laughter was quiet and bitter. "I'm not alive. I'm as dead as your father."

"But you've got—"

"A body? Yes. I thought it was a privilege when I was alive. I thought it was something the dead might—just might—aspire to." He shook his head. "It's the same as being dead except that the living can see it. Food has no taste. The cold is stronger; nothing is warm. Every minute I'm here, I can see the way to the other side." He lifted his hands to his face. "The only difference is this: I can't be bound tightly to the Queen's side. If I'm to play at being alive, I have to travel. I can hear her," he added, his voice dropping, "but she can't command me to return; I'm willing to obey, but the constructs can't travel the way the disembodied can."

It took Emma a minute to realize that the construct he spoke of was his physical form.

"You can't be a—a power source for a Necromancer."

"No. I'm spared that. But that's all I'm spared." He rose. "People have always judged me. People have always misunderstood." It didn't sound like whining, but Emma had to bite back words. How did one misjudge the willingness to murder an infant? "But what I wanted, in the end, wasn't so different from what you want."

Emma was speechless.

Her father was not. "You wanted a place to belong."

"A safe place," Merrick Longland agreed. "Where love, not pain, is waiting around every corner. A place where I don't have to watch my back at all times and where power isn't the only hope of safety I have." He closed his eyes. "Someplace that wants *me*." When he opened his eyes again, they were almost blue in the living room light, but they retained their subtle shimmering transparency. "I see it every day. I *know* I don't deserve it—but whatever is waiting on the other side doesn't *care*."

Longland glanced at her father. "You *saw* the place we were meant to be. Your daughter opened the door the Queen has kept locked and barred."

"I didn't see her open the door," her father replied. "But, yes, I suspected she would. I wasn't certain that I would be as strong as I wanted to be; I left before she tried."

"But you know what waits—you could be there now!"

"Yes. But, Longland, if my home wasn't perfect, if my family wasn't flawless, it *was* a family. I'm human. Sometimes I was frustrated. Sometimes I was lonely. Sometimes I felt like a failure. All of these things are true."

"Dad, you weren't—"

He give a slight shake of head that meant he wanted to be uninterrupted.

"But I also felt loved, by my wife and my child. Even when I was failure. Maybe especially then." He smiled at his daughter, in almost embarrassing gratitude. "I can't—and won't—judge you. What I had, you didn't have. And, yes, I know what you see."

"Is it—is it the same? Isn't it better than what you had?"

"It's different."

Longland swallowed. In a voice that was painful and at odds with everything she knew about his life, he asked, "Will I be allowed to go anyway?"

"Yes," her father said. There was no doubt in his voice.

Longland turned to Emma. "Could you do it again?"

For the first time, Emma accepted the fact that Merrick Longland was dead. She'd been told, but the knowledge had been entirely intellectual. Now, it wasn't. Like her father, like Nathan, he was trapped here. What he wanted was out of reach.

And it shouldn't be.

"I don't know," she said, after a long pause.

When he flinched—which surprised her—she added, "I don't hate you enough to keep you here." But she had. She knew she had. If she tried, she could still see the gun pointed at the baby. And at Allison, in whose arms the baby was held.

"It wasn't personal," he told her. "I came here the first time to save your life."

She believed him. "Why have you come here a second time?"

"I don't know." When he saw the change in Emma's expression, he added, "It's the truth. I was sent here in the company of the Queen's Knights. I was given no orders beyond that. I was to accompany the Necromancers, and I was to find a way to meet you that wouldn't be suspicious."

"What orders were the Necromancers given?"

"They're not to kill you, except at need. They're here to make certain you arrive in the City of the Dead. The Queen is waiting."

"And you—you're just supposed to *talk* to me? This isn't about revenge for what happened to you?"

"There are whole hours when I forget whose fault my current condition is. I can't hold on to it when I look toward the light. Revenge doesn't matter— there's no way for me to come back." He hesitated and then said, "And if I could leave this place, I wouldn't want to come back. Your father's right. What he had—what he built—I didn't have. I couldn't build it. I couldn't even *see* it. Maybe that's why he's still here.

"When I first saw you, I saw a pretty, popular girl who had it easy. You had friends. You had potential. You even had a hunter on your side. Until I was found, I had no one. I was nothing. Being dead hasn't changed that. I was invisible until the Queen's Knights found me, and I'm invisible now.

"There's nothing for me here. Even if the Queen of the Dead were gone and I were free, there's nothing. You can speak with your father. Short of interrogation, there's no one who would spend the time—or the power—talking to me.

"You have everything," he added. It wasn't an accusation, but she knew that had he been alive, it would have been. Death changed things. "Everything I wanted was just handed to you." His voice dropped to a whisper.

And he could never have it, Emma though dispassionately. For a moment, Merrick Longland was painfully young in her eyes. She knew what he'd been willing to do, while alive. She hated it. At the moment, all she could see was pain. Pain, isolation, and a terrible loneliness. She glanced at her father, who nodded but said nothing.

"If I could—if I was certain I could—I would open that door again. But the last time—" she shook her head.

"What? What about the last time?"

Emma did not want to feel sympathy—or even pity—for Merrick Longland. He was the type of person who justified the concept of Hell. He thought about his own pain but never considered the pain he left in the lives of others.

But if she had been without a father for over half her life now, the father she'd had had loved her. She'd never doubted it. Who would she be if her father were a different man? What would she be like if she'd had Mark's mother?

Dead, probably.

"Necromantic power requires the dead. It doesn't necessarily require binding them."

He frowned. "That's not how it works—"

"It's not how you've been taught," she replied. "But it *is* how it works, or can work. My father is free to come and go as he pleases. I don't know where he is when he's not with me. I don't *own* him. He chooses to stay. But he can give me power if he chooses to.

"The dead have a choice. That's the thing you don't understand—and you're dead. The dead are people. They're people trapped inside a giant, icy waiting room, but they're still people. When I opened the door, I did it for

Andrew Copis. And for his mother. She would never have known a moment's peace if he'd remained trapped here. But it took—it took so *many* of the dead, and they gave me everything they had." She exhaled. "The Queen of the Dead has closed the way. I don't know how. I just know that the power it takes to open the door requires hundreds or thousands of the dead. Maybe more. I stopped counting."

He closed his eyes. His lashes were dark and long as they rested against pale skin. He *looked* alive, to Emma. But then again, so did her father. She felt a peculiar tightness in her throat as she watched him, because she knew that she could touch him and her hands wouldn't freeze or go numb.

"If the dead knew," he whispered, "they would come. You had thousands, but Emma—every person who's died in the last several centuries would come if you called them."

"I don't know how. How did you find the dead? Did you find them in the hundreds?"

He shook his head.

"The Necromancers who are in Toronto—"

"Two are already dead."

"There's a third?"

"And a fourth."

"Are they also at Emery?"

"No." He lifted his chin, straightening his shoulders. "I can teach you."

Her father stiffened. Neither he nor Emma misunderstood Longland's offer. "To bind the dead?" she asked softly.

"You don't understand what you can do with that power."

"I understand what's been done with it in the past," she countered.

"If you had enough power, you wouldn't age. You could be immortal. You're young, now. But in ten years, twenty, you'll be older. You'll understand why the gift is valuable, then."

She shook her head.

"I can teach you how to gather," he said, bending forward, his hands cupped before him as if he were waiting for them to be filled. "You said you need power to free us. I can show you how to gain it."

It hadn't done Longland a lot of good. Emma didn't point this out. Instead, she said, "If I don't get back to dinner, my mother's going to be suspicious. Or worried."

"Promise me you'll try," he said, catching her by the hand as she turned. She was right. His hand was warm. It felt like a living hand.

"I promise I'll try. I want something in return."

He stiffened.

"I want the other two Necromancers."

"What will you do with them?"

Emma looked down at the floor. "You already know," she said. "I'm not going to the City of the Dead. I'm not going to the Queen's Court."

"She says you have power," Longland whispered. "If you trained hard, you could become the Queen of the Dead."

"I'm going back to dinner." She turned, then turned back. "Will she summon you home?"

"She can order me home," Longland replied. "But without a Necromancer to create a path, it won't be instant; I have to travel the way the rest of you do." He rose. His expression shuttered, becoming smooth and almost lifeless. "Even at the height of my power, I couldn't have budged that door an inch. Untrained, you did what I couldn't." He headed out of the living room and into the hall, where he retrieved his boots and his winter gear.

"Does the cold affect you?"

His smile was strange. "I'm always cold. If you mean the weather, the winter, no. I imagine this body feels pain; that the flesh can freeze or burn." He spoke of it as if it were entirely separate from him.

"But—isn't it better than being dead?" She hated the hope in her voice, because she knew it was foolish. It was *wrong*. But it hovered there anyway. If Nathan were like Longland, she could touch him. Nathan could touch her. There wouldn't be pain and numbness.

"Emma, I *am* dead. Clothed in flesh or no, there's nothing that can change that." He turned and left the living room; Emma followed after taking one deep breath. She thanked him for coming, apologized in advance for Amy, and otherwise spoke as if he were the teacher he'd claimed to be.

She wasn't certain her mother was listening. But she wasn't certain she wasn't, either; the dining room had fallen momentarily silent.

After she'd shut the door, she leaned against the wall, her head tilted toward the ceiling.

"Em."

For a long moment, she couldn't speak. Her throat was too tight. "I'm fine," she told him softly. It was a Hall variant on fine. To stop her father from worrying about her, she said, "Do you think we can trust him?"

"He strikes me as a boy who's always focused on what he wants, to the exclusion of everything else."

"And he wants to escape?"

Her father shook his head. "It's not escape. He is standing outside his home in a snowstorm. He doesn't have the key, and the door is locked. He can peer in through the window; he can knock at the door. He can scream. He can't enter. But he has the right to be there. I think it's the only thing he wants, now.

I think, as long as you're working toward that, he will do everything he can to help you."

"But he was sent here by the Queen of the Dead."

"Yes, Em. Do you understand why?"

She swallowed. Shook her head.

Halls did not accuse each other of lying. They respected each other's privacy. Her father was concerned enough to ask; he wasn't concerned enough to break Hall family rules. Not when he'd worked so hard in the early years to establish them.

"I have to get back to dinner."

"Jon is worried."

"Jon? I was thinking about Mom."

Her father's smile was brief. "She's not naturally as suspicious as Jon appears to be."

Emma turned, and then turned again. "Dad, you're really okay with this?"

"I am far less worried about your mother and Jon than I am about you," he replied. It was a very Hall answer.

She thought a lot about death at dinner, where the dead weren't. And she thought a lot about life, as well, watching her mother, watching Jon tease her mother. He never excluded Emma; she chose to step back, and he acknowledged it. It was subtle. Emma wasn't used to subtle adults. Most of the adults in her daily life were teachers, and subtlety was generally a lost cause on the student body.

But she thought her father was right: Jon was suspicious of Longland. He was suspicious, but he mostly kept it to himself because in the end, it wasn't his house, and she wasn't his daughter. He was willing to follow her mother's lead. Emma was polite, because she could be and still be preoccupied. If her mother noticed, she left it alone, and when dinner was done and cleanup started, Jon actually helped. He was better at washing dishes than her mom, which was a disloyal thought, but also true.

But even helping, he didn't seem particularly eager to please; the dishes were dirty, he'd eaten, and he therefore helped clean up. It seemed natural, although her mother tried to shoo him out of the kitchen three times on the grounds that he was a guest. He pointed out that a decent guest helped out.

Given that Emma had been told exactly this for most of her life, she found the disagreement amusing. She held on to that because there were now two things she had to face that she desperately wanted to avoid.

One of them was waiting in her bedroom when the dishes were done and she could retreat to give her mother some privacy.

Mark was sitting at her desk in front of her computer. "How is it," she asked, as her father also materialized to one side of that desk, "that he can use the computer?"

Her father shrugged. "I don't know. Before you ask, I don't know how I can, either."

"That's not like you."

"Not knowing?"

"Not caring enough *to* know."

"When I was alive, knowledge made a difference. Knowing how things work now doesn't give me the ability to fix any of them."

"Dad—"

Mark turned in the chair. The chair didn't turn with him. "Are you finished dinner, now?"

Emma surrendered. "Yes. And the cleanup. You'll have to give me a few minutes to get my dog ready for a walk." She fished her phone out of a pocket and hit the speed dial. "Eric?"

"Emma?"

"I'm about to go take my dog for a walk."

"Where?"

She glanced at her father. "Where does Mark live? Can I walk there?"

"We can walk," Mark began.

"Dead people don't take as long to walk between places as living ones," her father told him. To his daughter, he added, "But it's not that far."

It couldn't be. Not and be close to the ravine. Mark had said his mother had taken him for a walk, not a drive. "My dad says it's within easy walking distance."

"You're taking Mark home."

"I'm going home with him, yes."

"To do what, Emma?"

"I honestly don't know." She hesitated and then added, "Merrick Longland paid me a visit during dinner."

There was a long, silent beat. "Tonight?"

"Yes. He left about an hour ago."

"What did he want?"

She exhaled. "He wanted me to force the door open again, the way I did for Andrew Copis."

Silence. "That's it?"

"He was sent here to talk to me. He wasn't told what he should talk about. He wasn't sent to aid the Necromancers, but said he arrived with four. Two of them are dead."

"The other two?"

"Not dead but not at the school."

"Do you trust him?"

Did she? "It would be stupid to trust him," she replied, hedging.

"But you do."

"I trust what he said tonight. If you know of a way to bring the dead back to life, tell me now—because if there is, and that's what he's angling for, he'll lie."

"There isn't."

She swallowed. It took her a little longer to dredge up a reply. "He looks alive to me."

"He looks alive to anyone living. The dead know the difference. Did he try to tell you—"

"No. He told me, flat out, that he's dead. He's wrapped in a—a construct. It's like a cage of flesh."

Eric exhaled. "He was at least that honest. What did you tell him?"

"The truth. If I could open that door for him, I'd do it tomorrow. I'd do it now."

"You can't."

"I don't think I can, no. Every person gathered at the door—every dead person," she amended, "was willing to give me everything they had on blind faith, and I still only barely managed to pry it open a crack. I'm not sure I could gather that many of the dead together again. And if I did, I think she'd know."

"She?"

"The Queen of the Dead."

"Did you tell him how you gathered the dead?"

"The lantern? No."

"Good. Don't mention it if he doesn't. Don't talk about it even if he brings it up." He exhaled. "Tell me the route you'll be taking with your dog. I'll meet you on the way."

"I don't—I'm not sure that's a good idea."

"Fine. If you're not sure, I am. Do the other Necromancers know where you, Allison, or Michael live?"

Emma hadn't asked. She'd been so surprised by Longland—and by the rest of the evening—that what should have been the first question out of her mouth had never left it. "I don't know. I'm sorry—"

"It's fine. We're spread a little thin at the moment, but the old man is out making the rounds, and Margaret's with him." He hesitated, then added, "I've spoken with Allison. Chase has her back."

"Is she okay with that?"

"She's not happy about it, no. But she understands what's at stake. Give me five, and I'll meet you."

# Chapter 14

It was cold, even for November. Petal was heavy enough to break the thin layer of ice that had formed on the snow on the boulevard. Emma, wearing gloves and holding a scuffed lead, could barely feel her hands; her cheeks were numb. Mark walked to her left, her father, on the street side. Her father made a show of taking steps. Mark trailed in the air, his legs unmoving. The appearance of walking wasn't necessary in order to move, and he'd discarded it. He was dressed for winter, on the other hand; her father wasn't.

Petal's breath was a constant white mist. It was a wonder his tongue wasn't frozen. He didn't look up from his hopeful inspection of the frozen ground until Eric joined them. Eric patted Petal while he nodded to her father and Mark.

Mark said, "You can see me."

Eric nodded again.

"Are you dead?"

"Do I look dead to you?"

"How am I supposed to tell?" Mark asked. "The dead don't look dead to me. *I* don't look dead. To me. But you can see me."

"Emma's not dead," Eric said quietly. "And she can see you." Months of talking to Michael had given him some of the tools necessary to talk to Mark, but he wasn't comfortable. Then again, at the moment neither was Emma. She would have been in other circumstances, even given two dead companions and a half-deaf rottweiler. But with the dead came the living: the Necromancers and their Queen.

"Are you like Emma?"

Eric didn't hesitate. "No. No one's like Emma."

"Emma is a Necromancer."

Eric winced. "Emma has the latent ability of the Necromancers—but she's not one of them."

"Why not?"

"Fair question," Eric replied. "But I can't answer it."

Emma glared as Eric grinned. "Chase would love this conversation."

"He'd only get half of it."

"My half, which means he probably wouldn't be listening to any of it." She turned to Mark. "Having power is like—like having a knife. You can't cook without one, but not everyone who owns one uses it to stab someone else. I have the equivalent of a knife. But I want to use it in the kitchen; I don't want to use it to hurt people."

"People hurt people," he said.

"Yes. But mostly by accident." Mark fell silent, and she mentally kicked herself. She glanced at Eric, who was watching Petal as if the dog were fascinating. Things could have been more awkward, but only with the inclusion of, say, her mother's new boyfriend.

She followed her father's subtle lead, but asked Mark if he knew the way home. He frowned and thought about this. "I know," he finally said, "that I can go there."

"But not how?"

"The streets look different when you're dead. They change a bit. They didn't do that when I was alive. I can't tell you how to get there because you're not dead."

"Could you tell my father?" It didn't matter, but she found herself asking questions that had nothing to do with the mother waiting at the end of this walk. Partly for his sake and partly for her own.

"He already knows."

"Can he get there the same way you can?"

Mark considered this. Turning to her father, he asked, "Can you?"

"Yes," her father replied. "But Emma and Eric can't. Neither can Petal."

"Petal is a strange name for a dog."

"I thought so, but I didn't choose it."

Emma, remembering the reason she'd chosen the name, shrugged. It wasn't the name she would choose now, but he'd grown into the name, or she'd grown attached to it. "I was eight," she told Mark. "My dad always called me Sprout. I thought Petal was a good name."

"For a dog?"

"Well, for this one. He doesn't seem to mind it." He did perk up, the way he often did when people were talking about him. Mostly because he assumed his name was synonymous with food.

"Is Michael like me?"

"Michael is Michael," she replied. "You're Mark. You have some things in common, but you're not the same person."

"Michael isn't happy."

She closed her eyes briefly. "Michael doesn't understand what happened to you. I mean, he knows what happened but not why."

"Me either."

"When things upset him, he needs to understand why they happened—usually in a lot of detail—or he stays upset. Sometimes we can explain things, but sometimes we can't. I can't explain this." She stopped walking, and remembered: she had promised to take Michael with her when she took Mark home.

But it was late. It was late, and she did not want an upset Michael at the door of the woman who had killed Mark. She hesitated, torn. Eric marked it.

"I told Michael he could come with me." She considered appearing on Michael's doorstep at almost ten in the evening, dog in hand. His mother would be worried—and with cause, even if they couldn't explain it all.

Sometimes, dealing with Michael was hard. If she'd promised Allison and she reneged, Allison would understand why. She might not be *happy* with the explanation, but she'd understand it. Michael tended to see things as black or white. But he was generally forgiving if there was a reasonable explanation. Or rather, an explanation that seemed reasonable to him.

Emma hesitated again and then said, "We need to take a slight detour."

Michael's mother answered the door, which was about what Emma expected; Michael often failed to register the doorbell when it rang. "I'm really sorry, Mrs. Howe," Emma said. "But I promised Michael I'd show him something the next time I went, and I'm going now."

Michael's mother nodded. She was a mostly practical woman, rounded with years but pragmatic about it; her hair was shot through with gray. Mercy Hall dyed her hair. Emma was certain that when she reached that age, she'd dye her hair as well, but Mrs. Howe's hair was dark enough that the gray seemed to add shine to it.

"I wouldn't be here," Emma continued, "but Michael's been a little stressed lately, and I didn't think a broken promise would help him much."

Michael's mother knew her son. "Let me get him. Are you—are you going to be long?"

"I hope not. In part, it'll depend on Michael."

"And the other part?"

"How long it takes for my hands to freeze off."

"Well, come in and wait. With luck, he'll decide to stay in."

Emma thought it would take more than luck, but agreed. The important part at the moment was that she was in his front hall, having remembered her promise. What he then chose to do with it was out of her hands; if he decided not to accompany her, no guilt accrued on her part.

Michael came thundering down the stairs. He'd never learned the art of walking quietly, and he generally took stairs two at a time in either direction. He wasn't carrying his computer, but headed for the closet to unearth his coat, his mittens—he disliked gloves—and his scarf. His mother found his misplaced hat and murmured something about stapling it to his forehead.

During this, he spoke very little; he kept peering out the door, as if he

might catch a glimpse of Mark, although he knew that without Emma's intervention—Emma, who was standing alone in his hall—that was impossible.

And Emma knew, from one glance at Michael's mother, that she was worried. "Eric's with us," she said, "and he has a car. If we're going to be late—I
mean, later—I'll call you."

"I don't think I've met Eric," his mother said.

"He's keeping the car running. He just started Emery this year, but he eats
lunch at Michael's table."

"And the gaming discussions haven't driven him off?"

"Not yet."

"Emma—" She inhaled. "Never mind. Keep an eye on him tonight?"

"Always."

Mark was quiet; his silence was not comfortable. Emma was generally comfortable with silence—it was one of the reasons she'd so liked Nathan. He
didn't *need* her to fill silence in order to be at ease. But this silence was different, and she knew it. It was a veneer over things that couldn't be said, even if
words were roiling beneath it.

She hated Mark's mother. Hated her, despised her, wanted to see her
hauled off to jail to answer for what she'd done. Not just the death, but everything that had led up to it. No one had forced her to become a mother.

But saying this out loud wouldn't help Mark. It wouldn't change anything.
Hating his mother had zero effect; it didn't offer him either comfort or support. She almost reached out to take his hand but remembered that he found
touch uncomfortable—at least while he was alive. He was dead, but that didn't
mean what it meant to her father. Or to Nathan.

She inhaled. Exhaled. What did she want from this evening? Why was she
quietly following her father's reluctant lead to take a severely unwanted child
home to the mother who had murdered him?

Because the child wanted to go there. This wasn't about Mark's mother, in
the end; not to Emma. It was about Mark. It was about the dead child. Any
mistakes he made here couldn't harm him further; he'd suffered the worst
already.

But his mother had gotten away with murder. When she should have been
caring for and about her son, she had abandoned him to die, instead—and no
one knew. Everyone thought she was the grieving, bereaved parent. If Emma
did nothing, said nothing—where was the justice in that? How was that fair
to Mark?

"Emma," her father said.

She looked up, as apparently her feet had gotten really interesting.

"That's the house."

*       *       *

It was about the same size as the Hall house, and if Emma remembered correctly, it also lacked a father. It didn't lack siblings, but it lacked anything as fundamental as a mother, in Emma's opinion. She inhaled, held her breath, and then turned to Mark, who was staring at the front door.

Eric said, quietly, "Are you certain this is wise?"

"I'm certain it's not," she replied. "Mark, is my father right? Is that the house?"

Mark nodded, never taking his eyes off the front door. Emma tried to imagine what it would be like to stand in front of her home in the same context. How would she feel if her mother had killed her?

She failed, because she couldn't imagine it. In her worst nightmares—the ones that involved her mother—her mother had either died or disappeared. She had never tried to kill her.

"You don't have to do this," Emma said, aware that she was partly speaking to herself. But the alternative—breaking her word to Mark—had seemed worse. It didn't seem worse now.

Mark frowned. "I don't have to do this," he repeated, as if trying to make sense of the words.

Michael, who couldn't see Mark, said, "He wants to do this."

Mark looked at Michael. To Emma he said, "Michael is your friend." It was a question without the intonation.

"Michael is my friend," she agreed.

"Why?"

"If you mean why do I like him, there are a bunch of reasons."

"He's not normal."

She hated that word more than she'd ever hated it before. "I'm not normal, either."

He frowned.

"I'm a Necromancer. I can see—and talk—to the dead. Michael doesn't hate me just because I can do these things. Michael finds it hard to deal with strangers. He finds it hard to talk to people he doesn't know. He finds it hard to talk to people he *does* know if they're speaking about something he doesn't really understand. But he's direct, he's honest, and if he says he'll help you, he will. Michael's easy to trust."

"Is trust important?"

"Very. At least to me." Petal shoved his nose into her gloves. She dropped a hand to his head; he was warm enough that she could feel the heat rising off his fur. She should have left him at home. But she'd needed a reasonable excuse to give her mother, and walking the dog was an all-weather, all-season necessity. Mark's home wasn't the place for him.

It wasn't the place for Mark, either.

"Can we talk to my mother now?"

Emma nodded. "It's late," she added.

"She's awake."

"You're certain?"

"That's her window."

"Awake doesn't always mean someone will answer the door."

"She'll answer the door," he replied. "Because it might be an emergency. She always answers the phone, too—even when it's late."

"Michael, can you stand on my right? Mark will be standing on my left, and I'll be holding his hand." She handed Michael Petal's leash.

Michael nodded, his expression as neutral as Mark's.

"And I'm chopped liver?" Eric asked, with just the barest trace of humor.

"No. Chopped liver is disgusting." Emma walked up to Mark's front door and stood beneath the fake lamp that encased the porch light. She carefully removed her gloves; her fingers were already cold, and her breath came out as mist. "Ready?" she asked, as she held out her left hand.

He smiled. It changed the entire cast of his face.

She reached out with her free hand and pressed the doorbell.

Mark's mother was, as Mark predicted, awake. She didn't answer the door immediately, but the door was thin enough that the thump-thump-thump of feet hitting stairs that little bit too fast could be heard. If she rushed to reach the door, she didn't rush to open it; it opened slowly, revealing just a thin strip of her face and body. She was wearing rumpled, dark clothing and no makeup; she had probably been ready for sleep.

And it looked like she needed it; the lower half of her eyes were shadowed by dark semicircles, and she was pale. "Can I help you?" she asked, in obvious confusion.

"Yes," Emma replied. "We found your son." She lifted his hand, and his mother's gaze drifted down to his upturned face.

Her hand fell away from the door, which swung inward to reveal a woman who was just a shade taller than Mercy Hall but much, much skinnier. To Emma's eye, she looked almost anorexic. Her eyes sported such dark circles she looked like she'd been hit in the face.

Emma hated her. But what she felt, for just that moment, wasn't hatred. Michael moved to stand on the other side of the boy, one step forward, as if to ward off any blows his mother might aim at her child. She didn't appear to notice. Her eyes were fastened to her son's silent face.

They rounded, exposing the ring of white around brown irises. The hand that had held the door rose to cover her open mouth. Her knees gave slowly—

or she knelt, it was hard to say which. "Mark!" Her hand fell away from her mouth.

Emma looked down to Mark. Her hand was not yet numb enough; it hurt.

"Mark, oh, god, Mark. Where have you *been*?" She reached out for her son, her palms up and open. Her son took one hesitant step forward, but he was anchored by Emma's hand.

Mark's mother moved, fully opening the door. "Mark?"

He looked up at Emma. The questions he wanted to ask had deserted him, as had the rest of his words. Emma swallowed. "Mark," she said quietly. "Should we go in?"

"Mark?" his mother whispered. She lowered her hands.

"Mom?" A voice called down from the top of the stairs. "Who is it?"

"It's Mark!"

"Mom," the voice said, both gently and with apprehension, "it can't be Mark." It was an older boy's voice. Not a teenager's, but not far off. Emma looked up to see Mark's brother descend the stairs. He turned and hollered back up. "It's just a neighbor!" before he caught sight of the door.

He froze, his eyes widening just as his mother's had. His expression was just as hard to look at. "Mark!" Unlike his mother, he noticed Emma, Michael, and Eric.

He hesitated, the way a child would, which made Emma revise his age downward.

"Hi, Phillip," Mark said, his eyes just as wide as his brother's. He lost years—and he looked young for his age to begin with—as he smiled. He had a heartbreakingly open smile.

Phillip looked at Emma. "Let go of his hand," he told her. "He doesn't like to be touched."

"It's okay now," Mark said quietly. "It doesn't feel bad anymore."

"Mom," Phillip said, in a quiet voice, never taking his eyes off his brother. "You're freezing the house. If we're going to let them in, let them in and close the door."

Mark's mother was still on her knees, but the sound of her older son brought back the rest of the world. She rose—unsteadily—and nodded. "Come in," she said, as if seeing Emma, Michael, and Eric for the first time. "It doesn't hurt when she holds your hand?" she asked her son.

Her dead son.

"Not anymore."

Phillip's surprise at seeing his brother shifted, as if he could read the truth that no one had yet put into words in his brother's expression. "Why?" he asked.

"I'm dead," Mark replied, in a tone that suggested his state was self-evident.

Emma was watching Mark's mother, although it was hard to look away from Phillip. She saw the moment the woman's expression shattered, but it had been so fragile to begin with. Eyes that were circled and dark seemed to sink into the hollows made by sharp cheekbones and stretched skin; tears added reflected light to her face—the only light that touched it. This was the face of a murderer, and Emma knew she would never forget it.

This was what her father had been trying to tell her.

Phillip stepped between Mark and his mother—or between Emma and his mother. Emma wasn't certain which. What she knew was that Phillip was afraid. Afraid and determined.

"You're dead?" he demanded. "You're sure?"

"Yes." He looked at Emma. "Emma heard me. Emma promised she would bring me home. Emma," he added, before she could stop him, "is a Necromancer."

She felt like one as she stood, her arm numb, Mark by her side. His brother was staring, his eyes wide and unblinking; his mother, half-hidden by her older son, was—was weeping.

Emma had wanted monsters. Monsters could kill their own children. And this woman *had*—but if she was a monster, monsters were broken, shattered, pathetic things that were to be pitied. Emma did not want to pity a murderer. She'd been so angry, listening to Mark. She could stir the ashes of that anger now, but it provided no warmth and no heat.

She couldn't accuse the woman of killing her own son—not when her other son stood between them. Because then he'd know. It couldn't break Mark's mother any more than she was already broken; it could injure Phillip in a way that simple cold couldn't.

Why had she even come here?

Because she'd promised.

Emma stepped into the hall, and Mark followed because he was attached. He didn't seem to be aware of her—not the way Phillip was. Someone closed the door; she thought it must be Eric. Her dog stayed more or less near her legs; he was generally well behaved in other people's houses. Something about Emma stopped him from sniffing around strange legs and hands, looking for food.

Phillip glanced at the stairs, and Emma remembered that Mark had had two siblings, both of whom were, in his opinion, normal. Whatever that meant. "Mom."

When his mother failed to answer, Phillip briefly closed his eyes.

Mark's hand tightened in Emma's. "Why is she crying?" he asked his brother.

"She's been crying on and off since the funeral." He spoke in a quiet, matter-of-fact way, as if his mother weren't present. "She went out to look for you—" He inhaled, held his breath, and smoothed the worry off his face, which made him look older. "Do you want to see your room?"

Mark shrugged. "Not really. Did you change it?"

"No. It's the same mess it always was." He paused and then added, "I beat your high score, though."

Mark yanked his hand free of Emma's and ran up the stairs. He ran through his brother, whose eyes were widening.

Emma tried to massage feeling back into her hand.

"Where did he go?"

"If I had to guess, he went to his room to look at the high score list. What game?"

"Tetris. It's ancient, but he liked it."

"You didn't beat his high score."

Phillip shook his head. "It's not possible. He's a monster Tetris player. It's like he's hooked directly into the machine. I tried, though. I can't see him, now."

"No."

"Will my sister—"

"No. Unless he comes back downstairs and takes my hand, she won't see him either."

Phillip swallowed. He slid an arm beneath his mother's arms and guided her toward the living room doors. "Can you—"

Emma crossed the hall and opened one of the two glass doors that led to the living room, and Phillip walked his mother in.

Michael was staring at his feet, or at the floor beneath them, when Emma turned. Eric passed them both, and offered Phillip the help that Emma, hands numb, couldn't. She couldn't hear what Eric said to the boy; she could hear the broken syllables of Phillip's response, but not clearly enough to make sense of them.

"I don't understand," Michael said.

"I don't understand, either."

"She left him to die," he continued, as if Emma hadn't spoken. "She must have *wanted* to leave him." Before Emma could answer—and it would have taken a while, because she had no words—he said, "Why is she crying?"

Emma was surprised to find her throat tightening. Without thought, she reached out for the other dead person in the hall. Michael didn't even blink when her father coalesced at her side.

"I'm not Mark's mother," her father said, although to Michael this was self-evident, "but if I had to guess, I would say she made a mistake."

"But Mark *died*."

"Yes. Some mistakes can't be undone. I don't know why she took him to the ravine. I don't know why she left him there and told him to wait. I don't know if she meant to abandon him to the cold."

"But she *did*."

Brendan Hall nodded. "Yes. Maybe she thought it would make her happy. Maybe she was having the very worst day of her life and she couldn't deal with any more stress. Maybe she meant it to be an hour or two. I don't know, Michael."

"But she's crying. And she—"

"She was happy to see him."

Michael swallowed but didn't deny it. "I thought she would be afraid. I thought she would scream or hide or try to lie—"

"You thought she would be like the guilty criminals on TV."

He nodded, blinking rapidly. "Why did she ask him to come in? She knows he's dead. She *knows*. I don't understand."

"No. People—even people we know well—are sometimes impossible to understand or predict. I don't think Mark's mother has accepted Mark's death."

"But she *caused it*!"

"Yes. And sometimes the mistakes we make ourselves are the hardest for us to face and accept. I know Emma felt Mark's mother got away with murder."

"She did," Michael replied, voice low.

"Did she?" He nodded toward the living room. "We should go in. Mark's coming back."

"What was he doing?" Emma asked.

"Playing a game."

"A game?"

"I think he's making certain that Phillip will never be able to beat his high score," her father replied, with just the touch of a rueful smile. "He's only eight, Em."

"My sister's not sleeping," Mark said, as he drifted through the floor. He'd automatically taken the stairs on the way up.

"What is she doing?" Emma asked, glancing up those stairs; if his sister joined them, she couldn't do it the way Mark just had.

"She was watching me play Tetris."

"She can't see you." But Emma's stomach felt like it dropped two feet. His sister couldn't see Mark, no. But she could see the computer.

"I think she's coming downstairs," Mark added, in a much smaller voice.

And she was. She was walking, wide-eyed, her arms level with the banister. She stopped at the top of the stairs and looked down to see two strange teenagers—and a rottweiler—in her hall.

"What's her name?" Emma asked.

"Susan. She doesn't like to be called Sue," he added. "I don't know why people do it."

"Your brother is not going to be happy."

Mark looked down. "I'm sorry."

She didn't tell him it wasn't his fault. "It doesn't matter. After tonight, she won't be able to see you again, and she might want to say something."

"What?"

"Good-bye."

"Oh." He hesitated for a moment as Emma looked up the stairs at the girl who stood by the banister.

"Hello, Susan. Your mother and Phillip are in the living room. My name's Emma and I'm a—a—" She hesitated as Mark held out his hand. Without a pause, she took it and watched as the girl's eyes widened.

"Mark?"

Mark said, "Hi, Susan." He looked very guilty.

"You *were* playing Tetris!"

"Phillip said he'd beat my high score."

Susan snorted. "Phillip is such a liar." She looked older than Mark, although she wasn't much taller. She also didn't appear to be surprised. "Has Mom seen you?"

Mark nodded.

"She's been a mess since you died." Susan then added, "Why is that girl holding your hand?"

"It doesn't hurt."

"That's not what I asked." She walked with much more confidence down the stairs. "Who are you?"

"Emma."

"I heard that part. Why do you have that dog?"

Emma blinked. "He needed to go for a walk. He doesn't bite people, and he doesn't usually destroy furniture." Petal headed obligingly toward Susan. "She doesn't have any food, Petal."

"Petal?"

"His name."

"That's a stupid name for a big dog." Stupidly named or not, Susan hesitantly patted his head. "But who *are* you?"

"Emma's a Necromancer," Mark replied. "Was Mom really mad at me?"

"At you? God, no. But she's been mad or sad about everything. Tell her

you're okay," Susan added. It was delivered as if it were a royal command and
Susan were the Queen.

"I'm dead."

"I *know* that." Susan reached out to take Mark's other hand. The fact that
Mark didn't like to be touched—at least when alive—was something she'd
forgotten. Or, given her personality, something she'd ignored.

Mark didn't seem to be surprised or upset, but Susan wasn't thrilled when
her hand passed through his. "Why are you holding *her* hand?"

"Because you can't see me if I don't."

"Oh. Well, that's okay then." She gave Emma another look and then headed
toward the closed doors of the living room. "Are you coming, or what?"

Mark's mother's name was Leslie. She was sitting in the corner of a long,
leather couch, a drink in her shaking hands. Emma eyed its contents with
some suspicion. Susan eyed its contents with loathing, which confirmed Emma's suspicion; the girl did not, however, march over to her mother and take
the drink away.

"Susan, why are you awake?" It was Phillip who asked.

"Mark woke me up," she replied, casually tossing her younger brother to
the figurative wolves.

He knew it, too, but accepted it. ". . . I was playing Tetris," he mumbled.

"Yes, because *someone* told him he'd beaten the high score," Susan added,
punting fault back into Phillip's corner.

Both Emma and Michael were only children. Sibling interactions had always been a bit mystifying, if sometimes viewed with envy.

"Have you tried to touch him?" Susan asked her brother. "Look." She
shoved her hand through Mark's chest, and then waved her arm around. Mark
was looking down at her hand, his eyes slightly rounded.

"That's pretty cool," he told his sister.

"Yeah. Cool and creepy."

"Susan likes horror," Mark told the room.

Phillip, far from looking horrified, now looked embarrassed. Emma wasn't
certain on whose behalf, but suspected it was theirs: Emma's, Eric's, and Michael's. "She's always like this," he said.

Emma thought she understood why as she turned to face Mark's mother.
Her eyes were still red, her lips swollen; she had crumpled tissues in her left
hand.

"So," Susan said, and Emma realized suddenly that Susan was like a miniature version of Amy, "Why did you come home? You didn't *need* to put up a
new high score; Phillip's too much of a klutz to beat the old one." She snick-
ered and added, "He's been trying, though."

She had asked the question that Phillip and Leslie couldn't. Or wouldn't. But they listened for the answer just as apprehensively as if they had.

"I wanted to come home," Mark told her. He turned toward his mother, who sat frozen, like a cornered mouse trying to avoid a large, hungry snake in a small glass aquarium. "I wanted to ask Mom why she left me in the ravine."

Emma had come here for Mark. For Mark. She reminded herself, because she needed the reminder. Phillip's face shuttered. His mother's couldn't crumple any further. Susan, however, lost some of her childish directness, but she didn't look surprised by Mark's statement. She turned to look at Phillip; her glance seemed to take in everything in the room that didn't include her mother.

Phillip was silent. He opened his mouth and closed it. Emma thought he wanted to deny the truth in Mark's words and realized that on some level, he'd known. He'd known. But he knew his brother, probably better than Emma knew Michael; he knew that empty words of comfort or denial would change nothing.

She saw the same thing in Susan's face and realized a second thing: Mark was, unintentionally, asking them to make a choice between himself and their mother. Mark was dead. Their mother was alive.

And her father was right: Mark loved his mother, even if she had killed him. Susan and Phillip loved her as well. She had done something monstrous—but to them, she wasn't a monster. Monster or no, they failed to look at her. They looked at Mark and then looked away.

Mark didn't notice. He looked at his mother and then tugged Emma's hand. She followed where he led in silence, although she could no longer feel that hand; it was numb. He stopped a yard away from where his mother sat, drink in her hand like a useless shield. The liquid shook.

"Mom, why did you leave me in the ravine? Did you forget about me?"

"I didn't—I didn't leave you in the ravine."

Emma couldn't even feel outrage at the lie.

"You did." The words themselves were all of the accusation his voice contained; he was stating fact and stating it inexorably, the way Michael sometimes did. "You left me in the ravine. You told me to wait for you. You told me not to move."

"Mark, baby—" She swallowed. Drank.

*Never drink when you're angry, Sprout. Never drink alone.* She glanced at her father, remembering his words, and remembering as well the sharp, acrid taste of his drink. She couldn't recall how old she'd been at the time, and his words hadn't made a lot of sense then; they made sense—as so many of his words did—now.

This, Emma thought, watching, was what she had wanted. She had wanted Mark's mother to face her crime. She had wanted his mother to know that people knew. But she felt no sense of triumph, and looking at Mark, she realized he didn't either. He was standing in place awkwardly, stiff with anxiety; he looked—at the moment—like a very young Michael.

He blamed himself.

Michael had often blamed himself. God, she hated this. "Leslie."

Mark's mother looked up at her, as if she were drowning and Emma herself was a life buoy that had been tossed just out of reach. Emma swallowed. She had come here for Mark. Not for Leslie. Not for Phillip or Susan. But Mark didn't need Emma's anger. He didn't, she understood, need his mother's pain, either. What he needed—and what Michael needed almost by osmosis—was to understand.

Not to forgive. Not to judge. Simply to understand.

## ⤳ Chapter 15

She let go of her anger, or at least untangled it. The wreck of the woman curled defensively on the couch in front of her helped. It had always been hard to stay angry at Petal when he lay, belly to floor, his eyes wide, his voice pitched in a pathetic whine.

*She's not your dog, Emma.*

No.

"Leslie," she said again, in a gentler tone. "Mark isn't here to judge you. It's not what he does. What he needs—right now—is to understand why things happened as they did." She exhaled. "He needs to know that it wasn't his fault. He needs to know that it wasn't punishment for something he'd done." And it couldn't be, Emma's voice implied. "You can't bring your son back to life."

"No one can do that," Mark told Emma.

"Believe that I know that," Emma replied, never taking her eyes off his mother. "You can't bring him back. You can't undo what's done—it's done. It's over. It's in the past. What you *can* do is give him a measure of peace. You can answer his question. It's the only answer he cares about, now.

"You took him to the ravine. It was freezing outside. You asked him to stay there. He tried to do what you asked of him, even if he didn't understand why. He needs to understand why you asked it." She glanced, then, at the living children.

They were watching their mother. Phillip looked tired or weary; Susan was a wall. They knew what their mother had done. Mark seemed oblivious to anything in the room that wasn't his mother. Even Emma, her entire arm now numb, was like a shadow.

"Mom?"

"I went back for you," his mother said, her voice breaking. "I went back. You were—" She looked at her empty glass, and handed it blindly to her older son. "I called the police. I told them you'd gone out and you hadn't come home. I didn't mean to leave you there to—" She looked at her two living children.

"But why did you tell me to wait there?"

She closed her eyes. Opened them. They were bloodshot, ringed, and almost without hope. Emma thought she would lie. A lie—if it was believable— might be a kindness. But Leslie had passed beyond the point where a lie had any meaning to her. She couldn't protect herself, and Emma realized, watching her, that she had given up trying.

"I was never a good enough mother for you," she told her son. "I don't mean that you thought I wasn't good enough—I *wasn't*. I was only barely good enough to handle Phillip and Susan. You needed someone patient. You needed someone consistent. I—I tried."

Phillip took a step toward his mother; Susan caught his arm. They exchanged a silent glare, but their mother didn't notice. She was staring at her dead son as if—as if she could engrave the sight of him into her vision so that she never lost it again.

"But it was hard for me. I'm *not* logical. I'm not mathematical. I've always reacted emotionally. Before you went to school, it was easier. If I didn't understand you, I understood how to work with you. I knew our routine.

"But school changed that. The other kids changed it. The other mothers." She shook her head. "They'd look at you, and then they'd look at *me*, like it was my fault you weren't—"

Emma said, "Please do not use the word normal."

Mark glanced at her for the first time since he'd entered this room.

"What word would you like me to use instead?" Leslie replied, with more heat and less pathos.

"Try 'like their children.'"

Leslie closed her eyes. "Mark was never like most of the other children."

"No. But he didn't have to be."

The eyes shot open. "He did if he wanted to have any friends! He did if he wanted to be left alone instead of being bullied. If he could have fit in—" She exhaled sharply. "He was lonely. He felt isolated. You probably have no idea what that's like."

"I understand lonely," Emma replied.

"No, you *don't*. Don't tell me you've ever lacked friends. I won't believe it."

"My father died when I was eight," Emma shot back. "My boyfriend died this past summer. I *know* lonely."

"You don't know it the way someone like my son does, and you never will."

Emma started to speak; Michael interrupted. Mark looked up at Michael, too. "I'm not like other children—or other people. I'm like Mark."

Mark's mother blinked.

"I don't know how to be like other people. I know how to be like me. But I have friends. I'm not always lonely."

"And people are never mean to you?" Mark's mother demanded.

Michael thought about this. "Some people are mean to me," he told her. "Some people are mean to everyone. It's impossible for me to like everyone," he continued. "I don't know anyone who likes everyone. So it's impossible for everyone to like me. There will always be people who can't."

Leslie opened her mouth, but Michael hadn't finished.

"If I learn to pretend—if I pretend to be someone else—the people who like me won't like *me*. They'll like what I pretend to be. That's not the same as being liked. Those people wouldn't be my friends because they wouldn't know me at all."

Mark's brow furrowed as he worked his way through Michael's words.

"Are you lonely?" Michael continued.

Leslie blinked. After a long, confused pause, she nodded. She held out her hand for the empty glass in Phillip's hand. Phillip kept it.

"Are you normal?"

"Yes."

"And you're *still* lonely. Being normal hasn't made you happier. If it hasn't made you happier, and you're the adult, why did you think it would make Mark happier?"

"Because," Phillip said, coming once again to stand between his mother and Michael, "she thought Mark would be happier if people liked him more. And he would have been."

"Maybe he wouldn't be dead now, either."

Phillip's jaw set. He couldn't see the way his mother flinched—but he didn't have to. Love was complicated. It was never all one thing or the other. But when he met Emma's eyes, he flinched, his expression shifting into almost open pain. Phillip hadn't killed his brother. Emma thought, if he'd known where Mark was, she wouldn't even *be* here tonight; Mark would. And he would be alive.

Phillip knelt, surprising Emma. He knelt in front of Mark to bring their eyes to the same level. "The day Mom took you for a walk, two things happened."

Mark nodded, waiting.

"Jonas broke up with her."

Mark glanced at Susan, and Susan nodded.

"And her boss sent her home from work with a warning."

"But—why?"

"Because she had to leave work in the middle of the day twice that week. Do you remember?"

Mark wilted. "To come get me."

Phillip nodded. "At school. The school called her. She had to leave. Her boss told her she wasn't committed enough to work."

"But she—did she lose her job?" Clearly work meant something to Mark.

"No," Susan said, joining both of her brothers and their conversation. "Because you died. Her boss wasn't very understanding about the school stuff, but she wasn't a monster. I think she felt guilty, after."

Oh, the words. This is what her father had meant. Monsters—no. People were people. They were capable of monstrous actions, yes. But they were still people.

"Did Jonas break up with her because of me?"

Phillip and Susan exchanged a glance. "Not just because of you," Mark's brother said. But Susan said, "Yes." When Phillip's eyes narrowed in her direction, she folded her arms across her chest. "What? Mark's different, but he's not an idiot. He's never been completely stupid."

"Mom?"

Mark's mother said nothing. Mark moved, dragging Emma with him.

"Mom, was it because of me?"

Emma saw the yes lurking in his mother's eyes. And she saw the no his mother wanted to replace it with. They were in perfect balance for just a moment. "I came home from work. Jonas called. We had an—an argument. I couldn't—I can't—afford to lose my job." She was crying now, but the tears trailed down her face like an afterthought. "He loved me. He said he loved me. But he needed to know that he was the most important thing in my life. That we had the same goals.

"He asked me to send you to your father."

Mark flinched. "Just me? Not Phillip or Susan?"

"He told me," his mother continued, "that I'd done enough for you. I'd done all the hard work. I was going to *lose my job* if I didn't turn things around. Ian had gotten off easy. It was Ian's turn. And Ian has a new wife. He has someone else to help him around the house and to help with kids."

"She *has* kids," Susan said.

"Well, so does your father."

"I don't *have* a father," her daughter shot back. "And I don't *need* one." She turned and leaped onto the couch and put her arms around her mother. Emma wanted to cry, because Emma remembered almost *being* Susan. And saying the same things to her mother, to Mercy, in the early years. But her father had died. In no other way would he have left them. Susan's father was still alive, somewhere. Alive and no part of his children's lives.

Emma looked across the room at her father; he was watching Leslie and her daughter as if—as if he wanted to step in and join them, to offer the comfort that an ex-husband and absentee father had probably never offered them.

"Why didn't you say yes?" Mark asked. Mark was probably the only person in the room who could.

Michael opened his mouth, reminding Emma that her count was off by one. But he closed it without letting words escape.

"What was I going to tell your brother and your sister?" his mother answered, putting an arm around that sister and drawing her close. "Jonas—wasn't happy. He pointed out that I do earn more and that if we—if we were going to set up house, he needed me to be employed. He—" she laughed. It was not a happy sound. "He needed a sign of commitment. From me.

"And I knew—I knew he was leaving. He was already gone." She closed her eyes. Opened them. "I couldn't—" she exhaled. "When you came home, I couldn't deal with my life. I couldn't look at you and not see the thousands of ways in which I've failed at everything. I just—I needed alone time. I needed the space." She swallowed. "I took you out for a walk. And I left you there.

"I didn't mean to leave you there forever. I didn't mean—" She pulled away from her daughter and rose for the first time since Emma had entered the room. But she didn't walk away; she walked toward Mark. "I fell asleep, Mark. I—"

"You were drinking." It wasn't a question and it wasn't—quite—an accusation.

"After my day? Yes. Baby—I'm so *tired* all the time. I'm so tired of doing it alone when I'm *no good at life*. I'm terrible at it. I never make the right choices. I never make the right decisions. I—" She came to stand beside her older son, rather than behind him. "You were my biggest failure. If I had been any good at being a mother, you'd've been happy. It killed me to see you cry. To see the way the world treated you. The way other mothers looked at you, as if you were stupid or alien. The way they looked *at me.*

"I worried *all the time.* I was always worried. I never knew when the school would call, when something else would hurt you. I never knew how to make it *stop.* If I'd been a good mother, if I'd done the right things—" She lifted her hands, palm up, as if offering to take her dead child into her arms.

And Emma saw the look on Phillip's face.

"But I didn't. I didn't. I tried to talk to your father."

Phillip said, "She didn't ask him, Mark. She thought about sending you away, but in the end, she didn't ask."

"Why?" Mark asked.

Phillip rolled his eyes. "Because she loves you. She loves us all."

"But she took me—"

"Yes," his mother said, voice low. "All I could see that day was failure. Everywhere. I couldn't . . . I wanted a few minutes of quiet. I wanted a few minutes when everything I saw didn't remind me of how useless I really am. I thought—"

"If I were different. If I hadn't been born." Mark had no mercy, but there was no anger in the words. His mother flinched anyway.

But Phillip said, "Sometimes we just—we want a different life. We can't *have* it," he added. "And we don't want it all the time. But sometimes we *all* feel that way. Even you."

Mark looked confused. "You think that?" he asked his brother.

Phillip shook his head. "Of course I do. So does everyone in the world. Except maybe Susan. When Mom woke up she ran out of the house. She barely put on a coat. It was dark. We didn't know where you were." Phillip's gaze hit the carpet. "Susan woke her up. Susan said, 'Mark's not home.' And, Mark? If *I'd* woken her up—if I'd woken her up *earlier*—you wouldn't be dead."

"But I knew about Jonas. I heard her talk about work, and what her boss said. I knew—I knew she needed to sleep. And I *let* her. So it's not just Mom's fault. It's mine, too."

Susan got up off the couch and came to stand on Phillip's other side. "Are you mad at us?" she asked Mark.

Mark looked confused.

"Are you mad at Mom?"

"I think I was. I think, before Emma brought me home, I was angry. But I was more afraid."

"Of what? You're already dead."

Phillip and Leslie flinched. Mark, of course, didn't.

"I don't know. I thought it was my fault. It was my fault I was dead. I thought I had finally done something so bad I deserved to be dead. If I were normal—"

"We agreed we're not using that word," Emma told him.

"I didn't." He turned to his family. "But now I know Mom was having a really, really bad day. The worst day ever."

Leslie began to weep. Mark reached out to touch her, the movement awkward and hesitant, as if he seldom offered comfort to anyone. His hand passed through her, of course.

"And it was my fault," Mark continued. "I didn't do anything on purpose. But—it was my fault."

His mother was shaking her head. "It wasn't—it was me. It's always been me. I'm not strong enough—"

"But it will be better now," he continued, and Emma realized he was *still* trying to offer comfort. "Because now I'm not here all the time. Jonas could come back."

"Jonas," Susan said, in a voice that was both ice and fire, "is *never* coming back. I'll stab him in his sleep. Through his eyes."

"Susan—" Phillip began.

She turned an unquelled murderous gaze on her brother, who thought better of the correction and fell silent.

"And your boss—"

"Mark," Emma said gently. "Your mother was having the worst day ever. If she could take it all back, if you could *be here* and be alive, it would suddenly be the best day ever." And she realized, murder or no, accident or no, it was the truth. It wasn't what she'd expected to find when she'd knocked on Mark's door. But it was true.

"Yes, but then she would have bad days again. The same bad days."

And that, Emma thought, was the truth as well.

"You lied to the police," Mark continued, his voice dropping as if lying to the police were the larger crime.

His mother nodded. "I didn't know what else to do. I couldn't tell them that I—that I killed you."

"But you didn't mean to kill me."

"Baby, sometimes what you mean to do doesn't matter. If telling the truth would have brought you back, I would've told them the truth. Telling the truth would've landed me in jail. I would have lost the job, possibly the house, and Phillip and Susan would have had nowhere to go." She blew her nose and straightened her shoulders. "I'm sorry, Mark."

Mark smiled. It was genuine, and even peaceful. "Then it's okay," he told his mother. As if he were a child. As if apologies somehow made everything better. Emma only vaguely remembered being that child; it seemed so far away. He turned to Emma. "I would like to stay here."

"Can he?" his mother asked.

Emma nodded. She couldn't tell his mother there was nowhere else for him to go. She didn't want to explain the complications the dead faced to someone for whom life was probably not a whole lot better. "He won't be able to talk to you. You won't be able to actually see him unless I'm here."

"Yes, we will," Susan said. "He can play Tetris!" she shoved her hands through her brother's chest, laughed, wiggled her fingers and then said, "Come on. Phillip!"

Phillip rose. He turned, hugged his mother that little bit too tightly, and then allowed himself to be dragged off by his sister and the once again invisible ghost of the brother whose absence had haunted this house since his death.

# Nathan

Necromancers can see the dead, but they have to be looking. Emma hasn't been looking. She hasn't seen Nathan once tonight at Mark Rayner's house. Nathan has done nothing to make himself visible, though. It's a trick he's learned, and he didn't learn it the hard way—which would be the way Emma's father did.

The dead don't always see each other, either. Mark would never have seen Emma's father without some prompting on Emma's part. Mark doesn't see Nathan.

Emma's father does. He says nothing, does nothing, makes no sign. He's never interfered in their relationship, not when Nathan was alive and not now. But he's worried.

And he should be.

Emma brought Mark home. Nathan didn't want her to do it; neither did her father. Eric was practically spitting bullets. People don't think of Emma as strong. No, that's not true—Allison does. But mostly, they think of Emma as *nice*, as if nice implied weakness. Truth is, Emma is kind. She hates to cause pain. All that Hall guilt works like a tunnel; she can't climb the walls and doesn't even see them most days.

She saw them tonight. She saw them, but she'd made a promise to a child. The fact that he was dead didn't matter. Or maybe, Nathan thinks, it mattered more. She was terrified, but the promise was more important than the dread. Emma doesn't generally make promises. But it won't stop her from making promises like this one. Emma sees the dead as people. She sees the living as people. The dividing line is so thin, Nathan wonders if she's consciously aware it exists.

He doesn't have the right to be proud of her; he didn't raise her, he didn't guide her, he didn't shape her. He spent the happiest months of his life by her side—but she was already herself.

Emma was afraid. She came anyway.

Nathan knows how angry she was when she arrived. He understands how much she hated Mark's mother before she'd even approached his front door. He felt the same way.

But what happened in the living room of Mark's home wasn't about anger or hate. It was about fear, and failure, and love; it was about loss, about the way pain can cause the losses people most fear.

Nathan goes upstairs to where Phillip and Susan are bunched around

Mark's computer, watching the screen come to life as if it were a bridge between the living and the dead. Nathan can see Mark; his siblings can't, but they know he's there.

Mark, however, isn't aware of Nathan.

Emma isn't, either. Nathan knows when to leave her alone. It's harder, though. She was his world while he was with her—but there were always things to do when she needed space for thought. Now there's almost nothing.

"You shouldn't be here."

Nathan turns. He doesn't recognize the voice. He doesn't recognize the woman it belongs to. But something about her tone and the texture of her words makes it feel like the heart of winter in this small room.

Mark looks up, frowning. He looks through Nathan. He doesn't look past the old woman.

To Nathan's surprise, she smiles at Mark, the many lines around her lips and eyes transforming her expression. She doesn't look terrifying when she smiles.

"I live here," Mark says.

"In a manner of speaking," Nathan adds.

"And this is my room," Mark continues, soldiering on.

"Yes, of course it is. But I wasn't speaking to you."

Mark's frown deepens. "They can't hear you."

The old woman pins Nathan down with a wordless glare that manages to make clear exactly what she wants him to do. He steps through the bedroom door as Mark begins an explanation of Tetris to a woman who was probably chiseling stone tablets when she was his age.

It's no surprise that it takes her a while to finally join him in the hall.

"You shouldn't be here," she says again, as the smile falls away from her face, leaving only the ancient behind.

"I don't have anywhere else I need to be."

If she has a sense of humor, she's not sharing it. "She sent you."

Nathan says nothing.

"She sent you to Emma."

"Does—does Emma know?"

"I don't know. Young girls in love are often blind and willful."

It's a typical thing for the old and bitter to say, but there's an edge to her voice that implies personal experience. "Were you?"

She smiles. Her smile is less barbed than anything else she's directed his way. "I was young once. A long time ago. All pain was new, then. All grief was sharper, harsher. All loss was the end of everything. But you learn that you survive what seems fatal."

He can't imagine her ever being in love. He can't imagine the courage it would take to love her; she seems so cold and harsh.

"Emma's seen you."

Nathan nods.

"When?" The question is cutting.

Nathan shrugs. He doesn't want to admit that he has trouble keeping track of time, not to this woman. He settles on: "Before tonight."

The woman falls silent. "Does Emma know," she finally asks, "why you're here?"

"I'm here," he replies, with more heat, "because I *want* to be here. I want to be with her."

"You're here because you were sent here."

He shrugs. It's the truth. But so is what he said. "She didn't tell me why."

"No?"

It's one of his biggest fears. It's not the only one, but being on the other side of death has made most of the others irrelevant. It's not as restful as it sounds. "If I understand being dead, this is where I would have ended up eventually. Emma said she was waiting."

"Emma probably didn't know where to find you," is the bitter answer. "There's far too much that girl doesn't know."

He slides hands into pockets out of habit; it's not like they can hold anything else. "How do you know Emma?"

"You ask about your Emma and not your Queen?"

"She's not my Queen."

"You don't call her Queen in her presence?"

Nathan is silent for a moment. "What we call her doesn't matter. She's what she is."

"Oh? And what is that, boy?"

"The Queen of the Dead. She's an old-style Queen. She might as well be a god."

"A bitter, small god indeed."

"A lonely god," Nathan replies. He's not certain why. Maybe it's the empty throne that's always by her side when she sits in her courtroom. It's not a lesser chair. It's not set back. It's beside hers, and to his eye—to his dead eye—it's equal. But empty. Always empty. An image of the man she would make King hovers there, but he's more of a ghost than Nathan or any of the rest of the dead.

The old woman says nothing for a long, long moment. When she speaks, she surprises Nathan. "Tell me about your Emma."

"She's not mine."

The shape of the woman's brow changes. "Not yours?"

"She's a person. Romantic words aside, we can't actually own each other. We can be responsible for another person if the person is a child, but even then, we don't own them."

She snorts. "Just the work?"

"Something like that." He shrugs. He doesn't like the old woman, but that's no surprise; she's hard and bitter.

"Tell me about the Emma you know," she says, giving ground. That's surprising.

"Tell me why you want to know," he counters.

"I took a risk with that girl. I took a risk I've never taken."

"What risk?" he asks, in spite of himself.

She glares at him. "You'll tell your Queen if she asks. You'll tell her everything."

He thinks it's true. But he's never tried to hide from her; he's never tried to lie. He doesn't argue. Instead, he looks at his feet. When he looks up, she's watching him, her glance no less harsh but mixed with appraisal.

"You understand what she wanted, sending you here?"

He doesn't.

"Your Emma sees the living. She sees the dead. She doesn't understand that they're not the same. The closest she's come was this evening, when she brought that boy home."

Nathan nods.

"She didn't want to bring him," the woman continues. "It was a foolish act. I almost told her as much—but I wanted to see how she handled herself. I wanted to see what choices she made, given all of the facts she amassed. Given," she continued, voice softening, "her anger."

"Emma has a temper," Nathan says quietly.

"Yes. She does. But so do we all. Do you understand her anger?"

"Who wouldn't?"

The old woman nods. "Walk with me, boy." She drifts through a wall, and Nathan follows because he can't think of a polite way to say no. Apparently manners still matter, even when he's dead.

She doesn't speak. She doesn't stop. He's almost afraid to follow her when the streets bank and end in a jagged line, as if half the city has been cut away by a madman with a gigantic ax. But the line, if jagged, has the quality one finds in dreams. There is no rubble, there are no bodies; there's just an uneven break.

"It is the memory of a city," the old woman says. "If you let go of yours, you will see a place that spans all the lives of the people who have ever lived here. You'll see open fields and plains and heavy forests; you'll see old log homes and the ghosts of small homes that were destroyed to make way for larger ones. You'll see streetlamps, streetlights, dirt roads, footpaths—and they over-lap, shifting from one step to the next."

"Sounds like a good way to get lost."

She nods, as if the words were profound. "But you are lost, all of you. You hold tightly to the lives you once lived, although they're no longer yours. What do you see now?"

Night. Night sky. Nathan thinks it's an open plain with edges of mountain or forest, but he can't tell; it never quite coalesces. He squints, frowning. "Night," he finally says.

"Just night?"

"There's not a lot of light here. Maybe it's because I'm dead."

"No. It's outside of your experience, and perhaps that's as it should be. This," she added, "is where I stay." She doesn't say "where I live."

"Your Emma can't see this place yet."

Yet. Nathan stiffens.

"But when she brought that boy to his mother, she saw the edges of it. She doesn't realize what she sees. She doesn't understand what it means; that much is obvious."

"And you'll tell me?"

The old woman grimaces. "I've been here a long time." She shakes her head. "Love is a tricky thing. It strengthens us and weakens us; it binds us and it liberates us. It makes us hold on too tightly; it colors everything we see.

"But the dead aren't bound in the same way."

Thinking about Mark—never mind Mark, thinking about *himself*—Nathan shakes his head.

"That boy doesn't understand that he's dead. He doesn't understand what it means. What you saw—what you still see, if I had to guess—he *doesn't* see. He would have been lost had Emma not found him. The wonder, to me, is that she *did* find him.

"Understand that there were always those, among the dead, who were lost. The light that beckons you, that beckons Emma's father, that devours the young Necromancer—Mark couldn't see it. He couldn't leave the literal forest in which he'd been told to wait, and had Emma not found him, he would still be there decades from now. Waiting."

"Would that have been much worse?"

"In my lifetime, yes. It would have been. In a way that most of the living don't understand, it would have been a tragedy. Now, there is only tragedy. The Queen of the Dead doesn't *see* the dead; she doesn't serve them. She offers no guidance; she does not lead them home.

"Emma has had no training. She has learned nothing. But she *sees*. What she did for Mark was forbidden in my time. Not finding him," she adds. "Not leading him out of the forest. But taking him home."

"Why?"

"Because we were already feared. The dead do not meet the living if the living can't see them and speak to them on their own. There have been no guides—not since the Queen of the Dead. Now, those who might learn the art are taught other things. They look inward always; they are strapped and bound by their knowledge of their own lives. They can't—and won't—look beyond them."

"And Emma did."

"Emma did. Without guidance."

Nathan shakes his head. "Emma doesn't judge."

"We *all* judge. It's part of the human condition. But it is not a part of the human condition that serves the guides of the dead well."

"Is there no hell?"

"I don't know," the old woman replies. "But if there were, it would look at lot like this. Life blinkers us. It is difficult to see beyond the walls of our own experiences. Emma is certain that she would never be Mark's mother. She was angry—she was more than angry—when she arrived. She had already decided what she felt—and thought—of Mark's mother.

"I don't know if that's changed," the woman adds. "But I do know this: In the end, it didn't matter. The child mattered. The dead mattered. What she needed to do to ease his transition, she did. She may have wanted justice. She may have wanted retribution. These are natural desires. They are human desires.

"But she chose. And I do not think she was unmoved, in the end, by what she heard. I have put the only power that remained to me in her hands. But I am an old woman. Older by far than you will have the chance to be; older by far than Emma. Fear is a constant companion, and hope is bitter, it is prone to so many failures.

"Emma has now made choices that seem promising to me." She turned, in the darkness, to face Nathan. "All but one."

Nathan swallows. "Me."

"You. You are now the heart of my fear, boy. I understand why she loves you. But I fear what that love presages. You should not be here. She is *not ready* for you, not yet. She is discovering—against all hope—the limitations of her power."

"She doesn't even understand her power yet."

"You will find that she does. She doesn't understand how to use it the way the Queen and her people do, but what she did for Mark tonight, they could not do. If she holds to that, she will be the first to do so since the end of all our lines so many years ago; she will be the only person born with her gift that has some hope of unseating the Queen and her Court.

"But what she did for Mark, she could do within the bounds of mortal compassion. What she sees when she sees you is the enormity of her own loss—and the enormity of yours. What she feels for you is tied in all ways to the interior of the life she lived—and wanted. That life is over, boy."

Nathan says nothing.

"And she has not yet accepted it. Seeing you here, seeing you *almost* in the flesh, seeing the boy she loved as if he had never died, she won't accept it. And if she can't, then there is no hope."


## ⤳ Chapter 16

Silence.

The silence of cars, of snow against streetlamps. The impersonal sound of wind in branches, the constant friction of leash, the rising white clouds of dog breath. Moonlight. Stars.

Emma looked at the time; it was almost 11:30. She hadn't lied to Michael's mother; Eric had brought his car. He just hadn't driven it to Mark's house.

"Your mother's worried about you," she said to Michael.

"I know."

"Do you think you'll be okay now?"

He exhaled and turned to her as if he'd lost ten years. She could see the echo of Mark's face in his. "I don't understand people."

"Do you understand what happened to Mark?"

Michael nodded slowly. "She didn't mean to kill him."

"No."

"But he died anyway."

"Yes."

"He shouldn't have died. It's not fair." He closed his eyes and stopped walking; Emma stopped as well. Her hands ached, but some feeling had returned to the one that had been Mark's anchor. "You're going to tell me life's not fair."

"I don't have to," she said, her voice soft. "I don't need to tell you things you already know."

Michael's nod was stiff. "There's no justice in the natural world." He said it without bitterness, as if stating fact. "Justice is a human construct."

"And humans aren't perfect." It was an old conversation. Old, familiar, and, tonight, painfully true.

"But if we don't keep trying, there's no justice at all." He inhaled, opened his eyes. "Thank you for taking Mark home. Thank you for taking me with you."

"I promised," she said. "But if I don't get you home, your mother's not going to be very happy."

Petal nuzzled Michael's hand, and Michael turned his attention to the dog. Emma did as well, but the sound of Eric's phone drew it away.

"Are you going to answer that?" Emma asked.

Eric grimaced; he was already fishing the phone out of a pocket. "I hate these things," he said, as he looked at the phone. His grimace froze in place. "It's not the old man."

Emma froze as well. She glanced at Michael, at Petal, and then back at Eric.

He answered his phone. "Hello?" Pause. "Amy?"

At the sound of Amy's name, Michael rose, his hand still attached to Petal's head as an afterthought.

"You're where? Now?"

Emma fished her own phone out of her jacket pocket; her hands were shaking. It was off. She'd turned the phone off before she'd entered Mark's house. It took her four tries to turn it on, and as she fumbled, her father appeared by her side.

"Dad—"

"I'll go to Allison's," he told her, understanding the sharp edge of her sudden fear.

"Can you get there—" but he was already gone.

Michael didn't carry a phone. His mother had tried to give him one. Or, more accurately, three. He'd lost each and every one. Emma checked hers. There were four missed calls, all of them from Amy.

Eric wasn't doing a lot of speaking—but he was on the phone with Amy, and in general, Amy did the talking when a phone was involved. "Where will you be?" Eric finally asked.

The tone of his voice made Emma want to grab the phone out of his hand.

"No, there were too many people, from the sounds of it, to be Necromancers." Eric sucked in air. "Yes, they're capable of hiring people—but it doesn't generally end well for the people they hire. Look—you're all right? Your family is—" He inhaled sharply again. Emma couldn't hear what Amy said, but she could hear Amy.

"Emma and Michael are with me. Emma just turned her phone back on. No, we weren't someplace where a phone would have—yes, I'll ask her not to turn it off again until we're all in the same place. Have you spoken with Allison?

"Okay. Meet us at my place. We'll head there immediately. Hello?" Apparently, Amy had hung up.

Emma was so cold she felt like warmth would never reach her again. "What happened?"

"We need to get to the car," Eric replied.

"We need to take Michael home."

"We can't."

"We need to—"

"Phone Michael's house," Eric told her, his voice that little bit too tight.

"Emma?" Michael said.

Emma turned to Michael and handed him Petal's leash. He looked at it as if it were entirely foreign.

"Emma, what happened to Amy?" Michael's voice was softer.

"Amy is fine," Eric said, voice tight.

"And my mother?" Michael asked, voice rising at the end.

*No*, Emma thought. *No, no, no.* "I need to go home," she whispered.

"It won't help. If your mother is fine—if nothing's happened—and you go home, it probably won't stay that way." Eric stared at his phone and cursed under his breath.

"Where's Chase?" Emma all but demanded.

"Good question. He's not answering his phone."

"I'll call Allison."

"She's not answering her phone, either. Not according to Amy."

*No.*


Emma called Michael's house. She called before she'd planned out what she might say if someone actually answered the phone. Michael was rigid with anxiety, and because he was, Emma couldn't afford to be. She almost cried with relief when his mother picked up.

"I'm glad you called," his mother said. "I was beginning to worry. Someone came to the door to speak with Michael about fifteen minutes after you left."

"Who?"

"I didn't recognize him. He said he's a friend of Michael's. He left homework for Michael. Michael's homework," she added. "He said he'd borrowed it. He apologized for being so late to get it back."

Emma wanted to tell her to burn it. Most homework was done electronically; it didn't *need* to be returned. In person. By a stranger. She covered the mic with her hand. "Your mother's fine. She's worried about you," she added, "but you kind of expect that from mothers."

"Michael is not going home," Eric said.

"Michael doesn't exactly do sleepovers. What do you want me to tell her?"

"Whatever you need to tell her." He turned to Michael. "Can you talk to her without explaining too much?"

Emma knew the answer, but she looked to Michael anyway. He was less rigid than he had been, his unvoiced visceral fear for his mother's safety giving way to a more common fear. Michael was not one of nature's liars. He was practically the anti-liar.

"Are any of us going home?" she asked softly.

"No." Eric exhaled as they reached his car. "I'm not going to kidnap you. Either of you. You know what's at stake. You know who your enemies are. If you insist on going home, I can't stop you. But, Em—I can't protect all of you either. There are too few of us."

"Could you protect Michael and his family if I don't go home? Could Michael go home?"

Michael said, "I'll stay with Eric. I'll stay with you, Emma."

"But your mother—"

"She's still on the phone," Eric reminded her.

Michael frowned. "I think she knows that." To Emma he said, "I don't want to make my mother worry. I don't want to scare her. But I don't want her to die. If I tell her—if she knows—she'll call the police. She'll call the school. If she calls the school, the Necromancers will know she knows."

"I don't think they kill people randomly."

Thinking of Allison's brush with death, Emma disagreed. "I don't think they care."

"They do, or they wouldn't have to kill people who know about them."

"Can I suggest," Eric said, unlocking the door and opening it, "that this is not the time for this argument?"

Michael frowned. "We're not arguing."

Eric slid behind the driver's wheel. Michael opened the back passenger door. "Can I talk to my mom?"

Eric stiffened. Emma said, "Of course," and handed Michael the phone. She didn't tell him what to say—or what not to say. His entire posture made it clear that he knew what was at risk. He probably saw it more clearly than Emma did; he had the ability to be both terrified and observant at the same time.

"Mom," he said, while Eric's jaw clenched, "I won't be coming home tonight. Something is happening. I can't explain it. But Emma needs me to be here. She'll be with me. I don't want you to worry. I'm okay. But we have to figure out what we need to do." He fell silent, listening. Emma couldn't hear what his mother said to him and was grateful. "I need you to trust me," was Michael's reply. "No, I can't explain—it would take hours, and even then it would be hard.

"But I *will* explain it, when it's over. I promise. I have to go. No, everything's not okay—if it were, I'd be coming home now. But it would be worse if

I did." He hesitated and then handed Emma's phone back to her, which she'd been dreading.

"Emma, what's happening?" Mrs. Howe demanded.

"I can't explain it. What Michael said is true. It would take hours, and even then—it would probably take more hours on top of that. I won't let him out of my sight." She started to say, *I won't let anything bad happen to him*, but she couldn't. Instead, she said, "The only thing Michael's worried about right now is you. And me, a little. He needs you to be okay."

"Where are you going? Where are you going to be?"

"We're—" She shook her head. "If I can, I'll call you and let you know. Everything's up in the air."

"Emma—"

"—I'm sorry, I have to go." She hung up.

"She's going to worry," Michael said, with quiet confidence.

"Love," Emma replied, "makes worriers of us all. Yes, she'll worry."

"Are you going to call your mom?" he asked.

Emma compromised. She tried to call Allison.

There was no answer.

Amy was at Eric's when they arrived—or at least her SUV was. They walked past it; Eric hadn't chosen to park in front of the house. Petal was antsy; it was clearly past Emma's bedtime, which meant it was past his. She let Michael handle the leash and handed him the last of the Milk-Bones that served as dog bribery.

Eric didn't lead them directly to the house, either. He didn't exactly skulk—something bound to cause suspicions in anyone who happened to look out their window at the wrong time—but he walked with purpose in the wrong direction, dragging Emma and Michael in his wake.

"Em."

She turned at the sound of her father's voice. The world was all of night, and the single syllable he'd made of her name made it too cold, too harsh.

"Ally?" she asked. The word made almost no sound.

Eric slowed. Michael couldn't see her father—but he could see her. He stopped. Petal wound the leash around Michael's legs.

"Allison's alive. She's with Chase. Chase," he added, looking briefly at Eric, "is also alive."

"And the rest of the Simners? Her brother? Her parents?"

Silence.

"Dad? Dad!"

"Her brother was shot."

"Is he—"

"Emma, I'm not a doctor. I don't know. Emergency crews are on the way."

"How do you—"

"The neighbors. You don't shoot guns in that neighborhood without raising alarms." His hands slid into his pockets; they were fists. He hesitated, then said, "you'll have to tell Allison about her brother. She wasn't there when they broke into the house."

"How do you—"

"I found her. Chase got her out. Allison heard the gunshot, and she tried to go back. Chase . . . wouldn't let her. I wouldn't want to be that boy if her brother dies."

"Was Chase hurt?"

Her father nodded. "Not by Allison, not yet. I think he meant to bring her here."

"Where are they now?"

"Chase didn't drive."

Eric cursed. "Can you take me to them?"

Her father nodded.

Eric turned to Emma and Michael, who were so silent they might not have been breathing. "Stay here. Go inside, and do whatever the old man tells you to do. Don't argue with him. Don't argue with me."

"If Necromancers are there," Emma began.

"If?" Eric said, with a laugh that was worse than his swearing. "You don't have the training. I do. Chase does. Go into the house, Emma. Amy's probably waiting, and we can't afford to have her kill the old man. I'll bring them back."

## ᔥ Chapter 17

Allison couldn't breathe.

It wasn't the running—although she wasn't much of a runner, and her sides had been cramping on and off for the last half hour. It wasn't the cold; she was numb enough now that the air no longer chilled her or shocked her when she drew it into her lungs.

She couldn't hear her own breath. She couldn't hear Chase.

She could hear the echo of the gunshots. She could hear them over and over again, shattering the quieter noises of a normal night in a neighborhood that saw violence on television, contained in a frame, made distant because it was meant to be entertaining.

She knew Chase was bleeding. She'd asked him why; he hadn't answered.

He was a redhead; his skin was normally pale. Tonight it looked ashen, his eyes too dark.

He had come to save her life.

She *knew* he had come to save her life. She was certain that he probably had. And she hated him for it. Right now, right in this moment, fear had turned any gratitude she might have felt to ash. Her face bore the mark of his open hand; his bore the smaller mark of hers—and a scratch that had welted.

It was silent. It was too silent. If she broke the silence, she'd scream. Or she'd cry. Or both. And even if she hated herself for her cowardice—because that's what it was, this running, this silence, this abandonment—she *wanted* to live. Another thing to hate about herself.

Chase checked her coat; he checked the heavy necklace she'd been given what seemed a lifetime ago. His lips were almost white. He said nothing, but she knew what he feared: not men with guns, but Necromancers. He was certain they were here, somewhere. He was certain that they were hunting.

The snow didn't help. Its pristine, untouched surfaces held on to footsteps like accusations; there was nowhere they could walk—or run—that didn't leave an immediate, obvious trail. Only the sidewalks had been cleared, and Chase wanted to avoid them.

So did Allison. If they were seen—if their neighbors saw them, if anyone tried to help or interfere, there would be more deaths. No. No, not *more*. Not more. Please, god, not more.

She shook. In any other circumstance, she would have pretended she was cold; it *was* cold. Her hand was stiff; it was locked in Chase's, as if he didn't trust her to follow, as if he thought she'd turn and go home at any moment.

He had taken the lead. This was the neighborhood that had been home for all of Allison's conscious life, but Chase knew it too. He knew it at least as well—on a night when the world had gone insane—as she did, but saw it differently. The houses were obstacles; the driveways, the backyards, the cars parked in the street or the fronts, were cover for changes in direction.

Chase carried a mirror; he used it, instead of sticking his head out or up, where possible.

And he led them, in the end, toward the cemetery and the ravine. Allison knew there was no safety in numbers, but she felt exposed. Even the sounds of passing cars—and the intermittent whiteness of passing headlights—dwindled. Here, she could hear Chase breathe.

It was labored, almost as labored as her own shallow breaths. She stumbled twice. Her feet were numb.

"I don't care if you hate me," Chase whispered. "You probably will. There's nothing you could have done at your house except die."

She wanted to argue but couldn't—it was true. It didn't making running feel any better or any more justified. His grip tightened briefly, and then—for the first time since he'd slapped her, or maybe since she'd slapped him—he let go of her hand. Instead of his hand, she found herself holding the hilt of a knife; he'd placed it in the palm of her gloves, and her hands were so stiff she almost dropped it.

"I know you don't know how to use it," he said, looking over her shoulder, his eyes constantly scanning the shadowed trees. "You're not meant to kill here. If someone or something grabs you, stab it or cut it and run away."

"Chase—"

"I mean it."

"You're—"

"No, I'm not. I'm fine." He smiled. It was a lopsided expression; it contained a world of pain and very little warmth. "I'm not afraid of Necromancers. They'll kill me, one day. I'll kill them until that day. It's been the whole purpose of my life. Of what was left of my life.

"I know how you feel. I know why you hate me. I can't honestly tell you it's going to stop any time soon. The only thing I wanted on the day I didn't die—" He inhaled. Exhaled. "I shouldn't be talking. Stay here. Keep your back to the tree, breathe into your sleeve."

"Where—where are you going?"

"I need to put a few things on the ground. We're going to stay here, within this area, until they find us. Or until they give up. I'm hoping for the latter. Stay here. I won't be far."

She nodded. She didn't ask what she could do to help—he'd just told her. She could stay out of his way. She could be as silent and invisible as possible. She could breathe into her sleeve so her breath didn't rise in telltale, visible mist. Invisibility was something that came naturally to Allison, at least in her normal life.

But invisibility wasn't the same as inactivity. It wasn't the same as huddling in silent fear. She bit her lip, held her breath. She examined the knife Chase had pushed into her hands. It was simple, its edge notched in at least two places; the hilt was rough and worn. This had been made by hand by people who didn't have the time to prettify their work.

People like Chase. Maybe Chase himself. He probably knew how to slit a man's throat. He certainly knew how to kill. She closed her eyes. He'd killed Merrick Longland. But Merrick Longland hadn't *stayed* dead.

Allison had no doubt at all that she would.

That her parents, if killed, would. That her brother would never open his eyes and speak again. No. No. No. She took a deep breath and forced herself to exhale slowly into her sleeve; it was damp. She felt the tree at her back as if it were the hand of a friend. She could hear Chase moving across brittle snow.

She could feel the ghost of a tendril wrapped around her throat; could hear the echo of an equally brittle apology for her coming death.

And she could hear Emma's voice. The panic in it. The pleading.

She swallowed, bowed her head, and lifted her chin. If she died here tonight, it wouldn't be because she had just given up. She couldn't fight; it was true. It wasn't a skill that she'd ever felt a pressing need to learn. Reading about fighting—and she'd done a lot of that—wasn't the same. She was on the outside, looking in.

She promised she'd learn. If it came to that, if she survived, she'd learn.

A shadow cut across the snow. Chase had returned. He glanced at the knife in her hand and grimaced.

"It'll cut through anything but the fire," he told her softly.

His hands, she saw, were empty. She knew whose knife she carried. She tried to give it back, but he ignored it. "Do you know why I like you?" he asked. She blinked. It wasn't the question she expected.

"No. I always wondered."

"You remind me of home. Of the best things about home. I didn't appreciate them enough when I had them, and when I lost them—" He shook his head. Smiled. It was the first real smile that had touched his face since it had appeared at her bedroom window, hanging upside down.

"We don't get a chance to do things over. Things happen. They're in the past. We can see them—over and over again—but we can't touch them. We can't change them. I *need* you to survive. I need you—just you, I don't give a damn about anyone else—to make it out of here alive. If you do—if you can do that for me, if I can even ask it when I know what it'll cost you—then I'll feel like surviving myself had some purpose. Not dying won't be the end of my life. It won't be the worst thing about it."

She swallowed.

"You're solid. You won't turn your back on your friends. You won't lie—I honestly doubt you know how. Don't try on my account," he added, grinning. "It'll just be humiliating. You're not like Emma. You're not like Amy. People don't stop in the street to give you a second look."

It was true. People seldom really gave her a first one. "I don't need it."

"No. You don't. But the thing is, Ally, I don't need it either. I don't give a shit what people see when they look at you. I don't care what they miss. In my life—in the life I've lived since I lost my family—it's pointless. Most people would run screaming. They'd hide in a corner. They'd forget what they'd seen.

"It's safer for them. After tonight, you'll understand why." He turned away, and then turned back. "I hate that you're not one of them. But I like you because you're not one of them. You can't fight. You don't understand Necromancers. You really don't understand what we're facing.

"But even if you did, you'd still be here."

"And getting in the way."

He nodded. "And getting in the way." He reached up and brushed her cheek with his fingers; they were cold, but she felt them as if they were burning. "I'm sorry I hit you. My father would've killed me if he'd been alive to see it."

"I hit you first."

"I couldn't let you go back. I'm sorry. I couldn't. I never wanted you to be here. I wanted you to be safe. To be safe, to be an echo of the things home used to mean to me, where the rest of my life couldn't touch or destroy it. I hated your best friend."

"Do you hate her now?"

"Yes. Yes—but I understand why you don't. And I understand, when I try to be fair—and it's work, so don't expect too much of it—that she sees and loves what I see—and love. You're not superficial. You're not trying to be something. You're not trying to impress me or Emma or even random strangers. I can't expect her to walk away from you when she's known you for most of your life; I can't walk away, and I've known you for weeks."

His face was so close to hers. It was dark, but she could see his eyes, could see his expression. "If someone comes, if I'm not here—remember what I said. There's almost no binding magic that you can't cut through. You cut—and you run."

"Chase—"

"Please. Please, Allison. Promise." He hesitated and then said, "If you die here, it will kill Emma. It will break her. If you can't promise for my sake, promise for hers."

"That's—"

"Unfair?"

It was. It was so unfair.

"Maybe we haven't been formally introduced," he said, grinning again, his face pale. "I'm Chase Loern. Unfair is my middle name. I've been accused of worse when it comes to getting what I want." The smile fell away from his face. "They're coming."

Allison could hear nothing but Chase, yet she didn't doubt him. He stepped back, stopped, grinned again. Before she could speak, he kissed her. He was out of reach before she could react.

"If you want to slap me," he whispered, "you'll have to stay alive."

She would have stuttered if she'd had voice for words. Before she could find that voice, she saw a pale green light illuminate the snow on either side of the tree at her back. The Necromancers had arrived.

## ⌒ Chapter 18

The door opened before Emma could touch it, sliding in toward an ordinary looking front hall. Ernest stood three yards back; his eyes were dark, his jaw set. "Don't stand there like gaping tourists," he snapped. "Get in."

Michael obeyed instantly. Petal started to growl. Emma looked once over her shoulder and obeyed, stepping forward as if she were walking around the corner into a nightmare landscape. It wouldn't have surprised her at this point to see Ernest sprout horns, fangs, or guns.

Amy appeared in the hall at his back. Given the expression on her face, horns, fangs, and guns would have been gratuitous.

The door shut behind them. No one had touched it.

"Allison's still not answering her phone," Amy said, first up.

Emma nodded. "I don't think she has it with her. I turned mine on," she added quickly.

"Where's Eric?"

"He's gone to find Ally. And Chase." Emma closed her eyes. "Ally's brother was shot."

"So was my father," Amy replied. "They mostly missed."

"Your mom?"

"She's terrifying the police."

"She knows you're—"

"No. I told her I was going to Nan's. I had hysterics and told her I couldn't deal with the police." That was not—in any alternate universe Emma could think of—a remotely believable lie. Sometimes she wondered at the optimism of parents. "There were no Necromancers at my house. There were guns, possibly knives, and a lot of noise—but no Necromancers. If Allison's someplace without her phone, I think the timing is a bit coincidental for a random, armed break-in."

Ernest said, quietly, "We warned you. This isn't a game."

"Michael's mother seems to be okay for now. But they know Michael's not at home," Emma said, speaking past Ernest to the most dangerous person in the hall.

Amy nodded. "I took the liberty of packing." She turned and headed into Ernest's living room while Ernest shut his mouth. "I don't have much that'll fit Allison, though."

Michael opened his mouth.

"I raided Skip's closet," she told him. "You're not the same size; he's fatter. But it'll do."

"Where are we going?" Michael asked. It was the sensible question.

"Someplace else." Amy exhaled as she remembered who she was speaking to. "I borrowed keys and a pass card from my dad's office. We've got cottages and small chalets a couple of hours outside the city in a bunch of different directions. Inside the city isn't safe at the moment; if they want us, we'll make them work for it. They're not going to be able to pillage our information from the school records."

"And our parents?"

"I don't think they care whether or not our parents live or die," Amy replied. "It's just us they're gunning for." She grimaced. "At least that's the hope."

"Your parents—"

"Yes. My parents are probably safe. My father can afford to hire a small army, and has the smarts to figure out how to do it legally."

"My mother can't," Michael said quietly.

Amy didn't argue. "I'd tell my father," she finally said, "who to look out for. But to tell him that, I'd have to tell him pretty much everything *and* make him believe it. And he won't leave it alone if he does. He'll go to the police. He'll go above the police. It'll be all over the place inside of a week." She glared at Ernest, who had come to stand behind a suitcase the size of a small fridge. "This is the best I've got. I'm willing to entertain suggestions. From you guys," she added, pointedly excluding the man in black.

And he was in black. He had shed the old-fashioned tweed look that made him seem older than he was; to Emma's eye, he now looked like a lived-in version of Chase. She grimaced. Chase was not the person she wanted to be thinking about now.

But Chase had gone for Allison. He had, according to her father, saved Allison's life. He might be keeping it safe even now—something Emma had no hope of doing on her own.

"Earth to Emma," Amy said.

Emma shook herself. Amy's implied criticism was deserved. There were decisions that she could help make, things she could do. Better to do them than to become paralyzed by the things beyond her grasp. "It's going to look suspicious if we all disappear together."

"We're not. We're going on retreat together to an unspecified location. I'm obviously so shattered by an armed break-in into my own home that I needed the time away to put myself back together."

Michael frowned. Amy looked angry; she didn't look shattered. "We're supposed to help you . . . recover?" he asked.

"Exactly. I'll call my mother before we leave, and I'll tell her that I'm heading out of town for a few days because I don't feel safe at home." She folded her arms. "I'll tell her I need my friends with me. My mother can call your parents first and get their permission. Would that work?" She was mostly looking to Michael. She assumed everyone else could just *make it* work.

Amy wasn't above telling Michael what to do—she was Amy, after all. But she didn't particularly enjoy his version of panic, and she understood she'd be facing it soon if he wasn't handled with care. Amy's version of care, but still.

Michael turned to Emma. Michael, who had already called his mother.

Emma swallowed. "My mother would buy it if your break-in hits the news. She won't be thrilled—we'll be skipping school—but she'll understand it. I think Mrs. Howe would be worried—"

"Duh. Mother," Amy snapped.

"—But I think, if your mother talked to her, she'd actually be relieved. Michael's already phoned to tell her he isn't coming home." She exhaled and fell silent.

"You're not telling me something," Amy replied, voice flat the way the side of a knife was.

"Allison didn't answer her phone because she didn't have it with her. She's not at home."

"And?"

"Yours wasn't the only home that was targeted tonight. Chase—Chase somehow got Allison out of hers, but he didn't take down the people who were targeting her family. Her brother was shot. Unlike your father, whoever shot him didn't mostly miss. Ally's mother is probably out of her mind with worry—for Toby *and* Ally. I don't think your mom's going to be able to talk her down if she doesn't know where Allison *is*. And if she knows that your place was hit as well . . . she's not stupid. She might decide that the timing isn't coincidental."

"How? You *know* the timing wasn't coincidental. How is her mother going to know that? The two probably look entirely unrelated." Amy frowned. "Let me think about this. We're going to have to sell it differently." She swore softly and added, "Ally's not going to want to leave the city if her brother's really hurt."

Emma nodded, but added, "She'll go. If she understands that her brother was in danger because she was there, she'll go anywhere you tell her to go. I just think her mother will have a harder time with it, because Toby will be in the hospital." *If he survives.* She couldn't bring herself to say this.

Amy as a force of nature was a fact of life for the teachers in Emery; she was for the parents of her many acquaintances and friends too. If Amy wanted you to do something, you did it. Unless, Emma thought, you were Michael. Michael's sense of reality often collided with Amy's sphere of influence.

But he wasn't arguing now. He was nodding. He was nodding a little bit too quickly. Hall guilt asserted itself. She should never have gotten Michael involved. She should have taken Chase's advice—his bitter, heated advice— and left town when she could, without dragging all of her friends into isolation with her.

"You know," Amy said, "you should have been Jewish."

Emma blinked.

"You're so good at guilt, you don't need a mother reminding you of all the reasons you should feel guilty. If you feel guilty for dragging me into this mess, spare me. No one makes me do anything I don't want to do. And no one stops me, either." She glanced at Michael. Opened her mouth. Closed it. "We'll need clothing for Allison. I think she'll fit some of Skip's stuff—width-wise, at least. I've got money. I've got credit. I've got a car—I don't know if we want to ditch it or not.

"But we're going to have to decide what we do going forward. I for one don't intend to let some random Queen of invisible dead people dictate the course of *my* life. I don't intend to let her kill me or my friends.

"She needs to go."

"You make it sound so simple," Ernest said, his voice dry as kindling in winter.

"It *is* simple," Amy replied, folding her arms. "The logistics might be more difficult. I don't know how many of you there are. I assume all of you aren't here, in my city. I assume you've thought of all this before, and you've never managed to take her out. I even sort of understand why.

"Doesn't change the fact that she has to go."

"You are all schoolchildren," Ernest replied, folding his arms in the exact same way Amy had, although Emma didn't think the mimicry deliberate. "You can't fight. You don't understand Necromancy. You can't—without Emma's help—talk to the dead. You have nothing to contribute to the mission you so cavalierly dictate."

She lifted a brow and then turned back to Emma and Michael. "We'll need to talk to Eric. And Chase, if he makes it back."

Ernest's lips thinned; so did his gaze.

"I understand that you think we're useless," Amy said—without bothering to look at him. "Understand that we're not. We won't approach things the way you do—we can't. Doesn't mean we can't do anything. The first thing we're doing is getting out of the city for a bit. You can come with us, or you can stay here. I personally prefer that you stay here. We're going to take Eric and Chase with us."

Margaret said, "I like that girl." She had materialized—at least in Emma's view—beside the fireplace, between where Ernest and Amy stood, bristling at each other. "Her manners leave a little to be desired, but these days, it seems everyone's do. You understand that Ernest is not wrong?"

Emma nodded. "But neither is Amy."

Margaret smiled. "We forget that our world is not *the* world. We couldn't predict you—yet here you are. You opened the closed door, dear. The dead see you as clearly as they see the Queen. You carry our hope with you, but I think that hope will falter if you're forced to carry it alone—or forced, by circumstance, to carry it our way. Ernest," she added, although Ernest had not once looked in Margaret's direction, "we've tried for decades, and we've failed. Perhaps it's time to consider different methods or different avenues of approach. If I understand events correctly—and I frequently do—the greatest risk we face has already been taken."

"It was taken without consultation," he replied, every syllable spoken as if he disagreed with the decision.

"Of course it was. The decision was never yours—or mine—to make. But it's been made. We're committed, whether we like it or not."

He turned to Margaret. Amy, frowning, turned to Emma. "If the other half of this conversation has anything to do with us, I'd like to hear it."

Emma nodded and held out a hand to Margaret. Margaret glanced at it and shook her head. "That will not be necessary, dear," she said, smiling at the tail end of the endearment. "I don't require your hand. I'm bound to you; you hold me. If you desire it, I can appear at any time."

"Do you need my permission?"

"Yes. But permission is not a legal contract. It's not a ritual. You don't have to say the words if the words themselves trouble you." She turned, once again, to Ernest—but this time she also had Amy's attention.

Allison watched the pale green light grow brighter; her sleeve covered her mouth and nose, but it wasn't doing any good—she was only barely breathing. Chase, across from her in the shadow of the nearest tree, nodded brief encouragement before his gaze went elsewhere. He drew two knives from the folds of his jacket. They were longer and slimmer than the blade he'd given her, but reflected no light at all.

She closed her eyes.

This wasn't the first time she'd faced Necromancers, and at least this time there was no baby involved. She didn't have an infant to worry about; she didn't have responsibilities to fail. There was only Allison.

Why was it so much easier to fail yourself?

The light on the snow brightened, and the snow began to melt. No, she thought, watching, breath held. It wasn't melting; it was sinking and breaking, the crystals across its hardened surface surrendering territory to familiar, burning vines. Those vines shed light, and the light cast shadows. None of those shadows bore the familiar, attenuated shapes of people.

She lifted the dagger, remembering the way the vines had wrapped—like tentacles—around her exposed throat. She wore a necklace now that might protect her from the worst of it. She wore a jacket that would have her on the outs with Amy for six months under any other circumstance—not that she was ever "in" with Amy—that might stop the soul-fire from instantly devouring her.

Neither of these was armor. Neither of these was skill.

She listened. She glanced at Chase and saw an odd expression cross his face, just before she heard the first evidence of actual people. Someone screamed. Someone shouted a warning.

Someone laughed.

None of these voices were familiar. One woman, by the sounds of it, two men. How many Necromancers had Chase and Eric said there were? Three? Four?

As if he could read her mind, Chase held up a hand in the darkness. Four. He lowered two fingers. She'd heard three distinct voices. At least one could use Necromantic magic. The snow broke again, as if it were glass; small crystals fanned outward in a cold spray. The vines began to move, creeping along the ground and breaking snow as they traveled. Breaking it and melting it.

The sickly green fire did nothing to stem the chill of the winter air in any other way.

The voices drew closer. "We can't move at this speed. The ground's trapped."

"I noticed," the woman replied.

Chase slid away from his tree, gesturing for Allison to stay put. He couldn't move silently, but their enemies were making enough noise it probably didn't matter.

"Don't approach the areas where the vines have withered. It's the only safe place for our enemy to stand."

That, Allison thought, had to be the Necromancer, or at least one of the two. Her fingers curled around the knife Chase had given her; she could barely feel it. She hesitated, then removed her right glove, shoving it into her pocket. The air was cold.

The vines spread as green fire encased their circular, twisting forms. But they spread in a narrow line that seemed to travel straight ahead. As they did, they began to gain height. Watching in silence as she breathed into her sleeve, Allison realized they were forming a wall. A wall, a hedge of burning fire and thorns. She'd seen this before, and understood that they meant to enclose the area.

The area and everyone who was trapped within it.

"Come out," a male voice said. "Come out and I may choose to spare your lives. All we want at the moment is information."

She wanted to believe him. She wanted to believe that this might end without death—either hers or Chase's.

*All she loses is a few years. A few years, in the existence of the dead, is nothing.*

She couldn't. Fear was a horrible pressure against her chest and the insides of her throat—but it couldn't make her stupid enough. And if she were, Chase wouldn't be. Chase would walk out of here alive, or the Necromancer would— not both.

Voices drifted closer and then veered away. She pressed her back into the tree, willing herself to be invisible. The green light the vines shed made it harder, and Allison knew, as she watched them grow, it would soon be impossible. She'd be seen.

She checked the necklace at her throat. *Think.* One of the men had given instructions to avoid the areas where the vines had withered. Something Chase had done—something he'd planted, iron maybe—had killed the vines being powered by Necromantic magic.

By the dead.

She heard another curse—a woman's voice. It was followed by two gunshots. At this range, they sounded like firecrackers, but louder, fuller. "Longland," the woman said, as the reverberation died into silence. "You go ahead."

"I don't have your vision."

"You won't need it. You're already dead. If they damage your body, it doesn't matter; it can be fixed."

Longland was here.

"Those weren't the Queen's orders," Longland replied. After a longer pause, he added, "And I can't breach the barrier."

"The Queen's not here. *I* am. Go in. The ground's contaminated; cross in the contaminated zone; it shouldn't stop you. If the hunter tries to leave, he'll be leaving through those gaps; we're unearthing the iron we can find." The gun fired again, and this time, Longland cursed. "Your job was to find the kids. Ours was to clean up. Find them."

Eric stopped at the edge of the ravine. The snow was newly broken in several places; the air was cold, the night clear. Trees loomed like the broken pillars of ancient walls. From between those broken pillars stepped Brendan Hall, his eyes silver, like contained stars.

"They're here," he said.

Eric hadn't asked Brendan Hall to scout ahead, but he was grateful for his presence. He could see more or less what Emma's father could see: The ground was glowing a faint, sickly green, and the sky above the ravine was paler than it should have been at this time of night. "How many?"

"Two Necromancers."

"They did this with two?" He didn't ask Emma's father how long it had taken; the dead did not have a concrete sense of the passage of time.

Emma's father nodded. "Chase is wounded."

"Badly?"

"Not enough to stop him immediately."

Eric cursed. "Allison?"

"Frightened. Bruised, but otherwise whole." He hesitated.

"You went in?" Eric's brows rose.

"Chase had time to salt the earth. There are gaps in the barrier. I don't know how long they'll last. I can slide through them, with some effort—but if I breach the barrier, the Necromancers will know."

"If anything breaches that barrier, they'll know if they're paying attention." Eric looked into the darkness from which no sound escaped. *Hang on, Chase. I'll be there soon.*

Snow, rain, safe houses that changed from one minute to the next—these had been Chase Loern's life. He didn't have a home. He hadn't for a long time. If you asked him on the wrong day, he didn't have friends, either; he had enemies. He had a mission.

He glanced over his shoulder at a tree.

He'd learned a few things since he'd lost his home, his friends, and the life he'd taken pretty much for granted. He'd stepped into a world of kill or be killed, and he was fine with that. Killing? He'd make the bastards pay. They'd left him alive. They'd regret it, right up until the time they got lucky or he got careless.

Until then? He'd fight.

He'd learned how to do that. No sweat. He'd learned how to kill Necromancers. If he'd known then what he knew now—but no. No.

What he'd learned, the most important lesson, was that the world was a harsh, bitter place. You had to get its attention. It didn't negotiate with a man on his knees; no point. It had you where it wanted you.

Chase didn't beg. He didn't plead. He didn't pray. He'd tried that once, and he'd learned. He knew that the person with the power got to dictate the terms— any terms. Life or death. In Chase's world, power meant one thing.

But he glanced at the tree again, knowing who sheltered behind it.

In his old life, he wouldn't have noticed her. That was the truth. She was plain. She was surrounded by people who weren't. She was quiet; she didn't demand attention, and she didn't reach out—the way Amy did—and grab it with both hands, shaking it until she got what she wanted. She would never have crossed his path.

But the first night he'd seen her, she'd almost slapped him. She had been practically quivering with indignant rage. She was willing to say what her best friend wouldn't: He had come to kill Emma. The fact that Emma was demonstrably not dead didn't change her fury one bit. The fact that Emma didn't *want* her anger or the confrontation it would cause hadn't changed it either.

Among the hunters, tempers frayed. Life on the edge did that. It was all about the fraying. He'd seen temper before; he'd see it again. But not Allison's temper. Not Allison's rage. It wasn't for herself. It wasn't for her loss. She'd known what was right—and what was wrong. And Chase was wrong.

He wouldn't have raised a hand against her if she *had* slapped him. He wouldn't have raised his voice. For a minute—for just a minute—he could see the world as she saw it. And it felt familiar. It felt like—like home. Like the home he'd lost. Like the home he'd never tried to build again.

It was *stupid*. It was *wrong*. His entire life had proved that. Tonight would prove that to Allison. It would open her eyes.

And he didn't want that. He wanted her to live in the world she saw. He wanted her to have what he'd lost—what he should never have lost, if the world were sane. Because he thought Allison could somehow defend her corner of the universe. Not with knives. Not with cold steel, or silver, or guns, or weapons; those weren't her particular strength. She might be able to learn them; Chase had.

But even armed as she stood, sanity—angry, furious sanity—had roots that were deep enough, strong enough, to weather the storms that surrounded her.

He had no home. It was better to have no home; he'd only have to leave it. But he knew now that some glimmer of it had remained dormant in him, and she had touched it.

He couldn't pray. He couldn't beg. He couldn't plead. But what he wanted now depended on the things he had learned since the last time he'd tried. With his own hands, with his own power, he intended to protect the things he loved.

Allison looked for the gaps in the growing wall. She looked for the places where vines had, as the unseen speaker had claimed, withered. The tree she was sheltering behind was no longer good cover; green light had become too bright. She hesitated. Chase had told her to stay put. He knew Necromancers. He knew their powers. He'd given her the knife she held in a shaking hand, and he'd told her to cut and run if necessary.

But running with no destination was a disaster in the making. She didn't know where the Necromancers were, but their voices had drawn closer. She could see the wall of risen vines; it towered above her in the distance. As she narrowed her eyes, she could see gaps in that wall. The vines at these locations were brown and dark; the fire didn't burn around them. They were almost evenly spaced, and they weren't wide—but they were there. If she could make it that far, she should be able to push through them; they were just about wide enough.

She inhaled, held her breath, and then crouched, peering at half-height around the cover of the tree's trunk. She couldn't see Chase; she couldn't see anything but green and white.

She exhaled into her sleeve, although visible breath was fast becoming a nonissue. Chase had told her to remain where she was. But he'd also told her to cut and run if necessary.

"Over there!" The woman shouted.

Allison froze. She didn't have to hide her breath; she stopped breathing for a long, agonizing minute. But the voice was followed by footsteps—and the footsteps led away from the tree. Away from her hiding place.

She had no idea what Chase could do. She'd spent one afternoon with Ernest—and Michael—and all she'd learned was how to run. How to kick someone so she could run. How to hit them. How to cause enough pain to get away. She'd learned that she needed to wear a thick, ugly necklace that rode a little too high on her neck; she'd learned that iron links could be sewn into coat linings. She'd learned that silver was useful.

She hadn't learned why—and Michael had asked.

She knew that Chase could fight. Chase could use knives. He could use guns. He could use—in a pinch—crossbows. But she knew that Chase could do more than that; if she needed proof, she only had to look at the hedge wall.

She even understood—and hated herself for it a minute later—why he hunted Necromancers before they came into their power. Against people like that—against people who were *almost* normal, she might stand a chance. Against people who had magic, almost none.

She heard another curse, more shouting; she took a deep breath, bit her lip, and headed in a straight line toward a gap in the fire that limned the wall. She held the knife clenched in one hand, and it made running harder, somehow, but she knew it could cut through the Necromantic magic anyone was likely to spare for her.

And she knew, as she reached the dead vines that couldn't support fire, that she should push them out of the way. She did that, cutting in places. She made a gap for herself; she'd be scratched, but whole, when she came out the other side.

But she didn't push through the hedge. She did the stupid thing. She turned. She looked back.

Chase was facing two Necromancers. She could see the red shock of hair that made him visible no matter how many people surrounded him. She could see fire—green fire—enveloping his body like a bubble.

She knew he was struggling. His movements were slow; the fire had trapped him. It hadn't stopped him; it hadn't killed him. Without help, it was only a matter of time. She wasn't the help he needed. Running back to him wouldn't save his life; it would only end hers. She suffered no illusions and no false sense of her own abilities.

She turned back to the hedge, and then turned again.

She suffered from no illusions.

She wasn't brave. She wasn't kind. She worried about herself and her own needs far too much. She had been jealous of Nathan. She had wanted him to *go away.* And then, sickeningly, he had. She could spend the rest of her life making up for that one selfish thought—and it probably wouldn't be enough.

*Jealousy is natural. If you hate yourself for being jealous, you're going to spend a lot of time hating yourself. But now that you've* said it, *how do you feel?* She could still see her grandfather's teasing smile, and his voice was so clear he might have been standing beside her.

Terrible.

*Jealous?*

Afraid. Afraid that I'll lose Emma. Afraid that I *deserve* to lose her.

*Fear is natural, too. Your mother's not here, so let me put this the crudest way possible. Going to the bathroom is natural. If you never do it, you die.* He held up a hand. *Yes, you won't die if you never experience jealousy, but that's not the point of the analogy. You need to go to the bathroom. When you're an infant, you go anywhere. Your parents clean up after you. When you're a toddler, you're not supposed to drop your pants and pee on the sidewalk.*

*But you've seen children do it. You even laughed.*

Because they're *children.*

*Yes. But they're doing what comes naturally. They have to* learn *that there's a time and place to express what's natural. This is not about what you* feel. *What you feel is natural. It's understandable.*

*This is about what you* do. *Fear's the same. It's not about the feeling. It's natural. It's human. It's about what you* do.

Her grandfather was gone, but his voice came back to her as she stood, frozen, by the hedge wall.

*We all want to be good people,* her grandfather said. *But no one starts out that way. When we're infants, we're greedy little creatures. The only things that exist are our wants and our needs. We're not much better as toddlers. Becoming the person you want to be isn't an accident. It's not something that just happens.*

*We choose. We live with our choices. We make better choices. We learn to judge others less harshly when we understand the costs of our own mistakes. So here's my advice for the day.*

*Do your best to make the choices that will lead to you becoming the person you want to be. Accept the fact that you're human. Accept the fact that you'll fail when the days are long and harsh. And never knowingly make a choice that will make you think less of yourself. Make choices that will make others think less of you if you have to—but don't make choices that lead to self-hate.*

*There's enough hatred in the world. Don't add to it.*

## Chapter 19

Allison lowered her hands. For just a moment she could see everything so clearly it might have been noon. She could see Chase. She could see his scorched hair. She could see blood on his hands and steam rising from the snow beneath his feet. The woman was almost within his reach, but she no longer had a gun; the man was ten yards away from him, his hands spread in a fan at the level of his chest. He was the source of the fire; she was certain of it.

She had no illusions. She didn't need them, now. She wasn't going to run away while Chase fought. She wished—how she wished—she had taken her phone with her when she left the house through her bedroom window; it was on her desk. She had no way of calling for help; screaming probably wouldn't cut it.

But she wasn't helpless. There was no one holding her back except herself. Herself, her lack of experience, her fear. And if she gave in, Chase would die. Allison sometimes hated what Emma's sense of guilt did to Emma—but really, was her own so different?

She pulled back into the tree cover. She used what little of it there was. She crouched, which made movement agonizingly slow. Slower than Chase's. And she headed around him, as if her life depended on it. She didn't give much for her chances if she caught the attention of both Necromancers now.

Chase had it.

Chase had it, and she needed him to keep it while she edged her way around them to the man who was standing out of his range, controlling the fire.

And when she reached him—if she did—what was she going to do? She didn't look at the knife in her hand; it was the only weapon she carried. The "if" was big enough she was willing to concentrate on one problem at a time.

She heard the woman curse and demand more power from, presumably, the man; he didn't reply. But his focus was on Chase; Allison rounded a tree, forgetting to breathe into her sleeve, and she was ten yards from his back.

His exposed back. He wore a wool coat that fell past the back of his knees; it was either dark gray or black. She couldn't see his hands; she could see fabric stretched across taut shoulder blades. His boots were invisible, his legs ending in snow.

But he wore no hat. She doubted very much that he wore a necklace similar to her own. She ducked behind the tree again. She would have to run if she couldn't move silently. She wasn't certain how much attention the Necromancer's partner was actually paying to him—and wasn't certain if they had taken the time to trap the ground, as Chase had done. She was pretty certain they hadn't.

But what did she know?

Chase was in trouble. She needed to do something. She had a knife. She could stab the Necromancer with it—but probably only once; twice if she was lucky. She needed to make it count. And she needed to make it count in a way that still left a knife in her hands.

It was hard to breathe. If she messed this up, she was dead. They were both dead. But if she didn't try at all, Chase was.

*The worst thing that ever happened to me? Not dying.*

She hadn't understood it when he'd said it. But the gunshot—at her house—made it real in a way she'd never really considered. She could imagine Chase as a younger boy. She could imagine how powerless he'd felt; she felt powerless now, but she wasn't. She had a knife. She had silence. She had a Necromancer who was concentrating on the only person he thought might be a threat.

She had *something*. She had hope, a bitter chance. She intended to use it, because she didn't *want* to become Chase.

Allison Simner had never stabbed a man. She'd only hit one once, if you didn't count her brother. She hated causing pain. Even angry, she tried to avoid it. But she moved toward the back of a stranger she now hated, and she held on to hate, sharpening her fear rather than surrendering to it.

The Necromancer was taller than she was. His hair was dark, but snow-dusted where he'd come too close to branches. More than that, she couldn't tell. She practically crawled across the snow toward his exposed back. She couldn't see Chase at all.

She was almost in touching distance of the Necromancer when he turned, his hands dropping as she raised the knife to press it against his throat. "Stop the fire," she told him, her voice steady.

His eyes were gray light. Emma had told her that meant he was using power; she tightened her grip on the knife and drew it across his exposed skin. The blood that welled there was more of a shock to her than it was to him, judging from his reaction.

"Or what, little girl?"

"Allison!"

"Or I'll kill you." It was cold. It was *so* cold.

He smiled. That was the worst of it. He smiled. He was bleeding. She'd cut him. But not enough. If he was afraid at all, it didn't show. And she knew that she had to do more, do it quickly; that she had to make him bleed in earnest. She knew where the dagger had to cut.

But she froze.

The woman screamed; the Necromancer who faced Allison stiffened. She saw his eyes begin to glow as her hand shook, and she knew that her moment was passing. Maybe it had passed. But she also knew that Chase was free. Chase who wouldn't have bothered with threats. Chase, who wouldn't have wasted the one chance he was given, if he was given one at all.

She moved her arm before the Necromancer could grab her wrist; she held the knife. She wasn't surprised when his hands became gloved in the white brilliance of fire; this close, the fire wasn't so much tendrils of flame as the pointed, solid light of acetylene torch. And it was aimed at her.

She cut it with the knife—it was so much easier to use the knife that way. Fire didn't bleed. It separated, as if it were an extension of his hands; it fell away, as if it were solid. But it didn't bleed. It didn't kill. She backed away. *Cut and run.*

But she couldn't run now. She couldn't turn her back on the man. The air was dry; the walls of her throat clung together, making breathing hard.

And then she was hit across the face and her knife hand by something warm, and she looked at the underside of the Necromancer's chin—and the sudden, gaping wound where his neck had been. She froze, but her knife was nowhere near the open wound; it was nowhere near slick enough, or red enough.

"You really are a stupid girl," a horribly familiar voice said. The Necromancer toppled to one side, reaching for his neck as if to close what had been so brutally opened. Her hands shook and she forced the knife up, to point it at Merrick Longland.

He showed no more fear than the Necromancer had. "You've already made clear that you've no intention of using what you wield." He stepped toward her; she stepped back. "Your hunter had better be less squeamish than you are." He turned his back on her.

"Why?" she asked. Back exposed, she could have stabbed him. But she knew, now, that that was a wish, a dream. Whatever it took to knife a man in the back, she didn't have it. Not yet. Maybe not ever.

He didn't pretend to misunderstand, although he didn't turn to look back at her. Instead, he folded his arms across his chest; she could see small mounds of snow moving just above his feet, and realized he was tapping his left foot, as if impatient.

"Your Emma has something I need. She values you enough that saving your life might put her in my debt." He cursed and added, "I'd hoped my former colleagues would be competent enough to do away with the hunter by now. If you'd stayed where you were, I wouldn't be saving his life as well."

Chase.

Chase had killed Longland.

"I recognize him," Longland said, as if she'd spoken out loud. Maybe she had. She began to shake. It was cold. It was just so cold. "It's his fault that I'm here now. It's his fault that I'm powerless." He turned on her then, and she saw the knife he carried, saw the blood that darkened every crease in his exposed hand. "I don't intend to kill you, but I'll need you to stand between us for a few minutes."

When she blinked, he grabbed her arm and dragged her around—as he'd done once before. This time she wasn't carrying a baby. She was carrying a knife. And the knife was just as helpful in the end as the baby had been.

Chase was sprinting across the snow. He was bleeding; there was a cut across his forehead and his left cheek. His hair, which had barely recovered from the last bout of green fire he'd been forced to endure, was singed and blackened. He carried two knives, and the woman he'd been fighting lay face-down in the snow. The fire that burned around the hedges dimmed; the hedges themselves began to wither.

Longland lifted his knife to Allison's throat, and she let him. He didn't explicitly threaten her; the gesture was enough to stop Chase dead.

"I resent having anything to do with the preservation of your life," Longland said, in his chilly, even voice.

Chase looked above her head at Longland's face. With the guttering of the fires—both white and green—Longland stood in shadow, Allison his shield.

"Not half as much as I do," Chase replied. "Let her go."

"Put down your weapons."

Chase knelt and placed the daggers in the snow, where they became less visible with passing seconds. He rose. "Let her go."

"When we've finished our negotiations. I don't intend to harm her unless you attempt to harm me. If I'd wanted her dead, I wouldn't have intervened." She couldn't see Longland's face and didn't try; she watched Chase. "I wanted you dead."

"The feeling's mutual."

"You're not dead, I note; given the nature of your injuries, you're unlikely to die immediately. And given the risk the girl took, I doubt I could kill you without harming her first, which would defeat the purpose. I won't harm her if you—"

"If I what? Give you my word I won't try to kill you?" Chase laughed.

Longland didn't. "Yes."

"You know what that's going to be worth." Chase spit. "As much as yours would have been in similar circumstances."

"I'm already dead," Longland replied. "Which you understand, even if the girl doesn't. If you destroy my body, there's nothing keeping me here; I'll return to the City of the Dead at the command of my Queen, and I'll reach her side instantly. Nothing I know—*nothing*—will be hidden from her."

"You're hers—"

"I'm hers, but I'm not bound the way the dead are; I can't be and be reanimated in this fashion. You know this," he added again, his voice sharpening. "I don't wish to inform the Queen that I took a personal interest in preserving the lives of the people she ordered killed. I have a measure of freedom if you don't damage me so badly I have no physical anchor. And I assume you have an interest in keeping the knowledge of tonight's events contained for as long as they can be."

Chase hesitated.

Merrick glanced at the corpse to one side of his feet. "He didn't see who killed him." He nodded in the direction of the woman. "She didn't see anything but you. They can tell the Queen only what they witnessed—and only when she summons them."

"She summoned you."

"Not exactly. She found me. But I could be more easily found when I was not reanimated. I'm not alive; I exist in a half-world between the living and the dead. If she calls me, and I am compelled to return, I must resort to pedestrian means: planes, cars, trains. If you attempt to destroy me—and you succeed—I will be at her side instantly."

"Why did you interfere?" Chase asked. Some of the rage and the fear drained from his face, although he didn't exactly relax.

"Emma values this girl. I preserved her for that reason."

"And if—"

"What Emma did once, she can do again. I want her to open the gate. I want to escape this place. Without Emma, we don't stand a chance."

"We?"

Longland laughed bitterly. "The dead. You don't understand what it's like. The Necromancers who died tonight didn't. They will now," he added, with a strange mixture of both malice and pity. "To do what she did the first time, your Emma—"

"She is *so* not my Emma."

"Emma, then—she gathered more power than the Queen of the Dead has ever held. And what did she do with it? If rumor is to be believed, she used it all to pry open a door for a few precious minutes. Not to make herself immortal. Not to consolidate her own power in the face of her rivals; not to better her position in Court.

"I don't understand her. I try—but I don't. And it doesn't matter. What she did once, she might do again, and if she does, I want to be there. I'll give her everything I have—everything I've managed to retain—in order to be the smallest part of the lever she uses to open that door again.

"I'll kill if I have to. I'll save lives—even yours—if that's what it takes to convince her that I'm worthy of that privilege. I'll return her friend to her. I'll tell her everything I know, teach her anything I've learned—"

"She doesn't need to learn anything you learned," Allison said, breaking into their discussion for the first time.

Longland stiffened; Allison thought he would argue. But in the end, he didn't. "Maybe you're right. I wouldn't have survived my first week at Court if I hadn't learned some of it. But this isn't that Court, is it? And it *can't* be that Court, or I'll never be free. I have nothing else to offer," he continued, speaking once again to Chase.

"What were they planning to do to the rest of them?" Chase countered.

"The Necromancers came to this girl's house because they knew she knew."

Chase cursed.

"The others are in less danger."

Allison was frozen for one long moment. "What do you mean, less danger?"

"There are no Necromancers with them."

"But people were sent—"

"Yes, they were sent. You do not want our existence made public; you will force the Queen's hand. If pressed, she can usher in a new dark age. It's not without risk," he added, as Chase opened his mouth. "And it's possible she'll fail—but hundreds of thousands will perish before she does, with no guarantee that she'll be stopped."

Allison swallowed. "My family—"

"Most of your family is unharmed. They weren't concerned with your family; they wanted you. And the hunter, when they realized he was present."

Most. *Most* of her family.

Longland shook her and then let her go. He stepped back. "I don't understand you," he said. "You survived. There was *nothing* you could do there but die."

She glanced at Chase. "There are worse things than death."

"If you're dead, there's no chance at all that you can make people pay for what they've done to you."

Allison turned to Longland, but before she could answer, he lifted a hand. His expression was hard to read. She didn't try for long. Instead, she turned to Chase. He hadn't moved. His shoulders had relaxed, but he was watching Longland; he made no move to retrieve his weapons. Allison did; Longland didn't tell her to stop.

"I told you to run," Chase said, voice low.

"I know."

"Why didn't you do it?"

"Because I couldn't make myself believe there was nothing I could do." She lowered her gaze. "But you were right. There was nothing I could do. I couldn't—" She bit her lip. "I couldn't kill him. I couldn't just stab him without warning. I—"

He exhaled. "You'd better clean up before you see Emma again, or she'll kill me."

"You? Why?"

"You are covered in blood, and she's going to assume it's yours."

"But that's not your fault—"

"No, it's not. Fault isn't going to matter much." He reached out then and pulled her into his arms; he rested his chin on the top of her head, emphasizing the difference in their height. "I didn't tell you to kill and run. Not even I would be that stupid.

"You're not a killer. You're not Eric. You're not me. You're halfway Emma and your ridiculous friends."

"But not Amy?"

Chase chuckled. "Amy could have killed him."

Allison didn't laugh. "I don't think even Amy could have just slit his throat."

His arms tightened. After a moment he said, "No, probably not."

"You could have."

"Yes. I learned. I don't want you to have to learn what I did. I don't want you to need it the way I needed it."

"Why?"

"Because if it didn't break you, it would change you. I happen to like who you are right now."

"Even if I do something stupid."

"Even then. Maybe especially then. And you were right, for the wrong reasons. I'm not dead. They are."

"Chase—"

"We need to find the old man. We need to get back to Eric's."

"I want to go home."

He released her. "Old man first. I don't know if there were other Necromancers."

"There weren't," Longland said, in a tone that implied he should have asked. "But I wouldn't say it's safe. If I didn't think she'd go with you, I'd send you."

"I wouldn't let him go alone," a familiar voice said.

Allison turned, as Eric stepped around the trunk of a tree. He was carrying a gun. Not surprisingly, it was aimed at Longland.

Allison was shaking. It wasn't the cold. "He saved my life," she said.

"I heard."

"So please don't kill him."

He looked past Allison to Chase, and her gaze followed his. Chase grimaced but nodded.

"Amy is not going to like this."

"We don't have to tell Amy," Chase countered, which made clear just how little he knew about Amy Snitman.

"No problem," Eric said. "But she's at our place."

". . . Our place? The old man let her in?"

"I think he'd've been happier not to, but she's Amy." Eric glanced at Longland. "You have somewhere you need to be?"

Longland shrugged. "I have someplace to go. It won't last."

"Were they sending reinforcements?"

"Not yet. The two you killed a few nights ago weren't high in the hierarchy; the two you killed tonight were more significant. She'll call them home."

"The way you were called." It wasn't a question.

Longland nodded. He watched Eric for a long moment as Eric turned back to Chase. "Emma and Michael are also at our place."

"What the hell?"

"Allison's wasn't the only home hit."

Allison froze. Had this been the nightmare she desperately hoped it was, this is the moment that horror and adrenaline would have forced her to wake. Her heartbeat was a physical sensation, it was beating so quickly, but she was still standing in the snow in a ravine that was now up two corpses.

"Was anyone—was anyone hurt?" Allison managed to ask.

"We don't know," Eric replied. "But we know who their actual targets were. You're not going home," he added. "I'm sorry. Amy apparently packed a suitcase the size of a small freezer; we're leaving town."

"But our parents—" Allison swallowed. Her parents. Gunshots. Guns.

Chase slid an arm around her shoulder; she couldn't tell if he meant to hold her up or not. "I'm sorry." His voice was soft at the edges. It was cold at the core. "Their best chance of survival is your absence. Even if they worry. Even if they go out of their minds with worry. Even if they call the police and report you missing—it's better than going back. For them."

He didn't add, *This is why I told you not to get involved.* She was grateful for that. To her surprise, he said, "It's not your fault. Never believe it is."

"You warned me."

"Yes." He surprised her. He smiled. His teeth were slightly red—with blood. His. He didn't seem to notice. "But a question for you, and I want an honest answer."

"I'm not a liar."

"Not a good one, no."

"What's the question?"

"Knowing what you know now, what would you do differently?"

She was silent.

"Think about it in the car," Eric told her. "If these are the last two Necromancers, we've bought ourselves a bit of time—but not a lot."

The car was warmer than the air, but not by much, at least not for the first few minutes. Longland sat in the back—beside Chase. Chase had opened the front passenger side of the car and all but pushed Allison into it. He didn't trust Longland, but that was fair; Eric didn't trust him either. Allison was surprised that they'd chosen to take him along with them.

But she knew what Chase would say if she asked: Better to know where he is and what he's doing. Better to have him in easy reach; if necessary, we can kill him at any time. Even if, she thought, what he'd said about being dead was true. He didn't look dead to Allison; he didn't sound dead.

She met Chase's steady gaze in the mirror and looked down at her lap. What could she have done differently? If she'd known about the break-in, she could have started a fire and forced her family out of the house in time. Maybe. But that wasn't what he meant, and she knew it. She couldn't control what the Necromancers chose to do. She couldn't control what they wanted.

The only thing she could have done differently was take his advice at the very beginning. Walk away from Emma. Abandon her best friend.

She hadn't. She didn't know if all of her family was unharmed. *Most of your family is unharmed.*

Had she traded one of their lives for her friendship with Emma? Is that what she'd done? And if she had, and she could somehow go back, would she preserve that life and turn her back on friendship?

If a man had held a gun to her mother's head and offered her the choice, in *that* moment, she could have done it. *Speak to Emma again, and your mother is dead.*

She closed her eyes.

And opened them again. "No," she told Chase. "I wouldn't."

He was silent.

"Love is a weapon."

"Yes. In other people's hands. It's a weapon. It's a weakness."

"But, Chase—without it, what's the point? If love can be used to force us to abandon everything we value, what do we become, in the end? If we turn our backs on our friends, on our beliefs, on anything else we also love—what does that make of us? Cowards?"

"Survivors."

She was silent, thinking of the Necromancer—the man she couldn't just kill. Cowards, she thought, and survivors. "It's a stupid question."

"They're my specialty."

"I can't change the past. I can't change my decisions."

"I only wanted to know if you would."

"Why?"

He shrugged and looked out at the passing night. And then he smiled. He looked tired. He was always pale, but his eyes were dark, and his skin looked slightly sunburned. Or windburned. "Because I don't want you to give up on me."

"We were talking about Emma."

"Yes, and I was thinking about hypocrisy. I'm—I've been—angry at her for putting your life at risk. But if she didn't—if she hadn't—I wouldn't have met you, either. I don't want any more regrets. But I don't want you to be saddled with regrets like mine."

"People have regrets all the time, Chase. It's just—it's just a people thing. People who regret nothing have probably never tried anything. In their lives. Does this mean you'll stop hating her?"

"I won't hate her any more than I hate myself."

"So that's a no?"

Eric chuckled. "Hold out for something better than that," he advised.

"Pay attention to your driving," Chase shot back. "Or the entire discussion will be moot."

"It might be moot anyway. Amy wasn't happy."

This time, Chase didn't ask why Amy's happiness was a concern.

# ⌐ Chapter 20

Emma was already on her feet when she heard the front door open. Ernest was seated; he glanced up at the sound, but not in a way that made it a threat to anyone in the room.

She held her breath; if Ernest didn't rise to greet whoever was making an entrance, she couldn't; it wasn't her house. But she listened for the sound of voices. She heard footsteps instead.

And when Allison—when Allison, spattered in blood—walked into the living room, she almost wept with relief. Margaret was in the middle of saying something to a less and less happy Ernest when Emma cut her off and ran across the room.

Allison said, "I'm *fine*."

And Emma replied, "Yes, but are you okay?"

Allison laughed. "No, not really." She let her forehead drop until it rested on Emma's shoulder, and then, she shook. She might have stayed that way for a long, long time, but Michael had come to stand to their left, and he was agitated—if silent—while he waited.

"It's not my blood," Allison told him, without lifting her head. She knew him well enough to know why he was panicking. She also knew him well enough to know her brief comment wouldn't stop him.

"If the two of you could have your huddle someplace other than the door, the rest of us could enter the room," Chase told them.

"I'm not sure that would be a net positive," Amy replied. She started to say more, then sucked her breath in; the sound had so much edge it might have killed a lesser person. Emma looked up and met the eyes of Merrick Longland.

Allison disengaged. "He saved my life," she said, with a trace of defiance, knowing what had caught Amy's attention. She caught Michael's arm. "A Necromancer was about to kill me, and he—he killed the Necromancer before I died."

Michael was blinking. Emma sympathized; she was blinking as well. But she caught Michael's other arm, and she and Allison retreated to the fireplace, taking him with them. There, she took a deep breath. "Ally, come let me help you clean up?"

Allison glanced at Michael, but nodded.

*You'll need to tell Allison about her brother.*

Emma wondered, as she walked up the stairs at the side of her best friend, if this is what Nathan's mother had felt when she'd phoned Emma to tell her about Nathan's accident. She knew only what her father had told her: that Allison's brother had been shot. She didn't know if he'd survived. And she knew it would be the first question Ally asked.

But Allison said, "Chase knocked on my window. He practically broke it. I was studying with headphones on." She was watching her feet. "I opened the window; Chase was on the roof. Well, the part of him that wasn't in front of the window. He told me we had to leave—and we had to leave now. He didn't tell me why." She swallowed. "I didn't even grab my phone. I climbed up on the desk and he dragged me up to the roof. You don't want to know how we came down." They reached the second floor and made a beeline for the bathroom, where Emma picked up a face cloth and soaked it in hot water.

"Stand still," she told Allison, who obliged. Mostly. "You came down the old tree?" She began, carefully, to wipe the blood from her friend's face, pausing to dump her glasses into the sink; they needed at least as much cleaning.

"I almost missed it. I saw them from the tree," she added, her voice dropping again. "I saw them open the front door. I heard shouting." She closed her eyes. "We climbed down the tree—I was better with that—and Chase started to move us.

"I heard a gunshot. I tried to go back."

"Chase wouldn't let you."

Allison shook her head. "I was so afraid. So afraid. For my family. For myself. I don't know who was shot—" she stopped, meeting Emma's eyes in the vanity mirror. After a long pause, she said, "You know."

Emma swallowed. "Toby."

"Tobias was shot?"

"Yes. I don't know more than that. We were leaving Mark's mother's house—I promise I'll tell you all about that later—and Amy called." She ran hot water again to rinse the towel out. Steam rose in silence, like mist. "People broke into her house. Her father was shot. He's alive and he's mostly fine, according to Amy. Amy was enraged."

"And you—"

"She couldn't reach my phone; I'd turned it off. She couldn't reach yours either. And when Eric said you weren't answering—" Emma closed her eyes. Opened them again. "I asked my father to go to your house and tell me—tell me—" Her smile broke. "And tell me whether or not you were alive. He told me you were. But he said your brother had been shot, that emergency vehicles—and the police—were on the way."

Allison's hands were like ice as Emma set the cloth down and caught them in hers. "Amy has a car, a suitcase full of clothing from various members of her family, credit cards and keys to a number of her family's various cottages. We're leaving with her.

"Ernest thinks, if we disappear, our families will be more or less safe."

"Have you—have you talked to your mom?"

"Yes. Before you arrived. There was a break-in at Amy's house; Amy's father was shot. They mostly missed him—I don't know how. Amy staged a breakdown."

"Staged?"

"She pretty much came up with a reason that most of us can skip school for a few days. Or more. She flipped out and told her mother she was so terrified she couldn't be in the house."

Allison snorted, and they both managed a smile; parents could be so naive.

"I phoned home to tell my mother about Amy's break-in and Amy's subsequent breakdown. I said I was at Nan's, with Amy, and that Amy was hysterical."

"Your mother bought that?"

Emma nodded. "Enraged people are often hysterical; I didn't mention the rage part. My mother assumed she was justifiably terrified. I told my mother I needed to be with Amy and that I probably wouldn't be coming home for a couple of days."

"She was okay with that?"

"Not the first time—but she talked to Mrs. Snitman, and that seemed to help."

"Michael's mother?"

Emma bit her lip. "I'm going to phone her when Michael's sleeping, because I have to lie to her, and he's already so wound up it'll be messy." She exhaled. "It's your mom that we can't get around. Amy's terror at armed men showing up in her house makes perfect sense to all of the parents who *didn't* deal with the same.

"But your mother—"

Allison swallowed.

"I can ask my father to check in on Toby. I think he can do that from wherever it is we're going. But it won't be the same as being able to see him for yourself, and we won't know—" She stopped and closed her eyes. "We won't know how bad the injury was. We won't know. If he's—if he's dying, you won't be able to be there. Not with him and not with your mother."

Allison closed her eyes. Eyes closed, she said, "It's my fault he was shot. It's my fault any of my family was in danger at all."

"Funny, I was thinking the exact same thing. It's *my* fault that your brother was shot. It's *my* fault that any of your family—even you—were in danger at all."

Allison's eyes snapped open. Emma wasn't smiling.

"They're not going to kidnap us. If you choose to stay home, Chase will have a coronary, but no one's going to knock you out and dump your unconscious body in Amy's car. My dad didn't tell me how bad Toby was—but it's bad. If it weren't, I'm sure he'd've said so. Amy wants us all to leave—but she understands what's at stake for you. We're going to one of Amy's getaways. Chase and Eric will come with us; I'm sure Amy's telling them that right now.

"And Michael's okay with this?"

"He's as okay as the rest of us."

"Which means no."

"Which means mostly no. But none of us are exactly calm. I think you're about as clean as you're going to get if you can't take a long shower. Here, have a comb—there's dried blood in your hair; I think I got most of it. I can head downstairs if you need time to decide—and I can make sure people give you that time."

"Even Amy?"

Emma didn't smile. "Even Amy."

Allison fished her glasses out of the sink. "Can you ask your father to check now?"

"He's not here right now."

"No," a familiar and beloved voice said. "But I am."

Emma turned toward Nathan.

"Em?" Allison said; she had taken a dry towel to the surface of her glasses before she deposited them across her ears and nose.

"Nathan's here," Emma replied. Her voice came out as a whisper. Allison couldn't see him. Emma lifted a hand and held it out to Nathan—and Nathan dropped both of his hands into the pockets of his jeans, shaking his head. "Allison can't see you if I don't touch you."

"I know."

There was so much finality to those two words Emma let her hand drop to her side. "Ally," she finally said, "can you give us a couple of minutes?"

Allison nodded, opened the door and walked into the hall. Then she walked back in and said, "You might want to have this conversation in a room that isn't the bathroom, given the number of people in the house."

"Good idea."

Nathan was never a person to fill a silence, even when it had gone past the point of awkward into nearly painful. Emma could—but not with Nathan. She knew how to find small, daily things interesting when she needed to. But days when she could cheerfully do this didn't generally including two shootings and the near death of her best friend.

"Where are you going?" she asked.

"Back," he replied. "To the City of the Dead."

She nodded, as if this made sense.

"If I stay, I'll follow you. If I follow you, I'll know where you are. I might not be able to tell the living how to get there—but I'll know. And what I know—" he stopped abruptly. "You've been avoiding me."

She started to lie. Stopped herself. This was *Nathan*. Lies had never really been necessary, before. She couldn't quite make herself believe they were necessary now. No, she thought, feeling the cold of all kinds of winter, that wasn't true. But she hadn't been lying to Nathan—not directly.

Only to herself. And those lies were just as harmful, in the end. She exhaled. "Yes."

He didn't seem to be surprised; his expression rippled as he closed his eyes and waited, his *Why?* unvoiced, but nonetheless loud.

"You didn't find me on your own," she said, voice almost a whisper.

His eyes widened, and this time he looked away. But he answered. "No."

"You didn't find your way home on your own, either. My dad said it would take a couple of years before you could—" She swallowed. "Before you could tear yourself away from the door. But it didn't."

He said nothing, but he met her gaze; he didn't hold it for long, but to her surprise, the faintest hint of a smile touched his lips.

"She sent you."

He nodded.

"Do you understand why?"

After a long pause, Nathan asked, "Do you?"

Emma closed her eyes. Opened them again. "Yes." She wanted to look away from his luminescent, oddly colored eyes, but she didn't. "When I saw Merrick Longland, I was afraid. We were all afraid. Because we'd all seen him die.

"I wasn't there when you died," she added. "But it must have been just as messy, just as painful. I never expected to see Longland again. But, Nathan— until October, I never expected to see you, either, except in dreams."

"Or nightmares?"

"Or nightmares. But when I saw Longland again—it wasn't just the fear. It was the hope—" She had to look away. "It was the *hope*, Nathan. Longland was alive, and if Longland could come back to life—so could you." When she turned to face him again, he was watching her; his eyes were shining. It was a light that looked familiar to Emma, although she couldn't immediately say why. "I was angry. I was angry with Eric, because he must have known. He didn't even look surprised. He didn't react as if it was impossible."

"No," Nathan said, voice grave. "He wouldn't."

"Necromancers are supposed to raise the dead. We're Necromancers. He knew it was possible."

"Emma—"

She lifted a hand to her mouth, mute for a moment because her voice was becoming so quavery, and she hated that. "It was everything I *wanted*. If I could learn how to use this power—this power that I didn't ask for and didn't want—I could bring you back. You could be *with me*. I could hold you. I could hold your hand without losing all sensation. I could—" she stopped. For a long moment, she struggled with breathing, because breathing right now was too close to tears, and she was still Emma Hall. "But Longland isn't alive."

His eyes widened slightly.

"He's—no one living would be able to tell the difference, but Longland said it's different. He's not alive; he's dead, and he's trapped in a body that's not really his. He can interact with the world. He can pretend to *be* alive.

"But he's dead. He's cold. And the only thing he now wants—"

"That is *not* all I want from you."

She turned to face him. "Isn't it?" she whispered. "Can you tell me, honestly, that if I could somehow open that door—or remove the impenetrable glass from that window—you'd even be standing here now?"

Nathan had never, to her knowledge, lied to her. He was therefore silent. It was a silence that stretched and thinned, and Emma was almost afraid of what would happen if it broke. But conversely, she wanted it to break. People were just like that.

"No." He looked down at his feet. "If the way had been open, I would have gone almost immediately. I didn't know where I was. I didn't understand—not completely—what being dead meant. I was cold, Em, yes. And it's warm there. Don't ask me how I know—I can't explain it. I don't think even your dad could. I didn't think of going home after I—after. I didn't even think of moving. I didn't think of moving on, either—I was lost.

"And when I did see the light—and I realize how melodramatic that sounds—I walked toward it. I knew it was where I belonged. I wanted to go there, I wanted to be there. But I never tried."

"Why?"

"Because when I got close enough, I could hear the screaming. The wailing. The sobs. I knew—I knew if I tried, I'd join them, and I could probably howl there like a lost toddler for too damn long."

"How did you get back?"

"She found me."

"She?" But Emma already knew the answer. The Queen. The Queen of the Dead. She frowned, then, and approached Nathan. He stood his ground, but stiffened—and that surprised her. It also hurt a little.

"Why do you think she sent me back?"

"The same reason," Emma replied, looking at his hands, at his face, and then, eyes narrowing, at the center of his chest, "that she sent Longland."

"Em?"

And she closed her eyes. Closed them, because even closed, she could see Nathan. She had always been able to see him with her eyes closed, because while he was himself, he was also some huge part of her hopes and her dreams. Her daydreams. Only his death had plunged him into nightmares—and even in nightmares, it was his sudden, inexplicable absence that caused her to wake, crying.

She could no longer see the narrow halls of an older Toronto home. She couldn't see the white doorframes that had clearly been painted half a dozen times. She couldn't see the carpet, which was so neutral a beige she might not have noticed it at any other time. She could see Nathan.

And at the center of his chest, glowing faintly, the links of a slender chain. She lifted her hand, and she knew as she did, that Nathan was bound and that she did not hold him. Her hands closed in fists.

She opened her eyes. Nathan was standing before her, but the world reasserted itself around him, as much as it could.

"She sent you because she knew."

"About you?"

"About me. About—" She exhaled. "She knows how I feel about you."

"And Longland?"

"He's an offer."

Nathan's smile shifted. He looked tired, to Emma. She didn't know whether or not the dead usually experienced the exhaustion that comes from too much fear, too much stress—but Nathan clearly did. "People always underestimate you. I had no idea why she sent me. She didn't ask me to do anything. She didn't ask me to say anything or learn anything. She didn't tell me to watch you. She just told me—to come home."

"She knew—she had to know—that I would want to see you," Emma continued. "But it's not that—it's Longland. He was meant to be proof that I could—" she couldn't say it.

"You could bring me back."

Emma nodded. "But I don't know *how*. I don't understand the power I have. I don't know how to use it. I see the dead—but it's not a struggle. I don't *try*. It happens. It's like weather. Or breathing." Her voice dropped. She looked up at him.

When they'd first met, she hadn't really noticed him. He was one of a dozen people who drifted in and out of class. He played computer games. He read. He tinkered in the science labs.

But he was friendly—and entirely without condescension—to Michael. That had caught her attention. Held it a little bit too long. He wasn't classically gorgeous. He wasn't daydream material. But her daydreams were wild and incoherent; you couldn't build a life on most of them, because they couldn't bear weight.

Nathan could. While he was alive, he could. He could listen. That was a gift. But better, he could accept her. Not just the good bits. Not the parts other people might find attractive. She wasn't a trophy girlfriend, although she could have been. He was a quiet space. A quiet, accepting space. He saw her as she was, good and bad.

There weren't many people who saw her. Not as she saw herself; if he'd done that, he would have walked away as quickly as he could, especially on the bad days. But as she actually was. He surprised her with the small things he noticed. He surprised her by noticing things about her she hardly noticed herself.

She had never lied to him, not deliberately. If she didn't want to talk about something, she said exactly that: I can't talk about this right now.

"I don't think she thought Longland would actually speak to me. I don't know if she understands what it does—and doesn't—mean to him, to be half alive. And, Nathan—it would have worked if he hadn't."

"Em, don't—"

She lifted a hand, a signal between the two of them that he needed to let her finish, because she wouldn't be able to if he interrupted her.

"It would have worked. I know myself. Even now—if you asked me, if you said it was what you wanted, I'm not sure I could say no. Because even knowing what I know, it's what *I* want." She saw his expression, then, and before he could speak—and he wanted to—she closed the distance between them, put her hands on either side of his face, and kissed him.

It was not a short kiss. The shock of cold numbed her lips and the palms of her hands. Everything about the gesture caused pain. She let him go and saw that his eyes were closed.

Eyes closed, he said, "I would never have asked." And he smiled as he opened them. They were bright. Shining. She was sure hers were as well, but for entirely different reasons. "I know you mean it. I know you think you couldn't say no. I know what my dying meant to you—I left. I did worse than leave.

"But to do what was done to Longland, you'd have to become like the Queen of the Dead. Like Longland himself, before he died. You'd have to learn to see the dead—all of them—as sources of convenient power. You'd understand that power is necessary, because without it, you couldn't maintain what you'd built for me.

"You can't learn all that without changing something fundamental. The Emma who still walks Michael to school is not the Emma who could build me a body for her own convenience. Or even for mine. You'd do it because you love me.

"Because I love you. And it would change the nature of what love means to both of us. I didn't plan to die. I didn't want to die. I never wanted to be a source of loss and pain to the people I loved—the people who loved me." He looked past her shoulder for just a second, and then his gaze returned to her face, as if anchored there. "But I was. I was. I would change it in a heartbeat if I could—but not that way."

Emma placed a hand on his chest, her fingers splayed wide. It was solid. It was even warm.

He hadn't finished. "When I'm with you now, I don't see the exit. I don't long for it. I'm not drawn to it. I see you. I could spend the rest of your life seeing you, and I'd be happy. Believe that.

"I have to go soon. She's calling."

"You're bound to her."

His smile was slow and sweet. "Yes."

She reached into his chest, then. She reached for the slender links she could only barely perceive, curling her palm around them. Warmth became sudden heat; she could have flattened her palm against a live stove element with the same effect. She cried out, her hand jerking open.

"Don't worry," he told her. He lifted a hand and then let it drop. "I'm already dead. Nothing worse can happen to me." He was fading as she watched. She tried to grab the chains at his heart's center again. She didn't care if they burned. She had held onto fire before.

But her palm passed through them. She tried to grab his hand; it was no longer solid. "Nathan!"

"I'm sorry."

She tried to throw her arms around him. To keep him. She knew—she knew this was an echo of dying for Nathan. He didn't want to go; he didn't choose to leave. But choice or no, he vanished.

She was left—as she had been left the first time—holding nothing. But this time she knew, for certain, that Nathan was out there somewhere. She knew who or what had taken him. She had told herself for months now that death was impersonal, because it was.

But the Queen of the Dead? There was *nothing* impersonal about her. Emma clenched her hands, and she turned to head down the hall.

Her father was waiting.

"How do I get him back?" she demanded. She had no doubt that he'd seen everything.

He didn't answer the question. Instead, he said, "Amy's packed the car. She's waiting. Allison and Michael are with her."

Emma swallowed. She didn't want to go downstairs yet; she knew what her face looked like. She had to work to bring rage—and the pain at its core—under control; she had to stop her hands from shaking so much.

And that would take time, and it was time they didn't have. "Dad?"

"I'm sorry, Em."

"She won't send him back," Emma whispered. "I didn't do whatever it was she wanted me to do. She won't send him back."

"I don't think so, no."

She made it halfway down the stairs, stopped, and turned again. "Allison's brother?"

"He's alive. No—don't. He's alive, but he wouldn't be if it weren't for machines. They're not certain he's going to pull through; he hasn't regained consciousness."

Emma closed her eyes. She balanced a moment between guilt and anger, and to her surprise, anger won. "Amy's right," she said, as she continued down the stairs.

"She frequently is."

"The Queen of the Dead has to go."

# Nathan

The Queen is not in her throne room. The Court is not in session. The dead line the halls like rough statues; without the Queen's command, there's almost nothing for them to do—and nothing they dare to do. They don't speak. Not like Emma's dead.

Not like Brendan Hall.

Not like Mark.

Certainly not like Margaret.

These people have forgotten the life they lived; life might not have happened, for them, at all.

Nathan walks among them, avoiding them as if they were physical presences. As if he is. He knows he could walk the straight line through them, and through the walls themselves; nothing prevents it.

But the Queen doesn't care for it.

He walks the long way. She's not dead; she uses the halls. Many of the people who live in this great, fanciful edifice aren't dead either; they use the halls too. Her knights. Her Necromancers.

Some of the dead gathered here belong to them, but they don't wander the halls like handless puppets; they are hidden, invisible even to Nathan's eyes, until the moment the Necromancers choose to show their power. In the throne room, they take out their dead, displaying them like trophies or status symbols. No Necromancer of note or worth in the Queen's Court is ever without them.

The Queen alone doesn't choose to do this—but her power is absolute and unquestioned. She is never without it. If she died, this city would crumble—probably instantly. But he can see her in the distance. The stone walls do nothing to bank the brilliance of her light. He cannot imagine that she will ever die.

He didn't lie to Emma. He didn't tell her all of the truth.

But he didn't tell the Queen all of the truth either.

"Nathan." She is sitting in her outer chamber, on a chair as unlike the tall-backed official throne from which she rules as chairs can get. She is dressed in long, flowing robes, but they are looser and far less confining; her hair is unbound and falls in one long, glistening sheet down her back and over her shoulders. She wears no crown in this room.

She wears one ring.

He kneels before her, because she demands respect, no matter where she might be found. She doesn't stop him, but she tells him to rise almost immediately, and when he looks up, he meets her steady gaze. Her eyes are clear and shining; they are so much like Emma's eyes, it is hard to meet them. But once he has, it's impossible to look away.

"She saw you," the Queen says.

Nathan nods.

"She saw you and she attempted to take you from me."

He nods again.

"Do you wish to go to her?"

He does, and says, nothing.

The Queen rises. "I did not expect her to attempt to break my binding."

He knows that Emma almost succeeded. The Queen walks from the room, indicating that he is to follow; he does. She opens tall, wide doors and leaves the confines of the palace for a grand balcony that is longer than Nathan's former home. And wider. Above her, the sky is gray; beneath her, the sky is gray.

"Merrick Longland has not returned to me." She stands, back to Nathan, and gazes up, and up again, and Nathan knows what she is looking at: the only light that is bright enough, at this distance, to rival her own. He looks as well, but he schools his expression; all of the dead do. What they long for, what they yearn for, is beyond them; acknowledging it only annoys her.

"Is he dead?"

"No," Nathan replies.

"Ah." She seems amused; he can't see her expression. Amusement is no safety when it's in her voice. "Has she seen him?"

"Yes."

She turns, then, her expression haunted. "Did she speak to you, Nathan? Did she offer to resurrect you?"

He says nothing for as long as he safely can; he doesn't want to answer this question. And what he wants, in the end, doesn't matter. "No." Before she can speak, he adds, "She doesn't know how."

"Not yet. Not yet." The Queen smiles. It is cold. "You are certain, in the end, that she did love you?"

He says nothing.

She walks toward him, stopping six inches from his chest. She touches it with the flat of her palm; her hand is warm. It is the only warmth in the Castle. The only warmth he's experienced that is not Emma's. It is bloody hard to be cold all the time.

"Yes."

"And did she tell you that she loves you?"

He closes his eyes. It doesn't make a difference; he can still see her clearly. Eyes closed, she is the only thing he can see. "Yes."

"And you believed her."

"Yes."

"Then she will come, Nathan. She will come to me. I have not yet decided what I will do with her when she does." She looks at his face again. "You wanted to see her." She caresses his cheek. He meets her gaze without flinching because her touch doesn't make him flinch. It is warmth. It is life.

"Do you want to be able to hold her? To touch her?"

"Yes." Even more than he wants to crawl out of this conversation into painful oblivion. Love is not something to be pulled apart and dissected, not like this. Not by outsiders. There is no joy in it; there is a rough, painful voyeurism.

Her hand falls, and her eyes narrow. "Why?"

It is not the question he expects. And he knows he will have to answer it because the compulsion is almost painful. He doesn't have the words for it. He starts to say, *because I love her*, but he understands that this is not the answer she's seeking. And he understands that he doesn't have that answer, because in the end, the question has nothing to do with Nathan.

He has become so used to fear that he is almost too numb to feel it. "Because," he says, "she's alone." He can't look away. "She once made me promise that I would let her die first, when we were old. So she wouldn't have to face losing me."

"And you promised?"

"It was a stupid promise. I didn't want to make a promise I couldn't keep. But I know—I know what my death did to her. I know what it did, and I'd take it back in a second if I could. I want to be able to hold her when she cries—because she does cry, but only when she's alone. Only when no one living can see her."

It is all true. And he knows, looking at the Queen's face, that the Queen has also cried, and that she never cries where anyone living can see her. It is not safe for even the dead to bear witness to her weakness.

"Come," she says. "What your Emma is too unschooled to do, I will do."

His eyes widen, then.

"Yes, Nathan. I will resurrect you. I will bring you back to Emma alive and in the flesh."

# Grave

## Nathan

The Queen's meditation chambers are large. The ceilings are high enough you can't see them if you don't crane your neck. Looking up is a lot like falling; Nathan avoids it out of habit. The dead don't fall—even when that's what they want. They can jump off a cliff or the roof of a building and hang there, ignored by gravity. They've got no weight.

The Queen is not dead. She burns with life. She is luminous, beautiful; if the dead aren't careful, they are struck dumb at the sight of her. She doesn't know what she looks like in the eyes of the dead; she can't see herself the way the dead do. She's therefore incredibly impatient. She takes a dim view of disobedience.

She is the only law the dead know.

The Queen walks to the center of the round chamber. Elaborate chairs dot the circumference of the smooth, rising walls; there are cabinets with cut-glass doors that catch light and reflect it. Books line the shelves; books lie face-up across the various tables situated between the chairs. She touches none of them. Instead, she positions herself in the center of a large engraved circle. The perimeter of that circle contains runes or glyphs that Nathan would have found fascinating while alive. He barely sees them, now.

The Queen is not wearing her full court dress. She doesn't need it. If she wore sweats and sneakers, it wouldn't matter. People here aren't bowing or scraping at her dress. Nathan understands that bowing and scraping—when too obsequious—annoys the Queen. He doesn't do it.

But he doesn't speak, either, unless spoken to. He doesn't crack a joke. He doesn't ask her how her day went. Mostly, he doesn't want to know. And there are reasons for that.

She gestures. She doesn't speak. Or rather, she doesn't speak to Nathan; she can choose who, among the dead, hear her voice.

Four of the dead do.

They come to her as she stands, flowing through the walls as if the chamber were a vast, unmarked clock face; they trace the path from the quarter marks of time—twelve, three, six, nine—as they approach. Nathan closes his eyes, but it doesn't help. He can still see their faces. He can see their expressions.

There are two girls and two boys. They are all Nathan's age—or they were, when they died. Left to themselves, the dead tend to wear the clothing they spent their last living minutes in. But the dead in the citadel are not left to their own devices. They wear what the Queen dictates. Today—or tonight—they are wearing loose, flowing robes. The robes are a pale, luminescent gray, as is everything else about them.

They walk with a quiet, hopeless dignity. One of the girls struggles; he can see the strain in the lines of her mouth, the narrowing of her eyes. But he can't see it in the steps she is forced to take. She understands what is going to happen to her here. He wonders if the other three do. He can't ask. Literally. His mouth doesn't move.

That's probably for the best. Nathan is not a screamer. He's not a cryer. But the urge—the sudden, visceral urge—to do both is strong.

He understood, as he followed the Queen to this chamber, that she meant to "clothe you in life", a fancy way of saying "build you a body." He understood that all of the Queen's power is derived from the dead—and that the city itself is home to many of them. More come every day; overpopulation isn't an issue when your citizens can't eat, can't work, and don't particularly need a place to live.

He did not put the three things together. The building of a body. The power necessary. The source of that power.

She means to honor him. He knows this. He knows that this is how she sees what she is doing as she waits implacably for the drifting dead to reach her until she is the heart of their formation. Nathan can see her through the transparency of their bodies. No surprise, there; he can see her through the solid stone of her citadel's many walls.

She knows. She turns to him, smiling, her expression radiant. She looks—for just that moment—like a sixteen-year-old girl, not the ancient ruler of a dead city. The four surround her now. They reach out—to each other—and clasp hands.

They are already dead. So is Nathan. But he feels their fear; it's like a mirror of his own. He doesn't need to breathe—but even if he did, he wouldn't. She raises her arm, then raises her face, exposing the perfect line of a throat that clearly never sees sunlight. Her hair, loose, trails down her back, straight and unconfined. It is the only thing about her that reminds him of Emma.

No, that's not true. The Queen of the Dead reminds Nathan of Emma because she is, at this moment, everything that Emma *isn't*. Emma would never surround herself with unwilling victims. Emma would never reach out with her graceful, slender hands and *bury* them in the chests of the two young women, reaching for the hearts that they don't actually have anymore.

Nathan wants to scream. He wants to shout. He wants to beg the Queen to *stop*. To tell her that he'll take being dead—being invisibly, unreachably dead—because no form of life, no form of actual body, could be worth the cost.

The dead girls throw back their heads, just as the Queen did, but for vastly different reasons. Nathan can see only their profiles; their mouths are open in the silent scream that Nathan is certain shapes his own. When the Queen retracts her hands, the girls come with them, as if their bodies were made of cloth and she has yanked them out of shape. That cloth is like silk or satin; it has a sheen that catches light, implies color.

It doesn't look human anymore. But Nathan knows, watching, that it is. The Queen is radiant with color as she shifts in place. She turns to face Nathan, and as she does, she reaches out again for the center of two hearts. The two boys. They're braced for it; unlike the one girl, they don't struggle at all. Their eyes are wide, rounded; they watch the Queen—just as Nathan does. Like moths to flame.

She unravels them as well. Her arms are cocooned with glowing light; it's almost painful to look at. Nathan understands that the dead are there, exposed, rendered both helpless and potent; she has taken whatever they have left to give.

And she uses it now, as he watches. She works those strands of colored, brilliant light, as if weaving a basket or a wire dummy. He can almost hear the voices of the four as she does; they are weeping. They are so close to her, so close to the warmth of the light she sheds—and it makes no difference. Nathan wonders, then, if she can hear them at all.

But she must, because she can hear him. She looks at him now, as she shuffles threads, joining them, binding them, making their weave tighter and tighter until they seem solid to the eye. She then looks at her work with the critical eye of an artist. Her gaze pins Nathan and leaves him, over and over again.

Nathan has no idea how much time passes. No one comes to these chambers but the Queen. No one interrupts her when she works here. And she works now. She works, her brow furrowed, her eyes narrowed; she works until sweat beads her forehead and small strands of pale hair cling to it.

All the while, the voices of the four thrum; they have a pulse and a beat, an ebb and a flow, that are synchronized almost exactly with the work she does. It is the chamber music of hell.

Nathan, like anyone else alive—or, rather, anyone who was once alive—has no memory of being born. He has dim memories of childhood, and he believes some of them occurred when he was three—but he's aware that he might be wrong, even if they *are* his memories. He tries to sort through them now, as the Queen continues to sculpt: to shear off pale flesh from cheekbones, to elongate neck, to narrow the lines of chest, arms, hands.

When she is finished, it is the hands of her masterpiece she holds. "Nathan," she says, her voice softer than he has ever heard it, "come to me."

Like the single girl, he hesitates. He knows the hesitation could be deadly, but at this point, he almost welcomes it. He can *still* hear dim, attenuated voices, and he understands that they are part of the finished form.

It looks like Nathan, to his own eyes: like Nathan, but stark naked. He can't see the flaws. He knows they're there, but he can't see them for the light she still radiates. If he could plug his ears, he might even feel awe or gratitude. He can't.

Oh, he can lift hands to ears, but it does no good. His ears aren't actual, physical ears. His hands block no sound.

"Nathan."

He walks. He walks toward where the Queen clasps the hands of her empty, shining creation. He notes that the eyes—the body's eyes—are closed and wonders whether his eyelashes were ever that long. It's an absurd thought.

Absurd is better than horror.

He is not terrified of the Queen as he approaches her; horror and terror are different. But he understands, as she waits, why someone would run away from her no matter how much she loved them.

Nathan doesn't love her. If he had a choice, there is almost nowhere else he wouldn't be.

"Give me your hand," the Queen says.

He doesn't think; his hand is in hers before the echoes of her words die. Her palm is warm. It reminds him of Emma.

*Emma is a Necromancer.*

He didn't understand why Chase was so angry at Emma. He couldn't understand what Chase feared. No one who knew Emma could be afraid of her. They might be afraid of losing her—and the love she offers so steadily—but that was never Chase's concern.

He understands now. Emma glows with the same interior fire that burns at the heart of the Queen. Emma has as much power as the Queen of the Dead. Emma could—if she knew how—do exactly what the Queen has done today.

Emma would never do it. He knows. But he wonders what anyone could do to stop her if she did.

"Close your eyes, Nathan."

He does. He doesn't tell her that it makes no difference. She doesn't plunge her hand into his chest. She doesn't yank his heart out and stretch it into filaments. She doesn't destroy him for the raw materials she needs to create anything else. But he wonders, now, whether everything in her world—the citadel, the streets, the buildings that line them—was made the same way.

The warmth of her hand becomes heat, and the heat becomes pain. It is not a pain he associates with burning—he's burned himself before. It's not a pain he associates with physical injury. It's not localized. It's not confined to the hand she grips.

It travels through him. It curls up inside of him, as if he had swallowed it whole. It has no way to escape him; he has no way to set it free. Some small part of him thinks: It's better than feeling nothing.

He expects to be swallowed in a similar way; he's not. She attaches herself to him in a hundred little ways—in a thousand. As she does, the cold recedes. There's nothing sexual about her touch. Nothing predatory. She is alarmingly gentle.

It's the gentleness that almost does him in. If he couldn't hear the dim, distant voices of the others, he would surrender himself entirely into this woman's keeping. He is *so* tired. And he is warm. He almost believes he has finally come to a place of rest.

But the voices don't stop. They're quiet. They're dim. But they're inside him now. Or he's inside them. He opens his eyes. He blinks. The Queen withdraws the hands that held his—and they are his hands, now. The voices weep to let her go; they can't cling. Nathan could—but he doesn't. He has that choice.

He is standing before her. He's naked. He should feel embarrassed, but he doesn't; she recreated his entire body. There's no part of it she hasn't seen and no part of it she hasn't already touched.

"There is a robe on the far wall," the Queen says. "Take it and leave. Someone will be waiting to lead you to your rooms. You will require rooms, now; you will require food."

He doesn't ask her about sleep. He doesn't ask her about anything. He knows he should make some show of gratitude, but he can't quite force his knees to bend because he doesn't feel any. If he works—and he does—he can keep the horror from his expression. More than that isn't in him.

And he knows that there will be a bill for this, down the road. The Queen's generosity is never a gift. He is afraid that the bill won't be presented to him.

He puts on the robe and turns, once again, to face the Queen; she is standing, arms wrapped around her upper body, in the center of the circle. He looks away immediately. It is not—it is never—safe to see the Queen's pain, and it is evident now; she is a confused, lost girl, her fragility both her armor and her weapon. If he were a different man, he would go to her; he would slide an awkward arm around her shoulder; he would offer her comfort.

He doesn't. He knows there's no comfort she'll take from him. There is only one person she wants.

And that person has devoted himself to her death.

Nathan doesn't remember being born. He will never forget being reborn.

## Reyna

Reyna lives with the dead.

This wasn't always true.

As a child, living on the edge of villages, and once or twice, larger towns, she spent her days helping her mother in her various gardens, and helping her uncles when they went on errands for her mother. When she was eight, she took care of Helmi, her squalling, infant sister. From time to time, she played with other children, but in truth, not often; strangers always made her mother nervous.

Reyna has lived with the dead since she was just shy of thirteen. The dead don't frighten her. They can't do anything on their own. The scariest person Reyna knows is alive.

Reyna's mother is frowning at her over a circle etched in chalk. Reyna drew that circle. It's not good enough for her mother. Nothing is ever good enough for her mother. But the floors are rough here; it's hard to draw straight lines—or solid, curved lines—with chunks of chalk. Chalk is *not* to be wasted. Nothing is to be wasted. Reyna understands why.

She makes no excuses because she's learned, with time, that no excuse satisfies her mother and the attempt to offer one darkens a mood that is never bright to begin with. The circles are anchors. Without anchors, searching for the dead is not safe.

If she's to leave this house before sunset, these circles have to be exact. Her mother will settle for nothing less. Reyna works with deliberate care, even if her hands are shaking. If she makes mistakes, she will have to do it all over again—and that will take too long, always too long.

While she works, her mother talks about the only thing that matters to her: the dead. The dead who are lost. "It's cold," her mother says. "It's cold, where she is."

Reyna doesn't ask who. She knows. Somewhere—nowhere close to the village in which they've lived for almost a full year—someone died. Death didn't free her. She is trapped somewhere cold. She's afraid. The dead are almost always afraid.

"Did you see her?" she asks her mother.

Her mother shakes her head.

Reyna is surprised.

"She's not close enough for me. You're going to have to do it." It's said so grudgingly, it stings. Reyna swallows backtalk. Beneath her mother's words is the acknowledgment of the uncomfortable truth between them: Reyna's gift is more powerful than her mother's. Of course her mother's not happy about it.

But she has to be worthy of that power. "Can't you use the lantern?" she asks.

Her mother snorts. "We don't use it unless we have no other choice."

Daring more, Reyna says, "If you let me use it—"

"No. Not yet. You're not old enough yet."

But she *is* old enough to sit in a circle for hours, walking a path toward a stranger who died somewhere cold. Reyna doesn't say this. She tries not to resent it. Instead, she draws and redraws and tries to do it quickly.

Reyna has a secret.

It's never wise to keep secrets from her mother or the rest of her family—and it's *always* hard to keep them when Helmi is underfoot. But more than half of Reyna's life is a secret now; she's had practice. She knows when to speak, and she knows how to say very little. She knows how to let people fill in the silences and the spaces between words on their own.

And *this* secret is not a guilty secret. This is not a secret she keeps primarily out of fear, the way her mother keeps secrets from every stranger, every neighbor, everyone who might—just might—become a friend, otherwise. She keeps it because it is *hers* and it has nothing to do with the dead, nothing to do with the life the magar forces her family to lead.

This secret is about life. It's about living. It fills all the spaces that have existed as empty gaps and insecurities for as long as Reyna can remember. It is about love. Reyna's love. And the fact that Reyna is loved.

She feels she has never been loved before now. She has certainly never loved this way before. When she is with Eric, she never thinks about the dead. When she is with Eric, she isn't confined by circles of chalk and stories of death and loss. She barely thinks about the future. She wants every minute in his company she can get—because every minute is precious, and they seem to fly by, hours becoming minutes and minutes, seconds, until it's time to return to the darkness and the secrecy.

Reyna lives with the dead—but she's not dead yet, and she wants, she desperately wants, to *live*.

Reyna knows when Eric became so important to her.

She doesn't understand how it happened—but she thinks about it because it gives her joy. She thinks about every moment, from the first meeting to the last, every awkward word; she thinks about the fear of speaking, and the fear of touching, and the fear of being sent away. All of it—the anticipation, the insecurity, the hesitance—is part of the perfect story, because she knows how it ends. She loves the ending, so she has to love the beginning.

They talk about it in snatches at the end of the day or before the day starts; they have only stolen moments. Eric is the smith's son, and he is expected to work. They talk about the first time they met. They talk about how they saw each other. Reyna could listen to Eric talk about it all day, every day.

But she knows the important moment, for her, was his laughter. It was so open, so loud, so low, so instant—and so unguarded. He was laughing *at* her. That should have ended things right there. It had before. But his voice was so—so *joyful*. As though he had swallowed life and her part in it, and he had to let the happiness out somehow. There was no laughter like that in Reyna's life.

There was barely any *life* in her life.

Shade dappled Eric's face and hid the color of hers; even the birds fell silent. She can close her eyes and see Eric so clearly she could spend all day with her eyes closed. She can remember her own laughter, welling up in response to his, as if the sheer sound of him had opened a dialogue in a language she didn't know, until that moment, was her mother tongue.

"Reyna, *pay attention*."

Reyna opens her eyes. This is the wrong thing to do. She can see the crimped, weathered lines of her mother's face—her mother, who is just past forty and looks as though she's already at the end of her life. Age has withered her skin, and the pinched frown lines around her lips, eyes, and forehead are so different from the lines that transform Eric's face when he laughs.

If there is joy in this room, her mother will hunt it down and kill it.

"What are you *thinking*?" her mother demands.

Reyna doesn't tell. She grabs her joy and she holds it close and tight in the cage of her body, because if her mother finds it, she will take it away. She exhales and tries to wipe the vestiges of a smile from her own face. She is not supposed to be thinking of Eric, or of life with Eric.

She is not supposed to be thinking of life at all.

~

Reyna's mother only has eyes for dead people. Reyna remembers wishing, as a child, that she were dead—because then, her mother would come for *her*. Then, she would be the only person her mother could see. She would have all of her mother's attention.

The closest she ever comes is during lessons like these, but there's nothing unconditional about her mother's attention. She sits in judgment. She waits to criticize. Nothing Reyna says will be a good enough reason to wait. Reyna says nothing. She tries to focus. If she does what her mother wants done *quickly*, she will be able to see Eric.

Reyna listens. Eric's constant presence doesn't make her deaf; the reminder of life doesn't inure her to death. She understands the desire for home, for a place to belong. The dead trapped here don't have that, because no matter what they were in life, life has moved past them. The only people they can talk to are people like Reyna and her mother. Reyna doesn't understand why she can see the dead. She doesn't understand why her mother can. She knows it's a gift.

But tonight, it feels like a burden or a curse. Tonight, Eric will be waiting. If she could *explain*, it would help. She can't. If her mother is wrong about Eric—and her mother absolutely is—she's not wrong about villagers. People fear what they don't understand.

*Then let me tell them. Let me* explain *it.*

*What will you tell them? That you can speak with the dead? That there are dead who are trapped here? They already have ghost stories, girl. Stories of the vengeful dead are not going to make us welcome.*

*But the dead aren't vengeful. Mostly.*

*No. The dead are people who have become invisible. But the invisibility is necessary. No one wants to let go.*

Reyna thinks of the lingering dead who were killed in anger, or for greed.

*Even hatred is a form of attachment,* her mother said. She tries to remember this, but it's hard. She is not full of hatred, now; she is overwhelmed by love, and yes—she wants to hold on to it. There is so much that is hard and difficult and fearful, holding on to things that give joy makes sense. It makes all the sense in the world.

In the distance, Reyna hears weeping. She opens her eyes; her mother's are closed, her mother's brow furrowed in the etched lines of concentration.

\*      \*      \*

Reyna has always been powerful. It is her mother's pride—but also, Reyna knows, her mother's fear. The only thing her mother has is her role as magar. Take that away, and what defines her? Nothing. When Reyna was younger, she attempted to hide her power, to ease her mother's fear. It didn't work, and her mother didn't appreciate it. Reyna's power has only served to increase her mother's expectations and the harshness of her mother's lessons.

Helmi, Reyna's surviving youngest sister, takes lessons that are far less harsh, far kinder. Helmi, however, is too young to show even the traces of the power that came to Reyna when she was twelve or thirteen. Reyna can't remember her mother ever being as kind to her oldest daughter as she is to her youngest.

It's not a gift, Reyna thinks. She wants to tell her sister that. It's *not* a gift. It's just another way to fail. But maybe Helmi will be free of the curse. Helmi will be allowed to have friends, or maybe even fall in love. Helmi won't have to be magar.

Helmi won't hear the weeping.

It draws Reyna; it pulls at her while she sits in the confines of the circle she etched in such broad strokes. Safe in the circle, Reyna lets herself be pulled into the pit of another person's pain. Walking this path is hard. It's not like the first dead girl she met; that had been an accident.

She'd been working in the new field. The sky had been blue and the earth, brown; in the distance, trees blurred the horizon. Talking to the stranger had been natural, a part of the day.

Talking to this stranger is not. The circle defines the landscape, as Reyna sits at its center. There is no natural sky, no natural gardens, no trees; there are no people and no possibility of people. Reyna goes to the dead girl, but she walks the magar's road to do it.

She thinks the weeping voice belongs to a girl, possibly a young woman. The road takes the shape of the dead girl's memory. Reyna looks for some sign of her mother, but her mother is not present; Reyna is walking the narrow road alone.

There are trees in the distance, shadowed and gray. The magar has warned Reyna, many, many times, not to add color or substance to the world she sees while she sits in the heart of the circle. The circle is supposed to be both guide and anchor. It is a reminder of the life that exists outside the world of the dead. But it's hard not to add traces of color to what she sees, to give strength to the echoes of another's memories. She does it without thinking, as she walks. It's easier not to do it when it's night, because at night, there is very little color.

The path is familiar; Reyna realizes this only as she draws close to the voice itself. It's the path Reyna walks to see Eric. She is glad her mother has not yet found the girl; it gives Reyna time to let the natural landscape of the dead reassert itself. She stands very still until she no longer recognizes the turn of the road, the rise and the fall of the gently sloped land, the shape of the trees. She no longer hears the brook passing yards from her closed eyes.

She no longer feels the touch of Eric's lips or hands.

Instead, she feels cold. It is bone-numbing. She no longer sees earth, but something that looks whiter and softer. It covers branches, flecks bark, hides the rounded gnarl of tree roots entirely. It is hard to see past it. It is not hard to listen.

She walks across the ground, leaving no tracks; this is not reality. It once was, for the girl who is now dead. The cabin, such as it is, is covered in white. There are shutters; she can see their shape in outline. They're closed. So is the door. Neither matters. Reyna was no part of the girl's death. No part of death at all. Memories don't, and can't, contain her.

The girl is huddled in the corner of the room farthest from the shuttered windows. She is sitting in the dark—and it is dark here. There is a fireplace; it contains ash. There's no wood beside it. It is so cold in this room, breath is visible. She died here. She died alone.

There is a table in this room. Three chairs. A fireplace. There are plates on the table. Cups that look like tin. There is a door that leads to another room. Reyna skirts around the weeping girl and looks in. One large bed. One fire grate. One small table that contains shut drawers and the remnants of a melted candle.

This is where the girl died, but she didn't live alone. Reyna drifts back through the door and comes to stand a few yards away from the girl herself. This has always been the hardest part of the job for Reyna. The dead don't always pay attention to the living because they're so caught up in their own final moments. If she knew the girl's name, it would be easier. The dead often respond to their names.

She doesn't. The girl—and probably her family—died on the outskirts of an entirely different village.

Reyna tries anyway. But the girl can't hear her because her own pain, her own fear, is too loud. It has to be. If it weren't, she wouldn't be trapped here.

Reyna exhales. She then reaches out to touch the girl's shoulder.

In the heart of the circle in a distant, darkened room, Reyna flinches. The cold eats sensation in her palms, but not quickly enough: It *hurts*. She has to push past the cold—and quickly—or her arm will be numb for a day.

The dead are not meant to speak with the living. It's a natural law. The cold is a reminder, a sign that means: Stay out. But it's a thin sheet of ice. When one knows how to stand on it, it breaks. Beneath that ice, beneath the overwhelming cold, there is heat and warmth, a reminder that the dead come from the living.

The girl's eyes widen. She lifts her head, tightening her arms around her knees as she meets Reyna's eyes. Reyna doesn't know what the girl sees; what Reyna sees is a gaunt face, hollow eyes, pale, sunless skin. A threadbare dress, too large for the girl who inhabits it. The girl died when she wasn't much younger than Reyna. Or older. With the dead, it's hard to tell.

They don't age when dead.

"Who are you?" The girl asks. She lets go of her knees and rises. To Reyna's surprise, the girl is—was—taller.

Reyna doesn't give her name to strangers, even dead ones. "I've come to find you."

"Have you found my father? Is my father—"

"Your father," Reyna replies, "is waiting for you."

"How did you get here? With all the snow—" The girl shakes her head. "It's been snowing so long. You can always hear the wind screaming, just outside. We ran out of firewood."

And food, Reyna thinks, but doesn't say it out loud. She holds onto the girl, and the girl doesn't seem to notice; she walks, quickly, to the door. It opens for her, because it is not a door in a real house; it is the memory of a house. Just as the girl herself is the memory of a life.

The door opens into a howling snarl of wind and ice and snow. The girl struggles to close it. Reyna feels the undercurrents of her fear; it is so strong, it pulls her under. If the door is left open, they'll both die.

She shakes the fear out, almost literally. This death is *not* her death. She is not dead. The girl is—and doesn't realize it. She's caught in the moment of fear; it's all she can see. That and Reyna. Reyna takes shallow breaths. Her mother still hasn't found them, but she's closer, now.

There's only one certain way to break the dead out of the trap they've built for themselves—and it does take power. But it takes the power they carry within them. Reyna looks at the door. She looks at the room, and the empty fireplace, the empty table. To lead the girl out of this nightmare, she will have to alter what the girl perceives.

Fear is hard to shift. Reyna thinks, again, of Eric. She wants to be in his arms; instead, she is holding the remnants of a terrified girl, and she knows, looking at her, that there will be no time for Eric this evening. There might be no time in the morning, either, before the day's chores truly start. She swallows.

She swallows and accepts it. Yes, her mother could—and will—find this girl. She won't find her as quickly as Reyna because she's never been as sensitive. But even if she does find her, Reyna's not certain her mother could do what needs to be done. The winter and the isolation are both so strong it's hard to think of the circle and the summer that she left hours ago. And it has been hours.

"The snow will stop soon," she tells the girl. She takes a chair—an empty chair. "I brought food—it's cold, I'm sorry."

"The snow will never stop."

"The snow stopped long enough for me to make my way here," Reyna points out.

"Did—did my father send you?"

"Your father wasn't in any shape to travel," she replies, completely truthfully. If the girl's father left the house during this storm, he didn't survive it. Reyna's certain he couldn't see three feet in front of his face. He might have gone out, turned back, and been unable to find his way home. "I came instead."

Lying to the dead is tricky. Reyna thinks of it as telling them a story. It's a story they need to hear. It has to be believable, because if they believe it, they can step outside of the fear. Fear is a story, like any other story. Change the story a bit, and the ending shifts with it. The ending the girl faced was death—either by freezing or starvation. Reyna can't tell which, and it doesn't matter. She needs to shift the ending enough that the girl can leave the house. If she leaves the house, she should be able to see where she has to go.

That's the way it always works. It's no wonder her mother's not as good at it—comfort has never been one of her mother's strengths.

"If you're not hungry, I'll take the food with us. You'll need a coat," she adds.

The girl stares at the food; it's dried meat, hard cheese. There's nothing fresher than that. Her hesitation wars with her hunger—she doesn't get many visitors, and she's wary of strangers, here. But she's desperate. Sometimes that helps Reyna break people free of the spaces they create for themselves—and sometimes it makes things almost impossible.

The girl shakes her head; Reyna puts the food away. She does so deliberately, carefully; she takes no short-cuts. To be here at all, she's lost the evening with Eric, and if she's lost that, she might as well do *something* right. As she carefully slides meat and cheese back into the pack she's carrying, she concentrates on the weather. The howl of wind recedes; again, it's slow. She sits it out, waiting. She almost offers to build a fire, but she thinks that would be too much.

It's enough to still the storm. It's enough to stop the snow.

The minute her mother arrives, she knows; her mother remains invisible, watching. Reyna feels her fists clench; she feels her throat dry. It is always this way. She tries to focus on the poor, trapped girl, instead. When it's been quiet for long enough, she rises and walks to the door; the girl follows.

The wind begins to howl again, and Reyna says, "It's quieter, but we're not clear yet." She goes back to the table, knowing that this will happen again. No matter how quiet the cabin is, approaching the door brings the storm. Opening the door is death.

She doesn't tell the girl that leaving it shut was death, anyway. She works, and she waits. She offers the girl food each time they retreat from the door. The third time, the girl's shoulders slump, and she nods. She handles the plates; she tries to be host to a guest. When she begins to eat, Reyna thinks it is almost over.

She's wrong.

Five hours later—five actual hours—Reyna has fought the wind to a standstill. The girl has eaten. She has eaten everything. The fabric of her hunger is woven from memory, but when she has finished, she lets it go. She knows she is no longer hungry, because when she was alive, she wouldn't have been. It's enough of a change that she can—barely—believe that the storm that consumed her family will end.

She lets Reyna open the door. She has dressed, now, for a long trek in the bitter cold; she is prepared to step outside of her home. This should be enough.

It isn't. They can barely get the door open. It's almost as if the house itself has been buried. Reyna doesn't understand snow very well; she half suspects that the monstrous amount of it is also part of the girl's fear. She could make the snow vanish; she suspects she's skilled enough to do that. But the snow is just another wall, and if the wall isn't carefully deconstructed, the girl might never see beyond it; she'll build it again and again and again.

And so Reyna spends hours digging a path through the snow. It makes her arms and shoulders ache; she is so tired by the end of it she wants to crawl back into the imaginary house, into the imaginary bed—there's room enough for three—and sleep. There's a danger in that. Reyna almost made that mistake once.

She has never repeated it.

The girl, on the other hand, doesn't tire. She digs, and the memory of desperation lends her a strength the living don't possess. This could be another trap—a different one—if Reyna weren't by her side; the girl might spend eternity digging and never look up to see sky. It was evening when Reyna arrived; it is not evening now. She knows it is not night in the world beyond her circle. She can hear bird song and argument in the distance; she can hear crickets and the buzzing of dragonflies and other insects. She can hear the sounds of Helmi.

Helmi knows better than to interrupt Reyna or the magar when they sit in their circles.

*Mother*, she thinks, *where are you*? There is no answer, of course. This is a test. Another test. And Reyna knows what she must do to pass it. She must dig, as the girl is digging. She must become part of the girl's cage, the girl's fantasy. She must become enough a part of it that she can find the door and open it.

Find it too soon, open it too soon, and the girl will slip free of Reyna, not the cage; she will retreat, restructuring memory, and cloak herself once again in her uninterruptible fear. There *must* be another way. But if Reyna tries to make one today, she will fail.

So she talks while she digs. She talks about Eric.

The girl actually smiles. It's a shy smile, as if she's not quite used to talking to other people—and given the situation, she might not be. But she asks about Eric, about his father, about the village, as if she's hungry for news. And as Reyna is just digging, and she's tired, and she wants to stop and rest, she answers. Talking about Eric gives her energy. Talking about love makes the cold seem warmer, as if it could melt the snow just by existing.

Hearing the girl's tentative questions makes her seem like a real girl to Reyna. A living girl. Someone who has known loneliness and the fear of rejection, someone who can appreciate the gift that love *is*. Answering them—answering makes her seem almost like a friend. Reyna doesn't have a lot of friends. Living the life she lives, and moving from year to year, makes friendship impossible. She can't talk about what she does. She can't share it. She knew, before she could talk, that she was, and would remain, an outsider.

But the truth is, she doesn't want that. She's never wanted that.

What she wants is Eric. She wants to be loved, not feared. She wants to be understood. She wants to stand up and shout the truth to the world: She is here to *help people*. She is here to help the people that most people can't even *see*. She almost says as much to the girl, who is one of those people.

But the girl is talking about her father, now. He hunts and traps. She is talking about her mother, who died when she was very young, in a winter like this one. She is talking about her own dreams—of love and freedom and, most of all, summer. Summer, when the snow melts and the world is warm, and standing outside of four walls won't kill.

Her dreams are smaller than Reyna's, but she glows with them, and as she speaks, the tunnel through the snow expands; the digging quickens. She works—as all the dead do—without being aware of the work itself; by speaking of the things that she anticipates, the girl is pulling herself out of the hard shell of her fear. As she does, the tunnel lengthens.

The color of the sky shifts. The snow doesn't so much melt as vanish. The girl stops, midsentence, her mouth hanging open as if she's forgotten she was speaking. And she has. She is staring ahead of her, her eyes wide and unblinking. There is a look on her face that is almost painful; Reyna can't describe it. She struggles to find words for it, but the ones she comes up with don't work: love, desire, peace.

Reyna's mother says the dead don't cry.

She's wrong.

"What do you see?" Reyna asks. Her mother will be angry about it later—and her mother's anger never goes away—but she feels the sudden, visceral need to know.

The girl doesn't hear her. Reyna is holding her, and Reyna's hands tighten—just as they once did around her mother's skirts. "What do you see?" she asks again.

The girl whispers a word in a language Reyna doesn't understand. She's never had that happen to her before. She has always understood the dead, no matter where she finds them. They speak the same language. "I don't understand."

The girl then looks away from whatever it is she sees. "You can't see it?" she asks.

Reyna shakes her head.

The girl's tears fall again; she looks—with pity—at Reyna. As if it is Reyna who is trapped, or Reyna who is blind. "It is everything I ever needed."

"*What* is?"

The girl lifts her arm. Points. Frowns. "You helped me to come here. My father is waiting. And my mother. My mother." She looks down at her hand; Reyna is holding it. Reyna has been holding onto the girl for the entire, long night. "Close your eyes," the dead girl whispers.

Reyna does.

Eyes closed, for one long minute, she can see what waits for the dead. It is . . . like light. But not visual light; it's the essence of what light offers: illumination, vision, beauty. It is *home*. It is *warmth*. It is a place—at last, after so much struggle and fear and resentment—to *belong*. She cannot describe it because it isn't something that can be seen, even if she sees something; it is something that is felt. Here, all anger, all rage, all fear, all ambition, can and must at last be set aside.

She understands, then, why it is forbidden to look. If it did not remind her so much of what she feels for Eric, she is certain she would walk by the girl's side until there was no turning back.

And that she wouldn't regret it.

"There's no rain coming," her mother says, as Reyna works.

Reyna knows. The stream is so low in the bed beside the ring tree. This is not the first year the rains have been sparse. There is water, of course, for their own gardens. There will always be water for their gardens. But her mother doesn't like to use their gifts that way, even if it keeps them fed.

The villagers will notice.

The villagers, who know that there's been so little rain. Rumors will start. And eventually, someone will say, "They're stealing the rain!" It's not true, of course. It's never been true. If Reyna's mother weren't so afraid of people, she could make it rain for the whole village, and then, they'd be welcome. They'd be heroes.

But she doesn't. The only time Reyna was foolish enough to ask *why*, her mother slapped her. Her mother, bent and wiry, has a temper, but she almost never *hits* her children, not with her hands; she uses words for that.

"The power does not come out of nowhere!"

No, of course not. It comes from the dead. "If we're finding them *anyway*," Reyna countered, "they don't *need* that power. The only reason they have it at all is to help us search for them and free them. Once they're free of this world and their pain, why *shouldn't* we use that power to help the living?"

"Because that is where it would start," her mother replied grimly. "And it would not end there. It never does."

"And how would it end?" Reyna demands. "If we only want to help people—living or dead—why is that bad?"

"Why do you want to help the living?"

"What?"

"Why do you want to help them?"

"Because then *we* won't be hated. Then we can *stay*!"

And her mother shook her head and said, again, No.

# Emma

Snow clung randomly to highway signs along the 401, obscuring letters or numbers designed to mark the way. White borders absorbed white clumps; no one unfamiliar with the signs could be expected to read them.

No one tried, anyway. Amy was driving, and Amy knew where they were going. It was a comfort, to leave the driving to Amy—the only comfort in this small space.

Michael was on the right-hand side of the SUV's bench, head pressed against the window, chin tucked toward his chest. His eyes were closed, but he wasn't sleeping; his hand was running rhythmically across Petal's head. Petal, in theory seated in the middle of the bench, was actually sprawled across both it and the two passengers on either side of him.

Allison had his back end, which meant the stub of his tail as well as his damp paws. She didn't lean against the window; her head was tilted back, her neck almost rounding as she rested the weight of her head against the top of the seat. Her eyes were closed. It was dark in the car. Dark enough that her pallor shouldn't have been visible—but her expression suggested the absence of color; her lips were almost as pale as the rest of her skin. Her glasses, flecked first with snow and then with the water snow became, rested at a slight tilt across the bridge of her nose.

Emma was certain she was thinking about Toby, her baby brother. Toby, who was in the hospital, in the ICU, hooked up to god only knows how many machines, courtesy of a gun; it had been hours. Toby had been fine at dinner. He'd been his usual, annoying younger brother self until people broke into the house, looking for Allison.

Allison had escaped. Chase had made her leave.

Emma didn't know what to say to her. Allison hadn't shot her brother. But it was Ally the attackers had been after. Had there been no Necromancers—and no necromantic best friend—there would have been no break-in and no guns. Had Allison refused to get caught up in the lives of the dead, she'd be doing her homework or reading her latest amazing book.

Instead, she was on the run, trapped in a car with Amy Snitman, who had always made her feel uncomfortable, driving away from a brother who might die at any minute, instead of running in a frenzy of worry and fear toward him.

Ally couldn't phone. She couldn't ask how her brother was doing. She couldn't go home; if she did, it was only a matter of time before Necromancers once again descended on her home and family.

The only person who could feed Emma and her friends information about Toby was Emma's father, who happened to be dead. He'd promised to keep an eye out, to report any changes in Toby's condition. Emma didn't know if his absence—so far—was a good sign.

She wanted to believe it was, but she couldn't force those words out of her mouth. She wanted to comfort her best friend, but she didn't have anything to offer. If it weren't for Emma, if it weren't for that friendship, there would have been no home invasion. Toby would never have been shot.

Emma wondered if this awkwardness, this desire to help mixed with the certainty that *nothing* would be helpful, was natural; she felt like a failure of a friend. Was this how Ally had felt in the months after Nathan's death? Wanting to help, but awkward with uncertainty about how?

And the truth was, nothing had been certain to help Emma, then. Minute to minute, what Emma wanted or needed from her friends had changed. What she'd wanted was to have Nathan back. She couldn't have that. Some days, she'd wanted to go to the places she and Nathan had gone together, and some—she wanted to avoid them because all she could *see* there was loss and absence.

What had kept her sane? What had kept her *here*, as far as grief's gravity allowed that? The answer was contained in this car. Michael. Allison. Petal. Even, in her fashion, Amy. Amy could understand the theory of grief and loss, but Amy had never been big on sympathy—she considered it too close to pity, and no one who liked having a social life, however stunted, pitied Amy Snitman.

Had she cried on their shoulders?

No. Because she was a Hall, and Halls don't cry. Even at funerals.

What, then? She glanced out the window at snow that was almost horizontal, turning the question over and over in the terrible silence of the car. She almost asked Amy about her current rival in school, just to have that silence filled. But she realized that Amy, tight-lipped and active, wasn't in that much better a place than any of the rest of them, which was unsettling.

What had these friends given her, when she thought there was nothing of value that the universe could, anymore? She thought, although it was uncomfortable. Emma had always been taught, in subtle ways, that every request for help—or time, or attention—put pressure on another person. Asking was forcing someone else to say No, and given how much Emma hated saying No herself, asking for things became, as she grew up, a social crime.

She glanced at Amy's grim profile.

Amy asked—if by "ask" one meant demanded—for things all the time, but Emma didn't hate it, or her, most days. On the other hand, hating Amy would almost be like hating rain or snow. Amy didn't need anything to be Amy. Or rather, she didn't need anything from anyone else.

And that was beside the point. Emma looked at the rest of her friends in the mirror and understood what they had given her, in lieu of obvious, superhuman comfort. They had needed her. Even when she was at her worst, when she'd felt so empty she thought she'd crumble into dust and ash just trying to take a step forward, they'd needed her. They reminded her that she was necessary, even without Nathan. There was still an Emma-shaped space in the universe that had to be filled.

She would have said they'd asked for nothing. And, in words, they hadn't. Words weren't necessary to walk Michael to school. Words weren't necessary to walk and feed her dog. Words were definitely superfluous when listening to Allison talk about the most amazing book she had just read.

They hadn't asked.

They had assumed. No—that was the wrong word. They had *trusted* her. She had needed that silent trust. She still needed it. It didn't make her happy the way Nathan's presence—and silence, and speech, and actions—had. It merely reminded her, constantly, that she was still Emma Hall, even without Nathan. That even when she felt, when she utterly believed, that she would face the rest of the future alone, she was not, in fact, alone.

Emma Hall had been raised to ask for nothing; to be independent, to take care of her own needs without expecting anyone else to leap in and do it for her. She inhaled.

"Problem?" Amy asked.

Exhaled. This was not a discussion she wanted to have with Amy in the car. But Amy was in the car, regardless; if it weren't for Amy, they might still be huddling in Eric's house, numb with terror or grief. Silence was cowardice.

"I'm grateful," she forced herself to say. "I'm grateful that I have friends like you."

Amy had that "water is wet" expression. Allison, however, opened her eyes and lifted her head, meeting Emma's gaze in the mirror.

"Don't start apologizing," Ally said. "I won't be able to deal with it to-night."

"Emma always apologizes," Michael pointed out. His eyes were still closed, his cheek still pressed against the cold glass window.

"I didn't apologize to Nick after I dropped a book on his head."

"I would cut you from all my social circles if you did," Amy said. Michael did not respond. "But Allison is right—it takes a *lot* of patience to listen to you apologize for everything, and my patience is nonexistent right now. You were saying?"

Allison grimaced in the mirror, although it was brief.

"Even when things are crazy—or disastrous—you've always reminded me that I—I have something to give. Something of value." She hesitated.

Allison didn't. "You always did."

Emma shook her head, lifting one hand, a gesture that meant she had to continue now, or she would lose the thin thread of courage that kept the words coming. "When Nathan died, I thought the world had ended. Or that it *should*."

Michael opened his eyes; he was watchful now, although he could enter a conversation with his eyes closed.

"The world didn't end, of course. What I feel—what I felt—didn't change the rest of the world. Only me. I forgot. I forgot what it was like to be Emma Hall, on her own. And I didn't really want to remember. If I couldn't *feel* Nathan's loss, I felt as if I'd be saying he never mattered.

"But you needed me to be what I'd been. You knew me before Nathan. You knew me during. And you knew me after." She exhaled again. "I'm not sure I can do this without you. I know it's selfish. I know—"

"No apologies, remember?" Amy cut in.

Emma swallowed. "I don't know what's going to happen. But I'm grateful that you're here to face it with me. I don't think I could do it without you."

"Do what?" Michael asked.

"Find the Queen of the Dead," she replied, after a long pause.

"How are we going to find her?"

Allison said nothing, but she met Emma's steady gaze in the mirror. She even smiled, although as smiles went, it was terrible.

"That's the question," Amy said. "I'm personally less concerned with the question of finding her and more concerned with the question of how we handle her once we do. I don't suppose any of your invisible dead people have wandered into my car?"

"Without your permission?"

That dragged a brief laugh out of Amy. "We need to ask them what the odds of being discovered are. There are five or six places we can run to, if we have to—but that's not going to last if they're smart."

More silence. It was Allison who said, "We can ask Merrick Longland."

"I wouldn't trust a *word* that fell out of his mouth," was Amy's heated reply. She had not forgotten Longland's actions at her party. She had not forgotten what he'd done to her brother, Skip. "Even if we could, I'd just as soon not owe him anything."

"I don't have that luxury," Allison said, her voice thin and slightly shaky. "He saved my life."

"I haven't noticed that fact softening Chase's attitude toward him."

"Allison isn't Chase," Michael said.

"Thank god."

The snow let up forty-five minutes from Amy's destination, but by that point, it was irrelevant. Plows had come through what passed for main roads; they had also carved ditches out of the smaller side roads. The sides of those ditches were taller than Amy's SUV in places.

The moon was out, the sky was clear, and the snow reflected enough light that the sparsely placed street lights were enough to see by. Amy's winterized cottage was not so much a cottage as a very large, modernized house; they had their own generator somewhere on the property. They clearly had someone who maintained at least the drives. Driving to the garage was almost easier here than it was after a snow dump in the city.

"What?" Amy said, as they exited the car. "I phoned ahead and asked Bronte to take the snow blower for a spin."

That wasn't all she'd asked the unknown person to do; there was food in the fridge, and the wood stove was both full and burning. Also, coffee, which

Amy decided she needed. One glance at Michael, and she added hot chocolate to the impromptu menu while they waited for the second car to arrive.

Amy wanted to place bets on how many people would be in it when it did.

Eric, Chase, Ernest, and Longland were in the other car. Although he'd been cleaned up, Chase looked as though he'd been at the bottom of a game-deciding Hollywood tackle, where all the other players had also been given knives. He had not killed Longland. Longland had not killed him. Both of these statements hung in the air like unfinished sentences.

Longland, however, had saved Allison's life. For his own reasons, of course, which were almost entirely selfish—but they didn't matter. In the end, without his intervention, Ally would be dead. The thought made Emma forget to breathe for one long minute; when she exhaled, she exhaled white mist. Allison, shivering, was on the steps waiting for Amy to fish a key out of her purse.

Michael was tromping in circles in snow, one of which was rottweiler shaped, when the second car pulled up. Eric was behind the wheel. Ernest was beside him. Chase and Longland occupied the back seat, and both still appeared to be in one piece; neither looked best-pleased with the company, and they exited the car, putting anyone still standing outside between them.

Longland stayed close to Emma. Amy opened the door and ushered everyone inside; Longland, as he entered, was pale. He stared at Emma in a way that made her distinctly uncomfortable. He knew it and attempted to look elsewhere, but his gaze kept returning to her, and it stayed anchored there until she glanced in his direction.

Chase, for his part, went to Allison as if to ascertain that she was still breathing. He kept himself between Allison and pretty much everyone else, the exception being Michael and Petal. He didn't particularly care if Longland attached himself to Emma, because he didn't particularly care if Emma survived.

Emma, the Necromancer.

Amy immediately continued her stage directions once coats, boots, and other outerwear had been removed. She had already chosen the rooms in which her guests would stay and led them there, catching Michael's arm when he failed to follow immediately. She deposited Longland in the room between Ernest's and Eric's; Chase was, she told Eric, his problem. She commandeered the room her parents occupied when they were here and let Allison and Emma share a room across the hall; Michael was one door to their right. Petal, like Chase, was not Amy's problem.

Chase sourly noted the parallels between the designations.

"I should probably apologize," Amy told him, no hint of regret in her voice. "Petal actually *listens*. I am going to make coffee. I will also make hot chocolate for those who don't drink coffee." She then turned and marched down the hall to the stairs.

Chase, Eric, and Ernest did not join them in the kitchen. They risked the wrath of Amy by poking around the rooms in the house, and Emma privately thought Amy was right: there was no possible way Necromancers had come *here* first. Chase, between clenched teeth, pointed out that they were not attempting to destroy Necromantic foci, but Ernest cleared his throat. Loudly.

"With your permission," he said, "we would like to be more proactive in rudimentary defenses on the perimeter of your property. Or," he added, as Amy opened her mouth, "your house and the road that leads to it."

Amy nodded.

Chase said nothing, loudly. He could be sarcastic without saying a word.

"How likely is it we'll be followed?" She didn't ask Ernest. She asked Longland.

"The Necromancers with whom I arrived are dead." He hesitated. "It is possible—probable—that they were not the only knights sent. Emma is powerful."

"You didn't consider her a power the first time you met her."

"I did not see her then as I see her now."

"Neither will the Queen."

Longland nodded. "But the Queen's knights are not her only servants. She can, on occasion, send the dead to do her bidding; they are not capable of interacting with the mortal world—but they can observe and report directly to her almost instantly. None of the dead could fail to see the power Emma has."

"She could always use a phone." Amy folded her arms.

"She is not conversant with modern amenities, by her own choice. It is the only advantage the hunters have. Change, when it has come to the court, comes slowly through the knights. Had you joined us, your knowledge of things modern would inform both you and the service you offered; had your service—in pursuit of the Queen's goals, of course—been successful, she would review the mechanisms behind that success."

"Emma would not have survived to join the court," a new voice said. Emma turned toward Margaret Henney, who entered the conversation in a way that made the air cold. She was dead. She had been dead the first time Emma had laid eyes on her. She could make herself visible to the living, with Emma's help.

With Emma's unconscious help.

"Oh?" Amy said.

"She is too powerful. Had she been willing to learn what the Queen could teach, the Queen would have discovered this. Merrick is right: The dead see her just as clearly as they see the Queen; to our eyes, she looks almost the same. The Queen would have come to understand this within a handful of years—perhaps less. She would not have suffered Emma to live."

"How, exactly, do you know all of this?"

Margaret frowned and turned to Emma. Emma said nothing, but she clasped cold hands behind her back.

"I was a Necromancer, of course."

"Not a terribly impressive one," Longland added, with cool derision.

"Not terribly impressive to the Queen, no. It was only very briefly my life's ambition to be so. What I know of the Queen's court is not current, but the Queen was conservative, in her fashion. She did not value change for its own sake. Between my death and yours, how much did the composition of her inner court change?" The question was clearly rhetorical.

Merrick did not appreciate it. He glanced once at Emma.

Emma, however, nodded.

"I am no longer her servant."

"No. Are you mine?"

Everyone but Petal fell silent.

Watching his expression, Emma wondered if Longland had truly served anyone but himself. She had seen similar expressions in Grade Seven and Grade Eight. Fear, humiliation, desperation, the need to be seen as belonging. She'd often envied adults like her parents who didn't seem to have any of the same emotions.

"... Yes," he finally replied.

"Then please answer Margaret's questions."

"Is Margaret yours?"

Emma started to say no.

Margaret, however, said, "Yes. Until the door opens and I can leave this place, I serve Emma."

"Just in case there's any doubt," Chase said, "no one else here is bending a knee. We don't serve Necromancers."

Longland ignored Chase. Margaret apparently ignored him as well; she turned a severe glare on Ernest, who was leaning against the nearest wall looking even older than he usually did.

"Chase," he said, "we're doing a perimeter sweep." When Chase opened his mouth, he added, "Now."

Longland, however, continued to speak to Margaret—as if the rest of the living were of no concern. "Two of the Queen's knights—from your era—have died. Three, if you count me."

"And the citadel?" the older woman asked.

"There is one new wing, a small one."

"The city?"

"It has not changed."

Emma cleared her throat. "What is the city of the dead like?"

"It is not a city as you would understand it. None of the living occupy its buildings, although there are completed buildings. At some point, we believe the Queen intended her city to be occupied. The logistics were difficult. Food, in particular. She did not complete the city she had planned. Half of the streets are bare outlines formed of cobbles and forgotten intent. The dead wander there in numbers."

At the tightening of Emma's expression, Longland shrugged and looked away. "They have no power. Those that remain are not worth harvesting; the novices practice binding on them. You would not enjoy the city of the dead."

Amy glanced at the door. "We don't have our hunters. I think we should try to get some sleep; we can make plans over breakfast." No one in the hall mistook the suggestion as anything other than it was: a command. Amy was the closest thing they had to a queen, here.

"I want to know why you kissed me." Allison Simner squared her shoulders, lifted her chin, and spoke as forcefully as she could, given the subject matter. If the statement—which had started life as a shaky, confused question— sounded well-practiced, it's because it was.

"That was better," Emma told her best friend. "But you dropped the last two syllables."

Allison's shoulders were already bunched up so tightly they were practically at the level of her ears.

"Are you sure you have to ask? I mean—the answer seems pretty obvious."

Allison turned from the mirror, in which she'd been practicing the "right" expression. It was a small mirror, given that it belonged in Amy's family's cottage. "Why do you think Chase kissed me?"

Emma shook her head. "Because he *wanted* to?" When Allison failed to reply, she added, "He's Chase. He pretty much does what he wants. There is no way he would kiss Amy."

"But kissing Amy at least makes *sense*."

"If you're Chase?"

That pulled a smile out of Allison. "I guess it would be suicidal."

"Good point. Now it makes me wonder why he hasn't. It's Chase, after all."

Allison's smile became a laugh—the first of the day. The first, Emma thought, of two days.

Petal chose that moment to push the bedroom door open. It wasn't completely closed. He headed straight to where Emma sat, cross-legged, on the bed, jumped up, and made himself at home. But the blankets were wrong, the bedsprings were wrong, the bed was the wrong shape; the only thing that was right about this particular room, in dog terms, was that Emma was somehow in it.

For a rottweiler, he could make himself appear smaller and vastly more pathetic without apparent effort. He did have his leash attached by the mouth— at least until he dropped it in Emma's lap.

"Not now, Petal," she told him, setting the leash to one side before he dropped his head on it. "Sorry," she added, to her best friend.

Allison had been in Emma's life since before Petal came to join it. She shrugged off the interruption. "He wants to go for a walk."

"And I want to avoid a lecture." Emma scratched behind Petal's ears. "Eric's so tense the air is practically bouncing off him. I can pretty much imagine what he'd say if I told him I wanted to take the dog for a walk."

"The dog has to pee sometime." Allison glanced at Petal, and added, in a more dire tone, "Or some*where*."

This was absolutely true.

"I'll come with you."

Emma's face remained expressionless. If her first impulse was to avoid a lecture—and, sadly, it was—it was only because she'd refused to think about Chase and his possible reaction to Petal's needs. Chase wasn't tense the way Eric was—but he had a much shorter fuse and a much blacker temper. He had kissed her best friend. He clearly—to anyone whose first name wasn't Allison and whose last name wasn't Simner—loved her. And his love came with a stack of resentment for Emma, whose existence endangered her.

It had endangered them all.

Chase confused Allison. Emma had spent an hour listening to that confusion and the worry it caused; she offered advice only when Ally specifically requested it. Allison never talked romantically about boys; romantic boys were exotic creatures that other people had to deal with. They existed between the covers of books and on various screens. If she daydreamed about them, she kept it secret from even her best friend. Boys seldom gave Allison a second glance.

Confused or not, there were certain things that Allison was never going to willingly accept.

Emma knew that on any other day, in any other place, Allison would have kept her confusion to herself. But sharing it was better than the only other alternatives. She could talk about what had happened when she and Chase had faced off against two Necromancers without immediate backup. She could talk about the fact that she had escaped Toronto without talking to her parents, and her parents were probably frozen with terror. Or she could talk about her younger brother, Toby. Toby, who'd been shot, and now lay hooked up to hospital machinery of various types, in a city they had fled. They had no idea whether or not Toby would survive.

He might already be dead.

Emma and her best friend had grabbed onto Chase as a safe subject. Safe, in this case, was still dicey. Emma looked out the window. Allison's face was pale in reflection.

"If," Allison said, proving that all the work to remain expressionless was pointless, "you're worried about what Chase will say, don't."

Petal liked snow. He liked going for walks. Being outdoors while Emma carried her end of the lead had pulled out his internal puppy. Allison's presence confirmed for the rottweiler that *some* things were still normal.

Emma avoided the ravine in the winter, at least while walking her dog; he therefore bounded from tree to tree, practically dragging his tongue behind him. Given the utter absence of cars or pedestrians, she was tempted to let him off the lead. Instead, she gave it its maximum play.

She looked, as she always did, for her father; he wasn't here.

Neither was Nathan.

Nathan's death had been—until this past week—the worst thing that had ever happened to Emma. Worse—and she thought it with guilt—than her father's death half a lifetime ago. She cut one sharp, cold breath. Her eight-year-old self would never have agreed.

But her seventeen-year-old self had had time and distance. She had had her mother, her friends, school life, and her dog. Life's friction had dulled the edges of that pain until it no longer cut her anytime she returned to it. She could think of her dad now and remember the *good* things. The funny parts. The comforting bits. She could even remember the anger she sometimes felt.

Thinking about Nathan was still too painful.

For a brief couple of weeks, it hadn't been—because he'd been beside her. He'd been dead, yes—but death hadn't been the impersonal, silent wall at which she grieved. He had come back. He'd come back to her.

He'd come back to her at the command of the Queen of the Dead—and he'd left the same way. If he'd been like Longland—dead, but in possession of a body—he'd still be here. He might hear the Queen screaming orders at him in the distance, but he wouldn't have to obey.

"Em?"

Emma forced herself to smile.

Allison's exhale was just this side of a snort. "You know I hate the fake smile."

Emma shrugged. "Sometimes I'm better at making it look like a real one."

She shook her head. "Look at the two of us—we're both having boyfriend trouble."

"Only one of us is having boyfriend trouble," Allison replied. "I don't *have* a boyfriend."

"That's harsh," the non-boyfriend said, as he stepped around the trunk of a not particularly large tree.


## Nathan

Nathan doesn't see the Queen for three days.

He has his own rooms. They are not small, but they're not modern; he's not given a computer or a phone or a television. The rooms seem to have materialized from the pages of a stuffy Victorian novel or a Hollywood set. The bed, in particular. It has *curtains*.

Nathan can't actually tell what color they are, beyond dark. He understands that he is meant to sleep in the bed. His body theoretically requires sleep now. The problem is, Nathan doesn't. There's a disconnect. He lies down anyway. He lies down after changing into what might pass for pajamas. He closes his eyes. It makes no difference. He is not asleep, and he will not sleep. He won't dream.

He won't have nightmares. But if he refuses to lie down, if he refuses to *try*, he weakens. It's not exhaustion, not exactly—but it's what exhaustion would be if he were standing to one side of himself and looking in from the outside. His body requires sleep.

In the silence, though, it's hardest. When he is still, when he is not in constant motion, he can hear the voices of the dead. He thinks of them as his dead, because they're part of him; they surround him with their cold, their lack of life. He hears their muted whispers. They are not angry at him. He's not certain they're aware of him at all; he's not certain they're aware of each other.

The first night, he tries to speak with them. To speak to them. Mostly, he apologizes. He wants them to understand that he didn't ask for this, didn't choose it. That's guilt talking, and if Nathan's not Emma or his mother, it still keeps him going for at least an hour.

No one replies. Or perhaps they do: They cry. They plead. He can't make out most of the words, but he doesn't need them. They could be speaking binary and he'd still understand the meaning.

If he's moving, he can ignore the voices. They're so quiet that it's only in silence that they can be heard at all. But the body itself won't keep moving; it collapses in inconvenient ways, as if it's run a race that he somehow missed.

This is not living.

Maybe if he'd been dead for long enough, it might seem similar. He kind of doubts it—but sometimes the dead notice him, and they stare at him with a blank, silent *envy*. As if they can no longer tell that he's dead.

The living look at him differently. Or maybe he's overthinking because the living can see him now. He's not a mute, invisible spectator. He's a mute, visible one. The Necromancers of the Queen's court don't expect a lot of talk from the dead—even the resurrected. That's what they call Nathan: resurrected.

If they die in service to the Queen, they, too, will be able to escape death.

He doesn't tell them that there is no escape.

Nathan needs to eat. He needs food the way he needs sleep. He gets hungry, but the sensation is faint, and he doesn't, for the first day and a half, identify the fuzzy feeling *as* hunger. Food, however, is delivered to his rooms. The young woman who delivers the food is silent; Nathan thanks her, and she looks straight through him. Given that she *can* see him, he finds this surprising.

But she's dressed in a uniform that would be at home in the same universe the rooms are. And she's followed by a ghost. This shouldn't surprise him. It does, but it shouldn't. The Queen can't keep tabs on the living the way she can on the dead—and the dead, absent bodies, can't perform the menial tasks a living Queen requires. Even if they have bodies, they'd probably be terrible cooks.

So the girl in the uniform is either a Necromancer in training or a regular person who works for the Queen. But a regular person wouldn't be dragging a ghost behind her. The young girl grimaces as Nathan thanks the servant.

He frowns.

The girl sticks her tongue out. "I'm not with her," she tells him.

Nathan almost asks the child if the servant can see her. He doesn't.

"You're not very smart," the child continues. "I'm just keeping an eye on you. For the Queen."

Because he isn't certain that the servant isn't a Necromancer, he doesn't say anything. The dead child leaves with the servant.

He eats. He doesn't taste food. He is aware of the difference between textures, but everything about the experience is bland. He doesn't feel full when he stops. He has no desire to continue.

If he needs food, he probably needs water more. He doesn't feel thirst, but he drinks. He's never liked the taste of alcohol of any stripe—and he's clearly been given wine, judging by the shade of gray in the glass—but in this, being dead is helpful. Wine has no taste, either.

\*      \*      \*

He does bleed. He's apparently gotten used to walking through walls, and that doesn't work so well with a body. Gravity works far better than it did a few days ago, as well. He would have said that no one gets used to being dead, but he would have been wrong.

He doesn't feel attached to his body. He feels it as if it were a straitjacket. He has to learn its rules and its requirements, but they come to him second-hand, through observation and effort. He makes the effort. If the Queen is absent from the throne room, her presence is felt everywhere in the long halls; she casts a shadow the size of the citadel.

He doesn't ask to leave it. He doesn't ask for anything. Learning how to mimic life takes up most of his time. He does learn. He can read; there are books in his rooms. They're old, so he assumes they're musty; his sense of smell is—like everything else—poor. But he can read the words themselves. Reading was never one of his big hobbies. But as he becomes accustomed to the daily routine of life among the living, his fear and uncertainty gives way to boredom.

It is when he's reading that the young girl returns, peering through the door without actually fully entering the room itself. She watches him. He ignores her. It takes a bit of effort; there's something about her that is loud, even in the silence.

"What's it like?" she finally says. Her head, from the neck and shoulders, is now fully in the room. The rest of her is on the other side of the door.

Nathan knows what she's asking. "Same as being dead but less convenient."

The child frowns. "Really?"

Nathan's aware that she could be the equivalent of a hundred years old, by now; her appearance gives no indication of how long she's been dead, given the Queen's preferred style of dress. The dead wear what she wants.

The girl sidles her way into the room and sits. She sits in midair. "That's not how it's supposed to work," she tells him, folding her arms.

"Oh?" Nathan sets the book aside. He's seen Allison do this a hundred times over the years when dealing with Toby, her perpetual annoyance-in-residence. Except that Toby's not in residence anymore.

"You're supposed to be alive again."

"Do I *look* alive to you?"

The girl frowns. ". . . No. But she says you're alive now."

He doesn't ask who. "I don't understand how I can look alive to her—she's the *Queen*. Of the Dead."

The child shrugs. "She's always seen what she wants to see. It used to make our mother *so* angry."

If Nathan weren't already caught in the perpetual chill of the dead, he'd freeze. "Your mother?"

She nods. "It's funny. She *has* our mother's temper, but she *hated* it in our mother. Why are you staring? She's alive—she had to be born *somehow.*"

"You're—you're her sister."

"Yes."

"Her—her baby sister."

"I'm older than you are."

"How are we counting, exactly?"

She snorts. She is the only dead person Nathan's met who doesn't seem terrified of the Queen.

"Why don't you have a body?" he asks, before he can catch the words and reel them back.

"Because Eric's not here."

This makes about as much sense as half of what falls out of the mouths of children who look her age. "Eric can't give you a body."

"No. But she's saving her power. She said. And then she made *you* one. She's made bodies for her knights. Just not *me.*"

"Why?"

"Because she doesn't want to worry about me dying."

This makes about as much sense to Nathan as anything else the Queen has done.

The girl is not impressed. "I'm already dead," she points out.

"Duh."

"So she doesn't have to worry that anything worse will happen. If she resurrects me, someone could kill me."

"And then you'd be dead again. You wouldn't be any farther behind."

"No." The child is quiet for a long moment, and then she says, almost conspiratorially, "But I'd be *away* from her. It would be harder for her to find me."

"It would be easy for her to find you."

"How?"

"How does she find any of the rest of us?"

"She binds *you.*"

"But not you."

"No. *I'm* her sister." Just in case he is stupid, she adds, "*I'm* important to her. She trusts *me.*"

And not any of the rest of the dead. Nathan doesn't bother to put this into words. He tries to find the little girl charming. "She didn't kill you."

"Are you stupid?"

"Sometimes."

The girl snorts. "No. Other people did—but she found them. You're probably walking on some of them," she adds.

"I can't hear them, if I am."

"No. I can't hear them either. But she says she does. She hears them every-where." The girl shrugs. "She hates them, you know."

"And the rest of the dead?"

"What about them?"

"Does she hate them, too?"

"Probably not. It's because of the dead that she can build. The dead give her life. The dead," she adds, "give you life."

"This isn't life." Nathan lifts an arm. Flexes his fingers. Lowers his hand. "It probably only looks like life if you're living."

"So . . . why did she resurrect you?"

"She didn't tell you?"

"No."

"She didn't tell me either. And I'm not her sister. I couldn't ask."

The girl unfolds her legs; she doesn't bother to actually stand on the ground. If what she said is true, Nathan doesn't blame her. "Everyone's afraid of my sister but me."

"You have to admit she's pretty intimidating."

The girl shrugs. She shrugs a lot. She walks around the room as if inspect-ing it. She even puts her hand through Nathan's book. If she weren't dead, she would seem like a normal, bored child. Nathan doesn't believe it, although he tries.

"So," she says. "You have a girl?"

"I thought you said she didn't tell you."

The girl's smile is bright and feckless. "I lied." She reaches out experimen-tally and puts her hand through his right arm, which happens to be closest. He feels a wave of expanding cold at her touch, but it's not centralized.

"I don't have a girl. I don't have anything anymore. I have a cemetery plot. My real body is probably ash."

"Didn't the Queen tell you that love is eternal?"

Nathan is getting tired of the girl. "What about yours?" he counters.

"My what?"

"Your love. Did you never love anyone when you were alive?"

She stills.

"Is your love eternal? Have you found the people you loved? Do you talk to them, spend time with them, comfort them? They should all be dead, right? They should all be here somewhere."

He realizes he should shut up. Her eyes are like glass.

"They're not all here," she says, in a voice that no longer suits her body. For a moment her face ripples. Literally ripples—a reminder, if needed, that the bodies of the dead have an elasticity that the living don't. He looks, briefly, at his hands, and he shudders. "Some of them escaped, before the end. We're not like the rest of you. We're not stupid about death. Even if we have no power or light of our own.

"Some of us took too long to die." Her face has hardened. She looks like every demon spawn in every bad Hollywood horror movie Nathan's ever watched.

He doesn't step back. "You took too long to die."

"I almost didn't die. If I hadn't bled to death, she would have saved me. I would be here in the flesh. If I'd stayed quiet. Stayed hidden. If I'd made no noise. I was younger, then. I was afraid. So they found me.

"By the time she did find me, it was too late. You can see the door, can't you?"

Nathan has whiplash.

"It's closed. It was never closed before my sister."

The words sink in slowly. He knew the truth. Of course he did. But he's never heard it stated this way. "The Queen closed the door."

The girl nods. "She closed it so the dead couldn't leave. And she's never going to open it, either." She folds her arms and waits. Nathan's not sure what she's waiting for. "You're not very smart."

"No. Not usually."

The girl's eyes widen. She laughs. Her laughter is high and thin and as child-like as she looks. "You won't like it here," she says, with a touch of innocent malice. "But I'll like it. You can tell me about love."

Nathan's ambitions—in life *or* death—have never included long discussions about the nature of love with someone who died too young to experience it.

"But not now. I have to go."

"Where?"

"To find Eric."


↬ **Chapter 1**


Allison's face was already red from the cold. She told herself it couldn't get any redder.

Petal headed over to Chase and sniffed around him as if he were a tree. He didn't, however, mark him as if he were one.

"What," he asked, with his friendly, easy smile, "do you think you're doing?"

"Taking the dog for a walk," Allison replied, before Emma could. "Unless you'd like to have him pee in *your* room."

Chase wasn't biting. "He's an old, half-deaf dog. You're thinking he's much protection?"

"I'm thinking we don't need a lot of protection, at the moment. We're in the middle of literal nowhere, and we don't intend to stay."

Emma had been silent throughout. She remained silent, although she pulled the lead in when Petal wandered away from a person who wasn't offering to feed him. Chase didn't add criticism, which was theoretically helpful; he didn't add anything, which was awkward.

"I should head back," Emma predictably said.

Allison would have grabbed her hand if it had been closer. "You're not going back to the house by yourself."

"I'm going back to the cottage with Petal. If Chase is here, you'll be fine."

"It's not—" *me I'm worried about.*

"Ally, I'll be fine. You'll be fine?"

"She will."

"You," Emma said to Chase, "can barely speak without offending half the school. I'd just as soon let Ally speak for herself."

Chase's brows rose, the left one over a distinctly sallow eye. He'd survived two Necromancers—but not easily and not without injury. Allison could forget this when he was snarling at her best friend. Or, to be fair to Chase, at everyone. It was harder to ignore it now.

"I'll be—I'll be fine," she said.

"I'll make hot chocolate."

Chase said nothing. Neither did Allison; Emma felt like a traitor for ignoring her expression, which spoke the volumes she wasn't. But she knew Chase would never hurt Allison. And she knew Allison was, if not openly interested, fascinated by *his* interest. And intimidated by it.

Allison was a person who struggled, always, to live up to her promises. To live up to herself. There was no context for living up to someone else's inexplicable interest in her. Emma had seen Allison be nervous before, but not like this.

People were shallow. Emma herself was willing to admit she spent at least half her waking life—if not more—in the social shallows of the pool, with no regrets. She liked to look at attractive guys. Or she had, before Nathan.

That was as far as she wanted to take this thought. Allison didn't really understand shallows; she treated all of life as if it were the deep end. She jumped in only when she was certain she could swim—and jumping in for a dive when there was only a foot or two of water could be a disaster. But if you were drowning in the deep end, Allison *could* swim. She could lend you the hand you needed to drag yourself out.

"I have something on my face?"

"Too much of a chin, given the way you're sticking it out there," Emma replied. "I know I'm usurping your role here, but—I'll kill you if anything happens to her on your watch."

"Emma . . ."

"Sorry," she told her best friend, without meaning it. "Come on, Petal. I think Michael may have a Milk-Bone or two."

Allison would have followed Emma, but Chase stepped into the footprints her retreat had made. "She shouldn't be out here on her own."

"She's the only one they probably won't kill on sight, and we're in the middle of nowhere. I wouldn't let her go if I thought there was a real danger." He glanced once over his shoulder. "We're less than half a mile from the house; I think she can make it back without getting lost or freezing."

Since Allison was far more likely to get lost—mostly by not paying attention to the outer world—she said nothing. The nothing was painful and awkward, and she knew she should fill it. But she almost resented the fact that Chase looked so comfortable with the silence. He was grinning. At least, it looked as though he was grinning to Allison—but maybe she was seeing things in the dark; when she thought of him, it was that grin she could see.

And she could pretty much see it these days with her eyes closed.

"If we were in a different country," Chase said, relenting, "I could give you a gun and teach you how to use it." As an opener, it was almost what she'd come to expect from Chase, and she found herself relaxing.

"You're sure Emma will be okay?"

"We can follow her—at a distance—if you want. I just wanted to talk to you."

"You didn't much look like you wanted to talk to anyone."

He grinned—this one definitely wasn't her imagination. "I decided not to start a land war in Russia." The grin faded. "I'm trying to remember that Longland saved your life. I hate that he had to do it."

She looked down at her feet. Looked up again. "I'll apologize if you want, but I'm not sorry I didn't run."

"Apparently, neither am I. Angry, maybe. Sorry? No." His hands found his pockets and bunched in them. "I didn't give you the knife and tell you to kill someone with it."

She was silent.

"I didn't give you the knife to tell you to *threaten* to kill someone, either—with your training, that's just handing the knife to someone who'll kill you."

"I know." She exhaled. "I made it to the fence. I could have made it through."

Chase nodded. He took a hand out of a pocket to run it through what remained of his very red hair. "Believe it or not, I didn't come here to lecture you."

"No?"

"No—that part happens automatically. It would have been worse if I hadn't done the perimeter sweep. We're clear," he added. "I did salt the earth a bit here and there."

"Is it going to cause problems in actual cottage season?" Allison asked, cringing.

"I'm not spending the evening worrying about Amy's parents' reaction."

"I was worrying about Amy's reaction."

"Not spending the evening worrying about that either. I'll admit it's more practical, though."

"What are you spending the evening doing?"

He exhaled a plume of mist at a speed that suggested annoyance. Chase's temper didn't faze her. Other things about him did. "Thanking you." This was not what she'd expected—but Chase was never what she expected.

"Thanking me?"

"For the whole sticking around because you thought you could somehow save my life thing."

"Really?"

"No—it was stupid. I'm trying to be gracious. It's hard work, and I'm not seeing a lot of reward-for-effort."

Allison laughed.

His smile deepened, but it shifted. "Thank you for surviving. I mean that one."

"Still looks like you're having to work at it."

He laughed. The line of his shoulders became less rigid, and he looked—for just that moment—younger. Because he did, Allison took courage in her hands and clung to it for dear life. She stopped walking, drew clear, cold air into her lungs, and expelled it. With words.

"Chase—I want to ask you something."

He nodded. He didn't even look wary.

"When we were—when the Necromancers were coming for us and you—when you—" Holding on to courage, on the other hand, meant she let an hour of practice—much of it in front of a mirror—evade her.

"Yes?"

"We were—I was—it was after—"

He laughed again. It was louder.

"You're not being helpful."

"I have a reputation to consider. And given that I'm wearing one of Eric's hideous jackets, I have to work harder at it."

"It's too dark to see the jacket."

"Are you kidding? Look at this collar."

She did. As far as Allison was concerned, it was a thick, black jacket with studs. She didn't know enough about current fashion in any era that wasn't the tail end of the eighteen hundreds to have an opinion one way or the other. But it didn't look ridiculous on Chase—certainly not as ridiculous as it had on either her or Michael.

She slid her hands into her pockets, missing both Emma and Petal. Looking at her feet, which were mostly buried under snow, she tried again. She wasn't always good at finding the right words until long after she needed them—usually when she was on the way home and the opportunity to say them was long past. But she wasn't going home any time soon. "I want to know why you kissed me."

He didn't miss a beat. "I didn't have enough time for anything else."

Eyes widening, she looked up at him.

He laughed. "That's not how you make fists," he told her, reaching for her hands. "You'll only break a finger or two if you actually connect with anything."

"I wasn't trying to—"

"Thumbs on the outside." His hands, gloveless, were pocket-warm. She could feel their heat as he gently but deliberately uncurled her fingers. "And never, ever go into a fight biting your lip." He didn't let go of her hands.

She was aware of the difference in their heights, of the different textures of their skin—his was callused and rough; she was aware of the difference in their clothing, their attitude, and their lives. But mostly, she was aware of just how close he was standing. She wanted to pull her hands back. And she wanted to leave them in Chase's forever—as if she could extend the confusion of the moment, holding it for eternity.

"Do you really have to ask?"

She nodded. Having forced the words out of her mouth—and they were even the right words—she had none left; they were lost to a breathlessness that she would have said wasn't in her.

"Why? Is it really impossible to believe I'd want to kiss you?"

She closed her eyes. "No one else does. Except Petal, and while I love that dog, I could do without the dog-breath and slobber." It was embarrassing to admit this. "Have you actually looked at me?"

"A lot, actually."

"And I have a pretty face?"

"Pardon?"

"That's what they tell you. 'Such a pretty face.' It's like a consolation prize."

"I don't know," he said. She couldn't tell what he was thinking. But he released her hands and raised his to her cheeks, lifting her head gently. He met her eyes; she wasn't certain he was actually looking at anything else. Her eyes, on the other hand, were firmly behind her glasses. "Well, no. I wouldn't say you have a pretty face. But it's the face I want to look at. You understand that I don't care what anyone else thinks of you, right?"

Allison exhaled slowly. "What if I do?"

He grinned; his smile was much closer to her, now. "You're part of that 'anyone else.' I don't care what you think of you, either." His thumbs stroked her cheeks. "Why do you think people obsess about their looks?"

Allison shrugged.

"My guess?" He continued when she failed to answer. "They want to be attractive. They want to stand out."

Allison nodded, because that made sense. She was having difficulty, at the moment, making sense of anything.

"So, looks exist to grab the wandering attention. But once you've got it, what then?"

She really hadn't thought that far, because the first part of the equation had always been beyond her. "Chase—"

"Then it's all down to you. Who you are. What you want. What you demand. What you give."

"But it's not."

"Oh?"

"It's not just about the mythical 'you'—it's about what your friends will think. It's about what other people think of you for having an ugly girlfriend."

His hands froze. "What did you say?" His voice changed. It had become softer and much, much quieter. It was also more intimidating.

"It's about what other people think of you for having an ugly girlfriend."

He shook his head in exaggerated mock sorrow. "And there's that word again."

She closed her eyes. "Chase—I see myself fairly clearly. I don't lie to myself except in daydreams."

"We'll talk about daydreams in a minute," he replied. "Right now, we're talking about me."

She opened her eyes.

"I've been a student in your school. I hate it. I think it's a waste of time. I feel like I'm surrounded by idiot children who think they're almost-adults. Some of them think they're tough. It's not worth the time to set them straight. You expect me to care what they think of me?"

She couldn't shake her head, because Chase was still bracketing her face with his hands.

"Right. No. Who else does that leave? Let me tell you: It leaves only you. Other people are allowed to be idiots. I don't like it; Eric says I can't school them. Fine. But you? No. You don't get to be that stupid. Not when you're around me. So: You never, ever get to use the world 'ugly' again."

"She can if she's describing you."

Chase cursed. He didn't lower his hands. He did lift his head. "If she uses it at all, she'll use it the wrong way. It's why I didn't make exceptions, even for you. What do you want, Eric?"

"The old man wants a report on your portion of the perimeter sweep. He'd probably like it sometime tonight."

Allison could hear Eric's voice; she couldn't hear his footsteps. There was too much noise on the inside of her head. That and embarrassment. She pulled away from Chase, and he let her go.

"And Emma's probably worried about Allison, judging by her expression."

"If she were worried, she wouldn't have left her."

"Not that kind of worry, idiot. We might have a problem."

Everything about Chase changed at Eric's tone. Allison started to turn toward the cottage. Chase caught her shoulders. "We're only finished with this for now," he said, voice low.

Given Amy's suggestion that everyone get some sleep, Allison was surprised to see the fire in the fireplace to one side of the entrance hall. Michael and Emma sat side by side in exactly the wrong type of silence. Allison's glasses had become opaque enough that she couldn't make out their expressions.

Hot chocolate was, in fact, in cups on a tray on a low table beside Michael; he had a mug in his right hand and a lapful of mournful, sighing rottweiler. Petal and Emma looked up when Allison entered the room; Michael didn't. Firelight added color to his face and his almost vacant stare.

Allison sat beside him.

Michael, staring into the fire, said, "Emma's dad came."

Allison froze. After a long, silent moment, she rose and moved so she could stretch her hands out in front of the fire; she was cold. She was so cold.

"Toby is alive. Mr. Hall said he hasn't woken up yet. Your parents are at the hospital. So are the police." He spoke the words carefully, as if from a list. It probably was. Michael was not generally the person sent to convey important emotional information. Allison wasn't surprised when Michael started to cry. The tears were like an afterthought on his face; they didn't change his expression.

Emma slid an arm around his shoulder. "Thank you, Michael."

"I want to be able to help," he continued, still staring at the burning logs. "But there's nothing I can do."

"That more or less describes me," Allison told him. "I don't know how to fight. I don't know how to defend myself against people who do. I don't know how to stop the Queen of the Dead, and most of the people who might know are dead. Only Emma can see them.

"Do you want to go home?"

Michael shook his head. "I want to be *at* home. But I'm worried about Emma." He paused, and then added, "I'm worried about you."

It was never helpful to lie to Michael. "I'm not worried about me," she replied. "I'm terrified for Toby." Looking up at the ceiling, she added, "If I get him back, I will never, ever threaten to strangle him again."

Michael said, "Yes. You will."

She laughed. It hurt. "Yes, you're right. I probably will."

"But he knows you don't mean it." He paused. "Amy had an argument with her dad. On the phone."

"Her dad is a far braver man than I am. What about?"

"I only heard Amy's part. She's angry because her father doesn't trust her. But," he added, frowning, his face falling into more familiar lines of confusion, "she doesn't trust him enough to tell him the truth, either."

"She trusts him to be himself. But there's no way he's going to think that Amy is better prepared, more knowledgeable, or more competent than he is. It's just the way parents are. Except your mom," she added quickly.

Petal whined and looked hopeful. Allison took a deep, deep breath and held it, trying not to think about her baby brother. The last time she'd seen him—at dinner—she'd threatened to upend her plate over his head. He'd laughed. She wanted to ask where he'd been shot. She wanted to know what his injuries were. But her mouth was too dry, and she couldn't find the words for it.

Emma's eyes were red.

Allison found space on the couch between the arm and Emma and put an arm around her best friend's shoulder. She didn't tell her that everything was okay; it wasn't. They both knew it. She didn't tell her that things would *be* okay, because at this exact moment, she couldn't see how that would ever happen again.

She settled for a silence that contained them both: the arm across Emma's shoulder a bridge, a connection that said, *I'm here.* Or, in this case, *we're in this together.*

Amy joined them. Amy never looked frightened or uncertain; when she was upset, she looked angry. She was clearly upset now. "I swear, I am going to disown my father."

"He called you again?" Emma asked, voice strained.

Amy's lip curled. "I called him. Don't ask." She exhaled. "He threatened to call the police to drag us all home."

"Wow, he really *is* worried. He's going to being paying for that for—"

"The rest of his natural life," was Amy's furious response.

"You think he'll do it?"

"I wouldn't bet against it yet. He's—"

"Angry?"

"Enraged."

"At *you*?"

Amy snorted. "No—I'm just collateral damage. He doesn't understand the situation, and I can't explain it. This is not improving his mood any." She glared at the phone in her hand.

"He knows what happened to my brother?" Allison asked.

"I doubt it. I certainly didn't tell him."

"He's not a complete idiot. Do you think Skip talked?"

Amy's teeth snapped shut as the glare she was aiming at her phone sharpened. "I will *kill* him."

"If he did?"

"No," Amy snapped at Michael. "Just on general principle."

All in all, it was better to have Amy's restless anger aimed at someone who was in a different city. Amy was a lot like her father in that way. Allison had always envied her lack of fear and her ferocious self-confidence. Nothing that had happened in the past month had changed that. Her envy for Skip, however, had taken a nosedive and didn't look to be coming back, ever.

Emma stiffened beneath Allison's arm. Emma, always much more socially adept, could feign both delight and ease when she felt neither, and her expression, while a little more alert, gave nothing away. But her shoulders were tense, her neck, stiffer.

"Ally," she said.

They all turned to face her.

"Get Chase and Eric."

"Ernest, too?"

She nodded.

Michael was the only person present who asked, "Why?"

"I think—I think we're going to have visitors."

## ↜ Chapter 2

Allison left the living room before Emma had finished answering Michael's hushed question.

"Is Longland necessary as well?" Amy asked.

"If he's not part of this? Yes. But—I'm not certain he's not." Emma didn't look at Amy as she spoke. "So wait until Chase gets here and take him with you if you're going to find him." Amy didn't reply; that didn't bother Emma. Amy pretty much did what she felt was the right thing to do in any given situation, and anyone else's opinion was—unless asked for—superfluous.

"Emma?" Michael said, his voice closer than Amy's. "What are you looking at?"

"A dead child," she replied.

The child was between the ages of eight and ten, to Emma's eye; it was hard to tell because her expression was at odds with her age: It felt cold and ancient. Framed by dark hair that trailed down the side of her face in ringlets—with ribbons, no less—her skin was pale; she wore clothing that would have looked at home on the set of a period piece in which the director was not concerned with accuracy.

She should have looked cute. She didn't. Her smile—and she did smile—was slow to come, and when it did, it hardened an expression that hadn't been youthful to begin with.

"There really isn't much point in calling everyone to you," she told Emma. "They'll just die more quickly. But Eric *is* here, isn't he?" She paused and looked around the room, her snub nose wrinkling in disdain. It was the first expression that somehow matched her apparent age.

"Emma?" Michael asked.

Emma knew she could make ghosts visible by touching them. She *so* did not want to touch this one. She opened her mouth to say as much.

"Your companion's not a Necromancer," the girl said. There was a hint of question in the words, none of it friendly.

"No."

"And the loud girl?"

"No."

"The fat one?"

Emma folded her arms and stood. For a moment, she felt as if she were eight years old again, the desire to say, *you take that back right now* was so visceral.

"Do they serve you?"

"They're my friends."

The child snorted, and this sound also aligned with her apparent age. "You're a Necromancer. You don't *have* any friends." But she frowned for a moment, her forehead creasing. "You *are* a Necromancer, right?"

"That's not what I call myself, no."

"She is," Margaret Henney said.

Emma turned. So did Michael. Petal was too busy starving-to-death to do more than lift his head.

The girl's eyes widened. "Margaret."

"Helmi," Margaret replied. She turned to Emma. "We need to move, Emma. We need to move quickly."

"It won't help," Helmi said, staring first at Margaret and then—to Emma's surprise—at Michael. "They'll be here soon." She sauntered over to the fireplace and then turned to look at Michael again, her brow creased in faint confusion.

"What have you done?" Margaret demanded, in her most intimidating angry school teacher voice. Clearly, that voice was only effective on people who had lives to lose.

"The Queen ordered me to find Eric," she replied. "If I were you, I'd run. She won't be happy to see you."

"She's coming in person?" Margaret's voice was a bare whisper.

"Who knows? She told me to find him. I found him."

Michael rose as well. "Margaret, what should we do?"

"Gather anything you absolutely need right now. We may not have time to come back for it."

"Tell him to wait," Helmi demanded.

Neither Margaret nor Emma appeared to have heard her.

"Tell him to wait," the girl said again, "and maybe I'll help you."

"Michael. Wait," Emma said.

"Emma, dear, we really don't have time for this. I've spoken to Ernest, but if Helmi is here, the Queen—or her knights—will follow. We need to be away before they arrive."

Michael froze in the doorway. He turned back, his eyes darting between Emma and Margaret. Helmi's forehead creased; she looked at Michael and watched as he stood, indecisive, in the door.

"Ask him," Helmi told Emma, in the same imperious tone. "Ask him why he can see Margaret but not me."

"I can answer that," Emma said. "And I will. But let Michael go and get his stuff. Sorry, Michael."

Michael shot through the door and bounded up the stairs. He didn't weigh much, but he had never had a light step; he sounded like panicked thunder.

"Margaret can make herself visible to the living if she wants."

Helmi's small hands found her hips and rested there, in fists. She clearly did not believe a word Emma was saying. Emma would have found this annoying in other circumstances—no one liked being called a liar, even silently—but the air was getting colder by the second.

"And how exactly can she do that?" The child's voice dripped condescension.

"Emma is not precisely accurate. I can't," Margaret said, surrendering. The look she sent in Emma's direction, though brief, was pointed. She did not approve of any conversation with this particular dead person. "Not on my own."

Helmi turned to Emma, then. "She's yours?"

Emma said, "No."

But Margaret said, "Yes."

"Which one is it?" Helmi's fists tightened.

"I am not bound to Emma the way the dead are bound to Necromancers," Margaret said. "But I serve her while I have any choice or any say in the matter."

"*Why?*" The mask was off the child's face; the anger, the pain, the sense of betrayal were entirely exposed. It made her look younger. It made her look, for a moment, the age she had been when she died.

"Look at her," Margaret said.

"I *am.*"

"What do you see, Helmi?"

"You know what I see. It's what *you* see."

"No," was Margaret's surprisingly gentle reply. "It's not. Emma is not using my power. I am indirectly using hers."

The words made some sort of sense to the Queen's younger sister; they appeared to make more sense to her than they had made—and did make—to Emma.

"There is no point demanding explanations from Emma—she doesn't have them."

"She—she's giving *you* power?"

"Yes. She broke the binding that held me to Longland. She didn't realize what she was doing, at the time. Nor did I. But I understood it afterward, in a way that Emma cannot. I am dead. She is alive."

"Is this true?" Helmi asked. She asked it of Emma; her voice had dropped until it was almost a whisper. Her hands were bunched in her skirts, as if anchored there.

Once again, it was Margaret who answered. "I don't like to do it—but the choice is mine. If I leave, she can't force me to return if I have no desire to do so. If I choose to remain unseen by the living, she does not force me to appear. I am here because . . ." Her voice trailed off.

Helmi's glare had slackened, her narrowed eyes losing the sharp points of their edges as they shifted position. "Can they—can they touch you?"

Margaret shook her head. "What Emma gives is not what the Queen of the Dead gives. She cannot make me more than I am; she gives me the ability to be *all* that I am."

"How?"

"Helmi—"

"Tell me *how*," she said, voice low enough it sounded like an adult voice. Margaret appeared to be thinking; Helmi was not patient.

As Michael came thundering down the steps, Helmi turned to Emma. "Is it true," she asked, in the same low, intense voice, "that you opened the door?"

Emma saw some of Longland in this dead child. "Yes."

"How?"

Emma glanced at Margaret. Margaret did not come to her rescue. "I'm sorry," she said, the intense irritation at the girl's attitude evaporating, "but I don't know. The dead came to me, and they gave me permission to use their power to open the door. I needed all of it. I could only barely move the door, and it took pretty much everything they had."

"And that's enough of that," Eric said. He had entered the room; Allison was behind him.

Helmi turned to face him. If Emma expected triumph or sneering, Helmi ran counter to expectation. "Do you know what she did?" She was, on the other hand, still demanding.

"Yes. And I know she won't survive to do it again if they find her."

"Tell me."

"We don't have *time*, Helmi. If you've told her—or her knights—where we are, we need to move."

"If you don't answer, I'll just follow you until I know where you're going and tell her the new location. I don't *have* to tell her anything if I don't want to. You should know that well enough by now. If I told her everything, you'd never have escaped in the first place." She folded her arms.

Emma turned to Eric. "You recognize her?"

He didn't answer the question. To Emma, he said, "Allison and Amy are ready. It's just you and Petal."

"Is it true? Can she follow us and return to tell the Queen where we are?"

"Not as easily—"

"Yes," Helmi said. "It used to be harder. I've had practice. I've had nothing but practice." The words were laced with bitterness and resentment.

To Emma, Eric said, "Yes, she can follow us. She can leave for the City of the Dead and return almost instantly to the location she left from. But it is not trivial for the dead to navigate among the living; there are memories of streets and roads and fields and ancient homesteads that seem just as real to the dead as the streets you walk every day to get to school do to you. If there were a Necromancer here, he could build a kind of circuit that would serve as a beacon to her, but there isn't one."

"Longland is here," Helmi replied.

"Longland," Eric snapped back, "is dead. The dead—no matter what they were in life—can't *be* Necromancers. He might look alive to you, but he's just as dead as we are."

"But the Queen says—"

"The Queen has said many, *many*, things. You never used to believe most of them. Why have you started now?"

Emma understood why. It was always easy to believe the things you wanted to believe, because they gave you hope.

Helmi started to shout back, but no words come out. After a brittle and unexpected pause, she said, "So, Nathan was right."

"What did you say?" Emma found herself across the room and in arm's reach of the child before she could think about moving.

This did not terrify the child. "So you do know Nathan."

"I know Nathan."

The intake of breath in the room—and just outside of it—was sharp enough to cut. Of course it was. Only Emma—and the rest of the dead—could hear Nathan's name until Emma spoke it.

"Nathan is in the citadel. But don't worry—you'll be there soon."

"Emma," Eric said. He might have said more, but Amy appeared with Chase and Longland; Ernest was nowhere in sight. Amy was dressed for winter: coat, boots, scarf; her gloves were in her hands, her earmuffs looped over her right arm. "We have to leave. We have to leave *now*."

Longland's curt, sharp curse could be heard over Eric's steadier voice.

"Merrick Longland," the girl said, turning only her head toward him.

"Lady Helmi," he replied. He astonished everyone in the room by bowing. Even Emma. Only Helmi seemed to expect this as her due.

"Why are you here?" she asked.

"I was captured in a failed attempt to assassinate the red-haired boy and his companion." He spoke smoothly and without inflection, separating himself from Amy. Chase stood between Longland and everyone else, knives in hand. He was angry.

"You haven't escaped."

"I haven't had time, Lady. We have only just arrived. And I did not think that escape in this empty wasteland would be helpful to our cause. I have no transport. I was not allowed to return to my dwelling; I have no mirror and no easy method of communication. But I am the Queen's, and bound to her; I trusted she would find me."

Helmi snorted. "She hasn't. Well, not yet."

"May I ask why you are here, Lady?"

"She sent me. She *asked* me to come."

"To what end?"

"To find Eric. She knows where I am now, and her knights are coming."

Allison caught Chase by the elbow and held on with white-knuckled hands. Chase didn't take his eyes off Longland, so he couldn't see Ally's expression. But he didn't stab Longland or slit his throat. Emma wasn't certain how she felt about that, either.

"Ernest has the car ready," Margaret said.

"Michael, Ally, Amy," Emma said. "Go."

"I've got my car running," Amy added. "But I think we're *all* supposed to leave that way. Now," she added.

Helmi stared at all of them.

"I assume Margaret can follow on her own."

"And Longland?"

"Leave him here," Amy said.

"No." Everyone looked to Emma, who added, "Michael, can you grab Petal, too?"

"Em, if the Queen can track Longland—"

"But she didn't. She tracked Helmi."

"Who?"

"The dead child."

"Fine. We *all* leave," Amy said, folding her arms. "Don't even think of staying behind."

The hall was a flurry of coats and boots and too many people in too small a space.

"The road isn't safe," Helmi said, watching them all. She seemed almost

surprised at the words that had escaped her small mouth, but she didn't withdraw them; she stared at Emma.

Everyone who could hear her stopped moving. Everyone who couldn't noticed the lack of motion. Amy, who *was* worried, compressed her lips. "Emma."

Emma then turned to Helmi. Swallowing because her throat was dry in a
way that couldn't be blamed on cold winter air alone, Emma held out her left
hand. Helmi stared at it as if it were a dead fish. But she also stared at it as if
she were starving, and the fish wasn't dead enough to be poisonous. She
reached out and placed her right hand in Emma's left. Emma felt instant, searing cold. It was far, far worse than touching Mark had been.

But Helmi's eyes—Helmi's dead, oddly colorless eyes—widened and
blazed with light. For a brief instant, her eyes looked almost brown, almost
living. Ribbons fell out of her hair, and ringlets fell with them; the hair itself
straightened into a fine, waving fall around her shoulders and back.

She looked up. The dead didn't cry; Helmi's eyes seemed filmed with tears
she couldn't, therefore, shed. "It hurts," she whispered.

Emma's brows folded together; she tried to withdraw her hand, but the girl
tightened her hold on it. "I'm sorry—it's never hurt anyone else—"

Helmi shook her head. Her clothing went the way of her hair, falling into
something simpler and baggier, the sleeves too long and rolled up at the wrists.
Her feet were bare. Her eyes were bruised.

"Helmi," Margaret said, voice sharp.

Emma shook her head. "Let her be, Margaret."

"Helmi is older than any of the dead you have ever met," Margaret countered, once again using the angry teacher voice. "She has perfect control of her
appearance; she can take on the face and the features she chooses, down to the
last detail. It is not *necessary* that she show you—"

"Please. Let it go."

Blood trickled from the corner of Helmi's lips; those lips had swollen. The
whole of the left side of her face had become bruised; the blood that fell from
her mouth began to almost pour. None of it touched Emma; none of it reached
the floor. Emma looked.

Looked, and stopped. She was staring at a livid, gaping wound in the
child's chest. No, not one—three. She dragged her gaze away and was not
surprised to see a fourth wound, across the child's throat.

"*Helmi.*"

Emma was not afraid for anyone in the room but Michael, oddly enough.
Michael and Allison. They could see Helmi, because she held Helmi's hand.
What she had, by holding that hand, agreed to bear witness to, they might also
witness. Helmi was not kind.

"This is how you died," Emma told the dead girl. Her voice was steady, because Helmi *was* already dead. Knowing how she'd died might make Emma ill—but it changed precisely nothing. Helmi had been killed. Had Helmi died of—of scarlet fever instead, she would still be dead.

Still trapped here, where all memory seemed, at the moment, to be pain.

"Em," Ally said. "What are you talking about?"

Emma started. Blinked. Helmi once again looked like an eight-year-old child. Her hair was long and wavy, her dress, simple. But the blood and the bruising were gone. "You didn't—you didn't see her—"

"We can see her fine," Amy said.

For one long moment, Emma felt the edge of an absurd gratitude: Helmi had, at least, spared her friends. They weren't Necromancers. It wasn't their job to see the dead. *And is it mine?* She wondered. She set that aside. "Thank you," she told the dead child. "These are my friends. And this," she added, looking at the living, "is Helmi."

Helmi's frown softened, although it still hugged most of her mouth.

"I died."

"I know. And now I know how. Why were you killed?"

"Because my mother told me to hide, and I hid, but I could hear the screams and the shouting, and everything took too long," Helmi said. "So I came out of hiding too early. They thought we were witches. Or demons. Or something."

"You weren't."

"No. My mother was always afraid that that's exactly how we would die. It wasn't the first time it had happened to our people; it wasn't the last. Can you understand what that's like?"

Emma was silent for one long beat. "No, not really. No one has murdered my parents. I have no siblings—but my father died when I was eight, and my mother has never remarried. I have friends. Some of them are with me. No one was hunting them, either."

Amy said, "My great-grandfather almost died. Because he was Jewish. But—I'm like Emma. I've *personally* had a safe life. Both of my parents are still alive. I have a stupid older brother. The only person who's ever threatened him is me."

Helmi looked up, but this time, her gaze passed over Emma's right shoulder. In theory she was looking at the upper corner of the large room; in fact, she was looking at a very closed window. Or door. Emma knew.

"How did Nathan die?"

It had not been long enough that the question didn't cut. Given everything else that had happened since his death, Emma thought it should have been. But maybe there was no *long enough* at the end of which Emma Hall could calmly and objectively contemplate Nathan's death and what it meant for the rest of her life.

"He was in a car accident. He was hit by a drunk driver."

Helmi waited.

"I didn't tell him to hide." Helmi's dead eyes were almost alive as they once again returned to Emma's face. "You can't hide from life. He was in his car. He was on his way to meet me."

"What did you do to the driver?"

Emma blinked.

"Is the driver still alive?"

"Yes, the driver survived. He can't walk properly."

"Why did you leave him alive?"

"Kid," Amy said, "you're creeping the rest of us out."

Helmi's eyes didn't even flicker in Amy's direction.

Emma exhaled slowly. In her darkest dreams, the driver had not survived. He had groveled. He had begged for both forgiveness and mercy. His pleas had hit the wall of Emma's endless grief and rage. She shook her head, mute, and struggled to find her voice. "The reason," she said slowly, "that it's called an accident is because it wasn't deliberate. Your wounds—your death—were no accident."

"Do you think the men who killed me deserved to die?"

"Yes."

"Even if you *know* what waits for them at the end of their life?"

Silence. Profound and utter silence. Emma felt as if she had run a marathon.

Helmi turned then. She faced Longland, who was white and stiff; to Emma's eyes, he looked almost corpselike in the stillness. "You killed people. Deliberately. Does Emma know how many?"

Longland didn't answer. But his fingers curled until both of his hands were fists. He was, Emma thought, afraid. He was afraid of every word that was now leaving Helmi's little mouth.

"I don't need to know how many," Emma said. "I have no doubt at all that while alive, he was a murderer."

"And now that he's dead, it doesn't matter?" she folded her arms. The look she gave Longland was withering.

Longland waited, in silence, and the silence was cold. Did it not matter? Honestly? Toby was fighting *for his life* in the hospital because Longland, the substitute teacher, had had access to all of the student records—and therefore, their home addresses. If Toby died, his death could be laid in part at Longland's feet. Had she forgotten that?

"Does he deserve peace, Emma Hall?"

She looked at Longland, at his hands, bunched in fists, at the expression that was taking hold of the rest of his face. He knew her answer. He knew the only answer anyone reasonable had to offer. He had threatened to kill *Allison*. He had threatened the life of an *infant*. Without the unexpected intervention of a four-year-old boy, Emma was certain that he would have killed them both.

And Chase. Michael. Amy and her brother. Eric. Ernest would have survived, because he wasn't stupid enough to come out of hiding unless there was *some* chance. Emma would have survived—possibly—because she was a Necromancer, and Necromancers were the only people the Queen acknowledged *as* people.

She glanced at Allison, mute now, as the reality of Longland's actions once again took root. It was Ally who would suffer.

Who was already suffering.

This wasn't a decision that Emma could make on her own. She almost asked Ally for input or opinion. And Allison was not her best friend for nothing.

"You've already answered the question," Ally said quietly. "If you want *my* opinion, you already know it."

Emma felt her shoulders tighten.

"But I'm not God. If my brother—if Toby—" She faltered. She couldn't say the verb. Emma would never have demanded it. "I will hate Longland for the rest of my life."

"And you'll want him to suffer," Helmi said.

"Yes, I'll want him to suffer—but I'll want him to suffer what *I* suffer, and he *can't*. I don't think he's ever loved anyone. I don't think he's ever been responsible for anyone *else*. Maybe I could make him feel pain. Maybe. But *not* the pain I'll feel."

"But he'll feel pain forever if he can't leave," Helmi pointed out. "Maybe it's not the same pain. But it's as close as you'll get."

Allison's jaw hung slightly open for another long pause. Emma thought Eric was about to speak; Chase certainly wasn't, although he was staring at Emma's best friend, as if something about his own life hung on her answer. And maybe it did.

"It's not up to me." Ally punted. But then, because she was Ally, she added, "And maybe that's *why* it's not up to me—or to any of us. We shouldn't judge—and we always do. What I know is this: Longland won't be the only person suffering. My grandfather died. He's trapped here, just as Longland is. And my grandfather was not a murderer or worse."

Helmi frowned. "It doesn't matter what you think, anyway. You're not a Necromancer. Emma, what do you think men like Longland deserve? What do the people who murdered me deserve?"

*          *          *

Helmi waited. Emma understood that to Helmi, the response was critical, and Emma had never liked making instant, enormously important decisions—not when she *knew* beforehand what their weight was.

"Sometimes," she finally said, "We get what we don't deserve. And that cuts both ways."

"Pardon?"

"I can't—I literally can't—judge Merrick Longland. I didn't live his life. I wouldn't, from what little I know of it, *want* to live his life. And Helmi? He saved my best friend's life. If he hadn't been there, Allison would be dead."

This didn't seem to mean much to the dead child. The angry dead child. "He was powerful."

Emma nodded.

"And respected."

"Not by me."

Helmi said, "So that's your answer?"

"It's *my* answer, yes. Ask someone else in the room, and you might get a different one. I can't answer *for* people. I can't answer for—for society. I didn't demand an—an exit interview—when I asked the dead gathered nearest the door for their help—and their power—in prying it *open*. I didn't ask if they were murderers. I didn't ask if they were monsters. I didn't deem them worthy or unworthy. I knew—and they knew—that if I succeeded, they would finally go to the place they've been looking at since they became aware of their deaths.

"I needed to open that door, and they needed to leave." She exhaled. "Look, Helmi—if, to reach the land of peace and love and belonging, we have to be worthy, I'm not sure *any* of us would ever be allowed through that door."

Helmi said nothing. It wasn't enough.

Emma tried again. "What Longland deserves—no, let me try that again. What I think he deserves doesn't matter. Maybe, if he had lived in a world where there was no hatred and no fear and no pain, he wouldn't even *be* the Longland we both know. What I know is that Merrick Longland will never cause that kind of pain again—if he leaves.

"Right now, he *could*, because he has a body again, thanks to his Queen. But it's no longer what he wants. He wants what the dead want."

"Em," Ally said, "I think Ernest is going to die of apoplexy any second now."

"If Ernest doesn't, *I* will," Amy added. "And I'm not going alone."

Emma apologized. Sort of. "I have one question for you, Helmi."

"I don't have to answer it."

"No. I can't force you. But it's the same question. Does he deserve peace?"

"You already said he doesn't."

"I said I don't think he does—but I also said it's irrelevant."

Helmi nodded.

"Would you keep the door closed so that he would never, ever know the peace he doesn't deserve?"

Helmi didn't answer.

But Emma, continuing in that vein, said, "Is this part of the reason the Queen won't let any of the dead leave?"

## ᗡ Chapter 3

"They killed us," Helmi said, after a pause in which the air in the room dropped in temperature. "They killed everyone she had ever loved."

"You've already said that."

Helmi's brows rose.

Chase, who had been rigidly silent, said, "Your sister killed everyone I loved. She killed them *in front of me*. She *made me watch*. She even killed our dog."

"What had you done to her?"

"Nothing. I knew nothing—at all—about Necromancers or the Queen of the Dead until that day. Nothing. I have no idea if our ancestors somehow crossed paths with her—she didn't say. I asked. I asked *why*. I asked what we'd *done*. Do you know what she said?" His voice was low.

Helmi looked down at her hands. No, at her hand; at the hand that held Emma's. The dead didn't cry. Helmi was not, therefore, crying. But it seemed to Emma that she would. And she was eight.

"Chase—"

Helmi lifted her free hand and reached up to cover Emma's mouth. She shook her head; her hair was a spill down her back, her expression ancient. "I understood why she killed the villagers. She killed Eric's father. She killed Paul—and he was already sickened by everything the adults were doing. He didn't *want* to be there. He couldn't—" She shook her head. "I understood. I even understood why—in the moment—she slammed the door shut. She didn't want the rest of us to desert her—and she knew we would. We were dead.

"She was never very strong. She was just powerful."

Helmi looked at Chase.

Chase didn't blink. His knuckles were white; his eyes were narrow, his lips as pale as the rest of his skin. "She'd kill everyone Emma has ever loved, given half a chance—at this point, she'll probably kill Emma. If Longland doesn't deserve to pass on, your sister deserves a permanent hell of her own."

Helmi said, quietly, "Is that not where she's already living?"

And Emma understood all of the questions, then. All of them. "You love your sister."

"Yes. And I hate what she's made of herself. I *can* judge her. But it's not in my hands, and it never was."

"She's in pain."

"She's nothing *but* pain. She can't let go of it because it defines her. Without it, what does she have?"

"What do you want, Helmi?"

"I'm dead," Helmi replied.

"No kidding," Amy said. Her arms were folded tightly, her expression about as friendly as Chase's. Then again, Amy's father had been shot, as well.

"Helmi, it is time to let go of Emma's hand."

For the first time that evening, Helmi hesitated in the way Emma associated with the young. "It's warm," she said to Margaret.

"It is not warm for *Emma*," Margaret replied, radiating chilly disapproval.

"No?" Helmi looked up at Emma.

"It's—it's okay," Emma heard herself say. And then, because Michael was there, "The dead are a bit cold to touch, so I can't do it forever. You just said that the roads aren't safe?" Helmi was staring at their hands. Her gaze traveled up Emma's arm to her face and then shied away, for reasons that weren't clear to Emma. "The roads aren't safe. That's probably where the gate will open."

For one long moment, no one spoke. They had gathered their belongings in haste; they had every intention of piling into the two cars and gunning for a different destination.

"Why the road?" Amy demanded. She was the first to speak, which wasn't surprising.

"Because people who are trying to escape will probably drive." Helmi's expression shifted. "I've never driven. I've seen cars. I'm not sure you'll be able to escape by car; they'll be waiting for you. The gate is being conjured on the road near this house."

"By Necromancers."

"By the Queen's knights, yes."

"You told them where we are?" Longland demanded; his voice was both deeper and harsher than Amy's, his fear more palpable.

"I was sent to find Eric. They know that Eric is here."

"And Emma?" He said. "Did you tell them that Emma is here?"

"I didn't know her name." Helmi continued to stare at Emma, at the hand that momentarily bound them. "My sister knows that Eric isn't alone. I told her that there were hunters here."

Longland cursed.

"Well, there *are*. I wasn't lying. And I'm not lying about the road, either. They'll start at the road."

No one liked their chances of escaping on foot, either. A ripple went through the gathering as everyone silently considered their options. In the city, escaping on foot opened a range of other options. There were subways, yards, friendly houses or buildings, shopping malls or strips. Here, there was a lot of snow. The neighbors weren't close—and no one suggested neighbors. Well, no one but Chase, who asked.

"The cottages here are mostly winterized," Amy had replied. "I have no idea if people will be in them or not at this time of year. Probably not, given it's not a weekend—but if they are . . ." she let the words trail off. Everyone heard the "people will die" anyway.

"I'll tell Ernest." Margaret vanished to do just that.

Chase leaned against the nearest wall and cursed. His attention was divided between Helmi and Longland. Longland and Helmi, however, were now regarding each other with disdain, dislike, suspicion.

"Why are you telling them this?" he demanded.

Helmi's hand tightened again; Emma returned the grip while she could still feel hers, as Helmi turned her back on Longland. This did not please the former Necromancer. "You want to see Nathan, right?"

"Yes."

"He's in the citadel."

"I don't know what—or where—that is."

"It's the Queen's home in the City of the Dead."

"You cannot trust—" Longland began.

"And she can trust *you*?" Helmi snapped. "'But I am the Queen's, bound to her; I trusted she would find me.'" Her mimicry was savage and exact.

Longland was not impressed. The demeanor of respect—of obsequiousness—vanished as he looked down a very fine nose at a much younger girl. "Emma opened the door. She opened the way. Some of the dead are free and forever beyond the Queen's reach for the first time in their existence. She didn't do it for power. She didn't do it for status. I *do not* understand why she did it—and I don't care."

"You *have* a body," Helmi continued. "I have *nothing*."

"*You* have freedom—which is more than any of the rest of the dead have in the City. You can come and go as you please. You are the only person the Queen can command who has any choice in the matter."

"Yes. But you have *something*. If you're telling Emma that she can trust *you* because of what she did, why are you telling her she can't trust *me*? I've been dead longer than any of you." Her hand tightened. Emma did her best not to wince.

"Because you're the Queen's *sister*!"

"And I'm *still* dead. I'm *still* trapped here. I might be one of her family. She might profess to love me. But in the end, I suffer the same fate as the people she hated."

"You don't. You've never served as a source of power. You've never been forced to take the form or shape of furniture; you've never been a pillar or fuel to open a portal."

"She doesn't hate most of the people who have been used that way either. You served her, Longland. You obeyed her commands. You killed when she ordered it."

"You—" Longland's face flushed. "You did her bidding. You spied on *us*."

"Yes. She found you. She rescued you from the fate she suffered. And you would have happily killed her to take her place."

"Do you think Emma will *not*?"

"Emma will not take her place."

"Emma will kill her. She has no other choice."

Emma cleared her throat.

Longland and Helmi turned toward her.

"Well?" Helmi demanded. "Are you going to kill her?" She settled one fist on her hip, looking like a miniature Amy. She almost pulled her other hand free—but to do it, she would have had to let go of Emma. Her eyes narrowed. "You haven't even thought about it."

Had she?

No. Not really. She glanced at Chase, saw a flicker of contempt, and saw Allison turn toward him before he could open his mouth. Had she really thought that they could somehow neutralize the Queen of the Dead in a way that didn't kill her?

Or had she just assumed that somehow Chase would do it? Or Eric? Or Ernest? Someone who *had* killed Necromancers in the past? Had she assumed she could somehow leave it in Longland's hands?

"There is no way," Longland said, in a far less heated voice, "that you will escape this if the Queen of the Dead is still alive."

"Did you want to kill her just to—"

"I never wanted to kill her," he replied, before she could even finish her sentence. "She was the only one who saw potential in me. The only person, ever. She taught me everything I know. She gave me power I had never had; she gave me a home and food and an education."

"Why did the other Necromancers want to kill her, then? Didn't she give them the same thing?"

"Had you arrived in our city, Emma, she would have offered you what she once offered me, yes. But, like the Necromancers of very recent vintage, you have had no experience of privation, starvation, disease. You have lost no one to war or famine. Your entire experience is far, far freer than the life a Necromancer knows.

"It is always about context. In her early years, she gathered those with similar potential. Some of them already had status or wealth, if not respect." He hesitated, and added, "Historically. She had stopped gathering those when I was found; they were costly and ambitious. They understood her roots, and they despised them; they did not feel her fit to rule, or at least, not as fit as they would be. They are gone," he added.

"They are not," Helmi replied. "She is never safe from the machinations of the Court."

"She is *always* safe! There are things she has not, and will never, teach *us*."

Helmi's shoulders slumped. "She teaches you all the things she taught herself. She withholds only the things she was taught before she became Queen." She turned to look up at Emma. "He's right. You won't ever be free while my sister lives."

Emma had to retrieve her hand to put on her boots and her coat; she had to ask Allison for help to deal with buttons, zippers, laces, her hand was so numb. Helmi hovered by her side, her luminescent eyes a contrast to the rest of her pallor; she seemed shadowed and defeated. And she did so as an eight-year-old girl. Emma knew she wasn't eight in any real sense of the word, but it was hard to hold on to that knowledge.

Margaret walked through the closed door. "Ernest is in the car."

Amy immediately opened the door and walked into the winter night, clearly staking out her territory as the other driver.

"Has Ernest seen—"

"No. But I have. Helmi is correct. The gateway is not yet operational, but it will be soon. I could not approach closely enough to determine which of the Necromancers are present; there appear to be two." She glanced at Helmi, and added, "The only one of the dead who could approach them and be guaranteed either freedom or safety is the one who stands by your side. No Necromancer would be foolish enough to touch or bind her where the Queen has not."

"Emma," Helmi whispered. Emma automatically bent her head to bring her right ear closer to the girl. "Bind me."

Longland's eyes should have fallen out of their sockets. Margaret's surprise was less obvious.

"I can't," Emma said quietly. "I don't know how."

It was Helmi's turn to looked shocked. "What do you mean, you *don't know how?*"

"She means," a familiar voice said, "exactly what she says."

The dead young girl turned to face the magar.

Helmi left Emma's side in a heartbreaking rush of arms and fast limbs, as if she had forgotten that the dead didn't actually need to run. As if—and this was worse—she had forgotten that the dead couldn't touch anything, not even each other.

Only when she was inches away from the magar did she come to a sudden stop, lowering her open arms, closing herself off.

"I am not her magar," the older woman said.

"You must have taught her *something.*"

"No. Her life has done that, and better than I could. She cannot bind you. It's possible that Margaret or Longland could teach her, indirectly, what she would need to know—but not in time, Helmi. Even if she could do as you have asked, what use would it be to her?"

"Not *her. Me. Me.* She *has* Margaret. Margaret is bound to her."

The magar looked at Emma. "And how do you hold Margaret?" Which was the question Emma was expecting.

"I don't know. Maybe Margaret can answer."

If Margaret could, she didn't.

"What will you do now, Emma?"

That was the question, wasn't it? Emma looked to Michael and Allison. "We can't stay here. If we hit the road quickly enough, we'll be able to escape, at least for a short while—but we can't spend forever on the run. We can't go home if—if she hasn't been—been stopped."

Margaret nodded. "She cannot be stopped from Canada."

"Can she be stopped from anywhere in the world that isn't her citadel?"

"I don't think so, dear," Margaret replied.

"No," Longland said.

"No," Helmi whispered. The words overlapped, adding texture and certainty to the discussion.

"Is she coming, now?"

Helmi shook her head. "If there were more Necromancers, if she hadn't lost so many knights, she might take the risk. The Queen of the Dead is safe in her citadel. She won't leave it—"

"She's left it before," Chase cut in. Something in his voice caused Allison to raise a hand; it hovered a foot from his arm, as if she wanted to touch him to offer comfort and realized just how little that comfort would mean. Emma was surprised when he caught her hand in one of his.

"She won't leave if she doesn't feel her safety is guaranteed. In the past, she might have come here. But with cars and phones and internet, she's no longer certain to have uninterrupted time. So much has changed, so quickly." She turned, again, to Emma.

Eric, silent until then, said, "She's safe in her citadel. No one can touch her there."

Helmi's expression hardened further, and given the death glares she'd leveled at Longland, that should have been impossible. She said nothing, waiting as all eyes fell on Eric.

"She has, three times in the history of the court, come close to death," Longland said, when Eric didn't speak. "Once, before the citadel was constructed. To construct the citadel was not the act of a month or even a year. It required power on a scale that she had never before used. It required a gathering of the dead that she had never attempted. I imagine," he continued, when Eric failed to interrupt him, "that what Emma gathered in order to open the exit was the only gathering that might come close. How long did that take?" It was a rhetorical question; he knew the answer.

Helmi said, "You have the lantern." She turned, then, to the magar and said, in a quieter voice, "You *gave* her the lantern."

"And will you accuse me of betrayal, who are dead—and trapped—as I am?"

"My sister wants the lantern."

"She always did. And think of what she might have built if she had claimed it." She turned to Eric. "You are too silent."

He exhaled. "I have an idea."

Helmi said, with scorn, "And we know where *your* ideas lead!"

"Helmi," her mother said.

Eric ignored the interruption. He looked to Emma. "No one *could* touch her in citadel back then. But you weren't there. If you want—if you intend—to stop her, you'll have to go to her."

"How? I have no idea how to *reach* the citadel."

"The living need to eat. Very little grows in the citadel. There is some fertile land, but even that is only enough to feed a small family. She has to import food."

"Where does she get the money?" Michael asked. It was the first time he'd chosen to contribute throughout this lengthening emergency council.

"There is a long and complicated answer to that question. We can discuss it on the way."

"On the way to where?" Michael replied, an edge to the words. "Where are we going?"

"If you're willing to take the risk? The citadel."

# Eric

Eric has existed for so long he thinks he should be immune to pain, to fear. And perhaps he is; he is not afraid of Helmi. He is not afraid of Emma. He is not comfortable in the winter glare of the magar, but she never liked him, never accepted him.

And yet, for years, she has guided him. Years.

Longland is afraid of everything except Emma. Longland knows the fate of the dead who displease the Queen. So does Eric. But that fate might be peaceful, in the end. If he has no choice, he has no responsibilities—and he has shouldered responsibility, however imperfectly, since the moment he died. He is tired.

The magar offers no guidance. Her eyes—her dead eyes—burn with accusation and guilt. Eric wonders if his do the same. He is so tired.

"You want to return to the citadel," the magar says.

"No."

"There is a throne waiting for you. And a very lonely girl."

Chase curses, the sound familiar and almost comforting.

"You could have returned at any time," the magar continues.

Eric turns away from her. He turns toward Emma. He sees her as the dead see her. She is the brightest thing in the room, the warmest.

He came to kill her. He could not make himself do it. He had seen too much of Emma and her friends: Allison, Michael, the intimidating Amy Snitman. He couldn't imagine that Emma could become one of the Queen's knights. She might have the power, yes, but the potential didn't define her. If his target had been Amy? Maybe. Maybe Amy Snitman would be dead, and Eric would be in hiding, planning the deaths of Necromancers and longing for the moment when he might kill the Queen of the Dead and redeem himself at last—just as he's done for centuries.

On the night he made the decision not to kill Emma, Emma did not look like this. The seed of potential has grown, has flowered. The small light has become a miniature sun, a source of warmth. To the dead, there is very little difference between Emma Hall and the Queen.

As if she can hear the thought, Helmi lifts her hand. Emma's rises with it. "Can you kill my sister?" Helmi demands. "She loves you. Even after all this time, she loves you. She says love never dies."

"Love dies," Eric replies. He is not willing to have the rest of this discussion with Helmi. It's not a discussion to have with anyone who has spent centuries hating him, blaming him. Which is ironic, because Eric has spent those same centuries hating and blaming himself. Wishing, fervently, that he had never met Reyna. Wishing that he had never fallen in love and, failing that, that Reyna had never returned his love.

Love led them here. Endless pain. Endless regret. Endless guilt—a vortex that has destroyed not only Eric's existence but also the existence of every single person who has died since. It has been so long since he has seen Reyna. It has been so long since the girl he loved has existed in the eyes of the woman he has vowed to kill.

Every guardian has doubted that desire. Ernest doubted it—loudly—when they first met. But Ernest is not that young man; he is older, more fatherly, his fury burned to determined embers with the onset of age. He is so much younger than Eric.

*Love dies.* It's the answer he gave to Ernest, those many years ago. It's the answer he gave to Philip, the man who preceded him. It's the answer he's given to anyone who has known enough to ask. It's been a theoretical answer.

Eric is dead.

There is no action he can take against the Queen of the Dead on his own unless she desires it. She can immobilize him with a single word. All discussions about the nature of love, about his ability to kill the Queen, have been safely theoretical or philosophical. Until now. And now? Emma is here. The question is no longer theoretical.

Eric can return to the citadel at any time he chooses. But Emma and Chase can't. Emma doesn't even have the travel documents necessary to leave her own country, and Eric's not certain she'd survive the attempt if she did.

But if Helmi is right, if the Necromancers are truly coming in any force at all, there *is* a chance. There's a way. It's risky, and it means that Eric must return to face Reyna one last time.

"The magar is right. There is a place waiting for me in the citadel." He exhales and turns to Longland. Merrick Longland, the man he—and Chase—killed. "I have a plan."

# Nathan

Nathan spends his day reading, and when reading fails to keep his attention, he rises and heads to the door that separates his rooms from the rest of the citadel. He chafes at the clothing he's forced to wear because he's aware of every itchy thread; he feels the rough cloth and the edges of lace and wonders why a top-heavy wig hasn't been added to the almost comic assembly.

Being dead, it appears, is about discomfort and silence and boredom. And pain. Sleep still eludes him because he listens for the sounds of his body. Weeping is his heartbeat and his breath. He bleeds, and grows weak with lack of food or water. He will not, he is told, incubate many diseases.

Diseases are carried by the living. The only living person he regularly sees is the one who brings his food and leaves it in stiff silence.

Today, standing inside his door, he takes stock of the life he's been given. He considers the alternative. Being disembodied isn't pleasant, but there's freedom in it that being embodied doesn't have.

The door is heavy and opens outward; the hinges are on the exterior. The hinges are on the exterior of almost all doors in the citadel; only the doors to rooms the Queen occupies are normal.

No one moves in the hall facing the door, but the hall is not empty. Two of the dead stand at attention, framing the doorway. Nathan has been to London; he's aware that the dress guards at Buckingham palace will stand at attention as if they're carved statues. He doesn't expect the dead to notice him as he leaves—unless he has been ordered to remain in his room.

They make no sound; they make no movements. He nods at them anyway before he turns, arbitrarily, to the right and begins to walk. Other guards— dead guards—are standing immobile in the hall. They are furniture. They take no breaks.

Nathan wonders if they think. He wonders if they pass their hours and days trapped and encased with no escape; he wonders if they are still sane. And then, as he walks, he wonders whether the floors have ears or eyes or some way of seeing who passes above them and whether the walls are, like the guards, just more furnishings, but given no human shape.

He wonders, in short, if this is hell.

Helmi appears to his left in answer to the unasked question.

"Nathan," she says. "I need your help."

He continues to walk as she drifts by his side. He doesn't actually like her much, but she's company.

"What," he asks, voice tight with contained sarcasm, "could I possibly do to help you?"

"Emma is coming to save you, but she won't survive if you don't help."

*Emma.* Emma is coming here. The thought simultaneously fills Nathan with dread and desire. He holds up one hand. "Don't tell me this. Do not tell me another word." What he wants to ask, as well, is *when* and *where is she.* Those are the wrong questions. The answers are dangerous to know.

"You're worried about what you'll tell the Queen." It's not a question.

"Yes. If she asks—if she commands—I'll tell her everything." When Helmi fails to reply, he stops walking and turns to face her. "I *want* to know. I want to see Emma again. But—she can't come here. She'll die."

"Which is *why* I need your help. The citadel isn't the whole of the city. If the Queen and her court are distracted, Emma might be able to sneak in."

"How the hell do you sneak into a *flying city*?"

Helmi looks at Nathan as if he's too stupid to live. "You want me to answer *that* question, but nothing else?"

Put that way, she's right—and Nathan's not up to explaining that his question wasn't actually a question at all.

"The Queen hasn't summoned you today, and after I talk to her, I don't think she will. She'll be busy."

"Doing what?"

"Preparing," Helmi replies, with a hard, tight smile that is way too old for her face, "for Eric's return."

"Eric's coming?"

"Yes. Eric is finally coming home. If no one does anything too stupid, that's what will take up every single thought she has. We need you to run interference to make sure that the less-obsessed-with-Eric among the court don't call her attention to anything else. There might be people new to the court who would help with that, but I doubt it. They're not new enough not to be terrified of the Queen of the Dead."

"Neither am I."

"Does fear make you stupid?"

"Not exclusively."

Helmi says, "Well, save the rest of the stupidity for later. Follow me. Pay attention. You're only going to get one chance to get this right."

"But no pressure," Nathan replies. The irony is lost on Helmi. Then again, the citadel probably sucks the humor out of everyone who is forced to remain here.


## ◟◞ Chapter 4

The snow was warmer by far than the air above it. Amy, who had abandoned the warmth of an idling, large car, was exhaling what looked like steam. Eric and Chase had led them to within a hundred yards of the road nearest the cottage; given that they paused at even intervals to do something to mark the path—and to check it for Necromantic traps—it took longer than the combination of distance and snow dictated. No one was warm. No one was particularly happy, except possibly Petal.

Eric handed off the backpack he wore to Michael. Chase continued to shoulder his. They had packed all of the food that was easily portable, with can openers and the type of throw-away dishes taken on camping trips. If they managed to make it to the city, they wouldn't be dining with the Queen; Longland had implied that food could quickly become the biggest problem they faced if they survived. That, and water.

There was one permanent portal to the citadel, but it wasn't in Canada. They'd be able to access it from the citadel-side, but not easily, and the trip down might be one way. They would not have permission to be in another country, and they wouldn't have passports should that permission somehow be required. They would, on the other hand, speak the language.

Michael had asked how they would get home.

Ernest, however, declared that a non-problem. If they survived—if they somehow succeeded—he could arrange it with relatively little fuss. Emma wasn't certain she believed him. Michael needed details. Details were provided on the walk because the walk gave them time; Ernest would otherwise never have surrendered. He didn't *like* the plan, but he was confident that he could build the careful paperwork lies that would allow whoever survived to come back.

Whoever survived.

Petal was now Emma's biggest worry. It wasn't displacement worry, either; no one was safe. No one was guaranteed to survive. But every other living person present understood the rough, shaky plan that Eric had outlined. Some had greater belief in it than others. Petal, incapable of comprehension, was neutral.

He was not a poorly trained dog—Brendan Hall would never have allowed that, especially not for a rottweiler—but his hearing was not what it had once been, and his first tendency when going someplace new was to explore. Chase wanted to leave the dog, as he called Petal, behind.

Abandoning him here was almost certainly abandoning him to starvation and death. Emma's first suggestion—that Michael remain behind with Petal—was met with solid, logical resistance. Michael had not been affected by Longland's magic. Everyone else had. That resistance might—just might—save their lives if they somehow managed to arrive, as planned, at the citadel. Since the resistance had come from Michael, Emma swallowed and let it go. Allison would not remain behind either.

That left Amy.

Which meant Petal was either coming or being abandoned near a winter roadside.

"You understand what you're meant to do here?" Eric asked.

Chase nodded.

"Then Longland and I are heading back to the cottage. Wait. You'll know when it's safe. Helmi?"

"I don't have to leave yet. I'll come when you're closer." She glanced at Emma and at Emma's hands, now heavily mittened against the winter cold.

"Eric's plan will work," Helmi said, when time had passed. How much, Emma couldn't say. She didn't wear a watch, and the phone she used as a replacement was entrenched in a pocket she couldn't reach without removing her mittens.

"It doesn't make sense," Emma replied. Amy frowned but did not insist on being part of the conversation, which was good—Emma's hands still hadn't recovered from the previous one. "First of all, they knew we were here."

"They knew *you* were here," Helmi countered.

"Why wouldn't they hunt for me, then?"

"They can't afford to hunt and keep the portal open."

"That didn't stop them in Toronto."

"No. But in Toronto, you didn't have me. I have to go back to the citadel. I need to tell the Queen that Longland has Eric. The reason they've set up in the road is to catch you if some of you manage to leave by car. If she knows that Longland has Eric, she'll forget everything else—at least for a little while. She might tell her Necromancers to remain here to hunt the rest of you down. If she does, they'll be searching, but they'll start at the cottage, not the road.

"Even if they discover your trail here, it will end at the road. They're not going to guess that you went *to* the citadel.

"The portal itself will close. You could prevent that if you knew what you were doing; you probably can't on your own. Margaret will help you, so listen to her, and listen carefully. If you could bind me, I could do it."

"The Queen would know."

"No, she wouldn't. She doesn't own *me*." Helmi rolled her eyes before she continued what was, in essence, a lecture. "Let the portal collapse naturally—and step through before it vanishes. Don't worry about the portal after that. Worry about leaving the area you arrive in."

"What will happen to Eric?"

"Who knows? The most important thing you need to understand is that Eric's safety is guaranteed. No one else's is. That's why we're doing it this way." She frowned at Emma's companions. "I think you should leave them behind."

"I know."

"But Margaret told me how they've helped, and maybe, in the end, you can't do this on your own. Just—don't fall apart if they die, okay? I have to leave. I'll come back again when it's safe for you to move."

*       *       *

Chase was not happy. No one was, but Chase was one of the few people present who could actually *do* something in the worst case scenario. He had an arm around Allison's shoulder because Allison was shivering. Allison had an arm around Michael's shoulder because Michael was doing the same; only Michael leaned into the offered support. Allison was too stiff.

She bit her lip; she bit her lip when she was nervous. Had she been inside, she would have cleaned her glasses, because she did that a lot as well. Chase wanted to send her somewhere else.

"Don't even think it," she whispered, her words visible as clouds of mist.

"I'm not. I'm thinking about what we do when we land. Or how we do it. Longland bothers me."

Allison said nothing.

"Just because he's dead, we're trusting that he's changed sides."

"He has," Emma said. "By default. He's dead."

"He—"

"And the only sides he now sees are the dead and the living. We're all eventually going to be on the side he's on now."

"Or we'll be fuel for the side we're not on now."

"Or that. I wouldn't trust him with my personal happiness; I think he still resents any happiness that isn't his own—and frankly, he's a person who believes 'smug' is the definition of happiness. Normally, I'd find it a bit sad. Right now I don't care. He won't turn us in, and he won't have us killed because dead, we're no use to him. We'd be just as helpless as he is."

Chase could see Emma in the light that reflected off the snow; she was straight, narrow; her profile implied an edge that he had never seen in her. He didn't threaten her; he didn't disagree with her. No point.

Instead, he leaned in toward Allison and whispered, "I suppose kissing you is out of the question?" Her outrage was warming. He was fairly certain she wouldn't slap him while she was holding on to Michael.

"It is absolutely out of the question," Amy replied.

Allison stuck her tongue out—at Chase; Amy snorted. Michael pointed out that public displays of affection made people uncomfortable. Chase considered asking him why but decided against it because he wasn't up to the convoluted logic that would likely follow; he was sure he would find it amusing, but given Amy's expression, it wouldn't be amusing enough.

"Chase," Emma said. Wrong tone of voice. He let his arm fall from Allison's shoulder, surprised at how the cold rushed in. "Helmi says there's trouble."

"Necromancer?"

"Just one. The portal's not activated yet, but Helmi says he's by the road."

"Does she think he's remaining to hunt the rest of us down?"

"She missed a small part of the conversation, but—yes."

He smiled. "Did she recognize him?"

"Her. Yes. I think she knows all of the Necromancers at court. She says the woman is young." There was a brief pause, which ended with Emma saying, "That is *not* our definition of young, Helmi. Sorry. She thinks she might be part of Margaret's cohort."

"Is Margaret here?"

"She is now," Margaret replied. "Before you ask, no, I am not going to be a useful source of information; I'll be seen. Helmi occupies a unique role at court; the same courtesy is not extended to anyone else. If I'm seen and Helmi is correct, I'm likely to be recognized. Who," she said, turning to face nothing, "is it?"

Chase didn't hear the answer. Margaret, apparently, did. She turned to Chase. "She was in the citadel when I arrived."

"Is she powerful?"

"Yes. She is not powerful enough to be a concern if she is unprepared. I think," she added, "that's unlikely."

"No kidding."

Allison caught his arm. "She might leave—"

"She might, yes. But if she leaves, she'll be on the other side of the portal when we arrive. We don't want to face her there if we can avoid it. And we can." He glanced at Ernest.

Ernest nodded.

Allison's sudden stiffness had nothing to do with the cold. They were facing possible—probable—death. It made no sense to worry about her anxiety and her fear. But he did. "I'm not going to alert them to our presence; I won't take her down before Eric and Longland are gone. How many Necromancers in total?"

"Three," Margaret said. She blanched. "One of them is older than Longland. The Queen has lost many of her powerful knights in recent weeks; Longland was a significant loss. The man he killed to save Allison was similarly costly. In my youth, she would not have risked the man who is here. Be careful, Chase. He is canny and sensitive, and he's clashed with hunters before."

And clearly, if he was standing here, the hunters were the ones who'd died.

Silence. Silence broken by Petal, by breathing, by movement across the icy surface of old snow. Silence broken, more definitively, by the sound of a car. Helmi appeared in front of Emma, a foot above the snow, her eyes almost level with Emma's. "They're all in the car," she said.

"Eric—"

"Is safe. They won't kill him. They won't dare. Alraed might consider taking Eric as hostage—but it's risky."

"Should we—"

Helmi shook her head, the edge of a smile adorning her lips. It was the type of smile that could almost draw blood; she looked, momentarily, like a vengeful demon. Whoever Alraed was, she didn't like him. "I told him the Queen knows he has Eric."

"If he bound you," Emma replied, "would that change things?"

"She'd kill him," Helmi said. "She'd kill him slowly and terribly. Binding the dead isn't trivial. And it's not instantaneous. He won't have the time. She wants to see Eric. She'll be waiting to meet him. If it takes too long for Eric to arrive, she'll come in person."

Silence. Fear. This plan seemed so slight, so fragile a strong breeze might break it, shattering all hope. Emma inhaled and exhaled, her breath a mist between their faces. "Does she have any friends?"

"The Queen?"

"Your sister, yes."

"Would *you* be friends with her?"

Emma thought of Nathan. Of Allison and Michael. And, yes, of Amy, the most terrifying of her friends. She had no answer to give, because everything in her screamed No. But she had hated Mark's mother until she had finally met her, too.

"She blames herself for my death," Helmi said.

"Do you?"

"Do you always ask so many questions?"

Emma shook her head. "Usually Michael does. But he can't see you right now."

"I do blame her for my death. But not completely." Helmi shook her head. Her hair moved as if it were real. "Our mother would have been so angry at her. Our mother *is* angry. She wanted to leave the village; there had been no rain. People were afraid.

"My sister wanted to stay. They argued. They argued for two days. In the end, my mother agreed. But she didn't know—we didn't know—why my sister thought it would be safe. My sister had already gathered the power of the dead she found. She had kept them bound to her instead of walking them to the door. She kept them hidden."

"Why?"

"Because she wanted to make it rain," Helmi replied. "I knew. I watched her practice with small patches of land, in secret. She thought if she could make it rain in the middle of the drought, the villagers would love her. They would be happy to have her there. She thought they would accept her, and if they did, we would be safe. And loved. And welcomed.

"That's why she had power when they came. She had more power than the magar. She used it—but not for rain." Helmi lifted her face, gazing to the left of Emma's shoulder—to the left, and up. "She told me she killed the villagers before they could kill her. Those deaths were messy, but they were fast.

"I wasn't there," Helmi added. "I didn't see it. I went where the dead go. But I couldn't leave. No one could leave. No one has been able to leave since the day Eric died."

# Reyna

Reyna screams.

Reyna screams and screams and screams. There are no words embedded in the sounds because the screams are so visceral, so complete, she has no thought left to form them. She sees men, she sees clubs and torches and pitchforks and—yes—long knives. She sees the elderly, the aged who are not yet infirm, the men who, broad-shouldered and grim, have seen war and bandits and other deaths but have lived to father children of their own.

She sees the young men, men Eric's age. One is green-faced and shaking, but she doesn't remember his name; she doesn't remember the name of the father who stands, grim and proud, by his side.

She shouldn't see anything about them at all, because they're alive.

Her mother is not. Her mother was the first to die. Her uncle followed quickly, his raised arms meant to indicate that he meant no harm, that he was not a threat. Of course he wasn't. He wasn't armed. He had no power. He could not stand against the dozens assembled here. And Helmi is bleeding. Helmi, who might have survived had she stayed hidden. It is too much. It is *too much*.

Those deaths would make her weep. They would freeze her heart, her voice, her lungs.

But they are not real, not yet. Eric's death is real. Eric's blood is bright and dark and endless. Eric's eyes are fluttering, his chest is rising and falling far too quickly, far too shallowly; his skin is torn, his ribs broken; his lip is swollen because of his father's backhand. Eric is—Eric is—

Reyna screams in utter terror.

Eric is the only thing in Reyna's life that was *about* life and living. For Eric, she would have *saved* this village. For Eric, she had begged her mother. Defied her mother. Because her mother had wanted to leave. Her mother had wanted to leave a month ago, and Reyna had refused. Had refused to believe that her bitter, angry mother was *right*. Eric loves her. Eric's love was supposed to be the shield against the world. Eric's love was the promise of life—and his own people have destroyed it.

He will leave. He is leaving, even now, as she screams. All promise, all dream, all hope is a lie—a lie written now in blood, in a language too messy to read.

The end. The end. The end.

Rain falls, then. Lightning flashes. Thunder rumbles. The storm is her storm; it says—and does—what she cannot. If they want death, they'll have it. That is why they've come. To bring death. To end life. To end Reyna's life.

Let death take them instead. She doesn't need them here. She doesn't want them.

She looks up, and up again; rain washes blood from her hands, from her lap; she takes Eric's body into her arms, and bends, and kisses his open mouth. There is no response. She screams his name. *Eric! Eric!* Two beats, over and over. He has always answered her before.

He does not answer her now.

He is gone.

"How could you kill your own son?" she demands of the blacksmith. But the blacksmith, like Eric, will never answer that question; he lies face down in dirt that is rapidly becoming mud.

No, no, no. Eric. *Eric.* She gestures and the rain stops. The lightning stops. Silence falls instead, a blanket, a shroud. She *will not* gift the village and its fields with rain. Not now. Not *ever*.

He is still here. He is still here, somewhere. He has not left, might not leave. She has seen and spoken to so many of the dead. She has seen the door, the window, the exit to which they must all walk, in the end. She knows where the dead go when they accept the fact of death.

She rises. She rises and gently rolls Eric's corpse off her lap. She glances, once, at her mother, grimaces, and turns away. Her mother is dead. Her mother has no voice; her hands will never rise again, to either strike or caress. Her voice, her harsh, judgmental voice, is gone to silence, and Reyna will not call it back.

Reyna has always lived with death. She has accepted the wanderers and the lost; she has dedicated most of her childhood to finding and freeing them. But she has wanted life. *This* life.

Eric loves her. She loves Eric. Love is meant to last a lifetime.

But the dead don't linger unless they are frightened or trapped. They don't stay. They don't *want* to stay. Once they know they're dead, they leave. It's just a second stage of abandonment. She *believes* Eric loves her. She believes he will want to stay. But he doesn't know that she can see him. He doesn't know that she can talk to him.

And he won't know if he sees the exit. He won't have any *reason* to stay. Reyna knows.

She turns, walks into the home that will never be home again, and finds chalk. In a darkened room, she draws her circle, thinking that one day—one day—she will have one of stone, a place where she might sit and search as if it were both her duty and her right.

She does not cry as she works. Tears will smudge the circle. Tears will destroy the chalk. Her mother's harsh and angry voice reverberates in memory, and this time, Reyna listens. She will take what she needs, now. She is the last of her family. She is magar.

But she does not have the lantern. She does not have the light. Her mother would not pass it on to the daughter who was—and is—far more powerful than she. Reyna doesn't *need* it, to be magar. The lantern would make things easier, but in the end, it is up to Reyna. All she needs now, she has.

A circle. Chalk. Knowledge.

She has walked the path to the shining, brilliant warmth that is the promise at the end of life and death, and she will walk it now. She will walk it, she will reach it, and she will close it so that the dead cannot leave. Because otherwise, Eric might leave. He doesn't *know*. Eric might leave before she can find him.

They'll understand, surely. The dead will understand. And she will let them go when she has finally found Eric. But she needs the *time* because she does not have the lantern. And the dead are forever. A year or two won't harm them at all.

## ⌒ Chapter 5

"You knew he was dead, right? You're a Necromancer."

Emma said nothing. She didn't want everyone else to hear. But Helmi prodded and prodded until she spoke. "No. I didn't know until I spoke with Longland."

"You're not very bright."

Broken, iced snow cracked beneath Emma's boots; it sounded like glass. She froze, aware that no steps could be silent, here. "No, Helmi. I'm not very bright. This is still new to me. Margaret won't teach me anything—don't make that face, it's rude. I thought your mother might, but we've had *no time*."

"My mother gave you what she could," Helmi replied. Her tone was grudging. "I'd teach you if I knew anything. I only know how to draw circles."

This sounded like a non sequitur.

"Circles are for containment," Helmi continued, correctly interpreting Emma's silence. "When you go to find the dead, you sit in a circle. You have to draw the circle, unless you have a stone one. The Queen has one," she added. "I can show you how to draw a circle." Her expression grew remote and thoughtful. "Or I could show you where the Queen's is."

Emma's eyes widened.

"I don't mean right now," Helmi said. "I mean later."

"We're supposed to *avoid* the Queen."

"Not forever." The subject was clearly distasteful, and she dropped it. "Circles are supposed to keep you safe."

"How?"

The child's lips compressed. "I don't know. I died when I was eight. I can tell you how to draw a circle. I can't tell you why it works. But the circle is the way you root yourself in the world when you go looking for the dead."

The younger man in the distance waited until Longland disappeared. He then turned to the older one.

"Be right back," Helmi said, and she vanished.

Chase didn't return.

Instead, Eric's car did. They could see headlights in the distance, moving up and down as if the driver were drunk. But no: It was the road. The roads were thick with flattened snow, thick and uneven.

They hid behind trees, keeping trunks between the road and their bodies. It was almost impossible to believe that no one would see them, that no one would look. Helmi, watching, told Emma that there were four people in the car. Two Necromancers, two passengers. Eric was driving.

Longland was behind him, gun pointed at the back of his head.

Beside him, in the front passenger seat, a man—the Necromancer Helmi feared. To one side of Longland, a younger man.

"He's afraid," Helmi said, with obvious derision.

"He should be. Eric's probably killed a lot of Necromancers, in his time."

"Not enough of them," Helmi replied.

On the other side of the road, less hidden, was the woman. Chase would kill her. Emma's hands shook; she turned to Margaret, who shadowed Ernest. "Why did you stop?"

"Stop serving the Queen?"

Emma nodded.

"I met Ernest."

"Ernest talked you out of it?" Emma's words carried her disbelief. Ernest had certainly been keen to see Eric shoot Emma on an autumn lawn months ago.

"Not exactly, dear." A ghost of a smile—literal and figurative—moved Margaret's lips. "He tried to kill me."

"He failed?"

"He was using the wrong bullets at the time, if I recall correctly. Yes, he failed. The Queen was responsible for my death." She grimaced, recalling that death; she didn't offer details, and Emma would never ask. "I did not go willingly with the Queen's knights when they came to 'save' me. I didn't have your mother or your father; I didn't have your friends. And perhaps," she added, lifting her chin, "that was my choice. The friends, at least. I had no reason to trust people—but they had no reason to trust me, if I'm honest.

"I was trapped by life. I was doomed to serve the Queen; I was doomed to bind the dead and drain them of life and somehow keep myself alive. The schooling is both rigorous and treacherous; the peers—if you have them—are just as angry and just as untrusting. They understand survival of the fittest; they don't believe there is *any* strength in numbers. I could not leave the citadel; failure to comply or learn what was necessary would only harm me. I had always felt trapped by life. Ernest's intent—to kill me—was something I welcomed. It would have been a fast, relatively painless, death.

"I was perhaps five years older than you are now. I had burn scars up the inside of my left arm."

"The Queen?"

"No. Another student. He died. I do not believe I had ever been happy—it's hard to be objective. I meant to let Ernest kill me. Because I did, he didn't. I think he was confused—he was younger then, as well. He had lost much to Necromancers; he is like your Chase."

"So not mine."

"A figure of speech, dear. He thought it was a trick, of course. But I think he also knew it wasn't. We had no reason to trust each other. I was angry at the time. I didn't have the strength of will to end my own life, but it shouldn't have been necessary. Hunters kill us when we're weak. It's what they do. He was my only viable form of suicide." Her smile deepened. "I was so *angry* at him when he hesitated. It takes a very peculiar type of strength to hold still and wait for death; I was shaking. My partner, such as he was, was already dead.

"I believe I may have lost my temper, then. I may have shouted at him; I am not certain I remember the exact words, and even if I did, I would not repeat them. He was even more confused. I was already wounded," she added. "I fought until my partner died. Even then, I did not want to die and come face to face with the Queen. I knew what would happen after death."

"It happened anyway."

"Yes, dear, but later. By then I had truly earned her anger. I know very little of what occurred between my death and my meeting with you. Look at the road, Emma. It's starting." She turned to Ernest; he nodded.

Eric's car met road and stopped as it turned onto it. Four people got out; Eric was first, not last. He paused, gaze downcast. Longland looked, briefly, toward the trees. Emma held her breath, praying that Petal would remain quiet. No one spoke.

The air above the road, yards from where Eric now stood, began to shimmer.

Emma glanced at Allison and Amy; their eyes widened. What she saw, they could also see. Green light shot up from the snow-covered asphalt in two pillars; the pillars then bent toward each other, reaching and grasping at air until they met. When they did, they flared, in a green, twisting light that paled as it grew in brilliance until it was almost white.

The white light fell in a sheet from the height of what was now a very tall arch. At this distance, Emma could see only the shape of the portal; she couldn't see the dead who must be anchoring it. Her hands nonetheless became fists. She did not forget—could not forget—that people were its fuel.

She caught sight of the diminutive form of Helmi as Helmi joined the four. Longland stiffened; so did the older man. The younger did not, apparently, fear her, which made sense. Emma knew who she was but couldn't see beyond her apparent age; Helmi could irritate or annoy but not terrify. Not yet.

Helmi then vanished.

She reappeared by Emma's side. "Now," she said. "You won't have much time. Therese is holding the gate, but she's got no power. She's meant to come through it before she lets it go."

"If Chase kills her—"

"There's a bit of danger, yes. But the portals don't collapse instantly. If you have to, you can hold its shape long enough to get everyone else through—just listen to Margaret and do what she tells you to do. Are you really going to bring your dog?"

"I can't leave him here."

"We don't have a lot of dog food," Helmi said.

"I know." She swallowed. "Michael, can you hold on to Petal?"

Michael nodded and bent, hooking Petal to his leash. Petal was excited until he realized that Michael's hands were empty of everything but leash. No treats.

"Remember: When you get through, do *exactly* what I tell you to do."

"What happens to us if we're caught?"

"The Queen, in the end. You'll all die. Eric's job is to keep her distracted." This last was said sourly.

"Can he do it?"

"I don't know. She's been waiting for him for a long time. She'll probably be happy at first."

"And after?"

"She's pretty angry. It might get ugly." Helmi exhaled. "Why are you worried about Eric?"

"I don't want him to—"

"To what? Die? He can't. He's already dead."

Emma didn't ask what a bullet could to do the body the Queen had created. She knew that the bodies bled. She knew that they could be injured. She had no idea what the person who inhabited the body would feel at the moment the body was destroyed. Nathan now had a body that was very much like Eric's. Or Longland's.

Emma watched as what she assumed was a woman joined the two men; it was hard, at this distance, to tell. None of them wore distinguishing clothing, and the woman was not short. Chase was not visible at this distance; she looked for him, holding her breath.

She saw Helmi instead. Helmi was seated, midair, ten feet from where the three Necromancers gathered, in full view of the portal. Her arms were by her sides, her palms pressed down into a nonexistent bench. She should not have been so remarkably clear, given the distance—but she was. She was the only person who was.

As Emma watched, forgetting, again, to breathe, Helmi lost substance. She didn't lose clarity, although at first that was Emma's assumption; she lost shape. The blurred outline of her body—with her ridiculous clothing and her ringlet hair—remained, but it lengthened, gaining height and width. Without thought, Emma took a step forward.

"Emma." Margaret's voice, while quiet, was harsh. Angry-teacher harsh. Emma stopped moving automatically. "Your father told you about the ancient dead, did he not? Helmi is among the oldest of those that remain trapped here. She is not being bound; she is asserting herself in a different way."

Assertion, as Margaret called it, was transformation, in Emma's vision. Amy cleared her throat; she was annoyed. The fact that Emma couldn't gift her with vision didn't appear to lighten Amy's mood. She did not like—had never liked—being left out.

As if viewed through a ground-glass lens, Helmi's new form sharpened and hardened, coming at last into a different focus. Her face was no longer the face of an eight-year-old child; it was a woman's face—she was ten or fifteen years older than Emma Hall or any of her friends. She wore a dress that would have been at home in an old James Bond movie and gloves that ended at her elbow.

Emma couldn't discern the neckline of the dress and didn't try.

"Would she have looked like that if she'd lived?"

"I highly doubt it." Margaret's voice was dry. "The Queen prefers her sister to look familiar. Her sister chooses to honor the Queen's preferences. Her normal appearance is generally advantageous—it makes her look harmless, and people tend to ignore her. But Alraed won't; she could regress to the form of an infant, and he would still understand the danger she poses.

"This is merely an act of petty malice on her part. She does not—and has never—cared for Necromancers."

"Why would she? She's dead."

"Once, she would have," Margaret replied, voice neutral. "Her own kin—" She stopped.

Emma turned toward the road again. Ernest moved forward, waving everyone else back, although no one but Emma had moved.

The three Necromancers turned their backs to the roadside that Emma and her friends were so timidly occupying. Chase was on the other side.

"Ernest, don't."

The old man—as Eric called him—now carried a gun in his right hand.

"He knows there are—or were—hunters here. He is not a fool. You won't be able to take him with the first shot. You are unlikely to get a second."

Ernest didn't appear to hear Margaret.

"The children will die."

That, on the other hand, caught his attention. Emma didn't even mind being referred to as a child, but it wasn't making Amy any happier. "What is she telling them?"

"I can't hear her. Nor can I approach in safety. Alraed might not recognize me, but Therese almost certainly will. If I'm seen, they'll know that something is afoot. They almost certainly know about you."

"Longland."

Ernest lengthened the distance between himself and the group. Margaret looked at his back. "He is fond of Chase," she told Emma quietly. "He was fond of every hunter he managed to save and train. His life—since before me—has been about killing and death. If the citadel falls, I don't know what he'll become."

"And you?"

"Free," Margaret replied. "You've seen it. You've seen what is waiting for us."

Emma swallowed and nodded.

One voice rose in the distance. "I said *find him*."

"That would be Alraed."

No voice rose in answer but Helmi's. "Shall I ask my sister?"

"The Queen will not care; this is beneath her now. She has what she desires." The words were carefully chosen, carefully spoken.

"She doesn't. Eric has agreed to return to her side—but he has not been seen and has not been recognized by her court. Will you deny him that legitimacy now? If he means, finally, to join her, killing the hunters will be trivial in the future. Will you risk two of her knights when she is almost at the pinnacle of her success?"

"She's good," Emma murmured. She had been afraid that Helmi would tell them where Chase was, and she felt guilty.

"She was always capable of engendering hatred and rage," Margaret replied.

"What else did she have? From everything you've said, the Necromancers weren't exactly friendly or kind."

"No. But perhaps they might have been, in different circumstances. We will not know; they are, now, what they are."

Lightning struck the road. The sky remained clear.

Helmi was unmoved, but the Necromancers who had been wavering were not; they fell to either side of the great crack that appeared beneath snow and asphalt. The ghost of the Queen's sister then unfolded her legs; she appeared to be stepping down from an invisible chair. She approached the fallen man; the woman was already rising, unsteadily, to her feet. She knelt; her hair covered her face as she bent her head.

"The two of you, go," Alraed said, his voice thunder to the brief flash of lightning. "I will find the hunter. Play witness to your Queen."

"Their Queen?" a new voice said. Emma recognized it instantly. The winter chill became absolute. Ernest froze. Margaret froze; silence robbed every element of the night of warmth. "*Their* Queen?"

The voice emanated from the portal. The Queen failed to follow it. But Alraed turned to face her, and it was clear, as he fell to one knee, that he could see what Emma couldn't.

"My Queen," he said, his voice soft enough that it barely carried. That wouldn't have been enough for Amy—the only person Emma knew who could carry off this type of fury and make it look natural—and it wasn't, apparently, good enough for the Queen.

He knew it, too.

Helmi lost her adult look, becoming again the child the Queen recognized and preferred. She then vanished, to reappear seconds later by Emma's side. She looked worried, now.

Alraed lifted his face—only his face, he didn't rise—and said, "You have known for centuries how I feel about you, my Queen. I have—for centuries—endeavored to prove both my loyalty and my love. I have obeyed your commands. I have returned to your side, time and again. And I will return to your side now if that is your desire."

"It is."

"But it is difficult for me to watch him take his place at your side. Lord Eric is a *hunter*. He has killed my friends"—Helmi snorted in disgust—"and comrades. He has treated you as if you are an enemy. He is not worthy of you."

Helmi snorted again.

"Surely," the disembodied voice said, "that decision is mine, and mine alone, to make." But some of the anger had drained from the Queen's voice; it was cool now, but not icy.

"Of course, my Queen. I am being foolish. I am being . . . unworthy."

"You have never been unworthy," the Queen replied. "But I do not wish you to waste your time. We are preparing, and I want your counsel."

"My Queen." He bowed his head again, and this time he rose. Without a backward glance at the two Necromancers behind him, he strode into the portal.

"The stupid thing is, she believes him. He'd slit her throat if he thought he'd have any chance of surviving it."

"She understands jealousy and envy," Emma replied. "What he said is perfectly believable."

"It's not. If it weren't for her power, he'd find her contemptible. He already does." She glanced at Emma. "You thought I'd turned Chase in."

Emma closed her eyes and exhaled. "Yes. I'm sorry."

"I considered it. Sacrifice Chase, and the rest of you could all get through." Emma opened her eyes and saw that Helmi was looking down at her hand. At her palm, which was cupped and turned toward her.

"Thank you," Emma said, and meant it.

"I think like a Necromancer. I think too much like a Necromancer. It's not comfortable. Be ready. The minute the last Necromancer walks through the portal, you have to be there."

"The Queen is there. We can't walk through—"

"The Queen won't be there once Alraed joins her. She'll keep an eye on him. She might even attempt to offer him some sign of her renewed favor; the reasons he's given make sense to her. Eric *has* been killing her people." Helmi tilted her head to the side as she looked up at Emma. "Eric probably came here to kill you."

"He did. We don't talk about it much; it's in the past and it upsets Allison."

"But not you?"

"It doesn't quite feel real to me—and I guess I'd prefer not to think about it. Whatever might have happened, didn't. To be honest, I was more upset about my first meeting with your mother."

"She has that effect on people." Helmi looked up. "Go. Now."

Emma had seen a portal very like this before—on the night Allison had almost been killed. She'd never examined one closely. She approached it from what she assumed was behind, given the direction that Alraed had walked—but this ended up being a bad assumption. The portal had no front and back. From either side it opened into what appeared to be a large, plain room; the walls were lit with torches, and the light they cast was both gloomy and inadequate.

Emma couldn't see people.

She could, on the other hand, hear shouting. It wasn't close; it seemed to be receding. Random words caught her attention and faded as she clenched her hands in fists. She was shaking. It wasn't from the cold.

This was, she thought, the point of no return. She could enter the City of the Dead and leave her friends behind. They'd be safe without her. She glanced back, once. There was enough light in the room on the other side of this tall, standing rip in the air that the night seemed darker; she couldn't see her friends clearly.

"You want to leave them behind."

She could, on the other hand, hear Chase. He came from the other side of the road.

"I didn't think you were going to survive that," she said quietly. She lifted a hand; it hovered an inch above the surface of the portal.

"I had some concerns as well." His shrug was pure Chase. "You're changing the subject."

She was. She inhaled cold air, exhaled mist. She wanted her friends to be safe. "Would you stay with them?"

So did Chase. "I would—but she has Eric. I'm going." He hesitated. "Michael's not wrong. I don't know how he escaped Longland's original spell. Neither do Ernest or Margaret. But there's a decent chance he can do it again."

"Have you been there? To the City?"

Chase didn't answer. "I really wanted to hate you."

"I wasn't under the impression you were failing."

He chuckled. "Are you alive?"

"Point taken. If I leave—"

"I am not staying behind with angry Allison. I don't give a damn about Amy. But if you're going, you'd better decide quickly; Ernest's coming."

She wanted to leave them behind. That was the truth.

But she wanted them to come with her, and that was the truth as well. She balanced between two different types of guilt; she drew another breath. She needed her friends. She'd needed friends when her father had died, even if she hadn't really understood, at age eight, what death *meant*. She wasn't eight, now. She understood death: endless silence, endless absence, utter loss. But she'd needed her friends when Nathan had died, as well—she'd needed them more.

"I'm not you," she said quietly. "Sometimes I wish I were."

"You don't."

"I don't want—I don't want what happened *to* you. But if I were you, this would be easy."

"It's not worth it," he said, his voice so soft that she glanced to the side to look at his face. "I hated you because I love what Allison represents. But— without you, I would never have found it, never have recognized it. My life is all about loss. And fear. You don't get to be Chase Loern and have anything that you care about. I'm terrified that she'll die. Sometimes I can't breathe through the fear." He looked away. "Margaret said that you're not the Queen of the Dead because you have friends and family, and they survived. She doesn't think you can become the Queen—because of that. Maybe she's right."

"She's right," Allison said, taking the decision out of both of their hands. How long had they been talking? Emma hadn't even heard her approach, and it was impossible to walk quietly in this snow. "I think the portal's beginning to . . . fray."

It was.

Emma reached out to touch it and withdrew her hand, frowning. She walked past Allison, leaving her with Chase, and approached the portal's visible edge. Fraying was exactly the right description; she could almost see liminal threads as they lost cohesion and shape. Without thought, she caught those threads in a mittened hand. Nothing happened.

Her hands were already cold. Worse than cold. They ached. But she pulled off her mittens and shoved them in her pockets, thinking, absurdly, that she had no idea what the weather was like in the City of the Dead—as if this were a class trip or a not entirely welcome family vacation.

The air was bracing; she expected that.

The threads were like ice. She'd expected that as well but had hoped it would be different. They didn't pass through, or around, her exposed palm; she caught them. They began to glow.

Margaret appeared to her left. Helmi appeared to her right.

"What will she do with Eric?" Emma asked softly.

"Love him," Margaret replied.

"Does she even understand what that means?"

"No," Helmi said. "She can't hurt Eric."

"She can. She can turn him into another power generator."

"Do you think that's much worse than what he has now? After what you've said?"

Emma did. But she couldn't say why or how because she *wasn't* dead. She couldn't see the world as the dead did. "Will my father be able to find me?"

Helmi's jaw dropped. She turned to Margaret. "Is she for real?"

Margaret, however, said, "Yes, dear." To Helmi, she added, "Allison's younger brother is in the hospital, fighting for his life because of your sister's actions. Emma's father is the only information conduit they currently have."

"Did he—did he come out of hiding too early?"

Emma didn't understand the dead. She couldn't imagine that someone centuries old would think to ask that question—and in that tone of voice. She didn't know if death defined the dead in any way but state. Yet she heard the question clearly—and heard all that lay beneath it, and she thought that maybe the dead were not so easily changed as all that. She held out a hand not to the ancient, dead sister of the Queen of the Dead, but to the little girl who had been murdered by angry, terrified, villagers.

Helmi took it. And, oh, the *cold*. "You need both your hands," she said, but so quietly Emma almost missed it. Nor was Emma unkind enough to point out that Helmi was holding her hand regardless.

"I don't know what I'm doing with *one* hand," she told the girl. "But if I do end up needing two, I know you'll let go." She caught more of the threads, winding them, by simple motion, more tightly around her palm and her fingers. Cocoons in stories worked like this; the strands shimmered, impossibly delicate.

The more she gathered, the more slowly the portal frayed.

"Go through?" Chase asked.

Emma frowned. "Not yet. There's something—" She shook her head. "Don't let me fall?"

"What?"

She closed her eyes.

In the darkness, there was no road. In the darkness, there were people. In Amy's house, Longland had bound four; whoever had created this portal had bound two. They weren't like Margaret had been; they could see her. They could follow her with their eyes.

No, she thought, frowning; they weren't looking at her. They were looking at Helmi. Helmi, attached by the hand, was visible to Emma, even through closed eyes. Everything about the child was cast in sharp relief. The lines of her hair, her face, her hands and her clothing seemed harder, crisper. Light lent a glow to her eyes.

It was the light that drew the eyes of the two bound to the portal: a woman Margaret's age, with long, thick dreadlocks that fell down her back and around her shoulders, and a prim man who appeared to be much older and paler.

They could neither move nor speak, but their gaze fell on Helmi.

"It's not me they're looking at," Helmi whispered. She lifted her face and looked up at Emma. Emma was surprised at how much her expression hurt. When Helmi spoke to Longland—or to Alraed—she looked older and harder and just . . . meaner. But right now, hand in Emma's, she looked as if she *needed* an anchor, a guardian. She was a child.

She had seen things no child, in any sane world, would *ever* have to see. She hadn't come to Emma seeking rescue, not really; she'd come to find Eric. Possibly to torment Eric, she seemed to dislike him so much.

But she *had* found Emma. She'd found Michael. She had overcome her reluctance and fear for long enough to take the hand Emma offered her. It was literal, yes, the offered hand—but it was also metaphorical, because life could be, and often was, both. Emma's hand was cold. Emma's *everything* was cold. But she made no move to free herself.

Instead, she lifted Helmi's hand.

"You have to move *quickly*," Helmi told her, looking at the two dead people who powered the portal. "They'll be pulled back. This was never meant to last."

Emma had once stood, lantern in hand, and asked the names of everyone who approached her. All were dead. But all were human. She didn't hold the lantern now, and she was afraid to do so, this close to the place where the Queen of the Dead had stood, commanding Alraed. She had no illusions: The Queen of the Dead had more power and far greater experience. Emma had power, but it was a power she didn't understand. She'd never sneered at good intentions—they were better by far than bad ones, in her opinion—but good intentions here wouldn't cut it.

And yet.

She couldn't give up on them. "Come with me," she said to Helmi, as if Helmi were actually eight, and lost.

She approached the woman first; the woman's dead eyes seemed to see her, although they didn't move. No chain bound her, not that Emma could see. Margaret and the others had been bound together, roped in necklace-thin golden light that connected them.

Helmi, however, said, "Their feet."

Emma knelt. Helmi was right; the binding that held these two in place was anchored, somehow, to the road itself. "Do portals always require an anchor?"

"Yes. Here the road is best. It's much harder to open a portal without that grounding. Longland could do it. Alraed *can*. But it's a huge outlay of power, and it leaves the Necromancer vulnerable should he be attacked."

"By hunters."

Helmi nodded. "Or by other Necromancers looking to rise in the ranks. There are other ways to anchor, but those aren't taught now. They were, once. After she almost died, my sister changed what she taught the Necromancers she gathered."

"I've always wondered how she could find us."

"But not how Eric could?"

"I don't think Eric does—I think your mother does. But I can't imagine your mother helping the Queen of the Dead." She hesitated for a moment and then said, "I need my hand back for a minute."

Helmi closed her eyes. Nodded. It took Emma a moment to untangle their fingers, because her hand was numb. The winter air felt warm in comparison, but only briefly. She reached for the delicate chains that bound the woman's ankle. They were much tighter than the chains that had bound Margaret—and they were colder.

She opened her eyes and crossed the road to examine the chains around the ankle of the man. They were just as tight. Nothing seemed to bind him to the woman across the stretch of the portal.

"Emma?" Ernest's voice reached Emma as if from a great remove. She shook her head.

"Emma," Margaret said, her voice much clearer. "If you do not leave soon, you will not be able to follow. There has been some confusion on the other side of the portal; I believe we can take advantage of that confusion—but we must do it *soon*."

Both the man and the woman appeared to be serving as support pillars; the portal stretched between their still, bound forms, rising in a half circle above them. That, too, was collapsing slowly.

Emma frowned, and then, bending until her face was almost touching the dirt covered, flattened snow, she found her way in: a single, slender chain that ran from ankle to road and vanished there. This was short enough it was hard to grasp, but she managed; she could find no other way to pull at the chains that seemed almost a part of their skin.

These chains cut into her fingers as she tugged at them, but as she did, they loosened, falling away from ankles to float almost freely in the air. The man blinked and looked down at her—he had to look down—as she rose. She ran across the road again, back to the woman, looping golden wire around her palm before she did.

The woman was bound to earth the same way the man was; Emma freed her in the same way. Neither moved from the position they'd occupied, but they did move; they seemed to inhale as they noticed their surroundings. They blinked. They turned toward her and toward Helmi.

"I'm Emma," she told them, voice shaking slightly. "Emma Hall. And I'm sorry, but I need your help."

## ⤷ Chapter 6

The older man spoke first. "Where am I?" His accent was thick, but Emma recognized both the words and the confusion in the question.

"You're a couple of hours outside of Toronto. That's in Canada," she added, in case he didn't know. "It's winter." She wanted to ask him where he thought he was, or when he'd last been aware of his surroundings; she didn't. Instead, she turned to Margaret. Margaret spoke to the man quietly, as Emma turned her attention to the woman.

"What would you have of me?" The woman asked, her voice so worn and weary Emma's initial impulse was to say, *Nothing, you've done enough.* But it wasn't true; she wanted—she needed—something, and that something was not, in the end, different from what the Necromancers demanded.

"I need you to do what you've been doing until my friends and I can reach the—the City of the Dead."

"It is not someplace you want to be," the woman answered, with more force and less resignation. "You're not dead."

"I'm not, no."

"All that waits you there is death. It's where the dead go. It's where the dead *rot*." She looked up, past Emma's shoulder. Emma thought she would cry. Her lips twisted in a bitter grimace instead, which was better—but not by much. "I won't help you if it's my permission you require."

Margaret came to stand beside the woman. Her expression was frosty; she lost the carefully cultivated look of a matron as she regarded the woman. "She requires permission, but if you will not give it, you will not. Move."

"Margaret—"

"We *do not have time*, Emma. Short of agreeing to go with the Queen's knights, as she calls them, you will never reach the City of the Dead. And if you are accompanied by those knights, you will, in all likelihood, not survive an hour. Nothing you can do—nothing we can do—is effective against the Queen herself at this distance."

"I opened the door," Emma said quietly. "And I was nowhere near her at the time."

"Yes." Margaret's expression gentled. "But you could not *keep* it open. If you truly mean to free the dead, you must go to the Queen."

Emma looked at the glowing, slender chains around one palm. She reached out and offered her hand to Helmi again, and Helmi took it, even as Emma flinched at the cold.

"Eric will kill her," Chase said.

Margaret did not reply. The older man, however, said, "Ms. Henney is persuasive. I apologize for my disorientation. It is seldom that I both serve and am left to my own devices and my own form. We are here to anchor the portal. You can see it, yes?"

Emma nodded, throat dry, as Allison and Michael approached her. "You—you know what—what's done with your . . ." the words trailed off.

The man smiled at her gently—and as if she were four years old. *All of you look like babies to someone as old as me.* Who had said that? She thought it was Ally's grandfather but couldn't be certain; the voice was strong, but there was no accompanying image. Just her own sense of resentment at being treated like a child.

There was no resentment now. If someone arrived who could take the burden of this fight from her hands, someone responsible and—yes—adult, she would hand it over gratefully.

And yet, here she was, all the responsible adults in her life hours away. Ernest was here—but Ernest wasn't a Necromancer. Whatever it was he intended Emma to do, he couldn't do it or he would have done it by now, and they wouldn't be here. She was holding the hand of a girl who had existed for far longer than she had, and people were looking to her for guidance or even orders.

Emma's desire in life had been—and still was—to play a supporting role. She could imagine herself as the second-in-command almost anywhere, tending to the details and supporting the person who could deal with the big picture and make the decisions. All of the decisions she felt competent to make were small: what to wear, what to do with her hair, what make-up to buy, what to cook or eat for dinner, what classes to take. Even the question of which university to attend had given her hives.

This? This was too much. It was too much for her.

And this man seemed to know it. His smile was kindly, but it wasn't exactly saturated in respect, and oddly enough, right at this very moment, she couldn't resent it at all.

"I'm terribly sorry," he said. "I didn't introduce myself. There hasn't been great call for good manners for a long time. My name is Marcel." He glanced at the woman, who glowered. But she looked at Helmi, at Helmi's hand, ensconced in Emma's, and her expression gradually softened.

"Name's Belinda. Friends called me Belle, back in the day." She extended a hand. Emma glanced down at Helmi, who looked mutinous. She then lifted the hand that was bound in their chains—it was the right hand, anyway.

Belinda took it firmly; when she'd been alive, she'd probably had a crusher handshake. Her hand was cold. Emma expected that. What she didn't expect was the way the handshake changed the woman's features. Her brows rose, her mouth dropped open. No words came out for what felt like too long.

"Do we have time for this?" Amy asked. She added, because she was Amy, "I'm Amy Snitman, Emma's friend. We're in a bit of a rush because that portal isn't going to last all night."

The woman's eyes opened further. "You—you can see me?"

Sarcasm flashed, briefly, across Amy's face. Amy was not part of the welcoming committee, anywhere, ever. She managed to rein it in and said, "When Emma holds your hand, the rest of us can see you. It's not good for Emma, though."

Belinda shook her head. "It's so *warm*." She proved she was more adult than Helmi; she released Emma's hand. "What do you want with that portal?" Some of the wonder was still contained in the hard edges of her very practical tone.

"We need—all of us—to get to the City of the Dead."

"You'll die."

"We might. But we're all going to die one day, anyway."

"Not the way she'll kill you. You want to kill her?"

"We want—" Emma exhaled. "*I want* to stop her. I've led a pretty easy life. I've never lived in a war zone. I've never lived on the streets. Almost all of the violence I've seen, I've seen at a safe remove."

"Almost?"

"Long story. I don't know if I *can* kill another human being. But if she's not stopped, she's the hell that everyone I love is going to. I don't care if she dies. What I want is for the dead to be able to leave this world."

"It's what the dead want, as well," Belinda said. "Fine. If I tell you I don't want to help you, will you force me?"

Emma shook her head. "But . . . I have that luxury. Helmi is here. Margaret is here. They're willing to help even if you're not."

Helmi snorted. "She's testing you."

Emma nodded. "Wouldn't you, in her position?"

"Marcel isn't."

"Maybe he's just more trusting."

"Or more of a suck-up," Belinda snapped. Marcel didn't appear to be unduly upset by the insult.

"How can you help?" Emma asked.

"If it's true that we have choice," Marcel replied, "I believe that we can shift—slightly—the destination to which the portal will take you."

"I've arranged for a bit of distraction," Helmi told him.

"Yes. Perhaps our help is unnecessary or even unwelcome."

Emma shook her head. "Do you know the City?"

"I doubt I know it as well as the Queen's sister—but yes, I know it. The dead come to the City and not always because they are called. If they are wise, they avoid it, of course; some have even escaped it, once they've walked its streets. I was not so wise."

"Are you bound to the Queen?"

"No. And yes, the person who held my reins will know that I am gone. He will perhaps assume that I have finally been fully consumed. I cannot offer to take you somewhere safe; there is no safety in the City for the living."

"Or the dead," Emma murmured.

"Even so. But you must move quickly, as your friend says."

Margaret walked to where Belinda had been standing while she was bound. "Let me," she offered.

Belinda nodded. She came to stand by Emma's side, her hands behind her back. Yes, Emma thought, she was being tested. And yes, it made sense. Respect wasn't always given; sometimes it had to be earned. Belinda had no reason to trust anyone living who could actually see her—and many, many reasons not to.

Michael still held Petal's lead. Chase, red hair almost glowing with reflected light, joined them, as did Ernest. Amy stood slightly back, frowning, her arms folded.

"Where will the portal open?" Emma asked.

"There are buildings in the city itself that are no longer used—if they ever were. The dead don't need housing. The Queen did not pull those buildings down, and when she chooses to walk—to parade—in celebration, she orders the dead to fill the windows as she passes beneath them. That is where you will be going."

Emma repeated this for the benefit of the living. To Amy, she added, "Any last questions?"

"A lot. They'll have to wait."

Ernest went first, at Ernest's less than silent insistence. Chase followed, glancing once at Allison as if he were afraid to leave her behind. Maybe he was, but he was more afraid of what waited on the other side, because they couldn't *see* anything. Dim outlines and darkness, that was it.

She almost asked Marcel if the buildings were furnished, but Chase cursed loudly enough to be heard. Emma stopped breathing until the cursing stopped; it was followed by the right type of silence.

Helmi let go of Emma's hand. "I'll meet you there," she said. "I don't like portals, and I don't use them."

"Belinda? Marcel?"

"We will follow you before the portal vanishes," Marcel replied. When Emma looked confused, he looked, pointedly, at her right hand.

Emma reached out—with her numb left hand—and placed it gently around Michael's shoulder. "Let's go," she said quietly.

"And get Nathan back?" Michael asked, as Petal sniffed the hem of his coat—where the pockets were.

She nodded.


Stepping through the portal was not at all like stepping through an open door, which was what Emma had been expecting. It was very much like entering an old train tunnel, but without concrete or plaster or rock for walls.

It was gray here, charcoal gray. There were hints of light, but like faint stars, they could only be seen in the corners of Emma's vision; they vanished when she turned to look.

"No wonder Helmi doesn't like portals," she said aloud.

"Helmi dislikes portals because she understands the perversion that creates them."

Emma was not surprised to see an ancient, rag-covered woman walking by her side. She carried a cane, although it wasn't necessary. Nothing about her appearance was necessary.

"Oh?"

"Do you think we traveled this way in my youth? We could have avoided a great deal of danger had we done so. Travel was not for the faint-hearted; it was for the desperate. And we so often were."

"Yet you're here."

"Yes, Emma, I am here. This is a space that the living do not own; they can use it only if they have the power of the dead to anchor them. It is a space we once reached without the need to physically enter it; a space we traversed to find the lost and bring them safely to their new home." She looked, briefly, to her left, somewhere above Emma's head. "It is how we found the dead we could not touch or reach. It's not what you did when you went to the boy in the fire. It's not what you did when you found Mark. Were you trained, you could have done either from the absolute safety of your own circle, your own home.

"This path is not bound to, or by, geography, because the dead aren't."

"Andrew and Mark were, though."

"They were trapped; they believed they were still alive. When I was magar, boys such as those would have been my responsibility. They were lost.

"Belinda and Marcel are not. They are not trapped in the moment of their death. They know where they must go—and know, as well, that they cannot. They should not be here. In my youth, in my life, they would not have been."

"Are you here to guide us?"

"You have your guide at the moment. I am not bound to you."

Marcel appeared by Emma's side, gazing about the gray and featureless landscape as if he were on a nature walk. Emma wondered what he could see because, clearly, he could see something. She didn't ask. Instead, gathering courage, she said, "Marcel, are you bound to me?"

His brows rose, but his smile was gentle. "You are definitely unlike other Necromancers I have known. Yes, Emma. At the moment, I am yours."

"I don't know how to let go," she confessed. "Binding is supposed to take hours. This didn't." She lifted the slender chains.

"Perhaps," he said, "it would be best—for me at least; I cannot speak for Belinda—if you continued to hold me. I do not believe that Necromancers are taught how to release the dead they control, but I could be wrong."

"You are not wrong," Margaret said. "Divesting oneself of power was not a concern. Gathering it was."

Petal whined. If everyone else found the nothingness of the landscape unsettling, Petal found it frightening. There was very little as pathetic as a frightened creature the size of a rottweiler. Emma would have distracted him with food, but food was in backpacks, and they would need to husband it. They had no idea where they were going and no idea whatsoever how long they would be there.

"Marcel?"

"Ah, apologies," the older man said. "It has been some time indeed since I've been free to wander." He coughed a little, which Emma understood to be a type of punctuation, and added, "My apologies if I stare."

"At what?"

"You, Emma Hall. When I'm this close, what I see in you is enough to blunt the hunger."

She didn't ask what hunger meant; she thought she knew. She had seen what lay beyond the closed door she had, with so much effort and so much support, opened briefly, and she had wanted it for herself: an end to grief, an end to loneliness, an end to the weight of responsibility.

She did not, at this moment, want that. She wanted life, because life was not only those things. The man beside her would never have that life again.

Emma had mastered the art of small talk by learning to find almost anything superficially interesting. At the moment, that hard-won mastery deserted her; she had almost nothing to say.

But true to Hall upbringing, she felt slightly guilty about it. "Do you know very much about the Necromancer who bound you?"

Marcel was silent for one long minute. "Not directly, no. The Necromancers are not particularly interested in the dead as people; they are interested only in the power they can harvest. As a virtual slave, my interest in my master would be different: I want to pay attention and to understand them in the vain hope that that understanding will give me the key to avoid both abuse and punishment. But the knowledge the dead gain simply by being dead is about what you'd expect. You possibly know more about me now than the Necromancer did."

"I only know your name," Emma pointed out.

"Indeed."

"Do you know how much longer this is going to take?"

"I don't have the same sense of the passage of time as you do. The dead generally don't. It is perhaps one of the few mercies granted us in this world. I believe, however, that the passage through the portal is extended by geographic distance. It won't take as long to reach the destination as it would by boat or foot. Did you really open the door?"

"Not fully," she replied, "and not for long. And it took—it took hundreds of people's help."

"Dead people."

She nodded, and because there was no end to the walk in sight, she told him about Andrew Copis and the events that led to the opening of the door. She left out the lantern, because the magar remained by her other side.

When she had finished, he nodded, gravely. "I believe," he said, "we are here." He glanced at the magar.

Belinda, walking slightly ahead, snorted. "You always talked like this?" she asked him.

"In English, yes. It was not my mother tongue."

"It would drive me crazy," Belinda told him. "We're here, girl. Time to go back to the real world."

The real world, as stated, was a dark, large room, but by the time Emma entered it, it was crowded. The dead didn't need space, but the living did, and they took up a lot of it.

It was cold, in this room. Almost as cold as it had been in Amy's cottage before the electric baseboards had been turned on. There wouldn't be any source of heat here, if Marcel was right. This room was part of a building designed and created only for display. She was a bit surprised that there was more than just facade, a stage prop that could be brought out and carted off based solely on need.

"There should be windows," Emma said, into the darkness.

Someone moved past her, and something moved into her legs, at almost the same time. Petal whined. Emma knelt and hugged him, scratching behind his ears. Petal wasn't much of a barker, unless he was at home. This wasn't his home, and he knew it.

This wasn't anyone's home. A wall of harsh light broke the darkness as Ernest pulled heavy curtains back.

"That's a pretty serious window," Amy said.

Given the size of the room, it was.

Ernest stepped back, lifting an arm. "If we're standing in the window, we can be seen." That stopped everyone, even Amy.

It didn't matter. One didn't have to stand in the window to see out. On the opposite side of what Emma assumed was street was a two-story building with long, tall windows. Two-story buildings seemed to go on in either direction, although to the left, they appeared to end in a corner. Individually, they weren't impressive, but they were of a kind; there were no odd houses, no notable differences in architecture.

It didn't matter; after the first glance, they became irrelevant.

Towering above them at a height that almost obscured all of the sky was a building that defied imagination. A Tolkien artist might have created it in concept sketches before someone had to draw and render it, or worse, create it from scratch. It was both wide and tall; it had one spire that rose, narrowing slowly as it gained height. Beneath that spire were towers, all of stone, and upon those towers, flags had been raised.

The dead couldn't raise flags—and couldn't lower them, either.

"Yes," Margaret said quietly, when words failed them all—even Amy. "That is the Citadel. In it, you will find the Queen of the Dead."

"If she believes Eric," Amy said into the pause that followed, "will she decide that it's the right time for a parade?"

It was a good question. And Helmi, who had not accompanied them on their long walk, was the one who answered it. "Yes." Emma reached out and offered Helmi a hand, which Helmi took with almost alarming speed. She then, to Emma's surprise, repeated the answer so that Amy could hear it.

"Which doesn't make this the ideal hiding spot."

"No. But it might help us, anyway."

"How, exactly?"

"If she believes Eric will finally stay with her forever, she'll do two things. First, she'll summon her Court."

"Which means that there won't be random Necromancers on alert anywhere else."

"They're always careful," Helmi replied. "They use the dead to spy on each
other. The advantage of being dead—and bound—the *only* advantage, is that
the spies can't be killed. They can't be blinded, and they can't be bound by
anyone else. The older Necromancers use this to intimidate the newer ones.
Those that survive learn to overlook the presence of other people's dead." She
hesitated, and then continued. "If the dead are left to spy—and they will be if
Court is in session—they'll tell their masters what they've seen. They don't
have any other functional choice."

"I can stop them," Emma said, with more confidence than she felt.

Helmi nodded. "But if you stop them, the Necromancers will know instantly. The Necromancers who used Belinda and Marcel to sustain the portal
know that they've lost them both. They're not going to be particularly happy
about it, either. If it was Alraed—"

"It was Alraed, at least for me," Belinda said.

"—his concern will be replacing them. He'd be sweating if Longland were
still alive. With the absence of Longland, there's less to threaten him. Without
Belinda, he's still powerful. He doesn't have the power of the Queen, but the
Queen seldom kills her knights. She leaves them to kill each other.

"After she's enthroned Eric, after she's made a public display of both him
and his love, she'll probably leave the Citadel to go on parade. In other circumstances, you might even like the parade—it's pure spectacle. She'll expect every
attendant she has, every servant, every knight, and even the dead who personally serve her, to be lining these streets and filling these windows. During that
time, the Citadel will be empty."

"That's when we need to make our move."

Chase and Ernest exchanged a glance. "How many of the dead are used as
spies outside of the Citadel? How many could we expect to find in these
houses?"

"Here?" Helmi shrugged. "None. I told you: no one lives here. The Necromancers, especially the youngest, live in the Citadel. It's where they train, eat,
and sleep."

"Where does their food come from?"

"That," Helmi replied, "is a good question. It's not grown here. There are
no farms in the city. There's a greenhouse in the Citadel, but it's not used for
food."

"Food has to be brought here."

Helmi nodded. "Among the oldest of the Necromancers are those with less
power and less ambition. They see to the Queen's finances and the necessities
of the living—but they do it from the ground."

"Ground?"

Helmi frowned. "Ground." When this failed to sink in, she added, "We're in the air. The whole of the Citadel is a floating city. It is built on the dead, and of the dead—literally. There are very few structures here—including this one—that aren't composed entirely of people who were once like Belinda and Marcel."

"What do you mean?" Allison asked. She'd been silent since they'd entered the portal. "You don't mean we're standing *on* the dead?"

"I mean exactly that," Helmi replied; she looked annoyed. "You've seen—maybe you haven't. Emma has seen the shapes the dead can be forced to take. We only look human in our natural form—but we can be molded, blended or twisted into almost any shape. The beams beneath the floor; the planks beneath your feet; the stones in the street below. All of it. She built this city out of the dead."

# Reyna

The Queen is weeping.

She has sent everyone—living or dead—from her chambers and has sealed herself in the large, stone room into which, over decades, she has carved a fitting circle for a Queen. It was meant to bring her power. And peace. No tears, no act of human rage, can break it. Nothing can be erased by the accidental brush of skirts, of feet. The circle is complete and whole.

There, on the northernmost edge of the circumference, wind, air: the symbol for breath and thought. Opposite it, the most complicated of the symbols, water, for life: for tears of both joy and despair. The latter, she has shed for centuries, an ocean's worth.

She cannot be seen to be weak. When she is weak, people attempt to take advantage of the weakness; they think her stupid or shallow or vain. And perhaps she is, in part, all of those things—but only in part.

She has no living family. Of the dead, only Helmi remains by her side; those she did not bind left her, sooner or later. She bound none of her family. None. Their power was not meant to be a weapon. It wasn't, in the end, meant to be a shelter either—she knows the lie in that belief. They died. She didn't.

Her mother left almost immediately, abandoning her to her dreams of safety and freedom in angry judgment. And what, in the end, was Reyna's crime?

*She didn't die.* The power that she'd used to survive was the power of the dead, yes. But what had the alternative been? To die, as her mother had died? To bleed out the rest of her short life without ever *knowing* life at all?

*Yes*, her mother says. Even though she's not here, Reyna can still hear the word. She has lived the whole of her life under the cloud of her mother's disapproval. She no longer expects that to change.

No one, in the end, stays by her side.

And she has wanted it. Once, when she was young, she had had a brief dream of life, of love. She had planned to have daughters, but her daughters would not be forced to become seekers, as she was. Her daughters would have the life that she herself had wanted so badly and was denied.

There are no daughters, for Reyna. No children. The only person she has ever wanted to create a family with is Eric. And Eric, like her mother, refused her. She offered him everything. She changed the world to bring him back to life. He is alive now only because she loved him so much she was willing to do anything for him.

Anything.

She stops weeping; she inhales several shaky breaths. Eric is finally returning. It doesn't matter why.

She dresses. She has help dressing; the youngest of the Necromancers—two boys, one girl—have been trained to assist her when she requires assistance. They are sullen, bruised children; the smaller of the boys has a discolored eye. They are not as graceful as they will no doubt become—if they survive.

She thinks about Eric as she is dressed. She thinks about Eric and the village in which she met him, about love and death and abandonment. She thinks that she is lying to herself; why he's returning does matter. She worries at it in stiff silence. She has called for a full meeting of the Court, and her own attendants must be given time to prepare themselves appropriately—but she wants to look her best.

Her best involves powders and starches and oil. Her best involves complicated, intricate dresses. Her best involves the crown that she wears only in the massive audience chambers—it is too heavy to wear at other times.

She has a similar crown for Eric, if he will wear it. He has never once taken his place at the throne by her side. She does not know whether he will take it now. This is not the first time he has been in her Citadel. But it is the first time he has agreed to the escort of her knights without killing some of them first.

Why? Why now?

This should be her moment of triumph. This should be a moment in which life—the desire for life—triumphs. But a single word inserts itself into the stream of her thoughts, like a large rock in a small stream.

*Emma.*

She feels as if she is falling, although the ground beneath her feet is solid.

He has come home, yes—but is it a coincidence that he has come only at the appearance of this Emma, this stranger who she is now certain opened the door, however briefly?

She suspects that her mother has given Emma the single gift she had left to give. She did not pass it to her daughter; of course not. She passed it, in the end, to a stranger. A girl who would be here, helping her Queen dress, had it not been for . . . Eric.

How did he meet this Emma?

How did he meet her and fail to kill her? He has killed others before; some were younger than Emma, some a bit older. It makes no sense. What did he see in this girl? What did her mother see? She should have demanded more information from Nathan. She shouldn't have been content to let things slide. But she was, and now she is paying for it. She has all the time in the world—and so does Nathan, if she desires it.

But all the time in the world has become a very sudden now. This moment contains Eric. And she will face him without all the facts she suddenly feels she needs.

Reyna is afraid in the moment of her greatest happiness. She is afraid that he will not love her. That he might, instead, love someone else. That was her fear in the village, as well—but she never feared it when she was actually by his side. His smile, his focus, his dreams destroyed all but the shadow of fear.

He has not been with her for centuries, and that shadow is so strong it looks like night.

She will know. When she sees Eric, she will know.

## ᔣ Chapter 7

Emma knelt.

Her knees had locked for three long breaths as Helmi's words sunk in. This was probably good; it prevented her from collapsing.

In the graveyard in which Nathan's ashes were buried her dog had run across grass and inlaid stones. She hadn't thought twice about it. She herself, however, had never stepped directly upon the symbols of grief and memory that other families, other bereaved, had left.

Even so, there was a layer of stone and earth over ash—or coffins. She would not, in a million years, have let her dog walk across corpses. She would never have walked across them herself.

And yet, here she was, and the floor—which looked and felt like a normal floor—was composed of the dead. Not of corpses, not precisely; it was worse than that. She swallowed; her throat was dry in the cold air, and for just a moment, she wondered if she would ever feel warm again.

All of the dead she *could* see watched her: Helmi, Belinda, Marcel, and Margaret.

"Can you see them?" she asked, her voice almost inaudible to her own ears.

Everyone living looked at her then as well.

No one answered.

"Can you hear them?" she asked, her voice louder. Her hands were shaking, and not with cold, although Helmi's hand had numbed hers.

"Can you?" Helmi countered. She was the only person who spoke. The only dead person. Amy wanted to know what Emma was talking about.

Emma closed her eyes. She placed her free hand on the surface of the floor itself; the floors were cold, but not in the way that Helmi's hand was. She listened, but Amy's voice was too loud. That might have been a mercy in any other circumstance. Today Emma couldn't allow it.

"Amy," she said, eyes closed. "Give me a minute."

"To do what?"

"To listen to the dead."

Amy fell silent. Emma could imagine her expression.

Silence. The silence of the dead. The silence of the grave, which, no matter how personal the loss, was also unapproachable and impersonal: a fact of life. Death was. But as Emma listened, she could hear the attenuated, distant sound of weeping. There was more than one voice. There were no faces. Nor were there words. Not for the dead and not, at the moment, for Emma.

She pressed her hand into the floor; it fooled the senses. It was *floor*, with about as much give as any of the floors in her own home. For one long moment, Emma wanted to join the voices in their weeping and their grief.

That would help no one.

"What are you doing?" Ernest asked, taking over Amy's role.

"I'm trying to . . ." what? What exactly was she trying to do? "I'm trying to reach them."

"Reach *who*?"

"The dead, Ernest."

How had she reached them before? The lantern. She almost lifted it—how, she wasn't certain—but stopped. She was in the Queen's city, and she felt certain that if the lantern were raised here, the Queen would know. Hiding would be impossible.

Without its light, what did she have? Had Mark been a part of the floor, she would never have heard him. She could never have spoken with him. Who spoke to the floor? Or the walls? Who expected them to weep?

Emma reached.

She heard Helmi's sharp intake of breath—a breath that was cosmetic in every way—but didn't look up. The floor's texture changed; it became disturbingly less floorlike beneath her rigid palm. The weeping grew louder, more distinct. Emma reached again, as she had once reached for the mother of a dead four-year-old boy.

This time, she felt pain, ice, and nausea. And the voice beneath her hand grew ever more distinct. The weeping stopped, shuddering to a halt the way weeping sometimes did. A disembodied voice asked, "Who's there?"

Hope was carried in the two words: hope and fear.

"Emma," Emma said. "Emma Hall. I'm—" Words failed her. What could she say? *You're part of the floor and I'm standing on you?* No. No, she couldn't say that. She had no idea how much awareness the dead had. When Margaret had been bound to a wall in the Snitman mansion, she had seen—and heard—nothing. Or so Emma had assumed.

She forced herself to work free of those assumptions now. The dead were like clay. They could be molded and shaped into any form; they could be forced to fill any function. Here they were the floors. The floors, the roof, anything else in this unfurnished room. They weren't the windows—their absence was—but they were probably the cobbled streets outside the windows, the facades of the architecturally uniform buildings, the *stairs*.

Anything but the food.

This was a type of slavery that Emma had never conceived of in her life, and she'd spent a unit in school studying slavery until it had become very difficult not to be sick to death of humanity.

"Emma?" The voice was quavery, but Emma thought a young man spoke. Or perhaps a young woman. It was hard to tell, and at this particular moment, it was irrelevant.

She was sickened, yes. But that led to two places: despair, which she expected, and anger. She did not want to speak in anger now, not to this person, who didn't deserve it. Marcel had said the dead didn't really mark the passage of time the way they had when they were alive, and Emma fervently prayed that this was the truth.

"Yes. I'm Emma."

"Where are you?"

"I'm right—I'm right beside you. I'm holding your hand. Can you feel it?"

"I can—I can feel your hand. It's—it's so warm."

The dead always said that. To Emma, the floor was not as cold as Helmi. She didn't know why, and at this point, she didn't want to interrupt what little conversation there was to ask Margaret, who might be able to answer.

"Emma," Margaret said, speaking far more gently than she usually did. "I think I understand what you're attempting to do, but it is not wise. It is not yet time for it."

"And when *is* the time for it?" Emma asked, before she could stop herself.

"When the fall won't kill you or your friends."

This made no sense for one long minute, and during that minute, Emma willed herself to feel a stranger's hand, a stranger's fingers. She transferred part of her attention to Helmi, whose hand she did hold. The hands of the dead—even Nathan's—felt like hands with all the warmth sucked out. They had never felt like the flat, impersonal surface of the floor.

But these floors—if Helmi were right—weren't impersonal surfaces.

When the section of floor became a hand, she gripped it far more tightly than she had gripped the hand of anyone dead—except Nathan. And Nathan, she couldn't hold, in the end. She hadn't been prepared for the truth: The Queen had bound him, and the Queen could summon him, in an instant, across a geographical divide Emma could not easily traverse. Love didn't change that in the afterlife.

Love hadn't changed that in life, either.

Emma believed that love was eternal, that it could last forever. It was a thin belief, tested and damaged by Nathan's death, and before that by her father's; she had come, on dark days, to understand that the only eternity was death. Death and its endless silence, endless absence.

And eternity was being played out here in gutting ways. Emma wasn't always certain what she believed about the afterlife—and in some ways, she still didn't know. But this? This was hell. It wasn't the hell of demons or endless fire or endless punishment, but it didn't have to be. Human beings were perfectly capable of creating hell on earth. She just hadn't expected that they could continue to do so when their victims had died.

She meant to end it.

She meant to free the dead.

Thinking it, feeling the heat and the weight and the anger of it, she pulled on the hand she now grasped. She put weight behind it because she had to. She imagined that this was very like catching someone by the hand as they slipped off a cliff. Her arm strained with the weight of a stranger, and her hand locked with the visceral fear that if she could not hold on, they would be lost forever.

It wasn't true. They would be *here*. She could find them again.

But she didn't *believe* that, and she held on until she thought her hand would snap off at the wrist, it was so frozen. Held on to the falling weight, the weight of someone who would be lost if she couldn't maintain her desperate grip.

Michael said, in the distance, "Emma, you're crying."

Was she? She couldn't feel tears on her face—but she felt that particular thickness of throat that comes just before tears, when you're still trying to *talk*. She swallowed and realized he was right. She was crying. But she forced herself to speak, anyway. "Michael, what do you see?"

"It looks like you're trying to make a fist. But there's something in the way."

"You can't—you can't see a hand?"

His silence went on a beat. "Maybe?" he finally said, his tone doubtful. With Michael this actually meant uncertainty.

"You can see Helmi."

"Yes."

Emma found her voice after a long, thick pause. "I am holding someone's hand. I can't see them. I have no idea who they are. I just—I have their hand. It's like when someone's falling off a cliff or a building. I can't let go. But I can't—I can't pull them *up*. I'm not strong enough."

Michael was Michael. He trusted Emma enough that he was willing to try to help; trying sometimes paralyzed him. She almost told him, as he knelt beside her, that there wasn't anything he could do—but she didn't. Because as he reached for her hand, as he placed his *over* hers, interleaving their fingers, she felt *warmth*.

It was warmth she needed now. She closed her eyes briefly before tightening that hand and squeezing Michael's fingers. She didn't know what the dead person felt, if they felt anything at all. Maybe they were just too afraid of falling to have room for anything else. Michael was just afraid for Emma.

Petal nosed around them both; Emma opened her eyes to a face full of anxious rottweiler. The dog-breath she got anyway. But both seemed right, now. "Help me," she whispered to Michael. "Help me pull them up."

And he did.

Inch by inch, the hand that Emma had grasped so desperately became arm, wrist appearing first, and extending—agonizingly slowly—into elbow. She *pulled*, the force of her weight and Michael's almost knocking her off her knees.

"I can see an arm!" Michael said, loudly, in her ear. He had forgotten himself enough to speak loudly—his natural volume. Years of practice at lowering that volume deserted him, and Emma, ears ringing, didn't care.

"I can see it as well," Ally said. "Chase—"

Emma felt arms around her waist. Unfamiliar arms, in a very rough grip. Chase, she thought, surprised.

"What? I'm being careful."

She wanted to weep, but these tears were not tears of despair or fear. He was stronger than either Michael or Emma; he pulled Emma back while Emma held on. The arm gave way to shoulder, to elongated neck, to a face. A face.

Emma couldn't tell whether it was a boy's face or a girl's; it was a young face. Older than Helmi but not yet the age of Emma and her friends, long and thin with wide cheekbones and gaunt cheeks. Emma knew the worst was almost over; Michael's hands tightened—which shouldn't have been possible—as the dead person at last pulled free.

Her absence left an indent in the floor, not a hole, and she blinked rapidly, as if her eyes were real and she hadn't seen light for most of her life. Her lips, both thin and wide, trembled as she looked, at last, at Emma.

"Emma?" she whispered. Emma thought she was twelve or thirteen; she wasn't dressed the way the rest of them were, but Emma couldn't pinpoint her era from her clothing. Amy might have been able to, but Emma didn't ask her; it wasn't relevant.

"Yes," Emma told the girl. "I'm Emma. I'm sorry—I don't know your name."

"Furiyama Tsuki," the girl replied. "You speak my language."

Emma didn't. She spoke English with a smattering of French—French with questionable pronunciation.

"Dead is dead," Helmi said, speaking for the first time. "If she can see you, she can understand you—if you want to be understood." She glanced almost guiltily at Emma's hand—the one she herself was holding.

The girl stared at Helmi for a long, silent beat. "You . . . are dead?"

"So are you."

And Emma remembered that the dead—some of the dead—couldn't immediately see the others. She didn't understand how vision worked for the dead. Now was not the time to ask, and even if it had been, what could this girl tell her?

Helmi, to Emma's surprise, surrendered her hand, and drifted to the far side of the room—closest to the open window, the absence of the dead.

Emma, one hand free, began to shake. It was a mixture of rage and triumph and exhaustion—something had to give. But *not now*. Not now. She dropped her numb free hand to the top of her dog's head and glanced gratefully at Michael, whose fingers were probably stiff, they'd held hers so tightly for what felt like so long. "We did it," she told him. "Thank you."

Chase had released her waist the minute the girl had been pulled free. "No gratitude for me?" he asked, grinning. Before she could answer, he added, "It's okay. I'll get it from Allison."

Her brows rose—but so did the corners of her lips; they twitched. It felt as though it had been years since she'd actually smiled. Allison punched his shoulder, and that fixed the smile in place, allowing it to grow. Chase said 'ouch' in a deadpan tone.

Emma thought: I love these people.

"We're going to need to eat," Ernest said, before she could actually embarrass herself by saying anything out loud. "There's water—drink that. If you feel tired or short of breath, it's the altitude."

"Or raw terror," Amy added, looking as if terror were as far from her as it was possible to get.

"Or that, yes." Ernest exhaled. "Margaret. Explain what just happened to someone who is too old and fixed in his ways to understand it."

Helmi snorted, but this time, Ernest couldn't hear her. Just as well.

"I'm not certain that I have an explanation. I think, judging by expression, Helmi does. But Emma looks exhausted, and I don't think it's a good idea for Helmi to talk to all of us at this time." She looked at Tsuki and at Tsuki's hand. Emma had not released it.

She was almost afraid to do so. What would happen to the girl if she did? Would she somehow go back to being part of the floor? She looked toward that floor and froze.

"Em?"

What had been solid and flat beneath her feet—beneath all of their feet— no longer looked like floor. "Ally—what—what does the floor look like, to you?"

Allison frowned. "The floor? It looks—it looks almost the same. I'd say there's a slight warping, but I wouldn't notice it if I hadn't been here when you pulled Tsuki through it."

"I didn't pull her through the floor," Emma said, voice almost a whisper. "I pulled her *out of* it. She was part of the floor."

"Em, what do *you* see? What are you looking at?"

"Hands," she said, voice faint. "Just . . . hands and arms. It's like they're reaching up out of a dark pit. I can't see anything else. No faces . . ." She closed her eyes. Swallowed. Michael squeezed her hand, but he said nothing before he let her pull away. He then turned to look at the floor, and Emma, out of habit, let her gaze follow him.

The hands passed through Michael as he knelt; they grasped blindly at air. They were silent as they moved, the gestures of each individual and chaotic. Michael couldn't see them, which was a mercy. Emma couldn't *unsee* them, which wasn't.

But she hated it; she thought that Michael, of all people present, would grab each of the blindly grasping hands if he had the ability.

"Is the whole city like this?" Emma asked Helmi.

Helmi, like Emma, was looking at those hands; her own, she reflexively curled. "Probably. What you're seeing now—it's because of what you did. It's not the way the city looks, even to the dead. Not—not normally." She shook her head. "You want to help. But if you did—if you could—the entire structure would fray and disintegrate. While you—and your friends—are in it."

"But they—"

"We've been like this for a long time," Helmi continued. She wouldn't meet Emma's eyes.

"You haven't," Emma countered.

". . . No. Not like this." Helmi looked up. "I don't love my sister," she whispered. "I did, once. Sometimes I remember her as she was before—before they came to kill us. Before Eric died. When we were alive, she could never have done this. Before she met Eric, she would never have tried." In a softer voice, she added, "That's why I hate Eric."

"Eric didn't ask her to do this," Emma replied. It wasn't a question.

Helmi shrugged. "Does it matter, to the dead? If it weren't for Eric, she wouldn't have done it. That's our truth." She then looked at Emma. "You loved Nathan."

It was a blow, but it wasn't the body blow it would have been a month ago. Or two. Emma said, clearly, "Yes. I loved Nathan."

"Would you have resurrected him if you knew how?"

"If resurrection meant bringing him *back*, yes. Yes, I would have." She expected Helmi to sneer, and was surprised when she didn't.

"And now?"

Emma exhaled. "Now? I know the dead can't come back to life. I don't want to drag a pretty corpse beside me from here to eternity." She turned away from the floor to the girl whose hand she still held. "I'm sorry," she said, without thought, because social apology came as naturally as breath.

"Your hand is warm." The girl glanced around the room, her eyes wide and unblinking.

"This is Michael. The girl near the window is Helmi; that's Amy, Allison, Ernest, and Chase. Oh, and Margaret. And this," Emma added, as her dog nudged her hand with his wet nose, "is Petal."

The girl was staring at Emma; her eyes were luminous. They were also uncomfortable to look at; there was a hunger in them that made Emma want to retrieve her hand permanently—even if she thought she understood it.

Help came from an unexpected quarter: Helmi. "You need to let go of her hand."

Tsuki's hand tightened in response.

"She's here to help us," Helmi continued. "But she needs to conserve her power." When the girl failed to respond, she added, in a much sharper tone, "Let go of her hand."

This time, the girl obeyed. She didn't fade from Emma's sight; she did disappear from anyone else's. Or anyone else who was alive.

Petal whined.

"I know," Emma said, scratching behind his ears. "I find it hard, too."

Helmi grimaced. "Try being dead," she snapped. When Emma failed to respond, she shook her head. "Sorry. You don't deserve that. I have to go. Wait here, or as close to here as is safe."

Emma was too shocked at receiving an actual apology from Helmi to reply.

"And I mean it—wait. Stay hidden." She looked at Emma's friends. "Tell them. Tell them what happens to people who don't." And she lifted a hand, and the hand was momentarily red with blood.

"Don't be too angry with her," Margaret said, when Helmi vanished.

"Do the dead not change at all?" Emma asked her.

"They change," Margaret replied. "But death, in some ways, defines them. They don't let go easily of the fears they felt at death. They learn to see them differently. They learn context. They have regrets—but those thoughts and feelings remain central to their existence on this side of death. Even if the way they view them shifts, the fact that they view them . . . doesn't.

"Helmi is no different." Margaret smiled. Helmi rarely saw Margaret smile, and Emma wished, for just a moment, that the girl had remained. "She's seen you, Emma. She understands what you might mean to all of us. But she died because she did not hide. Hiding is second nature to her.

"She understands what your friends mean to you. She understands the event that *made* the Queen of the Dead. She is both fascinated and afraid of what you might become should you face the same losses. If the Queen finds you," she added, "you will." The smile saddened but did not leave her face. "You do not know what it means when you offer us your hand and we take it. It is costly—for you—but you do it, regardless."

Tsuki, who had not left, stared at Margaret and then at Emma. It was not entirely comfortable. She lifted her hand—the hand that Emma had clutched so desperately. "She is right," the girl said, in the softest of voices. "What will you do?"

"Eat," Emma replied. "We'll eat and we'll discuss our possible options. Margaret, you know the citadel. Tell the rest of us as much as you can?"

Margaret nodded.

Michael was not twitching; he was not walking in circles. But he might as well have been. His expression openly revealed what they were all feeling—but he had not yet shifted his focus. He was in an empty house that was built on— made *of*—the dead. He was afraid to sit on the floor; he felt guilty even standing on it.

Emma sympathized. There was, however, no alternative.

"I don't understand why she would do this," Michael said.

Allison—and Amy, who defined the word pragmatic in emergencies—had hit the backpacks; there was a brief and desperate search for a can opener while under the hopeful supervision of a rottweiler who clearly had never been fed in his Entire Life. Ernest eventually intervened, but Ernest was not yet one of Petal's people.

"You are a really, really stupid dog, you know that?" Chase said.

Petal wagged his tail.

"I don't understand it, either," Emma told Michael. "I understand that we have to stop her."

"How?"

"I don't know. But we're here, and there has to be something we can do. She's just one person."

"And her Necromancers."

"We've got Chase and Eric."

"Eric's not here."

"And Ernest. Michael—" Emma caught both of his hands. "We can do this."

Michael was silent.

"The Queen has never been able to find—and capture—Eric. Eric wouldn't be here if he hadn't made that choice. It doesn't matter how powerful the Queen or her Necromancers are. Eric doesn't have any special powers. He's normal, like we are."

"You mean, like the rest of us are?"

Emma did not grimace; she did bite her lip. "Yes. Yes, that's what I meant." She rose.

"Emma?" Michael rose as well, aware that he had said the wrong thing but unaware, at the moment, of why.

"No one wants to be seen as an outsider among their friends." It was Chase, unexpectedly, who intervened. Emma drew one sharp breath. "And no one wants to be seen as the only possible salvation—it's a lot of pressure. You're probably the only person here who won't—or can't—understand that Emma somehow thinks this is all her fault."

Michael frowned. It was the frown with which everyone in the room was most familiar. "How could it be Emma's fault?"

Chase rolled his eyes and ran one hand through his much shorter hair. To Emma's surprise—and growing concern—Chase tried to answer. "Try to see it the way I've seen it. Emma is a Necromancer. Emma—in theory, and given the rest of you, it's a pretty crap theory—could *be* the Queen of the Dead if she had the time. She could be taught. Or teach herself. She could do what the Queen has done." He held up a hand as Michael opened his mouth.

"I told you, it's a crap theory. I believed it when I first met her. But even I can't hold onto that belief. The Queen, however, will. She won't see anything else. The Necromancers will. They won't see Emma, and they don't know her as well as the rest of you do. Emma is thinking that the Necromancers wouldn't have come for her if she didn't have this power. And she's right.

"But neither Eric or I would be here, either. If we weren't here, you wouldn't be here. We wouldn't have the chance to somehow fix things or end things. I didn't see it that way when I met Emma, but I see it now. I've been fighting the Queen of the Dead—or her minions—for most of my adult life. This is the first time I've ever thought we actually have a chance."

"Why?"

"Because Emma *is* powerful. And Emma can do things that even the Necromancers would have said are impossible. She doesn't think the way they do. She doesn't—luckily for her—think the way Eric or I do. None of you do. And maybe that's what's needed. If we had the time, Emma could take the entire city apart without lifting a gun or shedding blood.

"And I think—I think she can open the door permanently. I think she can free the dead."

"Why?" Michael asked, again.

Amy, busy with food she would never have eaten unless she were camping, said, "Because she's already done it once. She almost died saving Andrew Copis. She didn't. Andrew Copis is wherever the dead are supposed to be. And frankly, I'm more than a little tired of all this, and we don't get to go back to real life if she doesn't." When Michael did not immediately nod, Amy added—with less patience than Chase had shown, "She's already proven that she can do it once—with just as little information or education on her part.

"I believe she can do it again, for real this time."

# Eric

Longland can't sweat. If he could, he would. The gun he carries appears welded to his hand. He is pale. Ernest and Chase don't trust Longland. They don't quite understand why Eric does. But neither of them are dead. Hurt, yes. Scarred, definitely. But they exist, persist, among the living.

Being dead has not inured Eric to the fact of death, the fact of loss. He does not want them to die. He has never wanted any of his comrades to die. But want or no, they all have.

Only Reyna is perpetual.

It has been so long since he's seen her. So long since he has dreamed of anything about her but her death, the death she avoided, the death that would free the dead, that would free Eric himself. He can't remember loving her, but he knows that he once did.

He stands in a small room composed of four walls and no windows. There is a door; it is closed. He faces it, Longland by his side. He looks for Helmi. He has often looked for Helmi; she is a flag, a warning that death is coming—but not for Eric. Never for Eric.

He wishes—as he has wished for centuries—that he had never met Reyna. He wishes that she had never loved him. He might have loved her at a distance; he might have felt the pain of rejection, of things one-sided, unfinished. But that pain would be better than this pain.

*Can you kill her?*

*Yes.* Yes, Helmi. That belief has been the pillar of his existence for so long that life itself seems the greater dream. He has never questioned it. Here, in the world Reyna created by dint of will and terror, it is the only way he can atone.

But as the door opens, as he sees the angry, stiff faces of the Queen's knights, he wonders: atone for what? He was a young man, barely more than a boy. She was a young woman—young, slightly wild, always open. Her smile was radiant. Small things delighted her: sunlight on the lake, shadows beneath the boughs of the tree that served as their meeting place, wildflowers. Toads. She liked toads. He remembers because the first time he saw her involuntary smile, he said, *I see. This is why you like me.*

He remembers—only now—the sound of her laughter.

He loved her as the young love the young. She was the center of his world. He believed, had believed, that his family would accept her. He had wanted to spend his life by her side. He had wanted what young men want.

He cannot imagine that he could tell that young man not to love that young woman, not with any hope of success.

"Lord Eric," a young woman says. She curtsies, her back stiff, her expression wary. "Please, accompany us." Before he can speak, she continues. "You will want to change before you meet the Queen."

She is wearing the robes that the Necromancers wear in the Citadel. She rises. Her eyes are living eyes, but they, like Longland's, are heavy and bright with fear. And he has earned that fear.

*Can you kill someone who loves you so much?*

*Yes.* He has always said yes. But he is aware that "yes" is a simple word, an easy word; it encompasses broken desires and self-loathing and memory. He is not certain how he would answer that question if Helmi asked it now.

But he will know, when he sees Reyna.

He'll know.

# Chapter 8

"Can we really trust Helmi?" Amy asked as they ate the world's gloomiest dinner. Allison didn't have much of an appetite, and neither did Emma or Michael. Ernest and Chase ate. No one cared to answer Amy's question; they didn't care for the answer. What choice did they have?

"You're used to this, aren't you?" Allison asked Chase, instead.

He shrugged. "Not really."

"No?"

"I'm used to eating when I have time. The breakfast we cooked at Emma's before we went to fetch Andrew Copis was so out of the ordinary it no longer feels real." Before she could speak again, he added, "I spend most of my life on the run. Running to something, running away from something. I don't expect to die peacefully of old age. I expect on some level that every meal I'm eating might be the last one.

"I don't sleep well. I *can* sleep standing up." He chewed what looked like canned pear, swallowed, and added, "I never want my companions to die. But all of my companions—until now—have been like me. Any of the ones who weren't didn't last very long. None of you are like me."

Ernest coughed.

Chase ignored him. "It's easy for me to contemplate my own death. It's been kill or be killed for years now—it's the only way of life I know." He caught Allison's hand in his, entwining their fingers. "So I'm eating what might be my last meal with people I actually care about. Love makes you weak." As Michael opened his mouth, Chase grimaced and said, "Love makes *me* weak. When I care, I'm afraid. I'm afraid of losing the people who are important to me. Fear makes me stupid. When facing the enemies we've been facing, stupid gets us killed.

"But I want you to *be* what you are."

"Please," Amy said, waving a hand in front of Chase's face. "The rest of us are eating."

"Amy doesn't like public displays of affection," Michael added. "They make people uncomfortable."

Chase laughed. Amy, notably, did not. Allison squeezed the hand that held hers but said nothing. She'd always found Amy intimidating. Nothing had changed that.

Allison wanted to know if her brother Toby was still alive. She didn't want Emma's father to come anywhere near the city of the dead. Caught between these, she retreated—but absent her shelf of comfort books, the retreat was doomed to be incomplete.

"Emma?"

"Margaret's back." There was a pause. "And Helmi's with her." Emma reached out with her left hand, and the younger girl appeared. Margaret, however, materialized on her own.

They didn't have much in the way of paper. They didn't have chalk. Michael had his computer, but there was no source of electricity; Emma wondered if the city of the dead possessed any.

Margaret outlined the city, sans actual map. "The Queen is in her audience chamber. She has summoned her entire court. Even the dead who would normally serve as her spies are in the chamber."

"For how long?"

"Hours," Helmi said. "Think of it as a kind of anti-wedding." She glanced to her left, to a space that appeared to be empty.

"Shouldn't *you* be there?"

"Yes. I can't stay. But I wanted to tell you: Nathan is in the audience chamber as well. He's been assigned to Eric. They're both relatively safe. If you're going to move, now is the time to start. If things go well, she'll be parading in the streets—and you'll be looking down at her if you stay here."

Ernest opened his mouth.

Helmi glared and said, "It is *not* the time to ambush her. She'll have the entire court walking behind her. You've managed to survive her knights so far, but you've never faced their full assembly. Move to a building that's closer to the actual gates of the citadel. When she leaves the gates, I'll come back." She glanced at Emma. Or rather, at Emma's hand. She didn't want to let go.

"Helmi."

But she did. "My sister has never been happy," she said, her voice barely a whisper. She appeared to be staring at her feet; she could have been staring at her almost ridiculous skirts. "You love your friends." It wasn't a question. But the nonquestion was offered to Emma.

Emma's hand tightened, as if to offer brief, wordless comfort. "Yes."

Silence. Extended. Helmi broke it. "The Necromancers believe," she finally said, "that if the Queen dies, the city falls. Anyone living in it will fall as well. It's a long way down," she added, in case this wasn't obvious. "The dead can't die. We'll be fine." The twist of lips that accompanied the last word said many, many things; "fine" wasn't one of them. She fell silent for another long beat, and then her gaze drifted to Michael, who was watching her with some concern.

It wasn't the type of concern she was used to. In the ridiculous dress, she looked like an evil, spoiled princess, and her expression did nothing to dispel that impression. She looked at Michael as if he were a species of animal—or plant—that she couldn't quite place.

"In the history of the citadel, only one man came close to unseating my sister." She glanced at Emma before her gaze was once again dragged back to Michael.

"What happened to him?" Michael asked.

"He died."

Chase grimaced. Since the Queen was obviously alive, there could only be one outcome. Emma lifted a hand before he could put the thought into words. She watched Helmi.

"I think you're all stupid," Helmi told Michael.

"Ignorant," Michael corrected her.

Amy liked neither word and cleared her throat to indicate as much. She didn't follow with words. Like everyone else in the room, she was afraid enough that she wanted to hear the rest of what Helmi had to say—if she said anything more at all.

"His name was Scoros."

More silence.

"He was like a father to her. She trusted him."

"She killed him." Chase's voice was flat, uninflected.

Helmi hesitated again, her gaze upon either her feet or something beneath them.

"Could he be part of the floor?" Emma whispered.

"You don't understand my sister's anger," Helmi replied, her voice no louder. "The floors mean nothing to anyone."

"They mean something," Michael said, his voice much louder than hers.

She looked as if she would argue but not as if she *wanted* to. "They meant nothing to my sister by the time she built them. She doesn't see the dead the way you do." She looked for comprehension in Emma's expression, but it was slow to come. "He wouldn't be floor or wall or anything else that was supposed to look normal. It wouldn't be enough for my sister. She trusted him. He betrayed her."

"Would there be anything left of him at all?"

"I don't know. But when he attempted to overthrow my sister, he had his supporters. I don't think all of them would have been willing to throw their lives away, even to be rid of her. Scoros, by that point, would have. I don't think he valued his own life much by the end.

"You won't be the only person to look. You might be the only person to succeed."

"Your sister knows what happened to him."

"Yes. But she won't share. Not even with me. If I knew where he was, I'd tell you." Bitterly, she added, "If I knew where he was and someone was foolish enough to bind me, I'd tell *them*."

"Which means she thought there'd be something to tell," Amy said, voice rising slightly toward the end of the sentence.

Helmi's glance lost hesitance as she met Amy's eyes. Her lips turned up in a half smile. "I like you," she said. "And yes, that would be my guess." The smile dimmed. "If you have any hope of—of surviving what you came to do, he's your best chance. He might be your only chance." Her hair moved as if in a strong wind; her eyes were the clear, bright eyes of the dead. "You need to get out of the city before the parade starts."

She hesitated, looking down at Emma's hand; her lips thinned briefly, as if she were swallowing pain. Before Emma could speak, she faded from view, taking the cold with her.

Chase was rigid with silence. His arms shook; his knuckles were white. He exhaled only when Helmi disappeared. He then released Allison's hand and began to repack their precious, scant supplies. While he worked, he asked, "Margaret, where does the food come from?" The question made almost no sense to Emma, given Helmi's information.

Margaret, however, answered. "There's a portal in what was once considered a fae cave. The portal is a fixed structure; the passage is two-way. It is small, and it is well hidden. In the history of the citadel people on the ground have stumbled across it—by accident—perhaps a dozen times. For that reason, the citadel side is well guarded. The cave itself, however, is only intermittently watched. If we could reach the door in the citadel, we could escape." This made Chase's question make sense.

Emma exhaled. "If the Queen dies, how much time will we have before everything disintegrates?" As she spoke, she glanced at the floor—at the small indent which was, to her eyes, a field of waving arms.

"According to the Queen? None. It was one of several threats held over the heads of her court. She was our savior, and if we did not wish to commit suicide, we could not unseat her. As attempts have been made regardless, I believe that some of the Necromancers thought she exaggerated for her own benefit; it would not be a first for her."

"How much do you know about those attempts?"

"Very, very little. I'm sorry."

Walking through the empty streets of a small, perfectly laid out city was almost surreal. There were no people except Emma and her friends. There was no traffic. The streets that existed between uniform and well-repaired buildings were wide enough for a large car but not for two, and, honestly, the driver of the large car would have had to be competent.

There were no birds, no trees, no grass—and no dumpsters, no recycling bins, no bushy rodents or rodent cousins. It was like walking through a professional photograph: everything sharp and crisp, everything evocative. As an image, the city invoked the *feel* of history, of things ancient.

That feel suited none of the people trapped in it. Even Margaret seemed withdrawn and tense.

Helmi was right. No one lived here. No one stayed here. If someone happened to look out from the vast reaches of the citadel's tower, they *might* see Emma and her friends—but only if they were looking. This didn't make Ernest or Chase relax, and neither of the two seemed impressed when everyone else did.

"We know what's at stake," Amy snapped.

Emma wondered whether they did. If the city streets seemed surreal, so did their mission. Not a single Emery student had ever killed a person. Or an animal, if it came down to that. Death was something that happened by accident—tragic accident. It was part of life. Murder was different: human beings interfering in the natural order. It implied many, many things: deliberation, malice, choice.

Emma had never lived in a war zone. Chase's entire life was one. But it didn't take Necromancers to create a war zone. Just people. In the end, Necromancers were people. The Queen of the Dead was a person.

And maybe there was a reason, some part of the intricate, messy, chaotic design of the world, that people—individuals—did not possess the powers of gods. Thinking this, she looked up to the sky; the air was thin and cold, but the sky was a clear sheet of blue that seemed to extend as far as the eye could see.

Emma wondered, then, what the Queen of the Dead was doing now. Eric had never been willing to speak about her much—but it was clear to Emma that the Queen of the Dead had been waiting for, searching for, hunting for, Eric. He was here now. What was the Queen of the Dead feeling? Was she happy?

If she had ever been happy, would this city and this citadel even exist?

Emma had not been born into a world that feared—and killed—witches. She hadn't been born into a world in which her family had been murdered before her eyes, in which the natural order was kill or be killed. She could forgive—not that forgiveness was hers to grant or withhold—the death of the villagers who had murdered Helmi, a helpless eight-year-old child. She was certain that had she been the Queen of the Dead in the exact same circumstances, with the exact same power, those villagers would still be dead.

What she couldn't understand was how Helmi's murder, Eric's death, could lead in a straight line to the death of Chase's family, among others. She couldn't follow the transformation of bereaved victim into callous mass murderer. Maybe if one killed, and killed enough—for any reason—life lost its value. All the good intentions, or at least the justified ones, couldn't preserve what life *meant*.

Emma shook her head to clear it. She paused, briefly, to talk to her traumatized dog. She felt a little like Michael at the moment: out of her element and very afraid to be so. She wanted the world to *make sense*. She wanted the world to be safe, or at least predictable. She didn't understand the Queen of the Dead, and because she didn't, she couldn't see the possible paths that led to a future in which they all survived.

It was the only path she wanted to see.

She lifted her face to Michael. "I think," she told him, "I understand a little bit better how you see the world. Nothing that's happening here makes any sense. And I hate it."

Michael met—and held—her gaze.

"Your mother is never going to trust me again."

The citadel was an impressively large and forbidding building. It looked like something taken out of a Lord of the Rings movie, but grimmer. And cleaner. There were no guards at the gates, although the gates were closed.

Margaret did not find this confounding. She took the lead, speaking quietly as she did. Ernest followed; Chase took the rear. Between them, Amy at their head, walked the rest of the Emery students. And Petal, who did not look any happier.

She should have left him.

She should have left him at home. She shouldn't have taken him to Mark's. She shouldn't have kept her promise to Michael. She shouldn't have—

Allison caught her left hand and held it tightly in her right, as if they were—briefly—five years old again, on a school trip. It steadied Emma.

Was it selfish to need people? Was it selfish to want their support and their friendship when things got unbearably hard? She wanted to reassure Allison. She wanted to tell Ally that she was fine. But the words wouldn't come.

Margaret walked around the gate; there was a peaked door to the left of the gate, so small in comparison it would have been easy to miss. "This," Margaret said quietly, "is how everyone but the Queen and her court leaves the citadel. Even when the gates are open, the apprentices and the novices are not allowed to use it; they exit before the Queen and move into their assigned positions in the streets.

"We'll need to move quickly; if she intends a parade, they'll be coming soon." She waited. After an awkward pause, she said, "I'll need someone to actually open the door for the rest of you."

The interior of the citadel was not, as Emma had half-expected, a grim, gothic dungeon. The first thing she noticed was the light. It came in from high ceilings and huge windows in spokes, the air so sterile no dust motes danced in its fall. The walls and the floors were a pale gray beneath carpets and runners and paintings; statues in small alcoves could be glimpsed at a distance.

She wondered if any of those statues were actual dead people, and the sense of evocative grandeur faded, the way safety sometimes did when sleeping dream turned sharply, without warning, into nightmare.

Her hand in Allison's to anchor her, Emma closed her eyes. She could still see the halls. The light, however, vanished. She couldn't see individual ghosts, but she understood that in aggregate, they were here. She opened her eyes again.

She wondered, not for the first time, where Nathan was and what he was doing—or being forced to do. He was, in the end, the reason that Emma had come. The thought—never spoken aloud—felt wrong and selfish. Less than an hour ago she had struggled to pull a total stranger out of a floor in an empty house; she had felt—in that moment—that it was the most important thing she could do.

*Nathan.*

Was love, in the end, just selfish? Nathan had loved Emma. Nathan still loved Emma—she was certain of that. But Nathan's love would not free the dead in the hundreds or thousands or tens of thousands. And Emma's love? Emma could remember a time when she hadn't loved Nathan because she could remember most of her life, when she hadn't known him. She knew that she hadn't fallen in love with him at first sight, but she didn't *feel* that, thinking of him now. He was—had been—Nathan. He had never been her whole world, but he had been her world whenever they were alone together.

And her love for Nathan wasn't going to save the world, either.

In truth, the world would continue even if Emma and her friends failed. The dead would live an eternity in servitude and slavery, but the world itself would barely register their pain or captivity. Emma had known nothing of what happened to the dead; she had known, deeply and personally, the cost of death to the living. The absence. The silence of the grave.

And the grave, she thought, would be silent again if they achieved their goal here. The dead—most of the dead—would leave. They would go on to whatever awaited them. Emma had no idea whether or not what waited was a giant scam, and until she joined the dead, she wouldn't. But she'd glimpsed it, and she understood why they wanted it. Why someone like Longland, who arguably didn't deserve it, could see almost nothing else.

"Margaret?"

Margaret had stopped; she was frowning. She turned to Ernest and said something that Emma could only barely hear. The actual words faded into the sense of syllables. Amy, being Amy, stepped in beside Ernest, folding her arms; Emma could only see the line of her back, but it was clear she was annoyed. Amy did not get left out.

Chase didn't move. "Margaret doesn't know where she's going," he said quietly, almost under his breath.

"Has the citadel been changed?"

Chase shrugged. "We can't stay in these halls. We're going to have to take a chance on a side hall or room and wait."

Allison and Emma were silent for a beat too long.

And Michael, in a fashion, rescued them. "Can't we just go down that hall?" He pointed to a stretch of wall, in the center of which was a small alcove.

Margaret said, "What hall, dear?" Ernest was only half a beat behind, but he dropped the "dear" at the end of his question.

The Emery students—and Chase, to Emma's surprise—turned instantly to look at Michael, following his gaze—and his slightly trembling hand—back to what appeared to be wall to their eyes.

"We don't see a hall," Allison told Michael. "We see a wall—with a small, curved alcove. There's a pedestal there for a statue—but there's no statue on it."

Michael said, "There's a hall." He looked momentarily confused, and then his eyes narrowed; he shed confusion as he gathered thought. He raised a hand, palm turned as if offering to shake the empty air in polite greeting.

Emma caught that hand. Michael walked, with obvious purpose, toward the pedestal and the alcove, Emma in tow. "What I don't understand," he said, "is why Margaret can't see it." He hesitated, and then he walked through the alcove's wall. Emma, trusting him, had to close her eyes. She wasn't surprised when she failed to hit stone, but only barely.

Michael released her hand and turned.

On the other side of what was, to all intents and purposes, a very secret door, she could see the hall and its occupants. It was like a one-way mirror. "Why would she do this?"

Michael shook his head. "I don't even understand *how* it works. Let me go get the others."

Margaret did not require Michael's help; she did require Emma's. But Margaret, like the rest of them, could see the grand halls of the citadel from this side.

This side, on the other hand, was vastly less impressive. Emma had read about servant's halls and servant's quarters—and had even been in a house that used those quarters as the nanny's living space—but she had never seen a hall like this one. It would have been at home in an ancient dungeon. It lacked the light and the sense of grandeur and open spaces that the citadel's grand hall had evoked; it was, in fact, exactly what she might have imagined the Queen of the Dead's citadel should be.

"I think we're more or less safe here," Chase said. "Margaret couldn't see the space; none of us could see it. Either the Queen created secret passages known only to her, or this was created by someone else. In the former case, the Queen's busy. In the latter . . ."

Petal whined.

Emma gently placed a hand on his head as a familiar pang of Hall guilt became a sharp pain. "I'm sorry, puppy," she told her dog.

Margaret seemed fascinated by the hall. She insisted on exiting it and trying to reach the corridor on her own. Emma, nervous, said nothing—it was Amy who granted necessary permission. Nor did Margaret react as if permission wasn't Amy's to grant.

"It might be useful," Amy told Chase, when Chase raised a red brow in her direction. "Helmi said the Queen uses the dead as spies. If even the dead can't find this place, we've got a base of operation for however long we've got food."

Ernest seemed to begrudge the fact that Amy's decision had logic behind it. Chase, once again surprising Emma, didn't.

Margaret did not return immediately, and when she did, she looked both relieved and perplexed. "If I were not bound—in some fashion—to you, I would not be able to enter this hall. I could, of course, pass through the walls and the doors of the citadel, as one would expect the dead to be able to do; I could not pass into this hall. There are rooms beyond it; if I walk through the walls of the great hall, I enter those. I seem to bypass this hall—and possibly what it leads to—entirely.

"We will consider this good news," she added, in a very teacher-like way. "Shall we see where this hall leads?"

Seeing was a bit of an issue, which was resolved the practical way: with flashlights. Since the hall itself was so narrow, they walked single file; they had three flashlights, and they were of the emergency variety: small and portable.

The hall didn't branch; it curved. Michael was the first to notice this, but Chase wasn't far behind. Chase thought it also descended but was less certain about that; it was a very gradual descent, if true.

Margaret could pass through the floor and the walls to either side, but could not return the same way. "Helmi won't be able to find us."

"That's a bad thing?" Chase asked.

"In this case, quite probably. If she is in touch with Nathan—if she can speak to him without the Queen's knowledge—she won't be able to tell him where we are. Unless she knows about this space. It's possible. If the Queen created it, she'll know. If it was not created by the Queen, she might still have some idea. I think, at one time, she loved her sister."

"I think she still does," Emma said quietly. "She just doesn't trust her anymore."

"Why do you think that?" Michael asked.

"When she asked me what I meant to do with her sister." Michael waited. "It was the way she asked. I think she wants to stop her sister. I don't think she wants her sister to—to be dead and trapped the way Helmi has been."

"There's a room." Ernest's voice drifted back. After a moment, he said, "Or at least there's a door."

Some of the light changed direction, effectively dimming for anyone in the line who wasn't near the door in question.

"The door," Margaret said, after a brief pause, "is impassible. I cannot walk through it." She sounded slightly irritated and slightly surprised.

"It's also locked," Ernest added.

Chase said, "That's my cue." He began to bypass everyone else in the line; given the narrowness of the hall, people had to squeeze into the nearest wall to let him pass. He stopped for a bit longer in front of Allison, but Amy appeared to have stepped on his foot; he didn't linger.

He did kneel at the door; he did demand one of the two remaining flashlights, and he did curse—a lot. When he finally rose, he said, "I don't think it's that kind of door."

"You can't pick the lock?" Amy demanded.

"There are locks I can't pick. That type of lock is a little high tech for the Queen's citadel."

"Then what's the problem?"

"It's not a lock, per se."

"So the door should open."

"It's not a normal door." When Amy failed to reply, Chase glanced at her and said, "It's a Necromantic door."

"What is a Necromantic door?" Michael asked. To be fair, it was the question in everyone's mind, but Michael got there first.

"I'm guessing," Chase replied. "This door has a keyhole. It's missing tumblers or any other mechanisms—at all—that I can see. Michael, come take a look."

Michael obliged, although he made it clear as he knelt that he had no idea how to pick a lock.

"That's because they teach nothing useful in school," Chase snapped.

"He means," Allison followed up quickly, "that they teach nothing useful about dealing with Necromancers in school. School works out fine for most of the rest of us."

Michael, however, rose. "I don't think that's where the lock is," he told Chase.

"Fine. Are you willing to allow that this is Necromantic magic?"

Michael nodded, lifted his hand about two feet, and touched the door. It wasn't locked, for Michael.

The door itself was better suited to a closet than a room. Emma half expected what lay beyond it to be a dungeon cell.

Nothing about the dead, or the people who lived with them, worked as expected. She entered the room at the tail end of the group, Petal squeezing her into the left part of the frame. Chase was talking to Michael; Michael seemed naturally focused and far more at ease than he had since—since before they'd left the city.

The door had opened into a large room that contained chairs, two long couches, and a low table. Beyond this room was an arch, and beyond the arch what appeared to be a dining room; there was a small kitchen off to the side. Emma had doubts about the kitchen, but she said nothing. There was no fridge, and the oven was not a standard, modern appliance. It looked very much like a wood stove.

Chase and Ernest left the sitting room and headed toward the dining room and apparently beyond. Everyone else sat, heavily, as if the invisible strings keeping them upright had been cut.

Margaret spent some time testing the walls. To her surprise, they were impassible, just as the door had been. She could clearly see them, but she could not drift through them. Some of what must have been ferocious concentration when she had been alive took hold of her eyes and her face, transforming her expression; she no longer looked vaguely teacher-like.

Chase came back and sat beside Allison. This put him almost squarely in Amy's lap; a bit of shuffling and a lot of Amy glaring, which everyone pretended not to notice, ensued.

"There are two bedrooms," Chase said, "one small office space—there's a desk in it, three cupboards, and not a lot else—and a library. Guess where I left Ernest. The library is probably the largest room in the suite. It's down a very narrow set of stairs from the office. There don't seem to be any permanent magical traps; we've done a clear sweep. Ernest suggests you touch nothing but furniture until we've had a chance to be more complete."

"Does anyone look like they're moving?" Amy asked.

Chase shrugged and continued. "There's no food in the pantry." He slid an arm around Allison's shoulder; she tensed very slightly but didn't ask him to remove it. Emma thought it was mostly because the arm was a very public—and casual—display of affection, and as Allison had never had to deal with that before, it made her nervous. Then again, Chase alternately made Ally nervous and angry. "Margaret?"

Margaret turned at the sound of her name, half her thought clearly somewhere else. "Yes?"

"Is it possible that this is the Queen's version of an emergency bunker?"

Margaret's lips compressed into a single thin line before she finally answered. "It would make some kind of sense—but I don't think so. The citadel itself was the Queen's version of an emergency bunker. I think this must have been created entirely by someone else. It has to be old—I can't imagine it was created in an off-hour or two, and the Queen trusted none of the Court in my time."

"Do you know what it would take to create this?"

Margaret shook her head. "A few minutes of uninterrupted thought might afford better answers."

Chase laughed. "This is the first time," he said, continuing his obviously unwelcome interruption, "that I can see you and Ernest as a couple." His laughter faded as he glanced at Allison. His very theatrical sigh drew everyone's attention, even Michael's.

"What?" Amy demanded.

"Allison wants to see the library."

The office desk was large and unadorned; cupboards were mounted on the wall opposite the door, and between them were a very simple chair and a desk. The desk's drawers weren't locked; they opened smoothly, but with effort. Pens of the variety Emma was used to were absent, but ink wells—long since dried—suggested that whoever had used this desk had used it to write. There was no paper, though. There were no books on the desk, no framed pictures, nothing to lend character or personality to the rooms' occupant. Or occupants.

"What we need is a history of the Necromancers," Allison said. To Margaret she added, "Was there some kind of official history or historian?"

Margaret shook her head. "History often disagreed with the Queen's personal memories, and she privileged her memories. She didn't intend to die; she therefore assumed that the only historical records she required, she contained. It's possible that other Necromancers left written accounts of their activities, but none would be official.

"In the case of traitors, none of those records would survive. I didn't keep records of anything but my lessons, personally. No opinion that was not the Queen's was safe to have. Shall we investigate the contents of the library? I admit a fairly sharp curiosity."

By the time they reached the library, they were talking in their normal tones. The tense, strained hush that had surrounded them all since their arrival in the city lifted, and with it, the harshest of their fear.

The library was, as Chase had claimed, the largest room here; it wasn't large, as far as libraries went. Emma's school had a larger library. Emma's *elementary* school had had a larger library.

"The Queen learned to read very late in her tenure. She could write—in a fashion—but the type of writing she had been taught was not to be found in the pages of books. She is not a woman who likes to acknowledge her ignorance, and if she couldn't acknowledge it, she had nothing to learn."

Emma nodded. "I can't read most of these."

"No. I can read perhaps a quarter. English was my mother tongue, but it was not the only language I learned. One of the few useful things taught to novices was languages. Emma? Emma, dear, what is wrong?"

## ↜ **Chapter 9**

There was a ghost in the library.

She had the same weathered look that Allison's grandfather had had, when he'd been alive; the same leathery cast to wrinkled skin; the same slight stoop to shoulders that would otherwise never bow. Allison's grandfather, however, had had a warmth to the many, many lines of his smile; if he had seen too much atrocity in his life, he had also seen joy, and he had chosen to believe in it. This woman had not.

Her clothing was both simple and restrictive, but after the first glance, awareness of it faded. It was the harsh, lined planes of her face that caught—that demanded—attention. Emma's attention.

"Emma?" Margaret stepped toward her, her voice heavy with concern. She frowned. "What are you staring at, dear?"

The old woman's gaze didn't falter—but it didn't actually move. She stood, casting no shadow, in the center of a carpet that had seen better decades; it might once have been blue, and there was a faded pattern woven into it.

"I'm looking at a woman—a dead woman. She's old, and she's standing in the center of that rug. You can see the rug?"

Margaret's frown intensified. She turned, not to Ernest but to Chase.

"I can't see her, either."

"Can you see the rug?" Margaret demanded.

"I can. You can't?"

Margaret's silence was answer enough. Emma wasn't certain what her expression contained; she found it difficult to look away from the old woman.

Ernest said, quietly, "Chase."

Chase swore. "Emma's the Necromancer," he snapped, resisting the unspoken command. "If she sees a dead person, who am I to argue?"

Ally surprised no one who knew her; she stepped quietly between Chase and Ernest. It wasn't a declaration of love or attachment but a sign of friendship; she would have done the same for Emma or Michael. She wouldn't have done it for Amy—but Amy might find it offensive, and Ally always tried—hard—not to cause offense.

"If Emma sees a dead woman," she said, "There's a dead woman here. There." Emma finally turned away from the dead woman toward her friends.

"Margaret can't see her," Ernest replied. Although he was clearly accustomed to command and authority, Amy had laid ground rules: His chain of command didn't extend to the Emery mafia.

"Neither can Chase."

"Chase is unusual. If he works at it, he can see the dead. It is not entirely comfortable, and he does not do it the same way the Necromancers do. But, when necessary, he can. It is no doubt a large part of why he's survived as long as he has."

Chase snorted and stepped out from behind Allison. "The old man is too terrified of Amy to actually ask you any of the hard questions."

Allison turned, her hands falling to her hips. Chase grinned. But beneath that grin and the yellowing bruises, he'd lost a bit of color—and given his redhead's skin, he didn't have that much to lose.

"She doesn't seem to see me," Emma said, stepping into the pause. "She's standing still, looking almost directly ahead. Oh, no, wait."

"She sees you now?"

"No, now she's looking around a bit. She doesn't seem to be seeing the same thing we see."

Margaret moved onto the carpet she didn't appear to see. "It's not uncommon for the newly dead not to see the dead," she said, but in a tone that implied that she didn't believe this was the case. She walked toward the center of the carpet and stopped a few inches in. Emma could no longer see Margaret's frown, but she was certain she could feel it.

"Margaret?" Ernest asked, using her name the way Margaret had used Emma's.

"I can't move forward," Margaret replied.

"Is it like the walls?" Michael—of course it was Michael—asked. "Like the hall and the hidden door?"

Margaret nodded slowly, turning back to offer him a rare smile of approval. "In fact, it is very like that."

Emma frowned. "Helmi said something earlier about circles." No one spoke. "I think the pattern on the rug is circular. Concentric circles. She seems to be standing in the center of it."

"I believe Helmi said the Necromancer was to sit in the circle, not the dead."

Emma nodded. "But it was supposed to protect the Necromancer from—from getting lost, I think? It was supposed to be a way of reaching the dead without actually physically walking to where they died." She exhaled. "I don't think the woman can see us because she's in the circle. I don't think you can see her because she's there."

"Be careful, Emma."

"I'm not afraid of the dead," Emma replied. "It's the living that scare me."

The circles embroidered into a carpet that was so worn were surprisingly sharply detailed. Although the edges of the weave were frayed and faded, the thread out of which the circle itself had been woven almost shone. It seemed to form a wall for Margaret; she could move around the circumference, but she could not move into the circle it transcribed.

Emma could and did.

The woman's eyes widened, changing the lines around the corners of her eyes; the way her mouth opened changed the rest. She could clearly see Emma, now.

"Who are you?" she demanded, her hands balling into fists. Emma had found Margaret prim and intimidating on first encounter. Intimidation was not fear; this woman reminded Emma of the magar, the start of this journey. She reminded Emma of death.

Ingrained Hall manners saved her. She drew one even breath. "I'm Emma. Emma Hall." Hall manners were clearly not reciprocated. The woman failed to introduce herself.

"Why are you here?" she demanded, instead.

Fair enough. Emma and her friends hadn't exactly waited for an invitation. "We're here to find our friend."

"Your friend?" The woman's lips thinned. "You've lost friends here?" Her eyes narrowed as well. "What on earth are you *wearing*?"

Since there was nothing remarkable about Emma's clothing—nothing terribly revealing, it being winter—Emma was momentarily at a loss for words. "Clothing. I mean, clothing from my country—and my time."

The woman was silent for one long, uncomfortable beat. "You're not dead."

"Not yet, no."

"Are you the new Queen?"

"God, no," was Emma's emphatic response.

"You remind me of her."

"Because you're dead."

The woman nodded. "Yes. Were you one of her supporters?"

"No. Until a few weeks ago, I'd never even heard of her. What I *have* heard—" Emma shook her head. "No."

"And the friend you're looking for?"

Emma hesitated. "She has him."

"Girl, you look soft. Young. I don't know how you came to be here, but this is not the place for you. Leave the way you came, and leave quickly." She hesitated. "Did my son bring you here?"

Emma shook her head.

The woman closed her eyes. If she had looked old before—and she had—she hadn't looked frail until this moment. "Then he is dead. He is lost."

"And you?"

"I am, as you see, safe. I am one of the few who are." She glanced at her hands and forced them to lose the shape of fists—fists that wouldn't be useful in any way. In a more conversational tone, she said, "Tell me, do the walls still scream?"

Emma decided then and there that she didn't like this woman. The question, casually asked, was barbed and pointed; it was meant to cut. And it did. She folded her arms tightly.

"Em?" Ally asked, the single syllable expressing all of her worry.

Emma focused on the dead woman. "Yes. And the floors. And probably the rest of the citadel too."

One gray brow rose, but so did the corners of her narrowed mouth. "You'll pardon an old woman," she told Emma. "I see there's some strength in you."

"Strength," Emma replied, "isn't measured by cruelty or anger."

"Here, it is."

"Maybe when you were alive."

A harsh bark of laughter followed. "When I was alive, girl? No. Had I been stronger from the beginning, there would be no Queen of the Dead. But that girl? She was kin."

"Her family died."

"Distant kin. Are you afraid, girl?"

Emma said nothing.

"This citadel was built on love and fear. Don't mix the two." Emma thought she meant to continue, but she fell silent. It was a haughty, bitter silence, from which Emma understood one thing: ferocious pride. Whatever her crime, she didn't want to expose it to a bunch of teenagers who were in no way kin.

"I cannot leave this place. I cannot leave the circle." The old woman closed her eyes. "I hear them, you know. I hear the dead. They shatter me with their accusations."

Emma shook her head. "They don't accuse."

"They would if they understood what I was in life."

"They don't accuse."

"Tell them what you know, and they will, girl. Death doesn't change the living—not when they're trapped here."

"It changes what they want." Emma's arms loosened; she dropped them to her sides. "You were taught what the Queen of the Dead was taught."

The woman inclined her chin stiffly. Everything about her was stiff. "Who was your teacher?"

"I haven't really had one. I haven't had the time."

"And you've come here to save your friend?" The obvious outrage in the woman's expression didn't quite reach her tone.

"Right now, there's no one else."

"You'll die."

"I'm going to do that anyway—hopefully much later. When I die, I'll be trapped just as you are. Even if I weren't, everyone I love, everyone I've ever loved or will love in the future, will be. I don't draw circles. I don't understand how they work. But honestly? You're safe from the Queen—but you're not any freer."

"In this city, safety is its own freedom." She looked down toward her feet. "It was not meant to last forever." Lifting her face, she said, "Is this now the eternity I face? It is the one I deserve."

"Maybe," Emma replied. "But I'm not qualified to judge that. And even if *you* deserve it, the rest of the dead don't. You said your son built these rooms?"

The woman nodded.

"Do you understand how? I mean—how he could make them impassible and invisible to the dead?"

The woman nodded again. Some of the steel had left her face, to be replaced by the weight of age.

"He didn't trust the Queen."

"He loved her, as a child; we do not trust our children to see wisdom when they are young."

"She's not young now."

"No? To me, she was only that, always that. But she had power beyond age and wisdom and nothing to prevent its use. I cannot teach you what you need to know; I am dead, and you will be dead soon."

"Then tell me about the circle," Emma said. "Tell me what it does and how it works. I've seen—I've touched—the dead before, but I've never done it from a circle."

"Then how?"

"I went to where they were." She hesitated and then said, "And I called them to where I was."

"Impossible."

Emma didn't argue. Helmi had mentioned circles, and there was clearly some safety in them. Unless the lesson took less than an hour, Emma wouldn't have the time to learn. But something about this circle, this private space, tugged at her. "What are the circles meant to do?"

"They are meant to protect us when we search for the lost dead. They bind us both to ourselves and to life. While within the confines of the circle, the living cannot be drained by the needs and the fury of the lost; they can approach the dead in safety.

"If the circle is broken or frayed, that safety is not guaranteed." The carpet on which the ghost stood had seen better days. "Yes," the woman said quietly, seeing the direction of Emma's gaze. "Nothing lasts forever except death."

"Is that why I could see you?"

Silence.

Emma reached out and offered her hand to the old woman. She couldn't say why, then or later; this woman was not the type of woman to whom one offered comfort. The old woman stared at that hand. She didn't take it.

"If you're here to bind me—"

"I'm not. I want you to talk to Margaret, but she can't enter the circle. And I don't think you can leave it, either. Not without help." When the woman failed to take Emma's hand, she lowered it. "I won't make you leave. I can't. I don't know how to bind you."

"Then you'll get no power from the dead."

"I don't want power—"

"You don't understand what you'll be facing. If you have no dead of your own, you have no chance."

Emma folded her arms again, disliking this woman. The woman was trapped—they were all trapped—*because* of the power the Queen had taken.

Emma believed she was a decent person on most days. Maybe she wasn't the best daughter in the world. Maybe she wasn't the best friend. She lost her temper sometimes. She said things she regretted later. But *everyone* did that.

Before Mark, before Mark's mother, she had been certain of herself. Mark's mother—and the death of her son—had unsettled Emma. She was no longer completely certain that she would always *do* the right thing. She was only certain that she wanted to.

But when you had the power of life and death—literally—a bad day could have consequences that lasted forever. One day. One slip. One terrible temptation.

If Emma had had the power that the Queen of the Dead possessed, she wasn't certain that she could have let Nathan die. The grief of his loss, his constant absence, had blighted every day that had followed it. Yes, there were good days—but even those had thorns and barbs; there were always reminders of Nathan wherever she went. A stray song. A specific store. A restaurant dish. A piece of clothing.

He had promised that she could die first.

And some promises should never be made. Should never be asked of another person. She bowed her head. "Stay here, if here is where you prefer." She turned to leave the circle and felt the ice of a dead woman's hand touch the back of her own.

"You are a foolish, foolish girl," the woman said, tightening her grip.

"So I've been told."

"But warm," the woman continued, as if Emma hadn't spoken. "Warm. You reek of life, girl."

"So does the Queen of the Dead." Emma reached out—slowly—and caught the old woman's hand in her free hand, shifting her grip.

"Yes. Yes, she does. She had so much power, so much promise; she could find the lost far more easily than anyone I have ever taught or encountered. She wasn't—she wasn't an evil child."

"No child is evil," Emma replied. "I can understand what she did, if I try hard—but it doesn't matter *why* she did it, because she never stopped. The dead want to leave. It's the only thing they want. It doesn't matter what kind of life they lived." Emma's hand hurt. It wouldn't, in a half hour; it would be too numb. She turned to the woman and found herself being intently studied. "People who are hurt cause hurt."

The old woman nodded. Her eyes, the peculiar translucent color that Emma wanted to call gray, were shining as if with unshed tears. "Will you let go of me if I ask you?"

"Yes."

"Will you leave me here if I ask it?"

"Yes." But Emma knew then that she would never ask.

"What will you do if the Queen is dead?"

"Go home with my friends. Except for the dead one," she added, her throat tightening.

"And him?"

"If he can't find his way to the door, I'll walk him there." And try, desperately, not to weep while she was doing it.

\*　　\*　　\*

Margaret's gaze sharpened when Emma stepped out of the circle. The hand that she held allowed the dead woman to cross the boundaries woven into an aged carpet with what appeared to be gold thread.

"The carpet is a circle," Emma told Margaret, half apologetically. "The living—Necromancers—would probably see her, as I did. But not the dead." Turning to the old woman, she said, "This is Margaret Henney." To Margaret, she said, "She didn't introduce herself, so I don't know her name."

"Names have power," the old woman said.

Emma didn't actually believe this, but Hall manners in a public space prevented any verbal disagreement. "She was hidden within the circle. I'm hoping she can tell us a little bit about the citadel or the Queen of the Dead."

"Or how these rooms were built?"

"Or that, yes."

The woman looked around the room, taking in all occupants at a glance. The fact that they returned her stare—some more politely than others—didn't seem to concern her at all. "This room, the rooms that surround it, are a circle."

"What *are* circles?" Amy seldom did something as trivial as asking where a demand would do.

"They are bindings," the woman replied. "Not chains, but—reminders. When we leave our bodies, we meet the dead in their own domain. It is easy—far too easy—to become as they are. It is easy to lose ourselves and the sense of our own lives, and if we do that, we lose our lives. We're no good to the trapped and the lost if we become trapped and lost ourselves." She looked down an angular nose at Amy with very clear distaste before her glance returned to Emma and the hand that bound them. She seemed to be making a decision.

"The dead have no choice. But the living do. We leave our bodies tethered to the circles of the living world. Every circle is therefore slightly different, but at base, the principles are the same. We write or carve the ancient symbols of earth, fire, water, and air. We carve the runes of birth and death. We surround ourselves with those symbols, and into that mix, we choose one for ourselves. A name, if you will. A name to join the symbols that speak of life.

"From there, from behind those protections, we can seek the dead. It is not a trivial undertaking, to draw a circle. It is not trivial to learn the mechanics of creating one."

"I don't mean to be a killjoy," Amy interrupted, in a tone that heavily implied the opposite, "but these rooms aren't exactly circular."

"The circle is a metaphor," the woman snapped, her expression as cold as her hand. "There is a reason that the dead cannot drift into this space. The Queen could, but magics of her own devising prevent the finding of the rooms by the living. And perhaps those magics are finally failing—you are here, after all." She glanced at Emma. "Or perhaps your queen—"

"*So* not a queen."

"It is habit; forgive me. How did you find this room?"

Everyone in the room very carefully avoided looking at Michael. Michael was silent as well.

The woman didn't seem to find the silence offensive. "The rooms were constructed by my son over a period of years. The Queen trusted him, as she trusted very, very few. She taught him everything she had learned, and he taught her everything he had learned. Yes," she added, glancing toward the floor, "he became the first of her supporters, the first of her knights.

"He believed—*we* believed—that time would heal the pain she felt. We committed crimes in the short term while we waited for that healing. And we did so from a place of safety. We were free to speak about our vocation. We were free to exchange information about both our successes and our failures.

"You cannot understand what that was like—to be free to be true to ourselves. It was a powerful, heady gift. For the first time in our lives, we did not fear to be murdered in our beds by the terrified and the ignorant." Her voice had grown in strength as she spoke; Emma could see her features shift, the wrinkles sliding away from the corners of her lips and her mouth. Those wrinkles were not laugh lines or smile lines; they'd been carved there by grim frowns.

"She gathered us from the corners of the land; found us in our tents and our homes. She brought us to her village. And the village grew." She was definitely younger now in appearance; her hair was a wild, tangled spill down shoulders that were no longer stooped. She was, to Emma's surprise, striking—even beautiful.

"We offered safety and shelter to our distant kin. And they were grateful, just as we were. They felt free, just as we did. But some were troubled by the Queen's treatment of the dead and the use of their power. Some could justify it, of course. Some could not. The disagreement grew heated, and the division, bitter. It did not stop with words.

"It was perhaps the closest the Queen had come to death, beyond that first terrible day. She took control of those who were loyal to her and banished the survivors who were not." The woman hesitated, and then added, "There were very few survivors.

"But the conflict started from a very simple question: How long? How long were the dead to be trapped? How long would they exist in a state of servitude?" The woman fell silent. Emma thought she had stopped speaking. She was wrong.

"It's easy to say: just a little while longer. It's easy to speak of the primacy of the living. The dead do not age. They have time."

It was *not* easy for Emma. She said nothing.

"We had seen death. We had lived in fear. We were drunk with the knowledge that we need not fear again." She shook her head. "But fear comes anyway. What we fear changes. I was not taught the arts of longevity. At that point, the Queen trusted very few, and I was not among them. I reminded her," she added, with a bitter grimace, "of her mother. And so, as all must, I died. But I died of old age. Of ill-health. Men did not come to murder me in my bed.

"And I existed thereafter as the dead exist. The enormity of what had been done—to the dead—became real to me only once I had joined them. I returned, not to the Queen but to my son. We spoke for some time. He asked me to wait. And what could I say to him?" She spread her hands, palm up. "Had I not decided the dead could wait when I was not myself among them?

"He would not listen to me, not immediately. I thought him cold and proud, and perhaps he was—but perhaps I was as well. He wished for the Queen to be safe."

"If he's dead," Margaret said, her voice oddly gentle, "He must have changed his mind."

The woman nodded; she wrapped one arm around herself, as if she could feel the cold. "Yes. The Queen required a legion of the dead to build her city, her citadel. She built a circle for herself, and she went out to gather them; she found them by the wall."

"The wall?"

"It is what I call what she has made of the only exit offered us.

"But it was not enough. Had the magar granted her daughter the one distinguishing item she possessed, it would have been much, much simpler. But if the magar loved her daughter, it was a harsh love, and it did not imply trust. She searched for her dead mother," the woman added. "For decades. For centuries, to listen to my son. She could not be found.

"And had I not come to my son, I would not have been found either. To the Queen, I was one of a legion of necessary tools. To my son? I was his mother. They argued, then. It was the first real argument they had had. In the end, the Queen relented, or appeared to relent; she agreed that I would not have the *honor* of becoming a necessary foundation for her future home."

"She didn't say that?"

"That is exactly what she said—to my son. My son did not agree. I make no excuse for him. He was willing to consign strangers—innocents, even—to the fate of being floor or wall for as long as the Queen reigned. He was unwilling to consign me to it. She acquiesced.

"But she was not happy to see his loyalty divided. The dead were dead. They did not have the primacy of the living. And even among the living, there was the Queen and everyone else. She did not wish me to continue to influence my son, and she attempted to bind me. I remember it. It was . . . unpleasant."

Margaret nodded.

"He came in time to prevent this, and she apologized; she said I had insulted her, that she had lost her temper. That was her excuse."

Emma could well imagine it was true.

"But he kept me by him after that. I seldom left his side. It . . . did not please her. She was always angered by lack of trust, even when the lack was deserved. My son proved not to be an utter fool; he had already built what he called a haven—this one. It was hard for him to come here in the latter days; they never completely recovered from the conflict. She was a child," the woman added. "And, as children do, she wished to be the most important—the only important—person. She wished to know that she, above all others, was cherished. He had given her that, for as long as he could.

"He created the circle you found me in. It is . . . clever. It can be moved or placed where necessary, in a way that the Queen's circle cannot."

"What happened to him?"

"I don't know. He left me here." She lifted her chin. "I do not think he felt certain he would survive whatever it was he intended; he did not tell me. He did not ask my advice; he wished me to be safe and beyond her reach—something he could not, in the end, guarantee for himself.

"He intended, I think, to destroy her."

## ⌒ Chapter 10

"How?" Michael asked. The woman was so unfriendly, he didn't follow it with the usual barrage of subsequent questions.

"I don't know. He didn't tell me. If he failed—if we were discovered—I would have told her everything. There were things he did not want her to know. And that was wise. If he failed—and he must have, if you are here—he might have had hope that someone else would eventually succeed."

"He was taught the old ways?" Margaret asked, her voice still soft and shorn of all judgment.

"Of course," the woman replied, her voice harsh.

Amy folded her arms, tilting her hip to the right. "There's no 'of course.' If he'd been taught the old ways and he'd *stuck with them*, we wouldn't be in this mess in the first place." The woman's face aged as she turned to Amy, but age wasn't going to garner any respect from that quarter. "Don't even," she said, glaring. "The only reason you've got regrets is that you *personally* suffered."

If the hand Emma held had been cold before, it became ice. Even the sense that she held something in the shape of a hand vanished. Time froze, in the same way her hand did; as if all warmth had been leeched from it, and warmth—like life—was required.

And yet, at the core of that implacable ice, there was heat—not warmth, it was too blistering, too unforgiving, for that. The sensation was both new and at the same time, familiar; Emma understood, just in time, what it meant. The fire wasn't meant for her. She was a conduit.

She had been a conduit for a dead child in just this way, and people had died. She'd had no regrets about those deaths; the people who had died had meant to murder Allison.

This was different. What she'd allowed a four-year-old child in her ignorance, she *could not* allow now; she knew who the power was aimed at. And if, on rare occasions, she'd strongly desired to kick Amy Snitman in the shins, that was the extent of her anger. Amy was, thorns and all, one of the best friends a person could have, especially when the chips were down.

After all, she was here, wasn't she?

Fire gathered in Emma's hands; she curled them into fists. That was simple; pain caused her to tense, to clench, to bite her own lip simply to endure. The only thing that was cold was her left hand. Without thinking, she reached for the cold—and to her surprise, it came, flowing up her arm and across her shoulders like a thin shell of sensation within which she could contain the rage of fire.

Her own rage was already contained because she was a Hall. She opened her eyes—when had she closed them?—to meet the older woman's and said, *No. I will not let you do this.*

The heat of the fire intensified, but Emma had cold, and as she applied it, the fire ceased to burn.

"Emma—" Margaret began.

Emma swiveled and Margaret fell silent—and not in the good way. The ghost took a step back, passing through Ernest before she stopped herself.

"Em," Allison said, at the same time. "Your hair is—"

"Standing on end," Chase finished. "What the hell are you doing?"

"Stopping a cranky old woman from turning Amy into an ash pile," Emma snapped back.

"That is not all you are doing," Margaret's voice was soft, almost a whisper, but it had an edge Emma had never heard there before.

Amy shrugged. Of course she did. "Emma's got my vote of confidence." She glared at Chase. "You asked a stupid question. She answered it, which is more than I would have done."

"Not noticing you're short of words right now," Chase replied.

"You asked her what she was doing. Rudely. She answered anyway. I personally don't care *how* she's doing it—I'm in favor of the end goal." She then turned to Emma. In a different tone of voice, she said, "Margaret's worried."

Since this was obvious, Emma nodded. "You remember what happened with Andrew Copis—the four-year-old trapped in the burning house?"

"Yes."

"She was trying to do what he did. She was going to lash out through *me*. I stopped her." Exhaling, she added, "I stopped me." Emma turned to the old woman. "Don't *ever* do that again."

The woman was utterly silent. What Emma had assumed was a glare because it was the woman's natural expression was something entirely different. She was staring *through* Emma, as though Emma was no longer visible. Or as though nothing was.

Emma had seen that look before. She yanked her hand back, and only when she did did she realize that she was no longer holding onto the woman's hand. She could still *feel* the cold, but it wasn't painful or numbing; it was almost pleasant.

She looked down at her hands. They hadn't changed. She was half afraid she'd see some sign of luminescence, of otherworldly energy; she didn't. She looked up, slowly this time.

"Em?"

"I think—I think she's bound. To me." She felt queasy, nauseated, even saying it.

"I think so too," Margaret replied. She had regained her composure.

"I didn't—I didn't have time to *think*," Emma said, voice dropping. "I recognized what she meant to do. I had to stop her."

"How did you recognize it?"

"It felt the same. I could feel fire. I could feel it in my hands. And I could feel ice, because I was still holding onto her hand. I used that. I used the ice to build a barrier between the fire and my fingertips."

"This is not the way it is normally done," Margaret said. "Normally, the binding process is much longer, much more onerous."

"Maybe they didn't have the incentive I did."

"No, dear, we probably didn't. We were concerned, of course, with our own survival—without power, it wasn't guaranteed. There are Necromancers who fail the many tests laid out for them. The Queen is not interested in failure."

Emma said, quietly, "I'm sorry."

The old woman stirred.

Emma faced her, uneasiness giving way to anger. "If the dead have power, it's meant to be used to *leave*. It's not meant to be used to kill the living—no matter *how* you feel about the living. You couldn't do it on your own—the only way you could do it is through me—and I'm not going to let you murder my friends because you happen to think they're too rude. I wouldn't let you do it if you were alive, either. Rude is not a death sentence in *this* world.

"And I think Amy's right. You think it's acceptable to kill someone because you don't like the way they talk to you? There's probably a reason that you were one of the Queen's early supporters. Or later, if it comes to that."

The woman's face lost the slack, distant look that had characterized the bound whom Emma had worked so hard to free. The fact that she was somehow bound to Emma—that it was because Emma had used her innate power when she had ceased to be aware of herself or anything else in the room—made it far, far worse: It was an accusation. It was proof that the power she had *was* the same power as the Queen's.

And she knew this. But the knowledge had, until this point, been entirely intellectual. Now it wasn't.

The woman's expression, however, was not one of horror; it was almost . . . smug. "So you've will in you, girl. You're not as weak as you look." She frowned and added, "Children had better manners in my day."

"Not if they learned them from you," Amy shot back.

As she couldn't reduce Amy to ash, she chose the next best option; she pretended Amy didn't exist. "What will you do with me now? I have power." She said this with a certain amount of pride.

"It wasn't *your* power you were attempting to use," was Emma's quiet reply. "Can you just stay here?"

"You do not require my permission to leave me here."

"No, I guess I don't." Emma flexed her fingers, paused, and examined her hands. The chains that bound Margaret—or Nathan—had been visible *as* chains to her eye. There were no chains around her hand or her arm. There was no visible sign that she had enslaved this woman. She winced even thinking the word—but she forced herself to call it what it was. Anything else was a lie, meant for her own comfort.

She did not want to become comfortable with what she'd done.

"What do you mean to do?" Enslaved or not, the woman asked questions the way Amy did.

"I told you. We're here to find our friend."

"And I told you—"

"And free him."

"You will not free him—or any of the dead—while the Queen lives."

Chase said, "The Queen surviving isn't part of our plan." He was the only person speaking so far who could speak of death—of killing—so naturally.

"You are all fools."

Amy folded her arms.

"You do not have the power to kill the Queen. I am bound to Emma—she has whatever power I have. It *will not* be enough. Emma will need to gather the dead and hold them."

"You're not the only one that Emma holds," Margaret told her, as Emma said, "There has to be another way."

"Do you think you're the only one to try to kill the Queen?"

She knew she wasn't, and, oddly enough, this lent her argument some strength. "No. And every other person who did try tried it your way. It didn't work for them, and they *knew* what they were doing. It won't work this time, either." She turned away from the angry dead woman, to Amy and Allison.

The woman said, "You must find my son." Had her expression not been so cold, it might have been a mother's plea. "My son witnessed many attempts against the Queen. He understood intimately how each had failed. He was not a fool. He would not have made the attempt if he thought there was no possibility of success."

"Finding your son," Emma replied, "is easier said—by far—than done. But . . ." she exhaled. "The Queen trusted your son."

The woman nodded, sombre now. "He had no living children of his own. She was the child of his heart. When you have children of your own, you will understand."

Emma hoped that this would never be true. "Was his name Scoros?"

Silence. It was heavy with suspicion, anger, and the bitter tang of fear. The woman did not acknowledge the question, but it wasn't necessary. *Names have power.*

"We were told that a man named Scoros might be our only hope." Emma's gaze fell to the floor. "Scoros attempted to kill the Queen."

Silence.

"He failed. Helmi was certain that he wouldn't be part of a floor or a wall—his was the greatest betrayal the Queen faced. She thought something might be made of him, but she couldn't tell us what. She has no idea where he is—and Helmi spent a lot of time with her sister. There's not a lot she didn't see. Scoros, however, was hidden."

The old woman's grimace of distaste could probably be seen from orbit. *"Helmi?"* To Margaret, she said, "Are they *all* fools?"

Margaret's answer—and her lips did move—was lost to the sound of music. Amy's response was lost as well.

Organs rattled the floor beneath their feet. The notes were dolorous, almost funereal; Emma raised her hands to cover her ears. It didn't help. The song went on for what felt like hours, and even when it had finally paused, she could still hear it, could still feel it.

"We probably don't have much time before the organ starts up again," Amy said, into the blessed silence. "Where are we going?"

Everyone looked at Margaret, and when Margaret failed to speak, they looked at the grim-faced, bitter stranger. Even Emma.

"Did the Queen's sister tell you where my son might be found?" She asked the question as if everything about speech was distasteful.

"No, sadly." It was Amy who answered. She returned a youthful glare for the ancient, weathered one. "Do you have any ideas?"

Silence.

And then, surprising everyone who was actually looking at her face, the old woman said, "Yes." She met Amy's gaze, held it, looking down at the Emery student in every conceivable way.

Amy, however, had played this game before, and she won it more often than she lost. She waited.

Having watched Amy play, none of the other Emery students were stupid enough to break in; none of them, not even Michael, asked the old woman anything. Seconds stretched. Amy folded her arms. She didn't open her mouth.

The old woman moved first, turning away from Amy Snitman to gaze at the far wall. "The Queen's personal chambers. If some clue exists, it is almost certainly there."

The music resumed, like an aural earthquake.


# Nathan

Nathan's first—and only—attendance at a wedding had occurred when he was six years old. Friends of his father were getting married; they had asked if Nathan wanted to be part of the wedding party. Parties, at age six, involved other children and loot bags, so of course he'd said yes.

He discovered that wedding parties were not like birthday parties. Either that, or adult parties were boring. The first night, he waited, playing with the flower girl under the watchful eyes of her mother while adults did their thing. And there was no cake.

But on the day of the wedding itself, it was different. He was required to wear a suit—and secretly felt that he had suddenly turned a corner into adulthood because of it—and to carry a small pillow that, on the *real* day, held a ring. It was his job—his single most important job—to make sure that ring did not get lost. Apparently the groom would be so nervous that he'd forget it somewhere or lose it if left to his own devices.

Nathan believed it, at six, but only because he trusted his mother to more or less tell him the truth.

He believes it in a different way now. He carries no ring. But he takes the position of attendant, and he stands beside Eric at the Queen's command. He stands one step behind as Eric is led to the thrones. He stands one step behind as Eric turns, at last, to face the audience.

They are mute for one second too long; they cheer and applaud on command. Nathan cannot see the Queen's face from his vantage. He can't see the expression she turns upon her subjects. He can guess.

So can Eric.

Nathan envied Eric, once. He envied Eric's ability to touch Emma without freezing her half to death, to interact with her, to *protect* her. It was stupid. It was stupid, and he regrets it now; he would apologize in a heartbeat if he could.

But he won't survive interrupting this moment, because it's the Queen's, and there's no room for anyone else in it. Not even Eric, who is theoretically the star of the show.

Nathan is not required to carry the crown. He's profoundly grateful.

Eric, however, is required to wear it, just as if it were a ring and this were a wedding, the end of a long romance in which obstacles to love have finally been vanquished. Nathan thought that the Queen loved Eric. That she loved him *so much*. And maybe, in her own mind, she does.

But the holographic image that once occupied the throne at her side was not Eric. It only looked like him. She had forced her Court, living and dead, to acknowledge his presence. She had cried at his absence, at his loss—although no one spoke of those tears. But that Eric, the Eric over whom she had grieved and for whom she had longed for centuries, was *not* Eric.

Nathan had not understood that until this moment.

He understands it now. He is terrified of the Queen, terrified for Eric, terrified, in the end, for himself. He told himself that the Queen loved Eric. He tells himself that Emma loves him. But if the words are the same, they mean entirely different things.

And the Queen of the Dead is not stupid. Malevolent, yes. Powerful.

Delusional in her fear. But stupid? No. There is no love in Eric's stony expression. There is no joy, no relief, no desire. He is dead and not-dead, like Nathan—but Nathan has seen more expressive corpses.

She must know. He is certain, as she speaks, her voice carrying an edge of the fear that has informed her entire existence—he won't call it life—that she *does* know. But in her universe, she has given her *life* to Eric. She has built a world for him. She has done everything she can in the name of love.

And Eric had better appreciate it.

Nathan is afraid, for Eric, for himself. For Emma, who is in the City of the Dead. He doesn't know what the Queen will do when she finds out that Eric doesn't love her, but he is certain he is going to find out.

The Queen lets go of nothing. Her ancient fears and hatreds are her armor and her cage, and she bears them proudly and defiantly. It is defiance he sees in her face when she at last finishes speaking and turns—briefly—to nod in Nathan's direction. It is a signal. Nathan moves to stand behind Eric, and one of the Queen's knights—a title that seems far less ridiculous in this opulent, cold hall—comes forward, bearing a cushion upon which the crown rests.

Eric kneels. He kneels like a condemned man facing a guillotine instead of a noose or a firing squad. The Queen's knight holds the cushion to one side of his head and looks daggers at Nathan. Nathan's hands—which are not in any way his own—tremble as he lifts them.

The crown is cold.

The crown is cold even compared to Nathan's natural state. He is inexplicably afraid to touch it. It looks as if it's made of gold, gold and gems. Nathan was never into jewelry and can't tell glass from diamond. He doesn't need to. This crown is gold the way Nathan is alive. He can almost hear it screaming.

She can't.

It comes to Nathan that she can't hear anything. She can't see anything. If she could, she would know that Eric was killed, died, and *is dead*.

As the crown trembles in his hands, he remembers his mother. He remembers her shut in his undisturbed room, weeping in isolation. Changing his calendar. His mother *won't* do that forever. She won't. She's in pain because the loss was unexpected; there's no way to plan for the death of a son. If it were cancer, if it were some lingering, deadly disease, she might have had time. But a car accident in the middle of the day?

No.

The driver of that car didn't mean to kill Nathan. Oh, he killed him—he and his joyriding friends. But there was no intent. The men who killed Eric hadn't killed him by accident. His mother probably hates the kids who killed her son—but the hatred has walls. There was no malice. There was no intent. They didn't shoot him or stab him or—or hunt him.

He's no longer certain what would have become of his mother if her grief and her anger had a justifiable target. His mother was always the rational pragmatist. His father had the big, wide streak of sentimentality. It's possible his mother could have let it go. At this very moment, Nathan doesn't believe it.

The Queen saw her family murdered.

The Queen has never forgiven the murderers—or herself. She fashioned herself into a weapon, and in the end there was nothing else left for her to be.

Nathan sets the crown on Eric's brow. Eric looks up, their eyes meet. Nathan sees a reflection of himself in Eric's eyes. And a reflection of his belief; Eric shudders, in silence, as the crown descends. When he rises—as King of this graveyard—he almost staggers under its weight.

The doors roll open. Nathan steps in to catch—and rearrange—the Queen's train. Helmi is at his side, showing him, with actions, what he's expected to do. She doesn't speak. If the Queen won't, no one else can—that's understood, even by her younger sister.

She doesn't look young at the moment. She looks ancient—as burdened by death as Eric. She watches Eric's back with a mixture of profound resentment and a hint of pity. It's the pity that almost breaks Nathan. He hasn't had Helmi's centuries of experience. He doesn't envy them. But those centuries are the foundation that allow her to go gracefully through the motions in which everyone present—everyone—is trapped.

If he knew nothing, this would seem like a fairy-tale wedding, a happily-ever-after. The Queen is beautiful in her flowing dress, and the King is tall, handsome, dignified. At a regal signal from the Queen, the crowds—living and dead mingled to Nathan's eyes—raise their hands and voices in cheers that never quite destroy the solemnity of the occasion.

But not even a fairy tale could contain the sound of the music that starts the moment the Queen takes her first step—and how could it? Fairy tales are words. Words on paper. He starts to look for the organ that plays these notes; it must be a monstrosity, and he doesn't understand how he missed it. But his gaze glances off Helmi, and her swift, definitive shake of the head prevents his search.

He walks instead. He walks behind the Queen and her consort. The aisle stretches out to eternity, and he wonders if that's an artifact of mounting dread or if it's literal—if the Queen intends this walk to be significant enough that she has elongated the hall that contains it. Even this, he can't ask. Shouting at the top of what passes for his lungs these days, he's not certain he could make himself heard over the music.

He walks, and walks, and walks. In front of him, Eric does the same, but he pauses to offer the Queen his hand. It is the only deviation from her scripted coronation, and it is therefore the only time she hesitates.

For one moment Nathan can almost see the girl she might once have been in the widening of her eyes, the slight opening of her lips. He can see the ghost of youth in the corners of her mouth, the sudden, almost shy smile. It is possibly the most shocking thing he's seen today.

She sets her hand in Eric's, but as she does, the smile vanishes; for one moment—only one—she is utterly still, her skin as pale as her dress, her eyes narrowing. She searches Eric's face; she looks up at the crown. Nathan thinks she might snatch it from his head and throw it to the ground, her anger is so sudden and so intense.

She doesn't. The music is the only sound in the hall. Her gaze is dragged to the hand that she now holds, to something that binds his finger—ah, a ring. Eric is wearing a ring.

By her reaction, it is not a ring that came from her at any point in their life. It is simple, a plain band. Her fingers tighten around his; she forces the bitter rage from her expression. Nathan is reminded that the worst anger is always rooted in pain. Hurt or not, she will not let Eric go.

Nathan wonders, then, if this is Eric's test. It's not a kind thought. But this isn't a kind place; it is not a city in which joy is easily made, found, or held. The Queen begins to walk again, Eric by her side.

If Nathan were still alive, this would put him off weddings for the rest of his natural existence.

# Eric

Graves are silent because the dead do not occupy them. There has been no silence in Eric's existence. It is silence, in his darkest of moments, that he yearns for.

The crown is screaming as it is placed upon his head by Nathan's unsteady hands; it is a chill band of sound that resonates with his body. His hands shake, and his legs almost fail to hold him as he rises, consort to the Queen of the Dead. King, as she has often called him. He remembers, sharply—terribly—the ceremony of his resurrection.

He does not remember the facts of his own death so clearly; he remembers the pain, not of the injury that eventually killed him but of his father's bitter rage, his father's fear, his father's ugly disappointment. He had believed, although his father was a stern, harsh man, that he loved him. Love. It's a silly, thin word, and it has caused endless pain. Eric knows there is joy to be found in it—but he knows there's joy to be found in narcotics as well, and he's been around long enough to see the price both demand.

He remembers the dislocation of seeing his own corpse.

He remembers the first—and only—time he referred to his body that way in Reyna's hearing. The madness of her grief, her rage, her *pain* . . . it comes to him as if it were yesterday. The dead don't experience time the same way the living do. But they experience its passage nonetheless.

She ran to Scoros.

Scoros came to him. Scoros, twenty years older than Reyna, himself childless because of the witch hunts.

*She is grieving*, the old man said. Eric remembers his eyes: brown, lined with wind and sun and echoes of a similar grief. *Please, Eric. Give her time.*

*What choice do I have?* The words were bitter. He feels them as if they are solid, textured, as if they've remained in his mouth all these centuries. He sees Scoros flinch. Scoros, who is long gone.

*You don't know what it's like to lose family*, the old man said, his face inexplicably gentle, his hands so warm as they rest, briefly, against Eric's cheeks— as if Eric is a child, not a man.

*I do. My father killed me. He had help*, he adds. And even saying this, he knows that had his father not come to Reyna's home, had Reyna's family not been murdered there, she would be free. They would all be free.

*Wait, Eric. I have no right to ask that of you. It is not what I was trained to do—but wait. She loved you, and when the madness of grief and fear abates, she will remember it.*

*And me?* Eric asked. He did not say the rest. He had no need. Scoros understood the question. *Will I remember that I loved her? Will I remember it when her madness abates?*

Scoros said, *It is easy to judge. It is easy for all of us. We judge the hunters. We judge the villagers. We judge each other. It is up to you. I cannot keep you here.* Scoros' voice was gentle, then. He was gentle with Reyna and with the young. He was careful and respectful of the dead.

Scoros left the decision in Eric's hand, and Eric—whose arms could not enfold his shattered girl—made the only choice he felt he could.

He remained with Reyna. He remembers her face, reddened with tears, her eyes, the same; he remembers the damp streaks left through the dust on her cheeks. She did not wear a crown then. Did not wear this dress.

He cannot remember her smile. It is buried beneath too many other memories. It is buried—as deeply as he can possibly bury it—beneath the weight of the lives she has taken and the distant, dawning realization that Reyna will never feel safe. No matter how strong her fortress, how high her towers, no matter how much power she gathers, safety will always elude her.

And because it does, the dead remain, chained to their Queen and growing in number.

He knows that he has one duty, today. Only one. To distract the Queen of the Dead long enough for Emma and her friends to infiltrate the citadel. Helmi does not speak, but it isn't necessary; Eric knows who, among the many dead, Emma Hall must find.

He is not at all certain she will succeed because he is not certain he can hold the Queen's attention for long enough. He tries to smile. He fails. In this almost unimaginable perfection, he sees nothing of the girl he once thought he loved. He was young then. So was she. Life had not yet become clear enough, real enough, to interrupt the force of their feelings. They saw each other and only each other.

But they are neither of them young anymore.

Had he not been graced with a second body for centuries, the touch of the crown would destroy all thought, all concentration. But Eric is accustomed to screaming. He glances at the Queen and sees that she wears a crown that is twin to his; different in details, but not in size, in weight.

She means to honor him.

It is hard. It is the hardest thing he has ever done. Dying was easy, in comparison, and he would do it again in an instant if it meant he would be free.

He lowers his chin, draws his shoulders back, remembers distant, ancient manners. He remembers the weddings of his childhood—noisy, bawdy affairs so far removed from this solemn coronation he cannot think of it as a wedding at all. But he offers Reyna his hand, as he once offered it.

Her eyes widen. It is the first expression he has seen on her face that stirs memory. She hesitates. Her lips part slightly, their corners in motion.

For one long moment, he thinks he has done the right thing, and then her eyes narrow, like windows slamming shut in slow motion. There is a ring on his hand. It is not, of course, a ring that she gave him.

There is no explanation that will suffice if she demands one, but she doesn't. And that, somehow, is worse.

# Chapter 11

This city, this citadel, was a prison.

Emma wasn't certain if the Queen was the warden or an inmate, and that was an odd thought. Ernest and Chase were as silent and tense as Margaret; Michael's silence was different. He was afraid, but he wasn't terrified. He walked beside Chase, scanning the walls, the floors, the ceiling. In some ways, this wasn't new to him. Michael was used to seeing things in a way that other people didn't. Sometimes he could explain the difference, and sometimes he couldn't.

Today there was no need for explanation.

Petal had been left behind in the safe rooms. He wasn't happy about it, but he was skittish and on edge. If Helmi was right, the citadel would be emptying, but the ceilings seemed to echo even the smallest sound. A rottweiler at full bark was not small. Chase had asked Allison to stay with the dog. He pointed out—courageously, Emma felt—that she had neither Emma's power nor Michael's unusual vision, she couldn't fight, and Petal was comfortable with her. Allison refused. No one had asked Amy to remain behind.

The halls widened; the walls rose; the ceiling once against suggested light and air above the heights of those walls. The residences, historically sized and situated or not, fell away. These halls were the domain of the Queen of the Dead. Not for the Queen small closets and stone cages. No. The Queen's halls were colorful, if sparsely decorated; everything suggested majesty.

"Margaret?"

"Beyond this point, you must exercise caution."

Emma didn't ask how.

"The doors at the end of the hall—the large ones—lead to the Queen's suite."

"You've been in those rooms?"

"Twice. No one who did not aspire to replace the Queen had any desire—ever—to see what lay beyond those doors." She hesitated. "The rest of the citadel has been astonishingly empty, which was expected. I am not nearly so certain that the Queen's suite will be likewise stripped."

"You don't want to enter."

"No, dear. I don't. But if I understand anything that's happened today, what we seek will be somewhere in those rooms."

\*    \*    \*

To Emma's surprise, the doors were actually locked, and the lock was mechanical. They were, Emma thought, real doors. They were wooden, and they were not in the pristine, like-new condition of every other door, rug, or stone the rest of the intimidating halls boasted.

Chase knelt, lockpicks in hand, and they huddled around him, looking down the hall and holding their breath. The hall remained empty.

Emma didn't hear the click that meant the doors were no longer locked; she heard the creak of hinges as Chase pushed one open. It wasn't a particularly quiet creak. Fear magnified it.

"Welcome," Chase said, "to the home of the Queen of the Dead." As they stared through the open door, he frowned. "Get in. Quickly."

Ernest and Margaret had already crossed over the doorjamb. Everyone else followed. Emma almost told Chase to leave the door open. She saw and sensed none of the dead; the halls were no colder than any other hall had been. There was no reason to leave the door open and plenty of reasons to close it. Chase, being sensible, closed it.

The halls behind these normal doors looked very much like the halls on the other side of it. They were grand, glorious, and almost sterile. Emma wasn't certain what she'd expected. She knew the Queen had made these rooms in the same way she'd made the citadel. Everything came from her.

All the same, she'd hoped for something different. She wasn't certain why. "Margaret? What are we looking for? Do you even know?"

Margaret nodded. She had drifted toward Ernest and stayed by his side, as if unconsciously seeking either protection or comfort. Emma shook her head. This was *Margaret*. Margaret Henney. She wasn't the type to seek either.

"Can you lead us there?" Emma asked softly.

"Can you lead us there today?" Amy demanded. Her arms were folded; she was no happier to be here than Margaret.

Margaret began to walk, the motion of legs and feet unnecessary but deliberate. "At the end of this hall is another suite of rooms. They are living quarters. When the Queen sleeps, it is there. Two rooms, meant to entertain more intimate friends, are behind those doors as well. I am not certain they are ever used.

"Down the hall to the right—and it is not a short hall—there is a library. I am not certain that the library has ever been used. The Necromancers knew of it; they knew that it contained books or journals that were not available anywhere else in the citadel. They assumed that the Queen's power resided in the knowledge therein."

"You didn't."

"The Queen learned to read late in life. Reading was neither required nor taught in her childhood. It was neither required nor taught when she began to gather her people. Most didn't read. The early Necromancers didn't either. It was only later that it became essential, as school and schooling spread. You all read, I assume."

Emma nodded.

"I'm not certain the Queen ever derived comfort—or knowledge—from the written word."

"Do you think we're looking for something in the library, if we're looking for forbidden knowledge?"

"No."

"What's down the left hall?"

"The resurrection room."

Nathan had been here.

Nathan had walked these halls.

Nathan had—if Helmi hadn't lied—been given a body.

Emma closed her eyes and inhaled the cool air. She opened her eyes. Everyone was watching her; no one had moved. She wanted to tell them that she wasn't leader material; Amy filled, and had always filled, that role, although sometimes the Emery mafia referred to her as the dictator. But even Amy was waiting on Emma. She wasn't waiting *patiently*, but no friend of Amy's expected patience.

Yet the expectation, the waiting, was a kind of support. Emma knew where they had to go. Margaret's expression, Margaret's tense silence, Margaret's almost obvious dread would have made that clear in any circumstance.

No one spoke as they approached the doors.

When Emma reached them, they rolled open.


# Reyna

The sky is clear.

This is the day Reyna has dreamed of for so long now she only barely remembers the first time she made the wish. She can't remember the details; she is certain that details existed, in the long-ago village in which her life almost ended.

What did she dream of, then?

She frowns. Eric's arm is beneath her hand; it is stiff and cold. He walks by her side, but he stares straight ahead. He is wearing a ring on his hand. He is wearing a ring that she *did not give him*. Today, of all days. She wants to tell him to take it off. She wants him to understand how painful it is to see it there. She has crowned him. She has opened the heart of her citadel to him—as she always intended. He has never really *listened* to her. He has never understood what she was trying to build.

Oh, in the past he had questions.

She answered them. For some reason he refused to accept those answers, twisting them into ugly things instead. He has always been better with words than Reyna.

Her hand tightens as they approached the gates. She remembers the stream and the tree against which she used to lean. She remembers the warmth of the sunlight; the shadows warm in a different way. She remembers, then, that her mother was alive. Her sister. She wanted to marry Eric.

She wanted to live in that village.

It was a small village. It was small, primitive, and ultimately savage.

What she has built for Eric—for the two of them—is so much better. There is knowledge here. There is *safety* here. They could love each other without fear of censure. Without fear of death.

But . . . for some inexplicable reason, she misses the trees.

She almost stumbles and casts a glare over her shoulder—but her train, her skirts, are perfectly placed. The stones beneath her feet are flat and smooth; there are no roots, no pebbles, nothing on which to trip.

This is not the dress she would have worn had she married Eric when her family was still alive. This is not the day she would have had. It's *better*. Surely it's better? This is something that Reyna has built for herself, with her own power.

But she remembers Eric's smile. Or perhaps the way his smile made her feel. She hasn't felt that way about anything in a long time. Not since Eric. Not since those days in the village when she fell in love and was loved.

She remembers sneaking out of her room when it was only barely dawn. She remembers the excitement, the giddiness, and the fear of her mother's anger, should she be caught. She remembers running all the way to the tree— but stopping a hundred yards away, because she didn't want to look pathetic to Eric.

But Eric was always there first. She would try to approach quietly, so as not to disturb him. She liked to look at his face, his expression, the half-closed eyes with their fan of lashes. He never seemed to be looking *at* something; he was alone with his thoughts. She liked that expression, but she loved best when he lifted his chin to look at her. No matter how quietly she walked, no matter which direction she approached him from, she could never surprise him.

She remembers the first time he held her hand.

The first time he hugged her.

The first time he kissed her.

So many firsts, to lead to this one. She almost lost him. Her most vivid memory of Eric—no matter how hard she tries to displace it—is his prone, bleeding body, his eyelids fluttering convulsively, blood spilling, without warning, from his mouth. He had no words for her. He had no words for anyone.

She had spent all her life interacting with the dead. She had cleaned and tended corpses in some villages. She had never, until that moment, come face to face with *death*. The dead, yes. She understood how they died; she understood why they were trapped, clinging to an isolated semblance of the lives they'd lived. But she had not *seen* them die. She had not experienced death itself.

Without thought, she shifts the position of her hand on Eric's arm. Instead, she reaches for his hand; it is so cold and so stiff when she touches it—

But he *wasn't* cold and stiff that day. She stumbles again, but this time when she does, Eric's hand tightens, his arm tightens, he offers Reyna support. It is silent. She wants to be grateful.

But he does not look at her. He doesn't meet her eyes. She has waited so long for the moment when he lifts his chin and meets her eyes and smiles. At this moment, on the day she dreamed of, almost everything is perfect.

But there are no trees. And Eric does not smile.


## ⤷ Chapter 12

The first thing Emma noticed when she opened the doors was the shape of the resurrection room. It was circular. It appeared to be open to the sky, given the quality of the light, but there was a dome above them. Windows in the shape of petals let in the startling clarity of blue sky. The ladders used to reach Andrew Copis wouldn't have helped them reach the sky here—the ceiling was that far away.

Emma's gaze fell from the impossible heights to the ground.

In the center of the room, in the heart of it, carved into the largest single slab of stone Emma had ever seen, was a circle composed of symbols. It reminded Emma of the gold thread on the faded and worn carpet in the hidden rooms. She wished, for a moment, she'd thought to bring that carpet with her.

"I think—I think this is like the carpet. I think this is a circle."

"It is," a familiar voice said. The old woman she'd found at the center of that carpet stood to Emma's left. Emma glanced at her face; it was puckered in something too intense to be a frown. "It is the Queen's circle."

"You were alive when she carved it?"

"No. No, by then I was dead. Tell me, Emma Hall, do you see anything unusual about this circle?"

Its existence, for one. Emma kept the words behind closed lips as she stared at the runes. She'd seen their like only once. They didn't look familiar. But where gold, in the hidden room, had glittered and caught light the way metal does, these runes were different: they had a light of their own.

It was a dull, glowing colorless light that she wanted to call gray. Even as she thought it, she froze, because if the shape of the runes wasn't familiar, the light they shed *was*. It was the color of the eyes of the dead.

"Margaret—can you see—"

"I see the circle," Margaret said. Emma glanced back at her; she stood beside Ernest—and Michael—against the far wall.

"Do you see anything unusual about it?"

The older woman, however, was the one who answered. "The dead are there. And you know it, girl. You can see them." Her tone was ice, but beneath that chill, there was fire; Emma could feel the heat of it, the pain of it.

"The circles," Emma said, her mouth too dry, "were meant to protect the living?"

"They were meant to allow the living to safely find the lost." Her tone implied that Emma should know this, because she'd already been told it once.

"But it's—"

"Yes, girl. Like everything else in the citadel, it's made of the dead." The woman's voice was lower, harsher.

Emma reached out with one shaking hand. She touched the nearest rune as if she expected it to burn. It didn't. She exhaled the breath she was holding. It felt like stone. But the floors in the empty townhouse had felt like floors until she had really touched them. Until she'd reached out and tried to pull them apart.

"Yes," the old woman said. "You could unmake this circle. You could unmake the citadel in exactly the same way, if you survived long enough to do it. And you won't—but it's possible. Say you succeed. How well can you fly?"

No one spoke. Michael stayed by the wall. But while everyone else was looking at the circle by which Emma crouched, Michael was staring ahead, a familiar frown puckering his forehead and narrowing his lips.

Emma rose. *We didn't come here to see this circle*, she told herself. She wasn't certain if this was cowardice. She didn't want to see a floor composed of clutching, frantic arms. She turned to Margaret, who was standing as far from the circle as the wall allowed. Margaret, prim, decisive, and unflinching, looked . . . afraid.

Fear made her look younger. And far more fragile.

Emma didn't want fragile, here. She had enough of her own to deal with. But fragile was better than broken. They'd come to the Queen's resurrection room for a reason. "Margaret."

Margaret met her eyes and nodded, staring just past Emma's shoulder at something that wasn't there. Or wasn't there *now*. "I see . . . nothing . . . out of the ordinary." The unspoken *for the Queen of the Dead* underscored her quiet words.

That was not what Emma wanted to hear, but Margaret wasn't the only person in the room who was focused on something she couldn't see. She turned. "Michael?"

He nodded; he didn't look at her. He appeared to be looking at a section of wall nestled between two ornate, standing shelves.

"What are you looking at? I can only see wall."

"A statue," he said, his voice very quiet. It was the wrong kind of quiet. He was stiff with tension, with concentration, and with apprehension. Apprehension was normal for Michael; it happened when he ran into something that made no sense to him.

"I don't think anyone else can see it." From Michael's expression, this was a comfort to everyone else. But it left Michael stranded. "It—I think it's supposed to be a man. A dead man."

She didn't want to ask him how he knew this. She didn't want to ask him anything else. She almost stepped in front of him to block his view, but he was taller than she was. He hadn't always been. And he wasn't a child. What he needed from her—what he'd probably always needed—was consistency and honesty.

And maybe, just maybe, working to give him what he'd needed had helped shape who Emma Hall had become. She didn't ask him to describe what he saw; given his expression, she wasn't certain she wanted to hear it.

"Margaret?"

"I see what you see," was the quiet response.

"I see a wall."

Margaret nodded. "The room is called the resurrection room. I was not here to be resurrected. I was not alone," she added. "Longland was here."

Ernest tried to put an arm around Margaret's shoulder. It passed through her without gaining any purchase, and Emma saw his expression shift, a brief, sharp bite of pain and regret, before he once again looked like a grim, older hunter.

Movement caught her attention; Allison's. She stepped into the narrow space between Emma and Michael, and reaching out, placed both of her hands beneath his, pulling them up.

And Michael said, "I don't think it's a statue."

"It's all right, Michael," Ally said. "We're here to help the dead."

"Not if you can't see them."

The old woman said, "It is something she would have done. She would not be abandoned by anyone else she loved." She exhaled ice; Emma could hear the air crackle around the single word that followed. "Scoros."

Emma approached the wall and touched it gingerly at first; what she felt mirrored what she could see: flat but gently curved stone. She grimaced; what she hadn't done to the circle, she now attempted to do here.

She listened for the voices of the dead.

The only one she heard was the old woman's; it was sharp and angry, but very thin. "What are you doing, girl?"

"If I'm right, I'm *trying* to reach what remains of your son." She regretted the words as soon as they left her mouth; they were harsh, unkind, a funnel for her own anxiety and fear, her own resentment. No matter how much she disliked the woman, no parent deserved to hear that.

And regardless, Emma couldn't find him. She could touch only the wall.

She rose and turned back to her friends, shaking her head.

"Don't even think it," Amy said, before Emma could speak. "We're not leaving."

"I don't know what I'm doing. I don't know how long it will take."

Amy snorted. "Does it matter? If you're still here when the Queen comes back, we're all dead. The only hope we have of getting out of here alive is you."

Allison was trying not to glare at Amy. She was wise enough to leave it at that. But Emma was aware that everyone was watching her. Margaret knew about modern Necromancy; she didn't know anything about the older stuff.

But the old woman who had tried to kill Amy did. And Emma felt certain that there was only one way to reach the trapped man—the statue that Michael could see. She was aware that they were running out of the time Eric had borrowed for them. She was aware that learning something new took time.

And she was certain that she could not reach that statue in any other way.

*Is it necessary?* she asked; the room was cold and she had started to shiver. But the man trapped here had created the safe rooms *within* the citadel the Queen had built, and those rooms had not been found, until Michael. This man, this former Necromancer, understood the citadel and its construction in a way Emma never would—and if he had planned to finally kill his Queen, Emma guessed he'd left the metaphorical equivalent of parachutes *somewhere*.

She did not want to leave the dead trapped here.

She did not want her friends to die. Or herself, either, if it came to that.

"Tell me," Emma said, turning to the old woman with her narrowed eyes and pinched lips, "how to use the circle." Speaking, she began to walk away from Michael's theoretical statue, toward the engraved runes that formed the circle's circumference.

"It is not your circle," the old woman said. She had managed to tear her gaze away from the blank wall, but it kept returning.

"No, it's not. But it's *a* circle, and it's the only one we have. Tell me how to use it."

"You—" The woman clearly wanted to sneer, but she kept it out of her words. But she stopped speaking. Maybe she wouldn't start. Maybe she'd offer no advice, no guidance.

Emma was willing to take that risk. What else was there she could do?

She walked toward the heart of the room and hesitated only once, her toes an inch from the engraved circumference. This wasn't her circle. If what she'd been told was true, each Necromancer—or whatever they'd been called before the Queen of the Dead—drew their own.

And if what hadn't been put into words was also true, a circle had been the beginning of the Queen's power. If the circle was unnecessary, it wouldn't be here. It was the centerpiece of the resurrection room. It was much larger than the circle in which the old woman's ghost had been hidden, which meant that size didn't matter.

This was the heart of the Queen's power, made grand—like the rest of the citadel—and ostentatious.

Emma was not the Queen of the Dead. Nor did she ever wish to be that. And that was the reason she'd hesitated on the edge of the circle: because she felt that entering it was to don—for however short a time, and for whatever reason—the Queen's crown.

She looked back at her friends, inhaled, and squared her shoulders. She took a step, crossed the line, and continued, aware that it had started this way for that long-ago sixteen-year-old girl: the need to protect and preserve what she could of the world she'd loved in the face of certain death.

Nothing happened when she came to stand in the center of the circle. Looking out, she could see her friends. She could see the curving walls of the resurrection room, and the shelves and small tables that huddled awkwardly against it. She could see the edge of the circle.

"Do I look any different?" she asked.

Ally shook her head. Michael said, "No."

Amy said, "Do you feel any different?"

She didn't. She hesitated for another moment and then sat, crossing her legs rather than folding them. She took a deep breath, held it, and let it go; she did this three times. Nothing changed. The air was cold, the silence oppressive.

On the fourth inhale, Emma closed her eyes.

From the heart of the circle, Emma could see the walls, the shelves, and two tables. She could see the engravings around the circumference of the circle in which she sat. She could see the floor. She could, eyes shut tight, see her crossed legs, her boots, her clothing. She could see her hands. She could no longer hear her friends.

What she hadn't expected was the sidewalk. Actually, that was probably the wrong word. It was a path, it appeared to be made of stone, and it wasn't wide enough to be called a road. It led to one of the walls.

It led, she thought, to the section of wall that Michael had called a statue. But even ensconced in the heart of this circle, Emma couldn't see what Michael had seen.

*Not yet*, she told herself.

"Very good, Emma Hall."

She almost opened her eyes again at the sound of the familiar voice, which would have been pointless. She could *see* the magar while her eyes were closed. She could see the woman who had given birth to both Helmi and the Queen of the Dead.

"I don't know where you learned to draw a circle, but you are sitting in one now."

"I didn't draw it," Emma replied. "It was already here."

"Here?"

"In this room."

"Ah. I am not where you are. I am not in a room."

"Where are you?"

The magar's smile was lined and harsh. "Where the dead are. If you have not been taught the rudiments, you will not be able to make use of the circle."

"Can you teach me what I need to know in five minutes or less?"

This predictably caused annoyance in the magar. "I could teach you what you need to know in a decade. And yes, I know you don't have a decade—not yet. Most of my pupils started far younger than you are now; they understood their roles and their abilities as they grew into them.

"You have done the inverse; it cannot be changed. Come." The woman drifted toward where Emma sat. She wore age far less heavily than she had on the first occasion Emma had seen her. When she reached the edge of the circle, she stopped and bent over the runes, as if she could not pass above or through them.

She held out her right hand. "Do not move anything but your arm—not yet."

Emma lifted her left hand and bent to place it in the old woman's.

"Now, pay attention. I will help you to stand. No, I did not *tell you* to stand. I said I would help."

"I don't really need help standing."

"You do. I have never interfered in this fashion with any of my own—it is risky, and if it's required, it means the pupil has *not* been well taught. My daughter could do this on the day she turned sixteen."

"I have no ambition to ever become like your daughter."

"No," the magar replied, with a bitter, bitter smile, which made Emma feel as if a bucket of ugly guilt had just been thrown in her face.

Emma's grip on the old woman's hand tightened. To her surprise—and confusion—Emma didn't feel the usual, instantaneous ice that came from physical contact with the dead. She *did* feel the old woman's hand; it was wide, warm, and obviously far more callused than Emma's hands had ever been.

"I bore five children," the magar said, which came almost out of nowhere. "Three died before they reached the age of five. Two survived."

"That must have been hard," Emma replied, Hall manners kicking in automatically. She couldn't see why the magar's comment was relevant.

"Hard? Yes. But children, then and now, are born weak and helpless, and mine did not have the advantages that you, as infants, had. Death was no stranger to me. Even had I not been magar, it would have been no stranger. It was no stranger to any of the villagers."

"The ones who killed you."

"Even so. They had no reason to fear us," she added, as if it were necessary. "But they feared. Fear is a very, very poor ruler—and its rule spans empires."

"You don't hate them for what they did."

"Why? Hate would change nothing. I wept when my children died. I wept when we buried them—and we did not bury them side by side. I knew that I *could* see them again, because I am magar. But I knew where they must go. I did not hope for them the torment and isolation of the trapped and the lost— and if they remained, that is all they would have had. I am grateful that they died when they did."

Emma was silent for one long beat. "Because they're not trapped?"

The magar nodded. "They are quit of the world. They went where the dead go and the living cannot. Helmi, my baby, has never had that peace; she understands that it waits and that she will never reach it. Not while her sister lives."

"Neither will you."

"No. But I carried the lantern for centuries, and its light kept me warm. It kept me safe."

"But—but you don't have it, now."

"No, Emma, I don't. You have it."

"Should I use it?"

"If you use it here, the Queen will know. She is living the moment of her greatest triumph; she is approaching the pinnacle of her dreams. But she has lived without that achievement for all of her existence; if she feels or sees the lantern, she will return. Are you ready to face my daughter now? No?" As she spoke, she helped Emma to her feet.

Emma stood.

Emma stood, turned, and saw herself seated, cross-legged, in the circle.

"You don't look surprised."

"I am, a little—but it's not the first time I've left my body. It's not because of the circle, is it?"

"No."

"It's you."

"Yes and no. It is your will, in the end."

Emma understood, then, why the containment circle allowed the magar and her kin to find the dead; they weren't constrained by what they could physically see and touch. What she hadn't understood until now was that she was almost effectively dead, which is why the magar's hand didn't hurt her. She frowned. "The dead pass through each other."

The magar nodded.

"How can you hold my hand?"

"Because you, Emma Hall, are not dead." The magar's lips thinned. "You are thinking of your boy."

She was. She was thinking that if she could find Nathan, she could touch him. He could touch her. They could hold each other and offer each other comfort in this world gone crazy. She was thinking of love, of what it meant, of why it meant different things to different people. She was thinking of the Queen of the Dead and Eric.

It was *easy* to think that she would never make the choices the Queen had made. But in truth, she wasn't certain. If she had *one chance* to save Nathan's life, one chance to save her own, would she truly have made a different choice?

The Queen hadn't saved Eric's life. If she *had*, if she *could*, things would have been different.

*Nathan*, she thought. *Wouldn't you have* wanted *to stay?*

*    *    *

The magar waited until Emma lifted her chin.

"Is there anything else you need to teach me?"

"For now, no. What I helped you to do, you should be able to do on your own. You did it once—foolishly, stupidly—without the grounding circle. You survived. Many, in our dim and distant history, did not. Do not leave your body if you are not confined; it is too easy to lose your way."

She inhaled—it was habit—and turned to face the wall. It was still all wall to her; leaving her body had not given her Michael's immunity to Necromantic illusion, if that was what it was.

"Can you see the statue?" Emma asked the magar.

Silence.

Emma turned; the old woman was gone. So much for help. No, she thought, that was unfair. The magar was at risk in this citadel. Mother or no, she was dead, and the Queen ruled the dead.

Emma listened. She couldn't close her eyes; her eyes weren't doing the seeing. She had hoped—somehow—that the circle would be her key to finding the door. And maybe it was; she just hadn't found the lock it fit. *Think, Emma.*

The only difference in the room now was the narrow path. It started at the edge of the engraved circle and led toward the wall. Emma thought that it led *past* it, but the wall obscured its final destination—if it had one.

She wanted—for one brief minute—to confer with Ally and Michael. Instead, she made a decision. She stepped onto the path and stood at the edge of the circle, listening. Silence. Either her friends weren't speaking at all or she had walked to a space that words and voices—living voices—couldn't reach. It wasn't a happy thought, and she glanced back at her body. She was still there.

And still here.

She began to follow the path.

The path did pass beneath the wall. Emma came to a halt in front of the curved stone surface, lifting a hand to touch it. And that was a mistake. The wall was not, as it looked, cool stone. It was warm. It was as warm as the magar's hand had been and as solid.

*You already knew this,* she told herself; her hand shook. The dead were here. If they took the form—unwillingly—of wall or floor or table, they were nonetheless *people,* far more trapped now than they had been in life.

She listened. After a brief pause, she spoke. "Hello?"

# 🙂 Chapter 13

Silence. The silence of held breath. Hers, of course. The dead didn't need to breathe.

She lowered her hands. The man trapped here—if the old woman was right—was only one of thousands. Or tens of thousands. He had stood beside the Queen. He had been a Necromancer in life.

Emma grimaced. Margaret had been one as well. If not for Eric and Chase, Emma would be a novice, imprisoned in a room that was, for all intents and purposes, a cell, trapped in a life that was designed and ruled over by the Queen of the Dead. Choice would be limited.

She wasn't here to judge. She was here to free the dead.

She was here to free Nathan.

She closed her eyes, which changed nothing. What she could see, now, had nothing to do with actual eyes. She couldn't free a man if she couldn't *see* him. Margaret, she had seen. The dead who had served as portable power generators for the Necromancers who had come to kill Eric and Chase, she had seen.

But . . . Andrew Copis she hadn't seen. She'd heard him. She'd heard him first. No, that wasn't right. She hadn't heard Andrew. She'd heard his mother shouting his name while a building burned, generating the smoke that would kill her young son.

She'd heard what *Andrew* heard. She'd walked into the fire that *Andrew* saw. He couldn't see anything other than the fire that had killed him. A four-year-old who had died in a terrible fire, he'd been jailed by his own fear and pain, trapped in the hour of his death.

Margaret wouldn't be here if the Queen of the Dead didn't exist. She would be wherever it was the dead were meant to go. Andrew would not.

He was gone now—but in truth, she *hadn't* freed him. He'd freed himself. She'd brought his living mother through fire and death and guilt. She'd provided a window through which he could see beyond flames and betrayal and abandonment.

The dead who were trapped by the Necromancers were trapped in an entirely different way. Chained, bound, taken out of their own lives, they were linked to the Necromancers who held their power.

She could break those chains.

She had.

But she hadn't seen them in time to save Nathan. She hadn't realized the truth.

In the other cases, she'd gone to the dead because she could see them. She could find the binding chains, grasp them, and yank them free. Those chains remained with Emma. She accepted that; Margaret didn't seem to mind so much.

But . . . she'd seen Margaret first.

She understood—barely—what the circle was meant to accomplish. Understanding the how was beyond her. And she had a queasy feeling that it was the *how* that would define everything that happened in this city of the dead.

How had she found Andrew Copis? How had she found Mark?

She'd heard them. She'd heard Andrew from halfway across the city, in a crowded classroom. The man she needed to free didn't have to be *here* to be found. But to be found, he had to be heard.

She almost asked him where he was, but she didn't. Nor did she ask the magar. She stood on the path that ended in wall, knelt, and examined the narrow, placed stones that seemed to continue beyond the wall itself.

Bowing her head, she listened.

She heard, first, the muted whispers that filled the room and realized that they were always present in the background—just as traffic noises were always present in Toronto. It was a terrible thought; in Toronto, cars were not sentient, and their owners were not trapped in walls or floors or furniture for eternity.

But those voices were not the voices she needed. If she survived, they would be. She swore they would be.

She rose, listening. Eyes closed, she retraced the path to the circle and watched herself, looking in. She was surprised by what she saw: Emma Hall, at rest. She felt separate from herself, enough so that she thought she looked young. Young, isolated, immobile. It wasn't a pleasant thought.

She opened her eyes—her real eyes.

She could see Michael, Amy, Allison. She could see Chase Loern, Ernest. Petal was in the hidden room, and she was both glad that he was safe, and afraid for him. But if he were here, the engraved circle wouldn't be much of a barrier for him; he'd lope across and dump his head in her lap and whine. He wanted to be home.

She wanted it as well. And there was only one way to get there.

She closed her eyes again. She listened.

Cemeteries were places the living gathered. It wasn't that people didn't feel grief anywhere else, as Emma well knew. Grief was sharp and unexpected; it could ambush her in the brightest and loudest of places. But in a graveyard, grief was expected, natural. It troubled no one else. It made no awkward pauses, no lurch in conversation. If there were tears, she could cry them.

Sometimes the tears were absent. Sometimes she felt anger instead—and guilt, because Nathan didn't deserve her anger. He hadn't committed suicide. He hadn't chosen to die. He'd intended to drive to her house to pick her up. To spend the afternoon with her.

The afternoon would never come. He was trapped in death—and she was trapped in *his* death, as well, because he'd been at the heart of her life. She was lucky. He hadn't been murdered. His death hadn't been an act of malice.

Lucky? She grimaced. She was lucky because his death had been an accident?

Her anger had no focus. On most days, she didn't want to find the boys responsible for his death. She didn't want to make them *pay*. Had they killed him on purpose, she would have. And she was a Hall. She wouldn't have *acted* on it, but the anger, the drive, would have been there.

Instead, she spent evenings in the cemetery with her dog. She could hear the familiar sounds of traffic, the occasional sounds of impatient drivers, the movement of leaves and long, weeping-willow branches. There were no people; she was almost in a world of her own.

The queen's city was a cemetery.

The walls, the floors, the vast windows, even the furniture—they were graves. But the living didn't come here for comfort. Not even the Queen. Perhaps especially not the Queen.

Emma wanted to speak to her father. Not Margaret, not the magar, the intimidating old woman who had started this journey. Not even Nathan. She wanted her father, because her father would know how to fix things. He always had.

And her father was in Toronto, in a hospital, watching Toby Simner's life bleed out.

She shook her head. Her father had been dead for half her life. He couldn't tell her how to fix things. He hadn't been able to fix things for her since she'd been just shy of nine. He hadn't been able to either hold her or offer her comfort.

She heard crying. For a moment, she thought it was her own—but Halls didn't weep in public, and she was, contained in a circle or no, in public. But the tears resonated with the ones she refused to shed, and instead of denying them, she let them in.

# Reyna

The streets are full. The old mingle with the young; she glimpses children between the full skirts of young women and old alike. Men bow their heads as she walks past. As they should, she reminds herself: She is the Queen.

Did she build these streets? They seem so long now, so full. They looked smaller, somehow, when they were empty. She thinks she would like to see them full, always full; she thinks she would like to glance out of her windows or down from her grand balconies and be surrounded by faces like these.

She glances at Eric, her hand on his arm. She expects his expression to be neutral, hooded. He is, however, looking at the crowd. He smiles at one or two of the people who catch his eye. She can't tell who those people are.

She can't tell if they're dead or alive.

Eric shouldn't be able to see the dead.

As she walks beside him, hand on his arm—and his arm is warm, her hand, cold—she thinks, clearly, *he shouldn't be able to see the dead*. And she wants, suddenly, to empty the streets of the dead. Because then, Eric won't see anything that he shouldn't be able to see.

Eric is not like Reyna. He never was. He didn't live her life. He hasn't lived her life for centuries. He couldn't see the dead. He didn't really understand them. He understood death—anyone alive in those days did—but he couldn't see what death sometimes left stranded, left behind.

She doesn't want to ruin this day.

She doesn't want to ruin this moment.

But this is not the first time since the day she lost almost everything that Eric has been by her side. She knows what love is. She has always known what love is. She has *waited* and *waited* for this day.

He does not look at her with reproach. He doesn't look at her with anger or disdain. The first time she saw him again, she expected both. She was so relieved to find neither. So relieved and so happy. But relief made her giddy. He is beside her now, yes.

But if he doesn't look at her with hatred or anger, he doesn't look at her *at all*. Instead, he gazes at the sea of faces to either side of this road. He hasn't aged—of course he hasn't aged. Neither has she. And it is *because* of her power that this is true. Their life together as it should have been was interrupted. It was interrupted by hatred and fear and ugly, angry men. She had never done anything wrong. She had never hurt anyone.

She had loved—had meant to love—Eric.

Why did he not understand that? That's what she thinks, her hand on his arm, the streets of a city she built for him, for *them*, surrounding them both. Why did he not understand that she loved him?

Does he not understand that she loves him, even now?

Does Eric not love her?


## ꙮ Chapter 14

It was a girl's voice. A girl's tears, made nasal because that's what tears did.

Emma wasn't searching for a girl, but this voice was the clearest sound in the room. It wasn't attenuated or distant. It wasn't stretched, thin, almost impossible to catch. The girl might have been in the room with her, even beside her.

She looked; the sobbing quieted. The room—the Queen's room—was empty. Emma could see herself. Only herself. She could see her hands, her legs, the clothing she'd worn in their run from Necromancers. She could see the path that led from the circle and ended in wall.

She couldn't see the girl—but the path itself was laid down in the wrong direction. She hesitated, but the hesitation was brief. She turned away from the wall, from the path, and even, in the end, from the circle and went in search of the voice.

She wasn't certain what she expected to find, but she hadn't been certain what she'd find when she followed the terrified, broken screams contained in Andrew Copis' memories, either. She only knew that the visible path was not for her; it wasn't the right way. There was no path in the direction of the voice.

But there'd been no path the first time, either. Oh, there'd been streets—but they'd been the wrong streets; she'd tried to make Eric drive through a house or two in her rush to reach what she'd heard so clearly. Eric wasn't driving. He wasn't here. The protective shell of his car was absent. If Emma wanted to reach her unknown destination, there was only one way to do it.

She walked. The geography of the room began to fade, the walls receding as she approached them. No, not receding exactly; they were still there, immutable edifices of the architecture of death. She could reach out to touch them if she concentrated. But as she listened to the sound of weeping—the sound of grief—they became remote . . . while somehow standing in place.

She inhaled. Her chest rose and fell, a reminder that she was—for the moment—alive. Unlike the dead, she could leave this empty plane; the almost artistically sterile walls were not her prison or her resting place.

And if she encountered fire, it wouldn't kill her. In theory, nothing would. Only the living could now do that.

She was surprised to see trees form—trees, tall grass, the sporadic shapes of flowering weeds. She heard—although she couldn't see—birds; she heard the bark of a distant dog and thought of Petal. There was no road beneath her feet, but as she looked, she saw flattened weeds that implied a rough, unplanned footpath.

She felt sun as she walked. She heard the effect of wind through this memory of living things, because that's what it was: memory. She wondered, as she walked, if her own death would leave this snapshot, hanging in what she now thought of as ether, if someone searching for the ghost of Emma Hall would hear—or see—the things important to her. Would they find Nathan, smiling or listening or speaking? Would they see the father whose face she remembered now as photographs?

She shook herself. Whatever they might find, it wouldn't be this. There were no obvious buildings, but as she walked, the sound of moving water—more of a trickle than a roar—laid itself over every other sound. To someone, this had been familiar.

She wondered then if the weeping she heard came from the person she sought. It was high, soft, and very, very nasal—but it was a girl's voice. It grew louder as she walked, pushing herself through high stalks of dry grass and almost feeling their slap against her arms and legs.

The weeds formed a type of wall, a corner, but they opened up as she reached the bank of a river. No, not a river—a stream, a brook, something winding and narrow. The brook itself seem dominated by rocks of various sizes, but the water was clear.

And like the plants, the earth beneath her feet, the shade of a sky that seemed cloudless, it was gray. The world was, unoriginally she felt, black and white. So, to her own eyes, was she.

She saw the girl. On her knees, legs curled beneath the bulk of her body, arms wrapped around her as if they were the only thing supporting her weight, she had folded into a shape, a closed, furled tenseness, that Emma would ever after think of as the *shape* of grief.

And it cut her, because she knew it so well. There was no stream, no forest, no wilderness, in which she might have hidden her pain. Only the graveyard, and even there she had not wept. Not for Nathan. Not for her father. She stumbled, righted herself, and stopped moving.

Grief was, had always been, personal. Tears—the tears the Halls did not shed in public—had, in some ways, been more personal than sex. Done right, sex was joy and life, something that grief could never hope to achieve.

No—grief was a black hole. If you were caught on the edge of its event horizon, you might never escape.

And she knew then who this girl was. She could armor herself against pity because pity was something she didn't want, and had never wanted, for herself. But crossing the boundary of privacy that grief demanded was much, much harder. She knew how she would have felt had someone—a total stranger—intruded in a moment like this. She did not want to do that to anyone else.

Not even the Queen of the Dead.

Perhaps especially not the Queen. *We want monsters*, she thought, frozen a moment by empathy and the bone-deep consideration that had been instilled in her by watching her parents over the years. *We want monsters because it means we're not* them.

Mark's mother had inadvertently killed Mark.

And in the end, in the face of her pain and her guilt, Emma Hall had taken her dead son home, and had left him there. It was what Mark wanted, and she could not, the moment she had seen his mother's face, do anything else.

But Mark's mother was not the Queen of the Dead. The Queen of the Dead *was* a monster. She had murdered Chase Loern's family. She had created the Necromancers, who were perfectly willing to threaten an infant with death. Emma had no doubt that they would have killed the child. No doubt that they would have murdered Allison. Or Amy or Michael.

All of it could be laid at the feet of this girl—if her feet could be found; they were invisible beneath her.

*People do monstrous things. People, not monsters.* Her father's words. Her father, who remained by Toby's bedside, unseen by the living, waiting to carry word to Emma.

She forced herself to walk; she approached the stream. Water splashed up her boots, dampening her legs. She cast a shadow in the fall of sunlight, and that shadow touched the weeping girl, who did not move. She didn't seem to notice Emma's presence at all.

And Emma couldn't see her face. She could see the crown of her head, her shaking body; she could hear her voice. And she thought she would never forget it; the sound stabbed her, tore at her, almost demanded that she, too, weep.

Her body responded. Her eyes. She felt tears gather, until vision was blurry. She couldn't force them to stop, and in the end, they rolled down her cheeks—and she let them.

She wasn't certain what she would have said or done—how did one interact with a memory, after all?—had the man not appeared.

She couldn't see him; she could see his shadow against the grass. Unlike

Emma, the stream, or the weeping girl, he failed to cohere into something solid enough for her eyes to grasp, to interpret. She was certain of his presence because grass wavered as he passed through it.

He had moved through the same grass as Emma, and he had stood—as Emma had done—just behind the thinnest screen of remaining weeds, watching as Emma had watched, caught in the same turmoil: the desire to protect privacy, to protect boundaries, at war with the need to do something—anything—that might help and being uncertain what *would* help.

But he wasn't Emma Hall, a stranger who had every reason to hate and fear this pathetic, sobbing girl. He broke through the barrier nature had made for him.

Emma could hear his steps. She could *see* their impressions in the soft dirt of the dry bank. But she couldn't see *him*.

The girl on the banks could, although not immediately; it was hard to see anything with your forehead practically in your lap.

He put his arms around hers—around the clenched shoulders, around the hidden abdomen. This, too, Emma could see—in the line of the girl's clothing; in the way she tensed and redoubled her efforts to fold into invisibility. Her weeping did not cease; it redoubled, humiliation entering a tone that had, moments before, been pure loss. She struggled; he did not release her.

He didn't speak.

He held on.

He held her as if she were precious and fragile and her pain could somehow be enveloped; he held her as if, by holding her, he could vanquish all pain, all loss. He didn't ask permission; he didn't allow her to reject what he offered. He didn't make the offer of comfort contingent on her at all.

For one brief moment, Emma felt two things: anger.

And envy.

This human, tiny tableau went on and on; she was a mute witness to it. She had been uncertain upon sighting the weeping girl; she had hesitated. She was not uncertain now; now there was no place for Emma Hall. She almost left.

But the water of the stream in which she stood seemed to harden, becoming first ice and then something with even less give. She couldn't feel the cold; she could feel the insistence that she remain, that it was necessary *to* remain.

What she witnessed now had happened—if she understood anything—centuries ago. Nothing she could do could change it. But waiting couldn't change it, either. And any hope of survival lay in change.

Andrew Copis had been trapped by his memories; they had been the whole of his world. But he had trapped himself; nothing existed for Andrew except the fear, the desolate sense of betrayal, and the fire.

The man trapped here had not trapped himself. He had been trapped, bound, hidden. This had been his punishment. She was certain that it was *meant* to be his punishment.

But as the sobs finally quieted, Emma couldn't help but wonder how. This was, in the end, a memory in which he had taken a risk—she could feel the whole of the risk, still—and had been rewarded by success. He had offered a rough, complete comfort, and it had been accepted.

She needed to understand why. But understanding wouldn't come unless she could reach the man—and at the moment, she couldn't even see him; she could see only that he was present, somehow, and that he had had an effect.

"Emma's crying," Michael said.

Allison nodded. She looked with longing and dread at the circle that separated Emma from the rest of them.

"Don't," Margaret said, before she could take a step.

To Allison's surprise, Michael nodded. When she looked at him, the question transforming the shape of her eyes and her brows, Michael said, "Emma hates it when she cries." That was all.

Chase slid an arm around Allison's shoulder, and she leaned into him without thinking; the room was cold. Everything in the citadel was.

The landscape dissolved slowly; the crystal water around Emma's ankles dissolved as well. It was the last thing to go. Gone was the river, the bank, the black and white form of a huddled, weeping girl. Gone, too, the footprints, the disturbances caused by the man Emma could not see.

So, too, was the man. But the landscape did not reassert itself. She could not see the walls of the Queen's room. She could see the odd, translucent gray that reminded her so much of the eyes of the dead. She was standing in or on it. She listened.

It was harder now. She didn't know what to listen for or to. She could hear, as permanent background, the whispered pain of the dead—the dead who were trapped, as the man was trapped, by the machinations of their Queen.

She wondered, then, if the dead had ever heard the Queen cry.

The urge to reach out, to comfort the dead, was powerful; she took three steps, staggered, circling. There were *too many*. Too many. And they were not the right voices.

She felt lost, as the dead must feel lost; even knowing that she could return to herself and leave this place seemed such a distant possibility that she shuddered. She might have remained motionless except for that involuntary shuddering, but a sound caught her.

She flinched.

It was weeping. But the cries were different in tone and texture; grief didn't underlie them. Fear did. And as she listened, the fear grew stronger, the voice more powerful; it formed words that she did not understand. But the meaning was plain, regardless. She began, haltingly, to stumble in the direction of the voice.

She did not expect to see the Queen when she at last found features of landscape. She wasn't certain why, and in any case, she'd been wrong. The Queen was there.

She did not look particularly Queenlike, not as she had looked the one time Emma had actually seen her. It wasn't the absence of a grand, storybook throne, although that *was* absent. It wasn't even her clothing, which was remarkable only in that it had nothing at all in common with the clothing Emma and her Emery friends wore every day.

Her hair was drawn back in a single braid that traced the length of her back, falling between shoulder blades so tense they could have cut. The floor beneath her was solid, worn wood. Before her, beneath two flat, stretched palms, was a table that was at least as worn. It was unadorned by carvings or flourishes.

She could not see Emma—and Emma was grateful. The intensity of fury in her face made death seem inevitable. The grief that Emma had witnessed the first time was buried so deeply beneath icy rage it might never have existed at all.

She was not the source of the weeping, now.

Emma walked, gingerly, to stand by her side before the table. *This isn't happening now*, she told herself, squaring her shoulders. *This is just another memory.* She had nothing to fear.

But there was something vaguely terrifying about a grown man on his knees on the other side of the table weeping in terror. Men stood on either side of him; another man stood in front of a closed door. The room was scantly lit—the windows were glassless and small—but not even full sunlight would have banished the darkness in this room.

He was not, as it had first appeared, begging for his life. Not his own life. He was the only prisoner—there was no other word for it—in this room. The people he wanted to save—if they were still alive—were elsewhere. But his pleading made clear that that elsewhere was under the control of the woman— the girl—who stood before him. Emma held her breath. She knew, given her reaction to Mark's mother, that whatever anger she felt, whatever hatred, and there was no other word for it, would crack in the face of his terror.

The Queen did not.

She spoke the Queen's name, but the voice came out in a whisper—and it was not her voice that uttered it. "Reyna."

There was another man in the room—one Emma couldn't see. Just as there had been a man at the stream by which the Queen of the Dead had wept. It was his voice.

Reyna didn't appear to hear it. She didn't appear to hear anything; even the man before her seemed insignificant. But not so insignificant that she was unwilling to listen. And listen. And listen. She did not interrupt the flow of his broken words.

Nor did she look up at the sound of her name. Could not, Emma realized, take the risk of doing so. She was listening. She was measuring the man's pain against some invisible, internal pain of her own. And when he had quieted—and he did, briefly—his fate, or the fate of his loved ones entirely in her hands, she said, "We will show you the same mercy your kind have shown ours since the dawn of time.

"You wish us to spare your children? We will spare them in *exactly* the same fashion as you spared *ours*." She smiled, then.

He screamed. It was a blaze of sound, a last blossom before fear gave way to despair. He would die. He knew it. And perhaps he thought that death would bring him a measure of peace. And it hadn't. It wouldn't. Nor would it bring that peace to the children who would predecease him.

She spoke to the men at his side, and they slid hands under his armpits, lifting him to his feet—feet that would not carry him steadily. Emma thought one was broken.

She was, and felt, sick with dread and horror. She wanted to retreat. She almost did. But her body would not obey the visceral commands she gave it; she stood, as much captive to the memory as the man who owned it.

Stood, she realized, in the exact same place as he had stood. He was frozen there, by the Queen's side—the only man to be allowed that privilege—when the Queen turned, the steady, narrowed gaze of her eyes pinning him, trapping him, the anger flaring, and flaring again.

She did not dismiss the man at the door as she had dismissed the other jailers. She did not intend her words—or her response—to be private.

Breath held, Emma faced her. Breath held, Emma waited for the commands that she was queasily, sickly certain would follow.

"You know who he was," the Queen said, her voice burning ice, her eyes a darkness that made brown seem a shade of death. "You know what he did. You know what he *would do* if he were to survive."

"I do not counsel his survival," the man began.

She lifted a hand; it was shaking.

So, too, was the man's. Emma couldn't see his hand—he was no more visible here than he had been by the riverbank—but she could *feel* it. She could feel both of them; they were clasped behind his back. "The children have done you no harm. It hurts nothing to leave them; they're unlikely to survive on their own."

"Then consider it a kindness—a faster death than starvation."

"Reyna, whatever their father is, they are not him."

"It is the only thing," Reyna said, "that will hurt him. It is the only way to make him understand."

"The dead understand very little."

Reyna's laugh was wild, almost unhinged. "Is *that* what you truly believe?" He flinched. Emma flinched.

"I want them dead," she said. "I want them dead before he is. He will watch. He will watch just as *I watched*." She turned away as the floor began to tilt beneath Emma's feet; she grabbed the tabletop to steady herself. "You will see to it."

Silence.

"Fire," Reyna said.

He tried only once more. "Your family was not killed by fire."

"Not mine, no. But some of yours *was*. And they will pay. They have to pay." She turned to the door, and then back. "Never try to interrupt me again. I am not a monster. I am justice—I cannot afford to be weak, to be *seen as* weak. You know what that cost me in the past." She closed her eyes. "Go. Do not start until I arrive."

It wasn't over. That was the worst of it. It *wasn't over*. This room, this darkness, the Queen's anger, was only the start of it. The door opened as Emma approached it; she felt it beneath the palm of her hand. Felt, as well, the look she was given by the remaining guard, the sole witness. The Queen ordered him out as well and remained standing by the table, in judgment.

Emma wanted to look back. She even tried. But the man she appeared to be inhabiting had not looked back, and this was his memory; he was captive to it. There was no freedom of movement, no way to effect any change. This had happened.

This was happening now.

She whimpered, moving. The sunlight was harsh, the sky cloudless; the whole of the horizon seemed to be one immoveable witness, and it watched. There were tents in the distance, a horse or two; she heard chickens—or birds, she couldn't see them. She saw, instead, the prisoner, and she saw the men to either side of him; she saw the beginnings of what might become a camp-fire—a bonfire—a thing by which she had sat or talked or listened to simple music, a place which typified the edge of adolescent parties.

But that wasn't what it would become. She knew.

She knew because she could hear the voice of a young child, shouting for her father. And she could see the father struggle now with his captors, with his injury, with the ultimate certainty of failure.

And she kept walking.

And as she walked, she summoned up reserves of bitter hatred, the dregs of a fear that would never quite leave, as if fear were a contagion, a plague, a thing that passed itself on, sinking itself into every corner of the mind and soul, thickening into something that was so dense, so loud, so much a part of you, it could *never* be escaped.

She called up images of laughing men. She called up memories of deaths—most often beating and bludgeoning, but once fire, much like this one. She remembered the audience, the ragtag gathering of men and women and their children, as if the event were some sort of celebration or fair. And, oh, she remembered the screams. The laughter couldn't kill them, couldn't mask them—and nothing could mask the *stench* of burning flesh.

And she remembered lurking in the crowd, pretending, dredging up some hideous reserve of will to voice something that might have sounded like laughter to the distracted. She remembered that she had abandoned friends in a desperate attempt not to join them on that pyre.

And those memories were so strong, they were enough to carry her to the piles of dry wood and the child belted to one standing log; the other waited beneath the heavy hands of guards, of men so much like those other men, a hundred miles or more away. She was silent, that child, dazed and uncomprehending, as if what must follow was so inconceivable it was simply impossible.

Emma approached the bier and paused there, the child's screams overlapping with the father's, adding a new color, a new layer, to memories of death. They were not her experiences; she understood this dimly, at a great remove. The understanding didn't save her. She was this man, now. She could not detach herself from him. She couldn't fight him—and, in truth, like the numb little girl whose life was going to end here, and horribly, some part of her felt it *must* be a nightmare. It must be. She would wake from it. She would wake and be safe and the world would be sane.

But she couldn't leave, couldn't wake; she was enmeshed in the memories of this nameless, faceless man.

He turned to Reyna, for even at this distance, he was aware of her; she cast a long slender shadow, more pillarlike than human. The sun was setting; it lengthened that shadow, until it touched the edge of the pile of wood. The child's sobbing had ceased some time past; she had given way to exhaustion and stood only because she was bound so tightly.

It was silent, for just a moment—one long stretched moment in which the man stood on the precipice of hell, teetering, uncertain. He reached, again, for the armor of bitter, bitter experience. He reached for that first moment in which he had realized, with utter finality, that justice was a lap-story, a lie told to children. Their prisoner, and men like him, had been the genesis of that. What right had they to end the lives of his kin?

They had killed women and children without cause and without mercy. He could still hear, echoing down the years, the ugly sound of their laughter. Why should they be spared what he himself had not been spared? Why? Because of his squeamishness? Because of his hesitation?

The thoughts were loud; the anger was real. It was real and it was *just*. And perhaps, perhaps if they saw this through, boys like he had once been, girls like Reyna had once been, would never be broken by the savagery of armed, human fear again.

It was worth the cost. He told himself it was worth the cost. He let anger burn, in the absence of fire—the fire would join it, soon enough.

Reyna's face, in the slow fall of night, was a mask so pale it might have been exquisitely carved ice.

But he knew her well enough to see what lay beneath it. She was afraid. She had lost family: mother, uncles, and a sister only slightly older than the girl on the unlit pyre. She intended to build a world in which she need never suffer that loss again. In which *none* of her people would suffer it a first time.

She would see this through.

And she would see it through by his side. She was committed; she demanded a like commitment from him. He could hear the cries of the dead that surrounded her; the cries of the living were brief and easily extinguished in comparison. He took the torch that was handed him; his hands were steady, his expression, as he turned to the bier, as remote as Reyna's.

He did not flinch when he set the fire to the logs; the man did that. And soon enough, the child joined him, her screams nearer and far, far harder to bear. He stepped back as the dry wood caught fire—it was not instant. Had it been in his power, it would have been; the wood would have taken the flames in an instant, and the blaze would have been so hot, so undeniable, death would come just as instantly.

It did not happen.

He did not step back. He did not flinch. He did not meet the screaming child's eyes. He simply waited. And waited. And waited.

And some time during that long, horrible wait, Reyna joined him, standing to his left, her toes even with his, fire reflected so strongly in her eyes that they were red and orange. He understood, then, why she had chosen the time of day she had chosen; he could see the tracks of her tears.

# Nathan

The Queen of the Dead is radiant.

Her title is both absolute and somehow wrong. As she walks down the street, her Eric finally by her side, the street fills. It fills with her subjects. They are not the newly dead; they can change their appearance, including their clothing. They are different genders of many races, many ages. They appear to see each other—at least enough that they are standing in the same space they might were they alive: they don't overlap. They don't sink through stone.

They look like . . . a crowd. A crowd from a period movie, yes—but a genuine crowd. They're the extras, but their presence isn't insignificant. They watch their Queen. How much fear rests beneath the surface of their composed faces?

And is Nathan's expression nearly as composed as theirs? He is less worried about that than perhaps he should be; the Queen is unlikely to turn her back and look at her attendants. Either of them.

Helmi walks behind Eric at Nathan's side. She prompts him when the long train of the Queen's dress needs adjusting; she can't—obviously—adjust it herself. But her expression is neutral, in the way stone is neutral. She glances at the dead without truly seeing them. Eric sees them.

Nathan sees them. But Nathan, seeing them, can understand Helmi's reaction. It is painful to know that they are nothing more than accoutrements, that they are accessories that will be put aside—or worse—without a second thought. He's not certain if that's because it's also the truth of his new existence, and they remind him of what he now is—but it doesn't matter why. It's uncomfortable.

Helmi has been dead for much, much longer than Nathan.

But then again, so has Eric.

Maybe it's because Eric has lived in the real world. He's met real people. He's lived as if he were still alive.

Nathan is watching both of their backs. The Queen turns to look—at Eric. Eric's gaze is elsewhere, moving and pausing. He doesn't notice the Queen's expression. He doesn't appear to notice the tightening of her hand.

But when she speaks, he hears her.

When she speaks, although her voice is so low it's barely more than a whisper, all of the dead hear her. The dead who are looking out the open windows. The dead who are in the streets. Nathan thinks—although he hopes and prays it is his imagination—the *street itself* hears her; it is rumbling slightly beneath the soles of his incredibly uncomfortable shoes.

*Eric, do you not love me?*

And Eric turns to meet her open, desperate gaze.

## ᴖ **Chapter 15**

"Something's wrong," Allison said. Emma's shoulders had curved toward the ground, her neck retracting; her arms trembled as she held them, stiff, at her sides. Her eyes were closed, but the tears hadn't stopped.

Allison made her way to the circle's edge; Amy's voice stopped her. Allison wasn't one of the Emery mafia. She wasn't one of Amy's inner circle. She was too stout and too unaware of fashion and style, which she'd assumed meant the same thing until Emma had disentangled the words for her.

But no one in Emery—at least no one in the same grade—ignored Amy Snitman when her voice took on that edge. And odd though it was, Allison trusted her. Here, at least. She turned back.

"She's in there for a reason," Amy said. To Allison's muted surprise, she appeared to be attempting to shift the tone of her words, to deprive them of—of whatever it was that made them so particularly *Amy*. "None of us know what she's doing. We know *why*."

"Emma doesn't know what she's doing either," Michael helpfully pointed out. He was as worried as Allison was.

Amy shrugged. "She got the kid out of the fire, right? And she knew even less then. Whatever she's doing now, she probably has to do it." She exhaled. "Look, I know you want to help," she said to Allison. "You've got 'Emma's little helper' written all over your face. But she's somewhere we can't go. I don't want our 'help' to pull her back before she's done what she needs to do."

"And you're sure she needs to do this?" It was Chase who answered. He came to stand beside Allison at the circle's edge—but not between her and Amy. Not even Chase was that stupid.

Amy's expression sharpened. What she wasn't willing to say to Allison, she was more than happy to say to Chase—and that came as a huge surprise to Allison. Amy wasn't known for either her tact or her consideration of other people's feelings. "I'm sure *she* thinks she does. I'm willing to hear rational arguments against," she added, in a tone that implied none of that rationality would come from Chase.

Chase swore under his breath. Clearly both Chase and Amy were strug-

gling to be civil in their own unique ways. It wasn't Amy who responded—
a glare from Amy didn't count—it was Margaret.

"I can't cross that circle," she said quietly. "Or I would. Anyone else in the
room *can* cross the boundary—but it won't change what they see." Before
anyone could respond she said, "I am not an expert in what Emma is now
attempting. I have no advice or wisdom to offer. But, Allison, I'm also concerned."

It was confirmation, but it didn't make Allison feel any better. She turned
back to Emma. "Will it *hurt* anything if I cross the circle?"

"I don't know, dear. I think it may disrupt things if you actually touch
Emma—but again, I am not an expert. I do not know what she's attempting to
do." She looked, again to Chase, as if it were against her better judgment. Or
any judgment of any quality, anyway.

"There's no guarantee I'll see anything either," Chase said, the words pulled
from him by an unseen force.

"No." Margaret waited. Ernest was watching Chase with hooded eyes and
the slightest hint of . . . pain. He said nothing when Chase turned to him. Not
a single word.

Allison was aware that it was the silence, the lack of words, that stung
Chase. Chase looked for all the world like a man who was determined to fight—
but Ernest wasn't going to be his opponent. If anyone was, it was Margaret, and
her usual prim and dour school-teacher demeanor was absent.

"She's a Necromancer," Chase said, but the words lacked the heated conviction that Allison found so very difficult.

Ernest said nothing. Margaret added a layer to the silence. She seemed
content to wait.

Chase demonstrated his ability to swear without repeating a single word,
which was impressive, given he hadn't paused for breath. Without thought,
Allison put a gentle hand on his shoulder; he swung round, as if struck.

"I don't know what she did to you," Allison said, voice only barely above a
whisper. "But you don't have to do this. Amy's right—we should trust Emma."

Chase's laughter was bitter, all edge. "Thanks to the Queen of the Dead,"
was his angry reply, "I'm the only one who *can*."

"You don't know what you're doing, either," Amy told him. "And this
might not be the best time for your bull-in-the-china-shop routine."

He ignored her. Turning to face Allison, he said, "I don't like her."

Allison could have pretended to misunderstand; she didn't. She simply
waited.

"I'm not doing this for her. Understand?"

"You don't have to do this for me, either. She's my best friend—but she
doesn't have to be yours. Amy's right."

"On the other hand? I could live without ever hearing those two words side by side again." He grinned. It was a pale echo of his normal grin, but it was there, and it was real. In front of everyone in the room, he bent and kissed her. It was not a fast kiss. It said a lot about something that it was, for a moment, the most important sensation in the world.

And that was just wrong.

Chase pulled back before she could, the grin stronger and a little more lopsided. "Wish me luck," he whispered. He stepped away from her, squared his shoulders, checked—yes, his knives, as if they'd do any good—and headed toward the circumference of the circle.

Allison watched him go. She was standing less than a foot away from the engraved runes; it wasn't a great distance. But it felt as if it were miles. Emma had gone where Allison couldn't follow—and it was Chase who was joining her.

"I don't like her," he said, without turning back. "But I can't hate her. God knows I've tried. And without her in my life, there would be no *you* in my life."

Emma did not come back to herself. She did not come back to the circle in which she was sitting, in a grand, sterile room blessedly free of the terrible sounds of death. No. No that wasn't right. It was *full* of the sounds of the dead. But not—not the screams of the dying. Not the screams of men who had given up on life and who looked death in the face as if death were the only mercy left.

And it should have been.

She knew it wasn't. She was sitting on the dead. But it was *hard* to remember that fact while the charring corpse of a child occupied the whole of her vision no matter what she did. The first child, joined by the second. The two children joined by the man. And yes, by that time, he had wanted death—but the pain of it, the pain of *fire* . . .

She looked up, almost wild with the need to escape.

The need to escape inverted itself in the space of a single scream. It was not the terror and pain of children—it was the nameless, faceless man whose memories had once again absorbed Emma Hall. She wished that some of those memories could actually be useful: that they would be memories of how the powers of Necromancers were used *before* the Queen of the Dead had broken everything.

But no, this was not to be one of those memories either; the scream was joined by shouting, by one other scream, and by metal. Metal. Emma frowned. Metal.

Iron.

He had been running—desperation lent him speed, but only a little. She was, once again, in the passenger seat of his careening, painful memory. She saw what he saw. She felt what he felt. She could not look away, could not change the trajectory of what had already happened.

He saw salt across the ground and recognized the lines into which it had been placed; he kicked them, displaced them, and realized that iron shavings, under salt, now clung to his feet.

Iron and salt here.

*Iron.*

He knew before he reached the end of the hall what the iron presaged. He knew, as he removed his sweater and dragged it across the precise lines of salt, what it meant—but the knowledge was almost too large, too impossible to believe.

Men with bows or swords or axes, men with torches, men on horseback— these, they'd faced as they grew. They were a fact of life, an almost natural disaster.

But those men did not understand what iron *meant*. And even had they, they carried it as weapons. They did not draw it in lines across the floor. They did not—and he saw, destroying as much of the pattern as he could, in safety, destroy—inscribe ancient runes, invoking their protection and power.

Only his own kin could do that.

Another scream. A shout of betrayed rage. He didn't recognize the voice, and perhaps that was a mercy: There was only one voice he listened for, now. Only one. From half the building away, he heard it; he dropped the sweater, left it, avoided the rest of the salt and the iron shavings that would cling to too much of his boots. He paused briefly and removed those boots; he could not carry weakness with him. Not now.

Oh, they'd prepared.

They'd prepared for this. They'd chosen the meeting of the moon at nadir. Here, they gathered: men, women, and the youngsters who teetered on the edge of adulthood and their adult strength. He did not know—not yet—what numbers they'd come in. He did not know how many traitors there were in the midst of this village that Reyna had struggled to build.

That there was one was enough.

He paused at the wide doors to the long hall; they were open. Light and noise spilled into the natural darkness of the hall; the small torches were not enough to provide more than scant illumination. This close, he could hear voices more distinctly.

"You have broken all of the ancient codes. You have betrayed the gift you were given. You have betrayed and enslaved the lost."

He recognized the voice; had he not come to a quiet halt, he would have stumbled. As it was, he froze for one long beat, into which more words were spoken. Stavros' voice was fire and fury.

And there was only one person to whom he could be speaking. Reyna was silent.

He wondered, then, whether she was dead. But no—Stavros would not speak to a corpse, and if Reyna was not dead, there was time.

Time.

His hands were dry. His throat, drier. He opened his mouth to speak, but no words emerged; words were a bitter, broken jumble, a useless thing. He needed to see what was happening. He needed to see where Reyna was and how the room was arranged. More than that, he needed to *know* who had betrayed her. Stavros could not be acting alone in this room.

*Reyna*, he thought. *I did not understand you, until now.* He wished, bitterly, for that earlier ignorance, but he knew he would never have it again. Because he *had* the power. He had the power that Reyna had had on that fateful day that had changed everything.

It was forbidden power. It was the reason that she was surrounded by her own kin, facing exile. Facing, he thought, death. Because she'd had that power, and she'd used it, and she'd saved her own life.

Not just her own life. She'd saved *all* their lives. She had given them safety and harbor.

Emma was firmly ensconced in the memories of the unnamed man; she understood that this was not happening now; it had already happened. Nothing she said or did could change the past. But she tried, because the strongest memory she now had was that of murdered children.

*That is not all she did.*

*It was for our safety!*

*Because young girls are* so much *of a danger. They died horrible, horrible deaths. It wasn't about safety!*

*It* was.

*You just tell yourself that*, she thought, her fury far, far greater than his. Far greater, yes—and his own. She could not speak to an echo or a memory. She couldn't argue with one. She wasn't arguing with him now. He was arguing with himself. And he was winning—and losing.

He loved Reyna.

He loved Reyna as a child, not as the sovereign she would become. He loved her, saw her as an injured, scarred girl, in need of support. In need of, yes, the love that he felt for her. She was not his child; he knew that. But unlike his own children, she would survive.

He had had children.

Emma knew it was hard for parents to judge their child. To be angry, yes;

that was natural. But to judge them? To exile them? To desert them? To let them be killed?

No.

But the scream she could hear building up behind his closed lips was almost her own. He held the dead, just as Reyna had shyly taught him to do. He held their chains, and he therefore held their power. He was not bound, as Reyna was bound; he was not yet captive—but he would be. No doubt, he would be. And he would then be as helpless as she must be now, for Stavros to speak so.

He had one chance, and he knew it. He had broken some of the confinement on his way to the hall; he had erased the patterns in which salt had been laid. None of these protections had ever been meant to be used against the living. Only against the raging dead.

And perhaps the dead were raging against Reyna now; they were certainly weeping.

He gathered their power, felt it infuse his hands with warmth; felt it lift him, although in truth he did not move from his silent crouch. He did not use the soul-fire; that would come later, much later. But he did summon fire.

He summoned death—because the dead knew death. He was limited by the knowledge of those that he had bound to himself. He was no longer limited by the promise he had made to them in that binding. They had given him the permission he required to use the power itself, and they had no choice now in how it was used.

He begged their forgiveness in silence. He gave them no voice and refused to listen to what remained—always—close to his own heart: the cries of the lost.

*If you start this, you will never, ever stop.*

He knew. But he could not live with the knowledge that he had stood mute, remained hidden, while she was murdered. It would kill him. He had the power to save her.

*It's not your power!*

But it was. He summoned fire, and it came, and it spread into the wooden slats of the open hall. It spread everywhere at his command, lapping with ease against the robes, dresses, tunics that it touched. As he entered, columns of fire rose; they were reflected in eyes that otherwise saw only one person.

She had turned toward the door; her legs were bound, as were her arms. She had been forced to kneel in the posture of the penitent. There was no penitence in her now; there was rage. Rage and gratitude. She struggled to stand, and he could not help her; he was too far away. Too far and too vulnerable.

He shouted her name. He could not break the barriers they had set up around her—not yet. But the fire would do that, and when it did, she would be free to act. Her face shone with tears.

They were the last tears she would shed in public.

He hesitated. He hesitated just once. Mira stood just behind Stavros. Mira, only a handful of years older than Reyna. Like Reyna, Mira had suffered for the crime of being born into the wrong family, the wrong *people*, and yet she stood in judgment.

And he did not want to kill her.

Did not want to light her ablaze. He was willing to do that to Stavros, for he was angry as well—but Mira was a girl. Barely older than child. Barely older than Reyna.

It almost cost him his life.

She stepped out from behind Stavros, she lifted a crossbow, and she pointed it—at him. She fired. He felt the bolt pierce his thigh. Her aim was not good—but the heat of fire was causing distortions in the air, and smoke rose in a quavering bloom. He ran—limped—to Reyna to cut her free.

"Do not approach me!"

He stopped. No, no, he wasn't thinking. She was right. Whatever power he had, whatever power their survival depended on, would not work if he was standing where she now stood. He had to trust that she would survive. The whole of the rough council could not be on Stavros' side.

He could hear shouts and screams—at his back, to his side—as the world dissolved in flame and noise. But he listened for Reyna, afraid to move, his leg throbbing as the world they had built ended.

She would survive. He was almost certain of it. But what she built in future would be different. What they built in future would have to be different. He had broken the only oath that had ever mattered in his long years of service to the shadows of death, and there was no restitution, no repentance, that would absolve him of that crime.

Reyna had to live, because if she died, nothing would remain to him.

The memory faded. The sickening lurch of guilt, rage, and fear remained in its wake. Emma struggled to breathe—as she'd struggled to breathe once before, in the fire that had killed a four-year-old boy in a distant Toronto townhouse.

His fear had been her fear for what felt like far too long. But it was not her fear, and she knew that were it not for his interference, the girl who would become the Queen of the Dead would have died in that long-ago hall. She knew—without knowing—that the men and women who had chosen to stand against her *had* died.

She didn't imagine that their deaths had been pleasant—and she was almost certain that she could see them all if she had any desire to examine them.

And she didn't. She could see the screaming girl on the lit pyre. Had no one else died, ever, that would have been enough.

*Enough? Enough for what?*

She frowned. Lifting her head, she looked once again into formless, shapeless gray. Nothingness surrounded her, with a texture of its own; she could see no walls, but she felt them all around her: high, forbidding, thick.

Without thought, she reached for Margaret—something she had never done before. The faintest ripple of gray appeared. She could see it only out of the corner of eyes too sensitized to colorlessness to recognize the subtle shift in the air. Like everything in her surroundings, it was formless—but she could now see that something struggled to *take* form, to don shape.

And it wasn't Margaret.

She rose, aware that she had been kneeling. Aware, in some distant way, that she had always been seated and remained so. It was hard to wait, and in the end, she didn't bother. She walked toward whatever it was that was coalescing. She knew that she had managed to find the man whose memories she had inhabited. She had chosen to search for him. She couldn't blame him for that experience, but not even Emma Hall could manage to be fair all of the time. She did blame him.

She struggled with anger, with rage, with disgust, with—yes—hatred. On some visceral level, beneath the *very justified* reactions, she knew she was not here to judge him. To judge him was to fail.

But he *deserved* judgment.

He deserved to be trapped in whatever personal hell the Queen had created for him. The people trapped in the walls and floors and rooftops *didn't*. Her hands were fists. Never mind her hands—her whole body felt as if it were a fist. As if it were raised and shaking. She couldn't find the words that would convey the whole of what she felt—and she wanted them, as the swirls of translucence began to combine in a way that reminded her inexplicably of basket weaving.

Her father had done that once—as an experiment. She could remember it, hazy and distant, because she'd watched him in the act of this odd creation. Wet strips of something, carefully threaded through other wet strips. Emma couldn't believe that it would eventually be able to carry anything.

But it had. It had dried. Her mother still had it, somewhere in the heap of discarded kibble that characterized the Hall kitchen. She shook her head to clear it and then changed her mind. *She* was Emma Hall. She had had an easy life compared to this man. An easy life compared to his Reyna. An easy life compared to so many unknown lives. Certainly easier than Andrew Copis in his brief four years, easier than Mark, in his less than ten.

She was not here to judge him, no matter how much he deserved it. Lowering her hands, she took a deep breath and exhaled, and as if that were a sign, the ghost solidified in front of her, a yard from where she had chosen to stand.

There was no other landscape around him. No other sounds, no other light. There was no color to his clothing, which seemed to have been painted in broad gray brushstrokes. His face was similar; he looked like a storybook ghost. She couldn't see any hint of his feet. She hadn't spent all of her life seeing the dead, but she'd seen enough of them to know that they didn't look like this.

*I do not recognize you*, he said. His lips moved, but the words were more felt than heard.

"I don't recognize you either," Emma replied. "At least not from the outside." She hesitated as Hall manners struggled with reality—and won anyway. "My name is Emma Hall. I don't mean to be rude, but . . . most of the dead don't look like you do."

*No. They would not.*

"Is this because of something the Queen did?"

*Yes, in part. It is also because of something that I did.* He stared at her. One painted hand rose, fingers and palms clear. He lowered it. *You should not be here, child.*

"I don't have any choice."

*There is always choice.*

Emma shrugged. "Sometimes there's only one choice to make. I wouldn't have made the choices you've made."

*You do not understand half of the choices I made.*

"I wouldn't make the ones I know you did make." She exhaled again. "I'm not here to judge you."

*And yet, you judge. It is the nature of mortality.* Silence. It was cold, here. *It is dangerous to come here in judgment, child.* He drifted closer, but he made no attempt to raise a hand again.

Emma did. She reached out to touch him.

*Do not—*

Her slow scream was all the sound in the world.

## ✎ Chapter 16

Emma wept. For the first time in living memory, she didn't care who saw her. She wanted to throw up. To curl in on herself, sink through a floor made of the dead, and let them swallow her entirely. She was overwhelmed by Scoros. She had no doubt that was who the stranger had once been. It was who she was, now. Every step she took or attempted to take led her into another fragment of his past. He'd lived far longer than Emma; she could experience bits and pieces of his life until hers naturally ended.

She wasn't certain he was aware of her at all, and as she walked through the patchwork fabric of his life, she began to lose that awareness as well.

She struggled to remember that she was Emma Hall.

She could feel his anger, his sense of duty, his determination, as if they were her own. And she could feel his revulsion, his growing self-loathing, the lies that he invented and repeated to himself, over and over, in the vain hope that repetition would make them true.

She was good at those. They were already a part of the Hall universe. That and guilt. And the guilt was too much. It was just too damn much. He had developed emotional calluses. He could almost will himself away from his own actions. He could wield knife or fire or soul-fire without so much as flinching—on the outside. But Emma was trapped on the inside, and she was no closer to the information she had wanted from him than when she had set out searching.

She could barely remember what it was.

Pivotal events in his life caught her as she attempted to extricate herself, deadly undertows that pulled her back, again and again. There were *so many* memories. There were so many atrocities. There was no light, no hope, no joy.

She could shelter, for moments at a time in his humiliation and pain—in his arguments with his mother, for instance, in his guilty sense of relief at his mother's passing. Relieved or not, he had begged leave to teach that woman the arts of longevity, as it was styled by the Queen, and he had been refused. The Queen had never cared for his mother.

Death had not freed him of maternal conflicts or anger. Short of binding her and silencing her that way, nothing would. An eternity of her regret, her anger, and her abiding contempt awaited him.

And he deserved it.

*I did not choose Reyna over family*, he said—to his mother, perhaps, or his memory of her—*Reyna was my family. She was all I was allowed to keep.*

And he'd kept her. He'd kept her safe. He'd offered her comfort. He'd tried to offer her unconditional love—the love of a parent for a very small child. But a small child was not the Queen of the Dead. He'd done everything he could for her and in her name. He had forced himself, had proven himself, over and over.

And she had never trusted love. Not his. Not anyone's. She'd required proof of love, and when she raged or cried, he offered what she needed. Her tears then stopped and her smile returned—but it never remained there. Her eyes would lose their width, her lips would narrow, her brow would crease; doubt would shadow everything she said or did until he came, once again, to prove that she was the most important thing in his life.

Emma had never been a parent.

She had once wondered—briefly—what it must be like to be the parent of a murderer. She knew now. She didn't doubt that Reyna was daughter to this nameless man. She couldn't fathom his love for her, his memories painted her so clearly. She believed that he had loved her, and she hated him for it.

As he hated himself for it.

She could not escape him. Instead, dragged back once again by this brief harmony of thought, she opened her eyes and began to walk toward every single reason the man had for self-loathing. The children had been the start of it but not the end—and not, oh, god, the worst.

Something pulled at Emma; something tugged her sleeve. She was so accustomed to the man's life, she thought it another event, another death, another loss, another betrayal—of self, of kin, of belief.

But . . . most of the people in the man's memories didn't *swear* so much. She looked down without thinking—and found that she *could* look down. For just a minute, her vision wasn't a captive passenger; her eyes could move in a different direction.

There was nothing tugging at her sleeve. There couldn't be. She was facing Reyna—the Queen now, to all but the man himself—to report. The Queen met with him alone, dismissing all of her living guards; those guards—Necromancers, but not yet knights—glared at him but obeyed their Queen; they retreated to familiar doors, opened them, and closed them when they had crossed the threshold.

The town hall had long since given way to the opulent heights of bright, domed ceilings that let in clear sky and daylight. Scoros knelt in a room with which Emma was familiar. It had been the last room she had studied so carefully before she had set out on her search.

*Emma!*

She recognized the voice. She turned again, turned toward the doors, and knew that this was impossible; she was in the man's memories, and the man, kneeling, could not turn. He did not dare to take any part of his attention from Reyna, the Queen.

So it was not through his eyes that Emma saw the closed door. Not with his ears that she heard her name being called. She tried to move toward the door and failed; she heard the Queen's voice at her back. She didn't turn, but she didn't have to; the memories reasserted themselves, and she was once again on her knees before her Queen.

*EMMA!*

Reaction was involuntary. Something in the voice that was calling her name was so raw with fear that she couldn't ignore it, couldn't turn away, couldn't do anything at all but move toward it. After all she'd seen, all she'd heard, all she'd *done*, she should have been too numb.

But this voice was not one of Scoros' voices; it wasn't a voice he knew or recognized. It was no part of the guilt or shame he carried. It was part of her life, Emma Hall's life. Chase Loern had come to Toronto, and he'd been pretty pissed off to find out that she wasn't dead. He wasn't above sharing that anger. And maybe, if that's all she knew of him, she wouldn't have responded.

But he had saved Allison's life. He loved Allison, and Allison was so much part of the fiber of Emma's existence, Emma couldn't remember life before Allison. No matter how much Chase hated Emma, he'd actually had the brains and the perception to see Allison clearly. Anyone who saw her clearly would have to love her.

And that's what Emma remembered as she turned toward the pain and the fear in Chase's voice.

She had been anchored in the stranger's memories, trapped in his viewpoint; she had been a murderer so many times over—even thinking it, she shuddered, twisting away from herself. And of course she couldn't. She *was* herself. There was no escape.

"EMMA!"

She did the next best thing. She ran to the closed door. The Queen's monologue didn't change; the Queen didn't move. And the man's voice, in the few words of reply he could wedge in, didn't shift either. But they grew distant, blessedly distant, as Chase's voice grew closer.

She was almost at the door when she felt the ground shift beneath her feet.

*And will you abandon your duty?*

She almost didn't recognize the voice; had she not spent subjective months listening to nothing but its shades, its textures, she wouldn't have. The door was a foot away from Emma's outstretched hand. In the eye blink before that hand made contact with its surface, the surface shifted shape; it widened, thickened. Grandeur gave way to ugly practicality, vaulted arches gave way to rectangular frame. This was no longer the door to the most important rooms in the citadel.

It was a door to the hidden rooms, to the darkness beneath the opulence. It was a jail door, a dungeon door. The wood was heavy, thick; it was scored and scratched, no doubt from useless attempts at escape.

But it had what the palatial doors lacked: bars. And bars meant space through which Emma could see out. She reached up, gripped the bars, pulled herself toward them. She opened her mouth to speak, but words jammed up behind her teeth, and her throat was already so raw it hurt to speak. She hoped—she *really* hoped—that she hadn't actually been screaming in the real world, because she could just imagine what that would do to her friends. To Michael.

And then she forgot the eddies of guilt as she looked between the bars. She'd recognized the voice. She didn't recognize the person on the other side of this door, and her hands faltered, their grip loosening.

The boy on the other side reached out and grabbed them, curling his hands around and over them. He was maybe fourteen years old; it was hard to tell. His hands were red with blood. Literally red with it. And his hair was that bright red-orange that was so striking. It was also much longer than Chase's.

"Don't you dare let go," he said, voice grim. Fourteen; his voice had already entered adult territory.

"Chase?"

"No, I'm the tooth fairy." A tooth fairy with a bruised face, a swollen lip. All of the blood—on his clothing, on his face—was scarlet and crimson, and his eyes were almost blue. "What are you staring at?"

"The tooth fairy, apparently." Her voice was thin and quavering, and she tried to bring it back under control. The words, at least, were the right words.

"And I've got something on my face?"

Blood, she thought. She didn't say it. She wondered, instead, what Chase could see. She didn't ask. She asked the other question, the bigger one. "Why are you here?"

"To make sure you come back."

And she remembered that it had been Chase who had pulled her free of a sea of hands and arms that would otherwise have devoured her.

"Fine. *How* are you here?"

His hands tightened involuntarily; Emma's tightened as well. She could feel bars, and they had the consistency of metal—but the metal was warm.

He smiled. It was the first time she understood just how much of a defense that smile was. This fourteen-year-old version of the Chase Loern she knew hadn't mastered it yet; the lips moved in exactly the right way, but the eyes were so bruised and so haunted, they didn't match. "You know that thing about crying you have?"

"What thing about crying? I don't mind if people cry—"

"Not other people. You. Allison says you're very definite on that. Emma Hall does not cry in public."

"Yes, but—"

"Emma Hall has nothing on Chase Loern in that regard."

"I'm not—"

"You are, Emma. Look—can you just wake up? You're scaring the crap out of your friends. Except Amy."

Emma laughed, or tried to. "Can you?"

"Can I?"

"Wake up, if that's what you want to call it. Can you?" Voice dipping, she said, "I've tried."

The very modern cursing that had first caught her attention went on for some time. "I'm not leaving without you."

"Can you?"

"I'm not trying. I'm assuming the answer is yes—but if I wake up, you're still going to be here, and from the sounds of it, here is not where you want to be."

Emma shook her head. She didn't always trust intuition—especially not her own—but she thought she understood why Chase was fourteen. She didn't understand why he alone seemed to radiate color—maybe it was because he was alive. "I don't think you can," she said softly. Certainly.

"Is this some weird Necromantic thing?"

"I don't know a lot about Necromantic things. No one taught me how to see the dead. No one taught me how to take their hands. Chase—I don't think you can wake up either. You shouldn't be here. You shouldn't have come." Emma was viscerally certain that Chase Loern was just as trapped as she was. Chase Loern, who'd argued for her death, who'd wanted her killed—and who, she was certain, would once have been happy to be the killer.

He shrugged. He didn't let go of her hands. "Wasn't my idea," he finally said. His voice was blurred, thick. But it was his voice.

"Please don't tell me it was Ally's."

He laughed. It was not a happy sound. "It wasn't Allison's. She told me I should trust you."

"She's always been an optimist."

He laughed again, and this laugh was less wild, less terrifying. "She'd have to be, wouldn't she? Can you see any way to open the damn door?"

Emma shook her head. Took a breath and felt it enter distant lungs. Chase had bought her space to think. He'd brought her back to Emma Hall, to her own thoughts, her own pale worries. He was holding her steady, but she wasn't certain it could last; behind his back, she could see fire. She could hear the sharp snap of something that might—or might not—be gunfire.

She was certain it was not Scoros' past she was seeing because she wasn't the one shooting the gun or setting the fire. For the moment, she was herself. She was not passenger—or captive—to experiences she could not change and would never have chosen.

Gunfire didn't make Chase flinch. She wasn't certain he could hear what she heard or even see what she saw. He could see her. She could see him. But she saw him as she saw the dead—and she was certain Chase wasn't dead.

"Emma—open your eyes. Your real eyes."

"My eyes are open."

He opened his mouth—his bruised, swollen mouth—and shut it again. "Then we are so screwed."

Chase looked at the door, which was difficult given the level of his hands. He was afraid to let Emma go. From this side the door didn't appear to have a lock. Or a door knob. Or a handle. It did not seem designed to allow anyone entry. "Do you remember how you got in?"

A hesitation. "I walked. You?"

"I'm not exactly in—but I walked as well. The citadel's doing a really fancy impression of Dante's Hell at the moment."

"Which level?"

"No fair."

Emma's brows rose. Her color—and she had color—was bad, but her expression was almost normal. "What?"

"That was an Allison question."

The corners of her lips twitched. Her hands were warm. They were the only thing in this grim place that was.

"Is there a handle of any kind on your side?"

"No."

"You didn't look."

Emma's forehead creased, but confusion—of a certain kind—was better than pain or fear or—he shied away from the last description before it had fully formed. "I didn't, did I?" Her gaze shifted. Chase tightened his grip on her hands. He wanted to reach between the bars and grab her wrists, but his hands wouldn't pass between them.

"I think there's a handle—you need to let go of my hands."

"No can do."

She grimaced. "Then you need to let go of one of them."

He couldn't say why, not then, not later, but his grip tightened. It was involuntary, and he saw Emma wince. *I can't let go of you*, he thought. There was a desperation in it, a frenzy of certainty—and it was informed in all ways by fear. He looked at his hands, tried to get them to obey his commands. They almost seemed to belong to someone else.

They were red, sticky, gloved in dried blood.

"Chase?"

"My hands—" He met her gaze. "My hands are—"

She nodded, as if not trusting herself to speak.

He stared at his hands, at her face, framed between them by bars, and last, at the hands he was gripping so tightly his knuckles were white beneath the darkened crimson. "Emma—Emma, your hands—"

"What about my hands?" Her voice was thinner.

They were as red as Chase's. The blood was newer, and it was slicker; it made her hands slippery. He knew. He was trying to hold on to them. "Emma, can you reach through the bars?"

She didn't answer. He could see her eyes widen, could see the shift in focus as she looked through him.

"What are you doing?" he demanded.

She didn't, or couldn't, answer. He was no longer certain she could hear him, or see him. Or perhaps she could. Perhaps she could see—in this land of the dead and the trapped and the damned—past the Chase Loern she knew.

His hands were red, they were sticky, and as he stared at them, he felt blood fill his mouth, where his teeth had cut his lip. He knew the sensation. It wasn't the first time it had happened. It wouldn't be the last.

He told himself this, clinging to her hands, struggling to remember why he'd come here in the first place. What he remembered instead—

*No.*

But his hands were the *wrong* hands. He hadn't noticed it before. They were his hands; they more or less obeyed his commands. But they were, blood regardless, too young. They had no calluses. They had no scars. They were the hands he'd once had when—

*NO.*

He was frozen in place, hunted, afraid. This fear was the first fear, the worst fear; this was the moment in which he had learned the meaning of the word. He turned, or would have turned; his hands were stuck, clenched in fists, bound.

He could hear the dog. He could hear the faint echoes of his mother's voice. *What's upsetting him this time?*

His father: *Probably a raccoon.*

No. No, Dad—not a raccoon. Run. *Run. RUN.*

How many times had he had this nightmare? It ended—it always ended—

the same way. There was no hope. There was no chance. There was death, always death. And the only person to survive, the only person to be left behind, was Chase. No matter how hard he struggled. No matter how much he had learned. No matter how old he was or what weapons he carried. Nothing changed.

He could hear them scream. He could watch them die. He could be paralyzed by fear and the belief—the stupid, blind belief—that this *could not be happening.*

Emma saw the fire. It was small, but beneath it was kindling, and beneath that, logs piled high, in a rough pyre. Illuminated by its growing light, she could see the shape and outline of a woman. She recognized not the woman but the situation; she had experienced it so often.

The door with no handle, no knob, faded from view, except for the bars around which her hands—and Chase's—were wrapped. She looked at Chase and saw that he was fading as well, as if he had only been so much scenery, just another part of the nightmares of one dead man.

She tried to call Chase. Tried to shout his name. The name that left her throat was not his. She didn't recognize it and knew that the throat scraped raw by the force of those syllables was not her own.

Torches flickered, small whispers of flame; they were held by shadows, shades, their voices the only things that were clear and distinct. She could no longer see past them, could not approach them. But she *tried.*

Something hit her hard, caused her to double over. She had seen this fire before. But not these men, not these women. As the shadows grew sharper, she could see that there were children in the mix, their hands or shirt collars held by parents who otherwise paid them little mind.

"Do you *want* to die?" The words were a hiss of sound.

"My mother—I have to help my mother!" A hand was over her mouth, muffling most of the words, damping their volume. Were it not for the sound of the crowd, it wouldn't have worked—but the crowd was jubilant. Loud. Merry, even. It might have been a festival fire.

An old festival, a dark fire, a human sacrifice.

She struggled. She bit. Air rushed into her open mouth.

"Then go. Go and die. There is nothing you can do to save her."

She staggered. Her knees hit dirt, her hands following.

"Is that the death you want? Is that it? Do you think that's what your mother wants for you?" Again and again, the words hissed into his ear, his captor—who? Why?—unable to walk away, to let him go.

Her captor.

Her father. *No.* Not her father. Not Emma Hall's father. She was with

Scoros again. This man was Scoros' father. She turned to look, to glare, to
plead—and the look on his father's face killed all words. *You're just afraid. If
we go—*

*If we go, we'll die.*

His father's arms found him again. "We can't save her."

He heard the fear in his father's voice. The helplessness that had never been
there before. Against it, in the background, laughter. Laughter and the first
scream. And he stood, no longer struggling, as his father lifted him, understanding this one thing about himself: He was a coward.

He valued his life, his survival, more than the life of the woman who had
given him life. He would not do anything to save her. He would not lift voice
or hand. He would not lift weapon. He would do nothing at all but walk away;
he wouldn't even bury her.

He could not scream. Not out loud. But inside? The scream started then,
and it never, *ever* stopped.

Emma was, and was not, the boy.

Emma could scream.


The sound shattered Chase.

There was no part of his body that didn't feel it as a literal, crushing blow;
it drove him back in so many ways, staggering was the least of it. His mouth
wasn't open. He could swear it wasn't open, but he could feel the reverbera-
tions of that scream on his lips. He could lift his head, open his mouth, and
make the same sound, over and over.

He knew because it was the perfect harmony to his own scream. It was the
same cry, the same wordless eruption of noise that had left his own lips at his
mother's death. That was leaving it, even now.

It was not his voice.

He didn't hate Emma now. Chase Loern was tired, in this moment, of fear
and hatred. "Emma!"

The screaming continued; the voice grew hoarse with it, and as it did, it
became similar to the voice he recognized as Emma Hall's. Funny that the
sobbing always sounded like her, even if he had never seen her cry.

His hands tightened; they still clutched her hands. He could see them—
see *her*. And he could see the Queen of the Dead. He could see his mother's
body. He could see his father's, to the left and in the corner. His father had died
first.

And he knew, as he used Emma's scream as an anchor, that they couldn't
be killed or tortured to death more than once. They were already dead. The
Queen of the Dead could not kill them again. He struggled to find his own
voice, to dislodge the past from it; his throat felt raw.

If he had screamed like that in the real world, Allison was going to kill him. Or kill herself with worry. It was, oddly, a good thought.

It was the only one. He couldn't save his parents. Emma Hall was not a substitute for them; there was no redemption for him here. But he had come to save Emma; she was not dead, and he did not intend to leave without her.

He wasn't the same Chase Loern. The naive, shallow boy of memory was dead.

"Don't take this personally, but if you die here—or worse—it'll break Allison. I am not leaving without you. Are you afraid that you're helpless, that you're powerless? That's been *my* life. Do you want to be me?"

Emma heard Chase. Heard him, turned toward him, struggling to hold on to the thread of his familiar voice amidst the volume of all the other sounds: laughter, screams, shrieks of a glee so obscene it was hard to believe they came from . . . people. Monsters, yes. She knew about monsters. She'd walked through the life of one, watching as he emerged. Seeing his choices, feeling his fear, feeling his love and his desire to protect what was loved.

She understood that he had watched people he cared about die; his thoughts had touched on it before. She had never seen it until now.

She had never seen the thing that had broken him.

But she understood. He was a monster because of monsters. And monsters in this world started out as people, *were* people. It hadn't been all that he was, but that didn't matter; he couldn't escape the sum of his choices. Death had not freed him. It gave her no comfort to know how much they had tormented him, in life.

She could see the eddies of every monstrous action bleeding into the world, sinking roots in the hearts of other people and growing there.

"Emma! Emma, talk to me. Stop whimpering. It doesn't impress anyone, and it pisses Amy off."

She struggled against the imperative of death and death and death; struggled against the memories of the man she had come—she remembered this distantly—to save. To free. The thought of Amy Snitman helped enormously, because Chase was right: Amy would be angry. She did laugh, then. It was tremulous, shaky—it was too close to hysteria. But it wasn't a scream and it wasn't a whimper and it wasn't an endless litany of guilt and self-hatred.

"Tell me what you're doing."

She felt his hands once again; they were still locked around hers. Since neither of them were here, that was physically impossible—and she didn't care. Chase didn't look like he cared much either—because she could see him. Bruised, young, his eyes far too dark for the rest of his pale face.

She shook her head.

"Tell me," Chase said, his voice so soft it was more plea than command. Chase was not gentle. That was not part of his oeuvre. But he was trying.

And his voice was so much better than the voices of the crowd. The screaming had stopped—and that was worse for the man whose memories she still inhabited, although until the cries of pain and fear had ceased, he had wished so desperately that they would.

She didn't have an answer for him. She couldn't remember for one long, ugly moment. She couldn't remember because she was paralyzed by the death of her mother.

No. It was *not* her mother. Mercy Hall was alive, in Toronto, a world or two away. She had to remember that, because if she didn't, she would never leave this place. "I'm trying to find a man. A dead man."

"Which one?"

She struggled with the question. Chase knew. Chase should know. He had been there at the beginning. So had she. She tried again. "I'm sitting in the circle."

*Yes.*

"I'm in the Queen's circle. Where it was supposed to be safe."

"And it's not."

Emma grimaced. "Clearly." She fought, now. Her father did not restrain her; Brendan Hall was dead. She hadn't failed her mother. She hadn't walked away without even *trying*. This pain was not her pain.

And yet it was. It was, now. She could remember this stranger's life as well as she could remember her own. She took a deep breath, held it, exhaled. She could remember the *pain* and the *ugliness* of his life as well as she could remember her own. Her own life had not been painless—but it hadn't been joyless, either.

She was not the sum of her pain. She was—she had to be—more than that.

"I wasn't taught how to use the circle," Emma said.

*It wouldn't have made a difference.*

"Chase, your mouth isn't moving."

"Not the complaint I usually get."

Emma was silent for a long beat. She closed her eyes—or tried. It made no difference. "Let go of my hands."

"I don't think I can."

"I'm—I think I'll be okay."

"No, I mean I can barely feel my hands." He tensed.

"Chase?"

"Don't worry about me. There's nothing here I haven't seen before."

It was the way he said it. It was the fact that he was fourteen—or younger; that he was bleeding, that he was as yet unscarred. She heard a dog barking. From the sounds of it, it was an angry dog—the bark was territorial.

She couldn't see the dog. Neither could Chase; he was staring at her. But his fingers curled so tightly around Emma's they were painful. His shoulders tightened as if to ward off blows. His head snapped to the side; Emma couldn't see what hit him, but she had no doubt that Chase could.

Emma had never asked Chase about his life. She knew he'd lost his family at the hands of the Queen of the Dead; she knew he'd made his life choices because of that loss. And she knew, watching him, that he was just as trapped by those memories as she'd been by the memories of a dead man.

The difference—the big difference—was that these were clearly his own memories. Emma had some hope of separating herself from decisions she would never have made—if she managed to escape. She *had* a life, and if it wasn't nearly as long as Scoros', it was entirely her own.

Chase couldn't escape his own memories. Not that way.

"Chase. Chase!"

His eyes, unfocused, moved, widening until they were mostly whites. She tried to free one of her hands, but he hadn't lied—his grip was too tight. The dog's bark broke; it was loud and then it was nonexistent. No voice had ordered it to shut up.

And she knew, listening to the sudden silence, what would follow. She did not want to see it. She didn't want to be Chase Loern. She didn't want to watch her family die—again. But she didn't want to lose Chase here, either. He'd come to find her. He'd come to bring her back—and if back was to the heart of the Queen's stronghold, it made no difference.

"Don't make me do this, Chase. Don't. Please."

He didn't answer. Emma was afraid he wouldn't. She had no good choices here; no choice at all. And she didn't know *how* she was supposed to rifle through the memories of a living person. She heard a man's voice—adult. She heard a gunshot. Two. A scream, younger, female.

She wasn't seeing it through Chase's eyes—but Chase was.

Emma was, and remained, herself. The fear she felt was her own. The hatred—and it was momentary, visceral—was her own as well. Neither would help Chase. She could curse the Queen, curse Reyna. Or she could go back, curse the villagers who had killed Reyna's family and the man—no, boy—she had loved. She had no doubt, if she searched the citadel, that she would find other people to curse, other people to hate.

And again, it wouldn't help Chase.

Right here, right now, Chase was like Andrew Copis. He was like Mark. He was trapped, reliving the events that had destroyed his life. And she was standing outside of them, with the desire and the need to help, and no certain way of doing so.

But she *had* found a way. Both times.

## ∽ Chapter 17

Emma's hands were curled tightly around the bars of the door's grille. Chase's hands were clenched over the top of them. She couldn't shake him loose, and at this point she no longer wanted to try. It wasn't his hands that were the problem—it was the so-called door, a thick, wooden wall with enough of a hole cut into it that she could see his face.

She was shaking. It wasn't fear so much as exhaustion. No, she thought, that was a lie. She *was* afraid. She was afraid for Chase, who mostly hated her but had come anyway. She was afraid for Allison, whose brother lay in a hospital somewhere in Toronto because Allison's best friend was a Necromancer. She was afraid that Allison, who had never, to her knowledge, had more than a passing crush on anyone, would suffer the same loss that she herself had suffered when Nathan had died.

Toby's life was not in Emma's hands.

Chase Loern's was.

She had let herself be pulled into memory after memory, wandering almost aimlessly in the gray world of the dead, searching when she didn't know what she was searching for. She had been a passive witness to murder and torture. She'd been too horrified to think; she'd lost all sense of herself in the moment of each memory, struggling to reclaim it when the memory shifted.

She didn't struggle now. She was Emma Hall.

Chase Loern was not dead. He wasn't lost and invisible. Emma was not a Necromancer. But she'd been born with the power of one. She accepted it now. The power was meant to be used; she could feel the warmth of it, startling and sudden, as it flowered in hands that had lost all circulation.

The first thing she did was open the door. She didn't reach for a handle that wasn't there, because she couldn't free her hands. Instead, she refused to acknowledge the existence of the door. It wasn't solid. It wasn't a memory—or if it was, it wasn't a memory in which she consented to remain trapped any longer.

The door itself dissolved. Last to go were the bars that had become a kind of anchor; they weren't necessary. Chase himself was attached to her hands; she didn't need anything else. She looked at his face, his young face, at his eyes, at his slack jaw, his odd hair. This boy would become the Chase Loern she knew, but he wasn't there yet.

She couldn't prevent it happening. She understood that. She hadn't been able to prevent Andrew Copis' death either, although she could see exactly how he could have been saved. The fire had killed the four-year-old. The Queen of the Dead had killed Chase's family. She wondered if the Queen of the Dead had ever used the vast reservoir of her power to attempt to change the past.

Wondered why she even thought it.

But she knew, and she tensed, squaring her shoulders. She did not want to *be* Chase Loern. She didn't want to be trapped in his animal fear and fury. But she didn't want him to be trapped there either. Sometimes all choices were terrible.

Her hands still gripped in his, although they had been lowered without the bars to anchor them in place, Emma Hall stepped forward, into his life.

She knew, or thought she knew, what to expect. She had traveled through a shattered map of Scoros' life, jolted from memory to memory.

The sky above was dark; moonlight was clear and silver. She saw the dog first and flinched; it was dead, half of its head blown away. Gunshots. Its blood was too dark to be seen as a color. Listening, she heard nothing; her breath was sharp. Had she come too late? Was it over?

But no. No. She glanced down at her hands and saw them, empty. But she could feel Chase's hands. Unlike the hands of the dead, they were warm. Chase was here. He didn't know that Emma was with him. As Emma had been, he was trapped in memory—but it was worse. These memories were his.

And Emma was herself. She was not chained to Chase. As if she were a grim tourist, she could move through the landscape his life had created.

She stepped over the poor dog's body and continued to walk.

She found a house next; lights could be seen through glass panes in the distance. But the house was not where she needed to go. She moved to the left, to the gravel road that led to the house itself, and she found what she was searching for.

She saw a man, lying face up, head pointing toward the house. Like the dog, he'd been shot, but unlike the dog, a bullet was not the only thing that had damaged him. She knelt by his side, touched his wrist; her hand passed through it. The death itself did not disturb her—not as it would have done before she had entered the citadel. She had watched two children burn to death.

She rose, continuing to walk.

Six people stood at the far end of the gravel path, and three people knelt, arms bound. Chase's mother, she thought. Mother, sister—and Chase himself. She understood, then, why the Queen's knights had chosen to congregate on the road; the house wasn't large, and she wasn't certain ten people would have fit in the living room or dining room.

Moonlight glinted off steel—not gun, but knife. The knife had clearly been used. Of the standing figures, five were men of varying ages; one was a woman. Emma recognized her. She was dressed as the Queen and not the girl; she wore an ornate, complicated dress, and her hair was pulled severely above her face and neck. Her hands were gloved, her feet confined by pointed, polished boots. There was no blood on her.

No one moved as Emma approached. No one seemed capable of moving. No one spoke.

Emma reached, hesitantly, to touch the man farthest back—the man who had, no doubt, just killed Chase's father. Her hand passed through his elbow. This was a memory in the same way photographs were: a snapshot through which she had found a way to navigate.

More than that, she didn't try. Instead, she walked through the remaining figures, skirting only the Queen of the Dead. She headed straight for Chase, and when she reached him, she knelt. Tears were frozen in tracks along his face, smearing blood; Chase's cuts were superficial, but his eye had swollen.

"Chase," she said, raising hands to cup his face. "I'm sorry. It's over."

His eyes flickered, his expression shifted. He lifted the face she had cupped; his eyes met hers. "Emma."

She nodded. "There's nothing here. Just you. And me."

He jerked back, pulling his face from the cradle of her hands, his eyes widening as he struggled to turn. Toward his sister, Emma saw. Time did not begin to wind again; his sister and his mother remained motionless.

"Kaleigh."

The girl didn't answer.

"Mom?"

"They can't hear you. The only person who is actually here is you."

He struggled. He struggled with bound hands and forced himself to his feet. "Save them," he whispered.

She understood. And she thought she could; this was not actually happening now. It was very much like the door: a physical object that existed only because she had somehow consented to its existence—as had Chase. When she had consciously refused her consent, the door had dissolved into gray, vanishing as if it had never been real.

She thought the Queen and her men might be the same, and she wanted—for one visceral moment—to do what he asked. To change the nature of nightmare. To give this boy, who was not yet the Chase she knew, a happier dream.

He had done nothing to deserve this, and it was clear that some part of him lived *in* it, constantly.

But even thinking it, she knew she couldn't. He had not deserved it, but it had happened. The dream she could give him was the daydream she had given herself, day after day, week after week. What if Nathan had come by a different route? What if he'd never left home, at all—if she'd called him before he'd reached the door? What if she'd managed to get to the hospital before he was beyond all reach?

And none of those daydreams, not a single one, could change what had actually happened. Nathan had not deserved to die. Emma had not deserved to lose him. Chase had not deserved to lose his entire family in a single, long night. And all of these things had happened. They could not be made to unhappen.

"Please, save them," Chase whispered again.

And it killed her to hear it, to know that she could change what they both saw *here* but that it would change nothing.

Maybe, maybe it would give him the strength to break free. Maybe. She willed herself to believe it; she failed. Swallowing, she said, "I can't, Chase. They died years ago. You're not really here, and neither am I. But we have to go back. You have to leave this place."

He shook his head, mute. "Untie me."

That she could do and did, without ever touching his wrists.

He rose, pushed past her; she turned, still clinging, in some way, to hands she couldn't see. He leaped toward the Queen of the Dead, who stood beneath moonlight like the Faerie Queen herself. He passed through her, landed, rose, and charged again. And again.

Emma changed nothing. Instead, she stood, and she bore witness, and she knew he would hate her for it later. She couldn't stop herself from crying, but it didn't matter; no one here would notice. She waited. She didn't attempt to touch Chase in his youthful frenzy; she didn't attempt to speak to him, to talk him out of the attempts.

She had no idea how time passed in the realm of the dead, and even if she had, she wasn't certain it would have mattered.

Only when he had exhausted the reserves that drove him, only when he had collapsed on the ground at the knees of his mother and sister, did she attempt to remind him that she was here at all.

"Chase."

He didn't look up.

She wanted to apologize—that came naturally to a Hall. She didn't. Instead, quietly, she said, "The first time I went to the graveyard after the funeral was the hardest. Nathan wasn't there. I went at night because no one else would be there either. Just me." She hesitated, because Chase hadn't moved, and she felt that comparing the two losses was wrong.

She had no other way to reach him. "He wasn't there. Of course he wasn't. His body was, and that shouldn't have made a difference." Her voice dropped. "And it didn't, not then. Nathan wasn't there. My loss was. My grief. Maybe even a little anger. I spoke to him." She had never said this to anyone before. Not even Nathan. "I spoke. I wanted him to hear me. I wanted him to know that he would never be forgotten. That he had been loved.

"There was no answer. Of course there wasn't."

Chase was silent.

"I believed the dead don't care. Until Eric arrived, I believed it. I didn't want to believe it." She began to move as she spoke. She knelt, briefly, in front of the woman she assumed was his mother; she shifted her position to study the terrified, weeping face of his sister. Younger sister, clearly. Her hair wasn't the red that Chase's, even cropped so close to his skull, was. "I wanted to believe that the dead were there, that they were waiting, that they watched. That they would *know*."

She stood, raising her voice as she headed through the tableau of Queen and knights to the splayed body of Chase's father. She knelt by his side. Even captured like a 3D picture, the lack of life was pronounced, underlined. In this memory, Chase's father had already been killed. His face, slack and open-eyed, was broken, literally broken. She tried to imagine what he had looked like in life and failed. She forced herself to try again. While she did, she kept speaking, although Chase had given no hint that he was listening.

"By the time I knew that that wish had been granted, I understood that even if the dead linger, they don't linger by their graves. Graveyards hold bodies or ashes but none of the life that defined the person. They're not meant for the dead. In a strange way, they're meant for the living. They're a place where loss is acknowledged, is meant to be acknowledged.

"Do you ever visit their graves?"

Chase was silent. But in silence he rose. Emma dared a glance at him, and her eyes remained on his hands, which were clenched fists. He shook his head. No.

Giving Chase advice was no part of whatever friendship they had. Emma had come as close as she could. She was surprised when Chase chose to join her.

Chase wondered what the dead saw when they looked at Emma Hall. She stood inches away from his father's corpse. He wouldn't have been surprised to find her weeping; she had a soft heart. A stupidly, enragingly soft heart.

There were no tears on her face when she turned toward him. She was pale, her lips were set, her eyes—her eyes almost reminded him of his own, not in color, but in expression. Was she angry?

Yes, he thought. But not at him. What she offered him was probably pity. He hated that. He didn't want it. He opened his mouth to say as much—with more words for color—but her words finally penetrated the miasma of his anger and, yes, his terror.

She was right. Of course she was right. They were dead and would remain dead. She couldn't save them—no one could. No one could. Thinking it, he turned again to where his mother and sister knelt. He both knew and refused to know; he believed and refused to believe.

He really had despised Emma. Oh, and feared her. Her life had been so easy, compared to his. Her loss had been pathetic. If his parents had died in a car accident and not like *this*, he'd be grateful. He had wanted her to see *his* life. He had wanted her to know it. He had wanted her to suffer his losses because then—

Then she wouldn't be Emma Hall, anymore. Maybe she'd be like Chase.

*Death is death.* He grimaced. He'd said that before, to himself. He'd said it to others. It was true. Dead was dead. But *dying* was not death.

Emma could content herself with the fact that Nathan's death was not on her hands. He turned to face her again and was surprised to see her hands behind her back. Her eyes were dry, her expression remote. He wasn't surprised when she began to speak, although everything about her implied a stiff silence.

"You didn't kill your family."

"You didn't kill Nathan."

She smiled. It was . . . not a happy smile. "No? Had you met the Queen of the Dead before she came here?" Her arm swept out to encompass the road, the house.

Here, at the heart of the destruction of his life, Chase was not going to offer Emma comfort. He was raw with death, with loss, with the curse of helplessness. He had nothing left for a teenage Necromancer. He shook his head. She waited. "No. No one in my family seemed to recognize her either."

"She would have come here no matter what you did?"

He nodded. Grudging it.

"Nothing you did would have changed that?"

"How the hell am I supposed to know?" This was not the direction his thoughts took when he was forced to relive these events.

She waited. She waited until he said, " . . . No."

"The day Nathan died." She stopped. Blinked.

To his own surprise, Chase said, "You don't have to talk about it." He hadn't meant to say anything, but he was now afraid Emma *would* cry, and he'd never been good with tears.

"The day he died," she continued, not crying, "he was on his way to see me."

It was Chase's turn to fall silent.

"He was coming to my house. Coming to pick me up. I liked it when he drove." She looked down, to the wreckage of Chase's father, as if it would somehow steady her.

*Death is death.* But he couldn't bring himself to say it out loud because right now, he didn't believe it. He'd find belief again later. Maybe.

"I want to go back in time. I want to go back in time and cancel on him. I'd start a big argument if it'd help. I want to go back and tell him to stay home. He was coming *to see me*. And if he hadn't, he wouldn't be dead." She swallowed. She did not cry. "I know I didn't kill him. I know it. But I also know he died because he was coming to me.

"His death was so much better than this. And it was so much worse. Better, because he didn't have a lot of time to be terrified. Worse because—" She shook her head. "It was a lot of metal crushing a lot of metal, and he—"

"Emma, stop."

"Nothing you could have done—in reality, not in daydream—would have changed what happened here that night. Nothing. Even if you were the Chase Loern you are now, it wouldn't have changed a thing. There were five Necromancers *and* the Queen.

"Me? I could have made *one phone call*. And you know? I'm good at phone calls. My mother says I spend half my waking life on the phone. There is *nothing* about a phone call I couldn't handle. I don't have to be a Necromancer. I don't have to be the Queen of the Dead. Do you understand? There's *nothing* you could have done to save your family—and everything I could have done to save Nathan."

Chase stared at her as if he'd never seen her before. Or as if she had sprouted two extra heads.

The landscape in which they stood began to fade. It was a slow process. The Necromancers vanished first, leaving only their Queen behind, standing in the center of the bodies—dead and living—of Chase's family. The gravel road dropped out from beneath her feet; the grass, dark with night, sunk into the gray fog. In the distance, he could just make out the corpse of the dog before the fog rolled over it.

Chase changed as well. His face took on the subtle scars that she knew; his hair shortened into the tight crop he'd adopted after fire had burned patches in the greater length. His clothing changed as well; he wore the studded leather jacket that Amy despised volubly.

Without thought, he lifted both of his hands; with more thought, and more hesitation, she placed hers in them.

The land of the dead reasserted itself completely.

"You know you're being stupid, right?" Chase asked.

Emma smiled. Or tried to. "*I'm* being stupid?"

"I've never claimed to be smart." He tightened his grip on her hands. Exhaled. "There are no graves. Ernest found me. I didn't go back, didn't try to go back, for a year. When I did, I looked for graves. Believe that I looked. There were no graves. There *are* no graves. My entire family disappeared without a trace. The house was empty."

She didn't ask him if he had tried to go back to it. She doubted very much that he had. "You had friends?"

"Hard to believe?"

She shook her head.

"I guess not. You're friends with Amy."

The smile that pulled from her was more genuine. "She's a good friend. Just . . . harsh."

"She might be—she's never going to consider me a friend."

"Do any of your friends know you're still alive?"

Chase shook his head. "You've seen what happens to friends of potential Necromancers. Imagine how much worse it would be if they were friends of hunters."

"And you had no other family?"

He shrugged. She'd opened up. She'd given him her guilt—and inasmuch as guilt was a gift, he accepted it. Her hands tightened on his just before he withdrew them. "An aunt. Two uncles. Grandparents. Some cousins. And no, before you ask, none of them know I'm alive, either."

She didn't ask why. She thought she understood.

She was wrong.

He did not want to be here. Then again, he never did. "Even if I thought they'd be safe, what could I say? When they ask me why I'm still alive, what excuses do I make? How do I stand there and tell them that their children or their brother or their sister are dead when *I'm not*?" His voice had risen, which was strange given just how hard it had become to force air through his closing throat.

Chase, shaking with something that was like rage if you didn't look too closely, was rooted to the spot by the strength of Emma's grip. No, not Emma's. No matter how tightly she clung to his hands, it would be trivial to force her to let go.

He wasn't even trying.

More silence.

This time, when it was broken, it was not broken by Emma.

It was almost like hearing his own voice; for one moment, he thought it *was*. Most of what he'd just told Emma he'd *never* spoken out loud. He recognized his pain, his loss, his own hatred—and he understood then that if it had guided his life, if it had been aimed at Necromancers and the woman who had ruled them, it had also always been turned inward.

"It was not your fault. It was *not your fault*."


## Reyna

The procession comes, instantly, to a halt.

The air is cold, the sky is clear and merciless. It sees what Reyna sees. She lifts an arm; the streets empty. The dead vanish almost instantly; the living—and there are few—take time. Reyna wanted an audience. She wanted witnesses.

This was to be her moment.

She looks at Eric's pale, pale face; he might be carved of alabaster as he stands in the center of the street. Her hand is on his arm; she withdraws it. She wonders—for one brief second—why she is here.

And then she wonders, instead, why *Eric* is here. Joy and hope and relief freeze; they hang suspended somewhere outside of Reyna as she studies his face. She *knows* his face. She has never forgotten it.

She has never let herself forget it. But this expression is not the expression that she has captured in a thousand different images. This street is not the edge of a forest; it is not the banks of a brook, run low in its bed by lack of rain. There were more people here—until she dismissed them—than the entire village contained.

She made decisions. She made choices. She worked tirelessly. She has done everything, *everything*, for Eric.

Eric, who walked away from her once.

Eric, for whom she waited. And waited. And waited.

She looks at him now, and she is terrified, and she has never dealt well with fear. She can feel it rise like a wave, like bile, and she cannot will it away, although she does try. She has done *everything* for Eric. What has she not done?

*You have never asked Eric what Eric wants or needs. You have almost destroyed yourself to give Eric what you believed he wanted.*

And she hears the voice clearly, she *knows* the voice, although it has been centuries, literally centuries, since she last sought it out. Scoros. Scoros is speaking. He is not here. He will never be here again. She does not turn to look at him; she knows there is nothing to see.

She says, in anger, in despair, her voice as cold as she suddenly feels, "Eric, did you ever love me?"

But Eric is looking past Reyna. He is looking down the street, his eyes oddly shaped—not narrowed, not widened. Softly, softly, he asks, "Who was that?"

She realizes that Eric *heard*. He heard that voice from the dim and distant past; the voice that had promised love and understanding and in the end offered only judgment. And he *should not* be able to hear it. Wheeling, she turns to Nathan, to Emma's Nathan.

"Did *you* hear him?"

Nathan immediately folds into a bow that hides his face—and at the moment, shorn of disciples, she no longer wants that. She orders him, sharply, to rise—and he does. His face is the color of Eric's, his expression more strained. "He said, 'Who was that?'"

"And you heard nothing else?"

"You asked—you asked him a question." He does not repeat it.

Helmi says, "If you want, we can leave the two of you alone." Helmi rarely speaks anymore, although Reyna realizes this only because the sound of her voice is a shock. "You might want to talk about things too private for audiences."

Eric has not answered Reyna's question.

Or maybe he has. Maybe, over the passing centuries, he *has*.

*Reyna, you are asking the wrong question.* The voice is gentle.

Reyna stiffens at the weight of it, the weight of familiarity, the pointed reminder of things missing, things gone. She has almost forgotten. It has been so long. She should have known that he would wake and be present today, of all days.

Today is the day that she could finally prove him wrong.

And Eric doesn't answer her question. She turns to her sister, standing beside her sole personal attendant. "You may leave. Nathan. Return to my quarters and wait." Nathan bows again.

"And me?" Helmi asks, in her little-girl, trying-too-hard-to-sound-bored voice.

"You may keep him company if that is what you desire—but, Helmi, for the moment, I need him. Do you understand?"

Helmi says, sharply, "Because he can do things, and I can't."

Today is not the day to deal with Helmi's resentment, but Reyna tries. "There are many things you can do. You've saved my life at least three times just by being careful and listening. I would never have made it this far without you. You are the only one who's stayed by my side." She watches Helmi carefully as she speaks, although she wishes Helmi were someplace else.

Helmi shrugs, sullen. "You just want to be alone with Eric," she says. It reminds the Queen, sharply and unexpectedly, of the life she led before the massacre. Before she almost lost Eric. She loved her sister.

But she wished—as she wishes now—that her sister would just *go away*. Without leaving guilt in her wake.

"Eric and I have things to talk about. I promise I will come and find you when we're done." She speaks without much hope; this never worked in the past, when Helmi was actually alive.

Helmi's frown sets. She looks—with disdain—at Nathan and says, "Fine. I'll be waiting. Nathan can keep me company." When Nathan fails to move, she glares at him, finding a different target for her sullen rage.

"Nathan," the Queen says. "Please accompany Helmi."

Nathan bows. He is not like Helmi; he is not sullen or resentful. He is a much quieter, much less brittle presence. Perhaps that is why she will keep him, in the end.

But Nathan is not her problem. She dismisses him, with far less work than she dismissed her sister. She dismisses *everyone*, and the crowds, the triumphal witnesses to the end of her long and bitter struggle, also disperse with far less resentment than Helmi did.

And when they are alone, she turns to Eric.

But there is one person she cannot dismiss. *You ask the wrong questions. You have always asked the wrong questions.*

"Shut up." Eric's eyes narrow—and why wouldn't they? "I—apologize, I wasn't speaking to you."

He says nothing, and this is troubling; she has *apologized*, and he has failed to respond. Perhaps he doesn't know how seldom she apologizes. It has been a long time, after all. Perhaps he thinks she is as powerless, as stupid, as she once was. And that thought angers her.

No—it revives dormant anger. It roots anger to pain. She wants—has always wanted—Eric. But she wants him *here*. Not standing at her side as if he were still half a world away, and hidden.

And what, she thinks bitterly, did she expect? That he would grovel, that he would beg her forgiveness? No. Pathos is not what she wants.

And yet, conversely, he *should* do all of these things, because he *left her*. He is not looking at the city. He is not looking at the buildings. He is not looking at *anything*. She did so much. She built so much. And for what, in the end?

"Eric."

*Ask the right question, Reyna.*

"Go away!"

*If I could, I would. You know why I am here. You know why I am almost anywhere you choose to be. Child—*

"I am *not a child!*"

*Reyna, love, you* are.

She turns then. Turns before she can stop herself. She storms toward the nearest wall—the wall of a townhouse—and slams her fists into it in fury. The wall shatters. If she stomped, the ground would shatter in the same way.

She turns again; the building's facade lies in shards, but the shards are not of stone or glass. She hears the distant wailing of living things in pain, and she realizes that some part of it is her own voice.

She does not look at Eric. She doesn't want to see his expression.

"Reyna."

She looks at her feet. At her magnificent skirts. At the stones she took so long to figure out how to make. At the fall of her own shadow.

"Reyna." Eric's voice is not harsh, not angry. She can't look up to meet his eyes. "Reyna." She doesn't look up until his fingers touch her chin, until he lifts her face. Until his thumbs wipe tears—inexplicable tears—away.

"Who are you shouting at?"

"It's not—it's not important."

He looks at the melting hole in what was once wall; at the shards that had once been all of a piece but now lie, becoming amorphous as the seconds pass, at her feet. He closes his eyes.

## Nathan

Helmi leads Nathan out of the streets. She walks slowly, turning every so often to look over her shoulder. She even ditches the dress. Nathan wishes he could ditch the suit in the same way, but the suit isn't an integral part of what he is.

If the Queen notices, she says nothing—and Nathan is fairly certain she hasn't noticed. He is not Helmi. He is not the Queen's baby sister. He doesn't give much for his chances if he strips off his clothing, even in the ruins of her victory parade. Nor does he give much for his chances if he glances back and sees something he is not meant to see.

Helmi knows.

It's why she takes so damn long to clear the street.

He can't decide if her sullen resentment was put on or not. She isn't a child anymore—she just looks like one. He can't tell if she wants—as the dead do— to be ceaselessly near her sister's light and warmth, regardless of the fact that it burns to ash anything it touches. Given the Queen as the only choice, Nathan isn't certain himself.

But she isn't the only choice, not yet.

He suddenly wants to race down the streets. To race back to the citadel. Emma is here, somewhere. In life, Emma was his choice. In death, she is even more so. But he keeps pace with Helmi; it's a type of invisibility.

Helmi isn't in a rush. She doesn't appear to notice Nathan at all. Either she's the world's best actor, or things are complicated. Nathan goes with complicated.

"I can't help it," Helmi says, when they've turned a corner and put several solid walls between them and their Queen. "I hate Eric."

"Why?"

"If it weren't for Eric, none of this would have happened."

"Wrong. It had nothing to do with Eric, in the end."

"She loved Eric!"

"Is that what you call it? Love?" He lowers his voice, tries to still his hands. He is shaking with something like rage. "You can hate him—you're going to do what you want, anyway—but none of this is his fault. He didn't kill himself. You're blaming the wrong person."

"Really?" Sarcasm of the ages—all of them, ever—in that voice.

Nathan falls silent. He's been dead for weeks. Not years. Not centuries. To his knowledge, no one he loves and trusts has ever been guilty of murder, let alone Necromancy. He doesn't think it's Eric he'd hate, in Helmi's position—but how can he be certain?

"You didn't have sisters," Helmi says.

"Is it that obvious?"

"Yes. You want to ask me if I still love mine."

Nathan is silent.

"And the answer is no." It sounded like yes. "And yes." Which conversely sounded like no. "I don't remember what it's like to be alive. I *want* it," she adds, voice a burning kind of cold. "I *almost* remember when I'm with her. And that's irony, for you. I wish she had never fallen in love. I wish Eric had treated her the way most outsiders treated us: with suspicion and contempt.

"I never understood *why* we had to avoid people who were kind. People who liked us." Her face, her expression, is uncomfortable; it is not a child's expression, but it is informed in all ways by a child's features.

Nathan doesn't know what to say. He wants to tell her that this is *wrong*, that it is not the kindness that has to be avoided. Or the love. But he understands—and he hasn't understood this so clearly before—that the kindness and the love, like the anger and the fear, are not divorced from the *rest* of the person. He doesn't doubt—he cannot doubt—that Eric once loved the Queen of the Dead.

"Sometimes," he says carefully, "people can turn anything to crap. Anything. It doesn't mean that it started out as crap."

"And some days," Helmi says, as if Nathan hadn't spoken, "I want what she *didn't* give me then. Or ever. I want her time, her attention, her affection. Even now." She exhales. "How stupid is that?"

He doesn't answer. Instead he says, "Do you know where Emma is?"

"No. I know where she was, but she's not there now."

"How can you tell?"

"I can't see her."

"Can you find her?"

Helmi says nothing. She closes her eyes. Nathan is aware that this is cosmetic for the disembodied dead. So is breathing. But he holds his breath, his constructed, artificial breath, until the moment her eyes widen in something akin to horror. "What is *she doing*?" she hisses.

Turning to Nathan she says, "The Queen told us to wait in her chambers. I'm going ahead." Turning, she marches—there's no other word for it—through the wall. Nathan, embodied, has to take the long way.

He runs.


## ᓚ Chapter 18

Emma's hands felt almost numb, but not with cold. She turned first. She moved, subconsciously attempting to put herself between Chase and the stranger who had just spoken. Clutched hands made it almost impossible, but she wasn't certain she could let go of Chase's hands even if she wanted to.

And there he was: the man she'd stepped into a carved circle to find. He was older than Brendan Hall had been at the time of his death—if age meant anything to him; he was not newly dead and could change his appearance at will.

He was not looking at her. He was looking at Chase. Chase, who didn't appear to see him.

"Chase, you have to let go of my hands."

Chase's eyes found hers and narrowed; he shook his head, as if not trusting his voice.

"One of my hands, then."

He managed that, but it took time, and time had returned, at least for

Emma. What she wanted, right now, was home. Home, peace, and even her mother. She wanted her half-deaf rottweiler. She wanted safety.

She had no idea how to get home from here, but she knew that home would never be safe while the Queen of the Dead ruled. Or lived. In the quiet of her thoughts, she accepted the truth that she had shied away from. While the Queen of the Dead lived, there was no home that would be safe—not for her, and not for the friends who'd been dragged into the world of Necromancers because they refused, in the end, to be left behind.

Because they loved her, or needed her, or some combination of both.

Hall manners asserted themselves as Chase released her right hand. She turned to the man who had spoken—and who looked, to her eye, as shattered as Chase. She had lived through so many atrocities as a voiceless passenger—most committed by him. But the start of his path had been the same as the start of Chase's, and she wondered if that was the inevitable destination for anyone who was forced to walk it.

She held out her free hand.

The stranger stepped forward. He looked like a ghost, unlike the undead Emma was accustomed to seeing; he was entirely transparent. Even when he attempted to take her hand, his fingers passed through hers.

"I am Scoros," he said.

"I'm Emma Hall. This is Chase."

"Yes." It was at Chase he was looking. "It was not your fault." Chase blinked. Focused. He could *hear* the man and, with effort, could see him. "You didn't kill them."

"I didn't save them either."

"No. You couldn't. You didn't run."

"I couldn't. Why did she do it?"

"I do not know. I was not alive when it happened. You see me."

Chase nodded.

"And yet you are not one of the people."

"Neither is Emma."

Emma's eyes widened at the words. It was the first time Chase had said anything remotely like this. She wished that Allison could hear it.

"Why do you look like a ghost?" she asked.

The man turned to her. "Do I?"

"To me, yes—a storybook ghost. I can see right through you."

"With practice, Emma, you could see through anyone."

She grimaced. "Everyone else looks like a living person." When they weren't floors or walls.

"Ah." He looked past Emma and Chase, his eyes narrowing. Emma looked in the direction of his gaze and saw nothing. Nothing at all.

"I am not . . . all here."

"What do you mean?"

He smiled. "You are no part of the many, many memories it has been my task to keep. You are not the first person I have spoken to since my long confinement, but you are the first to hear my voice."

"I'm not," Emma replied. She didn't accuse him of lying.

His smile deepened; it was bitter. "But you are, Emma. My Reyna has not heard my voice for a very long time. I have heard hers." He lifted his head. "Eric is with her."

Emma nodded.

"I can see them."

"I can't."

"No. You are alive. You are not woven through the citadel. You are not embedded in its walls and towers and streets. You are not part of the bitter history of its creation."

"And you are?"

"Yes."

"Voluntarily?"

"No. No and yes. I knew what she would do. Reyna has always feared abandonment. I at least could never leave her."

"You tried to kill her." It wasn't a question.

"Yes. It is not one of the memories in which I've been imprisoned. She could not believe that the attempt would bring me nothing but pain, and she desired pain. Chase said you are not of the people."

Emma nodded.

"He was wrong. I can see it in you. You are very like Reyna."

"She's *nothing* like the Queen of the Dead."

"Is she not, boy? But I forget. You are not yet dead. You see the dead, but you do not see the living as the dead see them. To the eyes of the dead, she is no different."

"Not to the eyes, maybe," Chase said. "But what she does for the dead is different."

"Is it? I see that she has bound the dead. At least two; perhaps more. They are not with her, now."

Chase cursed. Stopped. "Can you see who she's bound?"

The man's expression rippled. If Emma could have, she would have kicked Chase; she was staring daggers at the side of his face. This man had tried to kill the Queen of the Dead *because* the Queen had attempted to bind his mother—and his mother was now bound to Emma. This could go bad very fast.

She stopped. How? How could it go bad? There was no longer anything this man could do to her. He was dead.

"The dead are not with her."

"Not here, no."

"Where are you, child?"

She resisted the urge to argue with the word 'child'. "I'm sitting in the center of a big circle that's been carved out of runes into stone floor. And I'm here with Chase—and you."

"And you found me through the circle?"

"I don't know. I was trying to find you—but you weren't where I expected you to be."

"When you say circle, what do you mean?"

Emma exhaled. "There's a big circle on the floor in the center of the Queen's—room." She could not bring herself to call it the resurrection room.

The ghost's eyes widened. "You are sitting in *her* circle?"

"I only had access to two, and we didn't think to bring the other one."

"It is not safe for you to use her circle."

"It's not safe for us to be anywhere near her rooms, let alone her citadel, no."

"That is not what I meant. Take me—take as much of me as you can—back to the circle."

Emma didn't tell him that she didn't know how to get back to the circle. She didn't want to tell him anything. She didn't want to take him to where her friends—her living friends—were waiting.

"Could I meet Reyna here, where we are?" she asked.

Silence. She met the man's gaze, seeing his eyes rather than the gray that lay beyond them, stretching out to eternity.

"You cannot harm her here. If you met here, it is you who would be in danger. She is not more powerful than you, but she is vastly more knowledgeable. Take me back to the circle." He looked down at the hand into which he had placed his own; his hadn't gained solidity. "There is, perhaps, something you can do—but you must act quickly. Reyna is aware of me, now."

"You said—"

"And she is not happy. I have perhaps spoiled her day." He tilted his face, as if he were listening. "Helmi is coming."

Emma opened her eyes. She saw gray; she saw Chase; she saw a ghost. She tried again.

"This will not do," the man said. "Have you forgotten?"

"Forgotten what?"

"That you are alive."

"No."

"Then remember what life *is*, child. Open your eyes."

She tried again. She failed again. What was life, exactly? She felt alive here. She had felt alive in the memories of the dead man. She had felt alive when wandering around the frozen tableau of the worst day of Chase Loern's life. She had felt alive—uselessly, pointlessly alive—in the cemetery to which she had retreated in the evenings with her dog.

She had no experience with death, except as an observer. Talking to the dead was almost exactly the same as talking to the living. This landscape wasn't life; she knew that. She had no idea how she was to leave it because opening her eyes changed nothing.

*No.*

She tried, after a long pause, to close her eyes instead. Closing her eyes, she could still see the man. And she could still see Chase. What she could no longer see was herself. She wasn't sure if this was better or worse—it was certainly different.

She kept her eyes closed, and she listened. The old man had fallen silent. He was motionless, his gaze fixed on something beyond where Emma assumed she was sitting.

Sight hadn't helped. She chose to listen instead.

Listening was an art; she was an amateur. She had learned—with time—to hear the textures in spoken words; the words had meanings, but they were imprecise, and the voice in which they were spoken compensated for meanings words alone couldn't convey. The same sentence could have multiple meanings, depending on who spoke.

Silence was the same—but it was harder to understand. Sometimes it was a well, sometimes it was a barrier, and sometimes it was the only response one could offer.

Sometimes it needed to be broken.

"Michael?" The single word was rough, patchy; her throat felt raw.

"Emma?" Michael's voice.

She nodded, or hoped she nodded. "I'm having a little trouble opening my eyes. Can you keep talking?"

Pause. "About what?"

"Anything."

"Margaret says to tell you that the statue I saw before isn't there anymore."

"You can't see it anymore?"

"No. I—I think you did something. It . . . broke when you were . . . upset." She could hear Michael choosing his words with care.

"When I was crying?"

"When you were screaming," he corrected. "It's gone now. There's no statue. But there's a door, now."

"Can anyone else see the door?"

"No," Amy said, before Michael could answer.

To the man, Emma said, "Can you hear them?"

"If he can't," Chase replied, "I can."

"Can you see Michael?"

"No."

"Why can't you open *your* eyes?"

Chase exhaled. "Because I'm probably not conscious. I don't know how long we've been here. Look, I can see the dead—but it doesn't come naturally. The Queen did something to me—I thought it would kill me." He had probably hoped, at the time, that it would. "She left me alive as a message to Eric." Chase laughed. It sounded like a controlled scream.

"Why did you need to be able to see the dead to deliver a message?"

"I didn't think to ask."

Emma winced. "Sorry—that was a stupid question."

"Spending too much time with Michael?" He grinned.

"Margaret is worried," Michael said. "Allison is worried."

"Is Amy?"

"I think so. It's hard to tell with Amy."

"Amy," Amy said, "doesn't appreciate being talked about in the third person."

Chase muttered something under his breath.

Amy said, in a distinctly chillier voice, "I heard that."

And Emma opened her eyes.

Michael was standing outside of the circle; he was much closer than he had been. Then again, so was Allison. Margaret, Ernest, and Amy remained closer to the wall. Amy's eyes were narrowed in a very particular way, but their edges were largely aimed at Chase. And yes, Amy was worried.

Amy Snitman didn't do worry—or rather, if she did, she used it as a springboard for confrontation. She liked to face her fears. And stomp them flat. Unfortunately, if there was nothing immediately stompable, her foot sometimes came down anyway.

Chase was lying, cheek to stone, in a curl against the floor. Mindful of Ally, Emma reached out and poked his shoulder. He opened his eyes and pushed himself into a sitting position. On any other day, Emma would have told him not to bother. His complexion was almost gray, his lips the same color as the rest of his skin.

"Thanks," Emma said to Michael.

He blinked rapidly but nodded. "Did you find him?"

Emma unfolded her legs, stood, shook them out. "How long have I been sitting here?"

"Nineteen minutes," Ernest replied. "You have not been entirely silent."

"Amy? Care to explain that in normal English?"

"You've been screaming your lungs out or sobbing so much we were afraid you'd throw up. Better?"

Emma winced. "Sort of." She offered a Chase a hand; he glared and refused to take it. It took him longer to stand, and he didn't look particularly steady on his feet when he did. Allison also offered him an arm—but this time, his pride didn't get in the way of accepting aid.

Emma turned.

The man was standing behind her; she could see him if she concentrated. He was no longer transparent; he was so diaphanous she couldn't be certain he wasn't a trick of the light. And the light, in this room, was bright and endless.

She reached out to touch him and wasn't surprised when her hand passed through his arm. She had no idea how to make contact with him, beyond the visual.

"Scoros, can you hear me?"

She thought there was a ripple in the air. Chase left the circle, attached by arm to Allison. Emma hovered at its inner edge. She was afraid to lose Scoros. "Helmi's coming, by the way."

Margaret stiffened. "When?"

"Now," Helmi said.

"Now," Emma repeated. She wasn't touching Helmi, so no one but Margaret could see her. She doubted Chase was putting in the effort, given he was standing and his color had gone from gray to white.

Helmi looked like a bruised, underfed child. She wore a very simple shift, with a tunic hanging loosely from scrawny shoulders; her hair was long but not tidy. Helmi could choose her appearance.

Emma didn't think her current appearance was a conscious choice. Her expression was thunderous; she'd entered the light-filled, cold room, and she'd brought the storm with her. It flashed in the eyes she turned on Emma; they'd widened.

"What do you think you're *doing*?"

"Finding a man called Scoros—which is what you told me to do." She might have grown an extra head with less effect on Helmi than the words she'd just spoken.

The fact that the advice had come from Helmi was not enough of an excuse. "Are you *insane*? Do you think my sister won't *know*?"

Emma had no answer.

"Leave him alone."

*Helmi.*

The child's eyes widened further. Emma heard Scoros' voice as an echo—something easily missed if one wasn't listening. Helmi, clearly, did not.

*You saved the Queen's life the last time we met.*

Helmi did not reply.

*Will you save it again?*

"There's nothing you can do, now. You're dead."

*So are you. Do you feel there's no harm you can do because of it?*

Helmi folded her arms.

"Can you *see* him?" Emma asked the girl.

Helmi didn't answer. Instead, she said, "You can't use another person's circle. Whatever you tried to do, it was just as dangerous as having no circle at all. You really don't know *anything*."

Emma nodded. "You said the circle—"

"You have to draw *your own*. You don't use someone else's. This is the Queen's. It'll keep her safe. It won't do squat for you."

*Helmi is correct.*

"If it was yours," Helmi continued, "you would never have found him."

"But . . ."

"But what?"

"The circles were meant to be used so we could find the dead safely, weren't they?"

Helmi snorted. "There's no safe way to find *him*. You need to let him go. Or make him go."

"Why?"

"Because you're alive. Most of your friends are alive. I'm assuming you'd all like to stay that way."

"He can't hurt us. He's dead."

"Outside of my sister and her stupid knights, he's the only person who *can*."

*I cannot hurt any of them,* Scoros said.

"She doesn't understand what was done to you. She doesn't understand how the citadel *rose*. Almost no one does."

*You do.*

"I was there." Helmi turned to face Amy and Margaret and Ernest. "Scoros attempted to kill my sister. He failed. His betrayal actually hurt her. It hurt almost as much as Eric's. Maybe more."

"She killed him."

"Yes."

"And then she bound him."

"I don't think it's as simple as that. What did he tell you?"

Emma said, after a thick pause, "He's told me almost nothing. What I know of his life, I . . . lived."

She wasn't certain what she expected Helmi's response to be—but it wasn't a derisive snort. "Of course you did. There's no other way to find the dead. But Emma, you need to understand something. Most of what was done to him was done *before* he died. It was done with his consent."

Emma turned to face the thin impression in the air; it hadn't moved. "Is she right?"

*Yes. The dead* are *dead, Emma Hall. But what remains of them when they no longer draw breath was in them before they ceased to breathe. It is how Chase Loern can see the dead. It is how you can see and touch the dead. There is part of you that is already dead. It is how the Queen can make bodies, how she could build a citadel that can house the living.*

*We are what you are.*

"What does Helmi mean?"

*She was lonely, she was afraid. She understood that she was not valued by her knights. They did not love her. They did not revere her, although she had given them their power. They betrayed her and would have continued to betray her.*

*I see the citadel. I saw its streets before I attempted to kill her. I saw its halls, its rooms. There was only one room I could not—could never—see.*

"This one."

*Yes. She trusted me more than perhaps she trusted any living person—but she was not given to trust. She needed a place in which she might rest, in which she did not need to worry that someone would see and disapprove of her. It made sense that it would be this room; this room was the heart of her power.*

*And now you are in it. She will come.*

"What does Helmi mean? What is she afraid of?"

*If I had to guess—and Helmi did not love me—she is afraid that you will die.*

"And will I?"

*If I am consumed, if I am recalled? Yes. But Emma, so will Reyna. She is like a god, but she is human.*

Emma had her doubts.

*She cannot fly. Disentangle me from the citadel, and the citadel will fall.*

Emma turned toward her friends.

*Yes. No one will survive.*

"You're bound to the Queen of the Dead?"

*I am bound to the citadel.* He paused. *And yes, some part of me—the part that was not built into the foundation of her current life—is bound to the Queen. But one part of me is not. When I threaded myself through the citadel, I created one space which would be my own.*

"You left your mother there."

Silence.

"Emma, maybe this isn't the right time," Chase said. His voice sounded normal. His color, when Emma spared him a glance, was better. He probably wouldn't achieve good for a couple of hours, if then.

She inhaled and stepped out of the circle. Nothing had changed if you didn't include the presence of Helmi. The girl had traded the expression of outrage for a mask that denied emotion.

"Is the Queen on her way here?"

Helmi said nothing.

Scoros said, *No. Not yet. You have time to escape these chambers.*

"What did you do?" Helmi asked again. "Why did you come to *this* room?"

"I thought there was a man trapped here." She turned to Michael and added, "Can you still see the door?"

Michael nodded, lifting an arm to point at the frustratingly blank patch of slightly curved wall.

Helmi, following the direction of his arm, frowned. "There's no door there."

"There's no man there, either. Or if he is, that's not where I found him." She exhaled and added, "You might as well come out. I know you're there."

Another ghost materialized. She became far more solid than the almost invisible form of the man who had been her son.

Emma wasn't certain what reaction she'd expected from either Scoros or the older woman, and at least in Scoros' case, it didn't matter, as she could barely make out his face. The old woman, however, was dour and grim; she wasn't exactly welcoming.

"He was always a fool," she said, confirming the lack of joy. "But we all want to think well of our own sons. I could not imagine how *much* of a fool."

She felt, rather than saw, Scoros' surprise and almost shied away from it. Lifting her hand, she turned it and examined the palm she had offered to what remained of Scoros. It was empty, but she felt something—a texture, a subtle weight.

He was demonstrably capable of speech, but he said nothing.

"You'll help her, of course," the woman continued.

"She's talking about you," Helmi told Emma, her face expressionless.

Scoros did not answer.

"Yes," the old woman continued, as if he somehow had. "I'm bound to the foolish child. Did you know that? Did you suspect?"

*Yes.*

"I can't find my way back to my room. I've tried. For me, there is only one possible safety now. Reyna will not be happy to see me. How did the girl find what remains of you?" Nothing in her voice wobbled. She was as lifeless, as joyless, as vacuum.

*She searched.* This was clearly not enough of an answer, and Scoros knew it. *She searched the old way.*

"In a circle not meant or drawn for her use." Flat, almost disbelieving tone.

*You must ask her, then.*

"She couldn't answer. You can."

*I was not in a position to observe her progress objectively.* There was now a sliver of irritation in his reply.

"Even when you were, you were never objective," his mother snapped back.

Amy's brows rose; she looked to Emma. "I want to know who he's talking to."

"You can hear his voice, but not his mother's?"

"No."

"Be grateful," Helmi told her. Amy couldn't hear Helmi, either. The leader of the Emery mafia folded her arms; she looked about as friendly as Scoros' mother, but infinitely more attractive.

*How did she find you?*

"You'll have to ask her."

*How did she bind you?*

The old woman fell silent.

*Emma.*

"Don't you use that tone with the girl," his mother said, before Emma could even think of answering.

Silence. Surprise.

*She is not controlling you.* It was a statement with a hint of question at the end.

"What do *you* think?"

*I think I do not understand Emma Hall. You are bound to her. There is at least one other.*

Margaret said nothing.

"I told the girl she'll need more."

*She will. But she does not have the time. I very much fear that Reyna will do to Eric what was done to me.*

"At least then she'd finally have to admit that he's dead." Cold, harsh words.

Eric had been dead long before Reyna had become the Queen of the Dead. He'd been dead for centuries, possibly longer. She had built this place for Eric;

it was to be their home. She knew this without examining any of Scoros' memories—or her memories of them.

How fitting, then, that this was built of the dead; it was built for the dead. Grief and loss and rage and helplessness had entombed a girl scarcely younger than Emma. All of those things, Emma thought, but also a bitter, terrible hope.

She understood it so well—and hated herself for the understanding—because the door opened and before anyone could think to panic, although both Chase and Ernest were suddenly armed, Nathan ran in.

# Nathan

He turns to shut the door behind him. There are no bolts or he'd bolt it, for all the good that would do. If the Queen of the Dead seeks these chambers, nothing will prevent her entry. Nothing.

And he cares now because he sees Emma. She glows so brightly; she is the only thing he sees for one long breath. He is across the room, he is almost at her side, before thought catches up with action. He stops, then, lowering arms he had no intention of raising.

They're *all* here. Michael, Ally, Amy. The only thing that's missing is the dog. He almost asks. He doesn't. Emma has turned to face him. She is frozen but burning. He almost can't see her expression. But when she moves, he doesn't need to see it.

He has lowered his arms, and he keeps them by his sides. He wanted—wants—to hold her. But he can't. Not like this. Maybe she doesn't see what he is now. Maybe she doesn't understand. He knows he can touch her and she will not freeze. He will even feel the contact in some fashion.

But she can see the dead. She's sensitive to their presence. And he cannot believe that if she holds him, she won't see what now comprises his body. The dead, the weeping dead, are what she would be holding; he doubts that her actual touch can reach him at all. He wonders if it will help the four who are bound and trapped and almost voiceless.

She sees him pull up short. She moves.

He raises a hand, palm out, and she stops. Her eyes widen, her brows drawing briefly together in hurt surprise. He hates it.

"I can't touch you," he tells her, trying—and failing—to keep his voice steady.

"You have—"

"I have a body, yes. But Em—it's not mine. It's made of . . ." He really does want to hold her. He knows the look on her face. He watches it transform as she does what she always did: finishes the thought so he doesn't have to put it into words.

"It's made of the dead."

He nods. "I can control the body almost as if it were actually real. I'm told it even bleeds. But—" He inhales, exhales. "It wouldn't be me who'd be holding you."

"I don't suppose they volunteered, either."

He shudders. It was in this room that he watched the Queen create the cage that houses him. "Em—what are you *doing* here? How did you *get* here?" And then, before she can answer, he asks the only question that really matters. "Can you get back home?"

"Probably."

He doesn't believe her. He can't. Being dead doesn't change the fact that he knows her. It's only been a couple of months—and an eternity. If she's changed in that time, she hasn't changed enough to make her doubt invisible. "How?"

"That's Ernest's job," she replies. "We only have one job, now." But she looks at him.

And of course he knows what she doesn't say. He knows what that job is. He wants to tell her that it's impossible for her. He knows it's impossible. Power isn't knowledge. Knowledge is power. Emma lacks knowledge. But looking at her with the eyes of the dead—his own eyes now and forevermore—he can't believe it. She is a light, a fire, to equal the Queen's—the only such light in the citadel.

The only such light, Nathan suspects, in the world.

"Where is the Queen?"

"She's in the streets outside the citadel, with Eric. They may be arguing. She sent everyone away—dead or living."

"Will Eric kill her?" It is a harsh question; it is therefore not Emma's. Nathan's eyes glance off Chase's face. He's surprised. Ally is beside him, under his right arm, and the question didn't even make her flinch.

Nathan can't answer because he doesn't know. He knows that in Eric's position, he would falter—but he can't conceive of Emma *as* the Queen of the Dead. If she were?

If that's what she must become?

## ⮎ Chapter 19

Michael stared at Nathan. So did Chase. Amy, never one for expressions of shock, nodded once, grimly, before her gaze moved on. It came to rest on Emma. No one did judgment as well as Amy Snitman. Amy Snitman could make a test out of anything—but it was easier for Amy; she never failed. She wasn't judging yet, but Emma knew this was a test.

. Of course it was. Nathan was here. Nathan looked like *Nathan*. He was, to her eyes, alive. Even his eyes appeared almost brown. He was wearing very strange clothing, and his hair looked almost ridiculous, but none of that mattered.

She tried to see him as she saw the dead. She closed her eyes. Why had she never tried this with Eric?

"Em." Ally's voice. And Nathan's, overlapping it, maybe half a second behind. Emma had just spent a subjective lifetime trapped behind Scoros' eyes. She'd wondered, until Nathan opened that door, whether or not she would ever be just Emma Hall again.

The answer was yes.

Emma had loved Nathan, still loved him, still dreamed of spending her life in his company and the accepting warmth of his many silences. She wanted nothing as much as she wanted that. She wanted Nathan *back*.

It was a good dream. It had been the *best* dream. And it was time to wake up, to live—forever—without it. What was left was what-if, and she'd done that. She would probably continue to do that, in the quiet moments when she came face to face with her loneliness and the empty space where Nathan had once stood.

In the worst and the darkest of moments, she had wanted to die. Just . . . die. She had never had the courage to kill herself, and, in truth, death and suicide were not the same. Even if they had been, she couldn't imagine deliberately doing to her mother, and the friends who needed her, what Nathan's accidental death had done to his.

But in daydream, death was different. It wasn't about the loss other people would feel or suffer. It wasn't about the pain she would cause.

It was about the pain she would no longer feel—because if she were dead, it would be *over*. She would never need to feel loss again. She would never have to confront the emptiness, the black hole, that had once been filled by Nathan.

She had been lucky, she realized, standing an arm's length away from him.

She had been able to see him again, to speak with him again, to tell him all the things that she couldn't tell his corpse. His mother hadn't even had that.

She had been able to hear him tell her, again, that he loved her. But that was all she could have. It wasn't what she wanted. It wasn't *enough*. But it had to be. More was impossible.

Loving her, not loving her, wanting her, not wanting her—they were all in the past. They were etched in her heart and her mind. They turned joy into pain, over and over again. They turned *love* into pain. She wasn't certain she would ever love anyone again—not the way she loved Nathan.

She wanted love to last forever.

And this one could—but it could never grow and change. It could no longer sustain her. It could no longer sustain Nathan.

Nathan was dead.

She exhaled—she had been holding her breath. With her eyes closed, she could see Nathan clearly. He was wearing the clothing he'd been wearing the day he died—the day he was coming to see her. To pick her up. To take her away from the rest of her life. She'd loved, and still loved, that life—but it was the space they created when they were together that had given her the deepest joy.

And that was lost to death as well. Lost to Emma. She held out one hand.

He shook his head, but she didn't lower that hand.

"I see it," she told him. "I see it, now."

"See what?"

"The binding," she whispered. And she did. It was a slender, golden chain that pulsed with a faint light—as if it were a stretched, attenuated heart. It traveled away from Nathan, into the gray; she couldn't see the other end of it.

"Em—"

"Let me do this one thing." She couldn't tell herself that she was doing this for Nathan. She was doing it for herself. If she couldn't have Nathan back, if she couldn't have what had been irrevocably lost, she'd be damned if she'd let the Queen of the Dead have what was left.

He hesitated, his expression drawn; she realized she must be crying—and she didn't care. Just this once, it didn't matter. What were tears, after all, but the overflowing of pain when there was just too much of it for one person to contain?

"I don't want to touch you," he said.

"Yes, you do. You just don't want them to touch me in your place."

"Can you—can you see them?"

She couldn't. The only thing she could see with closed eyes was Nathan. She didn't understand the magic of the Queen's resurrection. But she was certain that she *could* reach the dead, if they were sentient, if they were some-how present.

She was certain of that if nothing else.

She smiled. She forced herself to smile. He knew, of course. He winced at her expression. "People tell you that love doesn't die as long as someone re-members," she said.

"I always thought that was bullshit."

She laughed, a blend of genuine amusement and endless loss. "Me too. Especially after you died. But it doesn't matter. It doesn't matter if it's bullshit. It doesn't matter if love dies with death or if it lasts for eternity. What we had was special, but it's *over*."

"Em—"

"And I don't want it to *be* over. I never, ever wanted that. But it is, Nathan. There's only one thing I can do for you." She opened her palm. Her arm was steady. "There's only one thing I can do for *me*."

He drifted closer, as if pulled by main force. Emma hadn't moved. "I don't want to let you go," she whispered.

He closed the distance, then. He placed his hand in hers. There, here, it didn't matter. She felt the warmth of his palm as it met hers—but she felt the ice, too. With her free hand, she reached for the golden filament, and as she'd done before, she snapped it.

It broke cleanly; there was no resistance at all.

She wanted to hold him. No, that was wrong. She wanted to be held. She wanted to lean into his chest, seek comfort and harbor inside the curve of his arms, rest her forehead against his shoulder. She'd done that before.

She'd never do it again, and never was almost too much. But too much didn't matter. Death *was*. It just was.

And she understood his hesitation. She could hear—or feel—something that was not quite Nathan in the curve of a palm that mimicked his hand al-most perfectly. She understood *why* he hadn't opened his arms to her, or touched her at all until she'd practically begged.

She thought about Merrick Longland. If he had not told her that the body he'd been granted was not actual flesh, that the spirit it now contained was still, and always, dead, would she have believed it? It *felt* like life.

Without thought, she stepped into Nathan; without thought, he enclosed her in his arms. He said nothing. Neither did she.

"Em," Ally said, at a great remove.

Emma couldn't talk. Not while she listened, while she struggled to listen. In his arms, surrounded by him, she could hear attenuated voices more clearly—but not without effort; it took effort. Concentration. She had to *try* to hear them, and she thought she might never have tried at all if she hadn't known.

She wasn't in Nathan's arms, now. She knew it. But they *felt* like his arms. She was certain that if he kissed her now, his lips would feel like his lips. But they weren't, and wouldn't be, and she shivered, thinking about it.

She listened, as she had first listened when they had arrived in a deserted building. And she heard what she had heard then—but it was weaker, softer.

"Emma?"

She grimaced. "Michael, Ally—I need you to be quiet for now. I'm trying to hear the voices of the *very* quiet dead."

"Why?" Michael asked.

"Because Nathan's body *isn't* a body, not like ours. It's made—it's made of the dead, like the floor in the townhouse."

"You want to free them?"

"Yes." One word. A single word.

"Nathan?"

"Yes," Nathan replied. "I want Emma to free them, too." The borrowed arms tightened, briefly, around Emma. "But—there's almost nothing left of them, and Emma can't hear them if there's any other voice."

Silence then.


# Nathan

He hasn't lied to Emma. He won't.

But in his arms—in the arms that are not his but look exactly like the arms that once were—she feels like Emma Hall. He remembers the first time he kissed her. He remembers the first time he slid an arm around her shoulder; he remembers the first time he held her. He remembers the nervous desire, the elation, the quiet. He remembers his own heartbeat, and he can hear it now.

He can hold her. He could kiss her. He doesn't know what that would feel like, but he suspects it would feel the same.

He's no longer certain he would be aware of the cost of it, because in her arms, he can't hear the dead at all. Their voices are silent, mute; their weeping has banked. And maybe, he tells himself, this is what *they* want, as well. They want to touch Emma. They want to be with Emma. They want to bask in the warmth of her light, because in that light, they are no longer alone.

It's what he wants.

It's what he wants more than he's ever wanted anything.

If he could *ask* them, if he could be certain—but no. No. He *is* dead. He's dead, and this is not where he should be, because Emma will never live if he's with her. Emma will never forget.

He shakes his head and then kisses the top of hers. He's certain Emma will never forget him. He's certain his mother will never forget him. None of his friends will forget, either. He's not sure why that matters now. He's not, after a moment, certain that it *does*.

But he thinks he would give the gift of forgetfulness to his mother, at least, if he had the choice—because then her pain would stop.

"It's not just pain," she whispers. Her voice is so much a whisper it's hard to catch the aural edges of individual syllables.

"You haven't seen her."

"I've *been* her, though, in my own way. You gave me so much. You made me happy. And I was happy in a way I've never been happy before. I wanted it to last forever. I was—I am—greedy. I wouldn't feel this pain, and neither would your mother, if you'd never existed at all."

"And sometimes that would be the better option?"

She nods. She doesn't lie to him. "I know what happiness is now. I can't unknow it. I'm afraid I'll never be happy again."

He nods. He knows. But unhappiness is not what he wants for Emma. It's never been what he's wanted. It's not what he wants for himself, either. He looks past Emma, through the walls of the citadel, through the emptiness that must be sky beyond it, and he knows what he does want.

He wants to leave, because *there is no place for him here*. He knows—as the dead know—where home is. He knows that he cannot reach it. He knows that Emma is the next best thing—and that's a terrible thing to think.

But he feels the warmth of her, the warmth of her light—a light she can't see herself. And he feels it more strongly as the minutes pass; he feels it become heat but not fire. It does not burn. It does not consume.

And he understands why he feels it so clearly, so suddenly: Emma is unmaking his body even as she stands in his arms, pressed against his chest, her head bowed, crying. She is setting them free: the four who were called, the four who struggled, the four who were consumed. She is unraveling what was built.

Soon he will not be able to hold her. Or, he will, but he'll suck the warmth from her, numb her, freeze her skin.

He knows that the four didn't volunteer. He knows they had no choice. He knows, but he thanks them anyway. She untangles them all at once in a flurry of gray, the whole separating instantly into four distinct entities.

They see her, of course. Nathan can see them clearly: two girls, two boys; their mouths work, but their voices are so quiet even he can't hear them.

Emma can. He can see, from her expression, that their voices reach her. He can see that she's been crying, that she might still be crying, and that it doesn't matter, now.

But he hears what she says, and if he could close his eyes, he would. She thanks them. She apologizes for what was done to them—as if it were done *for* her or somehow at her request—and she thanks them.

And then she tells them to go. To go and to wait.

She intends to open the door.

## ⤳ Chapter 20

The four didn't leave her.

They remained, almost circling her, as Nathan's clothing—the clothing they'd collectively worn—drifted, empty, toward the ground.

Emma inhaled, wiped her eyes with the back of her hand, and paused; a golden chain was wrapped around her hand. Looking up to Nathan again, she said, "Margaret says she can appear in front of the rest of the living without holding my hand."

"I don't know how," he told her.

She turned to Michael. To Margaret. And to the old woman, who was standing just beyond the four, lips pursed in a frown that was probably etched there.

"You have my son," she said.

Emma could only barely see him. "He's not bound to me."

"No, I can see that. What did he do?"

Emma shook her head. "If you mean right now, he didn't do anything. If you mean in the past, or in his life, I think you already know the answer. And if you want to question him, you can probably hear his voice as well as I can. The two of you can talk. Michael."

Michael nodded; he was staring at the space that Nathan had occupied minutes before. "Is Nathan gone?"

"No. He's here. I have him." She lifted a hand again. "I need you to stand in front of the door."

"The door that you can't see?"

She nodded.

Helmi was staring at the dead that surrounded Emma. She transferred her gaze to Nathan, disembodied once again. Her expression was almost unreadable—always disturbing in a child of her apparent age. "He was dead," she said, voice as flat as her expression. "He was always dead."

Emma nodded.

"What are you doing?"

"Trying to find the rest of Scoros."

"Emma, you're talking to yourself again," Amy said.

"Yes, sorry." She held out a hand to Helmi. She had not been willing to do so for Scoros' mother, but she thought Helmi's input might be necessary, and thinking often went better in a group.

Helmi hesitated. "Are you sure?"

Emma nodded.

"My sister will come. You took Nathan from her. She'll know."

Emma nodded again; she did not lower her hand.

"Margaret says it drains your power."

"You know your sister better than anyone here except Scoros. I don't want to have to repeat everything you say—I'll probably get half of it wrong, which will annoy either you or Amy."

"But she's coming, and you'll need all the power you can get."

"Power alone won't be enough. I don't *know* how to do what she does, and I can't learn it in half an hour—or however long we have. Our only hope is to think of something that we haven't thought of yet. Take my hand."

Helmi obeyed. Her hand was cold.

Emma followed Michael to the wall, and Helmi drifted alongside. She was silent. "Scoros tried to kill your sister at the end of his life. He obviously failed."

"He was nowhere near as powerful as she was."

"No. But he knew her defenses. He didn't have to use Necromantic power to kill her, after all. He could poison her. He could stab her. I don't think guns were much in use when he tried—but she's *alive*. There are a lot of ways to kill a living person. The Hunters do it, and they *don't* use the power of the dead; they don't have it."

"How did he try?"

"I don't know. I didn't see that part of his life. And before you ask, I've seen enough of his life to last several lifetimes; I don't think I could bear the pain of looking at any *more* of it."

Michael put his hand on the wall at just above waist height. "It's here."

"Is that a door knob? I mean, is that where a door knob is?"

"It's locked," Michael replied, which was yes.

Emma saw wall. Even in the confines of the Queen's circle, she'd seen wall. There was nothing like a door where Michael said there was. She wondered if the Queen had learned the art of hiding things from Scoros, or if she'd developed it herself after Scoros' death. She certainly hadn't discovered his rooms.

"Helmi, can you see anything here?"

"Wall. You're certain *he* can?"

"He found rooms hidden in the citadel that we're fairly sure your sister has never discovered."

"Which rooms?"

"Scoros' rooms. That's where his mother was."

"And you figured out how to bind her?"

"Not deliberately, no. I'm not sure it's repeatable."

"How did you do it?"

"Can you just—" Emma grimaced. There had been a reason she wanted Helmi in the group. "She was holding my hand—the way you are. Amy said something that annoyed her, and she tried to use *me* as a conduit to turn Amy into ash. I stopped her."

"How?"

"It's my power," Emma replied, placing one of her hands flat against the wall where the door was. "I get to decide how it's used."

"And then you bound her?"

"And then she was bound, yes. It wasn't deliberate. I didn't think that's what I was doing."

Amy coughed. "Is that how binding normally works?" she asked Helmi.

"I don't think so," Helmi replied—more slowly. "I haven't been bound. I don't know."

"You've watched, though."

The child nodded. "It—takes longer." She was frowning. "You said she tried to use your power?"

"Or me, as a conduit. I knew what was about to happen. It's happened before."

"You let the dead use your power?"

Emma exhaled. The wall was chilly, but not in the way Helmi's hand was. "Not on purpose, and I'm not even sure it was my power that was used. A dead four-year-old boy wanted to save his living baby brother. I felt the surge of that intent leave my hands, and a Necromancer died because of it."

"That's not the way it's supposed to work."

"Maybe the Necromancers do more when they bind than just harness power; maybe they build in limitations."

"But—that means the dead could use you. I mean, the dead who *have* knowledge." She looked, then, to Margaret Henney, who hadn't said a word since Helmi's arrival. The child who was not a child seemed excited now. "You wouldn't *have* to learn how to use the power if the dead you've bound know how."

"Margaret?" Amy asked.

Emma closed her eyes. She could see the wall. Her own hand vanished, as did Michael. Helmi remained, of course, her eyes a translucent almost-gray that shone, faintly, as if with reflected light.

"What are you doing?" Helmi demanded.

"Taking down the wall," Emma replied.

"You don't have time for that."

"Then we'll die," Emma replied. "Our only hope of survival is Scoros—and some part of Scoros is here. It's hers—but I don't intend it to remain that way."

Helmi turned, still attached to Emma's hand. She looked at Scoros' mother—Emma still hadn't asked for her name and felt no particular guilt not knowing it. It was unfair, she supposed, but she couldn't forgive her for her attempt to kill Amy.

*Longland*, she reminded herself. She frowned. "Helmi, where is Longland?"

"I don't know. He was with the procession until she ordered everyone to leave. Maybe he thinks he can kill the Queen, with Eric's help."

"I don't know that Eric will help," Nathan said.

"No," Emma said softly, glancing at Nathan, who drifted toward the wall. "I don't know that he will either. He loved her once."

"Then again, so did Scoros," Helmi pointed out.

"I don't think Scoros really stopped."

"He tried to *kill* her."

Emma nodded. "It's complicated."

# Reyna

*You have never been happy.*

Eric's eyes are narrowed in confusion; there are lines in his forehead; the shape of his brow has changed. Reyna, who knows every expression that's ever crossed his face, recognizes this one. He's worried.

He's worried *for* her.

He isn't armed. He has no guns, no knives. He has no iron, no salt. She loves him, yes. But love and trust are not the same. She's learned that bitter lesson, time and time again. Everyone she loves leaves her or betrays her. Sometimes, both.

It is not Eric's voice she hears. She struggles to ignore the words, but they come again.

*You have never been happy.*

But he's wrong. Scoros is wrong. She *has* been happy. She was happy with Eric, before the drought and the fear and the murders. She remembers it; how could she not? It was the only time in her life that she had ever been truly happy. She had dreamed of the future, of love extending into forever, of Eric by her side.

*Reyna, child, he* wanted *to be by your side then.*

He is by her side *now.* He is here.

But Longland brought him. Longland and her knights. He did not come here on his own. He did not call her, did not return. He would not even speak to her for centuries, no matter how hard she struggled for even a glimpse of him. Instead, he picked up weapons and whittled away at her Court.

And it's true that she sent the troublesome and the difficult after the Hunters first, but not only, and not always.

"Eric," she says, voice thick. "You haven't answered my question."

She is afraid that he will pretend he didn't hear it. Or that he will look away. She is afraid, she realizes, that he will lie.

She hears Scoros again. She can almost see him, his voice conjures so many tangled memories. *You haven't asked him, Reyna. You have not asked the question aloud.*

"I will unmake you," she whispers, her fury so intense it swallows volume.

*You have already done that,* he says. His voice is gentle. *No, that is unfair. We have already done that, you and I. Eric was a child. He attempted to save you because he loved you, and he died.*

*You were a child—*

"ENOUGH!"

The ground shakes; the road undulates beneath their feet. The buildings, the facades of which she had worked on so carefully, ripple; for a moment, the world is liquid.

Eric catches her when she stumbles. Eric.

"Reyna." Her name again. Her name carried by his voice, so close to her ear. "Who are you talking to?"

"Scoros," she says.

Eric's gaze sweeps the streets. Cobbles and facades have reasserted their existence. Nothing moves—nothing but Eric and Reyna.

She is angry at Scoros. She intends—after today—that he *never* have a voice again. She can't remember why she left him one. She can't remember why she wanted to be able to hear him. Or why she wanted him to be able to hear her. But . . . that had happened before his death, hadn't it? That had happened before.

Before, when Scoros loved her as a father.

"Why did you come back?" she whispers. She pulls away from Eric before he can answer. She doesn't want to hear his lies. She is certain they will be lies. She almost removes his tongue, but to do that, she would have to touch him.

"Do you remember," he asks her, "the first time we met?"

It's not an answer. But it's not a lie, either. Reyna is tired. She is *so* tired. She nods, her back turned toward him, her hands clasped behind it. She knows that Eric can't hurt her. Even if that's what he wants.

She believes, in this desolate moment, that it *is* what he wants.

"You can make anything," he tells her. "Why this?"

Why this city? Why this citadel? "It is safe," she replies. "It is safe for us." She glances over her shoulder; he is not looking at her. He is looking at the empty streets. There are no trees here. There is no stream. There are cisterns for water, but no natural sources; there are no rivers. There can't be.

She can make water of the dead, of course, but it has never seemed desirable. Today she wishes she had tried. That's what she should have done. She should have created the world in the image of those early days.

Neither she nor Eric could have met in a city like this; Reyna's kin wouldn't have been allowed to walk these streets if they'd existed in her time. Reyna and her kin wouldn't have been allowed to stand as audience to such a wedding, such a procession.

No. The only celebration they could join involved their deaths—and the audience was jubilant at the ugliness, their own cruel triumph.

*Why* had she made this place?

Why had she thought that this is what *Eric* would want?

She shakes her head; she recognizes the thought, and it is *not hers*. She has hated no one in her life as much as she hates Scoros in this moment.

She wanted to make the world safe for love. Her love and Eric's. She would have been happy, before the villagers had come so many centuries ago, to live *anywhere* with Eric. Anywhere. A hut. A wagon. Why should it matter, then, whether she has created a forest, a stream? Why is a *palace* worse than that?

Why does he not see her? Why does he not see only her?

*Why*, Scoros asks, *do you not see yourself?*

She ignores the old man. She cannot believe she has *ever* been happy to hear his voice. It is heavy with age and judgment. She thought of him, once, as a father—but now, she hears only her mother. The ground shifts beneath her feet, echoing her ancient anger.

She might destroy him, even now—but that would destroy the citadel. She has made each careful choice, has chosen each action, so that she might survive; she has no intention of committing suicide here. She opens her mouth to tell him as much—to shout it, to rage—but before the words leave her, something else does.

Nathan.

Nathan is no longer bound to her. Longland, she owns. She has lost none of the dead she's bound—none except Nathan. The streets are empty of everyone except Eric. Her knights have vanished, obeying her commands as if they were of the dead, and not sovereign over them.

If one of them has *dared*—

Eyes narrowing, she forgets Scoros, forgets weddings, forgets triumph. It is not as Reyna that she looks at Eric, but as the Queen of the Dead. It isn't even Eric's name that leaves her lips.

*Emma.*


## ᑐ Chapter 21

This wall was not like the floors of the townhouse. Emma could hear nothing in it, no matter how intently she listened. She could feel the chill permeate her palm, but all of the walls in the palace were cold. She had no idea how to unmake this one—it might actually *be* stone.

But no—it couldn't be. She could still see the wall when she closed her eyes. This, like the floors of the townhouse, was made of the dead. Everything in the room was.

"You have done well, Emma Hall," a familiar voice said. "You have done well. Better than I expected when we first met."

Emma didn't turn to look at the magar.

"You will not find what you require—not this way. There are two things you must do first."

Emma lowered her palm. She had not released Helmi and was therefore forced to offer the magar her right hand.

The old woman shook her head. "I understand what you are asking for. I *could* do what you desire; it is possible. But this is your fight. It is not mine—I am dead."

"That didn't stop Scoros' mother."

The magar nodded. "She and I have much in common; we might have been cut from the same tree. But even so, we were carved in different shapes, for different purposes. What she attempted, I will not attempt. You are alive. My child is alive."

"What must I do?"

"Draw a circle, Emma Hall."

"She doesn't have *time* to draw a circle!" Helmi shouted.

"No," her mother agreed. "Hush, Helmi. Hush. Emma understands."

\*     \*     \*

For a long moment, the magar was wrong. She felt Helmi's frustration and fear as if they were her own—because they were. But she turned toward the Queen's circle, looked at the curved, precise runes that comprised the anchors of its circumference, and understood.

The floor was not stone.

The circle was permanent only until the dead that served as building blocks were finally free. Her hand tightened around Helmi's. In fifteen minutes, she wouldn't be able to control her grip, her hand would be so numb.

But Helmi looked up at her, seeing the question Emma didn't quite ask, and she nodded. "I know how to draw a circle," she told Emma, radiating, for a moment, the proud confidence of a girl who has suddenly learned that her knowledge is both superior and necessary. As if she were a child in anything more than appearance.

"I don't," Emma told her, as she approached the Queen's circle—a circle she had used in ignorance, assuming it would provide safety.

"No, I guess you wouldn't. Everyone who could teach you is dead." She looked over her shoulder at her mother, but the magar didn't move.

"Was your mother always like this?" Emma asked, lowering her voice.

"Like what?"

"I just—I feel like she's testing us."

"Oh. She is. Everything was always a test with my mother. The only person she didn't test was Reyna, and look how *that* turned out. She wasn't always like this, though. Sometimes she was worse." The grin she turned on Emma was bright and ageless. She started to move faster, toward the circle's edge, dragging Emma with her, although that was technically impossible.

They stopped when they reached the circle's edge. "Can you even cross this?" Emma asked.

"Yes and no. It's like the rest of the physical world—it doesn't exist for me if I don't want it to. I can walk over the circle. I can sink through the floor."

"Then how is it different at all?"

"I can't harm you."

"You kind of can't harm me now."

Helmi stared at Emma's hand, which was very, very cold. "Point taken. When you leave, when you go to search for the lost, the lost *can* harm you. Because you have to leave the living to find them. So, in theory, if you leave the land of the living, I *can* harm you. I wouldn't because I wouldn't know where—or when—you were. Death is confusing like that."

"And this is supposed to protect me?"

Helmi nodded. "If you lose your way, if you lose your time or your sense of who *you* are, you come *back* to yourself in the circle. You're probably going to faint or collapse—but you won't die, and you will recover."

Emma nodded. "That's why I tried to use this one."

"This one wouldn't have saved you, though. All circles are almost the same—but the difference between them is big." For the first time, she glanced over her shoulder toward the magar.

Emma's gaze followed Helmi's; the magar nodded at them. She said nothing. The nod was enough for Helmi.

"This symbol is earth." Helmi pointed with her toes. "It's the first one that's drawn, if you draw it with chalk or coal. It's the simplest—but it's hard to get exactly right, because wrong is so obvious.

"This one is air. The position is important," she added. "It's to the right of the earth, a quarter turn."

"Does the orientation of the symbol matter?"

Helmi's expression brightened. "Yes." As if Emma were a child, and had done something clever. "The symbol for fire is to the left, a quarter turn."

Emma nodded.

"Of the four, the last is the symbol for water. It's in opposition to earth. Water is birth and life, but it requires earth and air and fire. All circles have these four." She traced it with fingers that couldn't feel its carved edges; Emma traced it with fingers that could. Helmi moved on. Emma knew they needed to hurry—but she also felt, in this moment, that she needed what Helmi had to offer.

Or that Helmi needed to offer it.

"If those were the only things that mattered, it would be easy to draw a circle."

"What else is necessary? There seem to be a lot of other characters embedded in the stone here."

Helmi glanced over her shoulder again. The magar nodded, but this time she approached. "There are. They are the ways in which we anchor ourselves; they are runes that describe traits of life that are not always immediately visible. The circles we use change with time. But there are characters that are immutable and unchanging. Those," she added, "like the elements."

"And the others?"

"I think, child, the others are runes *you* can use. They are not so different from the ones I would counsel you to consider and write were I your master."

Emma turned to Helmi. "What do they say?"

"This one is sorrow," she said. "This one is hope. This one is love. This one is peace, I think. This one is strength."

"So, spiritual or emotional things?"

The magar snorted. "Perhaps. They are supposed to describe . . . yourself. They are meant to be honest, Emma Hall. They are meant to be the truth."

Emma hesitated.

"Yes?"

"I'm not sure anyone sees themselves clearly enough to write that kind of truth."

"No. Is what we see of ourselves a lie, then?"

"I don't think so," was Emma's slow answer. "But what others see of us isn't necessarily less true, either. And if I understand what Helmi is telling me, we don't draw the circles by committee."

"No. We write them in truth, Emma Hall. Do you understand why they change with time?"

"Because we change with time?"

"Yes. The words that might describe you at three are not these words, although some elements of them remain. The words that Helmi would have used are not applicable to you now."

Emma frowned. "Sorrow, hope, love?"

The magar nodded.

"Anyone of any age can understand those, surely?"

"Yes, of course. But at certain ages they are not prized, and in certain frames of mind, they are goals; they are not what you *are*, but perhaps what you desire."

"Sorrow?"

"There were stone circles," the magar continued, as if she had never stopped. "But only five characters were engraved there. The four for the elements, the fifth for *being*. This one," she added. "We tell our students that it means 'spirit' or even 'soul.' That is not exact. It is immutable as a character, but it is rooted in the shifting descriptions of self."

"Which ones are these?" Emma asked Helmi, pointing to the only runes that hadn't yet been explained.

"Those? They're her name."

Emma turned again to the magar. "If I understand what you're saying correctly, you think I *can* use this circle. The runes here that I don't know are runes you think I'd choose."

The magar nodded.

". . . Except strength. I don't think I'd ever describe myself as strong."

The magar pursed lips; she spoke, but the sound of her voice was lost to the loud rumble beneath Emma's feet. Beneath *all* of their feet. It sounded very much like they were standing on thunder. The old woman held out a hand.

Emma stared at it. She couldn't remember if she'd ever offered the magar her hand before. She hesitated.

"I think she wants you to take her hand," Helmi whispered. Helmi's expression, when Emma glanced down, was not heavy with sarcasm. Nor was her tone. She had existed for centuries. She could shift her appearance without apparent effort. But she was a child.

Emma placed her palm, almost gingerly, against the magar's.

The world vanished.

Gray gave way to black, the transition slow and seamless. But in the black, Emma could see stars. She held Helmi by one hand and the magar by the other—but she was no longer in the Queen's chambers.

No, that was untrue. She was undoubtedly still in those chambers. But she was here, as well.

"This," the magar said quietly, "is where I reside. It is all of the home left to me."

As homes went, it was impressive. But there was no house. There was no tenting. There was no landscape other than the distant stars. As Emma tilted her head skyward, she saw the faint outline of the low-hanging moon. She wondered why it hadn't been the first thing she'd seen.

Helmi did not look around. Her head, like Emma's, was tilted, and moonlight seemed to be reflected in her widened eyes.

"Your daughter couldn't find you here."

"No."

"Why?"

"She was taught how to search for the lost. She learned. But the lost exist in a world of their own creation—and it is a pale shadow of the world in which they lived. This is not. I am not lost. I am well aware that I am dead. I have never suffered the confusion that governs the lost."

"Why did you not go to her?"

"I could not take that risk," the magar replied.

Helmi, however, said, "She did. She tried to talk to my sister. My sister wanted to know where the lantern was; my mother wouldn't tell her. They argued. I hid."

The magar didn't acknowledge Helmi's statement. "She was a fragile child, in ways Helmi was not. And she knew, then and now, how to hold on to pain. You have come to the seat of her power, Emma Hall. What will you do?"

"Open the door," Emma said.

"And how, exactly, do you intend to achieve this?"

"I opened it once before."

"That is not an answer."

Emma nodded. It wasn't. "I intend to free the dead trapped here."

"Better. You avoid the question I have avoided asking. I cannot do what must be done." Having spoken, she waited, her eyes unnaturally bright and sharp.

"Could you do what Scoros' mother attempted?"

It was Helmi who answered. "No, she couldn't. Scoros—and his mother—learned the arts of Necromancy from the Queen. The magar didn't. None of the people had the knowledge or the power to stand against my sister. To do it, they would have had to do what she did."

"I can't."

Helmi nodded. "I'm not sure what she expects from you. She doesn't have time to teach you what you need to know."

"I have time here," the magar replied. "Time does not touch this realm."

"It touches the one I'm actually breathing in," Emma pointed out.

"Yes. It is why we are here. You walked for Scoros. It was a long walk, a harsh one—and very, very unsafe. I would say your own ignorance is likely to kill you—but you have not died yet. Perhaps you will not die today. Perhaps you will. I think it likely that you will, and I have brought you here because you must remember this place. It is to here you must travel—and in haste; she cannot follow."

"She can go wherever I can go," Emma said. It wasn't a question.

"Almost. You have one thing she lacks. You have the lantern. You are here because you carry it. And I am here because you are here, and you are carrying me. It is not so easy to find this place without it; the darkness is more . . . absolute."

"What, exactly, does the lantern *do*? Why does she want it so badly?"

The magar said nothing. It was Helmi who answered. "She thinks it should have been hers by right. She was the magar's daughter. She was supposed to be the successor—and the magar was dead. She expected my mother to give it to her when she was still alive—my mother, I mean. But she wouldn't. She kept saying my sister wasn't ready yet.

"My sister was always powerful. Always. She saw the dead on her own. She didn't even need the circle; they came to her, spoke to her. She could find the lost far more quickly than any other student. More quickly than our mother. She knew she was powerful. Our mother acknowledged her power."

Emma waited.

Helmi turned to face the magar. "She wouldn't acknowledge her *as* magar."

"I was not wrong," the magar said. "Look at what she has done since then. I had the raising of her. I had the training." Her lips twisted. "The failure is mine. Had I given her what she desired, that failure would be complete."

"Why did you give the lantern to Emma?" Helmi asked. "You didn't raise her. You didn't train her. The only thing you could know about her is that she's powerful. What was the difference?"

"You are thinking that if Reyna were happy, she would not have become what she has become."

Helmi shrugged.

"I gave the lantern to Emma because of Eric."

Helmi's expression tightened. "He told you to do it?"

"No, of course not. But he could not kill her. Or rather, he did not want to kill her. What he saw in her—"

"He didn't want to kill my sister either. He thought he loved her."

"Yes."

"Then what's the difference?"

"If Eric could, now, go back in time—and he cannot—he would kill my Reyna. I think he would be content to die with her. He would not argue with his friends and his colleagues to preserve her life. But he did, for Emma. He was not in love with her. He could see her clearly. And I could see him clearly."

"She hasn't been trained!"

"If you had trained the Queen of the Dead, would you be eager to train someone who has as much power, and as much potential? I failed the people. I failed *my daughter.* I could not take the risk of failing again. The cost would be too high."

"She can't go out there without—"

"She has found two of the lost, without training. One could have easily killed her; it is by the slimmest of margins that he did not. She has opened the closed door. The only dead to escape since your death—and mine—she freed. I did not train her. No one did. She accomplished these things on her own."

"I didn't," Emma said quietly. "I couldn't have opened the door—at all—without the lantern."

The magar shook her head. "You could not have done *any* of it without the lantern. You could have seen the dead and spoken with them. You could do as you are now doing for my youngest daughter. The lantern has power, whether or not you choose to evoke it consciously, as you did to truly set that child free. You have used its power.

"You are using its power now. Bring it out. Illuminate the darkness."

"I don't think we're ready to face the Queen yet."

"She will not see its light here. Raise it, if you can."

"But—"

"It is here that its light is strongest."

Emma didn't ask the magar what the purpose of that light was in this place. She didn't ask how it was that the lantern's light would be felt anywhere but here. She didn't even ask why the magar had brought her here, although she would have, had she been allowed one question.

Her hands were not cold here. They were still clasped by Helmi on the one side and the magar on the other, but they weren't cold. She could feel the palms and fingers pressed against her own as if they were flesh.

"I have to let your hand go," she said, to Helmi.

"No," the magar said, "you do not."

"The lantern—"

"The lantern is not a physical object. It becomes physical at your discretion. You think of it as an object that must be lifted—and in the end, that is true. But it does not need to be lifted in your hands." She paused. "Neither do the dead. You offer your hand because it is what is natural to you, but it is not necessary.

"Helmi is not yours; she accepts what you offer but is wise enough to offer little of herself in return. That will have to stop."

Helmi frowned. Emma froze. "I don't want to use her. I don't want to use any of the dead."

"Oh? Did you not use the dead—as you put it—when you opened the door?"

"That—that was different."

"How?"

"For one, I had their permission. I had the permission of *every single* person there."

"Ah. Yes. Yes, you did. Do the bound dead not grant permission to their Queen?"

Did they? "I don't know."

"In a fashion, they do. It is the consent of the terrified, the consent of the terrorized, the consent of the lost. That is what she has created: a world in which *all* of the dead are lost." Her lined, weathered face compressed slightly. "The lantern, Emma Hall."

Nothing about the magar was comforting or encouraging. Emma, not used to being treated like an idiot, flinched and wished—not for the first time—that she were Amy.

"Helmi." The magar's use of the name was a command.

Helmi looked as rebellious as Emma felt. But she compromised; she transferred her grip on Emma's hand to Emma's elbow. In theory, this shouldn't have worked, because in theory, there was no contact between Helmi's skin and Emma's; the child was attached to sleeve. But she didn't disappear.

Emma lifted her hand.

She'd never really concentrated on summoning the lantern. When she wanted it, it appeared. She'd never stopped to think about how little sense this made; seeing the dead made little inconsistencies seem irrelevant.

The wire at the top of the lantern cut across her palm, tracing part of her lifeline as she lifted it. Its light was orange. Orange and blue. It was dense, much smaller than moonlight or the distant tickle of light at the corner of the eyes that implied pale stars. Her eyes acclimatized themselves to the brighter light as she looked around.

The magar remained by her side, as did Helmi.

They were not alone.

Emma wanted to ask the magar if she had made the lantern or if she had inherited it; the words did not come; she forgot them.

She wasn't standing in a field. She wasn't standing on a road or on a sidewalk. She wasn't standing anywhere; there was nothing beneath her feet. It was a solid nothing, like glass but without the texture. She didn't fall. Or rather, she hadn't fallen yet.

Neither had the people who lay arrayed around them. Some were curled on their sides, some flat on their backs, one or two rested on their stomachs, heads cradled in the crooks of folded arms. Some were entwined. They had no beds, but they didn't appear to need them; they slept. There was no rhyme or reason to their clothing, their ages, their appearances; there were both men and women, boys and girls.

Emma started to count, but gave up. There were too many.

"Why are they here?"

"They followed the lantern you now hold. I could not take them to freedom, as I might once have done while I lived. I could bring them to safety, of a kind. This is not a path that the circle can reach. Had it been—" She shook her head. "It was created by the lantern you bear."

Emma began to walk. There was room between the sleepers to place her feet, but she had to move with care. She didn't want to disturb them; they looked peaceful.

"There are no dreams or nightmares here," the old woman said, trailing behind Emma but above the forms of the sleepers. "They will wake only if you choose to wake them."

Emma continued to walk. The light that bobbed just ahead of her seemed, to her eyes, to brighten. "The lantern doesn't hurt them?"

"No, Emma Hall. It is one of the few things that brings them comfort when they wake. It is a sliver of the world to which the dead should belong. They can reach out for it, touch it, and find the promise of peace in its light."

Emma continued to walk; she wasn't even certain why. She trusted the magar's previous words—here, she had time. And maybe she should be using that time to learn what she could before she confronted the Queen. The internal voice that came to her courtesy of Amy Snitman was pretty much screaming that advice in her ear.

She wished that Amy had been the Necromancer. Amy would have been a better choice. Amy didn't dither. She was almost fearless, and the fear that did get past her natural self-confidence got stomped flat. She wouldn't be flailing here, terrified by her own uselessness. She wouldn't be wandering aimlessly through an almost endless field of sleeping people.

"What are you looking for?" Helmi demanded, and Emma smiled. She had thought Helmi very like a young Amy Snitman at one point.

Only people with a death wish lied to Amy. "I'm not sure."

"Maybe you should *be* sure."

"Helmi. Enough," the magar said, although her pinched expression implied strong agreement with her youngest daughter's sentiment.

"But she needs to know—"

"We don't know what she needs to know."

"We *do* know *some* of what she needs to know, and she's not going to learn it here!"

Emma, however, stopped walking. The lantern wobbled briefly, its light dimming as she knelt at the side of one of the sleepers.

"What are you looking at?" Helmi demanded. The magar said, or asked, nothing, but she released Emma's hand. She must have released it; Emma reached out with her left hand, and the magar didn't automatically come with it.

She recognized the child's face, although she had only seen it twisted in pain or fear. Just beyond the girl, another child slept; they were side-by-side, although the younger child had an arm flung across the chest of the older one. "How—how did you find these girls?"

The magar nodded. Emma couldn't see her and didn't look back, but she *felt* the nod. It should have been more disturbing than it was. "Scoros found them before the Queen did. He bound them, and he kept them."

Emma felt a sickening, visceral fury; not all of it was her own, but the part that wasn't was the weaker part.

"It is not what you think, child. Had he not killed them—had he not murdered them—perhaps it would have been. But he did. He set the fire. He watched them die. The death of their father hardly troubled his sleep. The death of the children broke something in him."

"He served for a long time after that."

"Yes. But he was aware that the children were blameless. He had been that child, as I think you must be aware. Vengeance against the man had some rough symmetry, some justice. Burning the children to death did not. And again, you know this. If you have found Scoros, you know.

"He found the children before the Queen did. I do not know if she would have searched them out deliberately—nor did he. But he wished to protect them in some small measure. He wished to atone. It was the start of his discontent, because he wanted absolution, and the only way he could have given it to himself was to open the door and usher the two children to what lay beyond it. And you are aware of how impossible that would be."

"If they were bound to him, how are they here?"

"He died. Before he died, he called me."

"But I thought—"

"I can hear my daughter calling me, even now," the magar said. "But I can choose my response. I could hear Scoros, and I chose to take the risk; it was a small risk. He did not and does not have my daughter's power. He has her experience. He called, and he asked me to protect the children. I almost refused."

"Why? They were blameless."

"He was not. I am not a forgiving woman. But he convinced me, in the end. He had kept the girls safe. He had bound them, but he had only seldom called upon their power; there were others he used in that fashion. He was not—he was *never*—a kind man. I think he was, in his youth, very like your Chase."

"Chase would never murder little girls."

"You are so certain that none of the Necromancers he found and killed were children?" The question was sharp, pointed.

Emma wasn't.

"He would have killed you if Eric had not intervened. He would have done it without regret or pain. He would have killed you had you been twelve or thirteen, boy or girl. And Emma, Eric would have killed them as well. What you know of them *is* true, but it is not the whole of the truth.

"Scoros released the children into my keeping, and I brought them here, and here they slept. And sleep. *What* are you doing?"

Emma cupped the older child's cheek in her hand. She heard the magar's question as if it came at a great remove. She whispered a name. *Anne.*

Movement returned to the girl's face; her eyelids fluttered, as if she were dreaming. They opened before Emma could withdraw her hand—although she hadn't even tried. She heard the magar's consternation and even understood it, because part of her wondered the same thing. The child was at peace. She was safe.

But her eyes did open, and they met Emma's. Emma thought the girl might scream or flinch, but she did neither. Instead, she sat up, stretched—very much as if she were alive. She then turned to the younger girl beside her and shook her gently.

She didn't wake. Emma reached out and touched the arm that was still draped across the older sister. *Rose.* The younger girl's eyes opened in a squint. Where Anne had turned to her sister, Rose turned toward the light.

Emma wanted to set the lantern down, to offer a hand to each child.

Anne, however, stood, and Rose joined her; their faces were turned toward the lantern's light, and the light was brilliant, now. Warm. "Are we leaving?" the younger girl asked.

Emma didn't answer. The magar did.

"Yes."

Rose seemed terrified of the magar—which was just sensible, all things considered. Anne forced her eyes away from the lantern to the face of the person holding it. "Are we going with you?"

"Only if you want to. I think—I think you've been safe here. It's quiet. It's peaceful. Where I'm going, it's not."

Anne nodded, and Emma felt her throat constrict. She'd told them the choice was theirs, and she meant it—but she realized that for these two, there was no choice. Offering one was just a sop to her own conscience; it wouldn't change the outcome at all for either girl.

"Yes," the magar said. "But conscience is necessary. They have been waiting. It is time. You must return to the Queen's circle, now. There is one thing you must do if you are to have any hope of using it."

"I don't need to use it."

"Yes, child, you do. And there is only one way to use it safely."


## ∽ Chapter 22

Emma returned to the Queen's resurrection chamber. She held two hands: Anne's and Rose's. The lantern was gone; the magar was gone. Helmi, however, remained. She wasn't attached at the elbow; Emma wasn't certain that she could still be seen by anyone else in the room.

The girls were silent; they seemed almost sleepy. Emma looked at them because she wanted a memory of their faces that was not pain and horrible, slow death. She'd never quite understood the idea of mercy killing before, although she'd heard all the arguments. She understood it now.

Had she had a gun, she would have shot them both to end a misery she couldn't otherwise prevent. But it wouldn't have mattered; they had died centuries ago. The deaths she had witnessed, she could do nothing to ease.

She stood on the edge of the Queen's engraved circle.

Michael approached her. Or rather, he approached the two girls. He stepped over the circle's boundary so he could face them, and he smiled. He had—he had always had—an open, unfettered smile, especially when dealing with children.

Anne stiffened. Rose, however, smiled back. It was a tentative expression that Emma caught in profile.

"I'm Michael," he said.

"I'm Rose. That's my sister. She's Anne. Your clothes are funny."

"They won't let me wear dresses," Michael replied.

Rose laughed at the idea of Michael in a dress. Anne hesitated, but her lips twitched in an involuntary smile. She didn't speak to Michael, though. She turned her head to look up at Emma.

"He's not like you." It wasn't a question, but there was a thread of doubt in the statement.

"He's not like me," Emma agreed. "There's nothing he can do to harm you."

Anne nodded. Her expression twisted briefly, but her face remained the same: a child's face. Emma's hand tightened around Anne's, a brief pressure, meant to comfort.

"Are you the new Queen?" the girl asked.

Emma inhaled slowly. "I really, really hope not."

"You look like her."

"Do I?"

Anne nodded.

"I don't think the dead need a Queen."

"But we have one, whether we want her or not." The last few words were lost to Rose's sudden laughter. "Why did you bring us here?"

Emma had no answer, and Anne seemed to expect one. "I don't know."

"You did bring us here?"

"Yes. I'm sorry. I—I saw you and your sister, and I woke you." She struggled with the rest of the truth but couldn't quite force it to leave her lips. She had wanted to see them, to touch them, to know that they were not trapped in fire for the rest of eternity. She had wanted to see them at peace, to quiet the memories she was certain would never leave her. She had recognized them instantly, had reached for them without thought.

It hadn't been for their sake.

*Why,* a familiar voice said, *did you bring them* here?

Ah, yes. Scoros.

Anne turned at the sound of his voice. Rose, absorbed in Michael's antics—he was on his knees in front of her making unfortunate noises—did not. The older girl didn't flinch or stiffen at the sound of his voice. She seemed—to Emma's eye—to relax. She didn't release Emma's hand.

For the first time since she had come back with whatever she could gather of Scoros, he seemed to emerge. He was not solid—Emma doubted he could achieve that—but he was clearly visible; he looked like a shadow, and as the seconds passed, the lines of that shadow hardened, as if the light casting it had grown sharper and brighter.

Emma felt his question as if she had asked it. She had no better answer than the one she'd offered Anne, but Scoros was not a child—and he wasn't the only one who demanded an answer.

"I need their help."

Anne glanced up at her. Rose did not. Michael was probably the most amusing thing she'd seen since she'd died. It hadn't occurred to Emma to do what Michael was now doing, and it wouldn't have; this was not the time for play.

Not for Emma.

She could feel Scoros staring at Michael and reminded herself forcefully that Scoros could do nothing to her friends. Nothing.

"You're dead," Anne surprised her by saying.

*Yes.*

"Did it hurt you too?"

*Yes. But not as much as I deserved. Emma Hall, what do you intend to do with the children?*

"Free them."

*How?*

Emma looked down at the circle's engraving. "Helmi?"

Helmi drifted toward her, passing through Rose; Rose didn't notice. Neither did Michael.

"It's these characters, right?"

Helmi nodded. "This is her name."

"What would my name be in this alphabet?"

Helmi snorted. There was no other word for the sound she made. "It doesn't matter. You don't have a name in our writing. But you do have a name in your own. If *you* wrote out the whole circle, you'd be using your own language. I think," she added, lowering her voice, "that the magar is wrong."

"Wrong?"

"I think the words my sister chose and the words that you would choose are different. She thinks you're both young girls—her words, not mine. She thinks young girls can be described in the same words because they lack experience." Helmi shrugged. "But I wasn't magar. These two are Reyna's name."

Emma nodded. "Anne, I'm going to have to let go of your hand."

"What about Rose?"

"I might need to let go of Rose, too." But not yet. Not quite yet.

"What are you going to do?"

"Erase the Queen's name."

Emma knelt. Scoros came to stand behind her, or possibly on top of her; she felt his shadow fall. It was cold. The other shadow that joined him was natural and belonged to Chase. Emma glanced up at him; he was watching Michael and shaking his head, his own lips tugging up at the corners.

"I wouldn't have believed he could exist if I hadn't seen him myself. Michael, you do realize the Queen of the Dead could be here at any second, right?"

Michael answered Chase without looking at him. "Yes. But I can't do anything about the Queen of the Dead. I don't have weapons, and even if I did, I wouldn't know how to use them. I can't do anything to help Emma, because Emma doesn't know how to do what she thinks has to be done. But I *can* talk to Rose."

"Fine. You talk to Rose. I'll help Emma. You ready?"

Emma nodded. "It'll be like the floor in the townhouse. I think."

The floor rumbled again. The dead didn't seem to notice it. The living did. Emma placed her free palm against the two runes, which steadied her until the floor was once again still.

"She's coming," Helmi said. Emma didn't ask who; she knew. She shook her head to clear it, although fear remained. She listened.

The voices she could hear were not, to her surprise, the distant and attenuated sobs she'd expected. They were clear, high voices that appeared to be lifted in . . . song. Two voices, one melody, one harmony. The song itself consisted of the same syllables, repeated over and over. A name.

"Anne, Rose, can you hear them?"

Rose ignored Emma in favor of Michael. Anne, however, whispered a yes. "Can you get them to change what they're singing?"

It would be the best option, in Emma's opinion. But before she could say so, the magar said, "No." Just that. Her single word was thunderous; it reverberated. Even Rose looked up.

"They would not hear you, Emma Hall. They would not hear your request." She glanced at Anne. "You hear singing?"

Anne nodded. "You don't?"

"No. I hear nothing. Margaret?"

Margaret's answer was wordless.

Emma surrendered the hope and concentrated instead on the voices. She could see the floor; she could see the engraved runes. When she closed her eyes, both were still clear. "I'm sorry, Rose," she said quietly. "I need my hand back."

Anne said something to her sister.

"Michael won't be able to see you for now. I'm sorry," she repeated. Rose was reluctant to surrender the hand—and why wouldn't she be?—but Anne made it clear that it was necessary. Older sister clearly trumped Necromancer in Rose's mind.

"Sorry, Michael."

She could hear the voices clearly. She couldn't see the singers. There were two; it would have made more sense to Emma if each name were held in place by a single ghost. That thought was followed, swiftly, by shame. These were *people*, not objects.

They were people, though, who couldn't hear her. She tried to break into their song, to introduce herself, to somehow catch the attention of people she couldn't see. She failed. There was no space between breaths, between notes. Her voice didn't interrupt them at all.

How had she pulled one girl out of the floor she'd been made part of?

She'd reached. No, it wasn't just that. The floor itself had become a sea of hands and arms when those trapped within had become aware of Emma. She needed to get the attention of these two singers. But this floor didn't change in composition. She could see nothing to touch, nothing to grab—no one who was reaching out for her. She could hear no sadness, no tears, no wails of despair: just the words themselves. The names.

All of existence, for these two, had been reduced to that. There was nothing at all that Emma could touch.

She placed her second palm beside the first; the stone was cold, but it felt like a natural cold, not the chill of the dead. And yet the dead were here, just beyond her reach. Her palms flattened as she spread them, pushing against stone as if to find purchase. Except for the indents engraved there, the floor offered none.

This wasn't working. Emma looked up and saw Michael and Chase. She thought she'd closed her eyes and couldn't remember opening them; she closed them again. She needed to see the dead if she was to have any hope of unmaking what the Queen had made here.

And if she succeeded, what then?

She shook her head to clear it. She couldn't afford to be afraid of success. She looked down at hands seen through closed eyes. She knew that the path she had walked when she sat in the circle attempting to locate Scoros was not a literal path; she knew that her body hadn't moved. But she had nevertheless walked through so many landscapes and so many memories.

The floor here was not a floor in any normal sense of the word except one:

It supported weight. It appeared to *be* stone. But if she had found Scoros—trapped in theory throughout the whole of the citadel, a complicated web that resembled nothing so much as echoes—it didn't matter. She was looking at it the wrong way.

She needed to look at it the right way.

Or she needed not to look at it at all. Nathan's body—the container into which he had been poured so that he might interact with the living—had not been difficult to unravel; she had done it while weeping. She had done it without thought. Intent? Yes, she'd had that. But she hadn't felt for arms or legs or the component parts of the bodies that were melted together. She had just . . . caught them, held them, let them go. They had dissolved.

She needed to be able to do the same, here. Her hands covered the majority of the carved runes, which was as close as she could come to achieving the same effect—but she could not penetrate it. She could *hear*.

She spoke. She raised her voice. Lowered it. She tried a different harmony; she tried to join her voice to theirs. Nothing.

And then, for one brief moment, she felt something smooth in a way that stone wasn't; smooth, cold—not ice, but . . . glass. Glass.

"Nathan," she whispered.

"I'm here. I won't leave you." He didn't say *I can't*, but they both knew it was true.

"When you look at the—the exit, you can see what's beyond?"

"Yes."

"But you can't reach it?"

"No. None of us can."

"I see—I saw—a door. I opened it. Until I did, I saw nothing of what waits. You saw it as a . . . window. A closed window."

"Yes. It's like there's a layer of unbreakable—"

"Glass."

"Yes."

Emma lifted her right hand and turned to Helmi. "You said your sister was coming?"

Helmi nodded. "You can't see her."

"No."

"She has to run the long way. She's not running yet. But she's moving. If you leave—"

"I can't." Emma turned then. To Michael, to Allison, to Amy. "But you can. I think you've got time."

Allison shook her head but said nothing.

"Michael, you have to go with them. You've got to take them back to the safe rooms."

"And you?"

"The Queen of the Dead is coming. I think she's coming to wherever it is she thinks I am. And she probably knows now. I'm not sure she knows about you yet—she probably will if I don't—" Emma exhaled.

"I'm going to do something that will grab all of her attention. I'm sure it'll hold all of her attention as well—and I think you guys can make it out of here. I'm worried about Petal," she added, which was actually true.

"If she finds you," Allison began.

It was Chase who cut her off. "Emma doesn't have what it takes to have you remain here. Before, when she didn't know what she was going to do—or how—she wanted advice. Support. She knows now."

"Care to share, Emma?" Amy asked. And it was a question, not the usual demand.

Emma shook her head. "I'm not sure it's a plan that stands up to scrutiny. You remember what I did after we got Andrew Copis out of the burned out building?"

Amy nodded.

"That, but—maybe bigger." She hesitated.

"And you want us gone because you don't want to have to worry about us."

"Pretty much," Chase said.

"Wasn't asking you," Amy replied. She pursed her lips, folded her arms, and met Emma's gaze head on. Emma had no idea what her face looked like; she had no idea whether desperation, fear, or exhaustion currently occupied her expression.

But whatever it was, Amy nodded. "You'd better make it out of here," she said—and that was the usual demand. "The rest of us probably won't survive if you don't."

"I think she knows that," Allison said. "Em—you're sure?"

"She's sure," Chase said. Allison wasn't Amy; she didn't demand the words come from Emma's mouth. She trusted Chase. She had never trusted his opinion of Emma before, but clearly, something had changed. She caught Michael by the arm.

Michael looked as if he would argue, but he didn't.

"It'll be over soon," Emma told him, trying—and failing—to be confident.

Michael nodded, and if the nod went on a bit too long, it didn't matter.

Emma hesitated. "Chase," she finally said. "Go with them."

It was Allison who said, "No."

And it was Margaret who said, "Ernest will go with the children." Amy didn't even bridle. To Emma's lasting surprise, Ernest nodded, grim-faced.

"You need me," Chase said. "I'm the only other person who can see what you can see."

"Yes, but you do it in a heap on the *floor*, Chase, and I'm not thinking that'll be useful. And if the Queen is on her way here, so is Eric."

"Unless she's imprisoned him. What does Helmi say?"

"Helmi says so is Eric," Helmi said. "She may well imprison him—or worse—when this is over, but she hasn't taken the time to do it yet. You guys need to *move*."

Emma repeated Helmi's last instruction. "I'll give you five minutes," she told them, staring at the floor.

The door opened and closed; the Emery crew were on the move, and they didn't take the time to move silently. Emma didn't watch them go; she turned to the wall that Michael had seen as a door. It hadn't changed. Neither had the floor. Chase moved briefly around the room, emptying his pockets as he did; he was silent, but it was the silence of intent. He armed himself only when he returned to Emma's side, and he watched the closed door.

Everything in this room was under glass. Metaphorical glass.

Emma turned to Chase. "Ready?"

He nodded. He didn't ask her what she was going to do. Neither did Nathan or any of the rest of the dead gathered here. Margaret, the magar, Anne, Rose, the remainder of Scoros. And his mother. They hadn't turned—as Chase had—toward the door; they were watching Emma.

Emma reached for the lantern. It came instantly to her hand.

Blue light radiated from its center. Not for the first time, she noted the words that were stacked in an even column. She had assumed they were Chinese letters because of the shape of the lantern. She'd been wrong.

"Helmi, do you recognize these words?"

Helmi failed to answer. The light grew brighter, and brighter still—but it wasn't harsh enough to cause Emma—or anyone present—to close their eyes.

"Helmi?"

". . . No." She was lying. She wasn't lying *well*, but only a small fraction of her attention was devoted to the attempt. The rest was drawn to, and held by, the lantern.

Emma said, "It's important."

It wasn't Helmi who answered. It was the magar. "She can't tell you, Emma Hall."

"Can you?"

"Yes. But it wouldn't help."

Emma frowned.

"It is the language of the dead. Anyone dead, from any culture, at any time, would recognize the words—even if they had not been taught to read or write or recognize writing. She could repeat them. I could. Margaret could. You would not hear them unless you yourself were dead."

"But I can—"

"You can visit, yes. You can occupy the memories of the dead who linger. You can act in the world they create. But you are not dead, and these words are not for the living."

"Even if they would help the dead?"

"Even so. I have made many mistakes in my life. Many. Making you the keeper of the lantern and its light might prove to be the biggest. But I will not do this. It would be murder." And the magar had enough on her conscience.

"What exactly are you trying to do?" Chase asked. Of course he did.

"You can't see it?"

"See what?"

She nodded, as if he'd answered, because he had. She guessed that the light growing steadily brighter as it dangled from her hands would be visible to Necromancers, but she didn't ask Margaret because it no longer mattered. Helmi had said the Queen was coming anyway.

And even that faded to insignificance as she studied the harsh, brilliant light. It cast no shadows. She turned toward Chase, the only other person who remained in the room who was also alive. The light revealed him in all his uncomfortable glory: shorn red hair, faded freckles, white scars, and yellowed bruises.

"Have I got something on my face?"

"Nose, mouth, eyes—the usual bits."

"Gallows humor is *my* job, thank you very much. Is it just me or is the floor vibrating?"

"It's been vibrating all along—"

"Not like this."

Emma frowned at him. "What do you mean?"

"If you were standing, barefoot, on the throat of a man, and he was speaking, this is what it would feel like."

To Emma it was a rumble like thunder, or the earthquakes of imagination, given she'd never experienced one in person. She didn't argue with Chase, though. If she couldn't feel the vibrations the way Chase did, she accepted that they were becoming constant.

"What are you trying to do?"

"Truthfully?"

"Let me get back to you."

She laughed, as he'd no doubt intended. It was a thin sound, but it was genuine. And it was miles better than whimpering or crying.

"But seriously, if you mean to dissolve the chamber, give me a bit of warning?"

"I'll try." She looked at the circle engraved in the stone of solid floor. To her eyes, the runes were now glowing, as if light had, like liquid, been upended into their grooves. "Oh."

"Oh?"

"I think I understand what you were saying, now."

"Is that good or bad?"

"Good," she said, although she wasn't certain. She could hear the words without apparent effort or concentration on her part. She could hear raised voices. It was hard to focus on one or two, because the entire chamber was beginning to fill with syllables.

What words could stone speak? What words could be uttered without throat or mouth?

These ones, she thought. She had touched a floor in this floating city, and she had *listened*. It had been a struggle to hear anything, and it had required the whole of her concentration. Now, she thought, the struggle would be the reverse.

In Toronto, the dead had come *to* her while she held the lamp aloft, drawn by its light. She had asked for permission to use the power they didn't even understand they had. She had asked their names. She had promised them that she would open the door. They had given everything that she'd asked them for. Maybe they'd given more.

The dead here were not free to move. They didn't roam city streets, trapped in memories of lives that steadily receded as people aged and died and the future became the present. They were trapped, instead, in one woman's dream.

Reyna had dreamed of safety. Of a place in which she would finally be free to love Eric. In which Eric would be free to love her. Emma knew this. She'd *heard* it, time and again, in Scoros' memories.

And she was aware that the dream of a girl in love had become a nightmare for countless others—some living, most dead. She didn't even wonder at it.

She had loved Nathan. Nathan had died. The dreams she had hoarded and guarded so carefully had been irrevocably shattered. She had tried to hold their shards when Nathan—dead—returned to her. She had been *so happy* to see him. So happy to finally be able to tell him all the things she'd wished she'd said before her words could never reach him again.

She could keep him here.

She knew she could do what the Queen had done. She could house his spirit in something that could pass for flesh. She could hold him, be held by him, be comforted by him. At heart, her *dream* had been the same as the Queen's. She had wanted forever, although she'd mostly kept that desire to herself because it was sentimental and sort of embarrassing.

She had wanted a love that never died and never changed.

As if he could hear the words, Nathan came to stand by her side. Guilt sat poorly on his face, but it occupied it nonetheless.

But she shook her head and smiled. She'd done her crying. She'd said her good-byes. If she could talk herself into being what the Queen was, she knew that Nathan would never forgive her. He loved her, yes. She saw that clearly; his eyes were almost shining with it. But he would stop loving her if she became like the Queen of the Dead.

Because he saw her clearly. He'd always seen her clearly. He'd seen her fears and her insecurities and her desire and her fear of that desire. He'd seen her anger, been exposed to her temper, and endured it all by her side, smiling or grave or angry himself. To do what had been done here she would have to be everything she wasn't, *except* wildly in love.

What he loved about her would die, just as surely as he had.

She would have taken his hand, but she couldn't. Even that, he understood.

The voices rose to a crescendo of sound, and Emma raised her voice above them, shouting to be heard. She couldn't hear her own voice over the din, but it must have been piercing, as all-encompassing to the masses of the dead as their combined voices felt to her. She reached out, one hand free, and touched the stone of floor, into which words had been carved *of* the dead.

Something shattered.

And just like that, the voices stopped, and there was an echoing silence.

## ⌒ Chapter 23

In the silence, two words rose from the stone, leaving no grooves or marks in their wake. They left a gap in the circle's circumference as they came to hover in front of Emma. No, she thought, in front of the lantern. They fluttered there, like moths in a form too cumbersome for actual wings; she could almost feel them battering ineffectually against the lantern's body.

They spoke.

Emma listened.

The Queen's name reverberated in the air for a long, long minute, and then it died into silence and stillness. She reached out with a hand instead of the lantern, and the letter forms came to rest on her upturned palm. She didn't speak. She didn't have to. The forms of lines and curves melted around that palm, changing as light spread toward the floor, until she held the hands of two young women; they overlapped in her outstretched palm.

They were her age, maybe slightly younger—or slightly older. She was not surprised to find that they were beautiful, or at least that they had been beautiful in life, with wide, round eyes, long hair, regular, perfect features.

She was also not surprised to see tears.

"Isabella," one girl said, although Emma hadn't asked for her name. The other girl didn't speak. Or perhaps she did and Emma couldn't hear her; her hand rested over Isabella's.

"I'm Emma," Emma told them both.

They nodded. She meant to ask them if they could return to the circle, if they could speak—or sing—her name instead of the Queen's. She didn't; she knew, although she wasn't certain how, that they couldn't. But there was no name on this circle. Not yet. Not until she could remake what had been unmade.

"This," the magar said, "is why you found the two."

But Emma shook her head again, mute now. She turned to the girls, Anne and Rose, both silent. Their attention was focused on the Lantern, not Emma, and something in their expressions made her want to weep. Scoros had kept them safe. He had murdered them. He had been responsible for their horrible, agonizing deaths.

And then he had found what remained.

Even if they were willing to do what the two freed girls had done, she wasn't certain how to take advantage of that. She wasn't certain how to force them to be what the girls had been: words. Names that weren't their own.

"I'm sorry," she told the magar—and she meant it. "I can't draw a circle of my own. Not yet. Not in time. But this one can't be used safely by Reyna, either."

She lifted the lantern, her arm aching, her heart louder now than her own voice.

And Nathan said, "Let me."

She turned to him. "I can't—" and fell silent.

"Let me, Em. They were her name, right?"

It was the magar who nodded, because Emma was suddenly paralyzed.

"Just her name?"

"It is more complicated than that, but yes. Her name."

"And the others? The other words?"

Even as he asked, symbols began to rise, just as the two girls had done. His fists tightened as these words also drifted toward the lantern, pulled, called by

Emma Hall. Isabella and the silent, nameless girl withdrew their hands, turning to watch the same transformation they had undergone: words becoming people.

All of these were also Emma's age—the age she imagined Reyna had been when Eric had died. They were also beautiful. She wondered if Reyna had made that choice consciously or unconsciously; she wondered, as well, if the girls had all been dead when she had chosen them, or if she had simply ended their lives to preserve their deathly appearance.

It didn't matter.

"What are you doing?" someone asked, sharp-voiced and outraged. Scoros' mother.

"I'm not doing anything," Emma replied. "They are." She watched as the words that described who Reyna thought she was lifted themselves from the stone circle and vanished, one by one.

Only the elemental words remained. They were simple engraving. They did not appear to be written in the ghostly bodies of trapped, dead girls.

"They do not change," the magar told her. "They would never change. But the other words might, with time and experience. The words that might alter, in time, are the words that are rendered in the dead."

"It's not much of a circle, now."

"No, Emma Hall. And that was foolish of you. You have power, but you lack knowledge; this would have been one of your most effective shields." But she looked unruffled. Scoros' mother made up for it. She looked apoplectic.

And Emma didn't care. Because Nathan's sentence had finally cleared the fog of her thoughts and fears. *Let me, Em.*

She was horrified. The words became the loudest thing in the room. And he knew. Of course he knew. He'd known her better than anyone except maybe Allison.

"Those words—they're a description of who you are, right? And the first two—your name?" Nathan continued to speak.

She couldn't even answer. She had taken Nathan's chain—if that was even the right word, but she hadn't taken it to *use him*. To consume him. She hadn't—

"Em—give me the choice, okay? Don't make it for me. You know I always had problems with that."

She shook her head.

"You could talk yourself into the worst places. You could believe that a moment's anger described the whole of you forever and ever, that a random bad thought somehow made you a bad person. You could decide that you weren't good enough for me on the bad days. You might not remember them. I do.

"I remember all the days, Emma. I wouldn't let you decide that you weren't good enough for me on the hard days. Remember? Because that was my choice to make, not yours."

She shook her head again. Words failed her utterly, but she *did* remember. She remembered the insecurity and the excitement of the early, early days. The fear, and the jealousies that she tried so hard to banish. She'd forgotten them; it was easy to forget because the loss had been so profound.

"Don't choose for me. I'd give my life for you if I still had it. This is as close as I come in the afterlife. Let *me* do this. I know you. I know who you are. And I know your name."

"I don't know *how*," she whispered. "I don't know how to turn you into—" something that looked nothing like Nathan.

He nodded and turned to the magar. The magar's pursed lips failed to move. But Emma heard her voice anyway. *You are not old enough, boy. You have not yet learned that form is habit and limitation.* She turned to look at her daughter.

Helmi snorted. She reached out with both hands for Nathan. Her hands should have passed through him. They didn't. Emma didn't understand why—but she realized that Helmi's hands were the same color as the light shed by the lantern.

"I know what to do," she told Nathan. "If you're stupid enough to do this on purpose."

His smile was crooked. "I don't want her to die." He stared at Helmi's hands. "Why can you touch me?"

"The lantern," Helmi replied. "And no, before you ask, it only works on the dead. You still can't touch her without freezing her. Are you going to ask stupid questions for the rest of her life? 'Cause if you are, that's going to be measured in minutes."

Nathan fell silent.

"You can stop him," the magar told Emma, watching her youngest daughter holding onto the only person Emma thought she would ever love.

She almost did. She had to struggle with her visceral reaction to do what he had asked: to give him the choice. To respect it. He wasn't Anne or Rose. He wasn't a child. He understood what would happen.

And he understood Emma. The magar had said the words that Reyna had chosen to describe herself were words that were also relevant to Emma. She had said it dismissively, as if those words weren't actually important.

They were important to Nathan. He walked to the periphery of the circle, knelt, and placed one hand on the rock beneath his ghostly feet. The rock began to absorb him. Helmi said, and did, nothing that Emma could see, but the light that was Nathan faded.

The dead didn't need to breathe; the living did. She forgot how.

Helmi turned to Emma and to her mother and shrugged. And then, to Emma's shock, Helmi also began to fade.

The magar said nothing. She simply watched. Emma glanced briefly at the closed door and then did the same.

Words began to emerge, recreating the circumference of the depleted circle. But they weren't like the words that had lifted themselves into the air in the lantern's light. They were English words. Words she recognized.

"It is not the form," the magar said, although Emma hadn't spoken. She couldn't. "It is never the form."

The first word was Love. The word that followed was Hope. The third word was Fear, and the fourth, Courage. The fifth—Loyalty—made her eyes tear. The sixth was not a word she would have chosen for herself—but she would have chosen none of them so far, except perhaps fear.

Responsible.

She smiled.

Kind.

The word that followed kind was Ignorant, which made her laugh out loud. That wasn't a Nathan word—clearly Helmi had opinions. And even if the word was unkind, it was true. Emma did not know what she was doing. She only knew the *why*.

The last word was Strength. She shook her head, denying it. She wasn't certain if Nathan was saying she was strong in his eyes, or if he was urging her to be stronger—but it didn't matter. This circle was like a love letter. Nathan hadn't been a big letter writer, but then again, neither had Emma. So, this was the first love letter.

She stepped over the circumference that was almost complete, and she folded her legs, sitting in the circle; she looked up at Chase and found that he was wavering in her vision in a dangerous way. But she didn't care.

He said nothing. He offered no sympathy, no advice. He shook his head. "Circle's not for me," he told her, drawing daggers.

The last two words to emerge were the words that completed the circle in which Emma sat. Her name. Emma Hall. She set the lantern in her lap and met the magar's steady gaze.

"Helmi," the old woman said, although no sign of her daughter remained. "I am proud of you. If you had lived, you would have become a better guardian, a better guide, than Reyna." Her lips twisted. "And perhaps better than your mother, as well."

The words were now grooves in flat stone. They had no ears, no faces, no way of receiving information, and no way of broadcasting it.

But a final word pushed itself into the circle, squeezed and cramped because it was not the shortest of English words. It was also misspelled.

GRATITUD.

Emma liked it. Death had made it hard to feel gratitude. Hard to feel grateful for what she had, the loss was so enormous, the pain of it permeating everything. But she still had her mother—who was not the magar. She had Allison. She had Michael and Amy and Petal. She had a school life she had once enjoyed and might enjoy again, given effort and time. She had a roof over her head, and food on the table, and a mother who made certain that both of those things kept happening.

She had so much more than Reyna had had on the day of Eric's death. None of it excused Reyna's choices or actions since that day, but maybe it explained some of it. Maybe. Broken people did broken things; it was an act of will to change the course that violence and death laid over a life. She'd seen it in Scoros, in his memories of Reyna, in Chase. Emma had been hurt. She hadn't been broken.

She looked toward the wall that Michael had seen as a door. She closed her eyes, although that changed very, very little in the room. But as she lifted her chin she saw, at last, what Michael meant. She remained in the circle, but she left it as well, just as she had done when she had gone in search of Scoros the first time.

She now went in search of him for the last time.


## ᔐ Chapter 24

None of the dead tried to stop her. None of them moved. As she left the circle, she turned back to look at herself; she was seated, cross-legged, in the circle, the lantern in her crooked lap.

As Michael had said, there was a door where smooth, curved wall had been. As doors went, it looked like something that belonged to a closet; it was neither large nor particularly impressive. Emma walked toward it.

"You will not be able to open that door," a familiar voice said. The magar.

Emma grimaced. "You can see the door now?"

"No. You can see it now. But you are not particularly opaque."

Emma reached the door and placed a hand against it. Her hand passed through its surface.

"Maybe I don't need to open it." But she frowned. What she had assumed were scratches and wear were, on closer inspection, badly carved words. She couldn't read them, but she recognized the etching for what it was.

"Those words," she said, to the magar. "The ones on the lantern. You said the living couldn't hear them."

The magar was silent. Emma took this as agreement.

"But we can see them."

More silence.

"Your daughter could see them. I think these words are meant to be the words on the lantern's sheath."

"They won't have the same power. They won't have the same meaning."

"This door can't be seen by the living. It can't be seen by the dead." Speaking, Emma lifted the lantern. She wasn't surprised when it came to her hand; it wasn't a physical artifact. "Reyna saw the lantern."

"When I held it, yes. She did not have it to study. If you are correct—and I allow the possibility—she wrote from memory. She had a very good memory for the things that hurt her."

"The lantern?"

"She wanted it. I refused to give it to her."

Ah. "The lantern *is* physical. You pushed it into my hands the first night we met." Frowning, she held it up to the door, to the less polished, less perfect words scratched into the surface, as if with a pen. "Magar—how was the lantern made?"

"We do not know."

Frowning, Emma turned to look over her shoulder. She saw Chase Loern, moving outside the periphery of her circle. She saw the dead; they had turned toward her—but of course they had. She held the light aloft.

Emma pressed the lantern into the door's surface. Light stretched and spread across wood that was far too irregular, far too blemished, to be anything but real. With her free hand, she touched the door again, and this time, her hand met resistance. It was not like the doors she'd opened—or tried to open, or beat her fists against—in Scoros' memory. It was solid, but it wasn't; it didn't feel like an actual door.

The handle—and it had one—didn't feel like a handle, either. Michael had been able to touch the door. He hadn't been able to open it. The only person in the room with a professed ability to pick locks hadn't been able to see it.

Emma gripped the handle. It was warm, which she hadn't expected. She opened the door as the light across its surface faded. In the distance, she heard Chase curse.

The room behind the door was the size of a closet. It contained almost nothing that Emma could see. It was dark; there was a small table, a single stool. Emma wasn't certain what she had expected to find. Memories, maybe. That was how she had gathered the rest of Scoros.

Walking into his memories had been involuntary. She'd done nothing except walk out of the circle—a circle that guaranteed no safety from the dead. She faced this room in a circle that now did. Maybe that's why there was nothing here but silence and stillness in a cramped, tiny space.

She couldn't imagine the Queen ever sitting in that chair; she couldn't imagine the Queen sitting at this table.

"Scoros," she called. The lantern in her hand rose as she spoke his name.

She felt his presence as he walked through her. He was still mostly shade and shadow to her eye, although he had the outline and general features of an older man. He approached the table; she thought his head was bowed.

He took the single chair. As he sat, he placed his forearms on the tabletop, entwining his hands. For one long moment, he seemed to study the tabletop. The table itself, like the door, looked old, almost unfinished; it lacked the grandeur of every other piece of furniture in these chambers.

It was real.

"Scoros."

He lifted his head slowly. He looked old, to Emma—much older than he had looked in any other memory. He was bearded, but the beard was patchy; his brows were a crust of iron gray above the bridge of his prominent nose. His eyes were brown—but a brown that was dark enough she couldn't distinguish it from pupil. He wore robes that seemed threadbare. She might have mistaken him for a monk of the kind that wandered across historical flashbacks on television.

"Scoros," she said again.

His eyes focused slowly. "Reyna."

"No," she replied, her voice gentling without effort. "I'm Emma." She held out her right hand.

Her named confused him, which Emma hadn't expected. She glanced over her shoulder; the door was still open.

"The candle," he said quietly. "The candle is not lit." He looked at the center of the empty tabletop. So did Emma. What he saw, she didn't see; there was no candle here. Scoros' memory didn't cause a candle to materialize, either. This room was real. The candle that he expected was probably real as well, and she didn't have one.

"What is the candle meant to do?" she asked him.

His eyes flickered again, brushing across her face as if he couldn't actually see it.

"Burn," he replied.

She approached him, moving slowly as if afraid to startle him. His gaze brushed past her as she did, coming to rest at the table's center.

"Magar, what was the purpose of a candle?"

"We did not use candles," the old woman replied. "We did not hide rooms, or mark them in the fashion this one was marked. We did not bind and imprison the dead—they did that to themselves. It was our duty to release them from bindings, not to add to them."

Scoros frowned.

Emma walked around the chair, searching for the thin, golden line that meant he was bound to a Necromancer. There was no such line.

As Emma searched with growing concern, another woman entered the room—Scoros' mother. She looked very much as if she wanted to either slap her son or push him off his chair. Anger came easily to her expression, nestling into lines carved there by use and time.

She couldn't slap her son, though. It was the first thing she tried; her hand passed through his face. He frowned, blinked. She bent and shouted in his ear, which was even less successful.

"I don't think he can hear you," Emma told the woman.

"No." She looked at Emma, and beneath the anger, there was a hint of fear. "He hears Reyna. He only ever heard Reyna."

Emma understood why Scoros' mother thought it; she even understood the bitterness in the statement. But she knew it wasn't completely true. He *obeyed* Reyna. In a fashion, he loved her. He supported her. He had tried to make her feel safe—and that had been an utter failure.

Emma turned toward the part of the Queen's chambers she could see through the open, narrow door. She spoke two names, and two young girls walked toward her. Anne and Rose.

The mother glanced at them, frowning. She didn't recognize the girls. Scoros, however, did. They were the first thing to truly grab and hold his attention; he could see Emma, but not clearly enough to acknowledge her.

His eyes widened as the girls approached him. It was the first fear he'd shown since she'd opened this door.

"Do you hate him?" Emma asked Anne.

Anne glanced at her. "Do you?"

She almost said she didn't know him well enough to hate him, but that was untrue. She knew Scoros better than she knew most of the people she'd ever met or interacted with. "No. But he didn't kill me. He didn't kill my sister."

"No?" she asked, and Emma almost said, 'I don't have a sister'. But she realized that it was the hatred the girl was questioning.

"No. To find him the first time, I had to live through a lot of his life. *As* him. I'm not sure you can truly hate someone you've been."

"He tried to protect us."

*After he'd murdered you both.* Emma nodded.

Anne took his left hand. Rose took his right. What Scoros' mother couldn't accomplish, the children could. "The lantern," Anne said. She smiled, her expression at odds with her age. Or maybe not; it was gentle and even protective. "That's what the other girl said."

Emma blinked.

"You gave the girls—and Helmi—your hands. You did not release them."

"I did."

"No, Emma, you didn't. You didn't bind them; they were free to leave you. Come. My daughter will be here in minutes."

Scoros rose. He left the chair. The two girls—one on either hand—dragged him to his feet, looking for all the world like young daughters ganging up on a favorite uncle. His expression shifted as he left the chair, his eyes sharpening, their color lightening. He looked around the room—the closet—blinking rapidly. And then he looked at the lantern, and he froze.

"Magar," he whispered.

Emma turned to her right, but the magar wasn't there. A voice from her left said, gently, "He is speaking to you, girl."

Emma shook her head. "I'm not your magar. I'm Emma. We've met before."

Anne reached Emma first. She held out her free hand, and Emma took it. Then Anne passed Scoros' hand into hers. Her eyes were shining. They were the eyes of the dead, but they were brimming with light, and the light looked, for a moment, like tears.

Emma realized then what was wrong with Scoros: His eyes were brown. Or black. Or some color in between. They were not the eyes of the dead. This Scoros was like a memory.

*Yes.*

"Scoros," Emma said—to the brown-eyed man. "I need your help." She held the hand; it felt weathered, old—but not cold. She wondered, then, whether this was a side-effect of the lantern.

"To do what?" the older man asked, eyes narrowing as he glanced past Emma to the doorway.

"To save the citadel," Emma replied.

"If the citadel's safety is your concern, magar, leave me."

She swallowed. "It's not. I don't care what happens to the citadel." That was also a lie. She tried again. "I do care what happens to the citadel. I want to unmake it. I want to free the dead. But I can't do that until the living are safe. If I try to destroy what the Queen has built now, we're all going to die."

He frowned.

"The citadel is flying."

"Impossible."

"No. Maybe it was impossible when you were actually alive."

Again he frowned, glancing at Anne and Rose, at the open door, and at the table. "I am not dead."

Emma grimaced. She had no time to argue with him, and she had no choice. But she didn't, couldn't, understand how he could be here, trapped in this semblance of life, and be *there*, everywhere, trapped as the dead were trapped.

"Magar."

Emma exhaled. "If that's what the lantern means, then yes. I need your help. I need it now. Will you give it to me?"

"Will you free the dead? Will you shepherd them to their final destination?"

"Yes," she told him. "Yes, even you."

"Will you save my child?"

*What?*

He tried to reach out across the table, but his hands were occupied. "Will you save my child?"

Emma stared at him. She met his gaze and held it. His eyes were brown. The lines of his face had shifted in place, deepening across the brow. He seemed old, tired, frail. And he seemed alive. But the girls could see him; they could touch him. She didn't understand.

And now was not the time for confusion.

*No, magar, it is not.*

"You're dead," she whispered, to the disembodied voice.

She felt his bitter, bitter smile—a smile that didn't touch the face of the man seated in front of her. *Yes. Yes and no. Death is complicated in this place.*

"So is life."

*No, Emma—life is not.* But she felt his attention shift to the man seated in the chair, as if he were an entirely different person. *Life is simply a struggle not to become one of the dead.* He stood by the seated Scoros, as if he were a shadow—his shadow.

"Anne?"

The girl nodded.

"Why can you touch him? Why—"

She looked confused. "I can touch you," she finally said.

"Yes, but I'm—" She stopped, shook her head, and turned toward the open door. "I think," she told Scoros, "it's time for you to leave this room."

"Why?"

"Because Reyna is coming."

He looked confused—far more confused than Anne had. "Of course she is." He glanced at the two girls and said, gently, "You must let go of my hands. She will see you."

Emma stood at the threshold of this tiny prison. The very vague plan she'd made—and calling it a plan was a gross overstatement—was gone. She had intended to open Michael's invisible door, to find what remained of Scoros—and to take over the bindings that held him here.

The memories, the gathered bits of Scoros, had said or implied that Scoros was woven throughout the citadel, that it was his essence and his power that somehow kept it together, kept it afloat. He had implied, again, that if she found the element of himself that was hidden and bound, Emma would gain control of enough of the citadel that her friends wouldn't plunge instantly to their deaths.

He hadn't, however, told her that he was *alive*.

She had no idea how to bind someone who was still living. She had no idea how she had found *any* of Scoros if he wasn't dead.

"Leave him," the magar said quietly.

"I can't—"

"You have two options. Kill him or leave him. He is of no use to you if he is alive."

"He's of no use to me if he's dead, either." She exhaled. "But he's not—he can't be—bound to the Queen."

But the old woman shook her head. "He is bound," she said, grimly. As Emma opened her mouth, the old woman continued. "I thought he was dead. No wonder I could never find him. Do you understand what was done?"

Emma shook her head. She approached the old man, and held out her free hand. "I don't know if I can save your daughter," she told him. "I hope to save everyone else."

He stared at her hand.

"I'm sorry, Scoros, but you must leave this room."

"It is my room," he said, with a soft smile. "It is hidden, defended; it is here that Reyna can flee if there is danger. It is here she comes when she requires comfort or guidance. I cannot leave."

"Are you bound to this room?" she asked him. "Do you come to life *only* when this door is opened?"

*Yes*, the shadow Scoros, the gathered Scoros, replied. *When the door is open and only then. It is a prison.*

But Emma shook her head. She thought she understood some part of what had been done. Parts of Scoros were dead, but he himself was—barely—alive.

"Which one of you," she asked, her voice clearer and harder, "attempted to kill the Queen of the Dead?"

*Do not do this.*

She couldn't meet the eyes of the parts of Scoros that were dead. The parts, Emma thought, that must be killed, bound, and hidden if the man seated in front of her was to love and comfort the Queen.

"You did this to yourself."

*No. But we were not enemies, then. I had given her all of my life that mattered, and it was not enough. I was not the first to attempt to kill her. I will not be the last. Perhaps you will be—because the attempts will not end while she lives. Perhaps they will become infrequent. Perhaps they will all be ineffective. When I suggested what was done to me, I wished to protect her.*

*I know what was done to the dead to build this place. This was my penance: to suffer what the dead suffer—and for just as long as they suffer it.*

*But I chose. I chose what to surrender. I chose what to bury. And I watched. I watch her now,* he added. *She is almost here. She has not stopped to gather her knights. Tell him—tell me—that Eric is with her.*

She realized that Scoros couldn't hear his own voice. He could see the dead. He could see the lantern. But he was of the people.

"If the Queen kills you, what happens?"

Silence.

"Scoros, I'm sorry, but you must leave this room. It doesn't matter now that the room is defended and protected against attack. Attack comes." She lifted the lantern, understanding what it meant to him. Understanding what it made her, in his eyes.

He rose. "Magar," he said, and this time he bowed to her. "We have waited. We have waited a long, long time."

She left the closet-sized room, and Scoros followed, trailed by a shadow that didn't conform to the fall of light. The room was no longer empty. Men and women of all ages, shapes, races, had gathered there; they were silent. The voices of the dead—those without form, without mobility—were not.

They fell silent only when the doors at the other end of the chamber rolled—slammed—open.


# Reyna

The Queen's knights do not reappear. She is too angry to call them. The mobile dead have vanished. Nothing stands between Reyna and the citadel except Eric.

"You will wait here," she tells him. Her voice is the Queen's voice, not the girl's, and there is death in it. Of course there is. Who disobeys the Queen? She storms through the empty, silent streets; the only thing she can hear is her breathing and the rustle of her train.

Eric does not obey. Were he anyone else, he would be dead, now. He almost dies anyway, so potent is her rage. Everything in her is angry. Everything rages, although she does not speak.

She thinks she has never been so angry. She thinks she will never be so angry again.

She is wrong.

She reaches the great doors of the citadel; they are open. They were opened for the procession, and they will not be closed until the ceremony is finished—if it is *ever* finished. She enters. The halls are as empty as the streets. Beneath the high, vaulted ceilings, her footsteps echo. Her hands have curved into shaking fists; she cannot loosen them.

She is certain that Emma is here. It is a sick certainty, an angry one. She meant, once, to bring Emma here as a novice. Later, she intended to bring her here for other reasons. She kept Nathan, resurrected him, with that in mind. She wanted to have something to offer Emma.

Why?

She almost can't remember.

But Nathan is *Reyna's* to offer. He is meant to be a gift, a magnanimous act. She will not allow him to be *stolen*.

She walks toward her chambers; her anger cools. Emma is an untrained girl. She is less, much less, than Reyna was at the same age. She has been taught nothing. She has no skill. How has she taken Nathan? How has she broken that binding?

She slows. *Longland.* She will speak with Longland. She takes a deep breath. Another. She needs to think. Turning, she sees Eric. He is watching her. He does not smile.

She is not smiling either. The day is ruined. The event, destroyed. But Eric is here, and there will be another day. A better day. Maybe she was foolish to begin immediately. Maybe she was too impulsive. Things hurried are seldom perfect.

But she remembers hurrying to the tree by the stream in the early, early hours of the morning. She remembers Eric, standing beneath its boughs, watching her approach. She remembers the urgency, the joy—both hers and his. She knows there is no joy in him today.

But is there joy in her?

She opens her mouth, closes it, waits for the right words to form. She isn't certain what to say. She doesn't want to appear weak. Even if Eric is here, she remains the Queen of the Dead, and weakness is not allowed.

She is never certain, later, what she would have said. She knows her mouth is open, and his, closed. She knows that he is standing a yard away. She can close that distance or preserve it; he has given the choice to her.

It is not what she wants—the choice, the responsibility of choice. What she wants is his joy and his desire and his love. Her love has never died; she knows that love can last forever. She means to say this—even if this is the wrong time, the wrong place.

But a sudden, brilliant light cuts across her vision, blinding her; it permeates the walls, the floors, rises to the heights of the vaulted ceiling—and beyond. Reyna knows that light. There is only one thing that can cast it.

She turns toward the lantern. She can see its shape; there are walls between the light and her eyes, but they are made of the dead, and even if they weren't, the light would still be visible; it is close.

It is too close.

She sees the shape of Eric's eyes change; she knows he sees what she sees. She feels the rumble of the floor beneath her feet; imagines she can see the tremor in the walls and the ceiling they support. The whole of her world seems to strain toward the lantern's light.

And of course it does.

*Emma.*

"Tell me," Reyna says. "Tell me about Emma." She walks. Eric shadows her. "What is she like? Is she beautiful?"

Eric doesn't answer immediately.

"Does she look like I look?"

"No. She looks almost nothing like you."

"Is she powerful?"

"How could she be?"

"She has the lantern." Her voice cracks on the last word. Cracks and lifts. "Tell me, Eric. What is she like?" She walks, dragging him in her wake. She cannot see where the lantern is, but she knows it is close.

"How did she find my mother? How did she convince my mother to give her the lantern?"

Eric says, after a long pause, "Emma is kind."

It is not what Reyna wants to hear. It is not, in truth, what she *expected* to hear. She laughs; it is a bitter, incredulous sound. "The magar gave the lantern to a child because *she's kind*?" She is shaking, almost in time with the floor and the walls, as if they echo her fury—and the longing and the rage and the disappointment—always, always, the disappointment.

"What does that *even mean*? My mother was never *kind*!" It is true. The magar was bitter and harsh. She despised weakness. She despised her oldest daughter. Every bit of approval she gave was grudging and qualified—and there was little enough of it. So little.

Reyna did everything her mother asked. Learned everything her mother wanted her to learn. Lived with the dead, because that was what her mother wanted. She learned *everything*. She learned *quickly*. She was more powerful than any of her cousins. She was more powerful than her mother. She did what she was told to do, time and again, even when it meant that she would lose the day with Eric.

She has never understood what the magar wanted from her. Even Scoros couldn't explain it. She has never understood why she was not, why she was *never*, good enough. Her mother doesn't know Emma. Her mother didn't raise her. Her mother didn't live with her.

But her mother gave the lantern to *Emma*. Emma is her mother's choice of magar.

Reyna coughs around words and gives up on them.

She will kill Emma Hall. She will take the lantern. She doesn't need her mother's permission or approval. And then, when she has it, she will find her mother, and her mother will answer every question Reyna has.

She lifts her skirts, hating the train, hating the confinement, hating everything. She doesn't know where Emma is—but she knows Emma is in the citadel.

It is Scoros who tells her, indirectly.

*What is kindness? What does it mean?*

She will banish him, too. She will kill him. She doesn't need Scoros anymore. Maybe she never did.

*It means vision, little one. Emma Hall sees what is laid before her. She sees— or tries to see—clearly. She does not judge.*

"And I *do*?" Reyna shouts.

Scoros doesn't answer. It doesn't matter. Reyna knows where Emma is. She knows where Emma must be. A bitter, bitter anger fills her, spills over; the floor beneath her feet almost unravels with the potency of her rage.

Eric tries to take her arm, and she pushes him away—without touching him at all. It is Scoros she wants to kill. Emma. But if she is not very careful, Eric will also be caught in the cauldron of her rage, her loss, her endless, endless sorrow.

For just a moment, she wants that. She wants to immolate everything. She wants to give up on love, because love has always, always betrayed her. She is tired of pain. She is tired of trying. She is tired of everything.

And angry.

## ⌒ Chapter 25

The Queen of the Dead stood beneath the arched frame of the open door.

She was, in a fashion, beautiful; in the light from the skylight, she glittered in a way that suggested sequins—or diamonds. Her dress was white, the skirts full and rustling behind her; Emma thought there was, or would be, a train. There were no attendants to carry it.

Her crown was gold, a shade warmer and darker than her hair, which had been pulled back off her face.

She looked beautiful, perfect. She looked like a bride. A bride made of living ice and rage. Her eyes, brown, glittered as Emma met her gaze. She stared at Emma, seated in the center of her own circle.

The royal gaze swept the room and came to rest not on Chase or Emma, but on the old man who was seated within the periphery of the circle. Emma's circle. From what she understood, the circle would afford him no protection.

But she wasn't certain that the circle would afford anyone in the room any protection from the Queen's rage. She trembled with it, swelled with it, embodied it; it seemed larger in all ways than she was.

"How *dare* you?" Her voice was thin—like the edge of a blade—her eyes, narrowed. Emma found her so compelling that she almost missed Eric as he entered the room behind her. It was Eric who closed the doors; the Queen didn't appear to be aware of them.

It was Eric who bent and carefully straightened the Queen's train. It was such an unexpected gesture, Emma stared at him. He failed to meet her gaze. But he failed to look at the Queen herself, either. He simply stood behind her, as if he were a guard or an attendant.

Maybe, she thought, love didn't die. Maybe it couldn't be killed. Or maybe it was just Emma's love that was so conditional. If she had ever loved Reyna, she would have stopped centuries ago; there would be nothing in the woman she had become that would keep the love alive and much that would kill it.

If Nathan had been the King of the Dead, if he had changed so much from the Nathan she'd fallen in love with, she wouldn't have been able to continue to love him. Love—Emma's love—needed some small embers to continue to burn. She wondered what that said about her, because she had believed—not intellectually, but emotionally, viscerally—that love was forever.

She accepted that love was not fixed. It wasn't diamond. It was organic. It grew. Like a tree it required soil, sunlight, water, and deprived of those things for long enough, it died.

Reyna's had not.

But Eric's?

"Scoros. Why have you left your room?" Rage lent a killing frost to her tone.

Scoros' expression was drawn, reserved; his shoulders drooped, his spine turned gently down. He was not a young man, but he had aged a decade or two since the doors had opened. A bitter mix of yearning, grief, and disgust twisted his lips, narrowed his eyes. He glanced briefly at Emma; the expression didn't change.

"Reyna."

If the Queen narrowed her eyes any farther, they'd be closed. "Your Majesty," she said, correcting him. "You will *never* use my name again."

But the old man shook his head. "You are Reyna," he said. "To me, you will always be Reyna. I failed you."

Reyna stared at the lantern's light. She was silent for a long moment.

"Get ready," Chase let the two words escape the corner of his mouth. Emma heard them but didn't respond. She looked at the cast of the Queen's face in the lantern light. The Queen seemed to be drawn to it, just as the dead were.

"You might redeem yourself," Reyna told the old man.

"I have failed every attempt to do so," Scoros replied. Even as he spoke, Emma heard echoes and harmonies fold around each syllable. But she saw his expression shift, and she realized that even now, knowing everything he knew, Scoros—*this* Scoros—wanted redemption.

Reyna saw this too. "Take the lantern from her hands."

His chin dropped. He moved his hands—slowly—and folded them in his lap. When he raised his face again, he smiled. It was not a happy expression. "Have you forgotten so much?"

Silence.

"If you want the lantern, you must now prove yourself worthy of its light and its burden."

"I *am* worthy of it! I always was!" She seemed shocked by the words that had escaped her. She couldn't retrieve them; she could control anything else that left her mouth.

"We don't get to decide our own worth," Scoros replied, his voice gentle. But beneath the surface of those almost fatherly words, Emma felt the slow movement of glaciers. "Emma did not decide that she was worthy of the lantern. The magar did."

Silence.

"And you will not decide you are worthy of it, either. Emma will. The lantern and its burden is now hers, to carry or to pass on."

It was clear that Reyna had no desire to prove herself worthy to Emma Hall. It was clear, as well, that she wanted the lantern—and that she could not simply take it. Her lips folded in what was meant to be a smile; it did nothing to gentle her ferocity.

"I would have trained you," the Queen told Emma, her voice quieter but no softer. "I sent my Knights to save you from the hunters. You repaid them with death."

Emma, stung, said, "They would have killed a *baby*. They would have killed Eric and Chase."

"They would not have dared to kill Eric. Even had they, I would have resurrected him."

"They tried to kill my best friend. Even after I said I would go with them if they released her. They tried to kill my best friend's family. They may have succeeded with the youngest. Nothing you could have offered me was worth that. Nothing."

"Is that what you were taught? Poor child. You have lived in ignorance of the gift to which you were born. Do you know how old I am?"

"Not to the day, no. I don't see how it matters."

The cold smile almost fractured; the Queen held it in place with obvious effort. "Perhaps not. But, Emma, I resurrected Nathan for you. I did, for you, what I did for myself. He loved you. He wanted to be with you. It is only me who could make that possible."

"By binding him to you?"

*Do not argue with her.*

"Yes."

"But you didn't have to bind Eric. Have you become less powerful with time?"

Reyna raised a hand—a fist—and part of the wall melted. "I would have returned him to you," she finally said. The wall didn't reform. "If you proved worthy of his love, I would have given him into your keeping. I resurrected him because I know what it is to lose the man you love. I expected—"

"Gratitude?" Emma asked, her voice much softer, much fuller, than the Queen's.

"I would have given anything to have Eric back," the Queen replied. "And I *did*. Where is Nathan?"

Emma kept her gaze on the Queen. It wasn't as difficult as it should have been. "He's dead," she replied. At this very moment, it didn't even hurt to say it, which was a first. "Nathan is dead."

Eric turned to Emma, his expression almost unreadable. It was the first time since straightening the train of a very beautiful, very impractical dress that he had moved. It was the first time since he'd entered the room that he looked *at* Emma.

"You killed him?" the Queen demanded.

"No. A drunk driver did that." Emma tried to return her attention to the Queen—the most dangerous thing in the room. But Eric's expression caught her and held her—there was pain in it. Pain and hope—but hope was so often painful.

"Don't play games. What have you done with him?"

"He's dead," Emma said again. Eric nodded. She turned toward the Queen, and as she did so, she rose. The lantern came with her, part of her right hand.

Scoros attempted to rise as well, and Emma glanced back at him, shaking her head. "You don't need to stand," she told him quietly. "This isn't about you anymore."

"If it weren't," he replied, accepting Chase's aid, "I wouldn't be here. I, too, would be dead."

But Emma shook her head. "It affected you. It affected Eric. It affected the dead. But it wasn't *about* any of you."

"It is not," he said, his voice gentle and thin, "about you, either."

At that, Emma nodded.

Reyna had lost the thread of words; they were buried beneath accusation, anger, and the familiar sting of betrayal. Her eyes were fixed on the lantern as Emma raised it. "Eric," Emma said. She extended her left hand.

The Queen mirrored the gesture as Eric moved; she extended that arm into his chest, restraining him. "Eric is *alive*," she said, voice low. "You have no power over him."

Chase laughed. It was an ugly, harsh sound. He said nothing, but the laughter was accusation enough.

"Reyna," Scoros said, speaking the most forbidden words in the citadel, "the boy is dead. He's been dead for centuries."

Fire erupted from the floor, scorching and blackening it. The fire was green, bright, wild; it seemed to require no wood, no spark. Chase flinched but held his ground; the fire didn't enter the circle that enclosed the three of them. Emma could feel it and was surprised: There was no heat in it. It was a wild, lapping green ice.

"You will destroy the citadel," Scoros told her gently. "Before you can destroy me."

Reyna cursed. And it came to Emma, listening to the rising fury of the Queen, that she could understand every word the Queen spoke. That she had always understood every word—even in memory.

Surely that was wrong. The language Reyna had learned from birth wasn't modern English. The Necromancers that she had plucked from their homes across North America couldn't be the only Necromancers born. Had Reyna chosen the language of her inferiors? Had she chosen to adopt a tongue that wasn't her own?

Emma would have. If it eased communication, if it helped to build—and hold—a community, a family, together, she would.

She stared at eyes that were markedly brown in a pale, white face. She stared at the contours of lips and cheek and jaw, at the color of hair that could be seen above the rise of a crown, at the perfect, smooth skin of her throat. And she remembered Reyna as Scoros had first seen her.

This woman was not that child. Not the girl that Scoros had vowed to protect. Her eyes were the same, but very little else was; her build was different, her nose a different shape, the curve of her forehead less pronounced, the point of her chin too delicate. In other people, some of the differences would be produced by age.

But the Queen had not allowed herself to age. She had maintained the semblance of youth because Eric was young.

Eric, dead, would be forever young. Unless the Queen chose to change his body, the form that she'd made for him, he would never age.

The dead couldn't. The dead didn't. They were trapped and held forever in memories that could no longer be added to.

Eric was dead.

But, Emma thought, so was the Queen. Dead enough that her words were clear to Emma, no matter what language she spoke. All of the dead spoke in a language that Emma could understand—because they weren't actually speaking. And when Emma answered them, neither was she. Speech was a function of an actual body.

Reyna had that.

But how much of what she now had was built—as Nathan's body had been built—of the dead? How much of her living self remained beneath the shell of the perfect form, made and remade, massaged and changed, over the passage of centuries?

Something must remain; her eyes were living eyes. But the rest of her? Emma lifted the lantern, extending her arm to its full height. The light weighed nothing.

"Scoros," she whispered.

The old man seated beside her didn't reply. But she wasn't talking to him.

"Preserve them. Please." She didn't mention her friends by name. If she failed, she didn't want to tell the Queen who'd been here. Stairs—familiar stairs—appeared in the circle, the lowest step an inch from her foot.

*I will,* he replied. *But preservation has never been my strength.*

No, it really hadn't. But Scoros was not yet dead. Living, parts of himself had been scattered through the citadel, underpinning it, forming a structure beneath the whole, like a spider's web.

*You understand what was done?* he asked her.

"No. But I think you keep the citadel in the air. Bring it to ground," she whispered. "Quickly. Safely."

It was the living man who answered. "Yes. I did not intend to kill her. I hoped to separate her from the power that destroyed her."

"Destroyed me? *Destroyed me?*" Green fire leaped and sizzled in the air around the circle; it consumed the walls of the resurrection room. "It *saved* me! It saved us!"

"Is this salvation?" he asked her, raising one arm in a slow, steady sweep. "Is this life? It is a *tomb*, Reyna. It does not return you to the earth; it doesn't offer peace to the living. It is not a place where memory brings joy. It is not a place that offers comfort—to either the living or the dead."

"It is *not* a grave. It is home!"

"It is not a grave, no," the living Scoros replied gently. "It is a tomb. It is a gentle tomb. A monument of stone and unnatural grandeur. A thing made of—and for—man. Emma has spent much time beside graves. She knows the difference." He looked beyond Reyna. "Eric."

Eric was staring at him.

"It is time," Scoros said. "It is past time. I do not ask you to harm her. You can't without her permission. I regret what was done to you and your kin."

"It's not on your head," Eric replied, his voice rough and low.

"I regret what was done to mine."

Eric shook his head again.

"The magar will grant you the freedom you have never had, if you ask it. But she will, I think, grant you that freedom even if you don't."

"Scoros!" Reyna shouted.

The old man winced. "I loved you, child. Not wisely and not well. I love you still. But I can see it, Reyna. I can see what waits. And, child, I am tired." His expression gentled. "Aren't you?"

Chunks of the floor fell away, in answer to the question. Parts of the wall eroded, thinning and becoming porous.

Emma took this in before she squared her shoulders and set one foot on the stairs. She looked across the room at Eric, who stood, empty hands by his sides.

"Where is Nathan?" he asked her.

She shook her head. "Here," she whispered. She began to climb.

How many of the dead did Reyna hold? How many had she bound? How many had she drained? With each step she took, Emma wondered. She didn't ask. She wasn't certain that the Queen of the Dead was capable of answering that question—not now. She raged against Scoros, against her absent mother, against Eric. Emma was barely mentioned.

Emma began her ascent alone, but as she walked, people joined her. They poured through—or from—the broken walls, the crumbling floor, and they followed her, almost unseeing. No, she thought, they saw. They saw the light she carried. They saw what waited at the top of the spiral stairs.

And they wanted it. Of course they did.

She didn't ask them their names; nor did she ask for permission to use whatever remained of their power. She did note that some of these dead appeared as ghosts and some as living people. It didn't matter. They streamed toward the door above Emma's head, and when it failed to open, they retreated, standing in the glow of the lantern.

They didn't reach for it, not as they reached for the closed door. But it didn't matter. The lantern's handle was cold, and it grew colder as she climbed.

Emma wasn't certain what the Queen saw. Did she see stairs as Emma did? Did she see the dead that the walls and the floor had released? Or did she see Emma Hall sitting in the circle?

The circle itself didn't fray. It didn't shatter. The Queen of the Dead stormed toward it, toward Emma, and only when she reached the circumference did she stop. Emma couldn't see her expression; she could hear the sudden silence. It was the silence of slowly drawn breath. She looked down, over the slender rail on which her left hand rested.

The Queen's face was raised. Silence was broken. "Do you think you have any hope of destroying what I've built?" Hysteria, anger, grief, were gone. Icy contempt remained.

Emma shook her head. She glanced at Eric, whose face was white and still. "No."

"I see you've attempted to remake my circle in your own image. Clever." The Queen knelt, her skirts an impediment; their hems brushed against the words she attempted to study, obscuring them. Impatient, she pushed them aside. "But if my mother is your adviser, you don't have the knowledge to defend what you've built."

"I am not her adviser," the old woman said.

Reyna rose, the circle momentarily forgotten. "You gave her the lantern." Her voice was ice; her eyes almost glittered with it. "You gave *her* the lantern. An outsider. How could you?"

"She is of the people, Reyna. She has power to rival yours. To eclipse it."

"She does not!"

"And power was never the issue. You knew this. You know it now. Emma Hall has walked through the fires of the dead to free the lost—without training, without a circle to protect her. She thought she was risking her life, but she took that risk. I did not guide her. I did not advise her. She had nothing from me."

Reyna's lips were white. "And without lessons she learned how to draw *this* circle?"

"No. Most of what she knows of circles," the magar continued, "I did not tell her."

Reyna threw Scoros a murderous glare.

"Reyna," he said, his voice softer than the magar's. "It is time. It is past time. The dead have been weeping for centuries. The gift we were given—"

"It was *not* a gift," Reyna said, her voice low. The heat that seemed to drain from her was contained in those words. "You think this is a tomb?"

"It is a place of death, of the dead. There is almost no life in it."

She laughed. It was not a pretty sound. "What do you expect me to know of *life*? All of *my* life was given to the dead. To death. I wasn't allowed friends. I wasn't allowed daylight. I wasn't allowed *love*. The only thing that mattered to my mother—to my family—was death and the dead. There was nothing of *me* in it, and none of you cared.

"You think I should have built something else? How?"

Scoros closed his eyes.

"You never cared about living. Only survival. And Scoros? *I survived.* I don't intend to stop now." She reached out and placed her hand against the gentle curve of letters. Emma looked down, halting her climb. She shook herself and started to move again. Reyna was right. Emma had no knowledge and no weapon that would prove effective against her. She had no defenses, and Chase hadn't had time to prepare any.

Chase.

He was watching the Queen of the dead; Emma couldn't see his expression. She wasn't certain what he would, or could, do; she was almost certain he would try something. But the fire that lapped at the edge of the circle hadn't reached him yet. Both he and Scoros seemed safe.

That safety wouldn't last when the Queen unmade the circle. Emma had no doubt that she could—and she could remake it once again in her own image. While it lasted, Emma climbed.

She reached the door.

## Reyna

Reyna recognizes the words. They are English. They are not the old tongue, with its compact runes; they are not the hidden language. The circle shouldn't *work*, written as it is, a mishmash of the words that remain unchanging and pure and words that should not be written in a circle at all.

She is shaking with fury, burning with it. Ice melts, cold fades. These words are not carved in stone; they are carved in the bedrock of death. Death is Reyna's domain. Her rule over the dead is undisputed.

And yet they stream past her as if she has become invisible. Those that can, all but fly; they do not stop. They offer no obeisance and no power; they do not recognize their Queen. Nor does the circle that Emma Hall has fashioned prevent their passage. They come at will, as if nothing is preventing them.

Did Emma learn nothing?

Perhaps not. Perhaps it is only the lantern that gives her the strength to defy Reyna. It doesn't matter. Emma *will* learn. Starting now.

Reyna breaks the first word, changing the shape of the offensive, foreign letters. She is not sure that she has chosen the right word to start with, but it doesn't matter; they are all wrong, the wrongness so obvious it practically burns.

As if anything could burn her now.

But the word struggles against her, as if it had will; its shape breaks and then reverts, resisting her commands. She is shocked for one long moment; she assumes there is a greater treachery here—and that should not surprise her.

It doesn't surprise her when the doors burst open. It doesn't surprise her that the steps she hears are heavy, audible. It has been a long, long time since she has been vulnerable to physical attack, and she is not concerned.

Not until Merrick Longland brushes past her, leaping into the circle she cannot instantly remake. Her heart rises at the sight; she believes, for the briefest of instants, that he intends to kill Emma Hall—and she knows that Emma

Hall is vulnerable to all manner of physical attack; she is not what Reyna has become.

But he does not kill her. The whole of his attention is riveted by what she holds in her hand.

Emma looks up at him—but everything in the gesture implies that she's looking down, as if from a height. Her eyes are glowing faintly, but it is not her eyes that catch the attention—it's her smile. There's something in it as she looks at Longland; some hint of recognition, of connection. Of warmth.

Was it Longland? Did *Longland* teach her?

But no, no; he couldn't have. Reyna never taught Longland this. And Reyna knows that Emma Hall is indirectly responsible for Longland's death. She's heard the report. She's seen the injuries, writ in the memory of the dead.

Longland kneels, or begins to kneel; she stops him, catching his arm. Reyna can no longer see Longland's face, but he bows his head, and Emma Hall lifts a hand to touch his forehead. She is still smiling.

"Merrick," Reyna says, weighting his name with the whole of her command.

His body stiffens; he turns to look over his shoulder, to meet the eyes of the woman to whom he *should* kneel. He is hers. He is bound to her. She cannot force him to return the way the dead do—but once he is in her orbit, he belongs to her. His eyes widen, and Reyna realizes that he has run here—he has run past her—without even *seeing* her. He has looked at, and for, Emma.

Emma, who has the lantern, which she could never have obtained without the consent of Reyna's mother. Emma is a stranger. She is not of the people. And yet somehow, she has obtained the approval and trust that Reyna was always denied.

The love, she thinks, hating Merrick Longland, hating Scoros, hating everything. Why? Why does it always work this way?

Merrick Longland kneels at her silent command. He kneels, facing Reyna. What Emma will not accept, Reyna demands. He bows to Reyna.

"Kill her."

He rises. She can feel him strain against the command, against the binding placed upon him. But he is powerless before the Queen of the Dead. He removes a gun from its holster, his hand shaking with the effort.

Even Longland, Reyna thinks. Even Longland, who died because of Emma, would choose Emma if he could. She almost destroys him, then. She will, later. But without a body, he cannot do what needs to be done. He levels the gun and turns to face Emma.

Eric moves then. He moves. Reyna lifts an arm; his chest hits it. She sees that he wants to go—as Longland did—to Emma. And, oh, the anger that rises, then.

## ⌒ Chapter 26

Emma didn't hesitate.

She didn't love Merrick Longland. She didn't even like him. But she understood that when he turned, he would do as the Queen commanded. He didn't have a choice. Lantern in hand, Emma could see the filaments that stretched from his core to the Queen's; it was bright, vivid, golden. And it was a chain.

What she had done for Nathan, she now did for Longland—and she did it without hesitation, without terror. She reached for him before he could turn from the Queen; he was standing in her circle. The height of the stairs did not prevent this. The paradigm of stairs faded. She didn't have to ascend. What the dead needed was not at a lofty, forbidden height. It was here.

The Queen was not.

The circle was proof against death and the way the living could lose themselves in the memories, the fears, and the dying, but Emma was certain it wasn't proof against knives or bullets. It was ironic that she had spent nights longing for death to sneak in and take her too. It was visceral and terrible, but she understood that it wasn't death she wanted. It was peace. It was an end to loss and pain.

And she wanted to live.

She wanted life. The only hope of joy in this world was in life; death was endless privation. And she wanted that to change, too. Because everyone she loved now—everyone she would *ever* love—would die eventually. She would die as well. And this could not be all that waited. This could not be eternity.

She wouldn't let it be.

She placed her free hand on the back of Longland's neck, feeling the taut cords of muscles that strained with effort. She could even guess what caused him to make that effort.

"Do it," he said, his voice the product of clenched jaw and minimal movement of lips.

She nodded.

His body came apart beneath her hands. She felt it unravel, but this time, she paid attention to how; she saw the moment his body became its disparate elements—not flesh and blood and internal organs, as her own would have been, but the dead. They were older than the victims chosen to house Nathan; almost of an age with Longland's physical appearance now. They were also two women, two men—their forms so transparent they could be lost in the light.

Or they could have been had the source of that light been anything other than this lantern. She heard their whispers; she knew that was all she would ever hear. But they looked beyond Emma. They looked up, transfixed.

The gun held in their collective, single hand clattered to the floor, forgotten.

She held them. She broke the chains that bound them to the Queen of the Dead, reaching for Longland in the same way. She wasn't surprised at the tensile strength of his binding; the woman who had created it was here, and she knew more about binding the dead than Emma Hall would ever willingly know.

But it didn't matter. Emma had closed a hand around Longland, and if the hand no longer held his neck, it held him. She felt a grim amusement at the idea that she and the Queen of the Dead were playing tug-of-war over a former Necromancer. She was probably the only person present who did.

The Queen's eyes rounded, her brow rising into the momentary folds of her forehead.

"Chase," Eric said. The Queen's arm was still level with his midriff, as if this could stop him from leaving her side. She was smaller, finer boned, less well-muscled; all she had was power. She had not bound Eric except in one way: She had left him nowhere to go.

Chase bent and picked up the gun Merrick Longland had dropped.

Emma didn't turn to look at him; she was watching the Queen of the Dead. She knew, before Chase fired the first shot, that the bullet wouldn't hurt her.

Given Chase's lack of verbal response—and the lack of follow-up shots—he'd known, too. He watched as the bullet was absorbed by her body. She hadn't even stumbled.

"Do you honestly think you can kill me—any of you?" the Queen demanded. Fire burned at the edges of the room, but it no longer raged in the center. "Do you think I would have left myself vulnerable to you?"

"Scoros," Emma's ears hurt.

"I make no guarantees," he replied, as if she'd actually asked a question. He rose on shaking legs. No surprise there; Emma's were shaking as well. "Do what must be done," he added softly.

Emma nodded and turned to face what she called a door. It was the only door in the room that mattered to the dead; it was the only one that now mattered to Emma. The dead watched Emma, pressing against it in urgent silence.

Chase drew two daggers.

"Chase," she said softly. "You don't think those will make a difference?"

He didn't reply.

"Don't leave the circle," she whispered. More than that, she couldn't say. She turned her attention to the door.

It was thick, heavy wood; it seemed scratched and scarred, but only superficially. It was a solid door.

It was a door the dead couldn't see. What she saw now was invisible to them, except in one way: it was closed. They approached it as if it were a window against which they could find no purchase.

Emma had opened that door once. She had no idea for how long, although *not long enough* was the only relevant fact. She had strained and struggled to hold it long enough for one four-year-old boy to escape an eternity of afterlife. To do that, she had called the dead, and they had come, in hundreds. In thousands. She had borrowed their power, and she had used it, struggling to give them what she had promised.

Freedom.

"Emma," Longland said.

And in the giving, she had—for one brief moment—seen *peace*. She had seen an end to loss and suffering and self-hate and guilt and emptiness. She could not describe it in words. She couldn't even recall how it had looked to her. But she knew how it had felt.

And she knew, as she struggled, that that was what she needed to feel. She needed to see as the dead saw, as if she were one of them. Opening the door wasn't what needed to be done—that was the wrong paradigm. There was a window, a thick, plate of impenetrable glass, laid across the only freedom the dead were promised—and it couldn't be opened.

She needed to shatter it.

"Emma, dear," Margaret said, her voice startling in its urgent clarity. "The Queen is unmaking your circle."

"She's trying," Emma countered. "Margaret—I need to concentrate. I'm sorry."

Silence. Emma thought of warmth.

"Emma."

She looked at Margaret because Margaret appeared to have stepped in front of her. And Margaret Henney was clearer than the rest of the dead who had also gathered there—clearer, brighter, much more *solid*.

"Not that way, dear."

"The door—"

"Yes. It's here. It's everywhere. But you cannot approach it that way."

"How do you even know what I'm doing?"

"I can see it."

"What is she trying to do?" Chase demanded.

"She is trying to die."

Emma was offended. "I am *trying*," she said, through gritted teeth, "to see what the dead see."

"Yes, dear. And there is only one way for you to do that. Whatever you feel you must do, this is *not* the way."

"I need to see what the dead see to free them."

"No. You need to see what they saw *when they were alive* to free them, if I understand everything I've heard correctly. And the circle?"

Emma shook her head. "I trust them."

"Trust who?"

"Helmi," she replied. "And Nathan."

The Queen's dress shifted in place, wedding white—and complicated train—becoming something metallic, ornate. The crown remained, as did the tight pull of her hair; her eyes glittered.

Chase, knives in hand, stepped between the Queen of the Dead and Emma, placing his back against the latter while she worked. He glared at Eric. Eric, his partner. Eric, his rival. Eric, the *reason* the Queen of the Dead existed.

He had hated Eric when they'd first met. Of course he had. He'd been sent to deliver a message to Eric. All the pain, the death, the torture—all of it—a message for Eric. Eric was the reason his family had died.

He wanted to kill the Queen. He had dreamed, and daydreamed, about this moment for years. The blades of these knives were a bitch to keep sharp; they were silver. But sharp didn't matter. What the bullet couldn't pierce, these blades could.

He was willing to bet his life on it. He'd been waiting so long to make that bet. But Emma had said only one thing: Don't leave the circle.

He tried not to care. He'd done suicidal things so many times since his family had died, it was practically all his life amounted to. If he killed the Queen, Emma would be able to finish whatever it was she'd started in safety.

*No.*

Allison would be safe. Michael. Amy. The Old Man. Eric? In some fashion, Eric would be safe. All of the dead would be. His mother. His sister. His father. He didn't know if dogs counted, but in his opinion, they should.

He could see the dead, with effort. But he had never seen *his* dead. He had never seen his family. He was certain that they would see Emma. They would see what Emma was doing. They would leave.

And he was fine with that. In every other way that counted, nothing could hurt them anymore.

Things could still hurt Chase. That was the problem with love and affection—once you had it, it was yours to lose. Life could hurt you without ever touching you. If Allison died now, it would kill him. It would do more damage than guns or knives when they didn't end life.

He wasn't certain what his death would do to Allison. It had been forever since he'd worried about the effect his death would have on someone else. In fact, this might be a first, because he'd never really thought about death as something that could happen to him or his family, when he'd had one.

"Chase."

He looked away from the Queen's rigid face, her newly formed armor, her ringed, cold hands. He met Eric's eyes.

"Don't step away from the circle while it still holds."

"I can—"

"I've seen that fire level small villages," Eric continued, his eyes strangely translucent. "It hasn't immolated you—or Emma—because of that circle. It's a power that's built on the dead."

"The dead—according to Emma—are already standing on top of her head."

"Yes. The dead she allows, the dead she welcomes. But she won't let the fire touch you. And there's nothing to extend that circle. There's no way to preserve your life. There's no point in throwing it away."

"Eric," the Queen of the Dead said, her voice like a blade's flat. "Do you not love me?"

Eric was silent.

"Why did you return?"

"Reyna."

She didn't turn. Her eyes would have frozen whole lakes. If her tone implied pain or tears, those eyes were never going to shed them. She flinched when he placed a hand on her shoulder, although given the armor, she shouldn't have felt it.

"Why?" she demanded, as she looked at Emma.

"Because I want you to leave this place," he said, voice low. "I want you to leave it with me."

She looked, again, at Emma. And then she shook her head. "I will never leave this place." But there was something in her expression—bitter, dark, yearning, and loathing—that spoke to Emma. Because Emma, looking at the door, could nonetheless see the Queen clearly.

She wasn't carved into it; she wasn't part of it; the door itself was simple, dark wood. But she was more than a superimposition.

"Scoros," Emma whispered, "What is this door?"

Chase shifted the grips on his knives.

*They cannot hurt her, boy.* He recognized the voice and glanced at the old man. The old man wasn't speaking. He wasn't looking at Chase, or even Emma. His whole attention was focused on the Queen of the Dead. His lined, weathered cheeks seemed to glisten with tears. There was no fear in him. No aggression. He sat as if bearing witness. Again. *Wait. Trust the magar.*

"The magar's dead," he muttered. "No one dead stands a chance against her."

*She is not dead; she is new, and she is too young.* He spoke of Emma.

"She'll die."

*Trust the magar.*

"Because that worked out so well for you last time."

The Queen gestured, and Eric flew—almost literally—from her side. Chase saw him strike the far wall and slide. He wondered whether anything was broken. He knew that it didn't matter. Eric's body was exceptionally good at healing itself.

He even thought he understood why, and for the first time—ever—he pitied Eric. Plotting against the insane version of the woman you had once loved at a distance wasn't the same as personally stabbing or shooting her.

Green fire enveloped the room, scorching every square inch of floor except the ones she occupied. He looked across to Eric and then away. The fire was too intense to see through. If she had decided to destroy him, it didn't matter. She *couldn't* destroy Emma yet, and Emma was the only responsibility Chase had now.

"None of you," the Queen said, "will escape."

She didn't bend to the circle, this time. In that armor, bending was probably impossible.

Instead, she lifted her arms slowly and deliberately. She seemed to struggle with the motion, her arms trembling as if she carried weight in her hands. The weight was invisible to Chase, at least to start, but as the movement continued he could see it clearly.

The words that defined the circle in which he was standing were rising. They were golden; they reflected soul-fire. Some of the words, he recognized; some he didn't. They trembled as they were dislodged.

Given that they'd been carved into stone, it should have been impossible to lift them; their shapes were the absence of matter. But they rose. They rose in concert, each word legible. Even the misspelled one.

The Queen's face was stone; if her arms felt weight, she didn't acknowledge it. Her eyes were the color of the fire that surrounded her. The words rose to the height of her chest in a ring. She brought her hands down in one swift, sudden motion, as if they were blades.

Chase expected the words to break.

They didn't. They hovered almost gently in the air, Emma Hall at their absolute center.

The Queen's brows rose, her eyes rounding in astonishment. When they narrowed, they became blade's edge—glittering with sharpness and the promise of death. She brought her hands down again; the circle rippled, the letters rising and falling as if they were buoyant. But the words they comprised held.

The air was hot with fire, but it chilled as the Queen of the Dead summoned her army: the dead. She had made a citadel, a home, of the dead—but not all of the stones and planks and windows were bound to her. They remained where they had been laid, but their voices grew in strength as the minutes passed.

The bound dead came through the walls. They came through the floors. They flowed like the coldest of winter air. Chase could see them. He could see them without losing his grip on the rest of life.

They circled their Queen, making obeisance in the lap of green flames as if the flames were wildflowers or stalks of densely packed corn. They rose at her regal nod—even armored and armed and in combat, respect clearly had to be received—and turned at once toward the circle of gold and words.

Emma had said that she trusted Helmi and Nathan. Chase had only half understood what that meant until he watched those liminal words. The dead approached them in a wave of motion, reaching for individual letters with a sea of arms, a sea of hands.

They shouldn't have had any effect on the words, but the words wavered as more and more of the hands of the dead reached them. The letter forms began to sag, to shift; what had been perfectly engraved all caps began to resemble writing, and not the careful, deliberate work of chisels.

"Emma."

She nodded.

"The words—she's going to change them. She's trying to remake them in the old image."

Emma stared at the Queen, although her back was, in theory, turned toward her. She could see the fires that raged around the Queen's chamber. She heard

Chase's voice. It had none of Margaret's pinched gravity or careful urgency. But she knew what the Queen was attempting.

And she knew it would, eventually, succeed. Helmi and Nathan could hold out for some time—but not against the power the Queen now brought to bear. Once the circle ruptured, the fire would blaze in, killing them all.

And the door wouldn't open. Emma strained against it, pushing, pulling, but nothing worked. And why would it? She'd been across an ocean the last time she'd tried. She was now standing in the seat of the Queen's power.

Margaret was talking, her voice lost to the rising crackle of burning flame.

"I'm going to try to distract her," Chase said.

Emma turned away from the door, away from the stairs and the thought of ascension. She shook her head.

"Emma—"

Because she understood why the image of the Queen was so clear when she looked at the door. She understood what powered the barrier. She understood what had to be done to destroy it.

*Yes.*

"Not yet, Chase," she told him, touching his shoulder. He was tense—of course he was tense. "I can't throw your life away."

"You aren't." He was frowning. Something in her voice made him turn to her. His eyes widened. Emma wasn't certain what he saw in her expression, because she wasn't certain what her expression was. "You can't." His voice was flat.

"Throw your life away? No. No, I can't." She was deliberately misunderstanding him.

He didn't want to allow it. She couldn't think how this red-haired, angry, violent person had come to mean so much to her. Maybe it was because she'd seen some of his past and understood how it had opened up the path he walked. Maybe it was because Ally loved him, or maybe it was because he loved Allison.

Or maybe it was just because he was here, and even disliking her, he was willing to throw his life—and possible future happiness—away to buy her time. And it wouldn't be enough time.

He looked annoyed. "You can't kill her."

She said nothing.

"You've never killed anyone. In your life. You won't be able to kill her."

She felt calm. "I have to kill her," she said quietly. "She's the barrier, Chase. She's the door. She's the reason the dead can't leave. And they'll never be able to leave while she lives."

*       *       *

"In case you haven't noticed, there's soul-fire across every square inch of floor. You step outside of this circle and you're ash. Less than ash. You *won't be able to kill her*. You'll just die."

Emma shook her head. "Look at the circle. Look at the circle, Chase."

He did. Emma knew he would have grabbed her arm or shoulder if he'd had a free hand, but he didn't. He had two hands full of knife, and he didn't intend to surrender them while the Queen lived.

The circle that the Queen had pulled up from the ground remained. But it wouldn't remain for long, not against the concerted effort of the Queen and her army of undead.

"Just a little bit longer," she whispered. "Just hold it a little bit longer." To Chase, she said, "You'd better help Scoros."

"Help him what?"

"Stand, Chase. I'm moving, and the circle will come with me." She wasn't certain what Chase did. She wasn't certain what Scoros did. She looked at the Queen and only at the Queen. The army of the dead and the fire it produced wouldn't kill Emma yet. A simple knife would if the Queen carried one. A gun would.

The only gun in the room was on the floor beneath Emma's feet. The man who had carried it would never pick up a gun again. It didn't matter.

Reyna's eyes were clear and cold and almost green as they met Emma's. She looked faintly confused. "What are you doing?" Her eyes fell on the lantern that Emma carried. Emma held it out to her, as if offering it. She reached for it slowly.

But Emma shook her head. "You gave me a few days with Nathan," she said. "I thought I would never see him again except in dreams. Memories. I got to say everything I thought I'd never get to say again—and he could actually hear it.

"I got to hold him." She swallowed.

Reyna was watching her, arrested, although the fires didn't diminish, and the thinning of the words that held the circle together—the circle that moved now, with Emma—continued.

"I spent a lot of time sitting in the cemetery. I spent a lot of evenings sitting beside what was left of him. Probably as much time as I got to spend with him, in the end." She inhaled. Exhaled. She was an arm's length away from Reyna.

In one hand, she held the lantern; the other was empty.

"I thought the world ended the day he died. I had plans, Reyna. *We* had plans. It was easier for me. His parents don't get to choose what he does, and mine don't get to choose what I do. When his mother found out about me, she didn't come to kill me. She wouldn't. Even if she hated me, she wouldn't. It would have killed Nathan." She swallowed, smiled. There were no tears left. "I wanted to go to university with Nathan. I wanted to spend years with him. Live with him. I wanted to get married, find a home, have children—I wanted that life."

Reyna was still, in the light of the lamp.

"I *still* want it. I want it so much, sometimes I can't breathe. I look at every other man, and I can only see the ways in which they aren't Nathan."

"Why—why are you telling me this?"

"Because you'll understand it," Emma replied. "Because you'll understand it better than my friends or my mother or my teachers."

"But I *gave him back to you*," Reyna said, voice low—but not loud.

"No. You didn't. Nothing can give him back to me. He's dead."

"I resurrected him!"

"You made him a body of the dead. He's as much alive as the floor is. He's *dead*. And I can stay here, and grieve, and want, and let it destroy me. But, Reyna, it's not what he wants. It's not what Nathan has ever wanted for me." She swallowed. "The only thing he wants—the only thing I can give him—is peace. He wants what waits for the dead. He can't want me anymore—and I hate it. I hate that I can't—" She shook her head. "Eric's dead, Reyna."

"He is *not* dead—"

"But because of the choices you've made, so are you."

"Do you think you can—"

Emma shook her head. "Right now, Reyna, you are more dead than alive. You've never stepped out of the shadows. You are as trapped in Eric's death as—as Eric is. There's peace, there is joy, there's something beyond pain."

"You don't even believe that!" Reyna's eyes narrowed. Helmi had said she wasn't stupid.

"I believe it. I don't *feel it*. I don't *know* it the way I know how to breathe. But I do believe it. There's peace and joy and belonging and love—that's what Merrick Longland said. And that's what I've seen. You must have seen it yourself."

"I *hate* death," Reyna said. Bitter, angry, and bewildered. "All my life. *All of it*. Nothing but death. The dead. Always." She shook her head. "Only Eric— only Eric was about life. He made me want to live. To be alive."

"It's what I wanted as well," Eric said. Even in her rage, she had preserved him. "It was all I wanted. When I was working in the forge, it almost killed me—I'd get so distracted. I wanted to go to the stream. I wanted to stand beneath our tree. I wanted to watch until you arrived—you were always so breathless. I wanted to watch you look up and realize I was there, waiting, because your smile—" He touched her frozen lips, his hand so gentle Emma was certain that he could never have forced himself to kill her. "This isn't where I wanted to live. This isn't how I wanted to live. There's no stream, no tree—and no joy, Reyna.

"You haven't smiled at me that way since I died. Even this time."

"But *I'm* here," she whispered.

"Are you, love?" He bent down, kissed her forehead gently. "Emma?"

Emma held out her arms, lantern dangling from one hand, stepped forward, and hugged the Queen of the Dead. She hugged the Queen as if the Queen were another teenage girl, new to gut-wrenching loss and wandering the halls of an empty school, weeping. She hugged her knowing that in seconds the circle that protected her would dissolve, and she would die in the fires of that girl's wrath.

And she hugged her knowing that her body was mostly composed of the dead, the way Nathan's had been. The way Eric's was. Immortality, of a sort, had been made just as a new body had been made. And it could be undone the same way.

It would kill the Queen. It would kill Reyna. It would free the dead. And because the last thing was true, Emma unraveled the dead bound to the Queen's physical form, releasing them as she did. She knew what would happen, or thought she knew: Age would rush in, and the semblance of youth—with nothing to support it—would vanish.

In an odd rush of something like sympathy, she would have spared Reyna that. Because no one wanted to look like that in the eyes of the man they loved. And it was stupid, and she knew it. And she hated the choices the Queen had made, the damage she'd done, and she knew that if there was any justice, this wasn't it.

But she no longer believed in Hell. And even had she, she never wanted to be Hell's ruler. It wasn't, in the end, up to Emma to mete out punishment or judgment. It was simply to find the lost and lead them . . . home.

And it happened as she had expected it would; the health and vigor of this pseudo-youth drained away from Reyna's living body as Eric held it, held her; the armor melted, and the heat of the fire slowly banked. Eric's arms tightened as he smiled down into a face that was sinking into age and ruin and decay, smiled as he gathered her tighter, as if he could hold her to him forever—as if he *wanted* to.

Reyna whispered his name. She lifted a withered, bony hand, skin draped over its sunken flesh, its atrophied muscle, and she touched his face and said, "Eric, you're crying." And she didn't seem to notice that her own hand was so old, that her arm was spotted and white, that her hair had fallen out and away. She was smiling.

She was smiling as she died.

## ᔐ Chapter 27

The green fire died when the Queen did, winking out of existence in the cold, high air so suddenly it left nothing behind. The floor wasn't scorched; nothing was burned. But the holes in the wall and floor remained. They weren't sharp-edged or jagged; they were rounded and smoothed, as if portions of the rock had melted.

Except it wasn't rock.

Emma looked at Chase, briefly, before she turned to Eric. "Your turn?" she asked, voice soft.

He shook his bowed head, his arms tightening around a wizened corpse. She was glad that she couldn't see his face, which made her feel guilty. But it was Hall guilt, it was small and normal, and she almost welcomed it.

Chase had sheathed his knives. "That's it?" he asked.

Emma shook her head. She heard the cries of joy, of jubilation; she saw the dead—those who could move—shiver in place. She had thought they would stream to the exit, because the door that was locked had been opened, and it would never close again.

But they didn't. They looked—they looked up—and they raised arms or hands, as if something were reaching for them. As if something were gently gathering them. She watched them vanish, their expressions etched in her memory. The joy and the tears and the relief were bright. They gave her hope.

She even recognized one of them. Merrick Longland. She was surprised when he turned—arms still lifted—to look over his shoulder. She had never seen him look like this: younger, stronger. Happy.

She knew he didn't deserve happiness. But in that moment, she didn't care. Because the people he had killed, the people he had trapped, the people he had used, wouldn't care either. Like Merrick, they would pass beyond all pain, and she knew that they would deny Merrick Longland none of the joy they themselves felt. Even if he didn't deserve it. It was not the type of happiness that depended on the unhappiness of others to shine more brightly.

He didn't speak. Neither did Emma. But she smiled at him and nodded.

And when she looked down, Eric was watching them. But he gently—gently—set Reyna's body aside.

"Where is she?"

"She's only just died," he whispered. "She won't be here yet." He stood. His legs shook.

"Can I—"

"Not yet. I know what it means for the dead who contain me. But they know, Emma. They've seen."

"But you could leave. *They* could leave."

He nodded. "We will. But there's work to do here—for me, for Ernest, for Chase—that you can't do. There's not much of it left, but the Queen of the Dead taught her Necromancers well."

"I can do what I did to—or for—the Queen."

"If it's all the same to you," Chase cut in, "no. Allison would kill me if anything happened to you. We know how to fight Necromancers— and now they have no Queen. We'll do what we've always done. Let us finish this."

"I want you to come home," she told him softly.

"Emma, this *is* home for me." He walked over to Eric's side. Eric met his gaze, and to Emma's surprise, it was Eric who looked away. "But I want a different home. And I won't trust it until the last of the Necromancers is dead. They'll come back. Allison's baby brother may already be dead. Who's next? Her parents? Michael's? Yours?

"I don't want that life for any of you. Even Amy. And I won't be able to believe in home until I believe that it won't happen again. You get that, right? There's no damage this hunt can do to me. Not anymore."

She hesitated, and Eric watched her. "Chase can see the dead," she finally told him. "I don't want to leave the rest of your dead trapped the way they've been trapped for so long. It's not right, Eric."

"Emma—"

"If I do it—if I do it for a good reason, I'll eventually do it for a bad reason. Good, bad—it seems so much of it is subjective. I know what you intend to do. I think it has to *be* done. But I don't think it has to be done by you."

Eric exhaled. "Magar," he said. It was what Scoros had called her. Eric's gaze, however, traveled to the left of her face.

The old woman, Reyna's mother, was standing beside Emma, her arms folded, her lips pursed. She no longer looked like a shambling, ancient, undead creature. She looked like a joyless, severe taskmaster. "It is not up to me," she told Eric. "It's not my decision."

"But you would allow it."

The magar said nothing, refusing to offer anything Emma might use as guidance. Refusing, Emma thought, to take any of the responsibility of decision off Emma's shoulders.

It was Margaret who said, "Ask them."

"Ask?"

"Ask the dead."

"They'll want—"

"I am still here, Emma. I believe your father will wait for your return. Nathan and Helmi are both here—because the circle is still, barely, coherent. You will need it," she added softly. "They had the choice; you gave it to them. I admit Helmi surprised me. Ask them."

"I can't do what she did. Even if I could find dead who were *willing*, I couldn't rebuild a body for him." And she didn't want to, either.

"No. But I believe Scoros could. If it is necessary, I will volunteer."

Emma was silent. "I think we need four."

They both looked at Scoros. Scoros shook his head. "Emma has the lantern," he told them both. "If Margaret is willing, and you are willing to use its power, Margaret will be enough. More than enough. She already draws sustenance directly from you, magar."

"I don't understand."

"No. Do you doubt me?"

Emma shook her head. To Eric she said, "Margaret won't be voiceless. Not the way—"

"They aren't voiceless," he said softly. "They weep constantly. Or they used to."

Scoros approached Eric. "Then come," he said quietly. "I understand what you intend, and I would stay to aid you—but it is my time as well. Past time, and for the same reason. Emma will free the dead bound to me, and I will vanish. Before I do, I will do this one thing. Understand that it is contingent upon Emma's survival. If she dies, it will unravel."

Eric nodded. "Ernest won't be happy about it."

Scoros said nothing.

"Ernest will not be happy," Margaret agreed. "But I'll deal with that if I'm still left a voice. There is no other way. Emma will not let you leave as you are—and Eric, I don't think she's wrong."

Scoros came to stand by Eric. He held out his hands, palm out; Eric placed his in them. "This isn't the way—"

"I do not wish you to leave if you do not wish it. And I have never attempted this—not without some element of living flesh. Mostly my own. The containment that the Queen created must be preserved, and I cannot do it from a distance. Reyna was the most gifted, the most powerful, of our number. What she could achieve, we could not achieve on our own." He smiled almost apologetically. "It is possible that your body will not be quite as functional as it currently is."

Eric shook his head. "I'd like to be able to sleep at night. It's been hard since—"

"Since your resurrection. Margaret."

Margaret came to stand beside Eric, and then, after a moment, she stepped into him, occupying the same space that he occupied, although they weren't the same height or general shape. Emma turned to the magar.

"Do not ask me for approval. Do not ask me for permission. Your guilt or your pride are things you must come to on your own. And, child—my daughter became the nightmare of the people, made flesh. If I were infallible or wise, none of this would have happened. You must make the choices that seem wise to you. And you must understand that no choice is without fear or doubt."

"It was forbidden to use the power—"

"Yes." She glanced at the circle, pale and luminous, that still floated around Emma. "My choices were not your choices. But it is not you who is using their power, Emma Hall. Helmi chose. Nathan chose. You are a conduit that allows them to express their desire in a way that affects the world of the living. You did not decide; *they* did. Now, I must go. But I will return. Scoros is finished."

Scoros was no longer holding Eric's hands when Emma turned away from the magar. Eric's hands were at his sides. He didn't look significantly different to Emma. Before she could ask, the old man said, "Brace yourselves."

Chase, however, said, "Lie down on a solid patch of floor. Now."

Since he was following his own advice—and at speed—Emma did the same. The floor was cold. Emma absorbed its chill. "Will the citadel dissolve?" she asked, voice shaking.

He answered the question she hadn't asked. "No. Not yet. Large parts of what remains will require your intervention. But your friends are as safe as they can be."

"The other Necromancers?"

"Some are dead; the Queen's fire was not contained to this room."

"The others?"

"They will not find your friends. It is the only thing I can guarantee. They may find *you*, but I do not think they will come looking. They will be concerned with their own escape. They will know that the Queen is dead."

"Will they find her?"

Scoros shook his head. "Not without both time and effort. And yes, Emma, they may look. She knew much, and she did not share all of it. But they will not find her yet. She is too new to death—as I will be."

Anything more Emma could ask was lost as the floor shook. She expected it to crack, to break, the vibrations were so strong. But the floors only looked as if they were made of stone; they weren't. They were made of the dead, just as the walls and the ceilings were.

When the shaking stopped, she pushed herself from the floor to her feet. She could see the words of the circle around her; they moved as she did. She wasn't certain anyone else could see them, but it didn't matter. She understood why Helmi and Nathan remained.

She was going to have to free the dead that were trapped here, not by their own memories or their inability to walk away from the lives that had ended, but by the will of their deceased Queen.

This was a temple, a cathedral, to grief and loss. It was vast and it was fortified and it was, in a fashion, starkly beautiful—but it was a grave. It was a grave that Reyna had dug, had lain down in, and had occupied for all but seventeen years of her existence, adding to it, enlarging it, but never emerging.

And Emma understood it. And understood that grief was not respect, in the end. It wasn't a testament to love, to *how much* Nathan had deserved love. It just was. And she had survived it—would survive it—because she had Allison and Michael and actual responsibilities. There were whole gray, empty days that waited—and she would fill them as she could bear to fill them.

But she would not be Reyna. She would not create the same space, albeit with vastly different decor, and attempt to remain in it, forever frozen, waiting for something that could never come.

She lifted the lantern again, and, circled by Helmi and Nathan, she turned to Scoros.

Scoros nodded. "It is done. The citadel is upon the ground, as you requested. Your friends have survived its landing, although I believe your dog is very upset. And loud."

She placed a hand very gently on the old man's chest, and she undid the bindings that kept his body functioning, freeing the trapped, mute dead, who streamed away from him, arms raised, faces upturned.

And she watched as elements of Scoros came together, as if rushing in to fill the space that the dead had occupied, and she realized that Scoros had been both alive and dead, and he was becoming whole. She didn't ask him how it had been done. It was enough that it would be undone.

She began to walk through the Queen's resurrection room, and as she moved, the floors became liquid; she could see arms raised, a sea of waving, frenzied limbs. This time, it didn't disturb her. She reached for a hand, and instead of being pulled under, she had the strength, the balance, to lift, to pull the dead man—it was a man—free. As if he were a tightly compressed piece jammed into a very strained, intricate puzzle, the rest of the dead began to follow; there was nothing to hold them in place.

She knew where they would go. She could hear their voices raised—a whisper of sound, but so sharp, so sweet, words would have been superfluous.

She didn't know if the ease of this dissolution was due to the lantern or the Queen's passing, and she didn't care. The radiant joy of the dead was enough to move her to tears, and she let them fall as she walked. She didn't need the circle. The dead trapped here couldn't trap her. But she felt Nathan's presence as a comfort and Helmi's as a sharp encouragement to continue until every last one of the dead was free to leave.

She found Allison and Michael near the end of that journey; they were pale and drawn, but they lost the look of shuttered tension the minute they saw her. They stood on overgrown wild grass, and as they moved, a black blur streaked past them heading for her legs and whining in that high-pitched, overexcited way of happy dogs everywhere.

She knelt into a faceful of tongue and dog breath and was grateful for it, and when she rose, she said, "Where's Amy?"

"Marshaling the rest of the living," Allison said. "And Chase?"

"Chase is doing something similar with the Necromancers."

"I doubt it; Amy is only terrifying the maids."

"Maids?"

Allison nodded. "Some of the living weren't novices. They were just regular prisoners. They did the cooking and the cleaning, things like that. Ernest is with them as well."

"He should be with Eric and Chase."

"And leave the rest of them to Amy?"

Emma laughed.

"He's trying to arrange for a safe exit for all of us. Some of us aren't on the right continent, and we have no passports, among other things." She didn't mention clothing or food, although that was in short supply as well. At the moment, they had their lives. "He's also trying to come up with some sort of cover story for how we got here—and an international slavery ring isn't going to cut it. Even if the rest of us were good liars, Michael isn't."

The rest of them were, sadly, not good liars—they only looked good in comparison to Michael. Allison glanced at Michael and added, "Michael called his mother."

Emma nodded.

"With Amy's phone. He told her that we were all safe, just—not really close to home. And that we'd be home as soon as we could. Is it over?"

"I'm not sure it's entirely over—but I think the worst of it is." She hugged her best friend, and held on tightly while Petal, feeling left out, whined and jumped.

But Michael said, "Where's Nathan?"

Emma released Allison. "He's here," she said. And he was: the thread-thin words of a circle still floated around Emma at chest level.

"Is he going to stay?"

She reached out, touched a word—the badly spelled "gratitud"—and shook her head. "No. He can't. He's dead." The word was cold in her hand, but she expected that. She wasn't even surprised when it began to dissolve, the letters fully fading as the words gave way for peace, in a way they hadn't for war and death.

Standing in front of Emma, when the words had vanished completely, were Nathan and Helmi. She felt a surge of gratitude at the sight of them. Gratitude and grief. But she accepted the grief.

"Thank you," she said—mostly to Helmi.

The child snorted. "You were never going to get it done on your own. Neither was he."

Nathan grimaced—safely beyond Helmi's line of sight. "She argues more than Amy when Amy's on a roll." But there was affection in his words—affection Helmi could see when she pivoted to face him, frowning.

"Can you—can you see it?" Emma asked them both.

Helmi nodded, eyes shining. "You would have made a terrible Queen."

"Thank you," Emma replied, meaning it. "I can barely manage my own life. I don't think I want to be responsible for anyone else's right now." Petal whined. "Except my dog's."

Helmi settled small fists on her hips and surveyed the landscape. Emma wasn't certain what she was looking at; the dead, as she well knew, saw things differently. "Hey," Helmi said, staring off into the distance. She frowned when Emma failed to answer and turned to glare at her.

"Sorry—I wasn't sure who you were talking to."

"You. I thought my mother was an idiot. I mean, I *still* think she's mostly an idiot."

"I have days like that."

"I had centuries. Don't interrupt me."

Nathan was grinning as Emma nodded silently.

"You did a good job. You did the *right* job. Thanks." Her urchin smile deepened around the corner of her lips, her eyes almost sparkling with mischief. She looked young, to Emma. Maybe because joy was youthful. "My sister was really broken."

Emma nodded.

"Don't hate her. I mean, if it's possible. Don't hate her."

Emma said, quietly, "She's dead. There's no reason to hate her now."

Helmi shook her head.

". . . I'll try, Helmi. I'll try hard. I think—" But she shook her head. Held out a hand. Without hesitation, Helmi placed hers across it, and beside Emma, Michael's eyes shifted.

"Helmi wants to say good-bye. And thank you." And to Emma's surprise, Helmi did, smiling up at Michael with unfettered, uncomplicated joy. When she released Emma's hand, she looked up at Nathan, waved, and walked away. Well, *bounced* away, really.

She inhaled, turned to Nathan, and held out a hand. Nathan shook his head, and looped both of his hands behind his back. "I have a favor to ask."

Emma hesitated.

"I want to talk to my mother."

"She's not here."

"I know. I want you to keep me by your side until you get home. I don't know what you're going to tell the parents—all of the parents—and I don't have good advice. I imagine Michael will tell the truth, Allison will say almost nothing, and Amy will lie. I don't know what you're going to tell Mercy."

"A lot of 'I'm so sorry, Mom.' "

He laughed. It was the most wonderful sound in the world. His laugh was one of the first things she'd noticed about him. "I know the dead and the living aren't supposed to meet. I know there are rules—but, Em, I want to talk to my mother. Once. Just once."

"She'll want—"

"No. She'll understand why it can only be once. Unless you keep me here, I can't stay."

Emma understood. Chains of grief had bound Eric for centuries. She felt that grief tighten. She wanted—for just a moment—to be loved so completely that she would be the only thing Nathan wanted. She wanted him to *want* to stay.

And she wanted to let him leave. She was not ready to die yet. She knew she would let him go. She would smile. And part of her would mean it. Part of her would grieve—but she accepted that, too. She had loved Nathan, had anchored her dreams in him. It was okay to feel pain at the loss. It was what the living did.

"I want her to know I'm okay. I want her to know where I'm going and what's waiting for me. And that I'll be waiting. Just that. I think—I think that'll be enough."

"If you're bound to me the way Margaret was," she told him, "you should be able to make yourself visible without touching me. I don't know if it works at a distance."

Nathan nodded.

"I—I don't want to be there when you talk to your mother. I don't want to do that to her."

He smiled. Nodded. "She'll cry."

"I know. I would."

## Emma

There aren't a lot of surfaces on which Emma can draw a circle in her house. Her room—all of the bedrooms—are carpeted. The dining room has hardwood floors, but the floors are heavily laminated, and they don't take chalk well. She knows from experience that they would take paint or marker, but she's not three anymore, and even when she was, that hadn't gone over *well*.

In the end, she settles for the garage. She bundles herself in heavy winter clothing although it's spring, and she heads out, a box of chalk in her hand. She's had some practice in circle drawing in the past two years. It's been interrupted by the usual things—end of school, graduation, searching in panic for a university that both wants her and that she wants to attend.

Allison has started to complain about her annoying baby brother again; apparently he was still stealing pens and paper from her room. For nine months, she didn't offer a single word of complaint; his lungs were damaged by the gun—almost everything was. He needed physiotherapy and time to recover, and he lost almost an entire school year.

But he didn't lose his life.

The first time Allison stormed into his room to retrieve her stolen supplies and threaten to kill him with one of them, he laughed. That was normal. And then he cried, which was not.

Allison's mother got teary. "Allison's been trying so hard," she said, with a fond, but watery, smile. "But he needs to know that he can annoy her. He needs to know that she thinks he's strong enough—safe enough—to threaten."

Emma privately agreed. But she didn't think that Toby was the only one who needed it.

She thinks of this, smiling, as she writes. The magar wanted her to learn the old runic forms but finally surrendered—gracelessly—when Emma had insisted on English. "It was fine for Helmi," she pointed out. "And it worked."

She'd been surprised to see the magar, two months after they'd returned to Toronto. The old woman had walked through her closed bedroom door while she was conversing with her father about her university choices.

Her father, of course, had stayed.

He was almost ready to leave, he said, because Mercy was *almost* happy. He didn't mind Jon. In fact, he seemed to approve of him. Emma wanted him to go—but while he remained, she was happy to have his company. Happy and a bit chilly.

She was less happy to have the magar's company—but she was not at all surprised to see her. She turned to the old woman as her father tactfully faded from sight. "Did you come for the lantern?"

"The lantern," the magar said, "is yours. It's up to you to pass it on." Her frown practically became a canyon. "What are you going to do, girl?"

Emma could have pretended to misunderstand. She didn't. She wasn't a Necromancer. She was, however, Emma Hall. She thought about Andrew Copis a lot in the quiet hours of night. Andrew Copis was a ghost who would have been trapped in the moment of his death for decades or centuries, regardless of the Queen of the Dead.

It had been so important to her to free him from that.

"I'll learn," she'd told the magar.

Emma doesn't misspell "gratitude," although she considers it every time she draws the circle. It's the one word she's certain she won't give up, no matter how much living her life changes her.

She writes in careful chalk and she waits. She doesn't have to wait for long. The garage door is open to the evening sky. She can see street and trees in the boulevard just beyond the sidewalk.

And she can see Eric walking up the drive. He almost heads to the house, but some instinct causes him to jog a bit. He approaches the garage.

"You knew I was coming?" he asks, as he looks at the circle that's nearing completion.

"The magar dropped by." Like a Sisyphean boulder. She looks up to see his expression; dusk hides most of it. Or it would, if he were alive.

"I don't envy you," he replies, with a grin.

"You've got Margaret."

"She heard that. She's trying not to be amused." He takes a seat, leaning against the only bare wall he can find; he stretches his left leg, folds his right, and rests his elbows on his bent knee. He then lowers his head.

"Where's Chase?" she asks.

"I left him at Allison's. If I know Chase, he's standing on the sidewalk out of line of sight of her house trying not to look as terrified as he feels."

Emma laughs. She fumbles in her pocket for her phone.

"That's cheating," Eric says, but he's smiling broadly as well.

Emma texts her best friend. *Chase is outside on the sidewalk. He's too nervous to knock on the door.* "I'll blame you. Besides, Ally doesn't always check her text messages."

Apparently, she's checking them tonight. *OMG.* She doesn't even ask Emma how she knows.

Emma looks at the source of the information. "You're ready?" she asks him quietly.

Eric nods. Emma doesn't ask about Necromancers; Eric doesn't volunteer the death count. She is *grateful* that it's not her job. But she has a job to do. Emma carefully steps over the perimeter of her circle. She holds out a hand to Eric. There's no hesitation when he takes it.

But he says, "Margaret first."

Emma nods. She doesn't pull out the lantern, but she doesn't need it. In some fashion, Margaret is still bound to Emma. It's far, far easier to unravel her current shape than it would be to create it. In a matter of minutes, Margaret Henney is standing before her, smiling.

They exchange a few words, and Margaret says, "I'm going to go speak with your father."

"Don't waste breath. I've already tried. He says he's not ready to leave."

"I'm not wasting breath, dear. The dead don't. And I think he'll be ready to leave when he understands—and believes—that the threat Necromancers pose to you is over." She turns to Eric, her smile diminishing.

"Eric."

He nods. He's never been demonstrative.

"Good-bye, dear."

"Don't waste good-byes on me. We'll be seeing each other soon enough. Go talk to the Old Man."

"He's a little far—"

"He's in the car."

Margaret nods and leaves him alone with Emma. To Emma's eye, Eric looks the same as he did when he entered the garage. No one else will see him that way. He's dead. But he's been dead for as long as Emma has known him. It seems a lifetime. It's been just over two years.

"Are you sure you can do this?" he asks.

She nods but decides on honesty as she answers. "If there were anyone else who could, I wouldn't." She doesn't tell him why; there are so many reasons to choose from. But her biggest is Chase. She has nightmares about what happened to Chase's family. She understands why it's hard to let go of hatred or judgment.

She's surprised when the magar appears.

"You don't intend to help me, do you?" she asks.

The magar's glare is withering, but Emma's built up a tolerance to it. "That is not the way the circle works."

Emma sits at the rough center of the circle. She closes her eyes. She listens. This is the peaceful part of her task. She is never certain what she's listening for. The dead aren't always loud. They don't always cry or scream or plead. Andrew Copis didn't. But his memories were so vivid she could hear his mother's screaming in place of his voice.

Tonight is a bit different from the usual searching: she knows who she's searching for, and she has no doubt that she'll find her.

When she steps outside of her circle—and outside of her body—she touches down in a landscape she refers to as gray. It's an inexact description of a washed out nothingness. It has no character, no features, nothing to give it form or shape.

Or at least that's what usually happens. Today, however, the landscape has one distinctive feature. Eric. His hands are by his sides, his expression too complicated to place. But his lips turn up in a small smile as she appears.

She doesn't offer him her hand; he doesn't attempt to take it. "You know where you're going?" he asks.

She nods. She begins to walk, and Eric falls in beside her.

As they walk, Eric speaks. Eric, who never talks about anything personal. Eric, who is the foil to Chase Loern's gregarious anger.

She's never asked Eric if he still loves Reyna. She doesn't ask him now. She doesn't ask him if he stayed for Reyna's sake because she knows the answer is No. He stayed to finish the job.

But she sees his restlessness so clearly now, she wonders if that's all of the truth. She's come to understand that truth, like the people who believe it, is complicated; it's never entirely one thing.

She notes the moment the landscape changes, gray becoming stalks of dry, wild grass and the trunks of distant trees; she sees the sky become blue with a hint of clouds. She hears the rush of water and thinks of rivers or streams. The shadow of birds cross the ground as it solidifies beneath her feet, their wingspans large and open.

Vultures.

She has seen so much death on these walks. So much pain. So much fear. She glances at Eric; he is grim now. He knows exactly where they are. She almost offers him a hand because she's not certain he will be able to remain here. He shakes his head with a rueful smile, and she understands.

She concentrates.

She can hear a girl scream. It stops her in her tracks, and for one long moment the scenery loses color. It threatens to lose stability, she is so overwhelmed by what she hears. It is not Emma's voice, but it might as well be; her throat aches, and her chest; her hands are shaking fists.

She fights for control, fights to push the feelings aside just enough that she can navigate. She's had practice by now. She's lost evenings—and even weeks—to the lives the dead lived. She doesn't want to lose this one, because Eric is with her. He provides incentive to master her reactions.

It's been two years. More. She hasn't seen Nathan except in photographs—and she will never see him again. It hasn't hurt as much as this for a while, and she knows why. The girl's loss is new. She is looking at death. She is looking at Eric's corpse.

She glances at Eric; he is looking at her, his lips slightly thinned. "I'm sorry you had to do this."

"I didn't have to do it," she replies.

"It was you or no one."

She smiles, meaning it. "Is this where you expected me to find her?"

He is silent as the roof of a small house comes into view. He pauses there. "I wasn't certain. Were you?"

Emma nods. "I was certain. I don't know that she would have been happy with you, in the end. I don't know that you would have been happy with her." She has her doubts, but they're irrelevant. What she knows is that Reyna never had the chance to live that dream, and Reyna was fragile enough—young enough—that it destroyed her.

It destroyed so many people.

"Are you ready?" Emma asks.

"I don't know." His smile is apologetic, and his hands are tight. He is watching vultures and hearing the ugly laughter of villagers. Emma doesn't know if they actually laughed; memory, she has discovered, is subjective.

And irrelevant. This is the past. This is the cage that traps the dead. They don't see it, can't leave it, without help. She knows that Reyna deserves this cage.

But she knows that Reyna did not, on the day Eric died, deserve this pain. She didn't deserve to lose her mother, her sister, her uncle, and the only man she would ever love. She didn't deserve the murderous cruelty of villagers goaded by fear into an act of madness. If she hadn't suffered, if she hadn't been victim to things *she* didn't deserve, there would never have been a Queen of the Dead.

And it is here that the Queen of the Dead was born. It's here that she will, finally, die.

Eric makes—has made—no excuses for her. Emma is certain that centuries of almost-life have killed the love he once felt. But maybe love survives, in some fashion.

Or maybe Eric is as trapped by death as Reyna has been. Maybe some part of Eric is still the boy that loved her, in this village, centuries ago—the person he was when he was killed. And he was killed, Emma knows, attempting to protect Reyna. He was willing to give his life for her.

He did.

Emma can see the body. She can see Reyna. The gown and the tiara that characterized her later reign are nowhere in sight, and her hands are covered in blood. Eric's head is cradled in her lap; she is bent over his face, the edge of her hair matted red and sticky. Emma can't hear what she's saying, but she can guess, and she's grateful for the distance.

Eric, however, shakes off uncertainty and fear as he sees her there, cradling his head. He walks—almost runs—to her side, and stands in front of her, looking down at her bent head. He kneels.

"Reyna," he says, as Emma approaches them both, moving slowly. "*Reyna.*"

Reyna doesn't look up. She's not aware of Eric's presence. Emma feels a pang of disappointment on Eric's behalf, but she shakes it off quickly and smiles at Eric as he looks up at her.

She feels her clothing shift as she becomes firmly rooted in this memory place. She knows her hair changes. She's not certain whether or not she retains her own face because she's not certain her face would be relevant to village life—or life on its outer edge.

But she says, as she approaches, "I've called for a healer."

Reyna looks up at the words. She doesn't see Eric. She sees his injured body.

"We need to get blankets," Emma continues. "And we need to build a fire. We need to keep him warm." She doesn't look at Eric's chest, at the gaping wound that appears to cover the whole of it. She looks, instead, at Reyna.

Reyna is frozen for one long moment. She looks at Eric's body and looks at Emma, and then she very, very gently lowers the memory of Eric to the ground. She stands, facing Emma, and as she does, the scenery fades.

The look on Reyna's face is one of recognition. Emma is surprised. She's not afraid. She knows the circle will protect her, if protection is needed. The dead she has guided to freedom never recognize her for what she is until they are almost at the exit.

But Reyna recognizes Emma.

\*　　\*　　\*

"I didn't think you would come," she says.

"If you could think that I wouldn't," Emma replies, "you shouldn't be here at all. You shouldn't be trapped here."

Reyna shakes her head. Her appearance remains as it was on the day Eric died and her world ended. There is a quiet dignity in her now that Emma never saw in the Queen. And there's pain—but it's an honest pain, not a pain transformed into anger or rage or hatred.

"I was always trapped here," Reyna says. "I can't escape it on my own. I know—I know it's not real. Who better than me, to know it? But it holds me anyway. I—I didn't think you'd come. Why did you?"

Emma says, truthfully, "Because there's no one else."

"I would have left you here."

"I know. But I'm not you."

"Because you're better than me?" There is no rancor in the question. No accusation. No fear.

"Because," Emma says, surprised at the tightening in her own throat, "I was *safer* than you." She smiles and adds, "And because I was asked, as a favor."

"My mother?"

Emma shakes her head. "Your mother doesn't ask for favors. In fact, your mother doesn't *ask* for anything."

Reyna winces, but she laughs, and her laugh is surprisingly warm. "You've spent some time with my mother, I see." The laughter fades slowly. "Who asked you?"

Emma reaches out for Eric.

Eric hesitates and then places a hand in hers.

It's clear that Reyna can see him the instant their hands connect. Her eyes are wide and luminous—with death, and possibly with the tears the dead don't shed. And her smile steals breath, it's so radiant. To Emma's surprise, Eric appears to *blush*.

"Eric?"

"I told you," he says, voice rough and low, "I want you to leave this place. I want you to leave it with me." He looks down at her—he has to, she's not tall—and he says, "There's my smile."

And he smiles back.

"I'm proud of you, Sprout."

Although the garage is chilly, the words are warm. Emma's not a child; she doesn't *need* to hear them. But some part of her is still her father's daughter and always will be. Even if he's dead.

She is silent as she leaves the circle; she doesn't scuff it or obliterate the binding words beneath her feet. She doesn't know the precise moment when Margaret leaves, but she knows when she's gone. Eric is gone. Nathan is gone.

Memories are a poor substitute for life—but regardless, they're precious. The memories are Emma's to hold on to for as long as she wants, and they cost no one.

"Thinking?" Brendan Hall asks, as she leaves the garage, falling in beside her.

"Mostly that I have to take Petal for a walk."

"Want company?"

She nods.

Petal is older and deafer, but he has the heart of a puppy. A puppy that no one has fed, ever. She takes dog treats, picks up his lead, pops her head into the family room to let her mother and Jon know they'll have to do without a begging rottweiler for a while, and heads out.

Her father keeps her company, although he stays out of the family room. The only thing Emma resents Jon for these days—and it's a tiny, tiny resentment—is her father's stiff reserve. But Jon makes her mother happy, and Mercy Hall deserves some happiness out of life.

And, if Emma is honest, she likes Jon. Jon can pull a smile out of her on days when that's harder than pulling teeth. There are still bad days, after all. But they're fewer.

She walks to Nathan's grave. The fact of the grave once felt like the end of her life, and for a while, it had been. Things that had been so important became, instantly, trivial. She had gone through all of the right motions, with no sense that they meant anything.

But if this marked an end, it marked a beginning as well. It was here that she first met Eric and the magar. It was through Eric that she met Chase. In the past two years, Chase had become as important to her as friends she had known since she was five, which was good, because now that he had returned to Toronto to stay, she was going to be seeing a lot of him. He wanted to marry Allison.

She glances at her father.

"You're okay, Sprout?"

"I am. I'll miss Eric—but it was time." Saying that, she runs the back of her hand across her eyes.

The tears are not for Eric. Her father knows. But she doesn't speak until she finally reaches the cemetery, and even then, it's hard.

"The worst thing about being dead," her father says, starting the conversation, "is the helplessness. I wanted to pick you up when you fell. I wanted to hold your mother when she cried. I wanted to be able to duck out to the store and buy the groceries I knew she'd forgotten."

"I did that."

He smiles fondly. "Responsibility is for the living, to the living. I wanted to know you were both okay. I wanted to know that you were doing well." He shakes his head. "Every bad day either of you had wracked me with guilt, because there was nothing I could do about it.

"And then you met Eric and the magar. I am not—I will never be—grateful to the Queen of the Dead. But the consolation was that I could speak with you again. I could offer you comfort. Cold comfort," he adds, with a slight smile. "I watched you for years."

Emma turns, then. "I'll be all right, Dad." She wills herself not to cry but fails.

"Yes. Yes, you will. Thank you." When she doesn't respond, he reaches out with his cold, dead hands and touches her cheek. The tears should freeze, but they don't. "The best gift any child could give their dying—or dead—parents is that: the certainty that they'll be okay. You'll be more than okay, Emma." His smile deepens; hints of pain change the shape of his eyes. "Part of me doesn't want to leave. Part of me wants to stay and watch what you choose to do, how much you'll achieve, from here on in."

Emma holds her breath. Exhales. "But no pressure."

He laughs.

Emma smiles. She understands the part of him that wants to stay. She was his daughter. He loved her. But she understands, as well, that he is tired. He is exhausted. The only thing that ties him to the world of the living is the daughter he loved—but they both know he can no longer be part of her life.

Life is hard, sometimes. But it continues. Having seen the result of one desperate woman's attempt to create an eternity of love, it's best that way.

Emma opens her arms, and her father hugs her. "Can I walk you there?" she asks.

"I'm not sure it's a good idea."

"I've seen where you're going. I've never followed any of the dead."

"You've had no incentive."

"The magar has been teaching me for two years, Dad."

He laughs again. And he doesn't say no.

"I want for you what you want for us," Emma says, before he can. "That's all. I want to know that you're safe, that you're happy, that there's some peace for you."

"You don't know what actually lies on the other side of that door."

"No. But no one living does. If I can see you off happy, that's enough. That's enough." She takes his hand; it's cold. Of course it is. "Thank you."

"For what?"

"Everything. Giving me life. Loving me while you were part of it. Watching me when you couldn't be. The usual." She stops speaking and waits until the tears are under control before she leads her father away.

He's smiling. She'll remember that later.

# Acknowledgments

**For *Silence*:**

This book was a bit of a departure for me, and with departures, I generally pester my friends, because I'm less certain of myself. Chris Szego, who manages the bookstore at which I still work part-time (because it's about the *books*), was hugely encouraging. And nagging. In about that order. So were Karina Sumner-Smith and Tanya Huff.

And, of course, Thomas and Terry had to read the book a chapter at a time, because that's what alpha readers are for.

**For *Touch*:**

This was possibly the hardest book of my career to write. I thought, going in, it would be the easiest. This is the occupational hazard of the writer's life. Usually, though, my hazards don't cause quite as many problems for my publisher. DAW has been, as always, fabulous. I'm sure there was hair-pulling and teeth-grinding in New York—but it stayed in New York.

So: Sheila Gilbert & Joshua Starr, *thank you, thank you, thank you.* You let me take the time to start this book four times from the beginning, to figure out where and why it didn't work, and to ultimately make it work, even though it messed up the schedule terribly.

Inasmuch as this book is any good, it's due in large part to that understanding and that space.

Also: my family put up with an increasingly stressed and depressed writer for way too many months—which is generally what happens when I keep dashing my head against the wall of writer competence. So they deserve your sympathy.

**For *Grave*:**

I feel, as of late, that my acknowledgements are a frantic, groveling thank you to people who have had to endure my flailing and my optimistic sense of my own abilities. And they are.

*Grave* is the third and final novel in a trilogy that has seen more revisions, more "throw away two-thirds of the book" author angst than *any* other series I have ever worked on. This was enormously hard on me—but that almost goes without saying. No one expects someone to toss out their year's worth of work multiple times and be overjoyed to do so, given that they've got to start again at ground zero. I mean page one.

Terry, as always, read every word as it was written. All four times. He probably heard all the whining more often as well. And he reminded me that making a mistake does not equal total permanent failure. Which, as things wore on, became unfortunately necessary.

But people who are not in publishing seldom see the effect it has on the publishers, the editors. It knocks books out of schedule, which means the entire schedule has to be reshuffled. It makes it harder to gain any reader traction, because of the gaps and uncertainties in the publication timing. It is . . . bad.

And throughout this, I have to say, if my editor was furious—and seriously, human, she must have had those days—she kept it entirely away from me. If she had a dartboard with my picture on it, I would accept it as no more than my due. My managing editor, Joshua Starr, has been unfailingly polite, helpful, and almost instant in answering my frantic emails. No, polite is the wrong word. He actually sounds cheerful most days, as if he enjoys dealing with people like me who are, let's face it, not making his job any easier.

Cliff Nielsen's art for the cover of the third book is perfect, and I felt blessed by it, which again has nothing to do with me, the writer, but is the first thing most people will see of the book.

And of course, if the book falls short, if there are problems with it, it is, in fact, on me, and not on the people who did so much to guide it to your hands.